The Death You Deserve — Wither the Waking World #1

THE DEATH YOU DESERVE

WITHER THE WAKING WORLD

BOOK ONE

By Jonathan Techlin

Copyright © 2014 Jonathan Techlin

The Death You Deserve is a work of fiction. Names, characters, places, and incidents either are the product of the author's imagination or are used fictitiously. Any resemblance to actual persons, living or dead, events, or locales is entirely coincidental.

The Death You Deserve — Wither the Waking World #1

THE DEATH YOU DESERVE

WITHER THE WAKING WORLD
BOOK ONE

The Death You Deserve — Wither the Waking World #1

This book is dedicated to Mom.

PROLOGUE

Theel turned the knife in his hand, aimed the point back at himself, and wondered if this was the day he would die. There would be no one to mourn him if he did it. Not his mother, whom he'd never known. Not his father, whose funeral gathering was just beginning outside the window. And not his brother, who remained at his side, but only out of a sense of duty.

Now with his father gone, Theel no longer owed anything to anyone. His life was now his to do with as he chose. Perhaps this should be his life's first and last free choice. Perhaps this knife, which had never tasted blood, should finally find its purpose, its home, in his hurting heart.

Theel turned the knife over, looking at its plainness. It was a gift from his father, the vaunted Knight of the Southern Cross. His father's name was known in each of the Seven Kingdoms, a hero to all the people of the old clans, from noblemen to smallfolk.

But Theel's father left two legacies. To the people of the Seven Kingdoms, he left countless tales of battlefield heroism. For Theel, he left a lifetime of dark memories, years of abuse suffered at the man's hands; the taunts, the curses, the beatings. This treatment was necessary, he was told, to teach him strength, to prepare him for battle. The great knight required his son to be just as great, and would accept nothing less. It was an impossible expectation to meet, and an impossible burden to bear, even now, after his father was gone.

Theel looked at the knife; looked at its sharpened point. It would be so easy. If he could only find the courage.

Theel's father gave him the knife the day he spoke the words of the Squire's Oath, the day he began his training for knighthood. He wore the weapon sheathed on his belt for years while he followed his father to every corner of the western kingdoms, his every action following a command. As a squire, his life was no longer his own. He belonged first to his God, second to his clan, and third to his masterknight. They walked together, ate together, and practiced swordplay together. But they never spent any meaningful time as father and son. The father did not speak to his son. Instead, the masterknight gave orders to his squire.

Theel's father was a cold and rigid man, but Theel loved him despite this, as a son loves a father. For years, he clung to the knighthood and to its religion, just to please his father, thinking one day he could make himself worthy, and find the love and acceptance he needed. But the promises of the knighthood proved false, just like the promises of its religion. Theel had long harbored grave doubts, but the last tenuous strands that bound him to his faith were severed by the blow that took his father's life.

The great knight was slain by a chieftain of the zoths, the ancient enemies of the old clans. The loss was a blow to the knighthood, to all the armies of Embriss. He was like a god to them; unbeatable, indestructible, eternal. He was a man, it was said, who could beat death, and had already done so once. During a battle years ago, Theel's father was stabbed through the heart, yet he lived. He had the damaged shield and scar on his chest to prove it. He'd beaten death once, but it was a feat he could not repeat.

Now he was dead, and Theel was confused by this new reality without his father. He both loved and hated the man. He'd both hoped for, and loathed, the thought of their future together. Now that future was extinguished, and their journey together as father and son was left incomplete. The knight's death guaranteed that their story was etched in stone. It could not be changed, no matter how ugly and bitter it was.

Theel knew he could not finish this journey alone, not when he never truly believed in its destination. And so he turned the knife, staring at its sharpened point. Today, the day of his father's funeral, was the first day the blade of this knife was bared in years. It seemed so perfect that as the kingdom celebrated his father's life, Theel would celebrate his own death. And he would do it with his father's gift to him. He would use this knife to kill his father's other gifts to him, the pain and despair that clouded his every day.

The funeral mourners would wait for him to arrive, but he wouldn't come. He would be lying dead, by his own hand, by his father's hand, by his father's endless demands for perfection, by his father's glittering example of imperfection. Such an appropriate legacy this would be for the great knight. His family, dead. His unloved son, dead. All that he fought for, all he believed in. Dead.

But what if Theel's father was right?

"Theel," the Keeper of the Craft said to him. "You earned your apprenticeship with words. Now you must earn your knighthood with deeds. The time of Warrior Baptism must come for every squire. Now, it has come for you."

The Keeper of the Craft, court wizard of Embriss, advisor to the rulers of the Seven Kingdoms, was a short, wrinkled little man with a round face and thick-rimmed spectacles. The Keeper's face, and his expectant eyes, flickered in the light of the white flame that burned on the top of his battle staff, a flame that never died, even if thrust underwater.

"You have earned the chance to prove yourself in the eyes of your king, Lord Britou, ruler of Embriss," the Keeper said to Theel. "Today you will mourn your father. Tomorrow you will journey at Britou's behest."

Theel didn't respond, only stared at the knife in his hand. *Today, you mourn my father,* he thought bitterly. *Tomorrow, you will mourn me.*

"It is the most important and sacred duty a clansman can owe his people," the Keeper said. "A squire to his knight, a knight to his clan, the clans to our God."

Theel looked at the Keeper of the Craft, knowing that to be in this man's presence was to be in a position of honor. A handful of people met the Keeper, and fewer still found themselves addressed by him. In many areas of the realms, the great sorcerer known as the Keeper of the Craft was considered a mythical being.

"This is the fulfillment of your oath," the Keeper said. "The final honor you will earn for your lord and masterknight, your father."

The Keeper had summoned Theel on this day, the morning of his father's funeral, to inform him and prepare him for his next duty, the great honor of Warrior Baptism. This was the ancient rite of passage that lifted a squire to knighthood.

"Tomorrow you will begin your quest for Warrior Baptism," the Keeper said. "You will follow in your father's footsteps, and those of so many great men who have risen to the ranks of the Knights of the Southern Cross. God willing."

The Keeper spoke of the glory and honor of the knighthood, just as Theel's father so often would. He spoke of Warrior Baptism as though this quest would be the answer to Theel's prayers, to the world's prayers, as though completion of this quest could take all that was wrong and somehow make it right.

"You will travel far beyond the borders of Embriss, to the south of Yarik," the Keeper said. "Beyond the cliffs of Tera Watch, to a small Outlander town called Ebon South."

Theel had known the Keeper since he was a child. A knight of high rank, such as Theel's father, often kept council with the ruler of his clan, his court, his advisors, and the leading wizard of the realm. When Theel was a boy, the Keeper of the Craft identified within him a unique and powerful gift.

"There you will find a priest who calls himself Father Brashfor," the Keeper explained. "He can help guide you on your quest."

Theel's gift gave him the ability to see things that weren't truly there; things that had happened years before, and things that would happen years in the future. Theel had the gift of Sight, so the Keeper told his father. It was an ability that rarely occurred naturally in humans, and was therefore considered a precious asset to the realm. The power was only in its infancy, but if nurtured properly, it would only grow in strength as Theel matured to manhood, and might one day make him a candidate for schooling at the Temple of Juy.

"Your quest is handed down to you from the throne of Embriss," the Keeper said. "Lord Britou himself has chosen the method of your Warrior Baptism. You must quest to fulfill the prophecy of Sun Antheus. You must find the man who is called the Blessed Soul of Man."

But Theel's powers didn't mature at all. They didn't increase in strength or variety. For fifteen years, the Keeper studied Theel's abilities, even tried to train him to use them. Now Theel was a man, a fully trained squire to the knighthood. He still had no control of his ability, its strength, or its frequency. He didn't control the Sight. It controlled him. He once thought the Sight might provide a means to freedom, to independence from his father, from the knighthood, from everyone's expectations. In the end, the Sight was just another master.

"Your gift makes you special. Your Sight will guide your steps," the Keeper said. "You are the only one among us who can undertake this quest. It is you who must find the Blessed Soul of Man. Do you understand what Warrior Baptism requires of you?"

Again, Theel turned the knife over in his hand. "Yes, Keeper," he answered. "I must fulfill the prophecy of Sun Antheus. I must find the Blessed Soul of Man."

"You will leave tomorrow," the Keeper said. "You must honor your father, fulfill the prophecy, and earn the rite of Warrior Baptism. You must do this. You must not fail."

I will fail, Theel thought. *I cannot fulfill a prophecy I do not believe in, no matter what Father said. Failure has become my friend,* Theel thought. *I will fail you just as I failed my father. If I leave on this quest, I will never return.*

"Honor your father and the Knights of the Southern Cross," the Keeper said. "Honor our God, and bring the Blessed Soul of Man to us. Find this man, and become a man yourself. Find him, and you will find yourself. Find yourself, and you will be a knight."

There is no honor to be found here, Theel thought. *I wish it wasn't so, but I cannot deny the truth. I cannot complete an impossible quest with an unattainable goal. I cannot find a man who doesn't exist. There is no Blessed Soul of Man. My father proved that to me with his death.*

Theel would never be able to forgive his father for what happened that day. Nor would he be able to forgive himself for being unable to stop it. Most of all, he could not believe in a prophecy that caused so much death, or a Blessed Soul that sat idly by while others fought and died for him.

Just as he'd been taught, Theel prayed throughout his childhood. He prayed that he would meet the expectations the knights had for him, that he would excel in his lessons as a squire, that he would learn to master his gift of Sight. He prayed that he would grow in these things in a way that would please his father. But his father was never pleased. Once Theel accepted that he'd never meet these expectations, he prayed that his father would accept him for who he was. When all hope for that was abandoned, he just prayed to feel loved. But this too, was denied him.

"Theel," the Keeper said. "Will you find the Blessed Soul?"

All the prayers were empty words. Theel's prayers could not save his father. The knight's prayers could not save himself. The fruits of a life lived in complete devotion to the prophecy and the Blessed Soul of Man were nothing more than a legacy of pain, suffering, and disappointment, both for the great knight and for his son.

There was only one rational conclusion. The prophecies were false, and everything the Knights of the Southern Cross believed in was emptiness. Theel's father wasted his life waiting for the coming of the Blessed Soul. He wasted his last breath proclaiming his faith in the prophecy. Everything he raised his son to believe was wrong. He was wrong as a knight, wrong as a father, and wrong as a man.

"I will find him. I will find the Blessed Soul," Theel lied. "I will not fail."

But what if Theel's father was right?

Chapter 1

It took almost an hour of walking in the drizzly, gray afternoon, slogging through ankle-deep puddles and street filth, before Theel and his brother, Yatham, finally stood at the edge of Six Corners, a wide smear of mud and stink located in the center of the poorest quarter of Fal Daran. Six Corners was a center of commerce for the lowest class, clogged by merchants and street venders working out of collapsible stalls with canvas tops, or the backs of carts, or even a few blankets spread out on the rare dry spot to display wares of such questionable quality that they would never pass muster in any other market in the city.

Customers crowded among the stalls, people of small means with little or none of the king's work to spend. Most had wares of their own for sale or barter, baskets of fruits or vegetables or herbs, knit blankets and homemade clothing, tools, tack, or iron of any kind, smoked meats, fish, grain or flour, a chicken still alive and clucking, or even a bottle of liquor. But mostly it was muscle and sweat that was offered, hours of the king's work spent cleaning chamber pots, carrying water, sweeping floors, and doing laundry. Six Corners had a reputation as the place to find cheap labor, which occasionally drew some highborn lord or his work foreman from elsewhere in the city, searching for men who were willing to spend a few days working a hammer, axe, or shovel in exchange for a few bowls of soup and a dry place to sleep.

For this reason, Theel and Yatham's trip through the market was neither easy nor quick. They were accosted by poor men and women who mistook their purpose in coming to Six Corners, who surrounded them and blocked their path, offering services of all kinds, boasting of numerous skills as well as a willingness to work.

It was an easy misunderstanding to make, for both brothers clearly came from the more affluent side of town. Finely crafted armor poked out from under Theel's rain poncho, supple bullosk leather tanned and cut with a practiced hand, held in place with laces and straps pulled through shiny steel rings and buckles, and expensive boots, custom-made with brass eyelets. The sword he wore on his hip was old in its appearance, well-worn and beaten, but despite its age and use, it was also clearly forged by a master craftsman, and remained under the care of a loving hand, with a shiny pommel and a freshly oiled scabbard that said the blade it contained was likely sharpened to a perfect edge.

Yatham carried none of the accouterments of battle, but like his brother, he was dressed richly, with fancy leathers and well-made boots, a tight-fitting white shirt with cuffs around his wrists, and expensive leather trousers with intricate decorative braids down his legs.

Yatham led the way across the clogged market of Six Corners, slogging through the mud, parting the people so his brother could pass, and also politely turning down every offer of work, many of them several times. Theel was silent, held close to Yatham, his head bowed so his wide-brimmed hat covered most of his face. He stared at his brother's back, watched the rainwater drip from the brim of his hat, and blinked hard, fighting the occasional gurgle of nausea. The voices in the market stung his ears and his head, each shout striking his brain like a hammer. He concentrated on the simple acts of following his brother, keeping his face shaded, and trying not to be sick.

Halfway across the market, Theel saw something that might serve as medicine for his malady on the kiosk of a spirit trader. His brother led him directly past it, giving him just enough time to drop a few coins and pull a pouch of seraphim under his poncho. The amount he paid was far more than the seraphim was worth, but he had no time to barter.

Criers lined the north and south ends of Six Corners, men whose voices were employed by the higher institutions of the city to bring the news of the realm to the illiterate smallfolk of the city. These were the voices Theel attempted to hear through the cacophony of the marketplace, listening intently for one particular piece of information.

"News from the Council of Lords!" a man shouted to his left. "The Iatan Army remains encamped just beyond the eastern walls of Old City. The council continues to negotiate with the Iatan leaders in the hope of reaching a peaceful settlement, however, the possibility of war grows with each passing day. The council once again assures the people of Fal Daran that, whatever the outcome of these meetings, our city will not be conquered as the Eastern Kingdoms were. The council implores every loyal child of Embriss to ready themselves for whatever may come ... "

"News from the Hall of the Seven Swords!" a man shouted to Theel's right.

" ... We must hope for peace, but prepare for war," the first man finished.

" ... it is with profound sadness that First Guardian Lord Britou must announce that our brothers east of the Dividers have lost their struggle with the Iatan!" the second man continued. "Fighting on the Plains of Aramorun has ceased, and all land north of Mella Fex is now controlled by the enemy. Lord Britou hopes negotiations with our enemy will bear fruit, but also understands the city of Fal Daran may not be spared from the ravages of this war. He begs all God-fearing children of Embriss to join together in prayer that we be delivered from this trial. And that if it is true that the Year of Revelation is at hand, that God will soon fulfill his promise to send his champion to lead us. The day may come soon when our only hope resides in the promise of the Blessed Soul ..."

"News from the Keepers of Law and Order!" another man shouted from Theel's left.

" ... We pray the prophecy will be fulfilled!" the crier for the knighthood said. "We pray that the Blessed Soul of Man will come!"

" ... A bulletin from the Offices of the City Overwatch, to alert all law-abiding citizens of the city of Fal Daran!" the man said. "A murderer is loose in our fair city, and even now flees the law. His evil deed was done just last evening, in the barroom of the Glad Sire's Inn and Hitch, a block off the east wall of Old City."

Theel tensed at those words, fighting more angry protests from his stomach. He grabbed a fistful of the raindrops running off his hat and rubbed them on his face. Yatham continued walking, so Theel continued following, his head still down.

"The victim was prominent citizen and noble son of Embriss, Quiddip Kile of House Kile, who served on the council of his uncle, Lord Hiram, the Lord Protector of New City!" the crier said. "The identity of Lord Kile's killer is not known, though officers of the City Overwatch were able to collect descriptions from witnesses at the scene, who identified him as a subordinate of the Southern Cross Knights, a servant or a squire, bearing both the tattoos of the knighthood as well as a glove with the old crown seal of the First Guardian!"

Theel stopped wringing his hands beneath his rain poncho and now moved his right hand to cover his left, hiding the intricate stitching in the glove he wore.

"He was said to have a thin, yet muscular build, brown hair, and green eyes. And he wore rich clothing, finely crafted leather armor, and expensive boots, and carried an older-looking battle sword showing much wear and use, but forged under the hand of a master craftsman."

Theel pinched his eyes shut, sickened at those words. For the first time since crossing the square, he was thankful for the peasants who crowded him and his brother. The press of dirty bodies helped hide him from the crier's eyes.

"The killer had an accomplice, who witnesses said he referred to as his brother. This man also had a thin build, with blonde hair and green eyes. He was not armed, but like his brother he was richly dressed, wearing a tailored white shirt with wrist cuffs, and expensive leather boots and trousers."

Theel kept his eyes shut, too frightened to open them. He now followed Yatham so closely that his nose nearly touched the back of his brother's neck, head down, trying to disappear within his hat.

"The Keepers of Law and Order ask all citizens of Fal Daran to do their part in bringing this killer to justice!" the crier said. "Any information regarding his whereabouts should be reported to the Offices of the City Overwatch immediately!"

The brothers were nearly across Six Corners, to the south end of the market where the crowd became thinner. The harassment finally slowed as those seeking work realized these finely dressed men had not come to hire or to offer anything of value. But now Theel and Yatham made their way through the beggars at the southern edge of the square, thin and sickly, emaciated bodies lying on filthy blankets or in the mud, crying out for help, arms outstretched, hands pawing at the legs of passersby. Nearby, Theel could hear the words of a priest of the Temple of Juy, who, with two of his followers, moved among the beggars, offering words of comfort and encouragement, and drinks of fresh water from a pitcher. These were followed by invitations to the temple, where food and blankets, and spiritual guidance could be found.

"Do not fear an uncertain future," the priest said. "Instead, trust in God's promise as stated in the prophecy of Sun Antheus. We must patiently, but earnestly, await the coming of the Blessed Soul of Man."

Yatham led the way through the beggars and into a narrow alleyway at the south end of the square. The sounds of the crowd and the voices of the criers faded as they entered the dark and narrow confines of the alley. They walked down a crooked pathway of mud and garbage between old, shabby buildings, some of them little more than glorified shanties. The worst of these was a tavern, and also the brothers' destination. Hidden from public sight, without a single street-facing wall, and a front door entrance to an alleyway guarded by beggars, it was a tiny and nearly forgotten shack, built in a nearly forgotten place, just as its owner preferred it.

Pounded together from gray wooden slats and rusted nails, the façade of the Three Mugs and a Bowl said welcome to no one, but rather seemed to want to be left alone in peace, its shape slumped and forlorn, and leaning against the neighboring buildings like a wounded soldier needing the support of its brothers. The building suffered from a complete lack of care. The only sign that it had not been abandoned was the dozens of flickering orange cracks in its wooden skin, scant proof that something inside still lived. The wind blew, the eaves rattled, and the building's rain-dirtied wooden boards groaned in pain, as if in greeting.

Theel walked to the front step stones, but did not ascend, instead pulling a pipe from beneath his rain poncho. The bowl was already prepared, packed with the seraphim he'd just purchased in the marketplace. He put the pipe between his lips and struck a match.

"Is that necessary?" Yatham asked from over his shoulder.

"Calm yourself, brother," Theel muttered. "I need this to go on living."

"We have both travel and trial before us," Yatham said. "You wish to face these with a dreamy brain?"

"What other way is there?" Theel asked, puffing away.

"You never burned leaf when Father was alive," Yatham said.

"I didn't need to, brother, when Father was alive."

Yatham looked sad. "There are other ways to salve your wounds."

"Yes, but none so effective, or as effortless," Theel retorted. "Now please go inside. I must know if I am welcome here."

Yatham sighed and turned to climb the front step stones of the tavern. Theel waited outside and puffed away, huddled in the shadow of the Three Mugs and a Bowl. He smoked his pipe with deep pulls, feeling the seraphim fill his blood, fighting the poison of the alcohol, and soothing the ache in his head and the sickness in his gut. But it also stayed his nervousness, relaxed his muscles, and stopped his hands from shaking. Travel and trials indeed.

He looked up at the gray sky, determining the time of day by studying the black silhouettes hovering among the clouds. They were ever-present, day and night, these islands of rock in a sea of air. There were one or two of them on most days, as many as a dozen at rarer times. On clear days they appeared as dark splotches against the blue sky. On clear nights, they blotted out the stars. There was nothing predictable about them, appearing in many variations of shape and size. Some were so high they were barely visible, while others so low that they looked like they barely missed the peaks of the Dividers Mountains as they traveled from the eastern horizon to the west. Legends said these were remnants of the pre-Sundering world, trapped in a perpetual orbit by the Craft weaves that blanketed Thershon. It was said that some of these islands were large enough that men might still live on them, remnants of the ancient civilization destroyed in the Sundering thousands of years ago. Theel's father agreed, saying there were islands far above the clouds large enough to support life, and even claimed to have battled visitors from one of these islands.

Theel shook his head just considering the foolishness of this claim. None of those islands were good for much more than their role as muses for bards who told silly stories. None of them, that is, except for one. It was called Behe Kang, translated as "Isle of the Damned" in the old Thershoni tongue. Behe Kang was the largest of the islands, and the only one whose appearance could be predicted, crossing the sky twice daily. Behe Kang was at its highest point in the sky at midnight and midday, eclipsing the sun every day at noon.

Noondark had already occurred on this day, and Behe Kang was well on its way to the western horizon, telling Theel the time was three after noondark falling.

Still plenty of time.

His stomach growled. He finished his pipe, and tapped it out. Then he removed his hat and walked to the overflowing rain barrel at the side of the tavern building.

"Visitors from another island," Theel snorted derisively. "Father, you were such a fool."

He stood over the barrel and plunged his head into the cold water. It was freezing, but the seraphim angels now flying through his veins made it more soothing than painful. For a moment, he enjoyed the loss of senses. He opened his eyes and saw nothing but the blackness of the barrel bottom, listened, but heard nothing but water filling his ears.

Then he straightened with a splash, rubbed his eyes and smoothed his hair. His senses returned to him, but not as before. The alley appeared the same, and yet somehow felt different, in a way he couldn't identify. His hearing returned to him, but now sounds of the city seemed distant, even though he remained well within its walls. The market was quiet. No more shouting. The merchants, the criers, the customers and beggars—all quiet. The birds didn't even chirp.

But children played. He could not see them, but he could hear their voices, speaking rhythmically, reciting a rhyme between bursts of laughter. The sound came from down the crooked pathway, snaked between the buildings. It entered his ears, enticing him, tugging him forward.

He put his hat back on his head and left the rain barrel, following the sound, listening to the words of the rhyme. He recognized them, as would any clansman who grew up in the city of Fal Daran. He'd recited them a thousand times as a boy:

Close your eyes, God's will be done
The Blessed Soul will one day come
The light will swallow up the sun
And all the world shall wither
All the world shall wither

He rounded a bend in the alleyway and saw them, standing in a circle, holding hands. He expected filthy, starving street rats, but instead saw clean and healthy children, well-nourished and wearing nice clothing. They weren't dirty at all, nor were they wet, as if they were immune to the mud and rain. That was Theel's first clue that these children weren't truly there, that he was experiencing another vision. His second clue was the halo of white light that surrounded them, dulling the colors of their hair and clothing, and causing the smooth skin of their baby faces to appear pale.

Close your eyes, God's will be done
The Blessed Soul will one day come
The light will swallow up the sun
And all the world shall wither

We all stand up
And we all fall down
For all the world shall wither

They repeated the rhyme, and Theel watched them cover their eyes as they said the first stanza, wave their arms in a wide arc during the second, then point to the sky during the third.

Then the final lines were spoken:

We all stand up
And we all fall down
For all the world shall wither

The children fell to the ground, laughing hysterically and clapping hands. Theel knew exactly how much fun that could be. He remembered when he and Yatham played the game as boys. Had his face ever smiled so large?

When they'd sufficiently laughed themselves out, the children picked themselves up and began the game anew, reciting the rhyme loudly in unison.

Close your eyes, God's will be done
The Blessed Soul will one day come
The light will swallow up the sun
And all the world shall wither

"All the world shall wither," Theel said to himself.

Chapter 2

"Brother!"

Theel looked to see Yatham standing on the step stones of the tavern. He turned from the scene of the children and headed back toward where his brother waited, choosing, as he often did, not to reveal anything of what his vision showed him.

"Brother," Yatham said. "We have haven here. Uncle Guarn is within."

"Has word of Quiddip's stumble reached this place?" Theel asked.

"The voices of the Overwatch have reached even the darkest alleys of the city," Yatham answered. "Everyone seems to know of his death."

"Is that all they know?" Theel asked. "Anything regarding you and me?"

"They know Quiddip's killer flees justice."

"There was no killer, I remind you," Theel said sternly. "Unless you count the oaf's clumsiness that killed him."

"I know that, brother," Yatham replied. "But the Overwatch does not have officers searching all of Fal Daran for the oaf's clumsiness."

"No, they don't," Theel agreed, walking up the steps. "Very well, then. Let us call on our dear uncle."

Theel had visited the Three Mugs and a Bowl many times in his younger days, back when it was housed in a different building across town, then known as the Three Mugs and a Bowl Inn and Hitch. That building was much larger, and built on an actual street where it showed its face proudly rather than skulking in shame as the tavern in this alley now did. That old building said welcome. That old building said life. But that place was no more.

When Theel opened the tavern door, he wasn't met with light and warmth, only quiet, dimly lit sadness. The light of late afternoon followed Theel through the doorway, causing the half-dozen or so patrons to turn their heads; some to see who this newcomer was, others to shrink away like rats fearing the light.

Yatham shut the door, causing the room to fall back to near darkness. Little could be seen by the soft flickering of two lanterns and a wood stove. Nothing but the outlines of a few men, each sitting alone, no part of their bodies moving but the arm that raised the glass to their lips.

The fire popped. Someone coughed. No one said a word.

The smell of this place was nothing like the inn that once bore the same name. There was no warmth, only coldness. There was no joy, only decay. The old inn was a place to make merry and feel alive. This was a place to get numb and feel dead, a giant coffin full of people long gone, if only their bodies would realize it.

"Don't stand there."

The voice came across the room from Theel's right. He looked to see who spoke, but his eyes hadn't yet adjusted to the darkness. Something hit the brim of his hat with a soft pat. He looked up and a fat drop of rainwater fell into his eye.

"Don't look up, either. Roof leaks there."

Another drop hit Theel's cheek before he could move out of the way. He started across the room, rubbing his face as he went. He could see firelight reflecting off some stools and a bar on the far side of the room, the direction from which the voice came.

"The whole place leaks," the voice said from behind the bar.

It was a voice Theel knew; a little older, a little scratchier, but still recognizable. It was the voice of the man he came to see.

"Uncle?"

There was a striking sound and a match flared to life, moving to light a lantern on the bar top. The hand that held the match had only two fingers and a thumb.

"Uncle?" Theel said, moving to sit upon a stool. "It is your nephew, Theel."

"I know who it is," the voice said.

The match was raised to light a bent and twisted tobacco leaf cigar held between the lips of a man who looked to be many years beyond his true age. His face hung off his skull in a cascade of wrinkles and creases, some ancient burn scars, and a large scowl. One eye looked from the lantern to the cigar, then to Theel, while the other eye remained still, dead, and staring straight ahead. His hair was gray and messy, uncombed and uncared for, with whiskers and eyebrows that resembled patches of white brambles. Though the man appeared older, rounder, and worn like an old pair of trousers, his face was still recognizable. That face belonged to the brother of Theel's father. It was his uncle, Guarn.

"How do you fare, uncle?" Theel asked.

"Do you really care to know?"

"I'll pretend to care if you'll speak with me," Theel said.

"And if I choose not to speak with you?"

"Suppose I buy a drink?" Theel suggested. "Then I am your customer."

"I don't care to speak with customers, either." Guarn slid a mug across the bar top toward his nephew. "And your coin is no good here."

Theel pushed the mug away, looking ill. "No liquor."

"I know that look," Guarn said. "You wine sick, boy? Has my brother, the valiant, God-fearing knight of Embriss, raised a drunk for a son?"

"Don't call me *boy*."

"You got butter in your belly," Guarn continued. "Winesick as an alley dog, you are. I recognize it."

"You recognize it because you know the feeling well," Theel said. "You're drunk right now. Don't deny it."

"I don't deny it. And there's more drinking to be done, I'd say," Guarn said, taking the mug back and sipping from it. "When the world knows you as a worthless, sodding drunk, there's no reason to strive for anything more. It's liberating, I say."

"Father was right about you," Theel said. "Your love of liquor ruins you."

"I'm no worse than you are, Theel, just older. Take a good look at your future."

"I'll never be like you."

"Then why are you winesick?" Guarn asked.

Theel turned his head away, refusing to meet his uncle's one-eyed gaze.

"How did you spend last evening?" Guarn pressed. "Did you say your prayers and go to bed early, like a good little squire?"

Theel was still looking away. "Perhaps I should have."

"Yeah, you should have, but you didn't," Guarn said. "And I know why. Because you are just like me. Because each family has its own allotment of worth. After my brother, the perfect man, was created, there wasn't any worth left for you and me, eh?"

"Father wasn't perfect," Theel said. "He was far from it."

"And yet he was a better man than we are," Guarn retorted. "It is a fact we both must live with. What do you think of that? Me and you, the old drunk and the young drunk. We're the chaff of the family. I'll drink to that."

Guarn smiled for the first time that day, an odd sight on that worn old face—one eye showing the warmth of amusement, the other still staring, still scowling.

"I am not a drunk," Theel grumbled. "I am a squire of the Southern Cross Knights."

"You may be a squire, but you're not walking the path to knighthood; not with your love of liquors and leaf," Guarn said. "Men of the Southern Cross have shinier attitudes than the likes of you, with your spiteful tongue and fighting fists."

"I did not come here to discuss last night," Theel said.

"I knew it!" Guarn slapped the bar top. "You drank yourself stupid last night and commenced to fighting. Don't deny it. You look away, but I can still see your face. I only need one good eye to see those bruises."

Yatham cleared his throat loudly. "Perhaps we should take this conversation somewhere else? Somewhere private?"

Guarn ignored him. "You can tell me. There was a time when your uncle enjoyed a good bar fight now and then. What happened? Did you win?"

Theel was looking away again. "I'd rather not discuss it with you."

Guarn sat back with a creak of his stool, calmly regarding his nephew. He took a long, contemplative pull on his cigar and exhaled a stream of smoke into the lantern light.

"You'd rather not discuss it, eh?" he finally said. "Then why have you come to the Three Mugs and a Bowl? You're not here to drink. You're certainly not here to wish good health upon your old, tattered uncle. You want something. What is it?"

Theel took a deep breath, then said softly, "I must leave the city."

"All right then, you must leave the city," Guarn said. "So why haven't you?"

Theel stared at the bar top, speaking tense words. "I need your help to do it."

"Why must you leave the city?"

"That's my business, not yours."

"Then you will tell me your business." Guarn stated, "If you wish me to help you."

"I will not."

Guarn leaned in. "Are you chasing your quest?"

Theel frowned. "What do you know of my quest?" he asked.

"You're a squire of the Southern Cross Knights, are you not?" Guarn said. "It's a fact you proclaim when it suits you."

"Of course I am a squire; but by the will of my father, not my own."

"Squires undertake quests," Guarn said. "It is how they achieve knighthood. Warrior Baptism, yes?"

"Yes, it's true," Theel sighed. "I was assigned my quest only a week ago."

"So I heard," Guarn said.

"You've heard?" Theel asked. "How?"

Guarn took a long time answering, as if he enjoyed his nephew's frustration. "Well," he said, flicking his cigar ash, then taking another drag. "It's the Keeper of the Craft, you see. It seems he is wondering why you are still in Fal Daran."

Theel's lips tightened with fear, the ache in his stomach growing. "The Keeper?"

"Yes, the Keeper; and that means the crown," Guarn said, taking another drink, throwing a sideways glance at his nephew. "Your eyes grow frightened, boy. Why would that be?"

"The Keeper came here?" Theel asked. "To speak with you?"

"The Keeper wouldn't dirty his pretty slippers on my floorboards," Guarn said. "He sent one of his stooges. I don't remember the name."

"What did he say?" Theel asked.

"He asked me if I knew of your whereabouts," Guarn said. "He told me the Keeper is distressed to hear rumors that you are still in the city, despite the orders you were given. He is upset to hear that you are shirking your duty as a squire."

Yatham shook his head. "I warned you this would happen, brother."

"In short, he asked why you're showing so little interest in your quest for Warrior Baptism, assigned you just a week past by Lord Britou and the Keeper of the Craft," Guarn said.

"This is terrible," Yatham said.

"That's the First Guardian himself, the King of Embriss," Guarn added.

"I know who Lord Britou is," Theel stated angrily.

"It seems the First Guardian thinks this quest of yours is rather important," Guarn said. "Everyone seems to think your quest is rather important. Everyone but *you*. You don't seem to care at all."

"That's not true," Theel said.

"But now you've had a sudden change of heart," Guarn said. "Now you wish to leave the city. Is that right?"

"Yes, Uncle," Theel said.

"All right then," Guarn said. "But you still haven't answered my question. If you need to leave the city, why haven't you done so? Why are you still here?"

"Because I need your help. War is coming."

"War is already upon us," Guarn said. "Perhaps you haven't heard, but the Iatan Empire has a good-sized army right outside our doorstep."

"Then you must understand my need for urgency," Theel said. "A desperate fight is not far off. There will be a large battle, and probably a siege. Yatham and I must be gone from this city before that happens."

"What help can I give?" Guarn said, flashing a smug smile. "I'm just an old, worthless drunk. Is that not correct?"

"We need your knowledge," Yatham said. "We have long trails before us. You've already walked many of those trails."

"You've made friends among the road traders and traveling merchants from your days as an innkeeper," Theel added. "You know many who might lend their aid. You know ways in and out of this city, ways that will help us avoid the Iatan."

"The Iatan have not cut off the western roads," Guarn said. "You can go that way. You can take the Swan's Gate out of Old City and, best of all, you won't need the aid of your drunken uncle to do it."

"We can't pass through any of the city gates," Theel said.

"Why is that?"

"We need a different route," Theel answered. "We need to go south by way of Trader's Cave."

"The Trader's Cave," Guarn said, taking a large drag of his gnarled cigar. "That's the way of smugglers and thieves, desperates and scoundrels."

"Then the way of smugglers is the way we must take," Theel said. "And you can show me."

32

"That's right, I could." Guarn scratched his chin. "I know the route to the underground rivers of the Trader's Cave, and I know people who live and work there who can give aid."

"Yes, Uncle," Theel said. "Thank you."

"Keep your thanks," Guarn stated gruffly. "I've agreed to nothing."

"You will not help us?" Theel asked.

"The Trader's Cave is a dangerous place," Guarn said. "It is a place you might go if you wish to avoid the officers of the Overwatch. Only a man with something to hide would wish to go to such a place."

"I have nothing to hide," Theel lied. "I wish to pursue my quest."

"I don't believe you," Guarn said. "You are not leaving this city to pursue your quest. If that were true, you wouldn't be interested in the Trader's Cave. You'd be heading west out of Old City, like everyone else. But you don't want to be seen by any authorities. Why would that be?"

"Why do you question me?" Theel asked. "I only wish to do what Father would have wanted."

Guarn spit on the floor. "You and I both know your father would have wanted you to embark on your quest when it was first assigned to you. He would not have wanted you to waste this past week acting like a damned fool."

"I didn't—"

"What are you running from?" Guarn pressed.

Theel looked away again. "Nothing."

"Only criminals use the Trader's Cave," Guarn said.

"I'm not a criminal."

"Really?" Guarn said. "Then why do you need my help? Why don't you seek the help of your precious knighthood?"

Theel sighed. "Because I can't."

Guarn's anger softened. "Listen to me, boy," he stated evenly, keeping his voice low. "You must answer me. Are you in trouble?"

"No."

"I can't help you if you refuse to be truthful with me," Guarn stated. "What have you done?"

Theel sat quietly, his eyes focused on the lantern flame to avoid his uncle's questioning stare.

"They're blaming me," he said slowly. "But I didn't do it."

Guarn leaned in close, touching Theel's hand. "What are they blaming you for?"

Theel didn't answer, only rubbed at his temples. He said, "My head hurts."

Guarn's face suddenly registered realization. "Are you the one the Overwatch is looking for? Did you kill Quiddip Kile?"

Theel didn't move, nor did he say anything.

"Answer me," Guarn pressed.

"He doesn't remember," Yatham said.

Guarn's one eye grew wide. "He doesn't remember if he killed a man?"

"I didn't kill him," Theel said. "He killed himself. I think."

"You *think*? You're not certain?"

"We were on the second floor of the Glad Sire's," Yatham said. "Quiddip fell."

"You saw this?" Guarn asked.

"Yes, I saw it," Yatham said. "Theel wasn't at fault. Quiddip fell off the balcony. He was drunk."

"Then why is the Overwatch saying he was murdered?"

Yatham looked expectantly at Theel, who turned his eyes away, saying nothing. When his brother didn't answer the question, Yatham said quietly, "Theel and Quiddip were fighting."

"Oh, no," Guarn said. "The son of a lord is no one to trade blows with."

"I didn't start it," Theel said tersely.

"But you finished it," Guarn stated.

"Quiddip spit on our family," Theel said. "And he called me a coward."

"I see," Guarn said. "And everyone drinking at Glad Sire's saw this happen?"

"Everyone," Yatham said.

Guarn sat back, nodding in understanding. "And now you're fleeing the law. You've been shirking your duty, avoiding your quest, and now you've killed a man."

"I didn't kill anyone," Theel mumbled.

"And not just any man," Guarn said. "You killed the nephew of Hiram Kile, Lord Protector of Fal Daran, and patriarch of the wealthiest, most powerful noble house west of the Dividers."

"I know who Hiram Kile is," Theel said.

"And now you have the Overwatch looking for you, the officers of the Keepers of Law and Order, every soldier loyal to House Kile, the Knights of the Southern Cross, and the First Guardian—all hunting you down," Guarn said. "And you've chosen to bring all of this to my doorstep? Had you considered telling me any of this?"

Theel didn't say anything.

"Do you realize what might happen to me if they discovered I gave you aid in fleeing the city?" Guarn asked.

"They would take away this palace we're sitting in?" Theel guessed.

"Now is not the proper time for mirth, boy," Guarn said. "If they discovered that I gave you my help, there'd be a noose waiting for me. They'd hang me! They wouldn't care who my brother was."

"If you don't help, they'll hang *me*!" Theel said.

"Has that sobered you up?" Guarn asked.

"Yes."

"I don't believe you."

"Please, Uncle," Theel begged. "I need to leave this city."

Guarn leaned back, lit another cigar, inhaled, exhaled, and took another sip of Theel's drink.

"Please," Theel repeated. "Please help me."

Guarn sighed and flicked his cigar with his three-fingered hand.

"What is your destination?" he asked.

"Show us the way to Trader's Cave," Theel said. "That is all we need."

"That is not what I asked."

"We travel to the Outlands," Yatham said. "To Ebon South."

Guarn's face twitched, then he looked into his drink. "Ebon South." He said it slowly, as if the words stung him. "That is a long walk."

"Have you ever traveled to the Outlands, Uncle?" Yatham asked.

"Yes, long ago," Guarn said, rubbing the stumps of his fingers. "Your father served House Stormdell in Ebon South for a time, many years ago. I paid him a visit once, much to my regret."

"Then you know the way?" Theel asked.

"Aye," Guarn said, looking sad. "I know the way. It is not a short or simple road."

"It is not a short or simple quest," Yatham said.

"Will you help us?" Theel asked.

"Perhaps."

"Perhaps?"

"Do you have what it takes to walk all the way to the Outlands?" Guarn asked.

"What do you mean?" Theel asked.

"Are you going to walk all the way to the Outlands?" Guarn asked. "Or are you going to quit and give up before you are halfway there?"

"I'll go wherever you want. Just get me started."

"Are you leaving this city to pursue your quest?" Guarn asked. "Or are you running from the law?"

"I'm running from the law, Uncle. Isn't that clear?" Theel asked. "If I am captured, I am dead. What does the quest matter if I am dead?"

"You cannot run from your problems, Theel."

"Yes I can," Theel said. "I'm rather quick when I wish to be."

"You can't run *from* bad things," Guarn said. "But you can run *toward* good things."

36

"What does that mean?"

"You should be chasing your quest," Guarn said. "Not fleeing the law."

"There is no difference."

"Yes, there is," Guarn said. "There is a difference because I say there is. If I help you, I will help you begin your quest. I will not help you flee justice."

"Call it what you will," Theel said, his exasperation growing. "Just help me."

"You will make a promise to me," Guarn said. "Both of you."

"Name it," Yatham said.

"I can show you the way to the Trader's Cave," Guarn said. "I can show you the smuggler's route under the mountains to the Toden River Valley ..."

"Thank you," Theel said.

" ... but if I do, you promise me that your journey will not end there," Guarn said. "Once you reach the Toden River, you will not go any direction but toward the Outlands. You will not stop, and you won't look back until you are in Ebon South, pursuing your quest for knighthood."

"I will try," Theel said.

"You will do more than try," Guarn said. "If the Overwatch discovers that I helped you, I will hang. Someone is going to pay for Quiddip's death. They won't care if it's the killer, or his uncle."

"I cannot keep you from the gallows by walking to Ebon South," Theel said. "My Warrior Baptism has no bearing on whether or not you are arrested."

"That is true," Guarn said. "But it does have a bearing on whether or not I will help you. If you do not promise to chase your quest, I will not show you the way. Instead, I will give you over to the authorities and ask for a reward."

"You would not do that to me!"

"How many wagons of coin do you suppose Hiram Kile would pay to see his nephew's killer at the end of a rope?" Guarn asked. "Perhaps enough to fix my leaky roof?"

"You wouldn't dare betray your own blood," Theel snarled.

Guarn waved Theel off with a trail of cigar smoke, unimpressed with his ugly tone. "Make me the promise, and you'll never have to know."

"We have no intention of veering away from the quest," Yatham said calmly, obviously trying to take the edge out of the conversation.

"You have a good and honorable heart, Yatham," Guarn said. "I have no doubt the quest has been your goal from the start. But it is not *your* quest. It is your brother's quest, and you cannot force him to do the right thing. If you could, you would have done so a week ago. This decision belongs to Theel. Promise me, boy."

"I don't understand why this is necessary," Theel said stubbornly.

"It is necessary ... " Guarn took a slow and deliberate drag of his cigar, " ... because I say it is."

Yatham poked Theel in the shoulder. "Promise him, brother. We have no time to bargain over this."

"Why do you insist upon this?" Theel asked.

Guarn's one good eye had never held so much seriousness as it did now. "Because it is time your wretched life found some meaning."

"And you presume this promise will give meaning to my life?" Theel asked.

"Not this promise," Guarn said. "Warrior Baptism. Your quest for knighthood. If you run away and hide like a frightened child, you have accomplished nothing."

"Not so," Theel said. "I will have accomplished the feat of not swinging from the gallows for a murder I did not commit. I will have saved my own life."

"Which means nothing if you choose to do nothing with that life you saved," Guarn insisted. "But if you fulfill this quest, you will accomplish something real. You will achieve Warrior Baptism. You will rise to knighthood. You will learn to be a man."

"Now you sound like my father," Theel said.

"That's because I agree with your father," Guarn said. "You have the potential for so much. It is time for you to realize that. So many have sacrificed for you. It is time you took all that was given you and used it for something. You must not allow your life to become a waste."

"That is a splendid thought, Uncle. Perhaps I should operate a tavern located in a collapsing shed with a leaky roof?" Theel suggested. "Perhaps I should serve watered beer to a room full of ghosts, simply passing the time until death takes me? What happened to *your* potential, Uncle? Have you not wasted it?"

Now it was Guarn's turn to look away in shame. He nodded his head slowly, studying his own bar top as if memorizing each crack in the wood.

"All my life I've wasted what was given me," he said sadly. "It is time for that to change. It is time for both of us—you and me—to change. It is time for both of us to grow up."

"And if I choose not to?" Theel asked.

"That is no choice at all," Guarn answered.

"Why isn't it my choice?" Theel asked. "Why can't I do what I wish to do with my life? Perhaps I prefer to be a worthless drunk like you, Uncle."

"I'm not a worthless drunk."

"Really? Since when?"

"Since now."

"What will you do now to make yourself worthy?" Theel asked snidely. "What will you do to realize your potential?"

"I will aid you in making the proper choices in this difficult time, since your father is no longer here to guide you," Guarn said. "And I do this despite great personal risk."

"What does that mean?" Theel asked.

"I will honor my brother's memory," Guarn said. "And I will show my love for his son by doing what I can to help him in his greatest time of need, even though it might mean my life."

"So you've agreed?" Theel asked. "You will help me flee the city?"

"I will not help you flee the city," Guarn said. "But I will help you begin your quest."

"Thank you, Uncle," Yatham said. "This is the right thing."

"I will help you to leave this city, to pursue your quest, once you make your promise to me that your quest for Warrior Baptism is what I now purchase with the terrible risk I take in helping you."

"Still?" Theel said. "Still you insist on extracting a promise?"

"Yes, I do. You will promise me," Guarn pressed. "You will travel south to the Outlands, and nowhere else. The only acceptable way for you to fail in your quest for Warrior Baptism is if you are killed or captured by the Overwatch."

Theel sighed. "I promise."

"You will not fail," Guarn said.

"Not unless I am killed or captured."

"That is what I wished to hear," Guarn said, satisfied. "I will show you the way out of the city, and more," Guarn answered. "If you promise me to do all you can to fulfill your quest, I promise to do all I can to aid you."

"Thank you, Uncle," Yatham repeated.

"I can top off your canteens with water and wine," Guarn went on. "I can give you some food, enough to keep your bellies full until you reach the Toden River Valley. You know how to work a canoe paddle?"

"Yes," Yatham said.

"No," Theel said.

"You'll learn fast enough," Guarn said. "I'll get you work moving freight through the Trader's Cave. You'll be less suspicious if you are transporting something. I'll see that it's something light of weight that will not slow you down. And you should shed your rich clothing. You must not make an impression. You want to be forgettable, to blend in with the smugglers and thieves."

Theel looked down at himself. "This is my clothing. This is what I will wear."

"Your armor is made from the hide of the bullosk," Guarn said. "Men dressed like you do not frequent the Trader's Cave."

"Have you forgotten, Uncle?" Theel said. "According to the promise I made you, I must pursue my knight's quest upon leaving the city. I will not do so without my armor."

"As you wish," Guarn said. "They don't ask a lot of questions in the Trader's Cave, but two rich buckleshoes paddling through in a hurry will get more notice than peasant oarsmen transporting crates, so at least cover yourself up."

"I appreciate your advice."

"Once you reach the valley, make for Axelhead," Guarn said. "There is still freight moving south, which means there are caravans and guides for hire. Find one who knows the land around Krillian's Cut, the Sister Cities, and the Gray Mounds. Avoid the Narrows. Go through the Sister Cities. From there, it's not long to Ebon South."

"Thank you, Uncle," Yatham said.

"Seek no help from the River Lords, the Alisters, or the Overlies. They're just as likely to send you back to Fal Daran in chains as help you," Guarn said. "I can give you places with good stops along the way where you will find people who knew and respected your father—the Trader Hoachim in Axelhead, Micka the Wheelmonger in Herr Ridge, Jarcet the Sentinel of Calfborn, Damazaar of the Temple of Evosk in Kansann, and Kildsa the Craftworker in Dwelthia. These are good people who will give aid if trouble befalls you."

"We will seek out those allies once we are free of Fal Daran," Theel said.

"Those aren't the only names to remember," Guarn went on. "Once you reach the Outlands, find a knight of Stormdell named Barzil the Blood Axe. He is a loyal Knight of the Southern Cross and holds respect for your father's memory. You'll find him in Storm Hall at the center of Ebon South. He will give you guidance, show you the way, and may even lend his axe to your quest."

"Thank you, Uncle," Yatham said.

"Yes, thank you," Theel said. "Now will you show us the way to the Trader's Cave?"

"One more thing," Guarn said. "You will be walking some very dangerous roads. You might never return to Fal Daran. And even if you do, the Iatan could storm this city any day, destroying this place as they did the Eastern Kingdoms, leaving nothing here for you to return to."

"What are you saying, Uncle?" Theel asked.

"I fear we may never meet again."

Guarn sat back, staring into the darkness, his face very sad and very tired. "Anything might happen after today. The three of us know as well as anyone that death is never far. You might freeze in the mountains. I might swing from the gallows. There is something I promised your father I would do, and this may be my last chance to do it."

"What is it?" Theel asked.

Guarn didn't answer with words. He put out his cigar, then pushed himself to his feet, his knees creaking louder than the floorboards. Then he shuffled away with stiff legs and a bent back, disappearing into the darkness behind the bar. He was gone for many minutes, leaving Theel more anxious with each second that passed.

"Where did he go?" Theel whispered.

"Quiet, brother," Yatham said.

When the old man returned, he carried a worn wineskin and three fine crystal glasses. He gently placed them on the bar top, one before each brother, the last one for himself.

"These are wonderful glasses, Uncle," Yatham said.

The flickering lantern light showed Guarn's grizzled old face stretching into a smile.

"You boys know I cherish elegance and beauty above all," he said.

This brought laughter from the brothers, a brief moment of something shared between the three of them. Almost like they were a family.

"Strange to see something so beautiful in a place such as this," Theel said. "What's the occasion?"

"We drink to our future," Guarn answered. He carefully held the wineskin under one arm and used the other to direct sipping portions into each of the glasses. "This, my boys, is wine from the Kingdom of Sidon. The last I have. And after what the Iatan did to Sidon, it's likely the last we'll ever see. It's the very finest."

"Thank you again, Uncle," Yatham said.

"I knew this was long coming," Guarn said sadly, sniffing at his glass. "I was a fool to deny it; a fool to think it wouldn't happen. I could never keep your father from his zeal for crusade. Couldn't stop him from pushing the knighthood on you. I've tried my best, but as you know, the drink always leaves my best in tatters."

"Uncle, this isn't a sad day," Yatham said.

"It's sad this day had to come," Guarn said. "I shouldn't let it grieve me, but I know what awaits you in the Outlands."

"Warrior Baptism is what awaits me," Theel said.

Guarn nodded. "I know that. It will not be easy. Nor will it be forgiving."

"It is only the beginning," Yatham said. "The responsibilities of knighthood are considerably more demanding."

"As the family of a knight, a family torn apart by his devotion to his duty, we know that better than most," Guarn said. "But let us forget that for now. Instead we will drink fine wine together and be a family once again. Just for one sip of wine."

"Thank you for this aid you give us, Uncle," Theel said. "I mean that."

"I give you my help because I believe in you," Guarn said. "You will one day be everything they expect of you. I do not doubt it. You will be a great knight one day. And if I'm not there to tell you, always remember that your pathetic, drunken uncle loved you. Remember that, despite all the uncivil things said between us."

"I will remember that," Theel said. "I promise you."

"Now," Guarn said, setting his glass down. "I, too, have a promise to fulfill. A promise to my brother, your father. I told him I would do this."

"Do what?" Theel asked.

"I must give you something," Guarn answered. "Something I've had for safekeeping for many years."

He reached down behind the bar and produced a sheathed sword and belt. The lantern light danced and flashed across the weapon's hilt as he lay it across the bar top before his nephew.

"You know this weapon," Guarn said.

Theel's eyes were wide and staring as he nodded in acknowledgment. It was the most magnificent sword he'd ever beheld, with a golden hilt fashioned to resemble an angel with her wings as the crosspiece. The angel's golden skin captured the light of the lantern and multiplied its effects until her face sparkled like sunlight on the water. And as he sat, transfixed by her beauty, Theel remembered the name that was given her:

Battle Hymn.

As magnificent as her hilt was, it was the blade that made Battle Hymn so extraordinary. Forged from the rarest, unbreakable steel, it was lighter than wood, but harder than diamonds. Shadowsteel, it was called, named so for the tricks it played on one's eyes as the ripples of folded metal constantly shifted in color with every movement of the blade. The process by which shadowsteel was created had been lost since before the Sundering of the World. There were but a few dozen examples of shadowsteel in all the Seven Kingdoms, but precious few as splendid as Battle Hymn.

Theel sometimes found himself wondering what fate had befallen the sword. He hadn't seen it in years, and always assumed his uncle had lost it or sold it. It was worth several lifetimes of the king's work, and could have been traded for enough coin to buy his uncle the finest inn of the city forty times over. Yet it seemed his uncle had chosen to keep one of the finest weapons in all of Embriss hidden away in his filthy little tavern with the leaky roof.

And now the sword was here again, gleaming, just as she had in Theel's memories when she was hanging on the wall of his uncle's home throughout his childhood, always a few inches above his straining boy's fingers. Now it was within his reach. He need only reach out and take it.

"The sword of your father," Guarn said. "I know how you admired it all those years, but were never allowed to touch it. I knew one day you would come to me as you have today. I knew on that day I would give you this sword."

Theel didn't take his eyes from his father's weapon. "Thank you, Uncle," he said softly, his voice full of reverence and sadness.

"It is time you carried Battle Hymn at your side," Guarn said. "She is your birthright."

Theel reached out and took the sword by the sheath, still reluctant to touch the hilt's golden surface. "Thank you, Uncle. I will care for her."

Guarn nodded his head, pleased. "Then she will care for you," he said. "Take her with you on your quest. Look at her every day, and remember who you are, where you came from."

"I will, Uncle," Theel whispered.

Then Guarn raised his glass. "To our futures."

"To our futures," Theel echoed. "To yours and mine."

"We are worthless, sodding drunks no longer," Guarn said.

"Even I will drink to that," Yatham said.

"Right now we must sip our wine together as a family," Guarn said. "We must use these last few moments we have to make merry and be grateful for one another, for the Trader's Cave awaits, and with it an uncertain future."

"To the quest," Yatham said. "To Warrior Baptism."

"To Warrior Baptism," Guarn said.

Three glasses clinked, and everyone drank except Theel. Instead, he only fingered his glass, unable to stop looking at Battle Hymn. The angel's eyes were closed, but it felt as if, through her, his father was still watching him.

45

Chapter 3

The boat was oddly shaped, not even symmetrical, reminding Theel of half a peanut shell split lengthwise floating in the water. It was further proof that Uncle Guarn had very limited resources. It was a vessel barely seaworthy by its appearance, created and maintained with almost no care. It appeared to be carved from one large piece of wood, a hollowed-out tree trunk, broken several times in many places, then mended several times with imperfect fixes that leaked noticeably.

Yatham sat in the front half of the peanut shell, a large pile of crates right behind him. Theel sat in the back, unable to see anything, not just because of the wooden crates stacked between him and his brother, but also because there was no sun where they were, no warmth, and no light. There was only silent, cold darkness, the sort one would find when traveling an underground river beneath a mountain.

The single torch they carried was fastened to the bow of the boat, offering Yatham a limited view of the direction they were headed, offering Theel no view at all. He saw nothing but the black, square outlines of the crates sitting before him. To Yatham's vision, the torch illuminated a small circle of black water in the immediate vicinity, which did nothing to show him which direction to go, only provided a last-second warning in the event the boat was headed toward one of the jagged rock walls of the Trader's Cave.

Actual direction was provided by a series of fires placed at intervals in the caves, some as small as lanterns hanging from the rock walls, others as large as bonfires burning on the many subterranean beaches. But most of these fires were large torches floating atop airtight barrels anchored down at intervals throughout the length of the river. The distance between these signal fires varied, but whenever a boat traveling on the river came upon one, its crew was able to see the next flaming beacon in the distance, another in a long trail that led through the Trader's Cave, under the mountains to the Toden River Valley.

The Trader's Cave was, in most places, dark and cold, and quiet as death. But it was not entirely lifeless. There were those who lived and worked there, a small but separate society of outcasts whose fortunes never quite bloomed properly in the light of the sun. They inhabited a small number of settlements scattered here and there throughout the caves, some as small as a few shacks built atop wooden stilts that rose out of the water, or a few wooden crates stacked around a campfire on a beach. The smallest of these was Candle Rock, home to a single man, the famous hermit named Two Times. The largest was Barter Town, built in a chimney cavern that left the buildings exposed to starlight and an occasional glimpse of the moon, but never the sun.

Theel and Yatham reached Barter Town just before noondark, the time of day opposite midnight, when the Island of Behe Kang, floating in the sky above Thershon, cast its shadow across the Seven Kingdoms, signaling to all that the workday was halfway to its conclusion. As they entered the chimney cavern, Theel could see the rays of the sun reaching down, cutting the darkness at a sharp angle. The light slowly crept down the cave wall toward the buildings of Barter Town, and was just about to touch the rooftops when the Island of Behe Kang passed by above and snuffed out the light, stopping the hole in the chimney ceiling like a cork in a bottle. Anywhere else on Thershon, the midday phenomenon known as noondark appeared as a black splotch in the sky, with the rays of the sun spreading out around Behe Kang like the petals of a black-eyed daisy. Not so in the Trader's Cave. Instead there appeared a hazy, brown ring of sunlight high above, as if a dirty halo crowned the rooftops of Barter Town.

It was one of the oddest sights Theel had ever seen—noondark in Barter Town. It was the first of many odd sights his quest would show him.

The brothers spent much of the previous evening following their Uncle Guarn's directions up the Southwall, a portion of the city that had overgrown the hills to the south, and partway up the side of the mountain known as the Sky Horn. Theel had hoped to enter the Trader's Cave via the canals at the base of the mountain, but, as Guarn explained, that was the way the water flowed into the city, not the way out. To take that route would be to paddle upstream against the currents, and against all other river traffic for miles. It would be a very difficult task that, if undertaken, would only serve to draw attention to their escape. Instead, they needed to climb the Southwall, then take the branch of Trader's Cave that flowed southward out of the city under the daunting peak of the Sky Horn, eventually joining up with the Toden River. The Toden flowed west, out of the mountains, and toward freedom.

Theel did not like this advice. It meant staying within the city walls for a few more hours while they traveled up the Southwall, a route which took them through some of the wealthier and better-guarded sections of the city. They would be dodging officers of the Overwatch every step of the way. But as Guarn said, the Southwall was one of the few areas of the city where Theel's rich clothing would help him to fit in, and the authorities would never expect the killer of Quiddip Kile to be hiding in plain sight. Much like all of Guarn's assurances, this did little to relax Theel's mind.

Climbing the Southwall provided a spectacular view of Fal Daran. Theel had seen the city from great heights many times before, but never from this perspective. Always before, he'd been looking down from the Hall of Seven Swords on the northwest side of the city. The view from Southwall showed him many sections of the city he'd never seen before, including New City and the plains of Clan Aramorun, where the armies of the Iatan were encamped.

It was the first time he'd seen the invaders, even from a distance—the first time he was witness to the immense size of the army preparing to subjugate Fal Daran. Theel and Yatham reached the top of Southwall at dusk, a time of day that provided just enough light to see the vastness of the encampment. It stretched in all directions, covering every piece of land in sight like a giant sore on the skin of Thershon. But it was also just dark enough that Theel could see the stars that filled the cloudless sky, covering the floor of heaven just as the campfires of the Iatan covered the plains below. The whole scene brought to mind something he'd heard a knight of Aramorun say to describe the numbers of soldiers he had seen marching under the banners of the Iatan Empire:

"The Iatan look upon the stars with scorn," he said, "For the light of their campfires burn brighter than all the stars of creation, and outnumber them twofold."

And that was not the worst of it.

When they reached the top of Southwall, Guarn's directions told them to keep climbing until they found a mule trail that would take them around the eastern face of Sky Horn Mountain. The trail led to a secret entrance to the Trader's Cave, Guarn said, one that neither the Keepers of Law and Order nor the Overwatch were aware of. Unfortunately, the trail wound its way up some steep piles of rocks and across the edges of several cliffs, forming a path so treacherous it could not be safely traveled in the darkness of nighttime. So Theel and Yatham waited for a few hours until dawn, trying unsuccessfully to sleep on the freezing, windswept mountainside.

It was a horribly uncomfortable night, and it seemed the sun would never rise. But after hours of shivering, chattering teeth, and numbed fingers and toes, the blessed morning finally did arrive, bringing with it some much needed warmth, as well as enough light to resume travel. But it also brought something very unwelcome; a view of what was happening on the plains below.

A column of soldiers separated from the main body of the Iatan Army, a long, dark line that slithered across the plains like a great serpent of war. They moved southward toward the Toden River Valley, thousands of men, carrying thousands of points of steel, with a thousand histories bathed in blood. Packed shoulder to shoulder on the narrow road, heads down to protect against the whipping wind, their tread spoke the imposing rumble of numbers, displacing dried earth, kicking up a storm of dust that defiantly hovered and obscured much of their strength from view.

Cavalry rode at their vanguard, riders numbering in the hundreds. As Theel and Yatham watched, these horseman picked up their pace, separating themselves from the column to lead the way into the valley, an action clearly meant to open a path for the infantry to march through the mountains and into the lands of Embriss. Once on the other side of the Dividers, these Iatan soldiers would be less than a day's march from the western gates of Fal Daran. They would be in a position to close the circle around the city, ready to tighten the noose, and ready squeeze the heart of Embriss. The oldest and most beautiful city on all of Thershon would be at the mercy of her enemies, waiting to be surrounded, starved, conquered, and destroyed. And there would be nothing in the world to stop it.

Those troops the brothers saw heading into the Toden River Valley represented yet another in a long series of promises the Iatan had broken. It was an undeniable act of aggression, a non-verbal declaration of war upon the largest of the Seven Kingdoms and its greatest city. And Theel knew he wasn't the only one to see it this way. When he looked up the mountain, he could see that the warning fires had been lit. The Knights of the Southern Cross had lookouts positioned in the mountains to the north and south of the city, monitoring the Iatan armies and all that they did. When the morning dawned, those lookouts saw the same thing Theel and Yatham saw, and those fires were meant to alert the city that the Iatan were on the move.

It meant terrible things for Fal Daran, but potentially meant something worse for Theel and Yatham.

"How many soldiers do you suppose there were?" Yatham asked from the front of the boat.

"More than enough," Theel answered.

He sat with his oar across his lap, struggling to pack his pipe in the darkness without spilling.

"At least four thousand in the lead column, I'd guess," Yatham said. "Probably twice that coming up behind."

"Probably," Theel said. "Do you have any matches?"

"I already gave them to you."

"Oh, sorry," Theel said. "You're right. Here they are."

He tried repeatedly to strike a match, failed several times, and finally lost it over the side.

"Damn the world," he said. "I dropped it."

"What is the matter?" Yatham asked. "Too inebriated? Too smoked to smoke?"

"I'm not smoked," Theel said indignantly. "Just can't see what I'm doing. It's so dark in here."

"That is because we are in a cave, brother."

"Are we?" Theel said, striking another match. "I hadn't noticed."

"Are you paddling?"

"Of course," Theel lied. He lit his pipe and took a deep drag, watching as the bowl flared in the darkness.

"Have you forgotten?" Yatham said. "It is *your* neck we are trying to save from the noose, not mine."

"I'm sorry, but I need this," Theel said.

"If your nerves are frayed from fleeing the law, you might consider helping me to paddle the boat," Yatham said. "That would be a more sensible response to the problem than smoking to forget the problem exists."

"I'm not smoking to forget," Theel insisted. "I'm smoking to calm my thoughts, to help me focus. I have many things on my mind."

"I have many things on my mind as well. Would you like to know what is helping me to focus?" Yatham asked. "Paddling."

"Good then, keep paddling," Theel said around his pipe stem. "Your focus is of the utmost importance."

He took one more pull on his pipe and emptied the bowl by banging it loudly against the side of the boat.

"There, you see?" Theel said, banging the pipe loudly. "I'm finished. And now I will paddle."

"Good," Yatham replied. "I'm glad for you. Perhaps now we will survive this."

"Perhaps." Theel picked up his oar and thrust it into the water.

"Perhaps you will survive long enough to become a knight."

"I no longer care to achieve knighthood."

"I know," Yatham said. "Liquors and leaf are all you care for."

"There is no reason to wish for anything greater."

"Yes, there is," Yatham stated tersely. "I wish you didn't have such a nose for trouble. I wish we weren't fleeing the city like two criminals. I wish we could have left through one of the eastern gates like decent clansmen. I wish we were on the roads, riding horses."

"Of course you do," Theel retorted. "Horses are all you care for. I'm surprised you weren't born with four legs."

"That's not funny."

"And hooves."

"Are these the heavy thoughts that have kept you from helping me paddle the boat?"

"No, it is the idea of death that troubles my mind," Theel said. "Yours and mine, specifically."

"We will not die," Yatham answered.

"We are trapped in a vice," Theel said. "The city Overwatch are behind us and the Iatan are in front."

"The Overwatch and the Iatan are small concerns."

"Small concerns?" Theel asked, incredulous.

"You are on a knight's quest, brother," Yatham said. "We travel toward your Warrior Baptism. The Overwatch and Iatan are minor obstacles compared to what awaits you."

"Minor obstacles?" Theel said. "Forgive me, but I was under the impression you were aware of that army of Iatan soldiers? The one that is marching south around Sky Horn Mountain as we speak?"

"Yes? What of it?"

"That army is no minor obstacle," Theel said. "It's a *large* obstacle. And it is headed to the same place as we."

"How can you know that?"

"That's where their horses are going," Theel said. "The infantry will follow the cavalry. They will try to cross the Toden River at Axelhead, exactly where this river is taking us."

"We will reach Axelhead long before the infantry."

"But not before the cavalry," Theel said. "You above everyone should know how fast cavalry can move."

"Then we will wait until the cavalry are gone," Yatham replied. "We'll have to slip through and cross the river behind them before the infantry arrives."

"That will be risky."

"A knight's quest carries with it some degree of risk," Yatham said. "Or so I hear."

"This is not a knight's quest."

"It isn't?"

"No, it isn't," Theel said.

"Have you forgotten already?" Yatham asked. "Was your promise to Uncle Guarn so worthless?"

"My promise was not worthless," Theel answered.

"What if he is arrested by the Overwatch?" Yatham said. "Our uncle might hang because he gave us aid. Does that not bother you?"

"It bothers me."

"You may just have two deaths on your conscience before this is done." Yatham said.

"Three."

"What?"

"Three deaths," Theel said. "My promise to Uncle Guarn was not worthless. I am grateful for what he has done, and I owe him much, but I can do little to help him now. And there are simply matters that are more pressing."

"What is more pressing than honoring our uncle? Than keeping your word to him?" Yatham asked.

"Remaining alive."

"Now you'd prefer to live," Yatham said. "But before you didn't care. You even talked of suicide. Which is it?"

"I do not wish to die, brother," Theel answered. "But I do not wish to live."

"Do you wish for anything?"

"Yes, I do," Theel said. "I wish to not drown in this cave. And I wish to be through Axelhead before the Iatan Army arrives."

"At least you've decided that much."

"I do not make my decisions for your convenience," Theel grunted. "My choices come when I deem necessary."

"Sometimes choices are necessary before you deem them," Yatham said.

"I'd hoped leaving the city would free me of such knightly rhetoric," Theel said. "If you insist on filling my ears with that talk, I might free myself from *you*."

"Then who will do the paddling?"

"This boat needs only one oar to move successfully," Theel said. "You've proven that already."

"I've proven I can move the boat successfully," Yatham said. "While you've proven only that you can smoke successfully."

"Very successfully."

"At least you are accomplished at one thing," Yatham said.

"Smoking?" Theel guessed.

"Running away from decisions," Yatham said.

"And drinking," Theel added. "Don't forget drinking."

"There is no difference," Yatham said. "Drinking and smoking is just another way of running."

"What must I do to please you?"

"Just like Uncle Guarn said," Yatham said. "Stop running away from things. Start running *toward* something."

54

"Such as what?"

"Such as your quest!" Yatham said, exasperated. "Such as Warrior Baptism."

"What would you have me do?" Theel asked. "Swim back the way we came? Jump off the mountain and run to attack the Iatan Army?"

"I would appreciate that," Yatham said. "It would mean you've made a decision and are acting upon it. That would be a welcome change."

"As you've said a hundred times before."

"Consider my words and I'll stop repeating them."

"Consider working your paddle and quieting your mouth," Theel said.

"I've never seen a man so in need of a knight's quest as you," Yatham said.

"I don't need anything."

"You need to believe in something," Yatham said. "You need to learn what it is to fight for something."

"You think my quest will give me faith and the will to fight?" Theel questioned. "This quest is about Warrior Baptism. It is about earning knighthood, and nothing more."

"Warrior Baptism is not just about earning the right to be called knight," Yatham said. "It is about *becoming* one. I've seen squires raised to knighthood, and so have you. Remember Yagmar? I saw him leave for his quest and I saw him come back. I saw the Keeper of the Craft give him his knight's shield, and when he strapped it to his chest, everyone saw it in his eyes. He was a different person. He'd found his heart."

"He found his heart?" Theel said incredulously. "Was his heart lying out there somewhere for him to find on his quest? Did he pick it up, stuff it back in his chest, and come back a different person?"

"Yes, he did."

"How do you know that?" Theel asked.

"I could see it in him," Yatham answered. "There was a change about him, more than just his adornments of rank."

"Well, if I hope to feel such a change in me, I'd better rush to Ebon South with all haste," Theel said. "The Keeper of the Craft must have seen my heart down there somewhere, floating in a mud puddle."

"You mock me."

"But what if my heart isn't down there?" Theel wondered. "What if it's up by Kara Moor? They might be knocking it around with their swords, playing a jolly game of yardspot."

"The Keeper is right about you," Yatham repeated. "I've never seen a squire so in need of a knight's quest."

"No," Theel said. "The Keeper did mention the Outlands and Ebon South specifically. He told me of a priest named Father Brashfor. Perhaps the good father has my heart squirreled away in his collection box."

"Who is Father Brashfor?" Yatham asked. "Why did the Keeper mention him?"

"Why do you care to know?" Theel asked.

Yatham sighed. "I know your quest for Warrior Baptism does not compel you to find some random priest who runs an Outlander church. Who is this man? What is it about him that makes the Keeper speak of him?"

"The Keeper explained little to me," Theel said. "He only told me to seek Father Brashfor in Ebon South, for the priest may give aid to my search. He must be a wise man of some sort."

"What is it Father Brashfor will help you find?" Yatham asked.

"In my quest for Warrior Baptism, I have been given the honor and duty of chasing one of the greatest myths conjured by the simple minds of men," Theel said.

"Which is?" Yatham asked.

"My quest for Warrior Baptism requires me to search for the Blessed Soul of Man, the little boy whose coming was prophesied before the Sundering of the World," Theel said. "He would be a man by now, for the Keeper tells me he came into the world twenty years ago."

Chapter 4

Twenty years before the Iatan invaded the Seven Kingdoms, the Outlander town of Ebon South experienced a period of seven days in which the sun didn't rise. The moon didn't appear during that time, either. Nor did any stars. In fact, the days and nights seemed to vanish completely, replaced by a featureless orange haze that lasted without relenting for the entire week. There was no sky, and no clouds; only the occasional glimpse of Behe Kang floating in the blur, as if the town sat at the bottom of a bowl of tomato soup. It was the last day of this week that an assassin named Aeoxoea fell from the sky.

She didn't know where she was falling from, where she was falling to, or even that she was falling at all until her feet struck the ground. Though she was naked and it was winter, she felt no discomfort as her toes broke the crust of the snow. She looked up at the orange sky and smiled, as if it confirmed something she was already suspecting.

"Now, Aeoxoea," she asked herself. "Where are you?"

Freezing wind and swirling snow told her she was in the middle of a snowstorm. A street full of blood and death told her she was in the middle of a war.

The bodies of dozens of men lay scattered in the trampled snow at her feet. Some were frozen and silent, with limbs contorted by their final moments. Some were still warm and moving, but loud with screams of pain and pleas for help. There were pale-skinned humans, but many more were of a race the assassin had never seen before.

These were short, bestial humanoids, with splotchy, gray skin and large, black eyes. Their facial features were dull and brutish, somewhere between a human and an ape, but they also had wide, dog-like mouths, slightly stretched and elongated, and filled with rows of sharp teeth designed for tearing and shredding. Though many of them appeared to carry spears forged from black iron, it was clear they had no aversion to using their teeth as weapons too, judging by how many of them had mouths and faces covered with redness. Aeoxoea noticed that most of them were barefoot, likely to allow the use of opposable toes.

There seemed to be a lull in the fighting, but it wouldn't last long. The assassin watched as more of the human soldiers rushed into the street, one of them lifting a green banner out of the bloody snow. The wind caught the fabric to show a white horned animal, the same symbol emblazoned on the surcoats of many of the men who now moved among the bodies. They gathered discarded spears and swords, pulled arrows from the dead, and dragged their wounded out of harm's way. A hundred paces distant, a group of women hurriedly gathered little children together to load them into a pair of mule carts.

Aeoxoea heard bowstrings and saw human archers on surrounding rooftops, firing down at unseen enemies. Drums pounded in the distance, a steady rhythm answered by a horn blast. A man with tattooed arms and a silver, hand-sized shield strapped to his chest stood in front of the green banner, swinging his sword above his head.

"House Stormdell, unite!" he shouted, his words puffing in the cold air. "Men of Ebon South, unite! Rally to me!"

The men hurriedly began to gather together, drawing their weapons and forming a line beneath the green banner.

"The zoths will come back to bring us battle once again," the tattooed man shouted. "We must meet them here and we must stop them here. We must not surrender any more ground, or we surrender our children. Stand here and die, all men of Ebon South. Stand and die together, for your children and for your homes!"

Aeoxoea saw fear in the eyes of the soldiers, but it was a fear they were familiar with, a fear they'd known many times before. They joined their voices to the shouting of their leader, banging their weapons together. The distant drums pounded faster, a horn blast answered, and black-tipped spears began to fall from the orange murk above.

Then a fresh wall of sound rose and crashed over the humans, hundreds of voices joined into one shrill scream. The enemy was coming up the street fast, and they outnumbered these humans ten to one. The green banner fluttered, the tattooed man waved his sword, and the men in the street roared back in a response so paltry that it was completely swallowed by the battle cry of their enemies.

The numbers of black-tipped spears flying from the fog doubled, then tripled, and still the human soldiers stood their ground. They maintained their line and weathered the freezing wind and torrent of spears that swirled and slammed into them like raindrops in a hurricane.

The shrill screaming reached a crescendo as the front ranks of the zoths burst from the fog. If the street were a riverbed, it was an ocean of zoths that filled it to overflowing, a tidal wave of gray flesh and black iron about to crash against this insignificant wall of humans.

At the front of this horde was the zoth chieftain, an enormous beast the size of two men. He dressed himself in the remains of his victims, their flesh as his clothing, and their bones as his armor. A horned skull served as his helm, the eye sockets his visor slits, the handles of two knives his plumage. He ran several paces ahead of his warriors, a battering ram of gray muscle and scarred flesh, swinging two whips of spiked chain links already colored red.

The line of soldiers in the street did not waver, but the eyes of each man widened at the sight of this creature. This was a fear they had never known.

"Men of Ebon South!" their tattooed leader shouted, deflecting a spear to the ground with his sword. "It is now time!"

He looked at the two carts full with weeping children, the bigger ones holding the little ones. He looked at the women struggling with the mules, trying to keep them under control as the last children were loaded. Then he looked at his own men.

"We fight!"

He turned and charged toward the enemy horde, the green banner fluttering in the air behind him. Two dozen men swallowed their fear and followed, jumping bodies, slipping in the snow and mud, waving their weapons and screaming with raw throats.

While this was happening, Aeoxoea noticed a death blossom falling toward her, its orange petals spinning as it drifted to earth. It was warm-weather flora, and had no place in this snowy land, yet Aeoxoea saw nothing strange in its appearance. She caught the flower in her hand and lifted it to her nose, inhaling deeply.

The battle lines crashed together like a peal of thunder, followed by the din of savagery—ringing steel, thudding, splattering, screams and grunts, and gurgling death cries. The human soldiers fought with remarkable courage, but they were only a row of pebbles in the bottom of the riverbed and their formation was quickly washed away. The green banner fell, was raised, then fell again. In a matter of moments, the street became a scene of slaughter.

The zoths descended in groups of five or more upon single soldiers so outnumbered they didn't have a chance. Wherever Aeoxoea looked, the men were hacked to pieces while their enemies hooted the joy of their victory. But the human soldiers were successful in their sacrifice. She looked up the street and saw that the two mule carts had vanished. The children had escaped, up some street or down some alley. They were safe, for now.

Aeoxoea looked back in time to see an archer fall from a rooftop with a spear in his chest. This was the last human defender, she was certain. There were no more living soldiers anywhere in the street. Then she saw the tattooed man with the silver shield, somehow still on his feet. He was all alone, in the middle of an army of his enemies. But he was still alive, and he was still fighting.

He was an expert swordsman, possessing a level of skill and discipline that no zoth would ever know. Though he should have been dead long ago, he didn't appear to have suffered a single wound. He was covered with blood, but none of it was his own. And the speed at which the zoths attacked him was the speed at which they died. Everywhere he left a footprint in the snow, he also left the corpses of his enemies. He appeared to have no equal on this or any other field of battle. Until the zoth chieftain attacked him.

The enormous creature swung his spiked chains in huge arcs, making it nearly impossible for the human to get close enough to use his sword. And yet he still managed to do it, patiently and deliberately, ducking and jumping as nimbly as a fly refusing to be swatted. The attacks meant for him went astray, slamming into the ranks of the chieftain's own warriors, crushing their bones, and sweeping them off their feet.

The human ducked yet another lash of the whip, then snatched a spear from the ground all in one motion. He threw it at the face of his foe, but the chieftain turned his head and the spear tip bounced off the horned skull. The human used the distraction to roll forward and open the zoth's leg, just above the knee. Another feint with his sword and he spun to the chieftain's rear, slicing open the tendons at the back of the same knee. Against his will, the huge beast was forced to kneel.

The spiked chains didn't stop whipping, but they still couldn't find their mark. Spears began to fly anew, and the human knocked two away with his sword. He caught a third in his hand just as he ducked another chain whip. Spinning, he drew his sword across the chieftain's stomach, opening the flesh effortlessly. But he also spun right into the chieftain's fist. The enormous creature, with his belly gaping, should have been on the ground dying. Instead, he didn't react to the wound at all, and fed the human a face-full of knuckles wrapped in spiked chain links.

The blow should have killed the tattooed man. He was knocked on his back in the dirty snow, with blood bubbling from his face. But it didn't kill him. He crawled to his feet, slower this time, but still holding his sword and spear, and still prepared to fight.

Aeoxoea watched as the chieftain rose back to his full height as if he felt no pain. She looked at his leg and saw that the wounds were healed and replaced by thick, gray scars. It was as if he'd just undergone many months' worth of healing in a few seconds. At the same time, she could see the gash across his stomach closing. It was as if the zoth chieftain could command his body to heal itself as easily as he could command his hand to make a fist.

The tattooed man saw this just as well as Aeoxoea did; his enemy could heal, while he could not. And yet he didn't seem surprised, as if he already knew it was possible, or perhaps even inevitable. Aeoxoea knew that man had entered this battle knowing he was going to die. And now, when death loomed as large as ever, he still continued to fight.

The human and the zoth attacked each other at the same time, a spear flying and a whip lashing. The human was too slow to dodge, and the zoth didn't even try. The spear tip slammed into the chieftain's eye just as the chain whipped the human in the head.

The chieftain smiled and the human screamed as the chain wrapped around his neck. The zoth didn't seem to notice the spear protruding from his head. He took the chain in both hands and jerked it tight, choking off the human's cry of pain as the spikes sunk deeper.

The human was defeated and moments from death, held by the chain and unable to escape his enemy. So he charged, threw himself into the air, and plunged his sword into the chieftain's chest. If this enormous creature had a heart, the human had just cut it in half. But the zoth still showed no sign of pain. The human held the crosspiece of his sword with both hands, twisting the blade inside his enemy's body, and still it had no effect. The zoth threw the human to the ground and put his foot on the man's chest.

But the man still wasn't finished. He began to shout at the chieftain. It sounded like he recited the words to a pledge, or a creed of some kind.

"I, as a son of the Silvermarsh Clans, do commit myself, body, soul, and spirit, to the earthly warriors of the Southern Cross, to the Seven Kingdoms they protect—"

The chieftain spat on the ground, then jerked the chain so viciously that the man's head was torn from his shoulders, spinning high into the air.

The zoth warriors immediately rushed in, tearing the body to pieces as their leader pulled the spear out of his eye. He shook it above his head, his blood-smeared face and gaping maw roaring his victory.

Aeoxoea ignored all this and calmly crossed the street, stepping over bodies until she came to the place where the human's head lay in a red spot in the snow. She picked it up in both hands, holding it so the two were face to face. As she did this, slippery white tentacles slid out from between her ribs. Long and thin, and wriggling like snakes, they bared their fangs just before digging hungrily into the base of the man's head, nosing through the mangled flesh, and searching for blood vessels. The assassin closed her eyes and concentrated, feeling her heart thump harder at the strain of sharing her blood.

She waited patiently, her tentacles writhing in the air as gracefully as if dancing on the ocean currents. They held the man's head as a mother would hold her child, as if he was an infant about to awaken from a nap. Aeoxoea passed the time by twirling the death blossom against her lips, smiling as if it tickled.

Suddenly, the man's eyes flared open, watering, and blinking with fear and confusion. His lips moved wordlessly, then he looked at Aeoxoea, and his eyes widened with shock.

"No, kitten, I am not an angel," she whispered to him. "Quite the opposite."

Aeoxoea could not be seen when she wished to remain invisible, but this was a rare case where she chose otherwise. The man's eyes drank her in, from her face, to her hair, then to her tentacles, his confusion turning to panic. She knew it was much more than her white tentacles that gave him alarm, or the obvious comfort she felt in her nudity, even in the middle of a snowstorm. He may have seen white hair before, but probably not on a woman so young, and certainly not the sort that appeared weightless, licking at the air like curling, white flames. No inhabitant of this town had skin that shined like molten gold, or milky-white lips like those that kissed the orange flower in her hand. The pupils of Aeoxoea's eyes often shifted in their appearance, sometimes disappearing altogether, as they did now, becoming a deep crimson to allow her to see variations of heat. To help calm the man, she changed her eyes back to their natural appearance; black pupils with golden irises.

"I know that you are frightened," Aeoxoea said to the man. "Neither you, nor any of your people, have ever seen a being of my kind. That is because I have come to you from another island. I am but one of many visitors you can expect in the coming days. You should be grateful that I travel quicker than the others."

The man responded by moving his lips and grimacing, eyes darting about.

"I know it is quite rude of me to bring you back as I have," she purred. "But I have needs more pressing than your desire to die. I have questions, and the first is this: What is your name?"

The man's lips moved, but made no sound. His answer came into the assassin's mind through her tentacles.

"Sir Jassamar of Yarik, sworn sword of House Stormdell," the man said. "A Knight of the Southern Cross."

"A rehearsed answer if I've ever heard one," Aeoxoea purred. "Tell me, Jassamar of Stormdell. What brought you to this street, seeking your own death?"

"I was sent to Ebon South by the Third Guardian of Yarik to serve House Stormdell in the war with the zoths of the Outlands."

"Do these zoths seek to conquer your people?" Aeoxoea asked.

"They seek to destroy us," the man answered. "It is a war of genocide, waged for generations."

"When did this battle begin?"

"The zoths attacked when the sky became orange," the man said.

"Tell me how long ago this was," Aeoxoea said. "How many days?"

"There is no day or night since the sky became orange," the man answered. "Yet Behe Kang has risen and fallen thirteen times."

"Is Behe Kang an island that crosses your sky?" Aeoxoea asked.

"Yes, twice a day. The zoths have attacked us for seven days."

"That is excellent news," Aeoxoea said. "Tell me about the human nations that cover this land. How many are there?"

"It is the Seven Kingdoms you speak of," the man said. "Born from the Clans of the Silvermarsh, both greater and lesser."

"As I hoped," Aeoxoea said. "Your seven nations have seven battles to fight, six to lose and one to win."

"What do you mean?"

"You might be surprised to hear that I was quite certain of the answers to my questions before I asked them," Aeoxoea said. "You see, our meeting was preordained. The sky disappearing in a cloud of orange, the days of battle that followed, your sacrifice and my arrival, were all meant to happen. We are leafs floating on a river of prophecy, you and I, unable to control our direction no matter how we try. It seems the boy called the Blessed Soul of Man has chosen to come to your island. He will arrive shortly, if he hasn't already. You can't stop that, and neither can I. But we can find him, and when we do, that is when we will regain control of our lives."

"I don't understand," the man said.

"Oh, but you will," Aeoxoea said. "Your time of service is not yet complete. I have a task for you."

"I cannot complete any task as I am."

"You can complete any task I wish," Aeoxoea said. "Your life was taken, but I have taken it back."

"Why have you done this?"

"Because I have no choice," Aeoxoea said. "All I can do is find the Blessed Soul of Man. And all you can do is help me."

Chapter 5

"My quest for Warrior Baptism requires me to search for the Blessed Soul of Man, the little boy whose coming was prophesied before the Sundering of the World," Theel said. "He would be a man by now, for the Keeper tells me he came into the world twenty years ago."

Theel's words were met with silence. Yatham was clearly shocked at what he said. He even stopped paddling. For many moments, the boat glided across the surface of the water on the power of momentum alone. An airtight barrel floated by, bobbing gently, the torch mounted on its topside crackling in the darkness.

"The Blessed Soul of Man?" Yatham finally said.

"Yes, brother," Theel said. "The Blessed Soul of Man."

"I don't believe it."

"That makes two of us."

"Your quest is to fulfill a religious prophecy?" Yatham asked.

"Yes, by finding the Blessed Soul of Man," Theel said. "It is an act of cruelty the Keeper has done in charging me with such an impossible task."

Yatham didn't say anything, only worked his oar in silence. Theel's pipe was back in his mouth. He scratched another match to life, burned another bowl, and breathed more seraphim.

"Some savior of the world this Blessed Soul must be," Theel said, puffing. "Only a man of true impotence would need to be found when destiny calls. Why does he not show himself? Is he hiding? Is he afraid?"

"The Blessed Soul is not hiding," Yatham said. "He will reveal himself when he is ready; when the world is ready for him."

"How do you know this?"

"Father told me."

"Father had a great many opinions and beliefs," Theel said. "Where did they take him? To an early death and orphaned children. To a funeral no one attended and a pine tree to mark his memory."

"Father said the Blessed Soul will reveal himself when the time is right," Yatham insisted.

"Father also said he was stabbed through the heart and lived," Theel said. "Do you believe that?"

"I do," Yatham answered. "I saw the scars on this chest and back. We've all seen his shield with the hole through it. He wore the shield over his heart when that hole was made."

"I once believed the same as you, and now I feel a fool for doing so," Theel said. "A man cannot survive after being stabbed through the heart. It is not possible, no matter how you wish it was."

"Father was an extraordinary man, capable of extraordinary things," Yatham said.

"What do *you* believe?" Theel asked. "You've told me what father thought. What do *you* think? Do you think the Blessed Soul will come?"

"Yes, I do."

"Do you think he walks the world as we speak?" Theel asked. "Do you think he is out there waiting to be found?"

"He will be found if that is what God wishes," Yatham answered. "Perhaps God is leaving it to you to find him."

"If that is true, then God has made a grave error, for I am not up to the task."

"If God has chosen you to find him, then you will find him," Yatham said. "Then it is up to you, despite your wishes."

"It's up to me and this priest of the Outlands, Father Brashfor, to find him," Theel said. "Or so the Keeper said."

"What is it about this priest that makes him the goal of our search?" Yatham asked.

"I don't know," Theel answered. "The Keeper told me nothing more than where to find him, in the Outlander town called Ebon South."

"Father Brashfor believes in the Blessed Soul, I'm certain."

"Many men believe many things, wise or not," Theel said. "There is something about the prophecy of the Blessed Soul that causes otherwise prudent people to ignore their own sound judgment."

"Lord Britou is a man of sound judgment, as is the Keeper," Yatham said. "It is they who sent you on this quest."

"Yes, the Keeper is a man of sound judgment," Theel agreed. "Which is why he doesn't believe in this quest any more than I do."

"That's not true," Yatham said. "I know the Keeper is a man of faith."

"Yes, he is," Theel said. "The Keeper has strong faith. He believes the Blessed Soul will one day come. But he doesn't believe I will be the one to find him."

"How can that be?" Yatham said. "You always said the Keeper was great and wise. He would not send you to quest for Warrior Baptism without careful thought."

"And yet he has," Theel said. "This, to me, is proof that he doesn't believe the Blessed Soul is out there. If he truly believed, he would be sending a Knight of the Southern Cross to find him, or ten knights, or an army of them. Instead he has sent me—one lowly squire."

"You are wrong," Yatham said. "He has sent you, not because he thinks you will fail, but because he thinks you will succeed. He believes in you."

"He doesn't believe in me," Theel laughed. "No one believes in me."

"I believe in you," Yatham said. "I have faith you can complete this quest."

"Your faith fails you, brother," Theel said. "You wouldn't say that if you knew the things I know. Do you know the words of the prophecy? Do you know what Sun Antheus wrote about the Blessed Soul of Man?"

"I know a little," Yatham said. "I know Sun Antheus prophesied the coming of the Blessed Soul."

"You are like so many who know the myth but none of the details," Theel said, "carrying around your foolish faith while knowing nothing of what Sun Antheus actually wrote."

"What did he write?" Yatham asked. "Tell me."

"He spoke of a great struggle between good and evil that took place many thousands of years ago. The final battle was fought in a place called the Plains of Gyatna, where twelve heroes sacrificed themselves so the armies of good could prevail."

"The War of Souls," Yatham said.

"Congratulations, brother. You know at least that much," Theel said. "After the War of Souls, the Lord of Devils and minions were banished to Hell by God and his angels. Men of good hoped this was the end of the struggle, but it was only the beginning. Sun Antheus predicted thousands of years would pass, and again the Lord of Devils and his Seven Angels of Doom would begin to gather their children for another great war—this one in the world of men. He said great nations will muster armies of spear and sword, light and darkness, each side led by a great champion. Men of evil would rally to the banner of man known as the Serharek. Men of goodness would follow their own champion, a soldier hand-picked by God."

"The Blessed Soul of Man," Yatham guessed.

"Correct," Theel said. "All this would result in another war for the heavens, a Second War of Souls. Sun Antheus prophesied that in the days before this great war, God would raise the twelve heroes of Gyatna from the dead to fight for him once again. The heroes will lead seven armies against the Serharek. The Serharek will be victorious six times, but in the seventh and deciding battle, the men of good will be led by the Blessed Soul of Man."

Again Yatham was quiet for a long time, his thoughts unclear. When he did speak, his voice was very soft.

"Do you believe this is happening?"

"Of course not."

"Do you think the Iatan are the men of evil Sun Antheus wrote about?" Yatham asked. "Do you think the Second War of Souls has begun?"

"Are you listening to me? I don't believe any of this."

"Does the Keeper believe?"

"Perhaps he does," Theel said. "But he would be a fool to think you and I are the key to all this. And the Keeper is no fool. He knows better."

"What does he know?"

"He knows if the Blessed Soul ever shows himself, it won't be due to anything you or I do," Theel answered. "He knows we will waste ourselves chasing this quest, that we probably won't even reach the Outlands at all. We have a better chance of being killed or captured by the Iatan, or dying of thirst or starvation in the Gray Mounds long before we find any priest of Ebon South. He knows the Iatan will destroy Fal Daran, and there is nothing he, nor I, nor anyone can do to stop it, despite what some prophecy says. The Iatan Army will kill the city and tear the heart out of the Seven Kingdoms. While they are doing it, the Blessed Soul will be missing, his prophecy unfulfilled. That is what the Keeper knows."

"Then why would he charge you with this task?" Yatham asked. "If the Keeper did not believe you could find the Blessed Soul, why would he assign you this quest?"

"Because it is what father wanted," Theel said. "The Keeper is fulfilling the last wish of a dead man."

"That makes no sense," Yatham said.

"It makes perfect sense," Theel said. "I know I wasn't chosen for this quest only days ago. It was decided I would search for the Blessed Soul when I was a child. I was schooled in the teachings and writings of Sun Antheus, especially the prophecies of the Blessed Soul, for as long as I can remember."

"Every squire training for knighthood must learn of Sun Antheus," Yatham said. "It is the way of the Knights of the Southern Cross."

"No other squire receives the personal attention of the Keeper of the Craft as I did," Theel replied. "No other squire is trained from the day he was born with only one quest in mind."

"Do any other squires have the gift of Sight?" Yatham said. "Your Sight makes you special. That could be why you were chosen."

"Perhaps," Theel said. "But perhaps this has more to do with Father than with my Sight. He taught me everything he knows about the prophecies of Sun Antheus. He spoke of the Blessed Soul ceaselessly from the earliest I can remember. He has been preparing me for this quest for years. I have no doubt about that."

"Why does that possibility anger you?" Yatham asked.

"This isn't about me. This is all about Father's legacy," Theel explained. "For years I mistook his obsession with the Blessed Soul of Man for faith in the prophecy. The truth is, he was tormented by his failure to complete the quest himself. The Blessed Soul represents the only black mark on his legacy. The people think he could do anything, even defy death itself—but everyone knows he could not find the Blessed Soul. How could he erase that failure and once again be remembered as perfect?"

"I don't know," Yatham said. "But I'm sure you will tell me."

"By having his eldest son undertake the quest in his stead," Theel said. "That is why I am sent to look for the Blessed Soul—not because of the Iatan invasion, or any War of Souls. The Keeper is simply honoring Father's memory. I am forced to do this because it is what the great knight wanted."

"Why would the Keeper commit any resources or time to sending a squire on such a dangerous quest for no reason other than to please a dead man? Especially at a time when the kingdom is in such peril. Why would he do that?"

"The answer to your question can found in the term *Anora la Jinn*," Theel said. "Do you know what it means?"

"It is the old Thershoni tongue," Yatham answered. "It means 'Warrior Baptism.'"

"Many wrongly believe the same as you," Theel said. "The correct translation is 'Warrior's Burden.' The origins of this term are from a time when law required all squires to have noble blood, and be the eldest son of a knight. If a knight perished in battle, his son and squire would be given a knight's quest to finish what his father started. The son was required to shoulder the burden of his father's failure, to accomplish what his masterknight could not. In most cases, the Warrior's Burden required the squire to avenge his father. But some squires were required to show their worth by completing some specific task left unfinished by their father's death."

"What does this matter?" Yatham asked. "That tradition was abandoned generations ago."

"Father was nothing if not a man who cherished tradition," Theel said. "He quested to find the Blessed Soul. He failed to complete that quest."

"Countless sons of Embriss have searched for the Blessed Soul over the years, knights and otherwise," Yatham said. "Father's failure in that regard was not unique."

"No, it wasn't," Theel agreed. "It is my quest that is unique. I was given an impossible task, one my father could not complete, on the day of his funeral. This is not Warrior Baptism. This is *Anora la Jinn*. This is the Warrior's Burden."

"What if it is? Why does any of this anger you?" Yatham asked. "It is an honor to be chosen for this quest. Why do you question the Keeper's wisdom on this?"

"I do not question his wisdom. I believe the Keeper to be a wise man," Theel said. "That is why I do not believe he thinks you and I will find his miracle man. He is too wise and intelligent a man for such small thoughts. This quest is what Father wanted. It is the only thing he has ever wanted. It was his greatest wish to find the Blessed Soul of Man, to fulfill the prophecy he spent his entire life defending. He sacrificed everything for his religion. He sacrificed his family for this prophecy. It meant everything to him."

"You say this as if I am not aware," Yatham said. "I know Father's faith was strong."

"It was more than faith. He was obsessed," Theel said. "His desire to find the Blessed Soul was so strong it lives on after he has died. This is why I am forced to quest in his footsteps, to preserve his dream of finding the Blessed Soul, even though he knew I would fail."

"Father, too? You think even he believed you would fail?" Yatham said incredulously. "Why would he wish you to quest for Warrior Baptism if he knew you would fail?"

"To keep his dream alive," Theel said. "He knew I didn't have the mettle to be a knight. Despite what he said, he knew I never had any hope of rising above a squire. And yet he forced me to swear the oath only because he wished me to undertake this quest. And when I fail, as he failed, his wish is for me continue this folly by burdening my eldest son, just as he did. He didn't care how many generations must be sacrificed for this dream, so long as it was *our* family who won the glory of fulfilling the prophecy."

"This can't be true," Yatham protested. "He never said anything like this."

"It's the only reasoning that works," Theel said. "It's the only logical explanation for his insanity."

"No, it isn't," Yatham stated. "Perhaps he believed in you. Perhaps he knew you could find the Blessed Soul."

"That is the greatest insanity of all," Theel barked. "I refuse to believe it."

"That is precisely your problem," Yatham said. "You do not believe in yourself as others do. That is why you need this quest."

"I do not *need* anything!" Theel said. "And I will not allow Father to rule me from beyond the grave. He is my masterknight no longer. Now *I* am my own masterknight. And I say it is foolish to chase an empty dream. I will not pursue the impossible. I cannot reach a goal that is unattainable. Not to please a dead man who never loved me."

"But you will," Yatham said. "Your Sight will guide you. You will not fail."

"I *will* fail," Theel said. "Because I will not try."

"If God has chosen you to find the Blessed Soul of Man, then you will find him," Yatham said. "It doesn't matter if you try."

"Don't be a fool," Theel retorted. "You are wrong about this, just like father. He was a tyrannical fool."

"You say this only because you resent him," Yatham said. "This has nothing to do with the prophecy, or the Blessed Soul of Man. You are still angry with Father for his methods of squire-training and child-rearing."

"I have a right to be angry," Theel said indignantly. "He wasn't a good masterknight. Or a good father."

"He was a good father to me."

"You think that only because you were his favorite," Theel said. "You didn't have the knighthood thrust upon you against your will. You didn't spend countless hours being beaten and cursed in the training room because you weren't good enough, because you didn't learn fast enough."

Theel's voice softened, his sharp tone now dulled by a deep sadness.

"You were the son he wanted," he muttered, staring into the darkness. "You were the son he loved. He never wanted me. He never loved me. I was just another of his duties."

"That's not true," Yatham said.

Theel tried to say something to his brother—a snappy retort, and angry reproach--but the words wouldn't come. He could only grit his teeth and try to blink the tears away, grateful the darkness of the cave hid his emotions from his brother.

"He loved you, Theel."

Those words stung. Theel felt decades-old pain and regret welling up inside him, reminding him of the lonely and hurting child he once was, the child who cried for his father, whose cries were ignored. It took all of Theel's strength to keep his voice from shaking.

"I wish that were true."

"He said so," Yatham said. "More than once."

Theel was desperate to silence the weeping little boy inside him, so he cursed him and beat him, just as his father once did. That boy was weak, and weakness was unacceptable. He must be strong. He sought strength the only way he knew how, by drowning out that little boy's cries with anger and resentment.

"I shouldn't be forced to listen to Father's lies any longer!" he barked. "And yet you insist on reminding me of his false claims. Father said a lot of things because he was a fool and a liar. It doesn't mean I have to listen to them, or willingly believe them as you do. Father didn't see me as a son. He didn't even see me as a human being. He saw me as a tool by which he could accomplish his goals. He wanted me to use my Sight to prove his religion true. He wanted me to add to his legacy." Theel's tone became derisive. "The son," he spat, "of the great knight."

"What has happened to my brother?" Yatham asked. "How have you become this way?"

"I don't know what you mean," Theel said.

"It wasn't that long ago that you claimed to believe in the prophecies."

"I was required to make such claims by my masterknight," Theel said. "It was my duty as a squire."

"Is this the person you've always secretly been?" Yatham asked. "Did you ever believe?"

"Yes," Theel answered. "But not anymore. Things have changed."

"I know that," Yatham said. "Father is dead, and everything is different now. This doesn't mean we must forsake all we believe in."

"You don't understand."

"You are correct," Yatham agreed. "I don't understand. Enlighten me."

"No one believed as strongly as Father did," Theel explained. "He did everything his religion asked of him. He believed in the prophecy. He believed the Blessed Soul would come. He believed so strongly that he sacrificed my childhood in order to prepare me. He sacrificed the happiness of his offspring, and he turned his back on the love of his family, all in anticipation of the fulfillment of the prophecy. What did it gain him?"

Yatham didn't say anything, allowing Theel to answer his own question.

"Nothing," Theel said. "I was taught to believe in the same prophecies as he was. I wanted the Blessed Soul to come and save us. I followed Father everywhere he went and did everything he commanded, thinking this would hasten the fulfillment of the prophecies. I prayed for the strength to succeed as Father wished. I prayed for the faith to follow the prophecies. Then I was forced to watch him die. Despite all my training I could not save him, because God turned his back on me that day. What did my prayers gain me?"

Again, Yatham didn't answer.

"Nothing," Theel said. "No one prayed harder and longer than Father and I. And the Blessed Soul is nowhere to be found. The answer to our prayers is silence. Despite all our hope, the homeland of our fathers is being destroyed by the Iatan. Despite all our prayers, Father is dead at the hands of his enemies. And still, with all this pain and suffering, the Blessed Soul will not show his face."

"This means he is not yet ready to show his face," Yatham suggested.

"It means he's a coward," Theel said. "Or that he doesn't exist. Either way, he is not worthy of all this faith and devotion he's been shown. He is not worth all the sacrifices made by so many of those who have sought him out."

"But what if the prophecy is true?"

"It isn't," Theel answered.

"What if we find the Blessed Soul?" Yatham asked.

78

Theel grunted and dropped his oar in the bottom of the boat. "Haven't you been listening? We won't find the Blessed Soul!"

Again Yatham was silent for a long time, the exact time required for Theel to pack the bowl of his pipe.

"Worse than all the beatings I took," Theel said, putting his pipe in his mouth, "is the knowledge that every one of those beatings was done in the name of God. In my father's perverted mind, the abuse of a child would somehow fulfill a false prophecy."

"But what if you are wrong?" Yatham asked. "What if the Blessed Soul is somewhere in the Seven Kingdoms right now, while we puff in argument over the question of his existence? What if he is waiting for us, right now, to find him?"

Theel sighed, striking a match. "If we find the Blessed Soul, I will wash our clothing for a month," he said. "That's a wager."

"And what will you say of Father?"

"I won't say anything, because I won't need to," Theel said, lighting his pipe. "There is no Blessed Soul, and there never will be."

"But what if there *is* a Blessed Soul?" Yatham asked. "And what if we find him?"

"I will say Father was finally right about something."

"You'll admit Father wasn't a liar," Yatham said. "You'll admit that he told the truth about being stabbed through the heart, and the truth about the Blessed Soul. You'll admit that, and *then* you'll wash our clothing for a month."

Theel extinguished his match with a wave of his hand, then tossed it into the water. He watched the tiny ripples expand across the blackness, then merge with the wake of the boat, all of it reflecting the orange light of the torch.

"Theel?" Yatham said.

"Yes?"

"If we find the Blessed Soul, you'll admit father's words were true," Yatham insisted.

Theel didn't answer. His brain was smoked, and he knew it, which is why he was confused about the firelight glimmering on the water. It reflected where it shouldn't be, within the shadows cast by the crates. This could only mean one thing. There was another light source.

"Theel?" Yatham said. "Is everything all right?"

"No."

He turned to look at the light behind him, thinking it was the flaming beacon they'd just passed. His vision wasn't perfect, but it appeared the fire must have broken free of its anchor and was now floating after them, keeping pace with Yatham's paddling. Theel blinked and rubbed his eyes. There was no longer one torch, but three. And they were not keeping pace. They were gaining.

"Theel?"

"Quiet, brother," Theel said. He dropped his pipe in the bottom of the boat, picked up his oar, and joined his brother's work in earnest.

"What is it?" Yatham asked.

Theel paddled as hard as he could, greatly increasing their speed.

"Someone is following us ..."

Chapter 6

There were three of them traveling together, three small canoes full of men, paddling their way through the Trader's Cave. The canoes were small, built for speed, not cargo capacity, and carried no freight, nothing but their crews. Each vessel contained four men who plied their oars as fast as they could, behaving as if they were in a race for their lives. The three canoes did not travel single file, as boats commonly did in the Trader's Cave. They moved down the river side by side, with torches mounted on bow and stern, combining firelight in order to illuminate as much of the cave as possible. They were searching for something. Or someone.

Theel tried to remain calm, tried to remind himself that he and his brother might not be the object of their search. The Trader's Cave was home to no small amount of intrigue. Every man who rode the river and breathed the dank air of these caverns had his own story, his own special reason for avoiding scrutiny and seeking the protection of the darkness. Perhaps these newcomers were searching for someone else. If the brothers paddled along calmly, acting as two nameless and unimportant paddlemen moving some merchandise down the river, they may have nothing to fear from these men.

Then Theel remembered he'd removed his overcoat earlier when he was feeling overheated. He looked down at himself, the weak flame of realization flickering in his drug-addled mind. He sat in his rich leathers, with expensive boots and trousers, and his sword sitting in the bottom of the boat. He no longer had the appearance of a nameless and unimportant paddleman. He now matched the description of the killer of Quiddip Kile in every way.

Worse still, he'd undone the shoulder buckles and back laces on this armor, baring his chest in an effort to cool off. The expensive bullosk-hide leather would give him away, while offering no protection from frontal attack. And now there was no way to fix it. He couldn't fasten the buckles without Yatham's help, even when sober. And he couldn't lace anything with fingers just as smoked as his brain.

Perhaps he could cover up. Where was his coat? In the front of the boat with Yatham. Could he climb over the crates and retrieve it? His brain was too smoked for him to move with any proper coordination. He'd probably fall. He'd probably tip the boat on its side.

Theel ducked down low within the shadows of the crates and looked back. Those men were traveling fast, four pairs of arms and four strong backs propelling each canoe. Their torchlight filled the cavern, illuminating the darkness, lighting the rock walls and rippling on the surface of the water. It also illuminated the leather armor each man wore, as well as the symbols of the Overwatch on their chests.

"Watchmen, brother!" Theel hissed. "There are watchmen following us. Paddle faster!"

There was no longer any doubt in his mind. There were twelve of them, men of the City Overwatch, traveling in the Trader's Cave. The Keeper of Order would not send so many officers in search of petty thieves and smugglers. Theel could see sword handles resting against the sides of their boats, spears on their backs, bows and quivers of arrows. These men were ready for a fight, and not a small one. Either they were seeking to confront a small army, or they intended to arrest someone they anticipated would possess significant skill at arms. Someone with top notch martial training, such as a Squire of the Southern Cross Knights. Someone such as him.

There was nothing to do but paddle for his life—no hope but the possibility that he and his brother might outrace them. For a moment, Theel wanted to laugh. This would be remembered as the most futile attempt at a knight's quest in history. He would be the first squire ever to fail at achieving Warrior Baptism before even leaving the city. And he had no one to blame but himself.

This wouldn't have happened if he'd helped Yatham paddle the boat. It wouldn't have happened if he'd not been drinking and fighting at Glad Sire's. It wouldn't have happened if he'd left the city to begin his quest more than a week ago as ordered. It wouldn't have happened if he'd continued south after his father's death, instead of fleeing back to Fal Daran like a coward. He could hear all these accusing words in his mind, stabbing at his brain like needles. They sounded like the words of his father.

An arrow zipped by, a wide shot, but close enough to cause discomfort. That arrow meant there would be no peaceful resolution to this. The watchmen didn't attempt to talk to him. They didn't ask him or order him to stop his boat. Instead they spoke with violence, giving him treatment only a wanted killer could expect from officers of the Overwatch. It was now undeniable why those watchmen traveled on this river. They were in search of the murderer of Quiddip Kile. And they now believed they'd found the man they were searching for.

That was fine, Theel decided. If those men wanted a fight, they would get one. The chase was on.

"Give me the torch, brother," he said.

Yatham pulled the torch from its mount on the bow of the boat. "Here, take it."

Theel stood up and immediately regretted it, almost falling over trying to stand on wobbly legs in a wobbly boat.

"What are you doing?" Yatham asked in alarm.

"Just keep paddling," Theel said, reaching over the crates to take the torch.

As his brother worked to propel the boat, Theel used the light to find his father's knife. Then he used that to pry the lid off the topmost crate, looking inside to see what it contained. Fabrics, just as Guarn had said.

Another arrow zipped by, reminding him to move fast. He pushed the flaming torch into the crate, igniting its contents, then picked it up and threw it into the water. The boat rocked crazily and he almost fell out, but he held on, and managed to get the next crate open. More cloth, and that too went up in flames. As he lifted the crate, an arrow thunked into its side, inches from his hand. It was close, but close wasn't good enough.

"You keep missing, you bastards!" he shrieked with a face full of smoke, tears running down his face. He threw another burning crate into the water. "It is not my day to die!"

Soon the river behind them was filled with flaming boxes. They didn't remain afloat for long, as they weren't watertight. One by one, the boxes began to sink, but before they did, they slowed the canoes of the Overwatch, and did much to help the brothers increase their lead. Theel threw all the crates into the river, then extinguished his torch. When the watchmen made their way through the flaming obstacles left in their path, their fire-burned eyes were met with nothing but darkness.

Theel sat down and again joined his brother in paddling. Now they were working together, moving a boat made lighter by its lack of cargo. There was no light but the torches of the watchmen behind them and a single beacon far ahead in the distance. The brothers could not see where they were going, but they paddled as if they could, working hard to propel themselves as fast as they could into a big, black unknown. There was no way Theel would be captured without a fight. He would row until his arms fell off. Then he would row some more, with his teeth if necessary.

More arrows zinged by to splash in the water, aimless shots directed at an unseen target. The watchmen were desperate to catch the brothers, so much so that they were shooting blind. The flaming crates slowed them somewhat, increasing the brothers' lead and purchasing them some time, but not enough. The canoes of the Overwatch moved faster than Guarn's boat ever could. The watchmen would overcome them. It would happen sooner, or it would happen later. But it was inevitable.

Theel was determined it would happen later—much later. Now he found himself grateful for the merciless fitness training he'd endured at the hands of his father. No one must outlast a squire, Theel was reminded daily, not in strength of will, nor in physical endurance. There was no shame in failure if all effort is spent, no shame in being bested, or losing to another of greater skill. There is always someone smarter, stronger, faster, better. But there was great shame if that failure was a result of a lack of physical or mental conditioning. They might outwit you. They might outfight you. But they must never, ever, outlast you.

Yatham grew up with the same father and was subjected to the same rhetoric on a daily basis. Yatham was tireless, and would not fail in doing his share. And though Theel had spent the last week outwitting himself, and outlasting little more than countless bottles of wine, he knew he could still outperform most men physically, even with seraphim-soaked muscles. He would put his brother and himself up against any other tandem with no lack of confidence. It would be very hard to catch them if they didn't want to be caught. And right now, they didn't want to be caught.

"Let us see how quickly the average watchman tires, shall we?" Theel whispered loudly.

The sleek canoes of the Overwatch cut the water with efficiency, gliding smoothly across the surface of the river. Guarn's oddly-shaped boat glided nowhere and cut nothing, only pushed its way through the water with the elegance of a slug, exhausting the arms of its crew with every stroke of the paddle. The watchmen had better equipment and more men—twice as many in each vessel. So the brothers had to row twice as hard.

The arrows stopped flying. With nothing but darkness in front of them, and nothing visible to shoot at, the archers dropped their bows and took up oars. Just as Theel expected, the watchmen gradually gained ground. The brothers were able to make up for much of their boat's inadequacy with supreme effort, but it was not quite enough.

One flaming beacon glided by in the darkness, then a second, then a third. Theel looked back, and still the watchmen were there, paddling tirelessly. They traveled miles, passed three more beacons, and still the watchmen were there, closer this time.

Theel hoped they could stay ahead of their pursuers long enough to reach the famous island of stone called Candle Rock. It was a place where the Trader's Cave split into two branches, two separate caves, with the Candle Rock sitting in the middle. The way to the left, the western route, was a safe and slow descent upon calm waters to the Toden River Valley. The way to the right, the eastern route, was an unsafe, terrifying descent down twisting rapids and eventually, a waterfall. It was unlit, it was in pure darkness, and it was suicide.

Candle Rock was also the home of the hermit Two Times, a person rarely seen, but whose presence was made known by the hundreds of candles he lit and placed upon the rock between the two caves. The tiny flames of these candles combined to make a beacon to travelers on the river, a crude underground lighthouse to direct them safely down the eastern passage, and away from the waterfall.

Theel decided Candle Rock might be a good place for this chase to reach its conclusion. If a fight could not be avoided, he'd rather it occur on dry ground, within the light of the candles. There were too many watchmen for him to face in the best of conditions, but if he and Yatham worked together and fought smartly, they'd have a chance. And with any luck, perhaps one or two of their pursuers, or even an entire canoe filled with them, could be sent down the wrong passage toward the waterfall.

Another beacon glided by. Theel looked back and saw the watchmen still there, now so close he could see the determined looks on their faces, even the sweat glistening on their foreheads. By the time they reached the next beacon, the current of the river had picked up, giving aid to the forward momentum of all boats, but also giving Theel hope they were finally descending toward Candle Rock. Then he looked back and his heart sank. The watchmen were now only feet behind. They would never make it.

The light of the beacon briefly made the brothers visible, and their pursuers took advantage. One of the men in the lead canoe knelt on the prow, swinging a small anchor at the end of a rope. Another threw a torch, which landed in the center of Theel's boat behind Yatham, threatening to burn him.

"They have us, brother!" Theel shouted. "Fight!"

He snatched up the torch just as the other man threw the anchor. It missed both brothers, but landed in their boat. Now the vessels were locked together, the watchmen reeling them in like fish on the end of a line. Both boats began to drift, no one rowing, but everyone carried by the swift currents of the river.

"Fight, brother!" Theel shouted again, as the canoe moved alongside.

Some watchmen drew their swords, others raised bows and aimed them. Theel stood up, raising his paddle above his head, then nearly fell as his seraphim-soaked brain struggled for balance. He was surely a laughable figure, fighting to stay upright, waving an oar like a sword, his unbuckled armor hanging open in front. But no one was laughing.

He swung the blade of the oar as if it was a blade of steel, awkward and off balanced, yet still managed to hit the first watchman in the face. Both boats rocked uncontrollably, and an arrow zipped past his ear. Another man stabbed at him with a knife but missed, and Theel fell on top of him, into the boat of the Overwatch. All balance was lost and the canoe overturned, sending everyone into the water.

Theel was thrust upside-down into a freezing blackness, with arms and legs flailing and bubbles rushing past his head. He could see the rippling torchlight and canoe bottoms beneath his feet, tried to orient himself, but felt someone clawing at his face. He responded by taking a mouthful of fingers and biting down hard.

The hand jerked away, and Theel was free of harassment, kicking as hard as he could to right himself, and to swim back to the surface. He could still see the boats, knew they were moving rapidly down the river, but he kept pace, swept along in the strong currents. With much effort, he was able to grasp the side of the overturned canoe and pull himself up inside it for a breath of air. The boats were all in a cluster, as if locked together. If Yatham was still up there, he was fighting for his life.

Theel took one more breath, then splashed back down, holding onto the canoe, maneuvering himself under Guarn's boat. He pulled himself up by the stern and there was Yatham, swinging his oar at four very determined watchmen who'd pulled their canoe along the other side. The one closest to Theel raised a crossbow, aiming directly at Theel's brother.

Theel pulled himself up, grabbed the canoe, then grabbed the man just as he loosed his quarrel. The bolt struck the back of another watchman just as Theel killed the one in his arms, using his knife to open the man's throat from behind. Both the crossbow and its owner fell overboard, and Theel took his place in the canoe.

Another man raised his sword against Yatham, but Theel swiped at him from behind, cutting his wrist and disarming him. Yatham broke his oar over the head of one watchman, while Theel stabbed at the other. The third canoe came up alongside, with more watchmen reaching out with torches and swiping with knives and swords.

The boats were all tangled together with anchor ropes, spinning in lazy circles down the swift-moving river. There was no one in control, just a group of men cursing and flailing, punching and stabbing, slipping on wood made wet with water and blood, falling on each other, falling into the river, some trying to kill, others merely trying to survive.

Theel had one watchman pinned beneath him in the bottom of a canoe, then another jumped on top of him, trying to choke him from behind. That was when he saw the light, another beacon floating by in the darkness. This one was very large, a bright orange glow cast by hundreds of candles. The boats were floating past Candle Rock. They were doing it with alarming speed, and there was no way to stop it.

He tried to see where they were going, catching a glimpse of a crudely made sign passing by over their heads, with two words painted on its surface:

Danger. Waterfall.

They were going down the wrong cave.

Theel had little time to contemplate this terrible realization. The watchman behind pulled hard on this neck, so hard it felt as if he'd soon rip Theel's head off. The other watchman fought to steal his knife, and they wrestled over it as Theel felt his life being choked away. His vision faded to nothing, then quickly filled with twinkling stars as his ears roared with the deafening sound of rushing water.

Then the world fell out from under him, and he briefly tumbled through a wall of mist, to crash hard upon the canoe again. Now he was facing up, but the watchman still held him from behind. Theel tried to stab at the man as the canoe rocked and tossed, filling with water. He was pelted in the face with a cold spray, then thrown into the air again. The watchman tenaciously held onto his neck, and they both fell into the water. Theel kicked his legs and stretched out his hand, desperately reaching into the darkness, and managed to get a grip on the side of the canoe. He tried to climb in, but the watchman held onto him, dragging him down.

Unable to do much else, he clung to the canoe with one hand, swirling and spinning and splashing, trying to breathe despite being smashed in the face repeatedly by walls of water. It was like trying to stay on the back of an angry bull while bearing the weight of another person. He knew he'd have a better chance of holding on if he'd drop his father's knife and use both hands, but he didn't want to lose it. So he found himself foolishly trying to sheath it on his belt with one hand, cutting his pants and repeatedly nicking his thigh. *Drop it!* his brain screamed. But for some reason, he couldn't do it.

"Yath—" he began, but his mouth filled with water.

Other shouts answered him, several voices calling out for help, but none were recognizable.

"Yatham!"

His canoe crashed into something solid, almost tearing it from his grip. Then the violent currents slammed him against the side. There was a moment of stability, and both he and the watchman tried to climb in at the same time. Another wave hit and threw both of them into the misty air. Luckily, they crashed against the bottom of the boat. For a moment, Theel thought he'd be safe. But amazingly, the watchman still wanted to fight, jumping on him with fingers clawing at his face. Theel stabbed at him and they fought over his father's blade, wrestling and kicking and cursing. The canoe hit another rock, then another, swaying violently, splashing up and down as they fought with the knife between them. The canoe took flight and he was spinning in the air, a human maelstrom of spray. His wet hands slipped off the knife, and he lost all sense of where he was. Then he fell back into the boat, landed on the watchman, and onto his own blade. The steel sank deep into his chest, just under his collarbone. Suddenly, he wished he'd kept his armor buckled and laced.

He gasped, sucked in water, coughed, then sucked in more water. He tried to pull the blade out, but only fell out of the canoe, feeling nothing but freezing cold and the inability to breathe. Then he exploded forth from the water, flying out into freezing air with his body trailing spray, curled into a fetal position, hands gripping the handle of his father's knife. His mouth gaped in a silent, horrified scream, all of its sound swallowed by the deafening roar of a waterfall. The feeling of forward movement died and was replaced by the sensation of falling, spiraling madly through a tornado of biting wind and water, down into bottomless blackness.

Chapter 7

Twenty years earlier, Aeoxoea strode briskly through the streets of the town called Ebon South. For the first time in seven days, nightfall had finally come to the beleaguered city, replacing the orange haze with a sky full of purple and yellow clouds that would have been beautiful if they weren't nearly obscured by two dozen plumes of black, the smoking gasps of a ruined city.

No matter how far the assassin walked, she wasn't spared the sights and sounds and smells of human misery. She stepped over frozen bodies, frozen limbs, and frozen faces with dead eyes. She sidestepped dead animals, sloshed through puddles of blood, and walked on a carpet of dead zoths. All around, buildings burned and collapsed into the street, throwing sparks and heating one side of her face, just as the wind and swirling snow chilled the other. Aeoxoea considered these things half-heartedly, instead keeping her eyes locked on a short figure in a dirty brown cloak who walked far ahead.

"Sir Jass, my puppet, wake up," she said aloud.

"Yes, mistress?" Aeoxoea heard the voice, not with her ears, but with her mind.

"You will use my eyes," Aeoxoea commanded. "What do you see?"

"I don't understand," Jass replied. "I cannot see."

"That is because you are attempting to see with your own eyes," Aeoxoea chided. "But you cannot, because they no longer exist. They were destroyed along with the rest of your body."

"My body is destroyed?"

"Unfortunately, yes," Aeoxoea answered. "A severed head can be cumbersome, not to mention unsavory, so I threw it into a fire. As for the rest of you, it appears to me these zoth creatures have little regard for the traditional rites of burial. Cannibalism seems to be their preferred method of corpse disposal. But don't fret, my puppet. I have acquired your thoughts and memories. You will live on within me for as long as I choose. Since your body is gone, you have no eyes, and therefore I will need you to use my eyes to see. So please. Look. What do you see? Where am I?"

"You walk the streets of the Ebon South near Storm Hall," came the reply.

"Am I near to the priest?" Aeoxoea pressed.

"You are nearing the place," Jass said. "You are two spokes from the Chapel of God's Grace. It won't be long."

"Very good," Aeoxoea said. "Tell me more of the priest you spoke of, the man we seek."

"He is called Father Brashfor," Jass said. "Everyone in town knows and loves him. A good man. One of God's children."

"What does he know of the Blessed Soul?" Aeoxoea asked.

"More than anyone," Jass answered. "He is not just a priest, but a prophet, an expert in the writings of Sun Antheus and the Blessed Soul of Man."

"He is trusted and respected in the church?"

"In the church, and by all the Seven Kingdoms and their rulers," Jass said. "He is a man of God but also a sage, and a very wise man. He will tell you he was sent to prepare the people for the coming of the Blessed Soul of Man."

"Do the people believe him?" Aeoxoea asked. "Do they await the arrival of their Blessed Soul?"

"Many do," Jass said. "All who fight for the Southern Cross believe, as well as I."

"Does Father Brashfor keep with anyone, a girl?" Aeoxoea asked.

"Two girls, sisters," Jass answered. "They are orphans who live at the church. He has taken them as his daughters."

"Look ahead. Do you see either of these girls?" Aeoxoea asked.

"The younger sister. She wears the brown cloak. Why are you following her?"

"My actions do not require your approval, my puppet," Aeoxoea said.

The girl in the brown cloak stopped in the middle of the street, looked down at her feet, then fell to her knees.

"Do you intend her harm?" Jass asked.

"Oh yes, puppet," Aeoxoea said. "I fear we will soon be at odds, she and I."

As the assassin grew closer, she could see that the girl was kneeling over a body lying in the snow, weeping.

"Brashfor's daughters are innocent girls," Jass said.

"I'm sure they are, but that no longer matters," Aeoxoea said.

"What do you mean?"

"I mean the war has begun,"

"The war for what?" Jass asked.

"For the Blessed Soul," Aeoxoea answered. "Sleep now, my puppet."

"Yes, mistress."

Aeoxoea stopped a few yards away. She saw that the priest's daughter was kneeling over the corpse of another girl of similar age. She clutched at the girl's skirt, her shoulders heaving with sobs.

"My sister!" the girl wailed.

"Such a sad thing to see," Aeoxoea said. "So much loss at this tender age. Do you need assistance, my dear?"

"Please," the girl wept. "Please help me. I don't know what to do."

"Of course you don't," Aeoxoea said. "Your sister was the only family you had left. You are lost without her."

The girl didn't answer, only buried her face in her sister's chest.

"I understand," Aeoxoea purred. "You need the sanctuary of the Chapel of God's Grace, some food, and a blanket and a warm fire, am I right?"

"Yes," the girl wept, her voice muffled by the folds of her sister's dress. "But I won't leave her."

"Would you like your father to come?" Aeoxoea asked.

The girl slowly nodded her head. "Yes."

"Of course you would like that," Aeoxoea said. "But let me tell you what I prefer. I would like to stab my tentacles into your neck and rip out the blood vessels so I can watch your terror-stricken eyes turn to glass as your blood soaks into the snow. That's what I would like."

The girl turned and looked, her eyes widening with shock. "W-what?" she stammered.

"You heard me."

Aeoxoea allowed herself to be seen by the girl, in all her nude, golden-skinned, white-haired glory. She enjoyed the fear her appearance elicited in her victim. This girl knew she was about to die, and Aeoxoea loved that.

"You are dead, little girl," she said. "And someone has taken your place."

"W-what are you talking about?" the girl stammered.

"I had a brother, once," Aeoxoea said. "And someone took his place."

"I'm sad for you," the girl said.

"Not as sad as I am."

"So," the girl said, wiping her eyes. "It seems you've found me."

"It seems I have."

The girl twisted to her feet, a pair of throwing knives flying from her fingertips. The attacks were precisely aimed and expertly thrown, and would have stabbed into Aeoxoea's eyes if they weren't snatched out of the air by white tentacles before they reached their mark. Those first two were followed by more, so fast and so many it was like a volley of arrows. But Aeoxoea's defenses were solid, and every knife was caught or deflected by a tentacle, then discarded into the snow.

"Lord Meherarc, hear my prayer!" the girl cried as she threw her knives. "I bear your weapon. I carry your banner."

She threw something that exploded into a sheet of flame before hitting Aeoxoea's face. The assassin sank to one knee, burned and blinded. For the moment, she was stunned, and in that moment the girl slammed a blade between her ribs. It slid effortlessly into her chest and cut her heart as though it were paper. She felt it inside her, felt the burning of the steel corrupting her flesh, the familiar sensation of the black magic working its evil.

An assassin's dagger blessed by the Cult of Meherarc, the Angel of Murder. It could only be used once by its wielder, but it was guaranteed to defeat any defense, and guaranteed to deliver a lethal blow to any normal human being. But Aeoxoea wasn't normal, nor was she human.

This was the girl's best—and only—chance to hurt Aeoxoea, and she revealed her desperation by wasting no time in using it. Fortunately for the assassin, this was not the first time such an attack had been wasted on her.

She knew this creature who pretended to be the priest's daughter; she had faced its kind before. It was a doppelganger, with the ability to appear as any person it physically touched, a trick which had successfully misled Aeoxoea in the past. That wasn't the case on this occasion, and the doppelganger knew it.

When Aeoxoea's vision cleared, she saw that the creature was already far away, running up the street, then turning into an alley. The doppelganger knew it was helpless against her. Its throwing knives were as dangerous to her as children's toys. And now that its greatest weapon, deception, was taken away, it attempted to flee. But there would be no escape.

Aeoxoea remained on one knee, her breath hissing between clenched teeth. Smoke curled around the place where the dagger had entered her, accompanied by a sizzling sound like cooking meat. Then her body expelled the weapon as if her chest spit it out into the snow.

A white tentacle reached out, lifting the dagger into the air. Aeoxoea took a moment to hold the weapon before her eyes, studying it to confirm her suspicions. The handle was black, and covered with runes of Earth Sorcery and arcane symbols holy to the Cult of Meherarc. The blade was featureless, a dull gray that refused to reflect any image. Aeoxoea knew this blade contained— and drew its strength from— the blood of countless murders. Even now she could see her own milky blood covering the dagger, boiling and sizzling as if the surface was scorching hot. The blood turned black and rapidly disappeared, like it was evaporating. But it wasn't evaporating; it was sinking into the steel, drunk in by the dagger of Meherarc. Until now, Aeoxoea's chest wound had not bled. The Angel of Murder didn't miss a drop.

A few more breaths, some deep concentration, and the assassin willed her heart to mend itself, to force the hole in her chest to close. This done, she rose to her feet, and the tentacle dropped the dagger into the palm of her hand. As her fingers closed around the handle, she smiled.

A dozen tentacles exploded from her body, striking at the ground violently, launching her high into the nighttime air. She landed on a rooftop, ran fifty feet to the other side, and the tentacles slammed down again, launching her across the street to another building, where she spotted her prey. She continued running, jumped again, and saw the doppelganger going up the front step stones of a small church. She ran to the edge of the rooftop, broke no stride, and glided like a bird over the town, above the streets, above the townspeople, the fires, and the fighting. Beaten and battered by freezing wind gusts, bit in the face by a hundred tiny snowflakes, she sailed straight as an arrow directly for the church.

She crashed through a window and landed on a wooden bench, smashing it to splinters. The place was filled with war-wounded men, and women who were screaming and fleeing with fright at the sudden disturbance. At the front of the building, near the altar, an old man wearing brown robes and priestly vestments stared, eyes wide with terror. He looked to the back of the church where the doppelganger, still wearing its little girl disguise, had just burst through the doors, filling the air with its throwing knives.

The doppelganger was trying to kill the priest.

Aeoxoea threw herself between the creature and its victim, white tentacles sprouting from her body. Every knife thrown was caught in the teeth of a tentacle then spit on the ground; every one until the supply of knives was exhausted. Not a single one reached its destination.

The doppelganger stopped, weaponless, the little girl's face looking at Aeoxoea with fear in her eyes. The creature knew this moment was coming, and knew there was no way to stop it. Aeoxoea stared back at the doppelganger, and the area between them crackled with magical energy. This energy concentrated into a ball, then struck the girl in the chest like an invisible hammer. Her little body flew through the air, spinning like a doll cast away by a child. She struck one of the church pews with a smack, and crumpled limply to the ground. She was still alive, but unmoving, gasping and whimpering in agony.

The church was now quiet but for the crunch of broken glass under Aeoxoea's bare feet and the hoarse and confused voices of a dozen wounded men begging for help. The assassin ignored them and turned to the priest, alarmed to see him lying on the floor, clutching at his chest. Cursing, she ran up the center aisle to the front of the church.

"Awaken, Sir Jass," she shouted.

"Yes, mistress?" came the answer from Aeoxoea's head.

"You will use my eyes," Aeoxoea said. "Where am I?"

"This is the Chapel of God's Grace," Jass answered. "It is Father Brashfor's church."

Aeoxoea knelt by the priest, propping the old man's head on her lap. She touched both sides of his head, then touched his chest. "His heart has stopped. Jass, is this the priest I seek?"

"Yes," Jass answered. "It is Father Brashfor."

White tentacles burst from Aeoxoea's body, burrowing into the old man's chest. They curled around his heart and squeezed it. But the flesh was dead. It was too late. Brashfor would not live.

"Sleep, Jass, my puppet," Aeoxoea commanded.

"Yes, mistress."

More tentacles emerged from between Aeoxoea's fingers, digging into the sides of the priest's skull. Inside, sticky white tendrils spread across the surface of Brashfor's brain, probing and sucking, and Aeoxoea began to fill with the dying man's memories. She was like a sponge trying to sop up as much information as she could before it all evaporated. But it was drying up too quickly.

The man's thoughts and memories were elusive, retreating every place she searched. She pumped her own blood into him in an effort to prolong his life, to give her more time. But she soon realized time was not the problem. The old priest was fighting her. It was as if she gripped his hand, trying to drag him toward life, but he clung to something else that was pulling him away into death. He had no desire to come back to her. He didn't wish to live.

He got what he wished for. He died right there, on the floor of his chapel, with his head resting in the assassin's lap. She'd done all she could, but was unable to save him, or even salvage many of his memories. Unlike with Jass, who had a strong desire to live, she was only able to gather a few scraps of information from the priest before he was dead.

When it was done, Aeoxoea retracted the tentacles and stood over Brashfor's dead body. She gazed coldly at the creature who murdered him, the doppelganger who still lay on the floor of the church, gasping for life. The assassin hadn't learned everything she could have from the priest, but she had learned enough. And now she understood.

Her tentacles slapped the floor and she flew over the benches, landing on top of the doppelganger so the two were eye to eye. In its pain and distress, the creature had lost control of its disguise, and Aeoxoea now saw its true form for the first time.

The doppelganger was a fyral, one of the primary races of the Iatan Empire. Fyral were recognizable by their dark and olive-colored complexion, black hair, and sharp, angular facial features. This fyral retained little of her original appearance, her curse having dulled the colors of her eyes and skin to neutral shades of gray. It had also robbed her face of its distinctness, making her features bland. She didn't look like anyone, not even herself. Very little about her was noteworthy. Even her shirt and breeches were plain, gray, and utterly without distinction. But her spiritual allegiance was displayed upon her person with indelible prominence. Ritual burn scars striped her face and arms, one for each mission of murder undertaken and completed. She belonged to a cult of assassins, and was a slave of Meherarc, the Angel of Murder.

She looked at Aeoxoea, terrified, choking on her own blood, tears running from the corners of her eyes. Aeoxoea had no pity, only rage, and with a single thought, all of that rage was balled into a fist; a large, invisible fist of magical energy that drew back and hovered, poised to strike. White tentacles seized the woman by the throat and dragged her to her feet.

"What did you mean to accomplish by coming to this island?"

The fist lashed out, released by the power of the assassin's mind, and the woman's head recoiled from a furious blow. She stumbled and fell hard on her rear, grimacing and bleeding. She had no time to answer before white tentacles curled around her throat, lifting her to her feet again.

"You meant to take my prize, did you?" Aeoxoea asked. "You meant to find the Blessed Soul first? Before I could find him? Before anyone could?"

The assassin didn't move, but the woman reacted to a punch to the stomach and folded to the floor, coughing and choking.

"You killed the priest's daughters and stole their faces to befriend him, hoping to gain his knowledge, hoping he would lead you to the goal of my search."

The woman's head snapped back, and blood flew.

"Then when you encountered me, you tried to kill him to deny me his knowledge," Aeoxoea growled. "You tried to kill my chance at finding the Blessed Soul."

The doppelganger tried to crawl away, but again, white tentacles seized her by the neck and dragged her to her feet.

"You intended to kill the Blessed Soul of Man before he could reveal himself." Aeoxoea said. "You wanted to kill him, and kill his destiny with him."

Another blow to the stomach. Then another to the face. The woman stumbled and fell on a wounded soldier, tipping the bench over and crashing to the floor.

"You wished to ensure that the Blessed Soul didn't live to face the Serharek in the final battle," Aeoxoea said, lifting her up again. "You intended to steal my victory, steal my glory."

This time she threw the woman, slamming her body against the side of the large stone altar near the front of the church.

"You meant to be the first of the emperor's assassins to reach the Blessed Soul, the first to do his will, to win the war before it starts." Aeoxoea crouched over her and smiled warmly, drinking in her fear, indulging in her blood-streaked face and bulging, panicked eyes. "But your zeal to do the emperor's will has only placed you between me and my goal. You wished to be the first to find the Blessed Soul, but this only means you will be the first to die."

Tears began to run down the sides of the woman's face as she choked and sputtered breathlessly, her face a swollen, pulpy mess.

"Sad little kitten," Aeoxoea said. She knelt before the woman, running her fingers over her face, touching the burn scars that striped her skin. "Look what your choices have brought you. You were beautiful once, before this curse took your face away. Let us use what time we have together to make you beautiful again."

She gently wiped the tears from the corners of the woman's eyes, the blood and spittle from her mouth.

"Sadly for you, the only way to make you beautiful again is to end this curse you enjoy so much," she said. "And the only way to end this curse is to end your life, but ..."

She smiled brightly and touched the woman's nose with her finger.

" ... you'll want to look your best when Lord Meherarc takes you to Hell."

Pulling the woman's clothing open, she touched the soft skin of her chest, tracing her finger around the brand covering the doppelganger's heart, the symbol of her slavery to the Cult of Meherarc. She touched the brand with her fingertip and could feel the woman's heart pounding beneath it, felt it quicken as she held the black-handled assassin's dagger before her eyes.

"Just as this dagger pierced my heart, it will pierce yours," Aeoxoea said. "You meant to meet your god with honor, but just as you tried to take my reward, I will now take yours. Just as you meant to condemn my soul to the prison of Dehen Yaulk, I now condemn yours."

At that moment, the doppelganger's features shifted in shape. They changed from a woman's gray-skinned face full of brands and scars to that of another, a little boy from Aeoxoea's past.

If her childhood was a vast nighttime sky, full of black memories, this little's boy's face was the lone bright star.

"Help me, sister!" the boy cried with pleading eyes. "Don't let them hurt me!"

For a moment, Aeoxoea's heart softened. It was a face she hadn't seen since in years, a face she never thought she'd see again. Hearing those words briefly caused her to forget where she was, to abandon all thoughts of the Blessed Soul of Man. She was reminded of all she once had, and how having her little brother ripped away killed the goodness within her, painted her heart black, and transformed her into a murderer.

"They are coming for me," the boy wept.

Aeoxoea spoke slowly, every word dripping with regret. "Yes, they are, dear brother."

"They are going to hurt me," the boy said.

"I know," Aeoxoea said. "But I can make them stop."

She smiled sadly, then took her brother's face in her hands, gazing into the doppelganger's eyes.

"You wear a new face to conjure sympathy within me, but your efforts are wasted," Aeoxoea said. "I used to know a person who felt sympathy, but then one day her brother was taken from her. That was the day she died, only to be replaced by the monster you see before you. Therefore, instead of sympathy, I give you my thanks, for it is a blessing to see the face of my sweet brother one last time. I'd forgotten what he looked like, and now I have the chance to do what I couldn't do before. After all these years, I will finally say good-bye to him."

"Help me, please!" her brother begged.

"I could not save you, dear brother, though I tried," Aeoxoea said. "I'll never know for certain when you died and that creature took your place, but I know who is responsible. I know who conspired to end your life and steal my future. And I will make them pay for what they did. They took everything away from us. So I will take everything away from them."

"But sister—"

She touched his lips to silence them. "Hush, little brother. Your big sister is talking right now," she said. "And I must also give my profound thanks to this wretched creature who wears your face, for in her stupidity she has revealed herself to me as one of those who participated in your murder.

"You see, my kitten, I've acquired some insight into the ways of your kind since my dear brother was taken from me. And I know that a doppelganger cannot take the face of another unless they have come into physical contact. That tells me something very special about you. I know that you touched my brother. I cannot forgive that."

Aeoxoea pressed the tip of the dagger against the doppelganger's chest, against the brand of the Angel of Murder. Smoke curled from under the blade, and her brother's face screamed an inhuman scream, cursing in the language of devils. White tentacles lashed out, pinning the doppelganger to the side of the altar.

"You would love to die by your master's blade, wouldn't you? This would allow you to meet your god with glory," Aeoxoea said. "Sadly, I can allow you no such glory. The method of your expiration is mine to decide, and I fear a death by your own blade is far too unimaginative. You helped kill my brother."

"But sister, I'm not—"

The assassin reached out and grabbed the doppelganger by the throat, choking off her brother's words.

"You do not deserve something so unimaginative as to be cut by knives or pierced by arrows, or poisoned, drowned, or hanged," Aeoxoea said. "You deserve something more intimate. You deserve the feeling of my fingers around your neck. You deserve the sight of my face as you fight for air, as your vision dims, as you remember what brought you to this end. Strangulation is such frightful work, but I will do it just for you, my kitten. Oh, and after you are nicely settled into the shackles of your damnation, I would like you to deliver a message to your master. The Blessed Soul of Man is accounted for. His fate has been determined, and no other assassins may interfere. The prophecies will be fulfilled by *my* hand, and no one else's. The Blessed Soul is mine."

The doppelganger's lips moved, trying to tell another lie, but there was no air to fuel the words. The creature's eyes blinked, and watered with tears, becoming more unfocused with each heartbeat.

"Please remember to tell him, my kitten," Aeoxoea said. "The Blessed Soul is mine. Do you understand that? Mine!"

She released the creature's body and it sagged back against the altar, not breathing, eyes staring at nothing.

"Mine."

Aeoxoea retracted her tentacles and stood, taking a moment to look down upon the body. It still wore the face of her little brother.

After a moment, she said, "You always were a beautiful boy."

It struck her suddenly, the realization that this was the last time she would see her brother's face. She couldn't let this moment pass unused. She reached out, lifted his chin, and straightened his hair. Then gently, she closed his eyes.

"I love you, my dear brother," she whispered. "Good-bye."

As death came, the doppelganger's disguise faded, once again shifting back to its true form. The little boy was replaced by the gray-skinned woman, and at that moment, a death blossom fell from the ceiling of the church. Its orange petals spun slowly as it drifted down, coming to rest on the dead woman's lap.

Chapter 8

Aeoxoea stood on the wall of Storm Hall, a small fortress at the center of Ebon South. She was on the battlements of the outer wall, a place high above the rooftops of the town where she couldn't avoid the harshness of the elements even if she wished to. The freezing wind buffeted her face and messed her hair. The snow stabbed at her skin with tiny ice daggers from head to toe. And yet she held perfectly still, as if physical discomfort didn't exist for her. If anyone was able to see her, she might have been mistaken for a piece of ornamentation adorning the wall, the statue of a beautiful young woman, cast in gold, gazing up at the heavens, transfixed by what she saw there.

The orange cloud that had imprisoned the city for so many days was finally gone, replaced by a clear and beautiful night. To the north the sky was black, its stars blotted out by a towering wall of rock that Jass called the cliffs of Tera Watch. But the southern sky was unobstructed; no clouds, and only one small island, its underside glowing soft and pale like a shard of moonlight. Beyond that, the clear sky showed the assassin thousands of stars twinkling against a purple eggshell sky.

The assassin stared at these stars with a face full of wonder.

There were countless constellations named by religions and cultures spread across the world's history. They were named for pagan deities, creatures of myth, and heroes of legend, all of them spinning slowly in the night sky, endlessly retelling their stories for all the world to see. But those were not what held Aeoxoea's attention.

There was something new in the sky, a fresh addition to this ancient and beautiful tapestry. When the orange blanket was pulled back from Thershon, it revealed a new group of stars, shining in the sky in places where there was only darkness a week ago. It was impossible to notice for all but a handful of people in the world who knew where to look. Aeoxoea had never seen it with her own eyes, but she recognized it with ease. Even though her body was born only decades ago, her memory reached back several millennia, to a time when the stars of this constellation shined brightest in the nighttime sky. Those stars had gone missing more than a thousand years ago, but now they were back, and the world was just a little brighter for it. The little boy had taken his rightful place on the sparkling floor of Heaven.

"Welcome back, my stars," she said to the sky.

The Constellation of the Blessed Soul of Man had returned.

She giggled when she thought of the reaction this would elicit, of the resources that would be expended, the powers that would be set into motion. All the minions of the Lord of Devils would now begin their search. Countless creatures of evil would soon be frantically attempting to reach the spot where Aeoxoea now stood.

None of them could possibly best her now. The only other assassin who posed any threat now lay dead on the floor of the Chapel of God's Grace, leaving Aeoxoea all alone at the finish line of a race her rivals were just beginning. All she need do is step across to claim her prize, the greatest prize of all: The Blessed Soul of Man.

The appearance of the constellation told her she was close to her goal, but it did not tell her where to look. Her eyes dropped from the star-filled sky above her to the smoking city below her.

She had a splendid view of Ebon South from where she stood on Storm Hall's outer wall. The streets reached out in all directions like the spokes of a wagon wheel, with the castle as its hub. They were little ribbons of snow that would have been pure and white on a better day, where people would see to their daily chores, men and women collecting their wood, their water, or calling their children in for the evening meal. But now the snow was dirty, trampled, and pink with blood. Where children should have been laughing and throwing snowballs, there was only a legion of corpses, both human and zoth, frozen and half-buried in the falling snow.

Below the wall where Aeoxoea stood, rows of broken and twisted bodies filled Storm Hall's courtyard, lined up like product on display at a butchery. Scores of townspeople moved among the rows with torches and lanterns, brushing the snow off faces, searching for missing loved ones. Despite the wind, the air was thick with the weeping of the bereaved, the screams of the wounded, and the silence of the dead.

"Sir Jass, my puppet," Aeoxoea said. "Awaken."

"Yes, mistress."

"Father Brashfor is dead," Aeoxoea said. "Slain by another assassin."

"A great loss to Ebon South," Jass replied.

"A great loss to my efforts as well," Aeoxoea added. "I was able to absorb many of the priest's memories, but unfortunately, most of the knowledge I require perished with him."

"It saddens me to hear that."

"I'm sure it does," Aeoxoea said. "I learned the priest entertained visitors today. A Knight of the Southern Cross called on him only hours ago."

"Gavin the Zealot."

"You know this man?" Aeoxoea said.

"Many know his name," Jass said. "He is among the greatest of my order."

"He brought a child to see the priest," Aeoxoea stated.

"The boy of the forest," Jass said.

"What do you know about this boy?" Aeoxoea asked.

"A townsman found him alone in the trees beyond the wall today, and rescued him from the zoths."

"The priest was very moved by what he experienced at this meeting," Aeoxoea said. "There was something noteworthy about this boy, something which made quite an impression."

"Ebon South has experienced some strange things these past days," Jass said. "But nothing so strange as that boy and the circumstances in which he was rescued."

"Who rescued the boy?" Aeoxoea asked. "And how was it unusual?"

"A trapper called Brody found the boy," Jass explained. "Brody was among a party of hunters and trappers who went into the forest a week ago, just before the sky was swallowed by the orange light. The zoth attack followed, and when they didn't return, we feared they'd perished. Then only hours ago, Brody returned without the others, and he brought the little boy with him."

"Did this Brody explain where he was for seven days?" Aeoxoea asked.

"That's the strangest part," Jass said. "He swore he'd only been in the forest an hour or so. It was as if these past seven days didn't exist for him."

"An interesting story."

"Any other day I would have declared it an impossible tale, the rambling of a liar or a drunkard—but Brody was neither," Jass said. "And I'd have said the same about an orange sky a week ago. Much has changed. These have been strange times."

"About to become stranger, my puppet," Aeoxoea said. "Where might I find your friend Brody?"

"I was told he was killed near the southern gate," Jass answered. "Like many of us, he died defending his home against the zoths."

"A pity."

"The zoths have brought us battle every day since the sun disappeared," Jass said. "But this latest attack came only moments after Brody appeared with the boy. It was almost as if they followed him out of the forest."

"Was it your friend the zoths pursued?" Aeoxoea asked. "Or was it the child he carried?"

"I don't know," Jass answered. "But after six days of fighting, this day was the worst of all. I fear that child may be the reason."

"Your fears have merit," Aeoxoea said. "Is there anything else you know of this boy? Did you hear his name?"

"They called him Eleod," Jass said. "I was told he is not a child of Embriss. They say his skin is golden, like yours. And his hair is white ..."

"Like mine," Aeoxoea finished. "The boy is darhan, a race of the Iatan Empire. He is the first of his kind to visit your land. I am the second."

"The Iatan Empire?"

"Your people will be acquainted with the Iatan Empire in time," Aeoxoea said. "More so than you wish, I fear. But that sad reality is twenty years distant. And besides, it can't be avoided, considering those pesky prophecies. Now tell me; where might I find young Eleod?"

"Find Gavin the Zealot, and you will find the boy."

"You believe the child is under this knight's protection?" Aeoxoea asked.

"There is no safer place," Jass said. "Gavin the Zealot is the finest swordsman in the Seven Kingdoms."

"Then tell me, my puppet," Aeoxoea said. "Where might I find the finest swordsman in the Seven Kingdoms?"

"In Storm Hall, most likely."

"Use my eyes to see, my puppet," Aeoxoea commanded. "Where in Storm Hall do you suggest I begin my search?"

"Not in the courtyard. Look up," Jass said. "There, in the central tower, a fire burns."

Aeoxoea looked across the courtyard to a thick, round tower of dark stone, one of four that sat atop the roof of the inner keep. What set this tower apart from the others was the large bonfire which burned brightly at the top, sending flames and sparks high into the night sky. Unshuttered windows in the topmost room glowed white like a pair of eyes from the blaze within.

"The townsfolk call it the Devil's Torch," Jass said. "They know the torch is lit only rarely, when the town is in the worst danger. But it signifies much more than that. The fire at the top of that tower is a means of communication. It burns only when the Knights of the Southern Cross hold council with their leaders."

"And you think the Zealot is present at this council?"

"If all things were normal, he would be," Jass answered. "I would be at council if I still lived. If all things were normal."

"But, my puppet, you should know this by now." White tentacles sprang from Aeoxoea's body. "All things are not normal."

The tentacles struck the ground, launching the assassin through the air in the direction of the tower. She sailed through the smoke and freezing air, high above the townspeople and the gruesome sights below, landing atop another wall, part of a system of walkways that rose above the courtyard. This one led directly to the base of the black tower with the burning eyes. Aeoxoea took this course, walking through the swirling wind and snowflakes, her bare feet crunching in the snow as she strode across the top of Storm Hall toward the Devil's Torch.

"The child is fortunate Gavin the Zealot was near when the zoths attacked," Jass said. "If not for the Zealot's sword arm, that boy would be dead."

"The Zealot's sword arm has nothing to do with it," Aeoxoea said. "The boy will not die today, or any day soon."

"How can you know that?"

"You still don't understand, do you, my puppet?" Aeoxoea answered. "Everything we do is a small part of a larger plan. It's a peculiar thing, God's will. He makes his plan very clear, but we mortals never understand until it comes to pass."

"You speak in riddles."

"Here is a riddle for you to consider," Aeoxoea said. "A child's nursery rhyme older than the Sundering of the World. I'm sure you know it."

Aeoxoea began to recite the words:

"Close your eyes, God's will be done.

"The Blessed Soul will one day come.

"The light will swallow up the sun."

"And all the world shall wither," Jass finished.

"You know the rhyme," Aeoxoea stated.

"Every child born of the old clans knows that rhyme," Jass explained. "It is a game we all played when we were young."

"Then you've no reason to misunderstand," Aeoxoea chided. "You've known God's will since you were a child, playing a game based on a song of prophecy. The light has swallowed up the sun, my puppet."

"What are you saying?" Jass asked.

"The Blessed Soul has this day come."

"The child of the forest?" Jass said. "The little boy under the care of Gavin the Zealot is the Blessed Soul of Man?"

"Who else would he be?" Aeoxoea answered. "We can't deny it. All we can do is find a good place of vantage and watch the world wither."

"You mock the prophecies," Jass said.

"I do not," Aeoxoea said. "I am dreadfully serious. That boy is the Blessed Soul of Man, and the goal of my search. Now to find him, I must locate Gavin the Zealot."

She walked onto the top of the central keep of Storm Hall, to the place where the Devil's Torch arose from the surrounding battlements. There she stopped before a door at the base of the tower, standing on a patch of trampled snow that squished between her toes. She looked up and could see the bonfire licking at the sky a hundred feet above her. She studied the top of the tower, looking at the windows, judging the distance.

"Will you do battle with Gavin the Zealot?" Jass asked.

"Perhaps."

"You must not," Jass said. "You cannot kill him."

"But I will," Aeoxoea said. "If necessary."

"If necessary?"

"Only if he interferes," Aeoxoea said. "I do not kill for pleasure."

"You killed that woman in the church for pleasure. With your bare hands."

"I've been known to make the occasional exception."

"Who was she to you?" Jass asked.

"Makes no matter," Aeoxoea said. "What matters is who she was to the Blessed Soul. She was but one of an army of killers who seek this boy, each with their own designs on his life. She was the first to arrive in your city, but I will be the first to find the Blessed Soul."

The tentacles swatted down hard against the stone and once again, Aeoxoea was launched high into the air. She flew straight up, whispering past a dozen windows in a rapid journey toward the top. Her momentum died only halfway up, far short of her goal. But as soon as she was about to begin falling, her tentacles lashed out, finding firm holds between the stones. Then her ascent resumed, the tentacles creating tiny showers of dust and crumbling masonry as they slammed into the side of the tower, walking her toward the top like giant, white spider legs.

"If you will be the first to find the Blessed Soul, then you will be the first to be slain by Gavin the Zealot," Jass said.

Aeoxoea giggled. "Oh, my sweet puppet. It tickles me so when you talk like a fool."

"I am serious."

"As am I," Aeoxoea said. "Your concern touches me so. But be reassured. Your knight will never know I am near."

"Stay clear of him," Jass warned. "Or you will regret it."

"I will go where I wish," Aeoxoea said. "I will blow on his ear. I will hold his hand. I will kiss his lips. And he will never see my face."

"The Zealot wields the deadliest weapons in the world," Jass said. "He is not a man to trifle with."

"Which is why I have no plans to trifle with him."

Near the top of the tower, Aeoxoea came to a window large enough for a man to walk through. All the windows she encountered in her climb to this point were much smaller, containing soft glows and no heat. But this window belched heat into the night, accompanying it with the roaring and hissing that said a large fire burned within. Aeoxoea knew she had reached one of the "eyes" of the Devil's Torch. Four tentacles slid inside the corners of the window, found firm holds, then lifted her through.

When the tentacles set her down, the soles of her feet touched warm stone, made wet by melted snow. The room was large and round, and without a roof, encompassing the entire top floor of the tower. There were six windows, including the one which gave her entry, providing a clear view in all directions. It also guaranteed at least two windows could be seen from the outside from any angle, explaining the tower's sinister nickname. The fire of the Devil's Torch burned in a large metal bowl suspended by chains high in the center of the room. Other than that, the room was without feature, with walls blackened by soot and completely free of any adornment.

Aeoxoea absorbed all this in one moment, then forgot it in the next, when she saw two men standing near a trapdoor in the floor. One was small and lean, with bronze skin, short, white hair and an eye patch with a large, glaring eye painted on it. He was bare-chested, clad only in plain leather breeches, and wore a simple but sturdy battle-axe on his back. The other man was taller but just as lean, with long, blonde hair and several days' growth of beard. He, too, was dressed very plainly, in leather shirt and breeches, armed with several large knives strapped to his thighs.

Both men bore all the signs of Knights of the Southern Cross, with muscled arms and shoulders covered with tattoos of rank, battle victories, and symbols of their clans. And each wore a small silver shield on his left breast, just like the one Jass wore.

Aeoxoea did not need to search the old priest's stolen memories to determine which knight was the one she sought. She immediately knew the taller knight with the beard to be Gavin the

Zealot, because of the large backpack made of furs he wore. Sleeping inside it, with his little head hanging to the side, was a small boy of three or four winters, with white hair and golden skin.

Aeoxoea knew that face. She'd seen it in the stars.

"It is the child," Jass said. "It is the Blessed Soul of Man."

The knights stood and watched as two other men worked the handles of a pair of large wooden spools attached to the floor. With a steady clicking of metal and screeching of pulleys, they unrolled the chains that suspended the bowl of fire, slowly lowering the gently swaying inferno until it rested on the floor of the room.

The flames roared and snapped and cooked the room, pelting Aeoxoea with heat, both natural and unnatural.

"The fire burns white," Aeoxoea stated. "Someone works strong magic in this tower."

"Summoning magic," Jass explained. "The knights seek council with their leaders, who are miles away to the north."

"Leave now," the shorter knight with the white hair said. The two laborers quickly climbed through the trapdoor and closed it behind them, leaving the knights alone with Aeoxoea.

"Who is the knight with the white hair?" Aeoxoea asked.

"He is Elkor the Hound," Jass answered. "A Battle Lord of the Kingdom of Yarik. He was sent to Ebon South to aid in the war with the zoths. He has command of the soldiers of House Stormdell."

"Does he command the Zealot?"

"No one commands the Zealot but the First Guardian," Jass answered. "He is Nonuc Dieum, champion of Embriss, and the highest ranking Knight of the Southern Cross, second only to the king. It is a position he has earned through his skill at arms. The finest swordsmen of the Seven Kingdoms revere him. There is none deadlier."

"You mentioned that," Aeoxoea said.

Aeoxoea blinked, and her vision shifted to the light spectrum which revealed magic to her eyes. The air was swimming with it; rainbow colors writhing and twisting like a living fog. Ever since she'd set foot in this primitive little town, she'd found it truly remarkable how strong the Craft presence was, and it was even stronger in this tower. All four elements pulsed and glowed and vied for space in a room utterly choked with magic. But as impressive as the other elements were, the strongest were the Flame Bringers, which glowed an angry red, pulsing as if alive with their own heartbeat. This room contained one of the highest concentrations of Flame Bringers Aeoxoea had ever seen. It was probably the sole reason why the tower was built, to support this room, to create a place where this awesome power could be tapped. Any wizard casting a spell of fire in this room would hold all the fires of Hell in the palm of his hand. The Devil's Torch.

Aeoxoea studied Gavin the Zealot, the man who protected the boy of the prophecies, the man any assassin would have to fight to reach the Blessed Soul. When looking upon him with normal eyes, he appeared no more impressive than any other warrior she'd seen. But with her enhanced eyes, she could see that warnings given by her puppet must be heeded.

Gavin the Zealot was strongly favored by the Craft weaves. It was a phenomenon the great wizards often referred to as "Craft Life." Some people were touched by the invisible mystic forces of the world, and some were ignored by them, but precious few were embraced by the magic as this man was.

The shifting colors gathered around him, fighting like jealous lovers to get near enough for a caress. But once there, they clung to him as if trapped by desire, unwilling or unable to let go. Aeoxoea had seen many people like this before, powerful men with dominant wills, such as the emperor back home. Most people's lives were ruled by the fortunes dictated by the Craft weaves, leaving them to be unknowingly and unwillingly swept along in their currents. But Gavin the Zealot was rare in that he was not moved by these external forces. The Craft weaves did not affect him. Instead, he affected the Craft weaves.

The skin on the back of her neck peeled open and a white tentacle as thick as her arm emerged, reaching high into the air, then curling in the direction of the knight. It moved silently and gracefully, cutting the currents of Craft like a water snake. She need only touch him and she would learn a great deal about this man. It would be the gentlest of probes; a caress, really. But long before the tentacle reached the knight, it was stopped by a magical barrier.

It was clear there was more than just physical prowess and Craft Life that made the Zealot formidable in battle. There was also an external power at play, something which gave him some measure of protection. Aeoxoea looked at the tattoos that graced the knight's arms, images of ancient runes and sigils, religious symbols and tattoos of rank among the knighthood. The Zealot had strong protections against assaults both magical and psychic woven into those tattoos, and unnatural strength and speed and stealth to complement his already awesome natural abilities.

Her puppet surely did not embellish when he called the Zealot the greatest swordsman in the Seven Kingdoms. It would take the greatest assassin alive giving the greatest fight of his life to best this man on any level of contest.

Aeoxoea learned all this by touching the wall of psychic protection which surrounded the knight, by giving it the lightest brush of her mind's fingertip. It was the gentlest probe imaginable, could never be detected by its subject, but when she pulled her tentacle away from the knight, he turned his head and looked at her.

She held still and met his gaze, certain he saw nothing. She didn't draw a breath. Her heart did not even beat. A stone statue could not have been more still as the knight looked her right in the face. For a moment, his eyes dropped to her naked body, then back to her face, his expression revealing nothing.

"Mistress," Jass said.

"Quiet, my puppet."

"It is the Blessed Soul," Jass said. "Why don't you strike at him?"

"Quiet!" she hissed.

Even though the knight looked directly at her, his eyes showed no reaction, as if he was seeing nothing. Then he turned and looked back to the flames burning in the metal bowl, as if nothing at all was out of the ordinary. Perhaps he hadn't seen her after all. Perhaps he'd only looked in her direction, and saw nothing. Aeoxoea exhaled slowly, and allowed herself to blink.

"Mistress," Jass said.

"Go to sleep, my puppet," she commanded.

"Yes, mistress."

"Keeper of the Craft?" The white haired knight named Elkor said, looking into the flames. "Have you come to the Devil's Torch?"

The hissing and snapping of the fire grew softer as the white flames burned lower and lessened in strength, and lessened more, and slowly weakened until Aeoxoea could see the figure of a man standing in the bowl. He seemed unhurt by the fires; not so much consumed by them, but composed of them, a man of white flame, with hands and face and clothing and hair made of fire.

The two knights bowed to him.

"Knights of the Southern Cross," the Keeper of the Craft said from the white fire, speaking in a hollow whisper. "The Seven Kingdoms need you."

"What does our Lord Britou command?" Elkor asked.

"This has been a desperate day, one that will be remembered for good and ill, Elkor the Hound," the Keeper said. "After centuries of waiting, the Prophecy of Sun Antheus is on this day fulfilled. It is the seventh moon day in the Watcher's Wait, and the zoths have answered the cry of their demon masters. They came with numbers to murder the children of Embriss today. Their slaughter soaks the ground in blood."

Gavin nodded his head. "They respond to the coming of the Blessed Soul."

"Everywhere the worshipers of the Lord of Devils and his Seven Sons of Doom lash out against men of good," the Keeper said. "They prayed to their demon masters that this day would never arrive, but it has. The stars of the sky do not lie. The Blessed Soul of Man has come."

"Father Brashfor's judgment is sound? The prophecy has been fulfilled?" Elkor asked. "The little boy Eleod is the Blessed Soul?"

"Father Brashfor was correct," the Keeper confirmed. "The boy called Eleod is the Blessed Soul. He must be protected, no matter the cost."

"It is done, then," Gavin stated. "Where does Lord Britou wish us to go?"

"You will seek the ancient weapon of legend called Gilligod, the Devil Device," the Keeper answered. "It is by this weapon of evil that the prophecies say the Blessed Soul will be slain."

"What manner of weapon is it?" Elkor asked. "A sword?"

"Gilligod is whatever it wishes to be," the Keeper answered. "Each time it has appeared in our world it has taken a different form, but this time, it will appear as a weapon forged for one purpose; to take the life of the Blessed Soul."

"We will find the Devil Device as you command," Gavin said. "But then what? Can we destroy it?"

"You cannot stop God's will," the Keeper said. "The Blessed Soul will be slain by Gilligod as the prophecy states. But we must fight evil as long as we can, as long as there is breath in our bodies. Take the Devil Device and keep it from those who wish the boy harm. Protect him long enough that he may grow to follow God's plan and fulfill his destiny. He is our Blessed Soul. He is our only hope."

"Where will we find this weapon?" Elkor asked.

"The Globe of Infinity has spoken to me on this matter," the Keeper said. "Gilligod will be forged by a disciple of the Angel of Death. He masquerades as a holy man among the bloodkin dycleth, who live deep beneath the surface of Thershon. You must travel down into the caverns of the Neversea Depths, find this dycleth, and find Gilligod."

"How will we find the bloodkin dycleth?" Elkor asked.

"You will travel east, through the Outlands south of Yarik, to the southern spur of Arka Moor," the Keeper explained. "There you will seek the shadow of Behe Kang on the western border of the Forsaken Kingdom."

"Illengaard?" Elkor asked.

"Yes," the Keeper said. "The First Guardian Lord Britou commands you to go to Illengaard."

"Is this the only way?" Gavin asked.

"It is the only way," the Keeper said. "You must travel to the heart of the Valley of Illengaard, enter the ruins of the Castle of Teardrops, and there locate the entrance to the lair of the lizard worm of dycleth myth. This path will take you to the Neversea Depths."

"And once there?" Elkor asked.

"I have no further information to impart," the Keeper said. "I have told you all that the Globe of Infinity has shown me. We must trust that God will guide your steps."

"We will leave as soon as we can," Gavin stated.

"But first, know well what lies before you," the Keeper said. "The Seven Sons of Doom even now scream for the blood of the Blessed Soul from their prison in Hell. They will muster their best and their worst to defeat him. All who worship at the altar of Meherarc, the Angel of Murder, all who commune with Dehen Yaulk, the Lord of the Dead, every corrupted and rotten soul who has sworn allegiance to the Twins of Chaos and marches to battle under the banner of the Lord of Devils is coming. They will fight you for the Blessed Soul. They will do anything to take his life."

"And we will fight them," Gavin said.

The Keeper smiled and nodded. "God has made a splendid choice."

The two knights bowed once again.

"Take great care," the Keeper said. "Assassins with designs on this boy's life watch you from everywhere."

"Yes," Aeoxoea murmured, licking her lips. "Everywhere."

"We will not fail you," Gavin said.

"Farewell," the Keeper said. "The prayers of our people are with you."

With those final words, the fire lost its shape, no longer resembling the Keeper of the Craft. It became a normal fire, burning bright yellow, gaining strength and filling the bowl as it had before.

Gavin removed the furry backpack from his shoulder and gently set it on the ground, then lifted Eleod out. He rested the slumbering child against his chest, softly rubbing his back.

The two knights looked at each other.

"The time of our proving has come," Elkor said. "This is why we don leather and carry steel. This is why we took our oaths."

Gavin nodded and said, "God has chosen us. We must prepare ourselves to go."

Elkor opened the trapdoor.

Aeoxoea turned to look out the window, her eyes on the burning town of Ebon South. "Jass, wake up."

"Yes, mistress?" came the reply.

"Our partnership is not yet at its end," Aeoxoea said. "We are forced to cling together as we tumble through the froth."

"What do you mean?"

"It seems the Blessed Soul of Man isn't the only thing your God has chosen to deposit onto this island," Aeoxoea explained. "Your Keeper of the Craft sends his knights to seek out the ancient weapon of prophecy called Gilligod, the Devil Device. I have no doubt Gavin the Zealot will succeed in this task. He will lay hands upon Gilligod, and when he does, I must be there to take it from him."

Chapter 9

"Gilligod will be forged by a disciple of the Angel of Death. He masquerades as a holy man among the bloodkin dycleth, who live deep beneath the surface of Thershon. You must travel down into the caverns of the Neversea Depths, find this dycleth, and find Gilligod."

At the very moment the Keeper of the Craft spoke those words, imparting the command of the First Guardian of Embriss to his Knights of the Southern Cross, another great warrior listened to the will his master.

Hundreds of miles to the northeast, deep beneath the surface of Thershon, the dycleth battle commander known as the Kuri Kii took a knee, bowing his head before the Speaker of Stones, the Most Favored Wizard Priest of the Temple of the Stone Fathers.

The Kuri Kii was among the greatest battle leaders in the Ur'zyik nation, commanding the elite First Honored Battle Company in the defense of the subterranean city of Youghiot. The unit had distinguished itself in countless battles and many wars over the years, but nothing was quite so impressive as the string of victories won since the Kuri Kii took command. In the ongoing struggle with the ghostkin nations for control of the waterways known as the Father's Blood, the Kuri Kii and his warriors never once surrendered the field to their enemies.

But today, the Speaker of Stones had a task for the First Honored Battle Company, one that would take them far from the war. They were to follow a trail called the Pilgrim's Path, weaving their way through many miles of tunnels and caverns to a relatively quiet area at the far south-down end of the Garnet Dens. Their destination was a small cavern with a hole in its ceiling, the entrance to the lair of the mua giou, the great lizard worm of the

Neversea Depths. This was sacred ground to the Temple of the Stone Fathers, the place where the temple priests communed with their gods and made sacrifice to the lizard worm, a creature holy to their religion.

The priests of the temple had made many pilgrimages to the lair of the mua giou over the generations. Each time they were accompanied by troops of the Ur'zyik Battle Corps, for the path was very long and difficult, and passed through areas of the Garnet Dens inhabited by dangerous wildlife, miagnos and spearheads, as well as the mortal enemies of the Ur'zyik dycleth, the Flying Rock drell.

But this journey would be unique in that it would be led by the Speaker of Stones himself, the highest ranking cleric of the Temple of the Stone Fathers. The Gray Hand was his name, a dycleth of such incredibly advanced age that no one possessed any knowledge of his origins. It was said that the ancient priest had lived to see many generations of dycleth grow to manhood, then return to their place within the deep stone as he lived on, continuing to serve the church.

Since the representatives of the temple who would undertake this trip included a priest of such eminent stature, the leaders of Youghiot decided to send the finest warriors of the Battle Corps to accompany them. Therefore, one of the units chosen to act as escorts for the pilgrimage was the First Honored Battle Company.

Now the Kuri Kii knelt before the Speaker of Stones in the holiest of places, the inner sanctum of the Temple of the Stone Fathers. It was a place where all but the most devout were denied their senses, and so the Kuri Kii was unable to see or hear anything but the words of the Gray Hand, who touched his head, blessing him as a holy warrior of the temple, and touched his weapon, blessing it as a tool of righteous vengeance.

The Kuri Kii carried a double-ended spear with hooked blades on the tips called the Sen Kil. It was a delicate weapon, and difficult to wield for the speed and strength it required. Few warriors could take up the Sen Kil, and none could do so with skill—none but the Kuri Kii, who had earned the weapon some renown by the victories won at the edge of its blades.

The Sen Kil would taste blood in the lair of the lizard worm, the ancient priest promised. It would not be mere herd animals such as the eidyu or the durke, whose flesh would make sacrifice to the mua giou. It would not even be the natural enemies of the Ur'zyik, the miagnos, spearheads, or drell. The Kuri Kii was promised battle with a race he'd never before encountered.

There would be invaders from the surface, that near-mythical place where the ground is scorched by the cursed sun. They would be two human knights sent by their leaders into the realm of the dycleth on their own religious quest. Their mission would bring them to the lair of the lizard worm, where they would brazenly defile the ground held sacred by the followers of the Stone Fathers.

The Kuri Kii must see that the humans did not complete their quest. He must use the Sen Kil to guarantee they never saw their cursed sun again. He must use the strength of the First Honored Battle Company to defeat them without mercy. But most important was the little boy who would be found traveling with the two humans; a boy distinguished by his white hair and golden skin.

That boy must be taken alive.

The Kuri Kii knew it would be done. He had never tasted defeat before. And now his efforts would be blessed by the church. By the grace of the Stone Fathers, he and his men would be unstoppable in their task. As he understood this, and accepted his role as set forth by the Speaker of Stones, his senses returned to him. He could see again, could hear again, and knew with absolute certainty what needed to be done. He rose to his feet and hefted the Sen Kil.

"I will defeat the knights," he swore. "And I will take the boy."

CHAPTER 10

Twenty years later, Yatham walked the muddy streets of Herr Ridge, a humble Embriss town positioned at the west end of the Toden River Valley. The structures he saw around him were modest, plain and squat, built of wood and painted a dull and somehow colorless shade of brown, with so disorganized a layout that the buildings resembled a field of large tree stumps. It didn't appear as though Herr Ridge could be a destination anyone would choose purposefully, yet the gray morning found a rain-soaked Yatham trudging between these buildings after a full day and night of carrying his brother across the floor of the valley.

The sun had risen, but Yatham didn't feel its warmth, couldn't see its light, and knew he wouldn't all day. Angry clouds blanketed, thundering and pounding him with rain that soaked its cold deep into his flesh. It also drove the residents of Herr Ridge indoors with shutters closed, leaving no one to speak with, no one to guide him to his goal. He was left to wander the town alone, keeping a watchful eye for the shop of the wheel monger his uncle Guarn described.

His stride was slow, his carriage filled with weariness. His boots sank deep into the mud, each step making his brother's unconscious body an even heavier burden to bear. It was with no small relief that he found the heavy swinging broad board with the image of a wagon wheel carved into it.

Micka's Wagon Works.

The large, square building that wore the sign appeared like all the others, with doors bolted down and windows shuttered up against the wind and rain. There was no light or warmth or smoke in the chimney, causing Yatham to fear he'd come to Herr Ridge in vain. He pounded first on the door, then on the shutters. Hearing nothing from within, he slogged around back to an open-air forge with a meager roof hanging off the back of the building. There was no fire, no wood and no tools, just walls covered with empty hooks and empty shelves, and a small mule cart half-filled with wooden boxes and small liquor casks. Yatham walked inside, dripping and shivering, yet thankful for his first respite from the rain in hours. He carefully laid his brother's limp body atop the cart's load, and positioned him on his side. Searching his clothes, he found a handkerchief, wrang it out, and tried to wipe the rain from Theel's expressionless face, happy to feel that warmth remained beneath his brother's skin.

"It is by God's grace that you continue to draw breath, brother," he mumbled. "I'll never know how we survived that waterfall; how you avoided drowning or bleeding to death from father's knife in your chest. Surely it was a miracle of God."

If it was a miracle that saved them, that miracle was not extended to the officers of the Overwatch. In the day since the fight in the Trader's Cave, Yatham hadn't seen a single living watchman, though he'd seen plenty of dead ones. The river was full of them; bodies floating among the wreckage of their canoes, some of them drowned, some of them slain. There were wounds from knives and swords and arrows, and there were cracked skulls and broken bones delivered by sudden chance meetings with the jagged rock walls of the Trader's Cave.

If any of the watchmen had survived, they'd given up the chase, perhaps because they were grateful for the chance to go back to the city with their lives intact. Or perhaps it was because Yatham took Theel to the only place they were certain not to follow—directly toward the column of Iatan soldiers who were moving across the floor of the Toden River Valley.

After recovering from the shock of realizing that he and his brother were still alive, Yatham did a quick search of the bodies of the watchmen and their canoes. He was happy to find some scraps of food, a skin of wine, and a few coins. He also found a piece of Uncle Guarn's boat, the aft portion where Theel had sat. It was with utter amazement that he discovered his brother's swords still resting in the bottom. The angel's face remained solemn as Yatham took Battle Hymn into his hand, her eyes closed and mouth open in song. Despite her watery passage through the Trader's Cave, her golden skin remained dry as a bone.

Next, Yatham was able to find a little-damaged Overwatch canoe and load his brother into it. He paddled his way out of the mountains, following the river until it joined up with the Toden. This would take them to the bridge town of Axelhead, which was their goal from the beginning.

Nestled in the fork at the joining of the Toden and Greenstone Rivers, Axelhead was the largest city controlled by the Embriss-born Alister family, known as the Valley Lords, who had ruled over the Toden for hundreds of years. It was in Axelhead that the brothers hoped to find a man who labored in the service of the Alisters, a tradesman named Hoachim, who was also a friend of Uncle Guarn. If luck smiled, Hoachim would be able to find them transport southward on a caravan bound for the Sister Cities, or even better, the Outlands.

But they were still miles away from Axelhead when Yatham could see something was wrong. There were signs a battle had been fought for possession of the river crossings—plumes of smoke and clouds of crows. And those signs worsened as the town grew nearer. To protect their holdings, the Alisters had built towers at each of the river crossings, which stood as sentinels over the town for generations. The nearest tower south of the fork smoldered as if it had been torched. Yatham searched for some sign the Alisters still controlled the town. Just one banner depicting the family sigil, a silver pike on a blue field, would have given him comfort.

Then he saw another tower built to the north of the river, which finally showed him the crest he was looking for—but not in the fashion he'd hoped to see it. The silver pike of the Alisters was prominent on the tunics of the corpses that hung from the tower's wall. One of them was dressed in the silver pike war emblem of the

Wards of the Valley, marking him as the commander of these men. Probably one of Lord Alister's sons, butchered and strung up like a trophy.

Yatham could see those who were responsible camped on the far side of the town, rows of white tents and horses to the north of the fork.

Iatan cavalry.

They'd taken the town, and her bridges with it. Yatham couldn't begin to guess how they'd done it so quickly. The Alisters must have been caught by surprise. But no matter. The Iatan were north of the river, and now had free range of the valley all the way to Korsiren. It meant their plans to accomplish the encirclement of Fal Daran were succeeding. So far. Yatham prayed they'd succeed no further.

But this presented a new problem. Yatham had paddled the canoe all those miles in an effort to reach Axelhead, hoping to find help there. Theel was gravely wounded, and needed the attention of a healer. They'd lost all their provisions in the Trader Cave and needed to resupply. Both of these needs could have been met in Axelhead, but there was no going there now, not with its streets full of enemy soldiers. There would be no finding a healer, seeking the aid of the trader Hoachim, or buying passage south on a caravan.

Yatham's path toward the western valleymouth was blocked, literally, by an army. The Iatan occupied not only Axelhead, but also all the main roads to the bridge crossings, choking them with horsemen and wagons. Most of these headed east, guarding columns of valleyfolk, commoners and soldiers both, once subjects of the noble house of Alister, now prisoners of the Iatan Empire. The brothers had escaped the city Overwatch only to risk falling into the hands of the Iatan.

Yatham decided to avoid the city and road altogether, and so he abandoned his canoe and headed southward on foot. But this presented yet another problem. He was exhausted. He'd paddled the canoe alone all night and all morning, then carried his brother's comatose body for miles, hoping to be relieved of his burden in Axelhead. He couldn't carry his brother forever, and Theel's wounds were never going to properly heal through the constant jostling of his strides. He had to find a wagon or a cart. Or simply someone who would help.

Unfortunately, there would be no friendly faces for miles around. Here, there were no free clansmen, only Iatan soldiers and plumes of smoke. His only hope was to reach Herr Ridge to the southwest of Korsiren in the valleymouth, and there meet with another of Guarn's friends.

He walked south until he could no longer see Axelhead, or its burning towers and hanging corpses. He walked until all evidence of the Iatan and the war was far behind him. Then he turned and began to walk westward. After a few more hours of trudging over fields and hills and pastures, through stands of trees and across small creeks, he finally found the road to Herr Ridge. He spent several more hours on this road, continuing to walk even as night fell and the sky opened up with a steady rainfall.

Sometime after midnight, the lights of the Fortress at Korsiren came into view. The great mountain fastness and home to the Alisters had stood for a thousand years, surviving countless battles and a dozen sieges. It had never been taken by an enemy force, not even when King Brougit sued for peace in the War of the Black Diamond, surrendering rule of the Eastern Kingdoms to Jermalin the Kinslayer. The Alisters did not surrender Korsiren then, and it was clear they would not surrender it now.

The mountain fastness was alive with light, bonfires and torches burning on the battlements and in the windows of the keep, transforming the home of the Alisters into a beacon in the night. And though they hung limp in the dead breeze, the Alister colors that were absent over Axelhead were displayed proudly over every tower and wall.

Seeing the fortress made it clear to Yatham why the Iatan cavalry chose to stop and encamp at Axelhead. Korsiren was positioned at the base of the mountains in the western valleymouth, effectively blocking access to the lands of Embriss. Any invading force attempting to follow the river westward would have a battle at Korsiren. The fortress's walls presented a daunting obstacle, even when defended by a small garrison. But all those fires burning in the night meant one thing: Korsiren was occupied in strength.

If the Alisters were surprised by the Iatan at Axelhead, they would not be here. The River Lords commanded a host of a thousand trained soldiers, and could muster many more from the lesser houses of the valley, if necessary. Such a force could hold Korsiren indefinitely against any army, posing an obstacle far greater than the Iatan cavalry could possibly challenge. The horsemen were wise to make camp at Axelhead and wait for their infantry to catch up.

The advance of the invaders was briefly halted. But unfortunately, it would not be for long. After what Yatham saw of the enemy's forces from his vantage point on the side of Sky Horn Mountain, he knew the Iatan would have tens of thousands marching through the Toden River Valley in a matter of days.

Yatham briefly entertained the notion of seeking aid at Korsiren. The Alisters were fiercely loyal to Embriss, and would have been honored to shelter the sons of one of the kingdom's most famous knights. He could have spent the night in a dry bed by a warm fire, and Theel would have a safe and comfortable place to rest and heal. They would take all the time they needed to recover themselves, then continue on their way, freshly provisioned. They might even be given mounts to carry them the rest of the way to the Outlands. It was very tempting. Yatham would have given nearly anything for a horse at that moment.

But there was no way of knowing whether the Alisters were aware of the death of Quiddip Kile, or if they knew who was to blame. Perhaps the Overwatch never determined the identity of Quiddip's killer. But perhaps they did, and the news had reached Korsiren. If that was the case, Yatham was sure they'd likely spend the night on a stone slab in a dungeon rather than a warm bed.

They'd probably find themselves clapped in chains and dragged back to Fal Daran rather than given fresh provisions and horses.

Besides, even if the Alisters knew nothing of Quiddip Kile and showed the brothers hospitality, the Fortress at Korsiren would likely be besieged by the Iatan soon. A large battle would soon be waged on the very ground Yatham walked on, and there would be no avoiding it if the brothers stopped for any amount of time. This was why Yatham chose to keep traveling through the rainy night, carrying his brother across the floor of the valley. Every step he took was another step farther away from the war, and another step closer to safety.

Eventually the lights of Korsiren faded into the darkness behind him, and he gained confidence he was making the right decision. In the end, he covered more than forty miles with his feet, carrying his brother a full day and night. When dawn came on the fourth day of the brothers' flight from Fal Daran, bringing its gray and rainy sky to the valley, it also cast its light upon the buildings of Herr Ridge, only miles in the distance. Yatham knew his exhausted body needed to rest, but he pushed through, hoping and praying for a meal and a warm fire courtesy of Guarn's friend Micka Dorn.

But the town seemed mostly abandoned, and so did Micka's Wagon Works.

Now Yatham stood in the open-air forge at the back of the building, knowing he needed to continue on, but unsure if he had the strength to do so. He was able to unshoulder the burden of carrying his brother by placing his body in the mule cart. But what to do next?

"There will be no help for us here, brother. It appears Uncle Guarn's friend Micka is long gone," Yatham said, loosening Theel's shirt to look at the wound in his brother's chest. "This place is abandoned. They took everything but this cart and fled from the Iatan."

He poked gently with his fingers around the makeshift bandages on Theel's chest, then peeled them off to expose the wound and the pink skin around it.

"They really stuck you good, brother," Yatham said. "When you awaken, you will see that you finally have a common experience with father. You both suffered mortal chest wounds and lived."

He removed his gloves and rolled his shirt sleeves, baring hands and forearms covered with tattoos of all shapes, sizes, and colors, pictures and words and symbols, some ancient, some magical, some holy. He placed his hands on his brother's chest, palms down, one on each side of the angry red circle, closed his eyes, and took a deep breath.

His scalp began to tingle, and a tattoo on his left arm grew brighter in color and began pulsing, as if alive. It was the Kel Arka Moor, a green weeper vine which was the sigil of the father of Arka Moor, the old Clan of Life. Yatham winced as he felt the power burning within the tattoo, as if he was torched from his left elbow to his left knee, with tendrils spreading out across his lower back, reaching out to touch his neck, and his heart.

It was only a brief moment, and the power left him. The burning ceased, and the tattoo stopped glowing. As this happened, Theel's skin stretched and grew a little more, mended itself a little more, and Yatham could feel his brother's heart beating strong beneath his palm.

Yatham slumped into the mud, wheezing like he'd just carried a horse for a mile, and leaned back against one of the cart wheels.

"That is all I have," he said, as if apologizing to the air. He sat still for a long time, resting and breathing hard, feeling the crushing exhaustion as it crept in and tried so hard to take him away to slumber.

He reached up and touched his brother's hand and said, "Theel, what have I done? Where have I taken you? Far away from our intended course, and too weary to continue on. No help but an empty building and a mule cart with no mule. Here's your quest for you, brother. If the Blessed Soul is to be found, I don't know how."

He sat quietly and listened to the drum of the raindrops on the roof, blinking at the intermittent flashes of lightning. He tried to relax his body to allow himself a few minutes of sleep. Just a few minutes, and then he would shoulder his brother's body and continue on. Just a few minutes.

"Dear God, please give me a horse," he mumbled. "I'd give anything for a horse."

He might have drifted off. His thoughts might have become dreams. All he knew was his mind filled with his fondest desire. If only he could find a horse. The war had robbed the valley of every creature with four legs—mules, pigs, oxen, and of course, horses. He would have taken any of these creatures, from the grandest thoroughbred to the most sway-backed nag, as long as it was sturdy. He would even accept an ox if necessary, or a team of mules that could pull this cart; anything that would allow him to travel faster to transport his brother to a safe place away from this war.

He would have accepted anything, but what he dreamt of was the muscled back of a white charger. He rode in tournament, in both speed and distance competitions, then jumping for height and length, and finally the joust. He could feel the great beast between his knees, muscles rippling as he took his lance in hand, and a peel of thunder startled him back to wakefulness.

He was sad to be back in the forge, leaning against the wheel of the mule cart, soaked and shivering. And now he could hear someone coming—two men, boots splashing, yelling to each other through the rain. He climbed to his feet and composed himself as they walked around the corner of the building toward him, both bundled against the weather.

One was larger, with sunburned skin and tufts of gray hair poking out from under a lumpy, misshapen hat. The other was younger, skinnier, scruffy and pale, with a stained white hood pulled tightly around his eyes. Both carried two small wine casks on their shoulders and stopped walking when they saw Yatham.

"You see this, Rasm?" the older, bigger one said. "Not a soul you can trust in this God-forsaken town. Not even the rats."

"Nope," the skinny man replied. "Not even the, um ..."

"Get away from my cart," the older man said to Yatham.

"Yeah," the skinny man added. "Get away."

"And if you been touching my booze, I'll pound your head down through your jackhole," the older man said.

"Excuse me?" Yatham said.

"Your jackhole," the older man repeated.

"My what?"

"Your ass," the skinny man said. "Listen closer next time."

"Never mind," the older man said. "Just shut your mouth and move away from my cart. Rasm, get the knife."

"Get, um ... " The skinny man looked confused. "The knife?"

"The knife!" the older man shouted.

"Um ... okay. Yeah." The skinny man nodded and set his casks down, removed a backpack and began to rifle through its contents. "The knife? Right. Okay."

"We're going to tie you up," the older man said to Yatham. "Can't have burglars rooting around Micka's Wagon Works, that's for certain. No, not your soup bowl, Rasm, you idiot. I said get the knife."

"Not the soup bowl?" the skinny man asked. "I thought you wanted the soup bowl."

"The knife!" the older man shouted. "You damned wool-head."

"Make up your mind," the skinny man whined.

"I mean no harm. I haven't touched anything," Yatham said, and stepped away from the cart. He watched as the younger, skinny man continued to look through his cluttered backpack, dropping things in the mud; a soup bowl, a book, some cheese, a shoe.

"Don't you have the knife?" the older man asked.

The skinny man seemed to give up searching, and offered a large wooden spoon as a substitute. The older man knocked it out of his hand.

"Damnit, fool," he growled. "What did I say about remembering the knife?"

"Ug, um ... you said ..." The skinny man shrugged. "... to remember the ... um ... spoon?"

"Of course I said to remember the spoon, but I also said to remember the knife," the older man chided. "We can't walk the roads without a knife. How are we supposed to peel our potatoes?"

"Um ... with the spoon?"

"Lord save me from this half-wit jackhole." The older man set his casks down and looked at Yatham. "You stand right there. Don't move. I'll deal with you soon enough. When I tell Micka I caught a burglar in his place, he'll shit a calf."

"Really?" the skinny man said. "A calf? Is that possible?"

"Do you know Micka Dorn?" Yatham asked. "He is the man I seek here."

"All it takes is a few Iatan horsemen squatting in the valley for everyone to lose his head," the older man said. "A man can't leave his place in lockup without some creekwalker coming to steal his work." He poked the skinny man with his finger. "Did you bring any rope?"

The skinny man looked incredulous. "Rope? Yeah. No. Where would I get rope?"

"You didn't bring the rope either?" the older man said. "We need rope. Where are we going to get rope?"

"Try shitting some rope," the skinny man suggested. "Yeah. Try that. Hehe."

"Why do you have that shoe?" the older man asked. "Where'd you get that?"

"Um," the skinny man answered. "I don't remember."

"You don't remember?"

"Um ..." the skinny man said. "Uh ... "

"Shut up," the older man said. "Forget the knife. Get the clobber stick. It's in the cart."

"Do one of you know Dorn?" Yatham asked.

"You stay where you stand," the older man said to him. "Don't move. Rasm, why aren't you getting my clobber stick?"

"We don't need your, um ... clobber ... " the skinny man said, pulling a large book from his bag.

"Why?" the older man asked. "Did you find the knife?"

The skinny man gestured to his book. "I have, um ... I have ..."

Then he made a strange sound like a hiccup had become trapped in his throat, then squirted out between his lips.

" ... ack ..."

"What?" the older man asked.

The skinny man coughed and tried again. "I have sp- ... ack ... ack ..."

"Oh no," the older man said, rubbing his eyes. "Not spacks."

"Spacks?" Yatham asked.

"I have the perfect sp- ... ack ... here somewhere," the skinny man said, leafing through the pages. "Sp- ... ack ... book will show me."

"No, no," the older man said. "You don't have the perfect spell. Put the book away."

"I have the perfect sp-" the young man choked on his words. " ... ack ..."

"No, you don't. No spellcraft," the older man warned. "Will you listen to me? Do you want to burn your face again?"

"Don't need a clobber stick," the skinny man said. "Not when I have the perfect ... ack ..."

"What are you talking about?" the older man asked.

"Sp- ... ack ..."

"Does he know spellcraft?" Yatham asked.

The skinny man looked at Yatham. "No," he said. "Yes, I'm a wiz- ... ack ..."

"You're not a wizard, you lumberhead," the older man scolded. "Don't even try it. If you catch fire again, I'm not putting you out."

"You won't have to put me out," the skinny man said, gesturing at the clouds above. "It's raining."

"What's wrong with him?" Yatham asked.

"Oh, nothing." The older man sighed. "And everything."

"Can he craft runes?"

The skinny man nodded. "Yes I can. I'm a wiz- ... ack ..."

The older man looked at Yatham. "Look, there isn't time for this. We both know the Iatan Army is coming this way, so if you'll just get your dead friend off my cart and get out of here, I won't tell anybody I saw you stealing Micka's stuff." He looked at the skinny man. "Put the damn book away. We have to go."

"Yeah but, um ... There is no need for us to allow this man to escape the justice he so deserves," the skinny man said, turning the pages of his book. "I will detain him. Yeah. Without the use of violence."

"Oh yeah?" the older man asked. "How are you going to do that?"

"Prepare to be amazed," the skinny man said, bright eyed. "Oh, yeah. Prepare yourself."

"I'm waiting."

"Watch this," the skinny man said, rolling up his sleeves. "I am about to call upon the arcane power- ... ack ... what I mean to say is I will craft mystical- ... ack ... Ahem, I'll use mag- ... ack ... I'll cast a sp- .... ack ... damnit!"

"You'll do what?" the older man asked.

"I'll turn him to salt."

"With magic?" Yatham asked.

"Yes!" the skinny man shouted, pointing at Yatham. "He understands. He knows what I mean. Yeah!"

"No, you won't use magic," the older man said. "You *can't* use magic."

"Um ... " the skinny man said. "Yes I can."

"Shut up. You always talk too much." The older man looked at Yatham. "He needs to shut up, don't you think?"

"I don't need to shut up," the skinny man said. "*You* need to shut up. I'm a wiz- ... ack ..."

"He fancies himself a wizard, but he's nothing more than a menace," the older man explained. "He blows bubbles out his ears and wets his pants on a good day. This is not a good day."

The older man reached over and pulled his companion's hood back, revealing a strip of bald skin running down the center of a head otherwise covered with a forest of hair.

"See?" the older man said. "He set his face on fire. Almost killed himself. Almost burned down the whole city."

"Hey, stop!" The skinny man slapped his companion's hands away and pulled the hood back tight. "You don't have to tell everyone you see."

"Why?" the older man asked.

"It should have worked," the skinny man complained.

"It should've worked, but it didn't," the older man said. "Because you're not a wizard."

"My sp- ... ack ... book told me wrong sp- ... ack ... that day."

"Your spell book didn't tell you anything because books can't talk, and neither can you," the older man said.

"I can talk."

"No you can't, you idiot."

"I am not an idiot." the skinny man said. "I'm a wiz- ... ack ..."

"You are not a wizard," the older man said. "Now shut up."

"Yes I am. I'm a wiz- ... ack ..." the skinny man said. "I'll turn him to salt."

"Do either of you know Micka Dorn?" Yatham asked.

"We don't have time for this. The Iatan are coming and we have to clear out." The older man looked to Yatham. "Look, boy, if you say you aren't drinking any of my booze, that's good enough for me."

"Is he a wizard?" Yatham asked, pointing at the skinny man.

"Yes!" the skinny man exclaimed, nodding his head.

"No!" the older man shouted, shaking his head.

"Do one of you know Micka Dorn?"

"Yes," said the older man, nodding.

"No," said the skinny man, shrugging.

The older man cuffed the skinny man in the head. "Shut up, you hammerhead."

Yatham sighed, speaking his words slowly. "Where is Micka?"

"What do you want Micka for?" the older man asked.

"I need his aid," Yatham answered. "He is a trusted friend of my family. It is important. It's crown business."

"Oh, sure," the older man said. "Crown business. That means the world. Rasm, get my clobber stick. I'm going to club this guy just for fun."

Yatham stepped back to his brother's side and snatched the man's club from inside the cart, hefting it with skill. "No clubs, no spells, and no more argument. Just answer me. Where is Micka?"

"We don't need any trouble," the older man said defensively, raising his arms. "Micka's gone, like everybody else. This town is near dead. All you got is me and the idiot here."

"I'm not an idiot," the skinny man whined. "I'm a wiz-"

"Are you with the army?" the older man asked Yatham.

"No," Yatham said.

"Are you sword sworn to the Alisters?" the older man asked.

"No," Yatham answered. "I am sworn to Lord Britou and the Kingdom of Embriss."

"Sworn to Embriss, eh? And you can handle a weapon, I see that," the older man said. "How about your friend there. Who's he?"

Yatham answered by reaching over to tug a glove off his brother's limp hand. He threw the glove to the older man who caught it and turned it over, examining the decorative stitching.

"This is a crown seal," he announced.

"That's right," Yatham replied. "It is."

The older man raised an eyebrow. "You killed one of the king's men?"

"Yes he did, without a doubt, yeah," the skinny man said. "A very good reason to turn him to salt."

Yatham shook his head. "I did not kill him. He lives."

"What's your business?" the older man asked. "You didn't travel this far only to see Micka. I'll wager that."

"Sp- ... ack ... components," the skinny man said, digging through is backpack. He pulled out a live frog and a half-eaten turkey leg. "Is this what I need? No. Yeah! Maybe?"

"My travels continue," Yatham said. "You two are leaving town?"

"This isn't our home," the older man said. "We're going south. Is that turkey leg still good?"

"Do you have a mule for this cart?" Yatham asked.

"No, I got better. Two mules," the man answered. "Stupid as hell, but strong and loyal, when they're going in the right direction."

"You stay there," the skinny man ordered Yatham. "I'm almost ready with my sp- . . . ack . . . Imagine what it is like to be made of salt, 'cause that's what's about to happen. Yeah. This is going to be great!"

"Hitch up your mules and leave this man where he sleeps," Yatham said to the older man. "The three of us must get him out of this town before the Iatan arrive."

"Sure enough, I'll help you. No one will say I'm not a loyal son of Embriss," the older man said. "But you and your friend are sure to earn us some ugly looks. There's bandits and worse riding these roads, Iatan scouts and spies. You any good in a scrap?"

Yatham gestured to Theel. "You see to this man's safety, and I'll see to yours."

The older man nodded. "It's a bargain then," he said, extending his hand.

"It's a bargain," Yatham said, and accepted the handshake.

"Help us load these casks and we'll get moving," the older man offered.

"Done," Yatham said.

The skinny man continued searching through his bag. "This will be great. I have the perfect sp- ... ack ..."

"Shut up and help us, you half-wit," the older man said. "And give me that turkey leg."

Chapter 11

The road Yatham followed south out of Herr Ridge was no more pleasant than the one he took into town from the north. It was gray and soupy, full of rocks that poked at toes, and each footstep was accompanied by a sucking plop. The road was surrounded by dead grass, dead trees, and patches of marsh that steamed and bubbled and stunk. The day was just as cheery, with the downpour slowing to a drizzle by noondark. The sky no longer spoke with volleys of thunder, but the rainfall remained steady. The clouds moved continuously northeast, but the blanket of gray was never quite pulled from Thershon for the rest of the day.

Though it was a bad day for travel, the road wasn't deserted. Instead it was filled with refugees of Herr Ridge and other towns at the west end of the valley, husbands and wives and families walking, pulling rickshaws or riding mules, with wagons or ox carts packed with children and possessions, driven out into the elements from their fear of the Iatan. Yatham trudged along beside the mule cart, beside his unconscious brother. He kept his head low and watched as his feet disappeared and reappeared in the gray muck with each step, listening as the older of his two new acquaintances made small talk.

"I'm Hoster. Just Hoster," the sun-stained man in the misshapen hat said. "I got no surname or sigil like any of those noble jackholes because I don't need the heavy cargo it brings. I don't need the cargo and I don't need the sigil, so I'm Hoster, just Hoster, and I cook booze. The wares in that cart there is all I have, and I'm thinking it'll get us whatever we need. I can trade with the best there is. I'll barter your balls off."

"Really?" Yatham asked.

"Yes, sir. Clean off." Hoster nodded his head proudly. "That's Rasm over there with his nose in the book."

The young man with the bald head walked along on the other side of the mule cart, holding his book, staring at the pages with glazed eyes, his jaw hanging open.

"You met him," Hoster said. "He's a no-good, half-wit lumberhead. Says he's a wizard, but that's a bunch of scatter, so don't listen to it."

Rasm kept pace with the mule cart, despite not watching where he was going. His eyes were locked on his book, causing him to stumble constantly. As Yatham watched, he tripped and fell face down in the mud.

"He'll be fine," Hoster said. "Those two stinking, mangy flea farms are my mules, Chigger and Ragweed. Chigger's on the right, and, uh ..."

"Ragweed's on the left?" Yatham guessed.

"Sure," Hoster said, and belched. "Shut up, Ragweed!"

"She didn't make a noise," Yatham said.

"She's cursed by God, I say," Hoster said. "The worst damned mule in all the clans. She's stupid and slow, and a general disgrace to four-legged creatures worldwide. Her daddy was a good pull, a good ride, and was sturdy. You couldn't move him. Ragweed is stupid as hell and good for nothing. She ain't sturdy at all. She don't even listen. Rasm says she's deaf."

"Your mule is deaf?"

"A deaf mule is the worst kind," Hoster explained. "Chigger farts a lot. See? You hear that?"

"Hear what?"

"He's strong and a good puller, when he's faced the right way," Hoster said. "He's pulled my old ass out of the fire all manner of times. But he's dumb, even for a mule. You got to let him know he's got to earn his keep. Let him know he isn't worth his weight in his momma's shit, so he'll keep stepping. Hey, Chigger, you keep stepping or I'll carve you up for my stew, damn you! He acts like he don't hear me, but he does."

"He hears you?" Yatham asked.

"Yes, he does," Hoster said. "But he acts like he don't. So who's the stiff sleeping on my cargo?"

"That's my brother, Theel."

"He's going to wake up hurting," Hoster warned. "I've slept on those crates before, and it can be unpleasant, let me tell you. I've awakened so stiff I thought I had a broken back and a broken ass."

"I can carry him no longer," Yatham said. "Besides, a stiff back will be the least of his concerns once he rouses."

"If that's what you want," Hoster said. "Do what you have to do. Pile up the crates and throw the stiff on, I say. Lord, this road is one endless skid. Poor Chigger's working his ass off. Good work, Chigger. You keep stepping, you lumber head. Ragweed, stay out of Chigger's way, damn you. Anyway, so where are you and your brother Theel headed?"

"The Outlands," Yatham answered. "Beyond the southern borders of Embriss."

"By God, I'm your man. You're headed straight through the mountain kingdoms, aren't you? That's Yarik country." Hoster thumped his chest. "You're looking at a proud son of Yarik, boy. I was born and raised in the Dividers, carried the spear for my clan for six years. Yarik by birth. Yarik by blood. I know every way through the mountains of Yarik. Every way to walk, and every way to run."

"Do you know the paths to the south of Yarik? Through the Gray Mounds?" Yatham asked.

"I been through the Gray Mounds bunches, up and down, in and out of every gray mound there is," Hoster said. "Chigger will curse my bones, but I just curse him back and still make him pound those rocks. There's the king's work to be earned. Even in the Outlands."

"I've never been to the Outlands," Yatham asked. "What is the country like?"

"It's a dark sky overhead, let me tell you. If you don't starve or get the plague, there's plenty of zoths to throw spears at you. No place will show you greater proof of how unkind the world can be than the Outlands. It's a big bucket of scatter down there."

"A bucket of what?" Yatham asked.

"Scatter."

"A bucket of scatter?"

"Yeah, a bucket of scatter," Hoster said. "Zoths, the plague, creeper's disease. You ever meet a creeperman?"

"No, I haven't."

"Me neither, but I hear it's terrible," Hoster said.

"Terrible?"

"Horrible," Hoster said. "It's a real hellhole. No God-fearing man can breathe that stinking air without a choke or two. Zoths and creepermen, like I said. You can freeze. You can starve. That's if you're good at dodging spears. But hell."

"You still go," Yatham said.

"Of course I go," Hoster said. "There's a living, and that means there's the king's work to be earned. Wherever there are men with troubles, there is the need for a good traveling booze-cooker like myself. It's a good thing we have the spirits to kill the cold stones in our bellies, am I right? So, where are you headed in the Outlands?"

"A place called Ebon South," Yatham said. "Do you know it?"

"Yeah, I know it," Hoster answered. "I've done plenty of business in Ebon South. I know people there. I can get you to Ebon South in two sucks of a beer bladder. I got some beer bladders in the cart if you want a suck or two. Takes the scratches away, you know?"

"I know."

"This is perfect," Hoster said. "You're headed to Ebon South, and I know people in Ebon South. I been there bunches. You'll do fine with me. Of all the sorry sods walking these roads, you sure picked the right one to talk with. Me. That's right. Holy scatter balls."

"Holy what?" Yatham asked.

"Scatter balls," Hoster said.

"Holy scatter balls?"

"Yeah."

"Scatter balls are holy?" Yatham asked.

"Huh?"

"I don't know what you mean," Yatham said. "What is scatter?"

"Are you serious?" Hoster said. "Holy scatter balls, you are serious."

"What does it mean?" Yatham asked.

"Well 'scatter' is a term we working folk use to describe shit," Hoster said. "It's what Ragweed did, and Rasm stepped in it when we were leaving Herr Ridge."

"How can you call that holy?" Yatham asked. "It isn't holy."

"I'm not saying it's holy. I'm just saying holy scatter, that's all," Hoster said. "Boy, you need to learn a thing or two about common speak before you get to the Outlands or you won't fit in at all. Those stoat-skinning Outlander bastards will have your ass."

"They'll have my ass?"

"On a stick."

"Sounds terrible," Yatham said.

"Horrible is what it is," Hoster said.

"Sounds horrible."

"You got to act common, speak like one of those godless Outlander bastards," Hoster said.

"And proclaim the holiness of scatter?" Yatham asked.

"Yeah."

"I'll consider it."

"The Outlands aren't a friendly place," Hoster said. "Especially to city sods like you."

"City sods?" Yatham asked.

"Yeah," Hoster said. "City sods. Limp-wristed daffodil dandies like you and your dead brother."

"He's not dead," Yatham said.

"Sure," Hoster said. "So, you boys must have good reason to be going to a hellhole like Ebon South. What's your crown business? You boys gonna crack some heads?"

Yatham smiled. "No cracking heads. We avoid fighting."

"You avoid fighting, huh?" Hoster said. "Doesn't look like your brother avoids fights."

"Well," Yatham said, "There are times when he doesn't."

"He didn't avoid this one," Hoster said. "And he left you to carry his stabbed, half-dead ass all across the countryside."

"Sometimes a fight is unavoidable."

"That is most certainly true, my boy," Hoster said. "So, how'd he do? How does the other guy look?"

"It wasn't just one," Yatham said. "There were twelve of them."

"How do the twelve of them look, then?"

"They are all dead," Yatham said.

"Dead?"

"Yes, dead."

"Holy scatter balls," Hoster said. "Now I see why he's laid up. Any good man will catch a bruise or two if he's fighting jackholes by the dozen, whether he can handle himself or not."

"Theel can handle himself," Yatham said. "He was trained in steel by our father, who was a Knight of the Southern Cross."

"A Knight of the Southern Cross?" Hoster said. "Now *there's* a rare breed. Plenty of folks like to talk about training with those knights, but it's mostly talk."

"That is because only the greatest fighters with the stoutest hearts are even considered for the honor of wearing the silver shield."

"They say a knight can kill a hundred zoths," Hoster said. "They say you don't cross a knight because he can kill you before you know he's angry. They say a knight is worth more than an army in a fight. Did your father ever kill a hundred zoths?"

"Thousands."

"Your father killed a thousand zoths? That's really something," Hoster said. "I only fought a few zoths long ago when I carried the spear, but I'm not a knight. And I sure as hell never could be. I don't like to run to the front when the zoths attack, like those knights do. So, where's your father posted these days? Back in Fal Daran?"

"He died some months ago."

"Oh, that's no good," Hoster said.

"His body was never recovered," Yatham explained. "It took some time for the news to reach Fal Daran. We planted his memorial tree only days ago."

"That's sad," Hoster said softly. "Did he die a hero?"

"He died doing his duty, fighting the zoths."

"That's good," Hoster said. "Better than dying in a ditch with the plague, or having a wagon wheel hit you in the head. I knew a guy who got hit in the head with a wagon wheel and died. Rasm got hit in the head with a wagon wheel, but he didn't die. So, where was your father fighting? Bloodstone Pass? Korsiren? The zoths are nasty up there."

"No, it was down south," Yatham answered. "In the Dividers Mountains somewhere. I hope to go there someday soon. His knightshield was lost in the battle."

"That's no good," Hoster said. "No telling where that shield is by now. Probably worn by some heathen zoth. Probably parading it around as a trophy."

"Perhaps," Yatham said. "It may be necessary to fight to retrieve it. We'll do what we must."

"Much luck with that," Hoster said. "No fun scrapping with zoths, I'll tell you. Especially if your brother doesn't wake up first. So he's a knight, huh? He doesn't look like a knight. He doesn't have a silver shield on him."

"No, he doesn't."

"Is that why you're looking for your father's shield?" Hoster said. "For your brother to wear?"

"Yes, but it is more than that," Yatham said. "I don't wish for my father's shield to be lost. It is sacred to my family. It deserves to be in an honored place, not in the hands of a zoth."

"That's good sense," Hoster said. "I wouldn't want that either."

"It is my hope that the honored place will be on my brother's chest, worn with pride, just as our father wanted," Yatham explained. "That shield is my brother's birthright to wear, should he fulfill his Warrior Baptism and rise to knighthood. It is only proper that he should have it."

"Should he fulfill his Warrior Baptism?" Hoster asked. "Your brother isn't yet a knight?"

"No, he isn't, but he's been through the training," Yatham said. "He fights as well as a knight."

"He can fight like a knight?" Hoster said. "I'd like to see that."

"You'll see it," Yatham stated. "Theel could best almost anyone in a fight. He is exceptional with a blade. He has all the strength of arm and back needed to be a knight. He has only to satisfy the requirements of Warrior Baptism. Then he will have earned the right to wear our father's shield."

"If his Warrior Baptism says he needs to get stabbed in the chest and nearly drown in the river, he's doing well so far," Hoster said. "Should have his shield by morning."

Yatham smiled. "Unfortunately, that won't be enough."

"Then what will be?" Hoster asked. "What's he supposed to do to earn that shield?"

"He's been charged with a knight's quest."

"Oh, I've heard of those. Isn't that where you have to kill a bunch of people?" Hoster guessed. "I hear they make you swear an oath to kill a bunch of people and if you don't, you're supposed to kill yourself."

"An oath is taken, but it is not a promise to do violence," Yatham said. "That's against the beliefs of the knighthood."

"So what do you promise to do?"

"Whatever necessary," Yatham answered. "When the First Guardian Lord Britou charges a knight with a quest, the knight takes an oath to dedicate his life to the quest until it is finished, or until he dies. When Theel returns to Fal Daran with his quest completed, Warrior Baptism will be achieved, and he will be granted knighthood."

"So, what is the final step?" Hoster asked. "What does your brother have to do to become a knight? Find your father's shield?"

"No."

"What then?"

"It is not my place to discuss it," Yatham said. "He will tell you if he chooses."

"Oh, I understand," Hoster said. "It's his business. But I'm telling you something. Fate brought us together in Herr Ridge, Warrior Baptism or not. Me and Rasm finding you was no chance at all, for certain as God wills it. And your brother is going to be a knight someday, and I get to tell people how I know him. Of course, right now he looks like big puddle of scatter, but that's fine. He'll wake up sometime. My brews are looking damned safe. Any highway bandits try to take our cargo, your brother can give them a whipping. He can carve up the bandits while I watch the cargo, and Rasm can stand in the bushes and look stupid and the booze will still be safe. Yes, sir. What a beautiful day. I'm feeling good. So, what's your story? Why are you going to the Outlands?"

"I'm doing what I can to help my brother in his quest," Yatham answered. "Where we're going, it's good to have someone to watch your back."

"The knife seems to have gone into his chest. Perhaps you should consider watching his front," Hoster suggested.

"That was a terrible situation."

"The Outlands are full of terrible situations."

"And my brother has the steel for it," Yatham said. "It's just that the ability to use the sword and the ability to know *when* to use the sword are two different things. It's not easy. Our father used to tell us that every fighter has much learning to do, from the lowliest squire to the highest-ranking knight."

"He's got to learn," Hoster guessed. "That's why you're going to the Outlands?"

Yatham nodded. "Sometimes a knight's quest is more about the knight than the quest."

CHAPTER 12

Twenty years before the Iatan brought war to Thershon, a wave of zoth attacks swept across the Seven Kingdoms, resulting in hundreds of battles over the course of seven days. Wherever these creatures of evil lived, they rose up to assault their human neighbors with unprecedented coordination. Tribes who were separated by many hundreds of miles, who had no contact with one another, attacked simultaneously, and with terrifying savagery, every day for a week.

For years after, these attacks would collectively be known as the Scythe of Fire. So many died in these seven days it was said that Dehen Yaulk, the Lord of Death, swept his reaping blade across the land, cutting down thousands of people as if they were stalks of wheat in a grisly harvest. This was the Scythe.

During these seven days, the Seven Kingdoms were covered by a glowing orange fog that blotted out the sun. The zoth attacks began on the first morning to dawn orange, and did not cease until after the fog receded on the night of the seventh day. No hope could be seen in the sky as the people of Thershon struggled for their lives. As they looked up from all the death and destruction, seeking aid and comfort from whatever god they prayed to, all they saw was the fog. No sun. No clouds. No moon or stars. Just a murky, orange glow. This was the Fire.

At the time, many thought it was the strange sky which stirred the zoths to battle. Later it would be revealed it was a certain boy whose coming the orange sky heralded.

On the southern tip of the western kingdoms, on the frontier of a region known as the Outlands, the town of Ebon South was not spared any of the zoths' wrath. In fact, some of the most ferocious fighting occurred in this little town, for it was here on the seventh day that the boy of the prophecies appeared, ending the Scythe of Fire and setting the prophecies into motion. He was a sweet-faced little boy named Eleod, with pale hair and golden skin. He was the Blessed Soul of Man.

Though the town was surrounded by hundreds of vicious zoths who craved his blood, the boy slept peacefully in the protective care of Gavin the Zealot. He was also under the vigilant watch of another pair of eyes, unseen in the natural world—those of the assassin, Aeoxoea.

The Keeper of the Craft had ordered Gavin the Zealot and his fellow knight Elkor the Hound to take Eleod from the city and travel in search of Gilligod, the weapon of evil which prophecy said would one day take the child's life. Though their task was urgent, the knights waited within the walls of Storm Hall for several hours before embarking on their quest.

The darkest hours of nighttime came and went before they emerged. The sky had become the deep blue that precedes the dawn, extinguishing all but the brightest stars. The Constellation of the Blessed Soul looked down upon them as they walked across Storm Hall's courtyard, taking their first steps toward fulfilling the prophecies.

Their quest required them to leave the safety of the town and take Eleod into the wilderness of the Outlands, not an easy task. First they would need to pass beyond the large wooden stockade that surrounded the town. Then they would have to cross a grassy strip of land that separated Ebon South from the tree line. It would be nearly impossible to accomplish either without being spotted by zoth sentries. The predawn darkness would provide some cover, but not much since, as Jass explained to Aeoxoea, zoths could see in the dark "like cats."

The knights' goal was to reach the cover of the forest unseen, but once this was done, their ordeal was only beginning. The warriors of a dozen zoth tribes were out there lurking in the darkness, all of them hungry to avenge the day's defeat. Aeoxoea could see them as she stood among the sentries on the top of the wooden wall. She shifted her vision to a light spectrum which showed her variances of heat, and there they were, hundreds of warm bodies contrasting starkly with the cold snow, especially their glowing eyes. All around the town, red zoth eyes watched from the tree line, staring lustfully at the wooden stockade, eager to finish what they began. The assassin could see they were already in the process of gathering the survivors of the first attack in hopes to hit the town again before the sun rose.

Aeoxoea shadowed the two knights from the moment they left the Devil's Torch, watching all they did as they prepared to leave the town. She saw their grim faces, saw they knew well what they faced, and noticed how they oddly talked of none of it.

Gavin held the Blessed Soul in his arms as he walked through Storm Hall. This boy was the answer to the prayers of generations of clansmen, the one whose coming was prophesied in the writings of Sun Antheus thousands of years before. Gavin literally held the hope of the world in his hands, and now he planned to carry that hope out of the city and into the savage Outlands, home to thousands of bloodthirsty zoths.

Yet the two knights felt no need to make mention of any of it. They discussed no plans for their escape from Ebon South, and exchanged very few words as they gathered their provisions and readied themselves for travel. It didn't seem clear whether they had any idea how they would get the child out of town safely until they headed to the kennels to retrieve the final two members of their party, Behe and Kang, Elkor's dogs of war.

They looked very much like shepherd dogs, with shaggy necks and pointy ears, but their coloring was different. And they were much bigger, with the larger of the two standing taller than a man's waist.

Behe was the female, younger and smaller. She wore a coat of white, with shades of auburn around her eyes and back. Kang, her father, was larger and more powerful. He was black as midnight from tail to snout, except for a few white hairs that had grown in around his mouth in recent years. A grizzled old veteran just like his master, Kang was one of the first dogs Elkor ever trained, and had the scars to prove it. He'd seen as many battles as many of the swords of House Stormdell.

Eleod immediately took a liking to Kang, who was so big, he was able to stand face to face with the little boy. The Blessed Soul looked at the dog for a moment, then his face brightened.

"It's a bear!" he announced.

When all was ready for travel, the knights took the animals to the southeast edge of the town. Here was an area where a section of the stockade was destroyed in the zoth attack, creating a gaping hole nearly twenty feet wide through which hundreds of the creatures gained entry to Ebon South. Aeoxoea watched as a large group of soldiers milled around the opening, watching and waiting for the attack they knew was coming, while others worked to position a previously constructed section of wall, a large wooden bandage that would temporarily mend the hole.

The knights walked calmly into this chaos, wearing battle leathers under thick furs, Gavin carrying Eleod, and the dogs walking at their side. Their presence caused a bustle as men began to cheer and salute, and wave their torches. Some raised their weapons in reverse, grips and handles and hilts offered forth as a sign of allegiance. Others simply knelt.

"Sons of Yarik!" Elkor shouted, eliciting a sharp cheer from some of the soldiers wearing the diamond-shaped war emblem of Yarik on their shirts.

"Sons of Embriss!" Gavin shouted. This brought another, louder answer from the men who wore the tree of seven branches for the Kingdom of Embriss.

"Swords of House Stormdell!" Elkor shouted. This brought the greatest response, bursting from the throats of all the men, especially those wearing green surcoats featuring the white-horned bullosk, the sigil of House Stormdell.

"The zoth will come again tonight, that is certain," Elkor began. There was a wave of murmuring and exchanged looks of resolve.

"He will come tomorrow, that too is certain." Many of the men nodded in understanding.

"And he will come every day the sun rises and sets until all our homes are destroyed. There is no greater certainty than that," Elkor said, bringing a rumble of anger from the assembled men. "None but the certainty that you men of the old clans, from the silver tree of Embriss and the black diamond of Yarik, to the white bullosk of Stormdell; you who have beaten them back every time, will *continue* to beat them back every time they come, until it is the *zoth* whose body rots in death, until *his* house is destroyed, and the Houses of the old clans, the Seven Kingdoms, and the Southern Cross stand strong, together, resolute, kinsman all!"

The men cheered wildly, banging weapons and shields.

Elkor let this go on for many moments before he interrupted his men, saying, "Many of you know that I am leaving you, and have declared the Battle Lord Barzil the Blood Axe your new Lord Commander of Storm Hall. Follow him as you once followed me." The men began shouting their allegiance, cheering the Blood Axe. "Know that I will return to Ebon South one day, and when I do, I'll expect to hear that you all stood behind the Blood Axe on this night, and every zoth who dared breach this wall was crushed in the effort!"

As the men cheered further and chanted the Hound's name, Elkor and Gavin moved through the crowd, shaking hands, saluting, and tapping the blades of their weapons against those of the soldiers, a gesture of good will among clansmen. When Elkor finished saying his farewells, the knights approached the hole in the stockade, stopping short of the section of temporary wall which lay flat on the ground where it waited to be raised to plug the gap. Elkor looked through the hole at the line of trees distant, and Aeoxoea followed his gaze. The zoths were moving, jumping, rocking back and forth, shaking their spears. They were ready for blood. Their desire to kill was so strong it required all the influence of their chieftains to hold them back until the order was given. Aeoxoea could see it. Elkor could sense it.

It was time.

"Behe!" Elkor shouted. "Kang!" The battle hounds tensed at the sound of their names as though they knew what was coming. Elkor spoke words of command, "Flank wall, left!" and the animals leaped forward, ran through the gap in the stockade, and disappeared silently into the darkness.

Elkor signaled his men and the soldiers rushed forward, putting as many hands as would fit on the new section of wall, cursing and grunting, straining a dozen backs to lift it from the ground and push it into place. More men rushed forward with logs and wooden beams, pushing one end of each into the ground, the other end up against the wall to brace it against the coming attack.

Aeoxoea turned back, searched the darkness for the battle hounds, and saw the red glow of their furry bodies already far away. Once outside the stockade, the dogs headed northeast, quickly and silently, staying close to the wall. Gavin and Elkor headed in the same direction, but remained inside the town, following a street that ran parallel to the stockade. Aeoxoea followed them around the southern edge of Ebon South, nearly a full mile to the other side of town where there was less commotion and all was quiet but the wind.

Here, where the stockade remained strong and unbroken, there were only a handful of human defenders on the ramparts, lookouts standing ready to sound the alarm should the zoths once again emerge from the trees in force. The knights joined these defenders by climbing a ladder to the top of the wall.

It was quiet on the wall, and Aeoxoea could hear the gruesome story that played itself out in the field between the town and the tree line. Zoth bodies, living and dead, lay scattered in the grass, a feast for carrion animals, mostly the birds, broke necks and black wings, honking, hissing, and pecking. The cries of the wounded zoths could be heard among the flapping of wings, shouting out to their deity, whom they called their Blood Goddess, begging her for death, and thanking her for the chance to kill and die.

Looking out toward the trees, Aeoxoea could see the enemy presence was just as sparse as the human presence on this side of town, with also just a few lookouts; some in trees, some on the ground. Those few zoths watched the town, scanning the walls, making certain no human had a chance to enter or leave Ebon South alive. They didn't know that in the center of the field, unnoticed among the flapping wings of the carrion and writhing zoth bodies, two pairs of canine eyes watched them back.

Elkor gave a soft, almost imperceptible whistle, and the battle hounds looked back. He flashed them a hand signal and again, Behe and Kang were off and running, this time with deadly purpose. Aeoxoea watched as Kang entered the forest, teeth bared and fur bristling as he advanced in the face of a zoth sentry. His heavy steps crunched in the snow, drew the zoth's eyes to him, while Behe softly padded a circuitous route around. She broke into a run and jumped, hit the zoth from behind, and drove it hard to the ground. She clamped her jaws on the back of its neck and didn't let go until it stopped struggling.

Kang was already after a new kill, this one sitting in the boughs of a tree. With a mighty leap, he caught the zoth's leg in his teeth and pulled it down, where it crashed in the snow hard, broke its elbow and dropped its spear. It only had time to groan once before Kang's heavy paws landed hard on its chest and canine teeth sank deep into its neck. The zoth tried to scream, but with a mighty shake of his head, Kang tore its throat out.

The knights stood on the wall and calmly waited while the battle hounds did their work, going from one enemy to the next, quietly killing, quietly preparing a path for their masters. They were well-trained and efficient, and Aeoxoea was enthralled as she watched them do their work. Sometimes they did their business alone, other times they worked in concert, through many methods and without direction from their master. The animals moved through the trees without a whisper, unseen by a single of their victims until death was at hand—crushing throats, breaking necks, and leaving little sign of their presence but shallow paw prints and droplets of dark zoth blood that dripped from their jaws.

After several minutes of this, Elkor said, "It's time. We go."

Ropes were thrown down and the knights quickly jumped over the wall, climbing to the bottom of the stockade. They hit the ground running, crossing the field at a full sprint, hurdling dead zoths, sending carrion birds fleeing before them. They moved just as quietly as the battle hounds, breathing evenly, with sword belts secured and weapons wrapped in blankets and furs. Eleod rode on Gavin's back, a bundle of furs, quiet in sleep, only mildly jostled by the knight's smooth stride.

When they were midway across the field, Aeoxoea heard a horn blast to the southwest. It was followed by another, and another. The horns were answered by the shrill scream of hundreds of zoths. Aeoxoea looked and saw them emerge from the trees—a large, whooping, yelling mass of bloodlust, moving across the field to hit the stockade where the town defenders awaited them. The knights paid them no mind, and neither did Aeoxoea.

She looked back to see Gavin and Elkor enter the trees, still at a full sprint, running as if they could do this forever. About a mile into the forest, the dogs caught up and loped alongside, flanking the knights and watching the forest as they ran. Aeoxoea thought the knights would slow or stop, but they didn't. After several miles, they kept going.

Branches waved in the breeze overhead and a thousand trees whooshed quietly by as the minutes dragged on and became an hour, then another hour. The knights continued running, carrying Eleod farther from the town, deeper into the wilderness. The sun rose in the sky, the little boy awakened, and still they ran. Footstep after crunching footstep, heavy breaths steaming in the cold air, they ran all morning and well into the day. They breakfasted on their feet, noondark came and went, and their stride never slowed.

Aeoxoea wondered if they would ever stop.

Chapter 13

It was exactly twenty years later that the quest to discover the Blessed Soul of Man began in earnest. It was the third moon day of the Watcher's Wait, 3144 AS by the common calendar, during a period later called the War of the Iatan by some, or the Second War of Souls by others.

Night had darkened the skies above southeastern Embriss, closing many eyes as the watcher waited. Within city walls, the smooth-faced children of free clansmen slept beneath layers of quilts while their mothers cleaned the evening supper's cook pots. Old men puffed tobacco pipes by the house hearth while young men sharpened spears and spoke of war. Night also halted the movement of the armies—invaders and defenders alike. The killing was done, but only for a few hours.

Travel was ceased on the road to Yarik, with most everyone camped, most everyone fed, and a few already slumbering after the exhausting day. Wagons and carts were parked in clusters on the wooded roadside as families made friends for one evening, combining resources for quicker campfires, bigger meals, and friendly conversation. The evening was almost normal enough to cause the people to forget they'd been driven from their homes by war.

Hoster's mule cart was one of the rare few sitting far from the others, alone in darkness with the occasional pale burn of a firebug for company. Quiet nearly reigned, all but the constant chirping of crickets, the faint chatter of the distant travelers, and the soft murmuring of a man's prayer. Yatham leaned against the cart, hovering over Theel's unconscious body, holding his own head in his hands.

"I know I should talk to you more often. I know I only pray to you when I need something of you. I know that makes me terrible, and I'm sorry. I'm sorry I'm so selfish. I forget you when I'm happy, and complain to you when I'm sad. Please forgive me for all these things. Please forgive me for my doubt. Forgive me for letting things tire my heart and mind when I should leave them to you. Forgive me for not trusting your wisdom."

Yatham sighed and touched his brother's chest, felt the warmth of his body, and listened to the even breathing. "Theel is healing. Thank you so much for keeping my brother in life. Thank you so much for delivering him from death. It is so important that Theel live to complete this quest. He must succeed, but he can't do it alone. Now he is hurt, and lies in healing sleep. I must do what I can while he slumbers. Show me the way, please. I am not a man of wisdom, and I can't see the path to the Blessed Soul. Give me the wisdom to choose properly. Shape my choices. Guide me as you did my father. I need faith. I need strength. I need your guiding hand. We must find the Blessed Soul, or our people will die."

Yatham looked at his brother's peaceful face, sadness washing over his own features. "Theel needs you now more than ever. He needs your strength. He needs to realize his own strength. He needs to complete this quest more than he knows. I don't understand many things, but I know his heart is broken, and I know only you can mend it. Please bring him back to us. Help him realize the Blessed Soul is out there waiting for him. Help him realize he has the ability to finish this quest. Help him realize what needs to be done. Father would say his lack of faith is shameful. Father didn't know the struggle in Theel's heart. He can be strong. He can be a hero. You can show him this."

Yatham rubbed his face, smearing away the beginnings of tears. "Please help Theel to realize his power. Help him to know Father loved him. Help him to know he is forgiven."

This last was met with many moments of quiet, of Yatham standing in silence surrounded by the crickets' song. His head was bowed, eyes pressed shut, lips moving silently in practiced prayer.

Finally, he grabbed a sword from inside the cart and fell to one knee. Holding the weapon by its scabbard, he offered the handle of the sword to the heavens as a sign of allegiance to his god.

"I, as a son of the Silvermarsh Clans, do commit myself, body, soul, and spirit, to the warriors of the Southern Cross, to the Seven Kingdoms they protect, and to the one true Lord of all Creation, that I might do his will, to love God's children, to lead God's Children, to protect God's Children, and that by these deeds, the Lord's blessings be given.

"I will care for God's children, by showing God's love.

"I will guide God's children, by speaking God's word.

"I will protect God's children, by wielding God's judgment.

"With his mercy, I will care. With his compassion, I will give.

"With his wisdom, I will speak. With his word, I will guide.

"With his shield, I will protect. With his sword, I will defend.

"I will serve the Lord with all my heart, my mind, and my voice, by learning and understanding his holy word, gratefully receiving his holy gift of faith, and always proclaiming his holy name. These things I hold dear. Amen."

Yatham remained quiet and kneeling for many moments, looking at the hilt of the sword, at the crosspiece where there was a small ornamental angel with spread wings. Her eyes were closed as if asleep, her golden face dulled by the dark sky. Slowly Yatham raised himself to his feet and returned the sword to Theel's side.

Hoster approached in darkness from behind. He tried to be quiet, but his heavy steps fooled no one.

Yatham pulled Theel's shirt closed, covering his brother's chest wound, and said, "Fine evening, master tradesman."

"Fine as they come," Hoster answered, leaning against the cart at Yatham's side. "Those were some fancy words you spoke. You've got a heavy heart, my boy?"

Yatham nodded.

"All is well," Hoster said. "A man needs a word with his creator now and then. It's a righteous thing to do," Hoster touched his chest. "For the soul."

Yatham nodded again. "Yes, it is."

"Now, enough of the deep thoughts," Hoster declared. "Time to relax and let God do his work. Want to get drunk?"

Yatham smiled. "Is my mood dampening your spirits?"

"Oh, it don't bother me, your mood," Hoster said, scratching his fingernails together, checking his work. "I just want someone to get drunk with."

"Do you really require a partner to aid your effort?"

"The sins of vice come easier with company," Hoster said. "Especially my favorite sort."

"I'm here to ease your conscience, then?" Yatham asked.

"No, boy," Hoster answered. "I'm here to ease yours."

Yatham smiled at that. "You've done that much already."

"Glad to know my words bear fruit. However ..." Hoster looked up at the stars. "A fine night such as this—crisp smell of God's creation filling a man's head, and a variety of the finest brews and potions Embriss has to offer, going to perfect waste right here at this roadside?" Hoster nudged Yatham with his elbow. "I may have just the thing to put a smile on your face, my boy."

"The finest brews of Embriss?" Yatham said. "Before, you claimed you were born of Yarik."

"Is that what I said?"

"A proud son of Yarik, you said, born and raised in the Mountain Kingdoms."

"I am, I was," Hoster said, clearing his throat. "And I'm proud, too. Of each of the Seven Kingdoms. Each one is most wonderful in its own way."

"You'll say anything for a sale, won't you, brewmaster?" Yatham answered.

"Nearly anything," Hoster confirmed. "Want to do some drinking or not?"

"My answer is the same," Yatham answered. "Drink as you wish. But I'll do no more than keep your company as you do."

"A fine offer, boy," Hoster said. "One I'll accept with thanks. Now, let's see what we have here. What has this old spirit trader been hauling across all the Seven Kingdoms in his mule cart? We have your standard fermented grape stock, only the best, picked and crushed in the valleys of Sidon. It'll put bees in your ears quick enough, but this brew is for taste, mostly. I prefer a potion of more ... complexity."

"Of course," Yatham said.

"I can see you have an eye for quality," Hoster said. "Now, the bubblers in this box hold something I recommend highly. A seraphim tonic with ground cockbird leaf and a hint of dale berries, best served warm. Takes the scratches away, my boy. That may be your drink."

"With your thirst, it's a wonder these wares ever reach market."

"Oh, I don't offer these at market," Hoster said. "These are very exclusive. I'll only offer these to a fellow clansman of Embriss, like yourself."

"Once again you're a son of Embriss?" Yatham asked.

"If you say so," Hoster stated. "Do you mind moving your brother's leg? There's a hell of a concoction under there."

"I'd prefer to leave my brother's sleep undisturbed."

"Oh, hell," Hoster said. "We always have the pig swill."

He held up a corked bottle full of dark liquid.

"This is the foulest liquid you will ever taste. This stuff is strictly for the drunk who's burned the taste off his tongue years ago."

"Like you?"

"Or someone like me," Hoster said. "The smell will make a God-fearing man question all things holy, but it sure enough knows its use and sets right to it. Two pulls on this and you'll be pounding the scatter hammer."

"You'll be what?"

"You'll be really drunk."

"Oh," Yatham said. "Sounds terrible."

"Horrible is what it is," Hoster said, twisting the cork free. "A horrible, nasty recipe. Even the finest varieties taste like crap." He took a swallow and wiped his mouth. "Yes, sir. This stuff is terrible."

Yatham smiled. "Terrible?"

"Horrible is what it is." Hoster took another swallow. "Are you listening?"

"I'm trying," Yatham said. "Are you certain it's so horrible? You seem to enjoy it well enough."

"Oh, I'm certain," Hoster said, taking another swallow. "Only a damned fool would drink this stuff."

"Then why do you cook it?"

"It's that damned fool son of mine."

"Your son?" Yatham said.

"You'll see what I mean soon enough," Hoster said. "Spend a few days in the company of my boy, and there won't be enough swill in the world to help you keep your sanity."

"How is that?" Yatham asked.

"You probably fancy yourself a patient man, am I right?"

"Sometimes."

"Then you haven't yet faced this test," Hoster said. "That boy of mine would drive the Blessed Soul himself to drinking."

"Your son?" Yatham said. "Do you mean Rasm?"

"My boy, bless his simple brain," Hoster said. "I love him, but I hate him."

"Rasm is your son?"

"No," Hoster said, taking a heavy chug. "I didn't birth him. I just found him. But he's the son I'll never have, the son I never wanted, damn him. Curse my bones."

"He causes you some difficulty?"

"The worst kind of difficulty," Hoster answered. "Worthless, scatterbrained lumberhead."

"And this difficulty he causes you, it is best faced with a head full of that ... ?" Yatham said.

"Pig swill," Hoster said, taking a drink. "You understand perfectly."

"Perhaps this difficulty is an excuse to enjoy your liquor?" Yatham suggested.

"I have no idea what you mean."

"You claim he forces you to drink pig swill," Yatham said. "But it is your hand that lifts the bottle to your lips."

"The presence of your brother's leg atop a case containing a more suitable concoction has left me with little choice but to drink this goddamned pig swill," Hoster said, taking another sip. "You have yourself to blame for my suffering."

"It is not because of me, nor is it my brother's leg," Yatham guessed. "It isn't even your son's fault that you drink."

"Yes it is," Hoster said. "He's a horse's ass."

"I was thinking I knew every way a father could show love."

"True love is honest," Hoster said. "Any man of God will tell you as much. I prefer to call a turd a turd."

"A turd?"

"Yeah, a turd," Hoster said. "It means the same as shit."

"Then your son must be holy," Yatham suggested.

"I choose to call a turd a turd, and I choose to call my son a no-good lumberhead, since that's what he is." Hoster tipped the bottle to his lips. "Am I to believe you and your brother get on like two angels? In agreement on all issues, with nothing but kindly spoken words and pats on the back?"

"That is far from the truth," Yatham answered.

"That is what this old spirit trader was thinking as he swished his pig swill," Hoster said. "So what is the truth? What makes two brothers, two city sods from Embriss, want to go stick their pretty asses out in the filth and stink of the Outlands?"

"As I said before," Yatham said, "my brother is on a knight's quest."

"Your brother is, but you're not," Hoster said. "And you're doing all the work. He's sleeping through his whole quest. They should give *you* the knighthood."

Yatham chuckled at that. "I'll never be a knight."

"So, what is the truth about you two?" Hoster asked, taking another drink. "What are you doing out here? Do you follow him everywhere he goes?"

"That is our business."

"You uneasy talking about that?" Hoster asked. "Is it a painful subject?"

"Ask my brother when he wakes."

"You don't like to talk about that," Hoster said. "You don't want to talk about your brother, but you can talk about my boy all night, all night until the dawn. Is that right?"

"We can speak on anything you wish," Yatham said. "I will not force a discussion of your son upon you."

"You're damn right you won't," Hoster grumbled. "Me and Rasm are good for walking, like a shirt and a pants, like two pairs of boots. Or one pair of boots. We're like a boot. I'm a boot and he's a boot."

"I've never heard truer words."

"Our business is our business and it's nobody's business. Like you and your brother. So we won't talk about my boy Rasm no more, bless his scatterbrain." Hoster took another drink. "You know what's wrong with him? He's a damn fool. Rasm has a log in his head."

"So you've said."

"You ever listen to him talk?" Hoster asked.

"I have."

"It's a curse on me trying to listen to that nonsense every day," Hoster said, sloshing his bottle. "It's God's thanks to me for being a no-good drunk, for drinking too much pig swill, to saddle me with a boy who talks a fool like that. You know why he talks like that?"

"No, I don't," Yatham said. "Why is it?"

"I won't tell you. Hell no, never. It's none of your business," Hoster said. "So listen close, because I'll only say this once."

"Okay."

"You listen to this," Hoster whispered. "Listen close."

"Okay, I'm listening."

"You know how he tells everyone he is a wizack, uh- wizard?" Hoster said softly. "You know why?"

"Why?"

"Don't tell anybody," Hoster said. "Curse your bones if you breathe while thinking it."

"What?"

"I said don't breathe a word," Hoster said. "Don't speak to anyone."

"About what?" Yatham asked.

"I'll never tell you," Hoster said. "Fine, I'll tell you. It's because he really is a wizack- uh, wizard. He's a wizard."

"He is?" Yatham asked.

Hoster dropped the bottle to the ground with a thud and a clink, where it fell on its side and began to spill out. "Curse the hell, these things!" he said, bending down. "Damn cheap wind-blown bottles. A swallow or two and it's the same as squeezing a greased frog."

"Rasm is a wizard?" Yatham asked.

Hoster straightened, wiping the bottle with a handkerchief. "Who said that? Did I say that?" Hoster asked

"You said Rasm is a wizard," Yatham said.

"I'll never admit to it," Hoster said. "You'll never hear me talk."

"I'll never hear you *stop* talking," Yatham corrected.

"That's for certain," Hoster said.

"So Rasm is not a wizard?"

"No, he isn't, but he was," Hoster explained. "But not anymore. Can't spin Craft runes if you squeak like a chipmunk."

"Rasm can craft magical runes?"

"He could once," Hoster answered. "But he can no longer. Now, he can't get a straight word out from under that fat tongue of his."

"Impossible," Yatham said.

"Oh, it's possible," Hoster said, putting the bottle to his lips. "And it's true. There's no denying the sadness of it. Can you figure what the good Lord was thinking when he decided to give the gift of Craft to a scatter face like Rasm?" The spirit trader looked up at the stars. "Lord, what were you thinking? I'd like to know."

"Wizarding is a very special talent," Yatham said.

"Don't I know that? There is only one wizard born into the kingdoms every few years."

"That's right," Yatham said. "The ability to craft runes is extremely rare."

"As rare as a thought in Rasm's head."

"The Keeper of the Craft senses all magic in the realm," Yatham said. "He seeks it out."

"The Keeper doesn't much take to liquor, though."

"Why hasn't the Keeper found Rasm and taken him to Fal Daran for training?" Yatham wondered.

"He doesn't like potions, either," Hoster said, talking to himself. "No. Magic potions are forbidden."

"Hoster," Yatham asked. "Why hasn't the Keeper taken Rasm for training in the Craft?"

"If the Keeper catches me with these potions ..." Hoster mumbled. "Probably magic me into a rat's ass or something."

"Hoster?"

"Never tried to sell potions to the Keeper." Hoster stared into his bottle. "But he does like good wine."

"Have you met the Keeper of the Craft?" Yatham asked.

"Yes, but he doesn't buy anything from me," Hoster said, taking a sip. "Probably makes it himself."

"When did you meet the Keeper?" Yatham asked.

"When he came to take Rasm for training in the Craft," Hoster answered.

"So Rasm really is a wizard?"

"You city clansmen are all the same," Hoster grumbled loudly. "It's like you don't speak the language. What have I been saying?"

"You've been saying he's *not* a wizard."

"That's because he is not. He would be a wizard if he could speak, but he can't even say 'spell' or 'magic' or 'wizard,'" Hoster said. "When the boy can't *say* 'wizard,' how can he *be* one? You can't craft spells when you can't spit out the words, when all you do is squeak like a chipmunk. It's a curse. He's a curse."

"But he once was a wizard. He could craft spell runes."

"Yeah, he was once," Hoster said. "Before he forgot how to talk."

"Was he schooled in the arts?" Yatham asked.

"I don't know what's schooled or not," Hoster answered. "The boy had Craft runes at his fingertips. He was writing them on the air."

"You saw this?"

"I saw it," Hoster said. "The Keeper had him bending light, making a spark by rubbing his fingers. Once he made pebbles roll across the floor by looking at them. He had a gift. He had opportunity handed down to him from God above, but he pissed it into the river and watched it wash away."

"What happened? What did he do?"

"What does he always do?" Hoster asked after another sip.

"I don't know," Yatham said. "What does he always do?"

"He does whatever he wants to," Hoster said. "That's what he does. No matter what anyone tells him. He's got a hammerhead, and that means he knows best."

"Did Rasm anger the Keeper?" Yatham asked.

Hoster choked a bit, spit out some brown liquid and coughed hard. "Did Rasm anger the Keeper?" he said between coughs. "He had the Keeper shitting pigeons. That boy never met a man he couldn't make a sworn enemy after an hour of conversation. Even his dear, loving father. The sun never sets on a day where I haven't wanted to belt him across the head and leave him for dead somewhere. I did that once, but he came back and found me."

"I've never seen the Keeper of the Craft angry," Yatham said. "He's not the sort to untemper."

"I saw him untemper for certain." Hoster took another drink. "He was really damned untempered. He was shitting a flock."

"A flock?"

"Of pigeons," Hoster said. "He was hacked off."

"Was Rasm disobedient?"

"Was Rasm disobedient?" Hoster said. "When is Rasm obedient? That boy is a horse's ass. And the Keeper knew it, too. I told him."

"I'm certain that is true," Yatham said.

"It is true. That's what I told him," Hoster said. "But the Keeper loved Rasm anyway. 'That boy will be great and powerful one day' said the Keeper. He didn't know what a lumberhead my boy is."

"The Keeper loved Rasm?" Yatham asked.

Hoster nodded. "The Keeper said he had great talent, a gift for one of the elements."

"Which one?"

"The one where he sets fire to everything in sight, including himself," Hoster said.

"Flame Bringers?"

"Or something," Hoster said. "The Keeper said Rasm might serve Lord Britou one day, in the royal palace or in the king's army as a WarCrafter."

"Magic is so rare and precious to our people," Yatham said, shaking his head. "What could Rasm have done to cause the Keeper to refuse such talent? It must have been terrible."

"Horrible is what it was."

"Horrible?"

"The Keeper made a mistake with my boy," Hoster said, fingering his bottle. "The Keeper had one unbreakable rule. That was his mistake."

"What do you mean?"

"Rasm is stupid. He don't understand rules," Hoster said. "I don't give him rules. I give him a crack on the ass. Rasm

170

understands a crack on the ass. Or on the head. That works fine, too."

"The Keeper doesn't strike people," Yatham said.

"No, he doesn't," Hoster said, popping his thumb in and out of his bottle. "He talks all day. He talks reason. He makes too much good sense for a fool like Rasm. By the time the Keeper saw he wasn't reaching the boy, it was too late. I told the Keeper a belt to the head was what Rasm needed, but it was too late. The Keeper talked too long."

"It was too late how?" Yatham asked. "What happened?"

"Damn fool broke the unbreakable rule," Hoster said. "That's what he did. Three times."

"Three times?" Yatham asked. "What did the Keeper do?"

"I told you. The first two times, he talked to Rasm," Hoster said. "The Keeper thought Rasm had too much potential to cast away, so he ignored his own rule. He thought he could talk the stupid out of my boy. But he couldn't, because no one can. The third time was the worst, and the final."

"The third time was the worst?" Yatham asked. "What did he do? What is the unbreakable rule?"

Hoster smiled sadly, took a drink, and for one moment seemed to sober a bit. "He created a forbidden spell."

"An illegal spell?"

"It was legal spellcraft, but forbidden to the students," Hoster said. "The Keeper can't just have them trying to spin whatever sorcery they wish."

"What spell did he cast?" Yatham asked.

"A language spell," Hoster said. "He wanted to talk to animals. Humans weren't enough for him. He wanted to squeak like a chipmunk, and that's what he got."

"The spell is why he speaks as he does?" Yatham asked.

"Exactly. You understand," Hoster confirmed. "I always said it's better not to talk to a jackhole. You have to talk like a jackhole to talk to a jackhole. Rasm took me too seriously."

"So he was once a wizard," Yatham said in understanding. "But not anymore."

"Because he brays like an ass," Hoster said, nodding. "Can't cast spells when you bray like an ass."

"Was the Keeper unable to fix Rasm's words with Craft?"

"He didn't even try," Hoster answered. "He just barred Rasm from the tower. I knew it would happen. I knew Rasm would shake the Keeper's britches. Time is all it takes. At first I thought my boy's talent might make him good for something. But, like always, the magic only made him a bigger menace than ever. I heard the roar above me, like the scream of a great lion. I was in the market square mixing some nice lady an herb bubbler, and that roar popped everyone's ears. People stampeded like cattle. They thought the devil was back to encore the Sundering of the World or something. But I knew what it was."

"It was Rasm that caused the roar?"

"It was Rasm," Hoster said, nodding. "I heard that confounding racket, and knew only my boy made misfortune in such a measure."

"What was the noise?" Yatham asked.

"He wove his runes in the towers above the Hall of Seven Swords," Hoster said. "The Keeper's sorcerers work up there above the city. It was like thunder on a sunny day. All of Embriss heard his failure."

Hoster took a few swallows and added, "The rune unraveled. He released the energy wrong. Boom. It was like God shouting from the heavens, telling me what a jackhole my boy is. I wanted to say, 'That's right, Lord. You've never spoke truer words.' That's what I wanted to say."

"Where in the towers was he?" Yatham asked.

"I know why you're asking that," Hoster said. "You're hoping he wasn't in the Oxiagot, where the Keeper keeps the Globe of Infinity. That's what you're thinking about."

Yatham rested his forehead in his palm. "He was in the Oxiagot, wasn't he?"

"My boy doesn't try a forbidden spell just anywhere," Hoster said. "He was in the very same room as the Globe of Infinity. He was within arm's reach."

"Within arm's reach of the most sacred magical artifact there is?" Yatham groaned. "Did he damage it?"

"At this moment, Rasm is not hanging upside down in the dungeons under the Hall of Seven Swords, so I figure he didn't damage it," Hoster said. "But they told me he destroyed everything else in the Oxiagot."

"Oh no."

"Oh yes," Hoster said, taking another drink. "A bunch of old books and scrolls, and even the Keeper's journal. All gone up in a whirlwind of fire."

"Oh no."

"Oh yes," Hoster said. "Burned his face off. Burned his hair off. Knocked some teeth out of his head. You've seen him. He even put the flames to another wizard who tried to save him. The Keeper was shitting a storm of pigeons. Especially because of his journal."

"I can only imagine."

"Now you know why we're walking the roads again," Hoster said. "Now you know why my boy talks a fool like he does. He did it to himself. He tried to mix up a spell that was beyond his reach, a language spell. And now he can no longer speak the language of magic. He can't even say the *word* 'magic.' He chokes on it every time. That's how you lose your wizarding, my friend. That's how you become plain."

"I'm sad for him."

"Don't be sad," Hoster grunted. "Rasm's to blame for his own suffering. He did it to himself because he's a horse's ass."

"You told me."

"He still says he's a wizard, like he doesn't remember what he did," Hoster said, with a hefty gulp of liquor. "But he knows he did it to himself. He knows the Keeper could have fixed his words. I think the Keeper left him this way as punishment. I think Rasm's not hanging upside down in the dungeons of the Seven Swords because the Keeper figured squeaking like a chipmunk and losing his magic is punishment enough."

"It probably is."

"Perhaps that dumbass will finally learn to listen to me," Hoster said.

"Perhaps not."

"You're not kidding," Hoster said. "He just don't know when to quit. The scatter-faced idiot prattles on about the cure. He wants his magic back."

"The cure?" Yatham asked. "What do you mean? What is he doing?"

"He sputtered and blubbered for the Keeper to fix that fat tongue of his," Hoster said. "The Keeper told Rasm no one could help him. He told Rasm only the healing powers of the Blessed Soul of Man could fix his words."

"Oh, really? The Blessed Soul?"

"Yes, really," Hoster said, draining the last drops from his bottle. "Or God himself."

"That's probably true."

"But God is harder to find. Don't see him walking these roads anywhere," Hoster said. "So Rasm's settled for the Blessed Soul. He thinks he's going to find the Blessed Soul and get his magic back. He thinks we'll find him in the Outlands. It's where we're headed."

"You're headed to the Outlands?" Yatham scratched his chin. "Where in the Outlands?"

"Ebon South is where we'll start," Hoster said. "But only God truly knows where this Blessed Soul is at." He looked up at the stars. "Hey, God, do you know? Would you tell this dusty old spirit trader where your Blessed Soul of Man is at?"

"Why are you starting in Ebon South?"

"There's business in Ebon South," Hoster said. "There's the king's work to be earned. That's the reason for walking, right? But I also know a fellow down there, a preacher."

"Father Brashfor?" Yatham guessed.

"That's the one," Hoster said. "You know of him?"

"Many know of him. His name is renowned."

"Yes, he is well known," Hoster said. "Different brand of fellow, Father Brashfor. He has his own story. Never stops talking of the Blessed Soul." Hoster sighed. "I'll introduce Rasm and he'll be shitting pigeons in no time at all."

"That's ridiculous."

"Ridiculous isn't a strong enough term," Hoster said. "We'll find nothing but zoths and bad beer in the Outlands, and that fool son of mine will still speak like a mule's ass."

"Nothing like hope to strengthen a man's stride."

"I know this is a waste of good time, but Chigger and Ragweed still have to pound the stones," Hoster said. "We have to find business somewhere. The Outlands are as good a market as any. Let the boy have hope, I suppose. The loghead."

"Perhaps you'll find the Blessed Soul," Yatham said. "Have faith."

"Oh, I'm sure we'll find the Blessed Soul, and all the daisies will bloom," Hoster said, shaking his empty bottle. "All will be perfect. Then Rasm will open his mouth. Then Blessed Soul will see, and the scatter will come raining down."

"Why are you so certain things will not go well?"

"Because a skunk will always stink," Hoster said. "No matter what you do, you can't change that. You can't cure the stink out of a skunk, and my boy is a skunk. There is no other way to look at it. A dirty skunk that I have to smell every day. I have to learn how to speak the language of Jackass, trying to understand that boy's words. Some days, he won't even speak at all. He'll just grunt like a half-wit. Try to understand him then! It's a big bucket of scatter. It's a curse. Do you understand?"

"I'm beginning to understand."

Hoster looked into his bottle. Realizing it was empty, he threw it on the ground. "Balls, this pig swill is good. I wonder if there's any more. Do you mind moving your brother's leg?"

"I think he's waking up."

Chapter 14

Theel brushed the last of the dirt into the hole, packing it around the roots of the tiny white spruce with his fingers. He did it slowly and solemnly, because he'd witnessed this ceremony before, and knew it was expected of the son of the slain. The sorrowful notes of a viol accompanied him in his task, as did the sounds of weeping behind him. Theel did not join the mourners in the shedding of tears, but while his eyes were dry, his heart was tearing itself apart.

A man's stern voice echoed through the trees. "Get up. Do it again. Climb the rope."

Then came the sound of a boy whimpering. "I can't. I'll fall."

"You can, and you will," the man insisted. "You will climb this rope. If you fall a thousand times, you will get up and try again a thousand times. Now climb."

A ceremonial carafe sat beside the newly-planted sapling. Theel took it by the neck, carefully pouring its contents onto the ground, giving the tree its first drink of water. As he did this, any of those gathered might have noticed how badly his hand was trembling. If so, they would likely misunderstand the reason for it, thinking the son of the slain was shaken by his grief. But none of those gathered possessed the gift of Sight as Theel did. Therefore, they couldn't hear voices from the past that filled his head in that moment.

"You must gain strength," the man commanded. "Climbing will make your arms strong."

"I will try again," the boy said.

"You will do more than try. You will succeed."

When his task was complete, Theel rose to his feet, looking around the Grove of Min Anginus. It appeared as any other stand of white spruce that grew naturally in the world, but the castle walls above the treetops, and the mountains beyond, reminded him that these pines were different. This grove of trees grew at the top of the Hall of Seven Swords in Fal Daran. It was sacred ground that nurtured these trees, each one planted to memorialize the life of a great warrior of Embriss who'd perished in battle. On this day, a new tree joined the rest, one that would honor Theel's tormentor.

"Father—"

"In the training room, I'm not your father." The voice was utterly without emotion. "Here, I am your masterknight. Now climb."

Moments of strong emotion brought Theel's Sight to him, and now was such a time. These emotions could be his own, or they could belong to others. They could even be the emotions of past visitors to the spot where he stood, emotions visited upon him as the Craft weaves remembered them.

Theel saw a thousand funerals taking place all at once, generations of mourners bidding farewell to their heroes. He saw mothers holding their weeping children, families huddled together to share their grief. To his right, a woman clawed at the grass, screaming her agony to the heavens. To his left he saw a wrinkled, white-haired knight, with tears in his eyes, kissing the hallowed ground dedicated to his fallen comrades.

The magic that lived in the Grove of Min Anginus was soaked in the sadness of thousands of mourners. And just as flames feed on oil, Theel's Sight fed on this anguish. The visions were painful and overwhelming. They couldn't be controlled, and they couldn't be stopped.

"You must not be weak," the man's voice commanded. "You must not be a failure."

"I am not a failure," the boy said.

"No more whimpering. Climb."

Theel could see a legion of warriors standing at attention among the pines, each one next to the tree that was planted in his honor. Some of these were men Theel knew, Knights of the

Southern Cross who had recently perished. Others he knew only from legend, they having died in conflicts hundreds of years ago.

There was a story to be told by each hero who stood in the grove—tales of the way they lived, and the way they died. Theel could have relived any of these if he chose to heed what his Sight showed him. But only one of these ghostly images held his attention: the knight wearing the damaged shield with the hole in its center, who stood next to the sapling he'd just planted.

Theel's father left a legacy just as strong as any of the other warriors memorialized in the grove. He would be remembered as a great champion of the old clans, known for countless acts of heroism and personal sacrifice. Theel, however, remembered a different story. And this was the story told him now.

"Climb the rope." The sound of a wooden practice sword striking the stone floor caused Theel to flinch.

"I'm not strong enough," the boy said.

"Yes, you are weak," the man said coldly. "But I must make you strong."

"But, Father—"

"In this room, I'm not your father."

Theel could hear the loud crack of a wooden practice sword striking a stone floor repeatedly. It was a sound that terrified him as a boy because he knew what was coming should he fail. Even when he was alone, away from the training room, he could still hear that sound. At night, he would awaken suddenly, drenched in sweat, his ears echoing with it. Even as a man, he could hear the sound when he was most afraid, and it only compounded his fear, froze him to inaction with dread. But over the years, he'd learned to deal with that fear by drowning it in his rage.

"Climb," the man ordered.

"I can't!" the boy cried.

Theel flinched as he heard the practice sword hitting the floor again. He glared at the image of his father, the anger within him growing to a level that was almost uncontrollable. His father's ghost stared straight ahead, his dedication to his duty leaving him unconcerned with his son's feelings, as cold in death as he ever was in life.

Theel felt the little boy's fear melt away, replaced by hatred, and he embraced this hatred for its ability to numb the pain. The terror of the little boy froze him to helplessness, but the anger and resentment gave him energy, made him feel powerful.

"*You* did this to me!" he growled in his father's face. "*You* are to blame."

These were the same words Theel said to his father before he died, with precisely the same vitriol. Those words hurt his father greatly, but Theel didn't care. It was a rare moment where he was in control, and it was his father who suffered. It was the only time Theel was able to give his father a taste of what he'd endured as a child.

The man may have been a great knight, but he was a bad father, and even though he tried to apologize, Theel wouldn't listen. A thousand acts of anger and a lifetime of emotional scars could not be undone with one apology.

Every time Theel began to entertain thoughts of forgiveness, he was quickly reminded why he could not.

"Weakness. Failure." The man's every word was covered with ice. "Unacceptable."

The wooden sword no longer struck the floor. Now it struck flesh.

"Mercy!" the boy begged.

"Your enemies on the battlefield will not show you mercy. Therefore, I will not. Climb."

"Please stop," the boy wept. "Father . . ."

"I am not your father here!"

The knight stared ahead impassively, just as he always did, and it only served to stoke Theel's rage. He would never forgive his father for this, even if the man asked for forgiveness a thousand times.

"I will never forgive you," Theel spit in his father's face. "I hate you!"

CHAPTER 15

Theel felt himself falling. He awoke with a start, coughing and grasping at air, trying to save himself. He tried to call for help, but only a croak emerged as wet grass rushed up and smashed him in the face. There he lay, coughing heavily, warm liquid squirting from his lips and nose. He reached for his sword, found it was missing, tried to rise, but got his legs tangled in blankets.

He tried to call to his brother but his lungs wouldn't respond. Then his stomach did, and emptied itself all over the ground. He coughed some more, vomited some more, and felt gentle hands on his shoulders.

"Calm yourself, brother," he heard Yatham say.

Theel couldn't respond, he could only cough and heave as his stomach twisted itself in knots.

"He'll yack like that for a bit, and cough for days," said a gruff voice. "You're not a fish, my boy."

"But he's strong." Yatham's voice. "Just relax, brother."

"Just ease yourself," the other voice said. "Breathe some of God's good, clean air."

Theel's teeth began a loud clicking as shivers slithered up his back. He looked through bleary eyes to see that he was lying on the ground amid a pile of blankets. It was dark, and it was cold. He pulled the blankets close, shaking and coughing, exhaling clouds of steam into the night. He could see the light of a fire far away, could see the spokes of a wagon wheel near his head, and the blurry shapes of two men hovering. He rubbed his eyes.

"What happened?" he managed between coughs.

"You fell off my mule cart, boy. You landed straight on your face."

"You breathed some of the river, Theel," Yatham added. "But you made it. You'll be fine."

"I drowned?" Theel asked.

"By your britches, you drowned, boy."

Theel rubbed his eyes again, blinking. "Who are you?"

"I'm Hoster. Just Hoster," the man in the misshapen hat said. "This is my mule cart you just fell off. I'm the one who's been hauling your drowned carcass halfway across the Seven Kingdoms."

"Halfway?" Theel asked.

"Not halfway really," Yatham said.

"How long did I slumber?"

"Tomorrow will be the tenth day," Yatham answered.

"Nine days?" Theel gasped. "Where are we?"

"We are far away from the city, brother," Yatham answered. "A day or two north of the Calfborn Crossroads."

"You carried me in a mule cart?" Theel asked.

"That's my mule cart we carried you in," Hoster said. "Chigger and Ragweed did the pulling. They're my mules."

"Many thanks," Theel said, still shivering, "to your mules."

"Let's get you to the fire, boy," Hoster suggested.

"Can you stand?" Yatham asked.

"With your help."

"One on each side," Hoster grunted, crouching down.

Yatham and Hoster carried Theel, stumbling, shivering, and coughing, to a campfire where they set him down, propped against a blackened stump. Hoster leaned over, holding the spout of a bottle to his lips.

"Give this a swallow," Hoster said. "She'll kick your chest and warm your balls."

Theel took a drink, coughed again, and grimaced as his nostrils burned.

"By God, that is foul," he breathed.

"Takes the scratches away." Hoster smiled, taking a drink himself. "My thanks for moving your leg."

"What?"

"Are you feeling better?" Yatham asked.

"No. I need my pipe."

"That takes the scratches away, too," Hoster said.

"We lost most of our things in the river, brother," Yatham said. "Including the seraphim."

"That's right, boy," Hoster said. "But much to your profound luck and personal benefit, your brother—soon after fishing you out of the water—managed to cross paths with one of the finest booze-cooking merchants of mirth pounding the stones of these Seven Kingdoms of ours, both greater and lesser."

"Meaning what?"

"Hoster gave us some seraphim," Yatham said, packing a bowl with crumbled leaf.

Hoster smiled brightly. "And a new pipe, too. As a show of friendship and brotherhood between sons of Yarik."

"Embriss," Yatham corrected.

"Whatever."

"What happened in the Trader's Cave?" Theel asked.

"I'm not certain," Yatham answered. "I think we lost our direction in the darkness and went down the wrong tunnel at Candle Rock."

"You rode a waterfall, my boy," Hoster belched, sipping his bottle.

Theel sneered at him. "Did I ask you?"

The spirit trader responded with a loud fart.

"I believe Hoster is correct," Yatham cut in. "We went over the waterfall."

"And the Overwatch?" Theel asked. "Did they follow?"

"The river claimed them as well."

"Did any of them survive?" Theel pressed.

"You can relax your mind, brother," Yatham said. "We are no longer being followed."

"That is good. And what of my swords?"

"They were saved," Yatham answered. "Uncle Guarn's boat was smashed, but a portion of it remained afloat long enough for me to recover your weapons."

"And father's knife?"

"I found it as well," Yatham said. "In your chest."

"Where?"

"Stuck in you," Hoster said. "Right next to your gizzard."

Theel touched his hand to his chest, feeling thick layers of bandages, then a deep throb of pain as the tender flesh around the still-healing wound protested at even the mildest touch.

"You were wounded badly," Yatham said. "I don't know how you survived."

"Your brother is right, boy," Hoster agreed. "A wound like that should have killed you. And how you didn't drown after, I'll never know. God was surely dealing out miracles in that cave. I'm thinking he'd like you to reach the Outlands with your life intact."

The pain in Theel's chest spread like ripples throughout his body, throbbing with the beat of his heart. It was so sudden and so harsh that it took his breath away. He couldn't bear it. He felt the urge to pass out just to make it stop, but he couldn't will such a thing. This left one option, the only way to dull pain in consciousness: by dulling consciousness itself.

He put the pipe between his lips.

"Your brother shouldn't have survived either, and yet he did," Hoster said. "You two are blessed, my boy. Truly blessed."

"Don't call me boy," Theel said, and pulled a burning stick from the fire to light his pipe. "Who are you again?"

"I'm Hoster, just Hoster, the finest spirit trader kicking these roads," Hoster said. "You spent seven days sleeping on some of the best brews in God's creation."

"That's wonderful," Theel said. He took a deep pull on his pipe, coughed, and rubbed at his eyes. That first drag didn't bring enough seraphim, so he sucked more and harder, begging the drug to enter his body and cleanse it of pain. This it did, but as always, it also brought side effects.

One of these was a more intense, but also tenuous connection to his psychic nexus, causing random and uncontrolled flows of his inner mystic will, called juy. It often resulted in confusing and unwanted visions of history mixed seamlessly with the current reality, leaving little distinction between past or present, dreams and reality.

Now he could see someone else sitting at the fire, someone other than his brother or the spirit trader. It was a young man so ridiculous in his appearance it was difficult to believe such a person could have ever existed at any point in time.

His mouth hung open with a prominent jaw, the result of an underbite so large it could only be described as an outcropping on his face. His forehead was also big and bulging, and appeared to have eaten most of the top of his head long ago. The result was a stripe of bald skin running from his eyebrows to the back of his scalp, splitting his thick black hair into two disproportionate halves. He sat with his legs folded under a large, dirty book, his neck bent as if reading, but his eyes were glazed, unfocused and uncomprehending, each one moving independently of the other.

As Theel stared in wonderment, one of the young man's eyes stopped moving and focused on Theel, while the other continued to move, as if reading the book.

"Hello," the young man said. "I'm, uh ... Rasm. Yeah."

Their eyes met, and in that moment, the Sight came to Theel. He saw the Keeper of the Craft's black glasses and smallish face, every crease and wrinkle lit by candlelight. He smelled old parchments, dust, and lamp oil, then ash and cinder. And there was the Globe of Infinity, a twenty-foot ball of polished crystal with runes covering its entire surface, shivering with fire and lightning. It could only mean one thing.

"Are you a wizard?" Theel asked.

Rasm's face brightened. "Yes, I am!" he exclaimed, climbing to his feet. "I am a wiz- ... ack ... I am a sorc- ... ack ... I can cast- ... ack ... Yes!"

As he rose, the young man's book folded shut between his legs and fell into the fire.

Rasm screamed.

Hoster cursed.

They both rushed forward to save the book from the flames, but smashed their faces together awkwardly. Yatham stepped in and kicked the book out of the fire with a shower of sparks. It rolled across the ground and finally settled in some short grassy weeds, a small flame licking around the edges of its cover. Hoster and Rasm ran to the book, shouting and arguing, and began stomping at its pages, trying to put the fire out.

"This is the company you've been keeping?" Theel asked Yatham.

"You can see that he is a sorcerer?"

"I see the Keeper of the Craft in his past," Theel answered. "He's seen powerful magic in his life; some recently."

"Quit stepping on it, you jackhole!" Hoster yelled. He cupped his hands, trying to throw dirt on the smoking book, but Rasm stomped on his fingers. Hoster yelped in pain, pulling his hands away. Finally, he grabbed the smoking book and smacked Rasm in the face with it.

Theel sucked on his pipe. "As a wizard, he's not very accomplished."

"No, he isn't," Yatham said. "He can't speak properly to recite the spells."

"A runecrafter without runes?"

Yatham nodded. "Hoster will explain if you ask him."

Rasm tried pulling the book away from Hoster, but Hoster put up a fight, and the two began to wrestle over it.

"I've got it," Hoster growled. "Let go, you horse's ass."

"Mine!" Rasm yelled.

"Why did you choose these two to guide you out of the valley?" Theel asked.

"I needed aid from someone," Yatham said. "This is who God sent to provide it."

186

Hoster finally won the contest, ripping the book away from Rasm's hands, but dropped it in the process. He bent over to pick it up ...

"If this is how God answers prayers, then he does not bless our travels," Theel said.

"God does bless our travels," Yatham said.

Rasm took careful aim and kicked Hoster square in the hindquarters, knocking him onto his face.

"But God also has a sense of humor," Yatham added.

Chapter 16

Aeoxoea leaned against the trunk of a white waterleaf tree deep in the heart of the snowy Outlander forest. Numerous were the trees, and even more so were their leafless wooden arms and fingers, poking into the frigid air to form a canopy that ensnared the glaring moon, putting tiny cracks in its face. The cloudless sky was bright with thousands of twinkling stars, joining with the moon to illuminate the snowy landscape almost as clearly as if it was daytime. There wasn't the faintest tickle of breeze, or whisper of sound, just a lazy snowfall of silent, fat snowflakes.

At any time, Aeoxoea could look above, through the tangled branches of the forest ceiling, and see the moonlit wall of rock that stretched a thousand feet above the tree tops, the cliffs of the Tera Plateau that marked the southern boundaries of the Seven Kingdoms. It was a constant reminder of how far they'd traveled into the wilds of the Outlander forest, miles away from any outpost of civilization.

After escaping from the besieged town of Ebon South, the two knights called Gavin the Zealot and Elkor the Hound carried the little boy Eleod on their backs as they ran for two straight days. They always kept those cliff walls just to their left as they traveled east, deeper into the territory of their ancient enemies, the zoths.

Harassment from those bloodthirsty creatures had been light, consisting mostly of the occasional scuffle with a small group who were often surprised and easily dispatched by the battle hounds before even coming within sight of their knight masters. Gavin and Elkor were able to accomplish this, Jass explained, through knowledge of the zoth territorial markings. Aeoxoea saw with her own eyes how the zoths warned possible intruders by decorating their borders with the bodies of those who ignored such warnings in the past, both human and zoth.

In the two days they'd been moving through the Outlands, these territorial markings appeared numerous times, seen both close up and from afar. Some were mounted, tied, or skewered to tree trunks. Others simply hung from the lowest boughs. Each one was made of a corpse, or pieces of them, arranged in every imaginable way. Some were fresh, still dripping blood. Others were long dead, watching the passing travelers with darkened eye sockets set into skulls grinning with cracked teeth. There were bundles of bones, necklaces of fingers, piles of teeth and ears. These garish monuments were called deathmarks by the people of the Seven Kingdoms, and rarely did any human set eyes upon one and live to tell about it.

The deathmarks were horrifying for more than just their appearance. So intense was zoth hatred for humans, Jass told Aeoxoea, so unforgiving were they of the intrusion of non-zoths onto their lands, that even if a lost child set foot on the wrong spot of ground, a horde of zoth warriors would arrive in only minutes to dispense justice in as cruel and merciless a fashion as could be dreamed of.

Gavin and Elkor shared a healthy respect for the zoths, and took great pains to avoid conflict. Therefore it was among their highest priorities to avoid the deathmarks, and to never set foot on any lands marked as zoth-ruled. Since the zoths dominated the Outlands, this was nearly impossible many times during their trek. But in those situations where battle was unavoidable, it was the battle hounds that made the difference. Many times Elkor sent his animals places neither he nor Gavin could go, running fearlessly past the deathmarks to scout for zoth sentries, bringing death to those who posed a threat to the knights and their precious cargo, the Blessed Soul of Man. Aeoxoea wondered how long it would be before a zoth shaman or chieftain recognized those dogs as something other than mere animals of the forest.

Day and night, without stopping for food or rest, Behe and Kang cleared the way and the knights pushed through. The hounds did the fighting, and the knights did the running. Now, after the sun had risen and fallen twice since leaving Ebon South, the knights finally stopped. No food, no fire, they just stopped, laid down, and went to sleep.

Gavin and Elkor slept with Eleod and Behe between them for warmth, all wrapped in one another's furs, a pile of slumbering human and dog flesh covered by a fresh layer of snow. The only alert member of the party was Kang, who sat in the same spot without moving in the hours since stopping. Sitting in the snow beside his companions, he was a black splotch against the white snow, watching the surrounding forest with pale eyes.

Only feet away, Aeoxoea leaned against the white bark of the waterleaf tree, matching stares with a small snow squirrel that had ventured down from his home among the blue leaves above. The creature had climbed onto her shoulder, then onto her forearm, its tail twitching as it sniffed the air as if trying to determine her scent.

"What are the powers of the zoth shamans?" Aeoxoea asked, smiling at the squirrel.

"They wield powerful Craft," Jass answered. "They are especially gifted with Wind Magic, known to be more adept than most human wizards. They believe it is a gift of their deity, whom they call the Blood Goddess."

"Shia Ka," Aeoxoea said almost absent-mindedly. "It is the Maiden of Chaos who births such creatures, and blesses them with Wind Magic for their warcraft."

The snow squirrel got braver, climbed out to her wrist, and sniffed at her hand. She reached out and stroked its back with her finger.

"But the zoth shamans aren't merely warcrafters," Jass said. "They are also the spiritual leaders of their tribes. The shamans lead the chants of their warriors, singing with the horns and drums as they enter battle, blessing their weapons even as they fight. Most importantly, they use their powers of sorcery to support their tribal chiefs in battle. A zoth chieftain with his shaman supporting his attacks with magic is a nearly unstoppable terror on the battlefield. Most often, the shaman must die, or his chieftain will be impossible to kill."

Aeoxoea turned her hand over as the squirrel climbed out onto her fingers, its furry back rippling as it strained to sniff at her face.

"Have you ever fought a chieftain supported by his shaman's sorcery?" Aeoxoea asked.

"Ebon South is a frequent target of enemy attacks," Jass said. "My brothers and I have faced chieftains many times."

"Did you ever fight a chieftain alone?"

She held the squirrel close, allowing it to touch her face, to sniff around her lips and nose.

"Only once have I ever faced a chieftain alone," Jass answered.

"What happened?" Aeoxoea asked.

"He tore my head from my shoulders."

Kang's ears perked and he turned his head, snorting softly. The snow squirrel reacted as well, sitting up on its hind legs and looking off into the forest. Whatever it was, the squirrel didn't like it any more than Kang did. The little white animal jumped out of Aeoxoea's hand onto the trunk of the tree and scrambled away among its blue leaves.

Aeoxoea turned to look in the same direction as the animals. After a moment's thought, her hearing increased in sensitivity to a level far more acute than that of an animal such as Kang, and she knew immediately what had the battle hound's attention. Though it was a mile away, each sound was clear and distinct to her newly over-sensitized hearing.

She heard the footsteps of dozens as they moved quickly through the forest to the south, fanning out to encircle the position where the knights slept. Bare feet padded in the snow, accompanied by guttural murmuring and the clinking metal of jostled spear clusters.

Zoths.

Aeoxoea looked back at Gavin and Elkor and saw that they weren't moving. Kang sniffed at the air, clearly agitated.

"Suppose these knights are attacked by a zoth chieftain eager to please the Maiden of Chaos by slaying the Blessed Soul of Man?" she asked.

"The prophecies say Gilligod will slay the Blessed Soul," Jass answered. "A zoth chieftain, if he does not carry Gilligod, cannot harm the Blessed Soul, no matter what army he brings."

"Even so," Aeoxoea said. "What would happen if a zoth chieftain attacked these knights?"

"A zoth chieftain would not best Gavin the Zealot," Jass answered.

"A zoth chieftain bested you, my puppet."

"I was alone, not supported by Elkor and his hounds," Jass said. "And I never possessed the fighting caliber of Gavin the Zealot."

"Is he so unstoppable in battle?"

"Yes, he is," Jass said. "He is Nonuc Dieum, the greatest warrior among the sons of Embriss. He wields the deadliest weapons in the world. And now he fights beside the Battle Lord Elkor the Hound."

"Also an accomplished fighter?" Aeoxoea asked.

"There is no Battle Lord who is not distinguished," Jass said. "The Zealot and the Hound are both better men than I was. If a zoth chieftain chose to bring war to these two men, I would like to see it."

"You may see it yet," Aeoxoea said. "A zoth war party approaches."

"You know this?" Jass asked.

"I know this," Aeoxoea answered.

"Will you warn them?"

"I will not," Aeoxoea said. "Like you, I wish to see what will happen."

"The Zealot and the Hound will slay them all."

"Will they?" Aeoxoea asked. "How can you know this?"

"My faith in these men is second only to my faith in God."

"Why then, do the zoths attack them?" Aeoxoea asked. "Do these creatures yearn for death?"

"They are fanatically devoted to their religion," Jass said. "They believe the Blood Goddess commands their shamans to war and they obey without questioning. They attack, even if it means their death. Especially if they have a chance to do battle with a Knight of the Southern Cross."

"They prefer to fight those of your order?"

"The zoths will always seek out the best among us in battle," Jass said. "Many knights are accomplished, but the Knights of the Southern Cross are the very finest. It is a great achievement for the zoths to kill a member of my order. The Head Hunter added to his legend the day I fell."

"The Head Hunter?"

"The zoth chieftain who slew me," Jass explained. "The Terror of the Outlands. The soldiers of the Seven Kingdoms call him the Head Hunter for his proficiency in claiming the heads of his enemies. And for the horned skull he wears as a helm."

"With two knives in its crown."

"Each of those knives represents a Knight of the Southern Cross who perished at his hands," Jass explained.

"Now he will have three knives," Aeoxoea suggested.

"I suppose he will," Jass said. "He took my head."

"And his followers fought over your flesh," Aeoxoea said.

"They meant to take my soul," Jass said. "Something you'd already done."

"Perhaps the Head Hunter has come back to finish what he started."

The assassin blinked, switching her eyes to perceive a different spectrum of light, one which allowed her to see the zoths by the heat of their bodies. They glowed red and orange against the black night, hunched bodies running close to the ground, bristling head to toe with spears and knives and long-handled adzes. This was a strong war party. There was a chieftain and a shaman, and nearly five dozen other zoths. They were fanning out to attack, moving with a precision that said they knew exactly where the knights were sleeping. The ring of warriors was nearly complete. Very soon there would be no means of escape for the knights, no way out but to fight their way out of the zoth encirclement.

"Go to sleep now, Jass."

"Yes, mistress."

Kang's senses had clearly told him enough. He padded in circles, woofing softly, causing the pile of snowy furs to stir. Finally he turned and stomped on his masters with his front paws, howling loudly. The furs were cast off in a cloud of white as the knights scrambled to their feet, axes and knives bared and ready, eyes scanning the trees. Behe bounded over to where her father stood and took a moment to shake the snow from her fur.

"One war party, one chieftain; a shaman, too," Elkor said, blinking his one good eye, sniffing the air like one of his hounds. "Sixty zoths. No more."

Eleod remained asleep as Gavin wrapped him in his backpack, covering his head with furs. Before lying down for the night, Gavin tied a length of rope to the backpack, throwing it over a branch high in the tree above him. Now he pulled on the rope and the slumbering Blessed Soul was hoisted high into the air, dangling, sleeping among the highest boughs.

The dogs were nearly frenzied, jumping up and down, eager to fight. "Remember, old man," Elkor said to Kang, touching the patch that covered his left eye. "Watch old Elkor's left. Stay on his left side."

The patch had the image of a glaring eye stitched into its fabric. Elkor flipped the patch over, revealing a more intricate decoration, the diamond-shaped war emblem of the Kingdom of Yarik. "By this hand, justice shall prevail," the old knight murmured to himself.

With their circle of warriors complete, the approaching attackers gave up all pretense of stealth. Two horn blasts, one on each side, stabbed into Aeoxoea's ears. Battle drums began to

194

pound, and a number of zoth throats joined in the chant. The circle of warriors broke into a run, closing in on the knights from all sides, their shrieking war cry echoing through the trees.

Elkor rocked back and forth from one foot to the other, banging his axe against the buckler he held in his left hand.

"Wait, puppies," he said to his dogs, who stood on both sides, fighting their battle instincts, waiting for the call to attack. "We fight together, and you know old Elkor is slow."

Gavin picked up a bundle of spears and began thrusting them down into the snow, forming a semi-circle of ten spear shafts around him. When he was finished, he knelt and bowed his head.

"Pray for me, Zealot," Elkor said. "And pray for my enemies."

Gavin stood and shook the knives in his hands, loosening his joints, jumping up and down. He looked at Elkor. "It is our time, friend," he said. "God has chosen us. Protect the Blessed Soul."

"Protect the Blessed Soul," the Hound answered with a grin, holding his axe out for his companion. "For Yarik."

Gavin nodded and reached out, tapping Elkor's weapon with the blade of his knife. "For Embriss."

Long before Aeoxoea thought the attackers were within range, Gavin pulled a spear from the ground and threw it, hitting a zoth square in the eye. That first was followed by another and another as the Zealot threw all his spears, fast and hard, each throw as perfect and lethal as the first, each throw splitting a zoth head.

The spear throws were effective, yet they did nothing to stop the shrieking tide of hatred and bloodlust, the giant wave of zoth bodies about to swallow the two knights and their animals. The humans stood their ground and watched as the enemy approached, the zoths jumping the bodies of their fallen comrades, screaming, swinging their weapons, moonlight flashing in their black eyes as the horns blasted and the drums pounded.

"Fight puppies, now!" Elkor shouted. "Fight!"

The battle hounds leaped at the first two zoths to approach their master, knocking them to the ground as Elkor rushed past, swinging his axe, shouting praises to his god and his clan. He waded through the mob of flashing steel, flailing arms and gnarled zoth faces, swinging his axe, punching his buckler with a speed and precision that demonstrated years of battle experience. The Hound's attacks were straight ahead—little finesse, all power, brutal and punishing. Nearly every swing was lethal, the heavy, sharpened axe cutting cleanly through zoth armor, flesh and bone, crunching, then screaming, then thudding as the bodies hit the ground.

Kang fought on his left side, protecting his master's dead eye, his left flank, and his rear, the two working together with a familiarity that showed they'd fought together a hundred times. Behe quickly separated herself from her companions, preferring to roam the immediate vicinity, using finesse attacks rather than power. Elkor trusted his dogs with his life, often leaving his back exposed, always pounding ahead, and they didn't fail him. They followed his lead, and went everywhere he did.

The battle hounds were an effective tandem. Kang, the larger and more muscled, fought much like his master, straight ahead, into the zoth's faces, his powerful jaws and rear claws leaving victims with torn throats and shredded guts lying all over the battlefield. Where Kang stayed with his master, Behe moved around much more, attacking from behind, often hitting victims in the back, repeatedly knocking them over and exposing them to Kang's claws or Elkor's axe.

Gavin the Zealot, the Nonuc Dieum, or Chosen Warrior of the Kingdom of Embriss, was everything Jass said of him. Fighting with two large knives, he moved about the battlefield with the flexibility, grace, and athleticism of a dancer, filling the spaces around his enemies as fluidly as water pouring through rocks. He jumped in the air, slid on the ground, rolled and kicked and punched, appearing everywhere his foes weren't looking. He found every unprotected flank, dealing death and disappearing so quickly he frustrated every attempt of counterattack. His knives spun and twirled in his hands with an elegance uncharacteristic of their purpose, leaving precise and calculated wounds, never too much, never too little. They didn't seem so much weapons of death, but adornments, ornamentation on the work of art that was the knight's body in motion. He committed ugly deeds with beauty.

Gavin the Zealot's abilities were amazing, and it wasn't difficult to see why. He was strong like a bullosk, quick like a mongoose, and possessed the balance, awareness and battle training to combine all these attributes to the best effect. Based on these things alone, he was one of the best fighters Aeoxoea had ever seen. But there was something else. He was also strong with Craft Life, favored by the magical forces which made the world. Most people had no idea these forces existed. They lived their lives passively, watching as their fortunes were ruled by a series of chance occurrences, choosing to attribute their own success or failure to what they called luck, whether good or bad.

Gavin the Zealot was not one of these. The Craft weaves did not affect him. He affected the Craft weaves. When he wanted something, the Craft weaves answered, bolstering the power of his will with the power of magic. He was a little quicker when he wished it, a little stronger; his senses just a touch more acute to potential threats. He knew what was happening all around him, knew what was about to happen all around him. He dodged spear throws he could not see, and blocked sword swipes before they occurred.

He was perfect.

He probably lived most of his life unaware that he was affecting the world around him, or how he was doing it. It was possible he still didn't know. But the truth was, men who possessed fighting skill of his caliber were one in ten thousand. Men who possessed his level of Craft Life were one in a million. This combination made his combat abilities almost inhuman.

There would never be another warrior like Gavin the Zealot.

It was a hard lesson for the zoths who challenged his knives that night in the forest. After mere minutes, the humans and their animals had carved their way through nearly half of the attacking zoths. That was when the enemy's elite took the field. Pushing his way through the ranks of his warriors, a large chieftain rushed into the fray, shiny black eyes locked on the Zealot. All muscle and scars, and covered in human battle trophies, he wore pieces of rib cage on his head like a crown. His hands gripped two long-handled adzes with hooked blades, both of them darkened by layers of dried blood. He loomed nearly a foot above the Zealot, but possessed quickness to match the smaller human. He charged straight at the knight, raining repeated blows with what should have been deadly accuracy. But with every attack metal met metal, a loud, repeated clanging, as the Zealot blocked everything the creature threw at him. He dodged, darted, and rolled, throwing up his knives over and over, creating a barrier of steel the chieftain couldn't fight through. He constantly retreated and rushed about through the trees as the zoth gave chase, knocking over his own warriors and stepping on them in the effort.

The duel seemed as though it would go on all night, with neither the human nor the zoth able to gain the upper hand. Then Gavin ducked an adze chop that stuck in the side of a tree, and used the second-long opportunity to slip a knife between the chieftain's ribs, neatly bisecting his heart. But the wound didn't bleed, and mended itself as quickly as it had opened. The chieftain pulled his adze free and resumed the fight as though nothing happened.

Once again, Aeoxoea changed the spectrum of light her eyes perceived so she could see the Craft weaves swirling in the night air. Just as she expected, brightly colored tendrils of magic could be seen clinging to Gavin the Zealot, all four elements flowing throughout his body, trailing his every movement as if his limbs were aflame. The chieftain also glowed brightly, his speed and power so artificially enhanced his skin appeared to be bursting with sunlight. But where the Craft weaves loved, protected, and aided the Zealot, they hated and reviled the chieftain, recoiling from him when not controlled otherwise. Someone was controlling magic, forcing it to support and protect the chieftain through the use of runes. Aeoxoea looked at the big zoth and saw the strand of glittering golden light that bound him to his shaman.

Wind Magic.

There was no way Elkor could see what the assassin saw, but battlefield experience told him what was happening. So it was no surprise to see the knight with Kang at his side battling toward the zoth shaman, a smallish and aged looking creature surrounded by a ring of drummers several yards away from the Hound. The shaman danced in circles and swung a tree branch with several skulls attached, each trailing smoke from the eye sockets. He was clearly working Craft, Aeoxoea could see, drawing a glowing rune on the air itself with spindly fingers. White lightning crackled up and down his arms as he shouted his chants, and shook his staff to the rhythm of the drums. The rune exploded in a blinding flash, and lightning streaked from the shaman's fingertips into the bodies of the ten or so zoths around him. They immediately dropped their drums and turned to block Elkor's path, electricity dancing across their skin. But the knight met them fearlessly, and so did Kang. Sparks flew and lightning flashed as Elkor parried the attacks of the charging zoths, disarmed them, crippled them, and otherwise dispatched them, one by one, until the bodies of his enemies were heaped on the ground and nothing stood between him and the shaman but several feet of bloody snow.

For one breath, the two stared at each other.

"Flank right," Elkor said, and Kang circled wide, hateful eyes staring at his prey.

Then a ball of lightning appeared in the shaman's palm, and several dead zoths laying on the ground raised their hands, throwing their weapons at Elkor. Spears, adzes, clubs, even rocks and tree branches flew at the knight as he dodged and blocked, knocking them down with his axe and buckler. He nearly avoided them all, but then a spear shaft cracked against the left side of his head, directly over his eye patch. The Hound growled like an animal.

"Kill, Kang!" he shouted. "Kill!" And the battle hound sprang forward.

The shaman struck the ground with his staff, a heavy thunderclap rocked the trees, and Elkor was knocked off his feet. Kang, likewise, was stopped short, tumbling in the snow with a yelp.

But the battle hound quickly arose, as did his master, rubbing his eye patch as if greatly annoyed. Again the zoth shaman summoned Craft energy from the wind, fashioning the intricate pattern of a rune that sizzled and crackled with raw Craft, ready to burst. And burst it did, just as Elkor threw his axe. Yarik steel thudded heavily into the shaman's chest, and the zoth staggered. But his spell was finished, and his skull-adorned staff burned with flame. Despite the blood gushing from his body, the shaman flashed a brief, triumphant smile, pointing his burning staff at Elkor.

At that moment, Behe appeared behind the shaman. Flying through the air, she struck the zoth in the back, knocking him off his feet. He fell face first into the snow, directly under the jaws of Kang. The burning staff clattered on the frozen ground and exploded, sending a streak of flame straight up through the tree tops. The magical attack intended for Elkor instead burned itself out in the nighttime sky.

The knight looked at this as if watching a shooting star. He produced a handkerchief, calmly wiping zoth blood from his face, while only feet away his hounds savaged the shaman's body. They didn't stop until all that was left was a pile of bloody ribbons.

"Good girl, Behe," Elkor whispered.

Aeoxoea turned to see how Gavin the Zealot fared against the zoth chieftain, who was now alone, unprotected, and unsupported by the magic of his shaman. The chieftain, with his size and strength, was still very dangerous, and would have made a frightening adversary for any knight, even without his shaman. But he was no match for the Nonuc Dieum. Now fighting on level ground, the Zealot wasted no more time with parries and blocks. In mere moments the chieftain was relieved of his weapons, his hands, and also the use of his limbs, due to several precise cuts of the tendons in this his arms and legs. Screaming in agony and frustration, the chieftain collapsed to the ground, where Gavin left him to be finished by the battle hounds.

The two knights met in the center of the battlefield and knelt together for a brief prayer of thanks. When they rose, Gavin went to retrieve Eleod from his haven high in the trees. He gently lowered the bundle of furs to the ground, only to find the Blessed Soul with tears in his eyes. He shook the child gently in an effort to soothe his fear, trying to hold him so he couldn't see the heaps of corpses all around. But the little boy kept turning his head and trying to see, digging his little fingers into Gavin's armor in his terror.

The knights who just a minute previous had been slaughtering zoths by the score, suddenly began to behave like nursemaids, cooing and tickling and making funny faces.

Elkor began to juggle the chieftain's adzes, throwing them into the air, end over end. Then he sang. It was an upbeat song of redemption, normally heard in barrooms throughout the Seven Kingdoms, but now it echoed through the trees of the snowy Outlands, a solitary voice, singing for an audience of one:

Lord have mercy on me, hear this dying clansman's plea
As I lie here on the ground, my fallen brothers scattered round

If you'll listen from on high, I now confess my every lie
I know I haven't earned your care, but still my soul I must lay
bare
I never tried to heed your word, I always lived life by the sword
I fought and stole for my own gain, and I misused your holy
name

Lord have mercy on me, hear this wretched sinner's plea

As I die here without friend, to face this dark and bitter end

I know that it is far too late, and this is my deserved fate
I have failed in every way, but please Lord take this pain away
And though my sins have made me black, I ask that you will take me back
I beg you, Lord to hear my plea, precious Father forgive me

Lord have mercy on me, hear this dying clansman's plea
As I lie here on the ground, my fallen brothers scattered round

Now that you have heard my plea, your undeserved love for me
Will lift me and my brothers round, to walk upon the heavenly ground
And now that you have redeemed me, I do not need my eyes to see
For though I die in this cold place, my soul is warmed by perfect grace

Gavin gently rocked the child to the beat of Elkor's song and the crying quickly softened, then died. After a few verses, Eleod only stared as Elkor performed for him, juggling the adzes and singing, and for the first time since Aeoxoea initially saw him, Gavin smiled.

Elkor continued singing as he dropped the adzes to the ground, then lifted the bundle of furs into Gavin's backpack, smiling at Eleod face to face the entire time.

When Elkor finished his song, he kissed the boy's forehead and said, "Beautiful boy."

Now Eleod's face brightened. He clapped his hands and said, "More! More songs!"

"No more songs," Elkor said, grinning. "Elkor loves to sing for you, but that's enough for now."

"That's right, no more songs," Gavin said, turning around. "We must go."

The Hound nodded and whistled to his dogs. The four of them once again disappeared into the night, running through the forest at a full sprint.

The trees echoed with one final cry:

"Want more songs!"

Before following, Aeoxoea took a moment to stand in the middle of the carnage left by the battle, marveling at what she'd just seen. Sixty zoth corpses lay in the snow, quiet and unmoving. Not a single one survived.

"Jass, wake up." Aeoxoea said.

"Yes, mistress?" came the reply.

"I no longer doubt your words," Aeoxoea said. "Gavin the Zealot is the most gifted fighter I have ever seen."

"He is the greatest in the world," Jass agreed. "And he wields the deadliest weapons ever forged."

"Your words are true," Aeoxoea said. "His ability with those knives is unsurpassed."

"I wasn't referring to his knives," Jass said.

Chapter 17

Theel sat quietly by the fire, shivering even though Yatham had wrapped him in layers of blankets, yawning even though he'd just slumbered for nine days, and throbbing even though painkilling angels filled his veins. He breathed slowly, and coughed some, regularly exhaling streams of hot seraphim smoke into the freezing night air.

Yatham was far away in the darkness somewhere, walking in slow circles, watching and listening so the camp would remain safe and undisturbed. There was nothing kindly to be said about the disturbance Hoster made in his sleep, lying in the grass flat on his back with limbs and maw splayed equally. It was good sense to have Yatham practicing vigilance; with the snoring, sputtering and farting the winemaker did, an army would have a fair chance of approaching the camp unheard.

Also near the fire was the boy wizard Rasm, lying flat on his back, with his book on his chest, asleep with his eyes open. He seemed to be dreaming of fantastic things, his mouth busy with snorting sounds and failed attempts to talk with his broken speech.

"Huh, yeah," he mumbled. "Whoa."

Theel had wondered much about Rasm since waking on Hoster's mule cart. He wondered who Rasm was, and who his drunk of a father was. Why were they walking the trails so close to the war? Why did they choose to give aid to his brother? What were the minds and motivations of these two fools Yatham had chosen to ally with?

Theel couldn't say whether Rasm truly touched the Craft or not. He couldn't command it; not with his inability to speak clearly. But it was obvious the boy wizard had seen the Keeper of the Craft recently, and had stood in the presence of the Globe of

Infinity. That was a rare thing for any man, let alone the addled son of a wandering drunk.

Theel would never get a straight answer from either of them. That much was clear from the brief time he'd spent in their presence. The boy would prattle on in his broken talk about inferno runes and turning people to salt, while the old man would try to sell Theel some of his wares, barking out the virtues of fifty different brews and liquors even while his own brain was curdled by the stuff.

Theel was a man of little patience, and these idiots always dashed it whenever they opened their mouths. They were two of the most frustrating people he had ever met. Just the look on Rasm's face often made Theel want to punch him. But not right now, thankfully. The boy was as annoying as ever. His face was as stupid as ever. But rather than frustrated, Theel was uncharacteristically amused by these things.

That was because Theel was smoked, and getting more so.

He looked dully at the bowl of his pipe as it flared orange, slowly disappearing into a curl of smoke. Saliva curled around the stem of his pipe, dripping off his lip as the angels entered his blood and sang in his brain. He shouldn't be smoking so much, but he'd started with good reason. He needed to ease the pain in his chest; needed to ease the pain of healing.

The wound was mending itself at an accelerated pace. Aided by the power of his juy, it was doing a week's worth of healing in only minutes. It would not be enough to close such a terrible wound completely, but it would help. The process had its drawbacks. It drained his strength and could be rather painful. But he decided it was worth it.

He did not have the power to do this himself, so weak was his connection to his juy. The power was given him by a tattoo. It was called the Life Sign.

The traditional name of the Life Sign was the Kel Arka Moor, a green weeper vine which was the sigil of the father of Arka Moor, the old Clan of Life. Many Knights of the King's Cross blessed by the Temple of Juy or any of the Seven Guardians of the old clans bore this tattoo. The braided weeper vine of Arka Moor went from his left elbow to his left knee, with branches reaching out to his lower back, his neck, and his heart. Created with both the powers of the Craft and the Method, the Life Sign gave a knight the ability to tap his own well of juy to heal himself. It was one of the first tattoos Theel was given by the Keeper of the Craft after he'd sworn the oath to squire. This was highly unusual, since most squires did not receive the Life Sign until they were risen to full knighthood. Theel wore the sign much earlier than any other squire under the Southern Cross, which was undoubtedly another privilege of his father's high standing in the eyes of the king.

Theel had rarely used the Life Sign; only a handful of times. He always relied on his father or his brother to help him in the past. But he knew the prescribed words, the prayer that needed to be said to invoke its power. It contained words from the Morning Supplication of the King's Cross, taught to every child of the Temple of Juy, and was required of each squire to be recited on his sixth name day, followed by the Knight's Creed.

Give this child strength,
That he might raise your banner.
Cleanse this child's wounds,
That he might carry your shield.

I, as a son of the Silvermarsh Clans, do commit myself, body, soul, and spirit, to the warriors of the Southern Cross, to the Seven Kingdoms they protect, and to the one true Lord of all Creation, that I might do his will, to love God's children, to lead God's Children, to protect God's Children, and that by these deeds, the Lord's blessings be given.

I will care for God's children, by showing his love.
I will guide God's children, by speaking his word.

I will protect God's children, by wielding his judgment.

With his mercy, I will care.
With his compassion, I will give.

With his wisdom, I will speak.
With his word, I will guide.

With his shield, I will protect.
With his sword, I will defend.

I will serve the Lord with my heart, my mind, and my voice, by learning and understanding his holy word, gratefully receiving his holy gift of faith, and always proclaiming his holy name.
These things I hold dear.
Amen.

Theel knew the words, even if they meant nothing to him. And now he was healing, through the power of the tattoo. It was sucking his juy away, sapping his strength, but it was making him well again. It was an exhausting process. And painful. But it was nothing a few dozen lungfuls of seraphim couldn't fix.

The Keeper of the Craft would have been upset if he knew Theel was burning leaf. For those weak of juy, or with little or no connection to their mystic will, seraphim could be relatively harmless. But for those precious, rare, few gifted with strong juy, leaf was not only counterproductive, the Keeper claimed, it could also be very dangerous.

Once in the blood, seraphim provided an easy connection to a person's inner font of mystic will, called his psychic nexus. For those with weak juy, this connection provided a pleasant euphoria. For those with average juy, it provided a stronger euphoria accompanied by mild hallucinations. These visions were much like dreams in that they could be either pleasant or frightening.

But those with strong juy could face much more intense effects. The euphoria could be overwhelming, but so could the nightmares. And while seraphim provided an easier connection to one's psychic nexus, it also interfered with control. A person with strong juy whose head was full of smoke was a danger to himself and those around him, unable to control his perceptions, unable to control his reactions to them.

The Keeper imparted to his students cautionary tales intended to frighten, of people who acted out dreams, whether light or dark, jumping from cliffs in an attempt to fly, or drowning themselves to extinguish nonexistent flames.

But most frightening were the stories of those who filled their head so full of smoke that they unintentionally sucked their well of mystic will dry. They were unable or unwilling to stop the flow of juy, and it drained them so completely, there was nothing left to sustain their life. Their heart stopped beating. Their lungs stopped breathing. They just stopped living. They would be found pale, withered, and staring. Their corpse would be smiling if they were lucky. But most often they were unlucky.

There were cases where people survived this, but it was rare. They would awaken after several days or weeks of restless slumber filled with hellish nightmares. And once they woke, they would suffer weeks of debilitating illness, as if poisoned; unable to eat or sleep. Even at this point, death was never far away, starvation the most common cause.

Most who smoked seraphim were unaware this was even possible, so weak were their connections to their psychic nexuses, so shallow were their wells of juy. But to those rare few with strong sources of juy, seraphim could be a very dangerous thing indeed, or so the Keeper insisted repeatedly.

Theel was cautioned many times, but he didn't listen. He began to dabble with the stuff shortly after his father died, and before long he was smoking it every day.

Soon he was smoking so much seraphim he didn't think it was possible to harm himself. He didn't heed the Keeper's warnings, and he often smoked as much as he could. As long has he could hold a pipe and handle a match, he smoked. Sometimes he smoked so much that he blacked out, a frightening experience, but also a welcome one. The sleep of a blackout relieved him of the burden of thought, of life, of responsibility.

It was a practice he called Dancing with the Angels.

And he danced. He danced to kill the pain of wounds the Life Sign couldn't heal. Nothing could heal them. And as his pain became greater, so did his attempts to dull it. For most, seraphim was a foolish distraction. But for Theel, it was a necessity of life. More misery meant more seraphim. The bleaker his hopes became, the brighter the leaf burned. Then it was about survival. And he danced with the angels more and more.

Most often the angels brought you back. But sometimes they took you away.

The angels took Theel away one night, and didn't bring him back for several days, long enough that Yatham feared he was dead. Afterward, he suffered sickness for weeks, but Yatham nursed him to health, as great a cruelty as was ever visited upon him.

Theel had learned a valuable lesson. He put down his pipe. And started drinking. He used liquor to help wean himself off leaf. It seemed to work for a few weeks, until the night at the Glad Sire, and the death of Quiddip Kile. Theel learned another lesson. He stopped drinking. And picked up his pipe. It seemed the lesser of two evils. At least with seraphim, he only risked harming himself.

"The problem is not liquors or leaf," Yatham would say. "The problem is you."

"You're right, Yatham," Theel said with a smile, clicking his teeth with his pipe stem. "The problem *is* me. And until I can find a solution to the problem of me, all I can do is strive to forget who I am. And what a wonderful way I've found to do just that."

He picked up his pouch of leaf and held it to his nose, inhaling deeply. He had to admit to himself, there was some value in waking in the mule cart of a spirit trader, even an insufferable one.

Yatham was able to purchase new seraphim from Hoster, a fresh supply of leaf to replace what was lost in the Trader's Cave. But it was only a small amount, not nearly enough to dance with the angels. Theel was certain this was done by design.

Yatham gave his brother the pouch just before starting on his self-appointed guard duty, clearly meaning for it to help Theel with the pain of his chest wound. It was a supply that should have lasted for days, if Theel had any self-control. But he had none. And now Yatham was gone, leaving Theel alone with no one to forbid him from smoking as much as he chose.

"This is your fault, brother," Theel giggled around his pipe stem.

He took an enormous suck on his pipe, holding it in with a stupid grin. His lungs wanted to eject, but Theel kept it in, allowing only the smallest amount to leak out between his teeth. And then an explosive exhale hit, as if someone was pushing down on his chest, and all he saw was the geyser of white smoke streaming from his face.

"You shouldn't have given me the entire pouch, Yatham," he said between coughs. "It's all your fault. And since it's your fault, the more I smoke, the more your fault it is."

He laughed at his brilliant logic. But the truth was, there was no reason involved in the decision to burn more leaf. He wanted to get smoked, so he was going to get smoked. Out here on the trails, under the stars, with no father, no Keeper, and no knighthood to tell him what to do, he decided he was going to fly.

So he smoked the bowl in his hand to help him decide whether to smoke a bowl. Then he smoked another because the decision was so difficult. He smoked one because the healing of his chest wound hurt. Then he smoked another because the wound hurt no longer. He smoked one because he was cold. Then he smoked one because he was hot. Then another because he was hungry. He hadn't eaten for days; so he smoked one for supper, then breakfast, then lunch. Then he couldn't remember why he was smoking.

Then he couldn't remember to smoke, and sat dreaming as his pipe bowl smoldered to ash between his fingers.

The effects of all this turned his flesh to liquid, his body now a puddle next to the fire, slowly seeping into the ground. Any desire he had to move any portion of his physical body was melted like wax before the candle flame, dissolved on the hot tongue of Narssic of the Nightscape, pagan goddess of dreams and visions, who legend said gave birth to the seeds of the first seraphim plants.

Up above him, the stars moved in slow, lazy circles. He could see them so clearly, so brightly, twinkling and dancing just for him. He could see the constellations of Samicus, the god of food and drink, and Thiaset, the god of music and dancing. And further to the north, Narssic beckoned to him sweetly. He could also see the constellation of the Blessed Soul of Man, its stars burning just as brightly, yet somehow appearing dull and uninteresting to Theel's eyes.

His father told him those stars appeared in the sky twenty years ago. Theel believed this lie with child-like trust. But now he knew better. He knew reason, and reason said stars did not appear out of nowhere. Preposterous was the idea that someone counted the millions of stars each night, then suddenly noticed a few more. Preposterous was the idea that if such a thing did happen, that it proved a prophecy was true.

"You will not be found, because I do not search for you, Blessed Soul," Theel mumbled to the stars. "You are a broken promise that no quest will mend."

Another exhale of smoke, blown spitefully at the constellation.

"You mean nothing to me," he added. "All I care for is Narssic, my lover."

At that moment, Theel's body was in as uncomfortable a place as it could be, lying on the cold, uneven ground, his flesh exposed to the frigid night air. But he felt none of this discomfort. He didn't even shiver, because the signals never reached his brain. His mind was vacant, elsewhere, spirited away to the bed of Narssic, where he floated weightlessly in the loving embrace of the Nightscape, his skin caressed by silky fingers, his face tickled by the hot breath of a goddess. Hot seraphim. Soft and green and sticky, hissing as it burned, a sweet song to both his ears and spirit.

Always faithful. Never disloyal. Endless love.

The heavenly breath of Narssic filled his lungs and filled his head with gobs of brain-numbing, muscle-relaxing, spirit-soothing seraphim, filling him up so much there was no room for annoying concepts such as thought, reason, or control. This was why he was helpless to stop it once he felt his juy beginning to flow.

He realized then he'd made a grave mistake in consuming so much leaf when he began to see wisps of Craft in the sky, little tendrils of rainbow swirling and flashing each time he blinked his eyes. He'd seen this many times before, and recognized it as the beginnings of a vision, unwanted, brought to him by his Sight. This would not be a weak vision, such as when he saw the Keeper of the Craft in Rasm's past; not with the amount of Seraphim swimming in his blood. He was so smoked he would be a prisoner of leaf for the next few hours, and that meant this vision would be intense, painful, and unstoppable.

No, it wasn't the Seraphim that betrayed him. It was always the juy, always intruding into his warm and cloudy realm, a cold and hard reality when all he wanted was softness and comfort.

Why would his juy not leave him be? Why must it always shatter his peace by forcing him to face responsibilities he was trying to flee, to relive memories he was trying to forget?

"Stop foisting life upon me!" he shouted at the heavens. "I don't want to live. Can't you see that? I never asked for this!"

But the sky didn't care. It continued defiantly shifting in color and shape, rippling as if the stars were reflections on the surface of a pond. The little rainbows of Craft swirled together to form a face; a bearded man Theel had never met, but who'd traveled this road years before. The bearded man was just the first of many.

Theel spent his next hours watching the ghosts of long-deceased clansmen walking the ground, as they once did when living, most long before Theel was born. Hoster's cart was parked and his campfire built along a road that had been well-traveled for years, and Theel seemed to see them all as they trudged by, heading north or south, day or night, through every season, rain or snow or sunny summer day. They were camping and cooking, singing and dancing, praying and cursing, living and dying. There were soldiers, merchants, traders, missionaries, women and children and families. Even zoth warriors came and went, leaving their mark on the land.

It was this mark that Theel's visions seemed to draw upon, the distinct, individual, and impossible to erase imprint left on the land by every living creature who ever walked there. The land remembered everyone. This was the magical Craft energy that kept the island of Thershon whole, or so the Keeper of the Craft said. It was the Craft energy that kept all the islands of the world in their orbits, floating in the air together, ever since the Sundering. The Keeper said when a footprint was left in the dirt, it was left in the magic. Though time would erase the imprint in the dirt, it could not erase the imprint in the magic, and those with the ability to see those prints—those like Theel—could see the past as it had happened, perfectly and clearly. The land didn't lie. And it wasn't lying when it showed him a recognizable man who'd made camp on this spot only months ago.

He was tall and lean, and wore numerous weapons on his person with ease. He was without question a high-ranking Knight of the Southern Cross. Anyone could see this by looking at the muscles and battle scars and the tattoos that graced his arms and hands, if they somehow missed the silver knightshield he wore strapped to his chest. This shield was famous, for it was the only one of its kind—it had a large hole in the center.

There he was, Theel's father, standing beside the road as clear as if he were still alive. And just as Theel recognized him, he turned and looked at his son with a stern eye. There was no way of knowing what he was looking at those months ago, or what thoughts made his face look so stony with frustration. But Theel had a strong feeling he was the reason. He knew he was a disappointment to his father, to the knighthood, to the Keeper, even to himself. He saw it all in that one look. His father's eyes were his own. It was as if he were looking in the mirror, and he was hating himself.

They'd traveled this road many times, the squire and the masterknight, most recently a few months ago, just before Theel's father died. His father appeared just as he remembered him—the muscles, the tattoos, the swords—but also the wrinkles, the tired eyes, and the patches of graying hair above his ears. The man had aged ten years in those months just prior to his death. No man could carry his load forever, no matter how strong.

The zoths had killed him, but he died because of his son.

The more this image tore at Theel's heart, the clearer it became. The dark night and the star-filled sky gave way to a late afternoon sun that bathed the road in its orange light. The trees sprouted green leaves, and the freezing air warmed to the heat of summer. Theel knew he was seeing a vision that was only months old, watching his father as he stood on this spot, only days before he died.

He was looking at a dead man. The thought sent a chill up his back, causing his jaw to tighten. His eyes watered, and he cursed them for betraying him. He looked away, unwilling to see his father, or to face the pain and regret it conjured in him. He raised his pipe and looked in the bowl. It was empty.

"The Keeper would be upset if he knew you were doing this," Theel heard Yatham say.

He looked up and saw his brother standing nearby. But Yatham wasn't looking at him. He was looking at his father.

"You are ordering me to break my oath to Theel," Yatham said.

It was then that Theel realized his brother was a part of the vision. He was witnessing a conversation between Yatham and his father that occurred months ago. These were probably the last words spoken in confidence between the two.

"I know your words carry the authority of the Keeper of the Craft," Yatham said. "But you ask me to dishonor myself. I must not leave Theel's side—"

His father's words were not made clear by the vision, but Theel knew the look on his masterknight's face as he spoke. He was speaking firmly, allowing no argument.

"What will I do?" Yatham asked. "Where will I go?"

Theel now understood the subject of their argument. Just before he and his father had traveled south toward Yarik, they'd split with Yatham and left him at an inn in a small crossroads town about a week's journey south of the valleymouth. Theel couldn't remember the name of the town, or the inn.

"The Temple Forge near the Crossroads at Calfborn," Yatham said. "What am I to do there?"

Theel's father told him they'd parted ways with Yatham because he had other business at the crossroads. While they traveled south together, Yatham would seek out a knight called Jarcet the Sentinel, who served the house of Overlie. Jarcet was considered one of the finest horsemen in the Kingdom of Embriss, a true master of the mounted fighting styles.

"I would be honored to train with Jarcet the Sentinel," Yatham said.

Yatham had always displayed an affinity for animals, especially horses. And, as if all the other ways in which Theel's brother surpassed him weren't enough, Yatham excelled in riding, while Theel could barely coax a horse out of its stall. For Yatham, the animals loved to run. For Theel, their greatest desire was to throw him off. Yatham could get a dumb horse to do anything. Theel couldn't get a smart horse to do anything.

"I wish to train with Jarcet the Sentinel," Yatham said. "But not without Theel. He must come to train as well. He could learn much from the Sentinel."

Theel watched his father shake his head, watched his lips moving, regretful that he couldn't hear the words. He knew he was somewhere nearby the day this conversation occurred. There was no way for Theel to remember this particular night on their journey, but he knew he was in these trees somewhere, probably standing watch, or building a fire. And while he did his duty, his father and brother had this discussion about him behind his back. Why hadn't they included him in their planning?

"I can't leave Theel's side," Yatham said. "He needs me. That is more important to me than learning from the Sentinel."

Theel couldn't stifle a familiar sadness upon hearing those words. Yatham was always faithful to him, never passing on an opportunity to sacrifice for his brother. It was a pure-hearted brand of loyalty Theel seemed incapable of returning, even when he tried. In the end, it was just another reminder that his brother was a better man than he.

"I know you will care for him and protect him," Yatham said. "But you don't understand how much he resents you. There is a reason he's never told you. Would you have listened to him?"

"You are wrong, brother," Theel mumbled. "I did try to tell him. And he didn't listen."

"No, he won't," Yatham went on. "This is worse than you know. You can't mend it with a few days of travel together."

Theel's father said more words, but Yatham only shook his head, disagreeing.

"You don't understand. His heart does not wish to soften to you," Yatham said. "He plays the role of squire as he was taught, but he does not respect you."

"You are right, brother," Theel whispered to his vision. "I did not respect him. He didn't deserve my respect and I told him so."

Yatham shook his head.

"Don't say that. You made mistakes but were a good father to us both. You were hard on Theel but you were right to push him. He has become an exceptional warrior."

The knight said something, but Yatham cut him off.

"That's not true. You've not ruined his happiness. You've not ruined his chances to become a knight. He can do it. He will do it. But this will take time."

His father continued talking, but Yatham only shook his head.

"Yes, but you will have to earn his trust first," Yatham said. "Why do you keep saying there is no time? What is the need for so much haste?"

Theel's father cut him off again, and Yatham only grew more exasperated.

"Why is it so important that I leave Theel's side?" Yatham asked. "Where are you taking him?"

"Yes, father. Where?" Theel said. "You never did tell me where we were going."

"Warrior Baptism?" Yatham asked. "In the Outlands?"

Theel was so shocked by those words that he wasn't sure he'd heard right. In fact, he wasn't sure he wanted to hear.

"Theel is not ready for Warrior Baptism," Yatham said. "You must not force him before he is ready."

Theel closed his eyes and covered his ears, but it was no help because the vision was not brought to his brain by his natural senses. Instead it was brought by a flood of juy, made uncontrollable by his overindulgence of leaf.

"Father, you can't make him face Warrior Baptism without me," Yatham said. "He needs me for such a terrible trial."

Theel knew his father intended for their journey to take them far to the south, but he didn't know they would go as far as the Outlands, and he had no idea the goal was his Warrior Baptism.

As far as Theel knew, his quest began with the Keeper of the Craft on the day of his father's funeral. But now he just learned otherwise. His father was planning for him to make his bid for knighthood months ago. The thought made Theel shudder, a physical reaction that should have been impossible considering the host of angels singing in his blood. Such was the effect this news had on him.

There were things Theel's father said to him in those days just before he died, things that led him to believe his masterknight somehow knew he was going to die. But he forged ahead despite this, determined to take his son southward. And now Theel knew why that was.

Theel's father died leading him toward his Warrior Baptism. He died so his son could complete his quest.

Theel felt around under his blankets until he found the handle of his father's knife. It was easy to bare the blade, as he had so many times before, and aim the point back at himself.

"Does Theel know of your plans?" Yatham asked. "When were you planning to tell him? When you reach the Outlands? Sooner?"

"On the bridge where he died," Theel said, holding the knife in both hands, the blade pointed at his heart. He was one dastardly thought, one moment, one breath away from doing it.

"Why do you say there is no time?" Yatham asked. "Why must Theel face these trials before he is ready?"

Theel watched his father put his hand on Yatham's shoulder, and his eyes were full of sadness. It was something Theel never saw from the usually stoic knight.

"We can do it together," Yatham said. "The three of us. He doesn't trust you, but he trusts me. He believes in me."

And for the first time, Theel heard his father's voice as clear as a bird call.

"It doesn't matter who he believes in," the knight said, "if he doesn't believe in himself."

Theel saw the look on his father's face and saw the same sadness he remembered. His father had looked so worn, so tired in those few days before his death, and so sad. Seeing that look confirmed his suspicions. His father had knowingly walked to his death. And he did it because Theel's quest was more important to him than his own life. He was prepared to die for his son's Warrior Baptism.

Theel gasped at the emotions this revelation brought. He was joyful, yet grief-stricken. He loved his father for sacrificing himself, but he hated his father for dying. The great knight died so that his son might live, so he could go on to complete his quest. This was an act of great love, and it filled Theel's heart with warmth. But it also filled his heart with shame, for he knew he wasn't worthy of that sacrifice.

Theel continued to finger the handle of the knife. His hands were shaking so badly he could barely hold it.

He'd done many shameful things in his life, but nothing was so terrible as what he did that day, the day his father died. He tried to blame everyone else for what happened—his father, the Keeper, the Blessed Soul, God. But this vision added to the truth he so desperately wanted to deny. No one was to blame but Theel, himself. His father wasn't dead because God willed it. He wasn't dead because the zoths killed him. He was dead because his son failed him.

"It is I who should have died on that bridge," he said to the image of his father. "My quest should have killed *me*, not you."

It was no longer just his eyes that were full of tears. Now his face was flowing with rivers of them. Overwhelming sadness and regret filled him to the brim. He couldn't handle the emotions so he buried them with his hatred, as he always did. There was so much hatred that it could not be contained, exploding from him in all directions, aimed at everything.

Even the seraphim, which normally gave him comfort, became the object of his ire. All he wanted was something to dull the pain, and now even his precious leaf could no longer be trusted. It was smoking that brought these visions to him against his will. The seraphim was to blame. A stream of curses exploded from his mouth, and he threw both the pipe and the pouch into the trees.

"I hate you for dying," Theel said to the image of his father, wiping his face. "I hate you for leaving a hole in me that shows I loved you just as much as I hated you. Why didn't you just tell me the truth from the beginning?"

Theel was alone, confused, and directionless, like a ship with torn sails and no moorings. No one knew resentment like he did. It was an old friend. It was the only companion he had left. The Blessed Soul betrayed him by being false, and his father betrayed him by dying for an empty promise. Now all he had left was his resentment and hatred for them both. And he clung to it dearly, nurtured and cared for it, because it absolved him of responsibility. He was no less miserable, but at least the blame belonged elsewhere. Yes, it was his father's fault. It was the Blessed Soul's fault.

Adrift as ever.

He knew this was wrong. He just didn't know what was right.

He felt so alone. He had his brother, Yatham, with him, faithful and supportive as always. But Yatham could not provide the love of a father. He could not provide the approval Theel wanted so desperately. All he provided was a constant reminder of what a failure Theel was, a reminder that their father always loved the younger son better.

Theel was certain his father would have preferred to have Yatham as his squire. He would have preferred to take his younger son south into the mountains of Yarik just months ago. The pain of this knowledge was acute, but it was nothing compared to the guilt Theel felt at his own actions on that trip.

The truth was, if his father had taken Yatham into the tunnels, he would have survived. If he'd walked onto the bridge with Yatham at his side, he'd still be alive. If Yatham had followed him into battle on that terrible day, he would not have been killed by the zoths.

But instead, the masterknight took his squire into battle. He trusted Theel, and he paid for it with his life.

It was Theel's fault he was alone. It was his fault he had no protection. He couldn't face the future or his past. He just wanted to die. But he couldn't face death, either.

So he smoked. And now, he couldn't even do that.

Angrily, Theel threw his blankets off and cast his father's knife into the dirt. Exhausted and weakened, he took his time shifting his body so his head rested against the top of the short, black stump that made his chair. The summer warmth of his vision had departed, and so did the orange sunset. Once again he was back in the autumn chill, looking up at the heavens and the stars that twinkled there.

But he could not find respite there either, only saw the constellation of the Blessed Soul of Man looking down at him, as usual. No matter what he thought or said, it was there. No matter where he went, or what he did, it was there. When he went to bed at night and when he woke up in the morning, it was there, the Blessed Soul, looking down at him.

"You are to blame for all of this. You will not be found, because I do not search for you," Theel said spitefully, staring at the constellation, willing it to disappear, to stop staring at him accusingly.

"You will not be found, because I do not search for you," he repeated, as if saying it a second time would force the Blessed Soul out of his life, to leave him alone forever.

"You will not be found, because I do not search for you," he said a third time. "And do not search for me. I will not be found."

He looked up at the constellation, and it simply looked back at him, refusing to go away. Nothing would relieve Theel of the burden of this quest, of the crushing weight of the destiny his father had laid out for him—not all the leaf he could smoke, not all the liquor he could drink, not all the denial he could muster.

Nothing.

"I hate you," he said, taking comfort in his hate. He wasn't sure who those words were directed at, his father, the Blessed Soul, or himself. But he said it again.

"I hate you."

Chapter 18

Three cloaked figures trotted through the snowy Outlander forest; three black marks on the white and gray landscape. Their furry cloaks swelled and shifted at certain points in a manner that suggested to the practiced eye that there was plate armor beneath. All three wore a variety of weapons with the sort of ease that showed they had the knowledge to use them. These men were soldiers, and they were in enemy territory. Their heads turned constantly as they scanned their surroundings, searching for something, hoping to not be seen themselves.

The lead man was smaller—the brains, not the muscle—and was clearly an accomplished tracker. He followed a day-old trail through the forest, one made invisible by several inches of blowing snow. He followed the trail left by the two knights—the Hound and the Zealot. He followed the trail of the Blessed Soul.

Aeoxoea crouched in the lower boughs of a sweetsap tree at the top of a large, forested hill, watching the men move through the trees. It was very unusual to see anyone moving alone through zoth lands such as this. Courage of this sort was more than most clansmen possessed. In the absence of courage, it would seem these three were in the grip of madness to take such a suicidal course. Anyone other than Aeoxoea would deduce this. But Aeoxoea saw things, and recognized others, that most did not. She saw that these weren't clansmen. She knew that they weren't natives of Thershon at all.

They wore a very clever disguise which gave them the appearance of Thershoni clansmen. They had the pale skin with all its blemishes; some pock marks, a scar, even a few freckles. Their hair differed in shades—brown, black, and blonde, with patchy stubble for the young one, and streaks of gray for the old. They even wore the diamond-shaped war emblem of the Kingdom of Yarik.

But it was all an illusion, one borne of some very intricate and expertly woven Craft magic. Beneath those façades, Aeoxoea could see that these men were not from Yarik. They were not from Thershon at all.

They were soldiers in the army of the Iatan Empire, Aeoxoea's homeland. And not just any soldiers—members of the Imperial Guard, with their crimson armor and black surcoats bearing the seal of the Serpent of Ans Madar, a pale snake head with seven black eyes. They answered only to the emperor and this hand-picked lieutenants, men such as the one who led them along the path of the Blessed Soul.

This man Aeoxoea recognized. He was a wizard called Azzrot, and bore the title Icon of the Empire. Adept in every school of the Craft, he was the emperor's representative among the people—his right hand, the single greatest enforcer of the emperor's will within the empire.

But this was not the Iatan Empire. These were the Outlands of Thershon, and these men did not belong here. There was only one reason the emperor's agents would come so far to risk themselves, to trod this dangerous ground. It was the same reason why Aeoxoea had come so far.

The Blessed Soul of Man.

The emperor knew the war was coming. He had enlisted the services of the assassins of the Cult of Meherarc, sending two of them to Thershon to kill the Blessed Soul as a baby, to end the war before it started. But it was now clear to Aeoxoea that more of the emperor's agents made the trip to this little island than she originally thought.

"It seems you do not think two of us was enough, Emperor," Aeoxoea whispered as she watched the soldiers approach. "Your doppelganger was sufficient to the task. Sending me was a redundancy. And yet you must send your dog, the Icon, to police us, to make certain the task is completed as you ask. It will be completed, but only as I see fit. And you will pay for your lack of faith."

As Aeoxoea watched, the men ran through the snow as fast as their armor would allow. Judging by their heavy steps and heavier breathing, they'd been running for quite some time. And they'd already seen battle, more than once. The black zoth blood smeared on their gloves and cloaks, a bandaged hand, and a slight limp gave that away. As they drew closer, Aeoxoea concentrated, focusing her hearing on the place where the men were. Her ears were filled with the sounds of heavy boots and crunching snow, clinking armor and labored breathing.

"They are a day ahead of us," Azzrot told his men. "Two knights and two animals; hounds I think. They are very quick."

"Can we overcome them?" one of the guardsmen asked.

"Not at this pace," Azzrot said. "We must use Craft, but not yet. It will be too dangerous in this unknown country. I must see our destination, or a teleportation might kill us all. Quickly now."

The men altered their course to head directly toward Aeoxoea, toward the large rise and the sweetsap tree she'd chosen as an observation point. As they crested the hill, Azzrot raised his hand, and all three men stopped a short distance from where Aeoxoea watched them. The wizard stared through the trees down the trail they followed. Aeoxoea briefly shifted her vision to Craftsight, and saw that Azzrot's eyes glowed with a fiery brilliance, the effect of powerful runes. He used magic to see over a great distance, and saw the trail of the two knights as it stretched for miles through the forest.

"The trail goes due east for many miles," Azzrot said. "I can cut the difference to less than an hour with Craft. We will have battle before nightfall. Prepare yourselves."

"Yes, prepare yourselves. I yearn to see you cross swords with two knights," Aeoxoea whispered. "Yet I cannot allow it. I cannot allow you to interrupt their search for Gilligod. Most importantly, I can't allow the emperor to feel there is benefit in meddling with my affairs. Rush to your deaths, fools."

She watched as the Icon of the Empire prepared to work the Craft, feeling bile bubbling in her throat. She felt the usual hatred well within. She'd crossed paths with this man too many times in her life. This time would be the last.

"I promise you, Azzrot," Aeoxoea muttered, "only one of us will return home from this island alive."

Azzrot worked Wind Magic, something Aeoxoea had seen many wizards do. The Icon of the Empire drew a rune on the air, upon the very fabric of the Craft that bound the world together. It was a very complex rune, glowing the brilliant gold of the power of ether, sizzling and crackling with raw Craft energy. Azzrot unstopped a bottle and waved it in the air, said a few words, and watched as flames grew out of the ground. His rune exploded with a bang, followed by a small shower of sparks. The flames spread out into a large oval-shaped ring, man-sized, a magical gateway. The surface of the gateway rippled like water, reflecting its surroundings like a mirror.

The three men approached the shimmering gateway with a familiarity that showed magical travel was routine to them. One of the guardsmen stepped inside and grimaced at the sizzling sound, at the pain of crossing the threshold. The Icon of the Empire was next, also clenching his teeth, but much more accustomed to the burning sensation.

The second guardsmen was about to step through when Aeoxoea sprang from her perch. Hands at her sides, she dove at the ground like a striking falcon, with blazing speed and murderous intent. White tentacles sprang from her sides just before she hit her prey. The two bodies crashed together and tumbled into the snow, rolling halfway down the hill in a cloud of white dust. The guardsman had superb battle instincts. He had one hand around the handle of a knife and the other around Aeoxoea's neck long before he could have possibly known what hit him.

He was strong and very quick; a trained killer. In a simple fight of muscle and steel, the assassin would be dead in moments, her flesh sliced into ribbons, or her neck broken. But no fight Aeoxoea ever joined was so simple.

A white tentacle curled around the man's wrist, tearing his hand away from her neck. Another gripped his hand holding the knife, squeezing it until his fingers crackled and the blade fell into the snow. She forced the man's arms helplessly wide while more tentacles struck at the guardsman's chest like serpents, splashing the snow with blood.

Aeoxoea was nose to nose with her victim as he struggled and wheezed. She planned to make herself visible to Azzrot's eyes, so she chose to be seen now. She didn't know this man, and so she took no pleasure in killing him. She did not enjoy the shock and fear his eyes showed when he looked upon her face.

"Poor kitten," she whispered. "In another life, we might have been friends; lovers, perhaps. But alas." She kissed his nose. "My need to take your life denies us that pleasure."

While she held him pinned to the ground, two of her tentacles bore into his chest, digging and slicing their way toward his heart.

"You see, I have discovered a most interesting skill, and I require your aid in its implementation. I've recently slain one of your emperor's doppelgangers. And as I've so often been accused of heartlessness, I chose to borrow hers.

"I've always had the ability to appear as I wished, but this has given me the uniquely valuable ability to shapeshift. Not only can I look like you; I can now become you. This is necessary because your master Azzrot is a difficult man to fool. He has seen through my most clever ruses in the past, but he must not do so today. That is why you are most valuable to me."

The man groaned in pain, his body twitching.

"Oh, I know it hurts, my sweet, but it must be done," she purred. "There is simply no convenient way for me to do this painlessly. To become you I must take your heart from your body while you still live. Please understand, I find this as regrettable as you do."

226

She ripped her tentacles out of the man's body with a spray of blood. They held a glistening, fist-sized ball of muscle between them, the man's still-beating heart, now sharing the assassin's blood as it flowed through her tentacles.

The man groaned again, his eyes losing focus as his cheeks twitched and blood bubbled between his teeth.

"Off to Dehen Yaulk with you, my sweet," Aeoxoea whispered. "I hear the Angel of Death can be quite pleasant once you get to know him. Give him my compliments, would you? He has done so much fine work for me in the past."

As Aeoxoea drew her two tentacles back into her body, they took their grisly prize with them. The skin and flesh of her chest peeled open to accept the guardsman's heart, then closed again around it once inside. Her body swallowed it entirely, leaving nothing but a few drops of blood on her belly.

A moment later, her appearance changed to that of a clansman native to this island of Thershon, with light skin and black hair. Her physical body shifted to that of the guardsman, but in stealing the man's heart, she also stole the magical illusion created by Azzrot, wearing it without the Icon's permission.

She rose to her feet and stood for a moment, looking at the man she'd just slain. His physical form reverted to his natural appearance, with the olive skin and sharp features marking him a fyral, one of the many races of the Iatan Empire. The furs of a Thershoni clansman became the crimson armor of an Imperial Guardsman, covered by a black surcoat with the seal of his emperor, the Serpent of Ans Madar. Aeoxoea stared coldly at that seal, at its pale, white snake with seven black eyes. And as she did so, a death blossom fell from the sky, spinning slowly as it came to rest upon the guardsman's corpse, directly on the face with the seven eyes. This brought a brief smile to her lips.

But she wasted no further time. She turned and rushed up the hill, stepping through the shimmering gateway. On the other side, she wasn't surprised to see that Azzrot was in the process of weaving more Craft runes—green for Earth Sorcery, and yellow for Wind Magic—pulling power from the earth and the ether to create invisible, weightless armor for himself, then binding himself to his guardsmen. These were runes meant to create a channel of physical trauma to another body. If the Icon of the Empire was harmed, his soldiers would absorb the blows in his place.

Leading away from the wizard's feet was the trail left by the two knights and their dogs. With only a thin layer of new snow to cover them, the tracks were now very plain, even to the untrained eye. They were probably less than an hour old.

Azzrot finished his runecrafting, then turned and looked at Aeoxoea, seeing his own guardsman. He didn't suspect a thing.

"Not far now," the Icon said. "They are not a half-mile distant. We will have them before the sun sets on this miserable island."

With that, the three set off at a hard run through the trees. They were now in an area that had fresh footprints all around, familiar ones that resembled large human hands with opposable thumbs pressed into the fresh snow.

"Keep a sharp eye for the gray-skinned creatures," Azzrot said between breaths.

"Yes, my lord," the other guardsman said.

"Yes, my lord," Aeoxoea echoed.

Azzrot led the way through the forest, crossing dozens of the fresh zoth trails to follow the clear path of two sets of booted feet, flanked by the paw prints of the battle hounds. For many minutes they ran, weaving their way through the trees in pursuit of their goal. Then they reached a flat-bottomed dip in the land, with the dark ice of a frozen creek that ran north to south. Here the trail seemed to end, indicating the knights took a detour across the ice.

Azzrot took one look and ran northward down the length of the creek. It would make good sense to the wizard that the knights would take this route, seeking to obscure their path on a hard surface that left no tracks. But it didn't make good sense to Aeoxoea. She'd watched the knights long enough to understand their ways. They were deliberate and precise. If they didn't want to leave a trail, they wouldn't have. Yet the trail was there, lacking all precision. It was plain as day to anyone with the most basic knowledge of tracking that it was just begging to be followed, begging for any pursuers to rush northward without questioning the sudden change of direction.

The Icon of the Empire didn't seem to suspect a thing. He led his men in the exact direction Aeoxoea surmised the knights wished their pursuers to take, half a mile up the creek bed, then suddenly east again. They ran over a small hill, then down through a bushy gully. They jumped another frozen creek, then climbed a low ridge.

As they approached the high point of the ridge, Azzrot spoke.

"We are almost upon them. Ready your weapons and ready yourselves for glory." He smiled brightly. "Tomorrow we present the Blessed Soul of Man to our emperor."

As they topped the ridge, a field on the other side came into view. It was a vast expanse of waist-high thorn bushes, every one dark and twisted, with branches frozen as if in agony. It was dead ground, what the suspicious might call cursed, or soured earth. No life would grow there, nothing but thorns. And the tracks of the two knights went directly through it.

Azzrot slowed his stride at the sight of the thorns, but didn't stop running, and didn't say a word as he followed the trail into the field. Aeoxoea was right behind, and found herself quickly covered in scratches. The thorns were long and needle-like, a painful nuisance perfectly suited for snagging clothing. Aeoxoea looked at the ground and saw fresh tracks, many newer than just those of the knights. Zoths. Dozens of them.

Azzrot slowed to a walk, then finally stopped, signaling his soldiers to do the same. Aeoxoea complied, looking up to see what had the wizard's attention. In the center of the field of thorns was a monument to the Maiden of Chaos, Shia Ka, whom the zoths called their Blood Goddess. Dead tree branches were hammered together, tied together and thrust into ground. More branches were attached to these, then still more, reaching up into the sky to create a large, deformed column of gnarled wood twenty feet high. It seemed to be covered with a carpet of fur, but upon closer inspection Aeoxoea could see that it was human hair of every color and length, long locks or short tufts and clumps, the scalps of a hundred victims.

But that wasn't all. Deathmarks hung from every available inch of space; skulls, fingers, and eyes, zoth trophies of war cut from their victims' bodies, some from the outside, some from the inside, the prizes of dozens of slayings. The territories of several different zoth tribes intersected at this spot, creating a place where the worshipers of the Blood Goddess made a contest of pridefully displaying the atrocities they'd committed in her honor. The tracks in the snow showed that the knights traveled within a few feet, through the very shadow of this terrible display.

"What is this place?" the guardsman at Aeoxoea's side said.

"This construction is surely the work of the gray-skinned creatures," Azzrot answered. "It must be meant to glorify their god."

Snow no longer fell. The wind had calmed to nothingness. A dead quiet settled over the field, challenged only by their own heavy breathing. Nothing lived for long on this ground; nothing that didn't praise the Blood Goddess. Aeoxoea looked up and saw a pair of eyes hanging from leather cords. They swayed gently in the wind and slowly turned toward her, regarding her as though they were alive, as though they could see her.

The zoth shamans were watching.

"Sir," the guardsman said, finally breaking the silence. "The Blessed Soul."

Azzrot seemed to sober and said, "Yes. We must go."

Then Aeoxoea heard a new sound, that of feet crunching in the snow. She looked to see shadowy figures emerging from the forest, entering the field to her right. She spun her head and saw more coming from her left, many more. They were coming in great numbers.

"The grayskins!" the guardsman shouted.

Suddenly zoth spears sang like buzzing bees, swarming the field, making the air deadly. Aeoxoea turned and caught one meant for her with a tentacle. Two more bounced off Azzrot's invisible armor with a loud clang, but the other guardsman took one in the thigh, grunting and cursing.

Loud whistling heralded the flight of another volley, and horn blasts erupted from the trees. A zoth battle cry answered the call, dozens of voices rushing into the field of thorns, their ranks forming a large circle. They converged on their monument to the Blood Goddess and the three trespassers who'd defiled their precious unholy ground with their presence.

"Close ranks," Azzrot shouted, fumbling in his pockets for spell components. "We will fight out of this!"

The guardsman pulled the zoth spear from this leg and drew his sword. "Protect the Icon's back," the man shouted through the screams of the coming zoths, knocking spear throws away with this weapon. "We must free him to craft runes. He is our only salvation. Serve the emperor."

Aeoxoea nodded in understanding. "Serve the emperor."

But as soon as the guardsman turned his back, white tentacles sliced into his body, driving him face down into the thorns. Aeoxoea leaped onto the man's back, pulled a knife from his belt and sliced open the back of his neck, killing the man with his own weapon. In that single thrust, Aeoxoea stole Azzrot's only remaining ally on the island of Thershon.

The Icon of the Empire did not see any of this. He was facing the opposite direction, vigorously working a pair of Craft runes as the zoth army closed in around him. The battle was about to begin. Now it was time for Aeoxoea to take her leave.

White tentacles sprang from her body and swatted the ground, launching the assassin high into the air. She landed atop the garish monument to the Blood Goddess, where she perched like a vulture, waiting and watching.

Below her, Azzrot stood alone against the army of zoths. Spears flew in from all directions, hitting the wizard, bouncing off his unseen shield. He worked furiously, weaving a spell that involved two powerful runes of Evocation to tap the elements of wind and fire. He traced a golden rune of Wind Magic with his left hand while bringing forth a Flame Bringer with his right. The Flame Bringer showed its eagerness to explode by pulsing a deep and angry red, and explode it did, wind first, fire second, then a blinding smattering of sparks.

A wall of fire erupted at the feet of Azzrot's enemies, engulfing the first rank of zoths who charged his position. The flames roared high, and shrieks of agony filled the air. Azzrot held his hands out before him, quickly turning around, spreading the wall of fire into a large ring of protection that effectively halted the zoth attack.

But the shock on the wizard's face showed that this victory was swallowed by the sight of the guardsman dead on the ground, with the other nowhere to be seen. A knife handle protruded from the guardsman's neck, undeniable proof that the Icon of the Empire had been betrayed.

A large chieftain leaped through the wall of fire in front of Azzrot, trailing a fresh rank of warriors. Other zoths followed his lead, breaching the wall as if they didn't care what the fires did to their flesh. The charge of the Blood Goddess' children had been slowed, but nothing could stop them from defending the monument to their Maiden of Chaos.

Azzrot was standing in the worst spot a human possibly could.

He tried desperately to complete more Craft runes, but didn't have time before the chieftain was upon him. This was a truly monstrous creature, hundreds of pounds of scarred muscle wielding a giant club with branches growing out of it, and iron spikes attached to these.

The great beast loomed above the wizard, his body smoking, tiny flames dancing on his head. The spiked tree branch slammed into the wizard's unseen armor with enough force to knock him to the ground. Azzrot, lying prone, unleashed more runes of Evocation, Wind Magic and Flame Bringers, and shouted the words of command as he fanned his fingers out before him.

The chieftain screamed in rage, bringing his club down again, where it bounced off the magical shield. The huge zoth readied for another swing when a light as bright as the sun shown from Azzrot's hands, so piercing, so mercilessly brilliant that Aeoxoea had to cover her eyes.

When she did look back the light was gone, but the zoths hovering over the wizard were standing dead on their feet, appearing as though the front halves of their bodies were melted, exposing internal organs, ribcages, and grinning skulls, staring with melted eyes. Only the chieftain remained unhurt by the spell, clearly saved by runes of protection woven by his shaman. He still stood, holding his giant club high, now with flames dancing among the branches.

That spell was an act of desperation, an attempt to kill all the zoths at once. Aeoxoea knew this because she could see that Azzrot was forced to drop his magical shield in order to cast it. It was a gamble. And the gamble failed.

As the corpses of his warriors crumpled upon themselves, the chieftain hacked away at Azzrot's prone form. The flames devouring his club roared as he slammed it down on the wizard's legs, crushing flesh and bone. The Icon of the Empire was trying to cast another spell, but his chant was interrupted by a scream of agony. Again the club came down, smoke and flame joining wood and iron to pound the wizard's outstretched arms like the chieftain was hammering stakes into the ground.

Azzrot had no means to defend himself. His fingers were mangled and torn, his hands broken and bleeding. He'd lost the physical ability to trace Craft runes, and the mental ability to maintain concentration enough to speak the words. The chieftain had taken Azzrot's spells, and with it, all his magical defenses.

But the Icon of the Empire was never out of tricks. As the chieftain raised his flaming club again, Azzrot knew he had precious seconds to live. And he intended to use them.

"Contingency!" he shouted, and Aeoxoea knew what this meant.

She'd seen this done by wizards before. It was a trigger word, meant to activate a spell cast previously and saved for a time such as this. The spell would require no runes to cast, and no spell components. Azzrot needed only to say the word, and his runes would take effect.

The Icon clearly meant to save himself by instantly traveling elsewhere by the means of magic.

"Telepor—"

But the chieftain dropped to his knee, bringing the butt of his club down onto Azzrot's face like he was trying to plant a fence post. The wizard's nose splattered like a crushed bug, and his body momentarily went limp. The Icon of the Empire was never able to finish the word. Now he was truly helpless.

Knowing this, the chieftain stood over his victim, smiling with his scarred and twisted lips. Azzrot was barely conscious, barely even alive. But he seemed to know what was coming. He began to weep in terror, blubbering twisted broken words from a twisted broken mouth. The zoth chieftain responded by spitting in his face.

More zoths burst from the trees, jumping and hooting like hyenas converging on a fresh kill. They congregated around the base of the monument, swarming over the Icon of the Empire. Singing praises to their Blood Goddess, they tore his clothing off and shredded his flesh, opening him up and taking his insides while he remained alive and screaming.

Aeoxoea watched all this from above, enjoying to a small measure the death of the emperor's most powerful henchman. Azzrot, the Icon of the Empire, was easily Aeoxoea's greatest rival in the search for the Blessed Soul. Now he was beaten, and feasted upon by dogs.

The assassin leaped down, landing near to where the zoths did their garish work upon her enemy. She stood and watched as the body of the Icon of the Empire was desecrated, his insides removed and his limbs reduced to mangled stumps. Then the man's bleeding torso was lifted up by the zoths and nailed to the side of the wooden column that stood in the field of thorns.

Seeing that Azzrot had survived this process, Aeoxoea allowed herself a moment of indulgence. After a moment's thought, her flesh peeled open and the heart of the guardsman emerged. It dropped out of her stomach as if rejected, plopping into the snow among the thorns. This took away the disguise created by Azzrot, but it was no longer needed. She shifted her shape back to her true form, that of a white-haired and golden-skinned darhan woman, perfectly comfortable in her skin and nothing else.

As the zoths began to cut the wizard's eyes out, Aeoxoea made herself visible to him. As Azzrot died, hanging from the altar of the Blood Goddess, he looked beyond his killers to see who did this to him, who betrayed him and fed him to the zoths. Aeoxoea knew the Icon could see her, could recognize her, and see that he'd been bested. The wizard's eyes widened with astonishment a second before the zoths cut them out.

Aeoxoea's face was the last earthly thing Azzrot ever saw.

"Welcome to the Outlands, my kitten," she giggled.

The vaunted Icon of the Empire was defeated. But Aeoxoea knew the credit wasn't hers to take. She looked down at the tracks left in the snow by the two knights and their dogs, a path leading directly across land sacred to the Blood Goddess and her children. Aeoxoea looked at this and could see clearly that it wasn't she who had offered up the Icon of the Empire to the zoths. It was the knights.

At great risk they'd walked this ground so sacred to the children of the Blood Goddess, but they clearly did it with purpose. Somehow they knew they were being tracked, and responded by altering their course. To this point, they'd smartly avoided zoth lands, but now they walked straight across the most dangerous spot of ground for miles around, leaving a clumsy, easy-to-follow trail for all to see. By the time the zoths responded to the invasion of their sacred ground, the knights were long gone, and it was Azzrot who remained to feel the wrath of the Blood Goddess. It was a trap he should have seen, but in his arrogance and zeal, he had abandoned caution.

The Icon of the Empire underestimated the Knights of the Southern Cross, and now he was paying dearly for it. Aeoxoea knew she must never underestimate them herself, or she might suffer a similar fate.

Still, it was impossible not to marvel at their bravery. Defiling this ground sacred to the Blood Goddess was certain to bring more attacks from their enemies. The assassin wondered if the appetites of the zoths would be satiated by Azzrot's blood. Likely not. When this gruesome business was through, they were sure to follow the same trail that led the wizard into this clearing.

Aeoxoea chose not to dwell on it further. She turned and ran through the snow, following the trail of footprints left by the knights to the edge of the clearing and back into the forest.

Eventually, Azzrot's death cries faded to silence behind her.

CHAPTER 19

On his first waking morning south of the Toden River, Theel was truly miserable. This was mostly due to the chilled air that stung at his face and reddened his ears, a cold that somehow seemed to grow worse at dawn—if it could be called a dawn. The sunrise didn't warm the land, or even touch it, but happened somewhere else high above a blanket of gray clouds that left the world in shadow.

Theel was too tired and lazy to stay on his feet for his morning smoke, so he sat upon a large rock with an unforgiving cold surface that froze his rear, sending unrelenting chills up into his bones. He was wrapped in his sleeping blanket from neck to ankles, which provided some warmth, but little comfort otherwise. That was because beneath the blanket he wore the same clothing he'd worn since the day he and Yatham had left Fal Daran. It was the same he'd worn under his armor as he drowned in the Trader's Cave, then slept in for nine straight days atop Hoster's ox cart while in a coma. The fabric was sweat-encrusted and stunk with whatever substance currently caused the fabric to adhere to his body like a second skin. He was desperate to bathe.

Now he sat upon his rock, warily eyeing the water source that Hoster told him provided last evening's cooking water; a dirty little ditch that was probably a bubbling brook during the spring thaw. But now in autumn, it was just a little mud hole with a meager trickle of ice-cold water in the bottom of it.

Worse still, between his rock and the edge of the ditch, a soft carpet of brown pine needles covered the ground, thanks to the forest of black fir trees all around. If it was possible to get down to the water before freezing to death, one could only do so with bloodied feet. Also, the ankle-deep footprints Hoster left in the mud when retrieving his cook water the previous evening were clearly visible. If it was possible to get back out of the ditch and across the pine needles before freezing to death, one could only do so by reversing all the effects of the cleaning that was just undertaken. Despite his longing for a good bath, Theel wasn't certain he wanted to make this trip clothed or naked, shoed or barefoot—or in any other state, for that matter. As usual, there was no perfect option.

"Being your usual decisive self, Theel," he said to himself, sucking on his pipe, shivering, and staring at the creek.

He'd thrown his pipe away in a fit of rage the previous night, casting it, along with his leaf pouch, into the forest near the campsite. He vowed in that moment to never smoke again. But his commitment to that vow, like so many others, proved weak. It lasted only as long as it took him to find the pipe and pouch among the trees that morning. He picked it up while on his way to the creek, and it had already blazed orange several times.

But the leaf failed him again, only making his mood worse. It gave him none of the comfort he sought; it only confused his brain. He cursed the morning, cursed the clouds, and cursed the wind for his discomfort. Then he cursed his quest, and the Keeper of the Craft for forcing him to be in such discomfort in such a God-forsaken place. Of course, his father wasn't spared his ire, nor was the Blessed Soul, for it was the prophecy and his father's unshakable belief in it that caused all of Theel's problems.

It was all in vain. His curses were just as ineffective at giving him comfort as the seraphim was. All they did was make the pain worse. All it did was force him to face the possibility that none of these things were holding him back. Perhaps he was holding himself back.

These thoughts brought feelings of guilt and shame, as they always did. The knowledge of his own inadequacy was too much for Theel to face. He could sense his father's disappointment, could hear his masterknight's voice chastising him. He needed to be stronger—not just physically, but mentally.

It didn't matter that his father tried to deny it in his final days, tried to say he believed in Theel's inner strength, and trusted him to be stalwart in his thoughts and actions. The knight could not, with a few simple words, take back years of a single message repeatedly sent.

Theel was weak. Theel was untrustworthy. Theel was inadequate.

Theel's father feared he was too emotionally soft for knighthood, and it was a fear that grew as his son grew. He tried to toughen Theel by being abusive, ignoring his successes, pointing out his failures, leaving stripes on his back as punishment. Theel knew he could have survived all of this, could have weathered these verbal and physical beatings and come out stronger in the end, if any of it was done by a loving father.

But it wasn't done by a loving father. Instead, it was done by a masterknight who treated his squire's training as toil. He didn't raise his son out of love, but out of duty, as if it came by order of his superiors in the knighthood. Theel never felt as if he was truly his father's son. Instead, he felt like a tool in the knight's hand, an unfinished tool that needed to be tempered. Theel's father acted like a blacksmith attempting to sharpen his son's edge by beating him with a hammer on an anvil.

The emotions conjured by these memories were debilitating, leaving Theel almost completely incapable, gasping for breath, exhausting all of his mental strength to keep from weeping. It was the little boy inside him who continued to cry for this father, begging to be loved. Theel would do anything to silence that boy. As he grew, he learned to seek solace in his anger and resentment. His hatred of his father and the man's foolish belief in the prophecies gave Theel comfort. When that no longer worked, he turned to leaf. When even that didn't work, he turned to liquor. When that didn't work, he attacked a man and caused his death.

Now he was even more confused, courtesy of a vision he experienced the previous night by the campfire, when his Sight showed him a conversation between his father and brother that had occurred a few months before. Through this vision, he discovered that his father wished to accompany his son on the quest for Warrior Baptism in the Outlands.

This was painful knowledge, and it brought even more feelings of sadness and regret. It was on this journey that Theel's father was killed. His father died for Theel's Warrior Baptism. And he did so willingly.

It meant his father believed in him. The great knight had faith that his son could complete the quest. Theel had always thought this quest was forced upon him by his father's pride, his selfish desire to add to his own legacy. But the things his father said in the vision proved otherwise. Theel's quest was not *Anora la Jinn*, the Warrior's Burden, where the son of a deceased knight must sacrifice himself futilely to cleanse his father's name. This was not a foolish diversion. This was a legitimate quest for Warrior Baptism. It meant his father believed in him. It meant the Keeper believed in him.

They told him his Sight would show him the way, and they meant it. They expected him to find the Blessed Soul of Man.

But it was much more than that. Theel's father ordered Yatham to stay in Calfborn because he wished to be the only one to accompany his son on his knight's quest. Theel didn't understand these actions at the time, but now his father's reasoning was clear. The knight didn't wish to travel with his squire. The father wished to travel with his son. This was because he hoped to begin repairing their relationship. He wished to walk together, and complete the quest together, as father and son.

It was as they walked together that Theel's father admitted many of the mistakes he'd made in raising his son. He tried to apologize for the methods he'd used in Theel's training. He tried to apologize for withholding his love, thereby never allowing his son to build a foundation of self-confidence. He said these things in a stiff and clumsy way, using words chosen by a military mind unaccustomed to dealing with emotional matters. But he still tried to say them. And his angry and bitter son failed to reciprocate. Instead, he saw his father's gesture as a sign of weakness.

"*You* did this to me. *You* are to blame," Theel said at the time. "I will never forgive you. I hate you!"

He was so wrapped in his bitterness that he enjoyed the pain these words inflicted upon his father. If Theel was a man, he would have offered his forgiveness. But he wasn't a man. He was still a child. An angry, spiteful, resentful child.

Theel knew he needed to start looking after himself. He'd neglected his own best interests for far too long, always laying the blame for his failure at his father's feet. But he could no longer blame his father. His father had worked to mend things, had apologized to him, even died for him. His father tried to do his best for him. It was now up to Theel to do his best for himself. He couldn't blame anyone else anymore. No one could save him if he didn't want to be saved. He must save himself.

He knew he needed to put down his pipe and work toward something. He needed to move forward with a clear head, and confidently face his future, uncertain though it may be. If that future included the Blessed Soul, he needed to embrace that. If not, then so be it. He needed to embrace *something*.

Just as soon as that thought entered his head, he shrank away from it. Even though it was never more clear what he needed to do, he was never more afraid of doing it.

He needed to stop burning leaf, and yet the pipe found its way to his lips over and over. The more he smoked, the worse his mood became, and the cycle of self-destructive anger and resentment began anew.

"You did this to me, Father," he muttered, his eyes smoldering. "You and your precious Blessed Soul. I hate you both."

Unfortunately for Yatham, this was the state in which he found his brother after making the long walk from their camp near the road.

"Hoster has the mules hitched up," Yatham said. "We're waiting on you."

"You'll wait longer," Theel muttered.

"Why?" Yatham asked. "What are you doing?"

"Smoking."

"We wait for you to smoke?" Yatham asked. "That's nonsense. We must go. You can smoke on the road."

"I'll move when I'm ready."

"Will you be ready sometime today?"

"Yatham, I'm going to die of cold before long," Theel grumbled. "I'm filthy and sick, and there is a hole in my chest next to my heart that will never cease its aching or bleeding. My tunic is ruined. It's stained with blood and torn apart, thanks to you."

"How else could I bandage you?" Yatham asked.

"You might have taken some care with my clothing."

"I could have left you to die," Yatham suggested. "That might have saved your tunic."

"This morning and this day are godforsaken," Theel said. "As foul and cursed as the day the Lord of Devils was born."

"A perfect day for travel," Yatham retorted. "Stepping feet bring warmth to the body."

"I'm quickly learning what knighthood is," Theel said. "Freezing and starving and days without sleep, broken only by the random opportunity to die. This is not noble. This is useless."

Yatham ignored his brother's griping. "Theel, we must get on the road the soonest we can."

"Are you listening to me?" Theel asked.

"I have no interest in listening to your griping," Yatham answered. "I have an interest in leaving now."

"You have an interest in leaving?" Theel said. "Then go. I'll find you later."

"We will not leave you," Yatham said. "You're not fit for travel on your own. You'll need to ride in Hoster's cart."

"I don't need Hoster's cart."

"We're not leaving you," Yatham insisted. "Waiting around will only bring us more Iatan scouts, or zoths, or worse. Let us leave this place."

"This spot is as good a place to die as the next," Theel said.

Yatham sighed. "Not more of this talk."

"It's the only talk I know."

"That will be perfect," Yatham said. "While you talk, I'll carry you to Hoster's cart."

"You won't touch me," Theel growled.

"I can and I will," Yatham growled back. "I carried you across the valley from the Toden River to Herr Ridge. I'll carry you all the way to the Outlands. Cry all you want, but I'll do it."

"Don't touch me," Theel said. "I'll move when I'm ready."

"Hoster is anxious to go," Yatham insisted. "He has no wish to wait any longer."

"I can't stomach that man," Theel stated. "I will not force myself to endure the ceaseless, witless prattle of those two idiots."

"Please, Theel."

"They're simple fools, the both of them," Theel said. "The father berates his son only to forget what a hopeless drunk he is. The son pretends to be stupid—for sport or attention, I don't know which. It would be impossible to understand him even if he spoke straight."

"I think Rasm's speech problems are genuine," Yatham said.

"What hopeless fools," Theel said. "They will wander until they die of thirst or starvation."

Yatham smiled. "Hoster will never die of thirst."

"I'm not interested in listening to your jokes."

"Fine then," Yatham said. "But it doesn't change our need for travel. Everyone agrees we must leave."

"This is *my* quest, don't forget," Theel said. "Neither you nor the drunk nor the idiot will decide how and when I pursue Warrior Baptism. Go tell them to leave without us."

"I mustn't break my word," Yatham said. "I promised to help protect his cargo until we reach Ebon South."

"I have no concern for your promises to others."

"It is best for us to stay with them," Yatham argued. "Hoster knows of the priest we seek in the Outlands. He can take us to Father Brashfor."

"How do you know this?" Theel asked. "Have you told him about my quest?"

"No, Theel, he said it on his own," Yatham said. "Rasm thinks the Blessed Soul will heal his words, so Hoster is taking him to see Father Brashfor."

"Hoster says he knows of Father Brashfor?" Theel spit. "Anyone could say that."

"He says he's friendly with the priest," Yatham said. "He knows where Father Brashfor keeps his church."

"Hoster speaks lies," Theel said. "He will say whatever he must to keep us watching his liquor for him. He's a wretch."

"I don't think he lies. Not about this, anyway."

"You ask me to keep with liars and drunks?" Theel said. "Tell them to leave us behind."

"I swore to him, Theel," Yatham pleaded. "I said I'd walk with him, and I will."

"Why do you make promises that are outside of your ability to keep?" Theel asked.

"I can keep this promise," Yatham insisted. "I will keep it."

"As a result of your ceaseless promise-making, you're now in a tight spot between your duty to me and your duty to this drunk," Theel said. "Why must you make unnecessary promises?"

"This wasn't an unnecessary promise," Yatham retorted. "I needed to get you out of Herr Ridge, and I could carry you no further on my own."

"So now I'm wed to your oath-making? My quest for Warrior Baptism is jeopardized by your," Theel wrinkled his nose, "promises."

Yatham's face was cold. "Your desire to fulfill Warrior Baptism sleeps and wakes at your convenience."

"Just as your noble pursuit of truth sleeps and wakes," Theel countered. "It is wakeful now, but it slumbers when the brainless idiot lies to you. It slumbers when the fat drunk says what you wish to hear."

"Hoster hasn't lied to me."

"Just as Father didn't lie to you?" Theel asked.

"That's not fair," Yatham said.

"It is most fair," Theel said. "Father lied about the Blessed Soul. He lied about surviving a stab wound to the heart. He wished for me to believe in lies. That wasn't fair either, brother."

"You dishonor our father."

"No more than he dishonored himself," Theel said. "He disgraced himself and his family with his lies, this great and noble Knight of the Southern Cross. If that is knighthood, I want no part of it."

"Stop pretending."

"What do I pretend?"

"That you have no care for the knighthood or for Warrior Baptism," Yatham said.

"You speak sacrilege, brother," Theel said, his tone dripping with mockery. "Father wanted me to be a knight. Why won't you listen to Father? Why won't you trust Father? Why don't you show respect for the knighthood, Yatham? Why? Did he not beat you enough?"

"I'm not going you carry you to Hoster's cart," Yatham said. "I'm going to leave you here."

"How can you leave me here, alone?" Theel asked. "I'm wounded and defenseless. If the zoths find me, what will happen? My blood will be on your hands, brother, and why? Because of your promises to a fat drunk and his blubbering idiot son. Then who will find the Blessed Soul? Who will save the world?"

Yatham did not answer. He only stared angrily.

Theel spit clouds of derision. "If you leave me to die, you break your oath," he said. "You show you do not respect my Warrior Baptism. You show you don't care for my life or my quest. None of these things are knightly characteristics, Yatham.

Father would be embarrassed if he was here to see this. You are an embarrassment. You are a failure."

Yatham still said nothing. Nor did he blink. But his fist lashed out and hit his brother's face with a loud smack. Theel tumbled off the rock in a jumble of kicking legs and blankets, falling to the ground where he thudded and groaned, blinking at the sky with shocked eyes.

"It seems that first wasn't enough," Yatham growled. "Get to your feet."

Theel groaned slowly. "Mmuh?"

"It may take one or two more tries, but I will succeed in knocking you out," Yatham promised coldly. "I'll put you right to sleep where you'll keep better company with your silent mouth, as you have for the last nine days. And with the help of the drunk and the idiot, I'll carry you down the road to Ebon South, since it is clear to me that you make the best progress on your quest for Warrior Baptism while you snore and dream, and leave the work to others."

Theel stared at the sky, eyes glazed and unfocused. "You hit me?"

"Yes, I hit you," Yatham said. "And I'll do it again. It's what your festering mouth deserves. From this point on, you will sweeten your words when you talk of our father. He was *my* father too, and I loved him. He was *not* a liar. He *did* survive a stab wound to the heart, and I will prove it. With or without you, I'm going to find the knightshield he once wore over his heart. In case you've forgotten, that's the one that has a big hole through it."

"Okay."

"I don't care what you think of your quest," Yatham said. "I don't care what you think of the Blessed Soul of Man, because this is more important than what you think." Yatham pointed at his chest. "I want this quest finished. I want to find the Blessed Soul. I want the Seven Kingdoms to resist the Iatan, and I want to win this war and, if Hoster can lead me to the Blessed Soul, I will follow. I will find the Blessed Soul, and I will find father's shield, and I

246

don't need you awake to help me do either. I will drag your comatose body down and back from the Outlands and finish your quest for you while you sleep. Now stand up like a man."

Theel didn't move. "I don't think I can."

Yatham sighed slowly, shaking his head at his brother's crumpled form. Then he bent down and gathered Theel's blankets around him. With a grunt, he lifted his brother's body and slung him over his shoulder.

"Stop squirming," he said, as he began to walk through the pine trees, back to where Hoster's cart waited by the road.

"I feel ill," Theel said weakly.

"I know," Yatham said.

Theel groaned. "Did you hit me?"

"Yes, I did," Yatham answered.

"May I have my pipe?"

"Shut up."

Chapter 20

In the Outlander wilderness, just to the east of the frontier town of Ebon South, a war raged. Twenty years before the time of the Revelation, the zoth tribes of the Outlands attempted to win the Second War of Souls before it could start, attempting to kill the Blessed Soul of Man before he could grow to fulfill his destiny. Thwarting these attempts were two Knights of the Southern Cross; Gavin the Zealot, and Elkor the Hound. They ignited the fury of the zoths by invading their lands, and by bringing with them the one person that all the minions of darkness feared and hated most. He was just a tiny boy, with big eyes and messy hair, but he would grow to be God's champion in the world of men. Before the end of this boy's lifetime, the greatest war the world had ever known would be fought over his soul. And the first battles took place as Aeoxoea looked on.

The first days of travel after leaving Ebon South had been uneventful for Gavin and Elkor as they slipped mostly unnoticed through miles of zoth-held territory. That changed after the first fight they survived in the forest with the chieftain and his shaman. It was as if this act awoke all the tribes of the Outlands to the presence of the humans. They attacked nearly every day—war parties with chieftains and shamans and scores of warriors almost suicidal in their tenacity. They forced the knights to fight for every step they took in zoth lands, and for every breath they stole of zoth air. The Hound and the Zealot dutifully protected the boy Eleod as they were commanded, cutting down their enemies by the dozens. Day after day, night after night, the zoths came to fight. It appeared as though every tribe of the Outlands was bringing war against them. Every zoth they killed was replaced by two more, each one as prepared to fight and die as the last. And die they did. The path of destruction carved through the Outlands by these two men and their dogs was enough to make it appear as though a small army had fought its way through.

But the carnage only seemed to stoke the zoth's battle lust. Early on, the knights couldn't get through a day of travel without a fight; now they couldn't get through an hour without a fight. As a consequence, their once impressive progress was now a painful crawl, as constant fighting stalled their movement and sapped their strength. Aeoxoea guessed the knights covered fifty miles that first night and day after leaving Ebon South, and only that same amount in the three days since.

On the fifth day of travel, progress was slowed even further when morning brought a blizzard that beat the knights and their dogs with swirling snow, ice, and a freezing gale that tested the thickest fur cloaks. Still they trudged on through the white onslaught, heads bent against the wind, Gavin holding Eleod tightly in his arms.

This went on for days. The sun fell, then rose. The Island of Behe Kang swooped by, casting its chill shadow, and the blizzard dragged on. The landscape became flat and the trees thinned out, causing conditions to worsen still. With few natural barriers to slow its momentum, the wind became a snarling, howling beast, attacking the knights and their dogs without mercy.

The zoth attacks slowed, presumably because of the weather, but they never ceased in their harassment. Now they came in twos and threes, using hit and fade tactics meant to annoy and frustrate, and to instill fear, reminding their foes of the constant, looming threat the zoths posed. Gray silhouettes appeared in the swirling ice, just long enough to throw a spear and then disappear again. Sometimes they were bolder, attempting to surprise the knights by charging straight into their faces, black steel flashing. Elkor countered with his dogs, and soon the zoths weren't the only hunters using the storm as cover. Then the attacks stopped altogether, and the knights again began to make steady progress, now surrounded by the sounds of killing—canine growls, snapping jaws, and the death cries of their victims.

The zoths never gave up. Those who did not fall to the attacks of the battle hounds continued to follow, tracking the knights, shadowing their every movement. And their numbers steadily increased. The children of the Blood Goddess seemed to be gathering, biding their time for one final large-scale attack.

On the eighth day of travel, the cliffs of the Tera Plateau turned south, jutting deeper into the Outlands, which forced the knights to take a southeasterly route. Now the trees all but disappeared and they were walking across a plain, though it was impossible to tell by looking around. The wind whipped so fiercely in big, white snowy gusts that visibility wasn't more than a few feet. No sun, no earth—nothing but a world of white. How the knights knew which direction to walk, Aeoxoea couldn't fathom, nor could she understand how the zoths continued to follow. But they did. And now they had a chieftain with them.

It was the same monstrous, scarred beast who'd slain Azzrot, the Icon of the Empire. He'd been tracking the knights ever since that encounter, refusing to allow those who'd violated the sacred, cursed ground of the Blood Goddess to escape unpunished. He'd gathered a war party of well over two hundred warriors, and brought them with him to join in his pursuit of the Blessed Soul.

These zoths were miles behind, but were closing the gap with impressive speed. They ran through the drifts as fast as they could, sparing no energy for the coming fight. The knights seemed unaware of this, continuing forward at the same pace as if there was no threat behind them. They soon learned otherwise.

The storm finally broke on the following morning. The clouds parted to reveal a bright, orange sun glaring at them from the southeast, doing its best, futilely, to warm this frozen world. Now zoths and humans could see each other, four tiny specks moving across a sheet of white, followed by a giant horde of black, less than two miles behind, and closing.

And now a chase began, a desperate battle of endurance that tested the strongest legs. The humans ran with all the speed they could manage, an agonizingly slow and exhausting pace through knee-deep drifts. The snow was topped by a thick crust of ice that needed to be smashed with each step, like a ship cutting its way through frozen waters. The dogs ran effortlessly across the top of the snow, and the chieftain used the footsteps already made by the humans, leaving all the work to Gavin and Elkor.

The knights had already proven to Aeoxoea that they possessed superb physical conditioning, and now they were proving it again, pushing through those frozen drifts as if they had fresh legs, as if they hadn't just spent more than a week running day and night with almost no food or rest. They took turns leading the way, one man making a path through the snow by smashing his knees against the ice while the other followed, resting, and awaiting his turn to lead.

This continued all morning, hour after grueling hour. The humans were slower, but not so slow that the zoths could catch them easily. They were going fast enough to drag this chase out all day. Clearly the gray-skinned creatures didn't think they had that long. The chieftain drove his warriors forward with every threat and oath that could be imagined. He demanded battle before noondark, swearing that the Blood Goddess would accept nothing less. He showed no mercy, even as some of his warriors reached their breaking points, collapsing into the snow, unable to rise again after several days of running without rest.

The creatures were further frustrated by the appearance of the Island of Behe Kang on the eastern horizon. Just as the zoths chased the humans, the black shape of the island chased the sun up the eastern sky. It would catch it shortly before midday, and cast its shadow across the icy plain. The knights knew they only needed to stay ahead of the zoths until noondark, then the chase would be over. This was evident by the few words they spoke to one another throughout the morning.

Gavin glanced up at the sun. "One hour before noondark rising."

"We're going to make it, Zealot," Elkor panted, glancing back at their pursuers. "They won't catch us in time."

This quickly became apparent to the zoths as well. As things were going, the pursuit would be over within an hour, and the Blessed Soul of Man would slip out of reach. So the chieftain changed tactics. His warriors would not overcome the knights before Behe Kang caught the sun. But he seemed to think he could do it. He could catch up to the humans and force a battle with them, slow their progress, and give his warriors time to join the battle. There was still time.

The great scarred beast picked up his pace, leaving his warriors behind in an effort to catch the humans before noondark descended upon them. Already the shadow of Behe Kang could be seen creeping across the snow-capped mountains to the northeast, falling across the cliffs of the Tera Plateau, then inching its way across the snowy plain, turning the white drifts blue as it inched ever closer. The zoths ran as if they feared this shadow, as if its darkness brought some unknown doom. The knights ran as if it provided sanctuary, as if they would be safe once they stepped out of the sunlight and into the darkness.

The chieftain ran as if the Blood Goddess would personally rise up from hell to punish him if he did not catch those knights before noondark. His legs moved with the speed of a horse and the strength of an ox, kicking up a giant cloud of white as he plowed through the drifts. He was moving more than fast enough to catch the knights in time. Elkor realized this and turned back, leaving Gavin alone to carry the Blessed Soul to freedom. The Hound backtracked, following his own trail on a bearing straight for the giant zoth, pulling his axe from his back and calling on his dogs to join him.

The battle hounds, almost gleeful at the prospect of battle, ran ahead of their master, circling the chieftain, growling and threatening, but not yet attacking. The zoth did not slow his pace as he pulled his giant club from his back, a heavy piece of wood resembling a tree branch with iron spikes attached to it. It was appropriate, since this zoth was as large as a tree and just as strong. Elkor looked like a little child attacking a grown man, yet he showed no fear, mouthing a battle chant as he rushed forward, flipping his eye patch to display the diamond-shaped war emblem of the Kingdom of Yarik. Behe circled around behind the zoth's rear, while Kang joined his master on his left side. The chieftain took a mighty swing with his spiked tree, and Elkor shouted to his dogs.

"Kill!"

The knight didn't bother with his buckler; there was nothing that could block this monster's attacks. Instead, he pulled a knife from his belt and retreated, letting his hounds do their work. The zoth's club whooshed by like a thundercloud just as both animals struck. Behe hit her target in the back while Kang slithered under the attack, going for his ankle. Behe's paws would have pushed over any but the stoutest man, but hitting this thing was like trying knock down a stone wall. Her father fared better, getting a mouthful of the massive beast's ankle, but the zoth only kicked him off like he was a rabbit, sending him spinning through the air.

Elkor threw his knife, hitting the zoth in the stomach. The great monster just pulled it out and cast it aside. It did as much damage as a mosquito bite, but was still a good sign for Elkor. If that blade was able to find flesh, then the chieftain was fighting without his shaman. This meant the knight had a chance, no matter how slim, to win this fight.

The club swiped again, and again Elkor was forced to retreat. There was no stopping that club, no way of blocking it. So he backed away, pulled another knife, and shouted again:

"Kill!"

The battle hounds moved in; he threw his knife, and the zoth swung his club. The knife thunked into the spiked wood as it roared by in another mighty swing, throwing up a cloud of white powder. Kang clamped onto the back of the creature's leg, just above the knee, while Behe climbed the zoth's back, finding footholds in his flesh with her claws. But the zoth only ignored them, rushing forward at Elkor, trying to get past him in order to continue the pursuit of the Blessed Soul.

The knight retreated further, throwing a third knife that stuck in the zoth's chest. The creature roared in anger, but still wasn't slowed, charging on as Behe sunk her teeth into the back of his neck, raking her claws across his back. He was coming faster than Elkor could retreat, and the knight knew there was nothing he could do to stop it. He was about to be knocked into the sky by that club, or crushed beneath the creature's feet like a gnat. He drew another knife, his last, but another swipe of the club knocked it from his fingers before he could throw it. So he threw his axe, putting all the strength of his arm into the attack. The axe blade slammed into the creature's face right as the club whooshed again—from the knight's left side. His blind side.

Yarik steel split the zoth's nose while the spiked club slammed into the knight's left arm. Bones were broken and flesh was shredded, zoth and human blood spraying in the snow. Elkor was slammed to the ground, buried under the weight of the club. The chieftain fell to his knees, knocking both dogs off of him.

In the distance, Gavin the Zealot ran without looking back, carrying Eleod into the shadow of Behe Kang and apparently, to safety. In the other direction, an army of zoths saw that it was too late to stop him. They looked up at the island with fear in their eyes, saw its shadow speeding toward them, and gave up their chase. As one, the entire army turned their backs and fled in the opposite direction, abandoning their leader to whatever fate the darkness would bring to him.

The chieftain pulled the axe from his face, looking at the bloody steel with dazed eyes. It was amazing that he was still alive. Enough blood to fill a man's body flowed from the cleft where its nose once was in the time it took him to rise to his feet. He was mortally wounded, surrounded by his enemies and about to die. But rather than admit defeat, he took three steps and threw Elkor's axe with all the strength he had left. Then he collapsed, his body limp before it hit the ground. He would never see the result of his throw, which sent the axe spinning end over end, covering a distance three times greater than any human would ever achieve, just far enough to thud in the snow several feet behind Gavin's heels.

It was over. There was nothing left but the barks and growls of two shepherd dogs as they ensured this zoth would never rise again. As they did this, the sun was swallowed by noondark and the chieftain died, having failed his Blood Goddess in the shadow of Behe Kang.

Aeoxoea looked on silently as Elkor pushed the enormous club off and picked himself up out of the snow. The knight was hurt badly, with an arm clearly broken above the elbow, and a puncture wound in his shoulder that bled freely.

For the first time in all these days of following the knights, the assassin saw signs of weakness. Elkor was many years Gavin's elder, but he never showed it—not until this moment. Now he looked old and tired, kneeling in the snow, staring at the ground with heavy breaths. He held his wounded shoulder tightly, blood trickling between the fingers of his glove. He seemed to be praying, as if asking his god to make the bleeding stop.

That was when Aeoxoea detected the explosion of a Craft rune, a sudden pop and release of magic that caused her skin to tingle. She quickly called on her Craftsight, changing her vision to the light spectrum which allowed her to detect magic, and suddenly the world was filled with the vibrant colors of a million swirling Craft weaves. And then she saw it. A portion of Elkor's left side was alive with magical energy. It was one of the knight's tattoos, one of the larger and more intricate images that graced his body. It appeared to be a vine reaching from his left elbow to his left knee, with branches reaching out to his lower back, his neck, and his heart. The entire thing glowed brightly to her Craft-sensitive eyes, hungrily drawing on the magic from all around—the blues of Water Witching, the greens of Earth Sorcery. This was the rune that Aeoxoea sensed. She only had a second to realize what was happening when the magic took effect.

Elkor was healed. The bones of his arm knitted themselves together. The hole in his shoulder closed and formed a red scar. It wasn't perfect. He still felt some pain, and he clearly hadn't regained full motion. But he'd just accomplished a month's worth of healing in one second.

The sight of the knight struggling to his feet told Aeoxoea that this healing had not come without a cost. Elkor now seemed truly exhausted. His back pained him, and his joints stiffened. His face was too tired to hold an expression. He may even have gained a few wrinkles around his eyes. It was almost as if the healing rune had aged him a few years.

But his spirit was just as strong as ever, and he forced his tired legs into motion. He retrieved his knives, called for his dogs to follow him, and set out through the drifts to reunite with the Zealot.

Aeoxoea did not follow, looking down at the dead chieftain, then up at the Island of Behe Kang. She wasn't certain what she'd just witnessed.

"Jass, my puppet," she said. "Why do the zoths fear the coming of noondark?"

"It is not noondark which stokes the zoth's fear," Jass answered. "It is what noondark brings to this plain, and where it brings those unlucky enough to be caught here within its shadow."

"Where noondark brings them?" Aeoxoea asked. "What do you mean?"

"The shadow welcomes us to an evil place," Jass explained. "A place with no sun, no light, and no hope. It is called the Forsaken Kingdom by some, the Land of Teardrops by others. It is a world locked in endless nightmare."

"Endless nightmare?" Aeoxoea asked. "Where are we?"

Jass said one word:

"Illengaard."

CHAPTER 21

Aeoxoea didn't know where she was, or how she arrived there, but felt certain Jass's words must be accurate. She took only one step, but it felt as if she traveled hundreds of miles in that single stride. And now she was in another place so far from where she just was, it might have been another island for all she knew.

It happened at the moment of noondark, when the shadow of Behe Kang fell across her. Nothing about the noontime phenomenon appeared to be different from any other she'd experienced since arriving on the Island of Thershon. She still stood on the frozen plain next to the body of the zoth chieftain. She could see the cliffs of the Tera Plateau to the north, and an endless world of white dunes to the south. Everything looked the same. But everything felt different.

There was something sinister in the air. It couldn't be seen, or smelled, or tasted, but it was there. And it seemed to sap the life out of everything. The first thing it killed was the afternoon. Noondark should have lasted only minutes. The sun should have reappeared, illuminated the island, and warmed the day. But it only grew darker as Behe Kang continued to travel across the sky. The sun never reappeared, and by the time the assassin caught up to the knights, the sky was completely black and starless, as if the world had traded midday for midnight.

The next thing to die in the shadow of noondark was the wind. Before it was a shrieking banshee sweeping across the plain, threatening to lay all things flat. But now the great gusts were reduced to soft breezes, then mere whispers. An hour after the sun disappeared, the air was utterly still, almost stagnant, and there didn't seem to be enough of it. No matter how much she gulped into her lungs, Aeoxoea was denied a fresh breath. The more she tried, the more she suffocated, and she could see the knights were no different. Even the dogs walked with weary steps, panting, their tongues hanging out with exhaustion.

Then the snow disappeared. What started as an ocean of white drifts slowly diminished. The tallest ones became waist-deep, knee-deep, then ankle-deep. The air grew no warmer, but something was melting the snow with all the effectiveness of the summer sun. Then they were walking on dry ground, crunching through yellow grass that would have been several feet high if it stood up straight, but instead it lay on the ground as if each blade was too sick to hold its head up.

As if this wasn't unsettling enough, the moon suddenly moved across the sky in mere seconds. One moment, the silver crescent shown low to the southwest. In the next moment, it shown high in the east, bright and full. It was as if noondark hadn't just changed the time of day, it had also changed the time of month.

Aeoxoea didn't know whether she could trust what her eyes were telling her. All of her surroundings looked real enough, but nothing moved—not a whisper of wind, not a rustle of leaf. Every object in her sight had the feel of an unnatural thing trying to appear legitimate, with little success. It was as if she was standing in an oil painting.

The knights were the only life to exist in this place. Their boots crunched in the grass, weapons shifted and clinked, and heavy breaths steamed in the frigid air. But these seemed to be the only sounds heard for hundreds of miles. And even near to the source, these sounds seemed muffled, partly swallowed by the heavy, stifling air of the place.

The flat plain became hills of brown grass, and forests of dead, leafless trees. They crossed a sandy riverbed so deep and wide it should have been impassible, beneath a cliff that was clearly once a mighty waterfall, but all of it was bone-dry, without a hint of moisture.

On the other side of the river, the untamed wilderness began to show signs of human settlement. Someone had built rail fences, many broken, but never mended. These surrounded fields that were planted and irrigated from the dried riverbed. But they were never harvested—full crops of wheat and corn lay neglected, dead, and rotting. There were roads with wagon ruts, covered with footprints made by humans and animals, but completely empty of travelers, home to nothing but piles of dried leaves. Aeoxoea began to see farmhouses in the distance. These were places where the knights should have sought refuge. They were exhausted, wounded, and hadn't slept or eaten a decent meal in days. But they kept walking, and the houses and farm buildings passed by on each side, their windows black and silent.

Then the knights came to what was once a village, a small number of homes clustered around a place where two roads intersected. The knights chose not to stop here, either, walking through the middle of town and continuing on out the other side. Aeoxoea inspected some of the buildings and saw that they were clean and well kept, but empty, and devoid of life. A fireplace was full of fresh logs, waiting to be lit. An iron pot hung in the hearth, clean and free of dust as if it was just put there. The kitchen table was set for dinner, but there was no food, and no people, the chairs just as empty as the plates.

There were stables in similar condition—everything neat and clean, as if the humans and animals had just disappeared without a trace. The bellows were open and ready to blow. The hammer rested sideways atop the anvil. Out back, there was a well with an empty bucket, both completely dry.

The knights crossed a cemetery on the other side of town, with nearly as many open graves as tombstones. All of these graves appeared to be freshly dug and were empty, with no sign of who they were intended for. There was even a wooden coffin, sitting open in the moonlight, a shovel thrust into the ground beside it.

Hours passed, enough that the sun should have risen. But it never did. There was no morning, no daytime. It was as if there was no time at all—no past and no future, just one long, endless night with no beginning or end.

It began to play tricks on Aeoxoea's mind. It was impossible to know how long they'd been walking, because there was no sense of time passing, no sense of distance traveled. Houses and trees and farm pastures passed by. They crossed hills and valleys, walked through forests and fields, took many different roads, through many different villages. But these sights were all the same, almost indistinguishable from one another—cold, dark, abandoned, and trapped in this eerie, starless night under a moon that refused to move. It felt to Aeoxoea as if she and the knights had become a part of the place, as if the artist decided to add them to his painting. They were no longer people, but oil creations condemned to walk without end, traveling from nowhere, to nowhere.

Then she saw a flower growing on the side of the road, a rare species of white tulip called a teardrop. The teardrop was made unique by the dark, tear-shaped mark on the side of each petal. It was a rare thing to see teardrops in bloom anywhere in the world, and never outside of warm climates. And yet it didn't appear sick or dying like everything else. It was alive and healthy, standing erect, with moist petals and a faint sour-sweet scent. How this was possible in such a frigid place, without water or sunlight, was a complete mystery. Stranger still, the first was followed by many others, clusters of them growing everywhere, covering everything, thriving where nothing else could.

The clusters became thick patches, which became fields of them—white teardrops as far as the eye could see. The patterns of the flowers' growth suggested they were spreading outward from something, emanating from some source. There was something at the center of all this, and the knights appeared to be heading straight toward it.

They descended from the hills into flatter lands, walking across a series of ridges, up and down, up and down, as if riding the waves of the sea, only this sea was made of teardrops. They crested one of these ridges, and Aeoxoea could see mountains in the distance. At the top of the next ridge, she could see more of them, brown and gray peaks resembling miniature versions of the Great Dividers that loomed to the north.

There were cliffs to the northeast, a pointed spur jutting out into the Outlands so far away that Aeoxoea could never have seen it while using normal human eyesight. Those cliffs were the southernmost point of the Tera Plateau, soil controlled and protected by Arka Moor, the smallest of the eastern Greater Clans. It was the first sign that the real world Aeoxoea remembered might still exist somewhere, that it might someday be found where she'd left it. She looked up at those cliffs curiously, wondering if time moved forward there, with the normal cycle of day and night, with a sun that provided light, warmth, and life, and air that provided oxygen. Or was Arka Moor trapped in the same endless night that blanketed this empty land at the bottom of the cliffs? There was no way to know from where she stood.

They walked down, then back up the western face of another ridge, and again, Aeoxoea could see the mountains and hills to the east. But this time, she also saw something else, something positioned in front of this range, much closer to where the knights walked. At first she thought it was an oddly shaped rock formation, fingers of black stone jutting up into the sky at a slight angle. She wondered what natural phenomena would have created these. Then she realized they weren't natural creations at all, but were the work of men. She was looking at the topmost towers of a castle.

Each time they crested a new ridge, more of the castle came into view, as well as the valley that it dominated. Like the lands the knights had already passed through, this was clearly once a lush place, spotted by farms and fields and villages full of people. But now it was cold and empty, devoid of any life but the blanket of white teardrops that covered everything like a fresh snowfall.

This was the place the knights had been searching for, the center of this land, the source of its darkness. The teardrops grew up to the base of the mountains, surrounding the castle as if they clung to its walls, somehow drawing sustenance from it. It was an odd juxtaposition because, in a land of cold, black emptiness, this castle was the coldest, and the blackest.

But it wasn't empty. Aeoxoea knew the second she looked upon those walls that someone, or something, was looking back. Whatever it was, it was master of this place. It was aware of the presence of the knights from the moment they set foot on its land, and it did not appreciate the intrusion.

Whether the knights shared this sense of foreboding, Aeoxoea couldn't be sure. Their faces showed nothing but their usual resolve as they walked through the fields of teardrops, scattering the white flowers as they descended deeper into the valley.

Aeoxoea studied the castle as it grew closer. She could see it was once a thing of beauty, an achievement of both design and construction. Its towers were built to mimic the appearance of the same white tulips that covered the countryside, each one splitting into smaller turrets growing to various heights, all capped with masonry resembling teardrops. The castle might have once resembled a giant stone bouquet, but now the flowers of that bouquet were dead, and sitting at an odd angle, as if the castle was knocked off its foundation by some powerful force. Some of the walls had collapsed, and some of the turrets crumbled, exposing the courtyard in places, leaving a few stems in the bouquet without a flower on top.

Whatever force caused all this damage was strong enough to rival the effects of an earthquake, shifting the ground beneath the castle, and causing much of the stone supporting its walls to peel away and fall into the valley. It looked as if the castle had once sat high in the mountains, probably tall and straight like a sentry keeping watch over the land. That was before some calamity befell it, before its walls were perverted by whatever evil now resided within.

Everything about this castle said unwelcome, yet the knights traveled straight toward it as if they were expected for dinner, following a winding road up the hillside to the place where the front gates once were. The road was smooth and graceful and flanked by hemlocks, rows of trees that once grew green, pointing skyward. Now bare limbs hung at their sides as they slumped, as if exhausted, looking mournfully at the carpet of brown needles at their feet.

This route up the hillside would have provided a splendid view of the valley years ago when the countryside was something pleasant to look at. It would have also provided travelers ample time to stare in awe and wonder at the majestic castle of teardrops as its front gates grew closer, as its walls towered higher and higher overhead. This was not the way to the servants' entrance, where supplies were brought in and garbage was carried out. This was once the castle's best face, put proudly forward. Aeoxoea could almost see rows of gilded carriages sparkling in the sun as they waited in line to enter, with teams of horses decorated with flowers, and crisply dressed drivers and footmen, bearing the crests of noble families on their way to a royal ball. The first impression for these visitors would have been the front gates, painted white and gold and carved in designs mimicking a vast plain covered with thousands of teardrops. The gates could be both welcoming and impenetrable, the combination of beauty and strength which epitomized the Kingdom of Illengaard.

That was once.

Now the front entrance was a gaping hole flanked by crumbling walls. The boots of the knights thunked on the rotting wood of the former front gates, once so tall and regal, now lying on their sides like two playing cards cast aside by a frustrated gambler.

The courtyard was unlike any other Aeoxoea had seen. The floor of most castle courtyards bore patches of bare earth pounded flat by thousands of hoofs and boot heels, marked by the occasional heap of garbage or animal waste. But once inside the walls of this castle, the knights walked across cobblestone paths that ringed a series of fountains, between hedges and gardens where flowers once grew.

Standing in the courtyard, Aeoxoea could see the illusion provided by the outer walls that this was a fortress of teardrops continued within. The walls of the inner keep were built to resemble the leaves and stems of tulips, gracefully twisting and turning and reaching for the sky. At one time this castle looked alive, as if it grew up from the ground and continued to grow just like the flowers after which it was fashioned. The stonework was almost too perfect, seemingly beyond the abilities of hammer and chisel. Some of these walls seemed to defy the laws of physics, remaining standing long after they should have collapsed under their own weight. Aeoxoea wondered if Craft, or perhaps even the Method, was employed in their construction.

But just as amazing as this castle was, so was the scope of its ruin. Only something which was truly great once could possibly fall so far. The assassin couldn't help but wonder: How could someone put so much effort into creating such a beacon of opulence, only to allow it to fall into ruin? What happened to this land? What happened to this castle? And where were the people who once lived here?

Perhaps they suffocated trying to inhale the stagnant air, she thought, so thick and foul and filled with the stink of evil. The more Aeoxoea walked, the more she could feel the oppressive sickness that infected everything, the residue of a thousand sins committed on this ground. Something truly terrible happened here, and now something truly hateful inhabited this place, glaring from the darkness, burning her skin like the sun. She longed for the sun—just a glimpse, some light and warmth to deliver her from the black despair that suffused the ground and clouded the sky.

Even angels couldn't survive on this ground. While many fortresses were guarded by stone gargoyles, this one had statues of cherubim clinging to its walls, with wings spread, preparing to spring into flight. Some gazed benevolently across the courtyard, others raised their voices in a silent chorus. Some worshiped the heavens above, others gave glory to God's creation below.

Many of these ornaments had broken off, and now their crumbled remnants littered the courtyard. As the knights climbed the steps to the grand entrance of the inner keep, they did so stepping over shattered arms and legs, wings, and the occasional face, cracked and broken, but still smiling.

Once inside, the knights made their way to the center of the keep, and into the largest teardrop of all. Aeoxoea had seen it from the outside; a giant tulip with sepals of limestone and petals of crystal standing three stories tall. Looking up at it from the courtyard, at this giant, pale ghost looming in the darkness, Aeoxoea wondered at its function. Now standing inside, it appeared to be a receiving hall of some sort, a place for feasts and banquets, dances and balls, a place for a king to receive his subjects, to hold court, to issue decrees—a place from which to rule. All of this was enclosed within the loving embrace of the world's largest crystal teardrop.

In the light of day, this would have been a place of staggering beauty. Its walls, which formed the petals of the tulip, were built of interlocking pieces of crystal, measured and cut with a thousand possibilities for error, but with each calculation made so perfectly that even the tiniest of drafts was refused entrance from the outside. The light of the sun would have been allowed entrance, but only after being captured and controlled by the crystal, and sprayed into the hall in a thousand directions. Many of the pieces of crystal contained impurities which gave them colorful hues. The artisans took advantage of this, fitting the pieces together to create pictures, similar to works of stained glass.

The subjects of these pictures were kings and queens, noble men and women, priests and laymen, acting out fanciful scenes that chronicled the building of a once great and beautiful nation. It was a nation that no longer existed, whose greatness was faded to history just like its beauty. Much like the rest of the castle, and the kingdom over which it once ruled, these pictures set into the walls of the receiving hall only hinted at potential unrealized. The walls were dead and colorless, with no sun to give them life, no light to make them beautiful. In the absence of light and life, there was only darkness and death.

A giant hole gaped in the floor at the center of the circular receiving hall. From this drifted the faint smell of moisture, the first sign of water Aeoxoea had detected since entering this land. The crystal walls contained images of the receiving hall in its former glory, and from these, Aeoxoea could see that a fountain once stood on this spot, tall and slender, and built in the shape of the tulip's stamen. Water bubbled out of the top, raining down into a round basin, and creating rainbows that added to the spectacular colors that regularly filled the hall. But the fountain was no more. Something, perhaps the earthquake, had caused it to collapse upon itself and crash through the floor to an unknown fate. Now there was nothing but a jagged hole.

Aeoxoea suddenly felt the mood of the room change, as if something was now there that wasn't before. With each step taken nearer this castle, the assassin could sense the presence of something malevolent within. It was in the distance, across the valley, up on the hill, within the castle—always there, always watching. It was true darkness, pure evil, and the source of the disease which had killed this land.

And now, it had just entered the receiving hall. It was right there, and it was looking at her. She didn't know how she sensed its presence. It was nothing her eyes could see, nothing her ears could hear. But something was pulling at her, demanding her attention. It was like a fishhook lodged in her brain, tugging gently but painfully, forcing her attention to a place on the far side of the hall.

There stood a staircase two dozen feet wide, rising up to a dais half as tall. It would have been a grand ascension for any visitor to the receiving hall, rising to the place where two bejeweled thrones of gold and platinum sat empty.

Until now.

Something now sat in the king's throne, something with a capacity for cruelty and hatred far beyond human capacity to possess, or even comprehend. And once again, as before, it glared at her like the sun, burning her skin with its blackness. Burning more than that. Searing her heart. Scorching her soul.

Aeoxoea felt her eyes locked on that throne as if she was hypnotized, drawn in by an irresistible magnetism. Whatever sat in that throne could not be seen, but it could be felt by the incredible force it inflicted on its surroundings, like a black hole trying to suck everything into it.

With some effort she tore her gaze away, gasping at the exertion. Desperate to look at something else, anything else, she turned her eyes upward, looking upon the crystalline images of Illengaard's past. She sought out the face of the king. And as she watched, the image changed before her very eyes. It was a subtle change, but it could not be denied. The image of the king moved its hand …

And covered his face in shame.

Chapter 22

Aeoxoea stood in the center of the receiving hall, listening to the crackle of the knights' cookfire as it echoed in the otherwise silent air. The flames did little to push back the darkness, but did do just enough to cast its flickering glow upon the crystal walls of the place, making the images there come alive. Not that they needed help to do so. In all the time the assassin had stood on that spot, she'd seen aspects of the scenes contained in the crystal undergo changes numerous times.

She used her Craftsight to look upon the swirling magic that filled the air, and saw concentrations of it imprisoned within the crystalline walls. This confirmed that magic had played a role in the construction of this castle, and that the artist behind the pictures on these walls was a very powerful sorcerer. The Craft was working within those walls to show images of the past, shifting from scene to scene, as if recounting the history of this castle. It was a tragic tale, of a people who labored to build a kingdom from nothing, and a castle which stood as a monument to greatness, only to be betrayed by their king. They lost everything—their land, their homes, their health, and their souls.

The knights slept on the marble floor near to where Aeoxoea stood, wrapped in their furs, with Eleod and Kang between them. Behe was the only one of the party who remained alert, sitting on her haunches, quietly and patiently watching over the slumber of her father and their human masters.

Aeoxoea found it odd that the humans chose to make camp within the walls of the castle. They expended so much effort to get here, risking their lives to transport the Blessed Soul of Man through miles of territory controlled by the zoths, a decision which brought them nearly constant battle. But they fought and struggled through it, running when necessary, fighting when necessary, all in an effort to keep Eleod safe. And now it appeared they did all this only to bring the child to the most dangerous place they could have brought him, to the very heart of a castle corrupted by evil. And once here, as if oblivious to the danger, they made camp. They built a fire, cooked some rabbit, and laid down to sleep. It was a curious decision, and a fateful one, for that is where the creepermen found them.

"What is a creeperman?" Aeoxoea asked.

"The creepermen are what has become of the people of Illengaard," Jass's voice said from inside Aeoxoea's head. "They are called the living dead, cursed by Miacnon, the Angel of Disease."

"Living dead from a disease?" Aeoxoea asked. "How is that possible?"

"It is a magical disease that grants a form of immortality," Jass explained. "It traps the soul in a body damaged beyond the point of death, leaving the afflicted in a state of eternal agony. It is said they are denied heaven, living hell."

"The victim lives on though their body has died?"

"The disease sustains them, yet is constantly attacking them physically and mentally, keeping them alive only to inflict more pain," Jass said. "It is an excruciating existence. There is no humanity in the creepermen. Most every one of them has lost his sanity long ago."

"And this is what has become of the people of Illengaard?"

"Those who still live."

But there was no indication any of them *did* live. The assassin looked around the receiving hall, just as she'd inspected all her surroundings since entering this land. There was no life of any kind;, no people or animals at all. And no plant life but the teardrops. Endless fields of teardrops.

Aeoxoea extended her hearing beyond the walls of the castle in an effort to detect something, anything. But there was nothing but darkness, silence, emptiness. This land nurtured nothing but white teardrops and feelings of sadness.

"Those who still live," Aeoxoea said. "Are they dangerous?"

"Very dangerous," Jass answered. "A creeperman's skin is covered with cracks and lesions which bleed constantly. This blood is toxic to those who are uninfected, and burns like acid to the touch."

"And it carries the disease to new hosts?" Aeoxoea guessed.

"It can spread to the uninfected through mere physical touch," Jass said. "The flesh of the new victim bubbles and melts as the disease eats its way into the body, attempting to enter the blood stream. It's an agonizing experience, but it's only the beginning. The disease itself is far worse. There are stories of healthy men cutting off their own limbs to stop it from taking root in their bodies. Or cutting their own throats once they knew it was too late."

"Truly, a desperate cure."

"The creepermen know the threat their disease poses to the healthy," Jass added. "They often attack the uninfected and use their blood as a weapon."

"What do they gain by fighting?" Aeoxoea asked.

"Death, some say," Jass answered. "Even a violent death may still provide peace."

"I would suppose," Aeoxoea mumbled, staring into the darkness.

"Others say the creepermen answer the call of Miacnon," Jass went on. "As if the disease controls their minds, making them fight and die against their will."

"Is there a cure?"

"None that is known," Jass answered. "Many healers attempted to find a cure when the disease first appeared. They only succeeded in contracting the disease themselves. Even the masters of the Juy Method found themselves powerless against it."

"Because no power wielded by mortals can stop the magical diseases of Miacnon," Aeoxoea said. "Only the voice of God can do that."

"Perhaps the Blessed Soul of Man will wield such power," Jass said. "The prophecies of Sun Antheus state that he will speak with the voice of God."

"That is true."

"Perhaps he will have the ability to cure the disease," Jass said. "When the time of Revelation comes."

"Perhaps," Aeoxoea echoed. "Where did this disease come from? Something so sinister is not naturally occurring."

"That's right," Jass said. "It is an abomination so great that God would never allow it into the world by Miacnon's will alone."

"Then how was it created?"

"There are old legends which say the Angel of Disease found a willing host," Jass answered. "The disease was delivered when the blood of the demon was supped, as if in some unholy communion."

"Who would do such a thing?"

"The ruler of Illengaard, Morgess Lolth," Jass said. "The man who conquered the valley and built this castle. The stories say he gave his kingdom to the Angel of Disease in return for the promise of eternal life."

"Miacnon cannot grant eternal life."

"But he can grant eternal disease," Jass said. "A fact which Morgess soon learned."

"What of the others, the people of Illengaard?" Aeoxoea asked. "Why did they become sick?"

"Morgess wasn't the only one responsible, therefore he wasn't the only one to suffer."

Aeoxoea looked up at the images imbedded in the walls of the receiving hall, for a moment watching as they shifted slowly through a series of scenes from Illengaard's past. There were many scenes depicting many faces. All of them looked down impassively, admitting no guilt.

"Who else besides Morgess was to blame?" she asked.

"His wife, Carisse, the Queen of Illengaard," Jass answered. "The stories say she tricked her husband into drinking the blood of the demon. She hoped to poison him so she could seize control of the kingdom."

"Carisse made a pact with the Angel of Disease?"

"Yes, she did," Jass said. "She sought the services of a witch, who brewed the poison that brought creeper's disease into the world. As part of the pact, she drank the poison. Then the witch presented the wine to Morgess, and he drank it."

"Fools."

"To put it mildly," Jass said. "Morgess and Carisse brought ruin to the kingdom they'd built, all because of their petty jealousies. Both wanted to rule the land. Both wanted to poison the other. Each got their wish. Or so the legends say."

"How did they get their wish?" Aeoxoea asked.

"Morgess wished to live forever. Carisse wished to rule Illengaard," Jass answered. "To these ends, they made deals with the Lord of Plagues. Miacnon rewarded them both with the only disease which grants eternal life."

Aeoxoea looked up at an image of the king and queen, sitting on thrones within the Castle of Teardrops, their faces stony, impassive, staring.

"They became creepermen."

"That's right," Jass confirmed. "Miacnon had found his willing hosts, and the King and Queen of Illengaard became infected with creeper disease. They were the first, and are therefore the oldest."

"The oldest?" Aeoxoea asked. "Do they still live?"

"The legend says they rule the land to this day," Jass said. "Miacnon fulfilled his promise. The king and his queen shall live forever, and rule together, even though there is nothing left to rule. Condemned to eternal life, condemned to pray for death. Trapped in the prisons of their diseased bodies."

"Denied Heaven. Living Hell," Aeoxoea whispered into the darkness.

"Indeed."

"Certainly they knew nothing of the consequences their actions would bring."

"No one who bargains with the devil knows the consequences," Jass said. "They toyed with evil forces and found themselves the playthings. It is how the Kingdom of Illengaard fell into ruin, how this valley and this castle became the domain of Miacnon. Now the land itself is diseased. The trees, the rocks, the soil, even the air. Locked in eternal midnight. And home to a nation of mad creepermen with crazed eyes and rotting flesh."

"Morgess and Carisse may rule the kingdom," Aeoxoea said. "But something else rules them."

She did not look at the throne on the dais across the room but she could still feel something there, sitting on the throne of Illengaard, glaring at her. She could feel the hatred, throbbing like a heartbeat. Now she knew what this presence was.

"Morgess gave his kingdom to Miacnon," she said.

"So the stories say."

Jass called them stories, but right then, standing in that receiving hall, Aeoxoea knew those stories to be true.

"A demon inhabits the throne," she said. "The Angel of Disease."

Once again, the assassin looked up at the crystalline images set into the walls of the hall. Now they had changed drastically, depicting the glory of Illengaard no longer. Now they were scenes of the fall of Illengaard, stories of lies whispered, daggers bloodied, and poison drank. She couldn't tear her eyes from the most prominent picture, that of the king sitting on his throne at the center of a lavish banquet. A young woman dressed in white presented him with a goblet of wine. She knelt before him, the face she presented one of striking beauty, but beneath her robes she hid clawed feet and a barbed tail. The king's eyes were closed as if he couldn't bear to witness his own deeds. He took the goblet in one hand and a candle snuffer in the other, extinguishing the flame of Illengaard while he drank.

Hovering above this scene was a creature with a dog's snout, the eyes of a snake, and the wings of a bat. Its skin was blackened and burned by eternal, unquenchable fire. But despite the pain this caused, the creature's face was gleeful as it poured out disease from a chalice, covering the land with it, so much disease that everyone stood ankle-deep in it, even the king and queen. *Especially* the king and queen. It was the scene of a kingdom descending into a darkness from which it would never recover. It was the fall of the Kingdom of Illengaard. It was the rise of the Land of Nightmares.

Disease everywhere. Covering everything.

Aeoxoea looked down, realizing she wasn't immune. She was standing in it, too.

CHAPTER 23

Several hours passed while the knights slept in the cavernous receiving hall of the Castle of Teardrops. Their campfire burned low, and as the glow of the flames lessened, the darkness and the cold crept closer. And with it came the creepermen.

Aeoxoea stood beside the slumbering knights, untouched by the cold, unafraid of the darkness and quiet, though she knew well what it contained. The time was long. Hours. It was more time than she needed to wonder at the oddity of this situation, of this place, all that had happened here, and why the knights had come. The hall was completely dark, but light wasn't required to illuminate the magic within its crystal walls. The ever-shifting patterns glowed like the light of the sun to her Craftsight as they told and retold the story of the kingdom, how a prosperous nation was built, then destroyed by the selfishness and greed of its rulers. She watched as the images changed to scenes which occurred in the very hall where she now stood, including a battle between the king's soldiers and those who were the first to fall victim to the disease.

The creepermen were depicted as hideous wretches covered with sores and lesions that bled freely. They attacked the king's men with their bare hands, overpowered the soldiers with superior numbers, wrestled them to the ground, and painted their skin with infected creeper blood. This they did to add to the ranks of their army of the cursed, an army which included men, women and children, even animals, with faces contorted by madness, and eyes that shown yellow.

Then the scene shifted again, to the future, a day of deliverance some time in the Year of Revelation. There was a man with white hair and golden skin, clearly the Blessed Soul of Man fully grown. He stood in the castle, and hundreds of creepermen bowed at his feet. He spoke with the voice of God, healed their disease, and cleansed their souls. It was a portrayal of the future of this land, of the day when Eleod would return to the Castle of Teardrops where he'd once spent the night as a little boy, sleeping under the watchful eye of the Angel of Disease.

Then the picture changed again, this time becoming much larger, a vast cyclorama spread around the entire inside of the hall. At the center of this picture was the Castle of Teardrops, sitting on the hilltop at an odd angle, its walls crumbling like wilting petals. Outside those walls, the land stretched away for miles around—the valley and the hills, the cliffs to the north and the mountains to the east. And up in the tree-covered hills, an army of creepermen was waking. They rose to their feet, turning their heads as if in answer to some silent call. Their mouths gaped as silent shouts of alarm burst from their throats while they rushed down the hillside, a dozen, a hundred, a thousand, as if the entire nation of Illengaard was coming. Every single rotted diseased thing that called this land home now converged on the Castle of Teardrops, and at the center of all this was the darkened receiving hall with the campfire burning in the center of the floor. Near to this, the image shown two knights and two dogs, and the slumbering Blessed Soul of Man. It was an accurate depiction of what was currently occurring within, and without, the castle's walls. As the knights slept, the creepermen were coming.

Behe, sitting still by the fire, keeping protective watch over her masters, sniffed at the air, whimpering softly. Something had her attention, and Aeoxoea quickly saw what it was. A pair of yellow eyes hovered in the darkness, watching from just beyond the firelight. They did not move. They did not blink. They stared at the Blessed Soul of Man.

The battle hound looked on curiously as the eyes began to creep forward, slowly but surely. Aeoxoea wondered why the animal sat still; why she didn't bark or raise the alarm. Behe just watched as this being approached from the darkness, glaring with burning yellow eyes.

The visitor paused for a moment at the edge of the glow of the campfire. Then a small and delicate hand, the hand of a female, emerged from the blackness and clawed at the marble floor. This was followed by another, both of them covered with open sores and blackened fingernails that marred otherwise smooth and perfect skin. Then came the face of a young woman with wide, maddened eyes, darting without focus, yellowed and bloodshot. She should have been beautiful, probably was once—but now her beauty was marred by the ravages of creeper's disease. The skin of her face was cracked like dried clay, oozing streaks of blood. So, too, were her lips, swollen and black, split and bleeding, a small portion of the upper missing, showing the teeth beneath. Slowly, this horrible creature emerged from the darkness and crawled along the floor on her belly toward Behe in near perfect silence. The battle hound just watched her approach, doing nothing more than sniffing at the air.

When the creeper was close enough, she reached a hand out to the animal, palm up, and Behe smelled it, shook her head and smelled again. Then she licked the creeper's palm and yelped in pain. At this sound, Elkor awoke with a start, jumping to his feet. With one hand he put an unlit torch into the coals of the fire. With his other hand, he drew a knife from his belt, holding it poised to strike.

"Creeper!" he shouted as the torch came alive. As light filled the room, Gavin and Kang rose in answer to his alarm and the creeper shriveled away from the light, screaming in fear and pain, raising her scarred hands defensively.

"No, no, no!" she cried, curling her body into a tight ball, pressing her face to the floor. "Mercy, mercy, mercy!"

The dogs barked and growled at her, which caused more screams of anguish, weeping, and groveling. "Don't hurt," the creeper said, tears streaking her face. "Don't hurt. Don't hurt. Knights of the Southern Cross. Don't hurt."

The two men looked at one another.

"Keep the hounds away from her," Gavin warned.

"Don't hurt," the creeper shrieked, deformed lips hissing. "Fear God. Love God. Don't hurt."

"I'm not going to hurt you," Elkor said, yet neither his torch nor his knife ceased in their threatening postures.

The dogs snarled and snapped and the creeper squirmed, terrified. "Don't hurt," she begged, hiding her face. "Must help. Please help. Creeper's disease. I'm dying."

"We can't help you," Gavin said.

"Knights of the Southern Cross," the creeper wept. "Must help."

"We can't help you," Gavin said. "No one can."

"Help me. Oh, God, please help me." The creeper's shoulders heaved. Tears fell from her face. "It hurts. It hurts."

Gavin pulled both of his knives.

"Don't hurt!" the creeper whined. "Don't hurt. Don't hurt."

"Leave now," Gavin said.

"No, no," the creeper said. "Please help. It hurts. Help me."

"There's only one way to help you," Elkor said.

"No, no, no."

"It's the only way," Gavin said.

"Don't hurt. Don't ... Oh, God, help me!"

"Then leave now," Gavin said sternly. "Leave or die."

"Oh no. Oh, God. Help me. I'm dying." The creeper wept bitterly, tears mixing with blood. Aeoxoea could see sadness and pity in the eyes of the two knights, and understood their feelings. This was a person once. Denied Heaven. Living Hell. She wondered why they waited, why they stayed their blades. They would regret their hesitation.

With ferocious speed, the creeper darted across floor, crawling straight for Eleod.

"Kill me. Kill me. Kill me, Lord of Devils!" she shrieked. "The Blessed Soul!"

Looking at her, Eleod screamed in terror. She didn't even get close to him. Gavin raced forward to block her path and kicked her in the face so hard her neck should have broken. She screamed and rolled across the floor, but otherwise seemed unhurt.

"Lords rise. Lords rise," the creeper hissed, once again crawling toward Eleod. "Silwayou Darmethou Meherarc Miacnon Dehen Yaulk Shia Ka Keremoc!"

Gavin was upon her with both knives. She sprang to her feet and lashed out at him with unnatural speed. She tried to scratch his face, but he deftly blocked the attack, allowing her to impale her wrist on his blade. The steel gleamed in the darkness, streaked with crimson creeper blood, hissing and smoking. The woman's hand was nearly severed from her arm. But she hardly seemed to notice.

"Deceit betrayal murder disease death chaos! Chaos! Chaos!" she laughed, and spit in the knight's face.

Gavin answered with a vicious slash that opened her throat. She fell onto her rear, but remained defiant, smiling at him as blood flowed from her neck like a waterfall. And when she spoke, it came as a gurgling hiss from two openings.

"Lords rise. Lords rise. The Blessed Soul of Man has come!" she roared. "Lord of Devils come! The Children of Miacnon come for the Blessed Soul!"

Suddenly a deep rumble shook the floor of the receiving hall; a small tremor at first, but quickly becoming something more intense. It was felt beneath their feet, but heard from every direction, an awful, mournful groan, as if the world was agonized.

"The lizard worm stirs!" Elkor shouted. "It is time!"

"Gather the Blessed Soul," Gavin replied to Elkor. "Down to the Neversea."

"Lord of Devils come!" the creeper screamed.

The ground shook. The walls shook. The castle made frightening sounds from foundation to turret, earsplitting crunching and crumbling of soil and stone. The air itself seemed to roil angrily, deafeningly, and the dogs, spooked, barked out their protest.

"Lord of Devils come!" the creeper screamed. "Rise, children of Miacnon, the Creeper God!"

Aeoxoea could hear them, a thousand creepermen rushing down the hillside, shrieking with madness as they emerged from the trees and into the light of the moon. She looked up at the crystal walls above to see the images now shifting constantly, depicting the creepermen running through the rows of hemlocks, then crowding through the gates, scaling the walls, and rushing between the fountains and hedges of the courtyard. They pushed and shoved and fell over each other as they ran as fast as their diseased legs would carry them. The earthquake shook stones loose from the castle's towers. Headless cherubim shattered on the cobblestones at their feet.

They entered the castle through several entrances, climbing through windows and breaking down doors. They filled the hallways, rushing from room to room. The earthquake thundered. The castle seemed to be tearing itself apart.

The walls of the receiving hall shook under the strain, and sheets of crystal dust wafted down like a sparkling rainfall. Collapse seemed a certainty, but it never came. Elsewhere, the castle was being destroyed. Towers and turrets, walls and battlements tumbled to the ground, burying creepermen under mounds of rubble. The centuries-old castle was pounded by the world with a relentless hammer, hit by previous earthquakes, never repaired, now hit again. But the giant crystal teardrop, which should have been the weakest portion of the castle, proved to be the strongest—flexing and groaning in pain, but holding together due to the magic imprisoned within its walls.

"Now is the time to go," Gavin shouted through the din. "Take Eleod and the hounds. I will protect your escape and follow you soon."

Aeoxoea almost laughed. The Zealot intended to protect their escape? Against the entire nation of Illengaard? But she didn't laugh, and neither did Elkor. Instead, he rushed to Eleod and swung the boy into his arms while yelling orders to his dogs. Gavin stared down the creeper woman, positioned between her and his escaping friends, as if daring her to move.

She had no intention of moving, but she looked him square in the eye and said, "You are going to die here, knight."

Gavin behaved if she hadn't spoken at all. He didn't say a word of answer, only remained in a guarding posture as Elkor threw ropes down, preparing to climb into the hole.

"Your god cannot help you," the creeper said. "He has no power here. In this place, there is only Miacnon."

And Miacnon's army was coming, legions of screaming, diseased madmen, rushing through the castle's crumbling hallways without regard for life or limb. They ignored the walls that buckled and crushed them, the windows that shattered and cut them, the floors that split open and swallowed them. They ignored everything but the one thing that mattered—reaching the receiving hall where the Blessed Soul of Man awaited. They wanted to scratch at his face, and tear open his skin. They wanted to suck the blood from his flesh, and the marrow from his bones. They wanted to eat him and laugh at him and spit in the face of God. And the only thing to stop them was a single Knight of the Southern Cross.

Gavin knew what was coming, yet he did not move. He stood in the center of the hall and prepared to meet an army of creepermen alone, prepared to fight while the world crumbled around him just to protect Elkor's escape, and Eleod's.

It wasn't so different from what the Hound had done for him on the plain south of Arka Moor. As Gavin had carried Eleod into the shadow of Behe Kang, and into Illengaard, Elkor had faced down a zoth chieftain and two hundred of his warriors. Now the Zealot was returning the favor.

The Hound climbed into the hole, then looked back. "See you at the bottom, Zealot."

Gavin replied with a salute, touching his fist to his forehead.

Suddenly the tremors lessened in intensity, as did the noises of disaster all around. The crumbling sounds continued, but the earthquake lost strength quickly, just as fast as it began. The earth stopped its spasms, and the castle slowly settled, once again becoming an unmoving pile of stones. Finally it was calm, if not quiet. All that could be heard was the soft and steady sound of dust settling.

"Your friend will fall," the creeper hissed. "The earth will swallow him and the Blessed Soul of Man will die."

Calmly, Gavin wiped the infected creeper blood from his knives and sheathed them on his belt.

"We will cut his ropes," the creeper promised.

"No, you won't," Gavin said.

The first pairs of yellow eyes began to appear in the darkness all around.

"You cannot stop the will of Miacnon. We will eat his soul."

"No, you won't," the knight repeated.

The creeper glared at the knight in silent hatred, breathing heavily, blood bubbling on her neck. Finally, she smiled with red teeth.

"We will try."

"You will fail."

Hoarse screams of madness and rage cut the dank air. The walls returned echoes of a hundred creeper voices, raging, pleading, even laughing.

"Kill me, kill me, kill me!"

"Flesh for our hunger."

"Lords rise! Lords rise!"

"Blood for our thirst."

"Chaos! Chaos! Chaos!"

"Souls to feed our Lord."

They came by the scores, flooding the receiving hall with yellow eyes flashing in the firelight, a veritable army of the diseased, answering the call of their Lord Miacnon. Shuffling and stumbling, running and crawling, the creepers rushed into the firelight, blinking and shrieking with bloodlust. Filthy and starved, dressed in rags, they came in every shape and size, as varied in appearance as were the potential hosts of their disease. There were men, women, and children, all wild-eyed, rotting, and bleeding. Armed with spears, picks, clubs and rocks, or even their own fingernails and teeth, they rushed headlong to their deaths. Perhaps death was their desire.

If so, they were obliged in short order.

Aeoxoea watched the images on the walls above her, saw them shifting to depict the attack of the creepermen. The diseased creatures filled the room. They surrounded the Zealot, reaching out to attack, blood on their hands, disease in the blood. If only one drop touched his skin, an eternity of agony awaited.

And then the image shifted again, becoming truly fanciful. Now Gavin the Zealot held lightning bolts in his hands, two white streaks of electricity that lanced through the army of creepermen, cutting them apart, sending heads and arms and legs sailing through the air.

Just as the image changed, a new sound filled Aeoxoea's ears, unlike any she'd heard in the midst of battle before. It sounded like soft voices, a dozen gossipy girls whispering under their breath, singing their tales with angelic voices. A choir of young women each sung their own hushed lullaby, a jumble of notes with no two voices carrying the same tune. Then a sound like a leather whip uncurling to snap, but somehow delicate, soft as a breaking twig. Then the voices. Then the snapping. The lullaby. And the creepers screamed.

Gavin the Zealot did not hold bolts of lightning in his hands, but he held something equally as frightening and majestic, and just as deadly. Each hand manipulated something resembling a party streamer, both of them whipping and snapping and flashing like moonlight on the surface of a tumbling river.

They were very long; greater in length than two average men head to foot, and as wide as human hands, and yet were so impossibly thin that they disappeared to the eye when turned sideways. They had little to no weight, behaving more like satin ribbons than anything made of metal. They flitted about as if carried on the wings of hummingbirds, riding the breezes as the Zealot swirled them about his head. They slithered through the air at his command, darting this way and that, zigzagging, hovering, and striking. And singing their hissing lullaby.

This was the whispering sound, the voices of the gossipy girls. It was the sound of the air gasping as it was cut so delicately by the finest, sharpest blades in existence. Jass had said the Zealot was master of the deadliest weapons in the world. And now Aeoxoea knew for a certainty that this claim was not false. And she also understood clearly, while listening to the voices of the little girls singing in their hushes tones, the meaning behind their name: the Silent Sisters.

They were beautiful, shining like quicksilver even in the darkness, two ballerinas flitting about with the Zealot as their partner. It was a display so magnificent, the true purpose of these weapons could easily be forgotten. Were it not for the creepermen, the Silent Sisters could be mistaken for the accouterments of a costumed dancer.

But the creepermen were there, and they gave proof that the Sisters were not created to amaze and delight, but to make war. The blades yielded to the air like a pair of satiny ribbons, but this was by choice. They yielded to nothing when the Zealot wished it; not to steel, not to flesh, and not to bone. They cut everything he commanded them to, slicing everything cleanly as if it was made of paper.

Likewise, they did not cut if he did not wish it. His command of the Silent Sisters was so complete that he also used the flats of the blades to push the creepermen back, to keep them away from him by tripping them up and knocking them down. He clearly did this in an effort to avoid as much bloodshed as he could.

Aeoxoea did not have to employ Craftsight to see how this was possible. Jass told her that Gavin the Zealot was the only fighter in the world with the fitness to wield the Silent Sisters; the only one who possessed the dexterity of both body and mind required to wield such delicate and deadly weapons. Certainly this was true. Any other man would have cut his own leg off just picking them up. But there was more, and Aeoxoea knew what it was.

It was the Craft that aided the Zealot. Some people called it luck, some called it skill, but the knight was not just favored by the Craft weaves. He was loved by them. They obeyed him. They clung to him. And they supported all his movements. He may not know it, but he employed magic in everything he did. And it was magic, just as much as the movements of his arms, which commanded the Silent Sisters. He manipulated the Craft with the power of his mind just as adeptly as most wizards did with runes and chanting and spell components. It was as if magic was a musical instrument to him. He played his song, and the Sisters danced.

The creepermen strove with all their might to get near to the hole in the center of the receiving hall, to cut the ropes so Elkor and the Blessed Soul would fall. They attacked the Zealot from every angle, rushed him with numbers, threw rocks and spears at his head and feet. But the floating, curling blades of the Silent Sisters thwarted each attempt with a gentle flutter and a hissing reprimand. Every spear or rock thrown at the knight was caught in mid-flight, wrapped in silvery folds and dropped, or laid almost lovingly, on the marble floor.

They curled around ankles, tripping the creepers. They slapped their faces, knocking them down. More than one of the creatures threw a spray of infected blood, or belched a plume of it. They spit their hatred and their disease at the knight. And the Sisters spit it right back at them.

Every creeper who approached and threatened, or brandished a weapon, or simply came too close was knocked over, thrown back, or cut to pieces. The children of Miacnon didn't have a chance of defeating this knight. They didn't have a chance of reaching the Blessed Soul. Gavin the Zealot and the Silent Sisters simply would not allow them passage.

Despite their numerical advantage, the creepermen were outclassed, mere butterflies fighting a tornado. The weapons in Gavin's hands were the most effective Aeoxoea had ever seen.

And the Zealot was a true master.

Chapter 24

Aeoxoea looked across the room and saw that one of the creepers was not attacking. It was the first of the creatures to enter the hall, the very creeper woman who caused all this by trying to attack Eleod. After that first confrontation she seemed to have lost all zest for battle, and now only stood by as Gavin fought with her comrades, watching impassively as they tried and failed, and died. Aeoxoea could see the gushing wound where the knight had slashed open her throat, an injury that should have been fatal. Yet the creeper seemed oblivious to it, showing no pain, no weakness, not an ounce of care as her life blood formed pools at her feet.

Now the assassin noticed another wound marring the young woman's skin, one that was not made by the Zealot's knives. It was clean and bloodless, a hole in her chest the shape of a small blade. That blade should have cut her heart and taken her life. And yet it did not.

Aeoxoea had a strong suspicion that the wound was self-inflicted, perhaps a desperate attempt to end the agony as creeper's disease took hold. Likewise, the attack on the knights was possibly another attempt to die, to end the disease that had no cure.

But despite suffering multiple wounds that should have been fatal, she was denied the relief death would bring. The assassin wondered why this was; why she went on living even as the other creepermen were able to perish at the edges of the Zealot's weapons.

Perhaps this woman was no ordinary creeper. Perhaps she was among the first.

Denied Heaven. Living Hell.

Once again, Aeoxoea looked up at the scenes reflected in the crystal walls, and saw the image of a new person reflected there. It was a young woman of darhan heritage, with golden skin and hair as white as snow. Her body was blurred and fractured, as if the crystal woman was broken into many pieces. Each piece was a different person, many different faces and identities coming together to form this young woman, indicating a very complex past.

The golden woman looked up at the walls around her. On the dais above her head, the king sat on his throne, still covering his eyes, afraid to look. At the king's side, the queen's place sat empty. She had descended from her high place to be among her subjects, and now stood before the golden woman. Aeoxoea was not surprised when she lowered her eyes to see the creeper woman a short distance away, near enough that she could smell the stink of her disease.

The creeper woman smiled, then her ugliness faded as if her disease was instantly cured. The crumbling skin and blackened lips were replaced by the face of a young woman, smooth-skinned, healthy, and beautiful. The tattered, rotting rags that hung from her shoulders were replaced by a luxurious gown with white embroidery on black silk, bespeckled with diamonds and teardrops of white gold. Her hair was likewise decorated, silky blonde curls held in place by combs glittering with diamonds and silver teardrops, and a golden crown with a large orange sapphire on her forehead. The Flame of Illengaard.

Aeoxoea was in the presence of a queen.

"Greetings to you, weapon of the Dark One's champion," the woman said in a regal tone, chin held high. "Greetings to your master, the Serharek, whose mark you bear."

"Greetings to you, milady, Queen Carisse," Aeoxoea replied. "Mistress of Castle Illengaard, ruler of the Valley of Tears, Queen of the Creepermen."

Carisse clasped her gloved hands of black silk together, smiling brightly. "It is my regret to inform you that the king is taken from our presence due to pressing affairs of state. However, it is truly an honor to receive a guest of such stature, and such a singularly striking creature, but one of the many fingers on one of the many hands by which the Serharek enforces his will in the world. It is an honor, truly, to make your acquaintance, Mistress ... "

The assassin smiled wryly. "Aeoxoea."

"Mistress Aeoxoea," the queen said. "Such a unique and wonderful name; how it taxes the lips and tongue in the saying, even as it delights the ears. Might I inquire as to its origins?"

"The High God of the Darhan people is called Aeo by his followers," the assassin explained. "My name is made from his to signify that I am a being created to mirror his image. I am called the Reflecting God by my master."

"How intriguing," the queen breathed. "You must truly be the envy of all whose names reflect merely the plainness of their parents' imagination."

"Truly."

"Now tell me, Mistress Aeoxoea," the queen said. "What brings you so far from your homeland to the Island of Thershon, to the Land of Illengaard? Who has the Serharek marked for death?"

"Marked for death?" Aeoxoea answered. "Why must murder be my intent?"

"Well," the queen said, "I'm quite certain the Serharek would not send his finest killer to the Kingdom of Illengaard unless a slaying was to be done. So tell me, what unfortunate soul will be the subject of his wrath?"

"The Serharek cares for the fate of only one soul, Your Majesty."

Carisse smiled in understanding, but there was no warmth behind it. The air, already cold, seemed to grow colder. "The boy."

Aeoxoea nodded. "The boy who is the Blessed Soul of Man."

The queen produced a fan, folded between her silken fingers. She tapped it repeatedly against her skirts as she spoke, as if anxious or impatient.

"It is admirable that you would take such pains, travel such a distance at the behest of the Serharek to influence the fate of the child; but I fear your efforts have been in vain. The Blessed Soul will perish as you look on."

"Your words are true. The Blessed Soul will perish as I look on," Aeoxoea replied. "But not in this place. And not by the hands of your creepermen."

The queen's smile was seen and not felt, like the sun on a frozen, arctic plain.

"In the land of Illengaard, the king and his queen take as they wish."

"In this instance, I fear the king and queen may do no more than wish," Aeoxoea retorted. "Tell me. Do either of the rulers of this land, or any of their subjects, wield the ancient weapon of evil called Gilligod, the Devil Device?"

The queen opened her fan, fluttering it under her chin, now raised so she could look down her nose.

"How quaint. You speak of prophecies ..."

" ... which state clearly the Blessed Soul will die by Gilligod ... "

" ... on the Day of Seven Eyes," Carisse finished. "The prophecies are known to me."

"So, I must ask you," Aeoxoea said. "Is today the day the prophecies speak of? Is this the Day of Seven Eyes?"

The queen pursed her lips. "It makes no matter what is prophesied," she stated. "These are empty words, written by mad fools."

"But backed by the power of God."

Now the queen held the fan before her face like a shield, as if she felt threatened. For a moment, her eyes burned a bright yellow.

"God." Her voice slithered like steel on a whetstone. "An odd gesture, one such as this acknowledging the power of God."

"Only a fool refuses the might of one's enemy," Aeoxoea replied. "I am no fool."

"Indeed," the queen muttered.

For a moment the two stood, their tongues as still as their bodies. Then the queen's tone changed drastically. She cocked her head as if something caught her ear.

"Do you hear that?" she chittered. "This is a wonderful song. One of my favorites. As old as the valley itself."

Aeoxoea heard no music, only the noise of the Silent Sisters and the havoc occurring on the edges of their blades. It was the sound of Gavin the Zealot dominating the army of creepermen, a sound somewhere between a rout and a slaughter. If this was the music Carisse heard, it was a tune she enjoyed. And it prompted her to dance.

Her movements were stiff, a proper dance with predefined steps. She took the hand of an invisible partner, walked several feet, curtsied, walked a small circle, bowed, took the hand of another partner and walked another circle, this time skipping. It was an eerie sight to behold, and seemed to tell the story of Illengaard perfectly in a scant few seconds. The people of the valley struggled and died while the queen danced, unwilling or unable to even notice their plight. Her lips were smiling, her eyes delighted. As Aeoxoea watched the queen's delicate slippered feet brushing the marble floor, dancing with no music, dancing to the song sung by the Silent Sisters, she couldn't be sure if Carisse took pleasure in the deaths of her people, or if she was completely mad.

Perhaps her mind was far away in a place and time where the kingdom had not fallen, and her people had not been crushed under the weight of disease; a time when there was still reason to dance.

The crystal walls above showed the battle raging in the receiving hall—a legion of creepers, filthy and crazed, marching forward, turn by turn, to lay down at the feet of the knight who commanded lightning with his hands. And now their queen danced among them. They were in a war, but she was on a dance floor. And her partner was an inhuman beast, the same dog-faced demon who'd brought the disease to Illengaard, who'd anointed the king and his queen with the blood from his chalice. His hands and fingers grew thorns that pierced and ripped the queen's flesh.

Likewise, her regal clothing was shredded, leaving her naked in his arms. It was a union she willingly joined, but quickly learned to regret. Now she recoiled from the creature's embrace, her eyes filled with horror and revulsion as he licked at her neck with his forked tongue.

It was clear to Aeoxoea. The king may have betrayed his queen, but she betrayed him first. Then Miacnon betrayed them all.

Carisse wept in the arms of the beast who had ensnared her. The people of Illengaard wept as they rushed unwillingly to a battle they could not win. And as King Morgess covered his eyes, teardrops fell between his fingers. He wept for his people. The people wept for their kingdom. And Carisse wept for herself.

But when Aeoxoea dropped her eyes to the face of the queen, she saw none of this agony. Carisse threw her head back and laughed as she danced, spinning around, twirling her skirts and spinning her fan. As the assassin looked on, the queen's appearance changed again, and she was wearing an immodest dress of white lace, tight in the bodice, with large, fluttery sleeves, and totally sheer in all but the most important places.

Once again, Aeoxoea could see the hole in the queen's chest, the self-inflicted wound that would never heal.

"Do you like my dress?" Carisse giggled. "I have several. You may have your pick if you wish."

She danced away from the assassin, hopping from one foot to the other, clapping her hands and smiling brightly. Then she glided in a circle, her arms wide, spinning her white skirt and lacey sleeves.

"This dress was a favorite of my Lord Morgess, the king," Carisse giggled. "He was powerless against white lace."

One of the creepermen approached her, a youngish-looking soldier in a surcoat bearing the Flame of Illengaard. His face was so deformed by the disease that he hardly looked human. One side of his cheek was so swollen that it split open like an overcooked sausage, leaking bloody fluids all over half his body, soaking his surcoat.

"Hello, my lovely," Carisse purred. "This is one of my favorite playmates, a boy of Dama Moor who served our king in the Army of the Valley. Kindly introduce yourself to the Reflecting God, young Master Spirgil."

The soldier didn't say anything, only bowed to Aeoxoea, then took the hand of his queen and joined in her dance. It was a step that Aeoxoea recognized: The Fox and the Vixen.

"A dress of white lace was a potent weapon against my king," Carisse explained. "But nothing pierced his armor, or pierced his heart, like the sight of his beloved wife in the arms of another man, even if it was among a crowd of couples on the ballroom floor. The king is a most jealous man. A jealous fool."

The queen and her lover knew the dance well, mirroring each other's movements with practiced steps. The fox sees the vixen in the dale, but he is shy and flees. The vixen sees the fox in the glade, but she is shy and flees. The fox and the vixen meet at the brook and share a drink.

"Of all my playmates, Spirgil was the one the king hated the most," Carisse said as she danced. "He was so jealous, he would do anything to win me back. All I wished for, I was given. It was I who truly ruled Illengaard, then."

The queen took the soldier's hand and spun gracefully into his arms, wrapping herself in his embrace. She beamed at Aeoxoea as a child would when showing off her toys to a friend. Then she spun away from him and her dance changed again, now becoming seductive.

"But my dear, young, Spirgil. He was an easier bee to control once his wings were stuck to my web," she said. "I promised him many things; even said he'd be my new king once we arranged for Morgess's removal. But he found no promises so intoxicating as those fulfilled in the queen's bed."

The soldier stopped moving as if the dance had changed to a step he didn't know. He now stood flatfooted as his queen danced around him, her movements growing increasingly erotic. Suddenly she was naked, all legs, hips, and hair, a tapestry of motion. These were practiced movements, learned through years of dealing in desire. This was no longer The Fox and the Vixen.

"Then my dear Spirgil became molding clay in my hand. I could do with him as I wished, and I chose to form him into the shape of a knife aimed at my husband's heart. The king had every reason to be jealous; every reason to fear. He thought he might lose his kingdom. And he was right."

Aeoxoea knew she was seeing each side of Carisse in turn. First was the creeper, dirty and dressed in rags, cracked and bleeding, her body and mind ravaged by the disease. Second was the queen, complete with all her pompousness and arrogance, wrapped in all the riches afforded her station—her jewels, her teardrops, her crown, and the Flame of Illengaard. Now was the seductress, the coquette whose greatest weapon was the weakness of men, who prostituted her way to power, now wearing the costume of her trade: Absolutely nothing.

While the queen put on her show, Aeoxoea looked beyond to the battle raging in the center of the hall. She saw a creeperman, a former soldier of Illengaard, attempt to lunge past the Zealot, reaching out for the ropes. He swung a falchion in an effort to sever them, to send Elkor falling to his death. But the Silent Sisters answered with a hiss and a whisper, licking at his arm and leaving a stump where his hand once was. The falchion spun away to clatter on the marble floor, still in the grip of the creeperman's dead fingers.

"Magnificent," she murmured.

"Aren't they? I love my people." Carisse beamed as she intentionally misunderstood the assassin's meaning. "Every last one of them, for they are vessels of the gift of Miacnon. Their blood is rich with his precious disease."

"You claim to love them, and yet you drive them like cattle to the butcher."

"I do not drive them," Carisse said. "They act out of love for their queen. The soil of Illengaard is threatened by invaders. Is it not the duty of smallfolk to fight in the defense of their homeland?"

"I invite you to open your eyes to what is occurring in your receiving hall, Your Majesty," Aeoxoea said. "This is not a battle of armies. Your people do not fight for their homeland. They are, one by one, walking the steps to the gallows. The Zealot is their executioner, and thus far, he has been patient with you."

"If they must perish, then so be it, for it is their purpose," Carisse said. "It is an honor for them to obey their queen, even if they are destroying themselves for her pleasure. It is an act of beauty."

"There is no beauty in this foolishness."

"Oh, but I disagree."

"You are wasting the lives of your people," Aeoxoea pressed. "The prophecies state the Blessed Soul will die by Gilligod in the Year of Revelation, not by the hands of creepermen twenty years before it is time. Neither Miacnon, nor his children, have any part to play in this plan. Withdraw your slaves."

"Do you dare to deny my children what is theirs?"

"On the contrary. It is the prophecies which deny them. The Blessed Soul of Man belongs to the Serharek," Aeoxoea said. "Therefore he belongs to me, not to you or your children. This is the will of God."

"In the Land of Teardrops, it is the creepermen who take what they wish," Carisse said. "The creepermen. No one else."

"Not so, kitten."

"You forget with whom you speak." The queen smiled sweetly. "You stand here only because I allow it."

Aeoxoea smiled back. "You exist only because the Serharek allows it. The Blessed Soul of Man will pass through your domain unharmed, no matter how many of your people die trying to stop it. You must suffer his presence, and that of the knights who protect him. You must tolerate my presence here because the prophecies say it will be so. Because God says it will be so. Withdraw your army while you still have one. And allow these knights to pass that the will of God be done as the prophecies state."

"No." The queen's eyelashes fluttered. "Not yet."

As Carisse said these words, her façade of beauty faded slightly. Her eyes yellowed, and the gash across her neck reopened; but her flesh remained perfect in every other way, smooth and pale and unmarked.

"You take pleasure in wasting your slaves?" Aeoxoea asked.

The queen continued to dance, caressing her own neck, painting her palm with blood.

"I'll find more," she purred, looking down at her body, admiring herself.

She traced her fingers down between her breasts, drawing a line of red southward across her belly.

"You'll find more?" Aeoxoea asked.

Carisse continued to trace her fingers across her body, drawing lines and circles of blood around her abdomen and thighs, then back up her belly and around her chest and shoulders.

"There are always more," the queen said. "Those who wish to serve the Angel of Disease by marching in the armies of Illengaard. There are always more."

"Like who?"

Carisse stopped dancing, and winked.

"Like you."

She flicked her hand, throwing a spray of infected creeper blood into the assassin's face. It hissed as it flew at Aeoxoea, as if alive, as if gleeful to attack her flesh.

She had no reason to fear. Her natural defenses were formidable enough. And from the moment she'd set foot on this island, she'd maintained her invisible shield around herself, projected by the power of her mind.

And yet she still recoiled in horror, stumbling backward, throwing her hands up to protect herself. She knew she was vulnerable the moment she saw the blood on Carisse's hand flying into her face. She knew she couldn't stop it as it hissed and smoked, bright and glistening, penetrating her shield, evading the army of tentacles that lashed out attempting to deflect it away. It beat every mystical defense she had, leaving no protection between the cursed blood and her bare skin. She felt each individual droplet as it splattered against her forearms, felt the pain of each tiny fleck that marked the skin of her cheek.

She couldn't keep her feet and fell onto her back, thrashing around as smoke rose from her arms and face. It burned like molten lead, sinking into her flesh, her skin offering as much resistance as parchment did to fire. She screamed as tiny cracks spread across her forearms like shattered glass, with blood droplets at the impact points. Then her flesh split open, hissing and steaming and leaking foul liquids. She could feel it inside her, flowing through her body like fire in her veins. She knew what was happening to her, knew the Angel of Disease was claiming her. She didn't need to be told. But she was told anyway.

The voice did not enter her ears, for it wasn't heard. Rather, it was felt, because it entered her being, like the poisoned blood entered her body. The words throbbed within her like her heartbeat.

Cherish the time that remains to you, wretched creature, for you are already one of us. Whether you will confess it or not, the moment you stepped into the shadow of Behe Kang, your lips were kissed by the Angel of Disease. You may be the property of the Serharek. Your actions may carry the weight of his will. But you are also, now, as of this moment, marked by Miacnon, the Lord of Disease.

For the first time since coming to this island, Aeoxoea was humiliated and humbled, lying on her back, writhing in pain as the Queen of Illengaard danced circles around her, smiling at her, and laughing. She couldn't see the crystal walls, but knew if she could, the image depicted was probably the bat-winged creature hovering above, tipping his chalice to pour the blood of the demon all over her body. And his voice thundered within her.

Wrap yourself in the warmth and comfort of your role in the prophecies, for your usefulness to the Blessed Soul of Man and his God can cease at any time—today or tomorrow, or a year from now. And when that happens, the seed that was planted within you today will bloom into a weeping tulip made sour by Miacnon's blood.

"The Serharek—" Aeoxoea groaned pathetically.

You are not the Serharek. You are merely his plaything. When he is finished with you, he will cast you aside.

She knew this was true. If there was some way the Serharek was watching, he was most certainly laughing. She was just a tool in his hand, to be thrown away when her usefulness was done.

You proclaim God's will cannot be denied, citing the prophecies as if they are the god you worship. Then surely you must know that the prophecies state that in the Year of Revelation, disease will be released upon the land. I tell you the gates of Illengaard will be opened and the legions of creepermen will march forth. Who will protect you then? You rely solely on the will of God for your protection from disease. But how can you, a mere speck of filth, presume to know God's will?

Aeoxoea tried to say something. Her lips moved, but no sound emerged. The pain was excruciating. And her ears were filled with Carisse's laughter.

Do you suffer, pathetic creature? Then surely you suffer by God's will. Does it hurt you? The disease? As it swims in your blood? Then surely this pain comes to you by God's will.

You may go forth from Illengaard and do your part in fulfilling the prophecies. You may play your role as the Serharek's slave in the search for Gilligod. But you will do it knowing that Miacnon has claimed you, that his disease sleeps within your body. From this day forward, he goes where you go, and he does as you do.

Because it is God's will.

All that you do will be done under the mark of Miacnon, speaking with black lips and seeing with yellow eyes.

Because it is God's will.

Aeoxoea rolled over, attempting to push herself to her hands and knees but she collapsed, crushed under an immense weight that pressed down between her shoulder blades, like the thumb of Miacnon. She was face down on the marble floor, fully prostrate before the Angel of Disease. She was forced to lay this way for many minutes before the pressure on her back relented, but even then she did not move. Slowly, after a time, the pain left her body; but it lingered in her mind, causing her to tremble with the memory. There were others who had treated her this way in her life, made her feel a slave, subjected totally to the will of another. It was a feeling she loathed, one that crushed her spirit, making her feel like a helpless little girl again, like when her brother died— when everyone and everything she knew and loved died. When her world died.

It was why her soul was now a charred, blackened thing of evil. Because when her brother died, and she felt the worst pain of her life, she understood well the cause of all her suffering.

God's will.

Those two words soured her stomach, tasting like bile on her tongue. This was indeed God's will. The knights were protected by their role in the prophecies. She was not. Miacnon could do what he wished to her, if God allowed it. And certainly, God had allowed this.

She raised her eyes and saw Carisse standing over her, looking down with a sober face.

All pretense was now gone. This was not the queen or the coquette. She was a wretched thing once again, appearing just as she had the first time Aeoxoea saw her. Filthy, starved, bleeding, and dressed in rags.

Aeoxoea could see that the queen's wounds had also reopened—the cut across her throat and the hole in her chest. Neither would ever heal, nor would they usher her into death where she might find relief. Miacnon would never allow that.

The assassin suddenly felt a twisted kinship with Carisse. Despite their verbal sparring, there was only one being in control of this situation: The Angel of Disease, who had bloodied and brutalized and cursed them both.

Carisse looked at Aeoxoea with sadness, almost pity.

"Welcome to Illengaard, my dear," she said somberly. "You may go now, as you wish. But never forget, this is your home forever. Wherever you go and whatever you do, you will one day return home. Your seat at the banquet table is reserved, here, in the Castle of Teardrops."

With that, she turned to walk away. And at that moment, as though they shared one mind, the creepermen did the same. They all turned away from Gavin and fled, staggering, moaning, and crawling away, back into the darkness, yellow eyes flashing back with fear and hatred. They left Gavin alone in the hall, standing beside the hole in the floor, surrounded by the bodies of creepermen who'd finally found peace on the edge of his blades.

It was severe, the contrast. One moment, the clattering, screaming cacophony of battle. And the next moment, a cavern filled with the quiet shuffling of retreating creepers. Aeoxoea watched them as they left, watched Gavin as he did the same. For many minutes, the knight stayed where he was, standing within the flickering light of the fire, waiting. He waited to make certain none would return while he followed Elkor and Eleod down into the earth. But Aeoxoea knew it wasn't necessary. The creepermen would not be back. Their queen knew it did no good to sacrifice more lives, no matter how accursed those lives may be. They left Gavin alone. They left him with the darkness and the silence of their dead castle. And they left him with the one being who was sure to succeed where an army had failed.

They left the Blessed Soul of Man to Aeoxoea.

It was an honor to represent the Serharek, to enact his will on this tiny island, to track the Blessed Soul and fulfill the prophecies by seizing Gilligod. It was a position respected by many, even the creepermen, even their queen. Even the Angel of Disease.

But it was the position that won the honor, not the person. Honor was lauded upon the position. Filth and misery was heaped upon the person. She looked at her arms, at the cracks in her skin and the wounds already beginning to fester. There was a perfect line of black sores where droplets of the queen's blood had struck her, from her chin to her left ear; little black holes that rotted and stank, marring her otherwise perfect golden skin. She was marked by Miacnon just as she was marked by the Serharek. And there was no honor to be found in either.

Standing all alone in the blackened and cavernous receiving hall, covered in diseased blood, she felt like a lost little girl again. For the first time since setting foot on this island, she felt every inch of her nakedness.

CHAPTER 25

By all appearances, Gavin the Zealot wore a pair of finely made, yet well-worn leather trousers with intricate, decorative braids down the legs. In reality, those trousers were the sheaths for the Silent Sisters. After the retreat of the creepermen, Aeoxoea watched as the knight stowed his weapons, a process that included folding the cloth-like blades accordion-style and tucking them into two compartments sewn into the sides of the legs. The compartments reached from his ankles to this hips and were held shut by a series of leather cords that had the appearance of decorative braiding. There was no way to know those braids contained the deadliest weapons in the world.

When he was finished, Gavin doused his torch and climbed into the hole in the floor of the receiving hall. He didn't need to use the ropes as Elkor had, and proved it by first cutting them loose so they could be reused. He found purchase in the rocks with his hands and feet, descending like a spider deeper into the bowels of the Castle of Teardrops.

There were more levels beneath the main one; another dining hall, and what were likely servants' quarters. Then a chapel, deep enough that Aeoxoea was sure it was underground. Beneath the chapel, many unfinished passageways and rooms suggested that the castle wasn't quite complete when the builders succumbed to creeper disease.

This was where the damage was most severe. Earthquakes, both old and new, had repeatedly assaulted everything the stonecutters and masons had made, leaving walls that lay on their sides, floors pocked with gaping holes, and more heaps of rubble than would be seen on a mountainside. But these piles of rubble were different, in that they showed signs of human habitation.

People once lived here, if only for a brief time. Broken glass and pieces of furniture were constant obstacles. The assassin saw wooden plates, a washtub, and some bedclothes. Then she saw a tome. The holy book of Sun Antheus. Not surprisingly, most of the pages were ripped out. And Aeoxoea knew by whom.

They no longer attacked, but they still watched from the shadows, glaring with those hateful yellow eyes. The creepermen now filled the castle, crouching among the rubble, yearning to attack, but restrained by the command of their queen. Aeoxoea could see them on every level as she followed Gavin deeper and deeper into the earth. There seemed to be creepermen hiding in every shadow, behind every heap of rubble, looking through every doorway.

With so much damage to its foundations, it was amazing this castle hadn't yet collapsed upon itself. The magic contained in the giant teardrop at its center was probably the only reason it hadn't. The hole that started in the receiving hall continued down through the ceilings and floors of level after level, as if a giant spear had been thrust down through the center of the castle. This was the route Gavin followed, climbing down with Elkor's rope coiled over his shoulder. The stagnancy of the air gradually subsided the farther down he climbed, death and decay giving way to the smell of earth, moist and fresh. It wasn't long before Aeoxoea saw why this was.

Once there was a fountain in the center of the receiving hall, carved from a single giant block of crystal to resemble a tulip stamen. Its remains were found at the very bottommost portion of the castle, on the muddy floor of a room that would best be described as an underground cavern. It was lying on its side, broken into several pieces, and half- submerged in the ground. Portions of it were as smooth as the day it was made, but most of it was dulled by years of grit, and splattered with dirt.

Three wells were built here to supply water to the castle. They had been formed by human hands, their stones glistening with wetness. Another rope hung down into the mouth of one of these wells, indicating that Elkor had climbed down into it. As he had done in the center of the receiving hall, Gavin cut the ropes and climbed down without aid, finding handholds in the rocky walls. The well was deep, and the shaft narrow. The knight climbed down for several minutes before coming to the bottom, where it opened into the ceiling of an even larger cavern, a hundred feet above the rippling waters of an underground lake. When Gavin reached this opening, he released his grip on the wall and allowed himself to fall, growing smaller as he dropped, until he made a tiny splash in the lake below.

Aeoxoea did not choose to fall, but instead used the power of her mind to gather air molecules about her body, packing them tightly to support her weight. Then she descended from the bottom of the well shaft, literally riding upon the breeze as it carried her safely down. A small sphere of light below guided her movements to the side of the lake, where Elkor waited on the beach with his dogs. He was dripping wet, shivering, and waving a torch to guide Gavin as he swam to shore.

Aeoxoea reached the beach as the knight emerged from the lake, just in time to feel the spray as Behe shook some water from her fur. Before continuing in their journey, the knights spent a few minutes ringing out their clothing, and checking their weapons and equipment. For light, Elkor placed his torch on his back, where he wore some straps like a sconce. This held the torch upright so it cast its light over his shoulder, leaving his hands free. If this were a common torch, the Hound would have burned his ear off, but this torch was anything but common.

Seeing there was no flame, Aeoxoea looked directly into the light, allowed it to fill her vision. Thought the torch was like a small sun, it did not blind or even sting her eyes, and she could easily make out the source of the light as being one of four small metal rods protruding from the tip of the torch. She did not need to use her external senses to know this was a work of the Craft, a magical torch that undoubtedly became a necessity after the soaking the knights and all their equipment had just been through.

While the illumination it cast was strong and constant, the small circle of pale light seemed almost insignificant in the large black cavern. It twinkled like one lonely star in a vast black night.

Suddenly, Aeoxoea turned and looked through the darkness at the lake for many moments. "Jass wake up."

"Yes mistress?" came the knight's voice from inside her head.

"Use my eyes," Aeoxoea commanded. "Do you recognize this place?"

"The Neversea Depths."

"What do you know of this lake?" Aeoxoea asked.

"Nothing," Jass answered. "I've never been here."

"Does it sustain life? Fish of any sort?"

"I don't know, mistress."

"Damn my old boots, Zealot," Elkor said, removing his shirt and ringing it out. "That's another story to tell. You staring down an army of creepermen. I fear you're mad, sir."

"As do I," Gavin said, crouching down to check on Eleod.

"Creeper's disease is nothing to trifle with," Elkor said.

"We all do our duty." Gavin lifted Eleod into his arms. "How are you? How is Eleod?"

"He took to the water like a fish," Elkor said, smiling. "I thought I'd have to carry him but he swam without aid, and well. Better than me, even."

"I can swim!" the boy shouted triumphantly. "I learned."

"You can swim, for certain. And you've no qualms about embarrassing old Elkor, leaving him spitting water in your wake, eh, my boy?"

"Good boy," Gavin said, bouncing the Blessed Soul in his arms.

"There's the water," Eleod said, pointing. "Over there. I am all wet."

"Yes, the water," Gavin said. "The water has Eleod all wet. We have a very wet Eleod today."

"Over there," the boy said again, smiling at Gavin's approval. "There's water in the castle."

"Yes, water in the castle," Gavin said. "Was the castle pretty?"

Eleod frowned. "It was dark." Then his teeth began to chatter.

Aeoxoea watched as Gavin pulled Eleod's shirt over his head, then rung it out. Then Elkor rubbed him down with a blanket.

"C-cold water in the castle," Eleod chattered.

"Yes," Elkor said, rubbing his white hair with the blanket. "The water was very cold."

The boy sneezed, but held himself still, allowing Elkor to dry him off. He looked around, distracted, eyes wide at the darkness around them.

The child couldn't know where he was, but he could feel the foreboding of the place, so deep inside the island of Thershon, a mountain of earth pressing down just overhead. Aeoxoea studied the vastness of the cavern, looked at the rock, the stone, and sand, the utter lifelessness of this sunless world. There were a hundred tunnels of all shapes and sizes in the cavern's walls and ceiling, leading to larger rooms, smaller rooms, to tunnels that wound up or down, with a dozen destinations, or just leading to nowhere. The inside of the island of Thershon was one spectacular maze, as intricate a world as any other. It was so porous an island that it could have been likened to a gigantic fossilized sponge. This vast underground had as much room to roam as the surface of several islands combined and, according to all Jass had told her, just as much life roaming there.

The knights didn't spend much more time drying themselves or their clothing after making Eleod comfortable. Gavin gave the boy a bit of dried meat to nibble on and lifted him onto his back. Elkor stowed his blanket and checked his weapons, calling for his dogs. When all seemed ready, they set off on a course meant to take them around the edge of the lake. No longer surrounded by zoths or creepermen, they took a more leisurely pace, moving at a brisk walk that came far short of all the frenzied running that had characterized the trip so far. Soon they'd rounded the lake and approached the other end of the cavern, where they found a small stream flowing away from the eastern edge of the lake into a large tunnel with smooth sides.

The other tunnels connected to this cavern were naturally created, the offspring of gravity, water flowage, and the occasional earthquake. They simply existed, leading to nowhere with their directionless, jagged walls and randomly determined features. But there was nothing random about this tunnel. It was perfectly round, twenty feet in diameter, with smooth, almost glassy sides. In contrast to its brothers it was straight, and took a slightly downward and easterly course, hinting that it might actually lead to somewhere.

Gravity pulled the small stream away from the side of the lake and down into the tunnel, where it disappeared in the darkness, deep in the earth. Gavin stepped into this tunnel, splashing through the stream. For a moment he simply stood and looked, with water bubbling around his ankles. Aeoxoea wondered if he hesitated.

"It is the lair of the mua giou, Zealot," Elkor said softly. "This is our course to the Neversea Depths, according to the Keeper of the Craft."

"Mua giou," the voice of Jass spoke inside Aeoxoea's brain. "Those are words of the dycleth language meaning 'lizard worm.'"

"Lizard worm?"

"The name of a mythical creature worshiped by some peoples who dwell in the depths of the Neversea," Jass said. "Many believe it is dead now, if it ever existed. Our dycleth allies tell us differently."

"It is large?" Aeoxoea said.

"It is very large," Jass confirmed.

The dogs sniffed warily at the sides of the tunnel, whimpering softly. Elkor scratched Behe's head.

"Are we certain the time is right?" Gavin asked, looking into the darkness.

"The earthquake tells us it is so," Elkor said. "The trembling of the earth marks the passing of the mua giou."

"Then we must go now?" Gavin asked.

Elkor nodded. "Yes, now. Or not at all."

"It is now, then," Gavin said, and began to walk.

Elkor followed, his torch burning brightly on his shoulder. His dogs took up positions at his side.

Aeoxoea did not follow them inside the tunnel. She just stood and watched as the light of their torch faded, watched as they walked deeper into the earth, and eventually out of sight. The cavern fell into complete darkness, yet Aeoxoea remained where she was.

"Why do you not follow?" Jass asked.

"Go to sleep, Jass," Aeoxoea answered, keeping her eyes on the surface of the lake.

"Yes, mistress."

Many minutes passed, and yet the assassin kept her vigil, her eyes on the water. The ripples created by the knights' swim slowly died, until the lake was as calm as a sheet of glass.

She had plenty of time to consider what had transpired in the receiving hall above, to think about it, and try to recover from the shock of what was done to her. Repeatedly, almost obsessively, she rubbed at the cracked skin of her forearms and on her left cheek. The spots on her face formed a near-perfect line from the corner of her lips to her ear lobe. As she brushed them with her fingertips, she knew the scars would never heal. They were now just as important and distinguishing to her appearance as her nose was.

Marked my Miacnon. Those scars would be a constant reminder that the disease of the creepermen lived within her. Perhaps it was dormant by choice. Perhaps it was held at bay by the will of the Serharek. Perhaps even by the will of God. But Aeoxoea was certain the words spoken to her in the receiving hall were true. Once her usefulness to the Serharek was done, and the prophecies were fulfilled, there would be nothing stopping the Angel of Disease from claiming what was his. And Aeoxoea knew it for certain. She was now his.

"Oh, but my dear, precious Angel of Disease," the assassin whispered to herself. "You will have to wait your turn, for I have made myself a servant of so many, and yet, in the end, I will hold the Devil Device in hand, and then, I will be master of all ... "

Aeoxoea's voice trailed off as she watched the smooth surface of the lake began to ripple once again, in a large V-shape, as though something moved beneath its surface. The apex of the ripples moved toward the shore of the lake, in the direction of the mua giou lair, growing more pronounced the closer it came. Aeoxoea saw a shape moving under the water, something unsubstantial, made of nothingness, or rather, the absence of water. She could see the water around it, but she couldn't see the thing itself, just a small pocket of something, the shape of a small man, walking on the floor of the lake.

This was no lizard worm.

Aeoxoea stared at this newcomer, different spectrums of light flashing before her eyes, until she settled on that which allowed her to see human juy. She looked through a gloomy, bluish world, devoid of all psychic energy but her own, which appeared as smallish, amber flame licking about her own body. None of it touched the water or the being that traveled beneath it. Then she searched for Craft, switching her vision to detect the weaves of magic that bound the world. Her eyes almost burned with the strength of the Craft that flowed there. The myriad of colors burned and sizzled and popped in the air of the cavern, or swam lazily through the waters of the lake, filling it to the brim with magic, touching every last drop of water, but not touching this man-shaped thing.

The Craft weaves were fickle things. They embraced some, but rejected others. They favored Elkor the Hound, but they made love to Gavin the Zealot. Eleod, the Blessed Soul of Man, was not surprisingly the most favored Aeoxoea had ever seen. His little body burned so brightly with Craft that his presence stung the assassin's eyes, almost as if he *was* Craft magic.

But this creature was just the opposite. The term used by many wizards to describe it was "Craft-death." The colorful weaves not only didn't touch it, they seemed to shrink away, rejecting it, and with loathing. And Aeoxoea knew why. The Craft weaves of this island did not touch the creature, because it was not of this island.

Not born of these Craft weaves. Not born of this island.

It remained invisible to every form of sight available to the assassin and to any Thershoni wizard who drew upon the Craft. It remained invisible through some power she didn't understand. Not the Method. Not the Craft. This left only one explanation:

Technology.

The creature's head appeared above the surface as it walked out of the lake, insubstantial on its own, given shape only by the rivulets of water streaming down its face, its chest, and arms. It walked onto the dry land, its feet pressing deep into the soft sand, water still running down the length of its body. It was a human shape, that of a small man, unclothed, barefoot, carrying nothing, no weapons or tools. There it stood for a moment, the invisible naked man, looking slowly around. After a moment, the creature disappeared from sight, and it took Aeoxoea some thought to realize the water covering its skin had evaporated, as though the creature somehow dried its entire body in one second.

Once again, Aeoxoea switched her vision to the spectrum which detected Craft, and again her eyes burned with the gleaming strands of colorful power that filled the room. This way she could see the man, this distinctly unmagical creature, by the space it occupied among the glowing Craft weaves—an empty, black hole in the shape of a person that stood before her. That stood before her ... looking directly at her.

It pointed in her direction, arm outstretched, hand balled into a fist. Aeoxoea had only a second to react before the space between them exploded with heat, scorched and distorted by some invisible weapon. The cavern was filled with a heavy throbbing sound, a deafening and repetitive drumbeat. Aeoxoea barely had time enough to throw up physical defenses, using the power of her mind to bunch up the air molecules surrounding her, creating a barrier of protection that could best almost any physical attack. Her defenses were obliterated in seconds by the creature's invisible weapon, pounded ruthlessly, and shattered. Her tentacles streaked out of her body, a last pathetic defense as she tried to scramble to the cover of a nearby cluster of stalagmites. The tentacles exploded with a sickening splatter, rent by an unstoppable force, spraying Aeoxoea's body with her own milky blood. All protection gone, the weapon pounded away at the assassin's left flank as she crawled for cover. It treated her arm much the same way as it did her tentacles, utterly destroying it in only a second, creating a small rainstorm of blood, shredded flesh, and bone.

Aeoxoea found cover behind the rock formation, purchasing a few moments to gather her senses. All around, the air seemed to boil with the heat of the pulsing weapon. The heavy throbbing continued on, booming in her ears, filling the cavern with thunder. The stalagmites were hammered and beaten. Rocks and dust filled the air as her protection crumbled. She rolled forward into a small divot in the ground. The remains of the stalagmites exploding all around her covered her with stony debris. The hiding place was just the correct size, large enough and deep enough for her to lie in, flat on her back, in a position where she could no longer be struck at by her attacker's invisible fire. At this, the pulsing of the weapon stopped, giving the assassin a moment of reprieve, leaving only the sound of a cloud of dust settling to the earth. Then the soft padding of running footsteps, growing louder, approaching from the shoreline.

The black shape of a man appeared above Aeoxoea, punching her in the chest with a large blade that slid cleanly through her flesh, cleanly through her heart—a perfect kill on any other victim. A dozen white tentacles streaked out of the assassin's body, striking at her attacker, at its chest, its arms, and its head. Every attack bounced off its flesh as though this thing was made of steel. She tried grabbing at the hand that held the blade inside her, using every tentacle to dig into its wrist and forearm, to force the weapon out. But the creature's strength was god-like, and Aeoxoea didn't gain an inch.

It didn't matter, for she would only need that one second to end this battle, to lay waste her attacker's mind. She gathered all the strength of all the mystic will she possessed in her body and launched a scathing psychic attack that would have sliced any man's mind to ribbons, relieving him of his identity, memory, and motives. Relieving his body of his mind, destroying his entire life in one thought.

But just as the creature's skin seemed forged in steel, strong enough to turn away every physical attack, a psychic barrier of unimaginable strength surrounded its mind, sturdy enough to turn away even the most fearsome of assaults, one after the other. This left Aeoxoea with nothing, all her most powerful attacks spent, useless against defenses much more powerful. Whatever this thing was, it was physically and mentally dominating the assassin in ways she never thought possible. The creature held its blade inside Aeoxoea's chest with one hand, making a fist with the other, pointing it directly at the assassin's face, intending to blow her head off.

Death was inevitable.

There was but one option left; one course of action so desperate it would only be considered by someone with precious seconds to live, someone who could already see the grinning face of Dehen Yaulk. There was a chance she'd be saved, but there was a price to be paid. It might mean selling a piece of her soul. But it might just mean survival.

A certain dagger found its way into Aeoxoea's right hand; a dagger with a black handle and a blade of dull gray, covered with the markings of the Cult of Meherarc, Angel of Murder. It was once carried by a doppelganger who died in the church in Ebon South. Aeoxoea had seen this dagger do its evil work before. She had felt inside her own body as it tasted her flesh. Now the dagger would taste new flesh. And it would do so by Aeoxoea's hand.

"Meherarc, hear my prayer," she muttered. "I bear your weapon. I carry your banner."

Holding the dagger backward in her hand, she jammed its blade into her attacker's wrist. Like all her other attacks, it bounced off like it struck a stone wall. But the attack seemed to hurt the creature somehow. It shrieked and reeled back, giving Aeoxoea another few seconds of living breath. Then it retracted its blade from the assassin's chest, seized her by the throat, and leaped high into the air. Brilliant orange flames roared from the soles of its feet, propelling the two out over the lake, soaring higher and higher toward the ceiling of the dark cavern.

The creature's grip on Aeoxoea's neck was sure, holding her tightly as it flew through the darkness. But it tightened further still, until the assassin felt her attacker's fingers penetrating her flesh, crushing her throat, rearranging her vertebrae. She was blinded, her tongue squeezed out of her mouth. She knew she was dying, but refused to leave the world without a fight, stabbing the cursed dagger at her attacker's head repeatedly.

Suddenly her back was crushed as she was slammed into the side of a giant a stalactite. Dust and rock flew everywhere, and streaks of lightning lanced across the darkness of Aeoxoea's vision as her head rebounded off the stone. Again, a large blade was slammed into her body, clean through her stomach, into the stone at her back.

"Meherarc, hear my prayer. I bear your weapon. I carry your banner."

The assassin's lips only twitched, unable to form the words conjured by her mind. But a prayer thought and not said is a prayer nonetheless, and Aeoxoea's prayer was heard. It was heard by the Lord of Assassins.

The creature's black face was inches from Aeoxoea's, regarding her without expression, possibly wondering how the assassin remained alive. All around the creature's body the colorful magic swirled and danced, touching every molecule in the room, but not touching this being, whatever it was. The creature was rejected by the magic of this island, unlike the dagger in Aeoxoea's hand, which glowed brightly. With each word of Aeoxoea's prayer, the weapon sucked more magic from the air, glowing brighter and brighter, gaining strength from the Craft weaves and from Meherarc, the Angel of Murder, who blessed the dagger's creation.

Aeoxoea's attacker retracted its blade from her stomach and aimed for another, more perfect blow, one that would sever her head and end this fight once and for all.

"Meherarc, hear my prayer. I bear your weapon. I beg it find this creature's heart."

Both lashed out at the other in the same moment, but Aeoxoea's arm moved faster, so magically enhanced, it found its mark first. The dagger thrust was accompanied by an explosion of Craft, white and hot. Aeoxoea was blinded by what she saw, a bolt of magical electricity slicing down her arm, through the dagger, and into the guts of the creature. She was punched in the face by the force of it, and every muscle and nerve in her body shivered and twitched uncontrollably.

The black dagger of Meherarc slammed into the creature's belly, cutting easily through barriers that before were impossible to breach, then finding the flesh beneath. Once inside, the evil corrosive steel dug hungrily into the creature's innards. In answer to Aeoxoea's prayer, the blade struck unerringly at its most vulnerable spot, dealing the perfect blow, and a life was ended.

There was no scream, only a soft sound, like the sigh of a child.

The attack on Aeoxoea fell short as the creature's arm went limp. As the creature's entire body went limp, they both began to fall. White tentacles streaked out of Aeoxoea's body, finding firm holds in the side of the stalactite, holding her in place. The creature, though dead, still maintained its death grip upon her neck, hanging from her like a limp marionette on a string. The assassin tried with her remaining hand to force its hold off, but it was too strong, its grip seemingly frozen onto her neck.

Then a strange noise emerged from within the dead creature's body, something like the ticking of a clock. It grew louder with each second marked, and it grew faster as it grew louder. Eventually it grew loud enough that she could make out a woman's voice speaking within each ticking of the clock. She spoke in one of the ancient dead languages. One word per beat.

"... twelve ... eleven ... ten ..."

Desperately, Aeoxoea began to tear at the creature's hand, trying to force it to let go even as the countdown grew louder, fueling her anxiety. But she didn't have the strength of mind or body. She was so badly hurt, she could barely maintain her hold on the stalactite.

"... nine ... eight ... seven ..."

She took the black dagger of Meherarc and slammed it into the creature's wrist, trying to cut the hand off. She hacked at it repeatedly, splattering her face with the creature's blood.

"... six ... five ... four ..."

Finally she was able to chop the creature's hand off. The creature's body fell away into the darkness, leaving her clinging to the side of the stalactite, the severed hand still hanging from her throat.

" ... three ... two ... one ..."

The words faded away into the darkness below, followed by a splashing sound that told Aeoxoea the body had hit the underground lake. Then a huge thump sounded from within the water, and the entire surface of the lake exploded into flame. A shockwave hit Aeoxoea, crushing her against the stalactite, nearly knocking her from her perch. Then a wall of hot water rose up and did just that, slamming her into the rocky ceiling, forcing her body into the tiny crevasses between stalactites. This was the last her body could take. Already hurting and weakened to near-death, she lost all consciousness.

Her last sensation was that of falling.

CHAPTER 26

Theel sat atop a beer cask with his legs hanging over the side of Hoster's cart, swaying back and forth as the wheels thumped over the uneven surface of the road. The bumpy road and springless axle conspired against his head, which was heavy with ache, and the hole in his chest, which hurt him far worse. Every breath he took was somehow even more miserable than the last.

Hoster's mules trudged along, pounding the dust with their hooves, the filthy animals jerking against their harnesses. This caused the cart to sway and lurch, denying Theel the smooth ride his head so desperately needed. There were few things in the world that Theel detested more than mules.

But worst of all was the splotch of purple flesh covering Theel's cheek, a patch of tenderized meat that was roughly the size of his brother's fist. A glob of pulp that used to be flesh, it throbbed with its own heartbeat and sent waves of agony crashing into his brain. This particular malady owed its thanks to Theel's brother, Yatham, for its existence. As if the constant discomfort afforded by his journey was not yet enough, Theel now had his own brother's fists to fear.

Yatham had gotten exactly what he wanted by punching his brother in the face. Theel hadn't said a word in hours, stunned into silence by the humiliation he felt. Now it seemed his brother was prepared to bully him just as his father once did, with one act making him feel the size of an ant, insignificant and worthless.

These emotions reminded him of a time years before when he was on the receiving end of a beating from three older boys, street rats who thought it would be enjoyable to torment the son of a knight. Theel was already years into his training as a squire, but he was unarmed, and all three of his attackers were much bigger.

There were many witnesses, but none who cared to intervene on his behalf—not even his father. Theel was on the ground, his mouth full of blood and dirt, and looked between the legs of his attackers to see his masterknight standing nearby. Theel cried out for help, begging to be saved, but the help never came. The beating ended only when the ruffians saw who he was calling to and fled rather than face the knight. But they had nothing to fear, because Theel's father was not looking at them. It was almost as if he didn't see his son's attackers. All he saw was his son, lying on the ground, unable to defend himself.

Theel never forgot the coldness with which his masterknight said, "Get up."

No soothing words, no consolation or encouragement, just the two words spoken within a layer of frost. But worse than that was the look on his father's face. Theel had seen him disappointed before. He'd seen him angry or frustrated countless times. But he'd never seen him embarrassed for his son. And he'd never seen him with a look of helplessness.

Theel's father looked at him as if he was a task that refused to be completed, like he was a sapling that would not grow. This was a man for whom things came easily. He was unable to understand the plight of a person for whom things were difficult. He'd been successful at every endeavor he'd ever undertaken, but he couldn't succeed at this. He could not kill his son's weakness. He could not strengthen his son's resolve. His best efforts yielded no results. The son of the great knight had no greatness in him.

Theel remembered the laughter and jeers he'd heard when he returned to the Hall of Seven Swords with a swollen face and a broken lip. His father heard it as well, but again, did nothing to defend his son. He didn't join in the laughter, but he did nothing to stop it.

Their next sparring session was memorable for its brutality. Theel was worked relentlessly for days. No food, no water, working shirtless in the snow. He lost count of how many times he collapsed, how many times he vomited. Not once was help or reprieve offered, not even when the training was done. He was simply left to himself, a heap of quivering flesh lying in the snow, covered with bruises and scrapes and knots on his head. He barely managed to drag himself to the stables, where he slept that night among the horses, too exhausted to climb the stairs to the squire's barracks.

That was when Theel realized there was no hope of escape. There was no diverting from this path his father had laid out for him, not until one of them was dead. The more apparent it became that Theel was not destined for knighthood, the harder knighthood was force upon him.

Even so many years later, Theel remembered these events as the harshest, most painful experiences of his life. Whenever he thought of those days, he could still feel the blows as if they were happening again, over and over. Not just the punches of the ruffians, or the hits from the practice sword, but the cold dispassion with which his father meted out his punishment. His eyes were like daggers of ice stabbing at Theel's heart. The father didn't view his son as a human being to be nurtured, but a piece of steel to be beaten and shaped.

This was not how Yatham viewed his brother. Yatham was loyal and compassionate, always willing to help. But none of these virtues prevented him from striking Theel in the face, and in that one act, dumping him into a sea of black memories. The little boy in Theel knew the meaning behind the abuse he suffered. It meant he was worthless. It meant he deserved to be beaten.

That little boy was weeping again. No one saw him as a person. They only saw him as a means by which the prophecy might be fulfilled. King Britou, The Keeper, Theel's father—none of them wished him happiness. All they wanted was for him to use his Sight to find their precious Blessed Soul.

This was why his father forced the knighthood upon his son. He believed with all his heart that Theel would be the one to find the Blessed Soul of Man. It was why he'd groomed his son for this purpose from the first day the little boy could hold a sword. His father wished for him to complete the search generations of knights and clansmen dreamed of by finding the elusive Blessed Soul of Man.

It was painful enough to know that his father cared nothing for him as a person, only how his Sight might be used for the purpose of completing a quest. But then to learn that all those years of abuse, the endless hours of strict training, the endless demands of perfection, and the lifetime of suffocating, emotional neglect were suffered in the name of fulfilling a fanciful prophecy … all to find a man who didn't exist. It was a bitterness that sat in his belly like a poison, growing with each passing day. And it was killing him slowly.

Worst of all, no one cared to help him. No one took steps to deter the great knight in his foolish obsession. As Theel's father trained him in bladework, the Keeper of the Craft schooled him in the Method. And when it was decided he was ready, the king decreed the goal of his quest. No one cared whether he wished to be a knight. No one cared if he was prepared for Warrior Baptism.

No one cared.

Yatham was the lone person who didn't place unreasonable expectations upon his brother. Yatham saw Theel as a person. Yatham showed him respect. He treated him as a peer, as a brother. Most of all, he was the only one who listened. But all that changed with one angry punch to the face.

The message was clear: Yatham no longer cared, either. Much like everyone else in Theel's life, he'd decided that worshipping an empty promise was more important. The prophecy was more important to him. The Blessed Soul was more important.

Theel spent much of the morning silently fuming, but eventually his anger cooled and settled into sorrowful resignation. Yatham was his last hope for acceptance. If he didn't understand, no one ever would. This left Theel entirely alone in his struggle. The more he thought about it, the more it made sense. He, himself, was the only person he could depend on to fix this. No one else.

And the more he thought about it, the more Theel was unable to deny the knowledge that he alone was the source of all his problems. No one else was to blame. Therefore *he* was the problem that needed fixing.

This left only one solution; one opportunity to mend the damage he'd done to himself and to his family. One way to relieve himself, and the world, of the burden of him. The number of times he'd considered ending his pain on the edge of his father's knife could not be counted. But he'd already decided it would not be done that way.

He resolved himself again, that morning, while riding on Hoster's cart, that he would not pass judgment with his own hand. Instead, he would seek justice in the only place he could find it ...

Chapter 27

"The Dead Man's Bridge," Hoster said over the creaking of the cart wheels. "That's the faster way across the canyon, but also the more dangerous."

"What's the safer route?" Yatham asked.

"The upper passes," Hoster answered. "Much safer than the bridge, but it will take us longer."

"Hey!" Rasm shouted, bending over to pick something up. "I found a turd!"

"How much longer will the safer route take?" Yatham asked.

"A week, at least," Hoster said. "And that's if the snows are kind. It's not a long walk, but it's straight up a mountainside."

"Straight up a mountainside?" Yatham said. "That doesn't sound safe."

"It isn't," Hoster said. "But the Dead Man's Bridge is even worse."

"It's a scurbat turd," Rasm added. "Do you know what this means?"

"That route goes further west," Hoster explained, ignoring Rasm. "It's a straight walk down through the Narrows, a system of tunnels through the belly of the mountains. You cross the Dead Man's Bridge and knock ten days off your trip. But lately, some folks haven't been making it across that bridge. Some folks been ending up swallowed by Krillian's Cut."

"Anyone care to guess?" Rasm asked, waving his hand. "About the turd I found?"

"Zoths live in the Narrows?" Yatham asked.

"Aye, my boy. More than enough zoths to fill your belly," Hoster answered. "Word on the roads is the Narrows are swarming with those roaches."

"I see," Yatham said. "It's the upper passes for you then?"

"I'm going to the Sister Cities by way of the upper passes," Hoster confirmed. "It's safer. No zoths. Nothing but snow. My mules will never make it across the Dead Man's Bridge, and not just because they're stupid. They're too fat and slow. We'll make supper for the zoths if we try. Besides, I got business in the Sister Cites. There's the king's work to be earned."

"Anyone listening to me?" Rasm asked.

"Still talking to yourself, you damned scatterbrain?" Hoster asked.

"Actually, I find that talking to oneself is integral to maintaining sanity," Rasm opined. "Especially when one's primary traveling partner is a jackhole."

"You're an idiot."

"You're fat."

"The bridge is faster?" Yatham interjected.

"Much faster," Hoster answered. "It's only two days to Tavern on the Lake from the bridge. From there it's straight on to Eastwall, then out of the mountains down to Tera Watch on the border of the Outlands. That's Ebon South, my boy. That's where we're headed. Fifteen days into the upper passes and across at the Sister Cities. That's if the snows are kind. Or only six days down through the Narrows, and across the Dead Man's Bridge. That's if the zoths are kind. Pick your poison."

"There is a knight's quest to be considered," Theel said loudly. "Will the needs of the quest be considered in this discussion?"

The question was met with silence, everyone staring ahead, marching along the road.

"I would prefer this decision to be made with my knight's quest in mind," Theel added.

Still no answer. For many tense moments. Then Rasm broke the silence.

"Hey, Theel. Wanna see my turd?" he asked joyfully. "It's magic—"

"No," Theel said evenly. "I do not."

"But it's a magical tur—"

"I don't care what it is," Theel said coldly. "Keep your filthy talk to yourself, you blubbering fool."

Hoster shot Theel a nasty look. "Don't talk to my boy that way. Nobody talks to my boy that way."

"Except you," Rasm added.

"I think we should take the safer route, brother," Yatham said. "Even if it takes longer. Hoster knows the way. We can trust him."

"Yeah," Hoster said. "You can trust me."

"Whether or not I trust you is irrelevant," Theel said. "We will cross the Dead Man's Bridge."

Hoster shook his head. "We will not go that way."

"You promised to show us to the Outlands, did you not?" Theel asked.

"I did," Hoster agreed. "But I didn't promise to kill my mules and lose my cargo in the process."

"Do you remember *why* we need to travel to the Outlands?"

"Many reasons," Hoster answered. "There's the king's work to be earned, for one."

"There is another reason, more important than all the others," Theel said. "We travel to the Outlands because I am on a knight's quest given me by the Keeper of the Craft."

Hoster sighed. "I can see right now I'm going to need some pig swill to help me see this conversation through to its conclusion. Rasm, fetch me some liquid diversion from the cart."

"I could turn him to salt," Rasm offered as he dug through the boxes on the cart. "Um, yeah. Salt."

"No," Hoster said, resigned. "The swill will suffice. The awful stuff. There it is."

"Are you listening to me?" Theel asked.

"I am, most certainly," Hoster said, taking the bottle from his son. "But God willing, I won't remember it tomorrow."

"Then I will tell you again tomorrow," Theel said. "You will take me to the Dead Man's Bridge as fast as your mules can pull this cart."

"Is that right?" Hoster smiled, taking a drink. "This morning you refused to move. Now you are hot for a gallop. Why the change of heart?"

"I've had some time to think."

"What could be filling your mind with such deep thought, I wonder?" Hoster said. "Is it your brother's fist? Was a good wallop to the jaw all that was needed to stoke your passion for travel?"

"No, not my brother's fist," Theel said. "The Dead Man's Bridge. I must go there."

"We won't go that route," Hoster said, shaking his head.

"It is important that you do."

"Nothing is so important that it's worth getting skinned by zoths," Hoster said.

"That's where you are mistaken," Theel said. "This is a personal quest."

"You may be on a personal quest," Hoster said. "But I am not."

"I've heard you claim you are loyal to the king. Are you a proud son of Embriss, as you say?"

"That depends," Rasm cut in. "Are you buying?"

"Invoke the name of your king all you like, boy," Hoster said. "And your Keeper of the Craft. I'm not impressed."

"In the name of King Britou, I command you to take me to the Dead Man's Bridge," Theel said.

"Britou is not here," Hoster countered. "And I don't have to listen to you. You're no lord. You're just a lowborn commoner like me, no better than anyone else."

"I never claimed—"

"You treat everyone as if you are lord of the world. As if all of us must bow before you, the Lord of Fancy Farts." Hoster asked, "What's your sigil, Lord Fancy Farts? A powdered ass?"

Theel's jaw quivered. "I'll not be lectured by a drunk who wanders the roads, telling lies to earn his—"

"You'll be lectured and you'll listen, too," Hoster said. "You act like a high lord, but you are lowborn, just like me. A common, lowborn peasant wretch, just like me."

"Me too," Rasm said. "I'm lowborn. And a wretch. Yeah!"

"As low as they come," Hoster muttered.

"You both disgust me," Theel said.

"Lord Fancy Farts of the House of Powdered Ass is talking again." Hoster shook his head and looked at Yatham. "That brother of yours carries on like he thinks he's the Blessed Soul of Man or something."

Yatham sighed. "I know."

"Do not talk about me as if I'm not here!" Theel growled.

"Stop being such a pisser."

"I will not be treated like a child!"

"Then don't act like one," Hoster said, and looked at Yatham. "Would you hit him again, please?"

"I'll hit him," Rasm announced. "Yeah!"

He reeled back with his fist.

"No," Yatham said, grabbing Rasm by the wrist. "There will be none of that."

"Don't act like a child if you wish to be treated as a man," Hoster said, bringing his bottle to his lips. "You have to show respect to earn respect."

"Are you going to strike at me too? Just like my father? Just like my brother?"

"Maybe I will," Hoster said. "Your talk of the Dead Man's Bridge has me thinking your brother's fist turned your brain to soup. Maybe I could fix you good with another belt."

"You would not dare strike me."

"I would, in fact, dare to strike you," Hoster countered. "Once I get angry enough. A few more swallows should do it."

"You'll try," Theel said.

"I might."

"You'll fail."

"I won't."

"Hit him!" Rasm yelled.

"You'd deserve it," Hoster grumbled, taking another drink. "Lord Fancy—"

"Do not address me that way again," Theel warned.

"Rasm, you hear someone talking?" Hoster asked. "Is the Lord of Powdered Ass issuing decrees again?"

"He wants you to hit him," Rasm answered.

"Who?"

"The cripple ... uh, Lord Fancy ... Powder- ... um."

"He'll get his wish shortly," Hoster said, taking a hefty gulp. "Good God, but this stuff is awful. Almost drunk enough. Any second now."

"Warn me before you hit him," Rasm said. "I don't want to miss it. So tell me first. Yeah."

"You'll see nothing of the sort," Yatham said, glaring at Hoster. "Drink all you want, spirit trader. Get yourself thoroughly cooked. But if your inebriation causes you to lay a finger on my brother when he is injured and unable to defend himself ..."

"Do not speak for me, brother," Theel stated, but Yatham ignored him.

"... then it will be your face that takes the next walloping," Yatham continued.

"I'd enjoy seeing that, as well," Rasm said. "Warn me before you do it."

"Then you can walk to Yarik without escort for your cargo," Yatham said. "Unable to pour any liquor past your broken jaw."

"Yatham, you are a very violent person," Rasm said. "Wanna see my turd? It's magic—"

"We'll be upon the crossroads at Calfborn soon and we'll face a decision there," Yatham said. "There are two ways to pass Krillian's Cut. Do we take the Dead Man's Bridge by way of the Narrows? Or do we go to the Sister Cities by way of the upper passes? This talk of drinking and fighting does not answer that question."

"There is no questions to discuss," Hoster said smugly. "It's the Sister Cities for me."

"I need to go to the Dead Man's Bridge," Theel insisted.

"That's suicide," Hoster protested. "My mules are too fat and slow to make it without a fight."

"We will split then," Theel said. "Take your fat, slow mules eastward through the upper passes. Yatham and I will walk the road west, down through the Narrows."

"You'll find your dead carcasses feeding the crows at the bottom of the cut," Hoster warned.

"We'll be to Tavern on the Lake four days from Calfborn," Theel said. "Then we'll be on to the Outlands while you're still fighting the snows in the upper passes."

"You'll not make it across that bridge," Hoster said. "If you do, it'll be with zoth spears decorating your head."

"Yatham and I can handle a few zoths."

"Nobody said there was a few of them," Hoster said. "The stones of Krillian's Cut are crawling with zoths. They say no one crosses the Dead Man's Bridge unless the zoths allow it."

"They will allow us passage," Theel insisted.

"Boy, are you addled?" Hoster said loudly and slowly. "You ever met a zoth?"

"I am a squire of the Southern Cross. I've encountered zoths," Theel declared. "And don't call me boy."

"The zoths of the cut are even nastier, if it can be said," Hoster said. "They'll carve you up for supper, then make a shirt out of your skin."

"So I've heard," Theel said.

"Obviously you haven't heard enough," Hoster said. "You ever hear of the Crowlord?"

"Yes, I have," Theel answered. "A renowned zoth chieftain."

"A renowned zoth chieftain that's keeping his tribe in Krillian's Cut these days," Hoster said. "Many a good man died trying to cross that bridge, thanks to the Crowlord."

"This doesn't concern me," Theel said.

"It better concern you," Hoster said. "The Crowlord has killed knights, both highborn and low. Good swordsmen from both sides of the Dividers."

"I know," Theel said.

"The whispers say he's even killed a Knight of the Southern Cross or two," Hoster added.

"He's killed three," Theel stated.

"Three?" Hoster asked.

"He's killed three knights," Theel confirmed. "He'll kill no more if we meet him on the Dead Man's Bridge."

Hoster stared for many moments, looking suspicious. "You're not going to that bridge looking for a fight with the Crowlord. That would be stupid."

Theel raised his chin. "Then call me stupid."

"You're stupid!" Rasm yelled gleefully.

"More than stupid," Hoster opined. "You have a thirst for death. You're talking suicide."

"Finally," Theel said. "Someone understands."

Chapter 28

Theel knew something was wrong even before he could see the buildings of the town of Calfborn. Strong emotions, his and those of others, often ignited the juy within him, even when he didn't wish it. Events of intense human passion, good and bad, fueled his Sight. Theel could not control the flood of sights and sounds his senses brought him, not by closing his eyes, not by covering his ears.

The Iatan had been through Calfborn—not just scouts, but cavalry. They'd traveled over the mountains, or through the valley and past the Fortress at Kosiren somehow. The numbers were few, no more than two hundred, probably only one unit. The group was small enough to move around the armies of House Alister undetected, but large enough to create havoc in their unprotected rear.

The present was quiet, without a word spoken by the four somber travelers. The only sound was the clinking of mule harnesses, the sloshing of Hoster's bottle, and the squeaking of the cart's wheels. But the past was alive with the disharmony of what had taken place on the ground where they walked. Theel could hear the shouts of the officers, the snorting of the horses, the thunder of their tread, jingling harness, creaking leather, screaming women and crying children.

The horses ran past him, trotting and whinnying and tossing their heads, while their riders bounced in the saddle, kicking at their flanks with booted heels. The sounds of the horsemen were split into two groups; first the men attacking the town, then those same men riding away victorious an hour later. This second group carried with it some of the women of Calfborn who had survived the fighting, along with all the children that could be dragged from under their beds or pried from their father's corpses. Theel could see them, riding in the saddles with the Iatan, held tight by their captors, little hands tied with rope. He saw their tear-streaked faces, screaming for help.

Theel looked to the mountains on the eastern horizon where the captives had been taken. They were only as far away as twenty hours on horse at the most, riding toward their new lives as slaves of the Iatan Empire. If they were lucky.

Only hours away. A knight and his squires, traveling night and day, could catch them in time; catch the Iatan sleeping around their campfires and bring them to justice before they could whimper once the name of their pagan god. Kill them all. And save those children. That's what Father would have done.

But Theel wasn't like his father. And there was no one nearby who was. There were no knights to be found in this country. No knights and no soldiers. Just an unprepared squire, his brother, and two idiots. Theel looked again at the eastern horizon, staring with sad eyes. His heart ached, speaking a silent apology to the children of Calfborn.

"Theel?" Yatham said, quietly. "Are you well?"

Theel nodded to his brother and tried to smile, but couldn't. He couldn't wash from his mind the terror he heard in the screams of those children. Without thinking, he loosed his sword in its scabbard. Then he produced his pipe and clenched his teeth around the stem, sucking on it for comfort even though there was no leaf.

As the town drew nearer, so did the sounds of her death, the sounds of the battle raging in her streets. It had been one-sided and barbarous, with men and boys on foot, outnumbered, ill-prepared, stabbed and hacked to death, crushed by the horses and trampled under their hooves. Flames roared and women screamed and it all melted together into a single mournful moan as though the town was crying. In the present, the four travelers trudged on through the streets with quiet resolve, stepping on broken arrows, avoiding puddles of blood, listening to the awful joy of the carrion-eaters.

Calfborn wasn't large, merely a crossroads village; a cluster of buildings gathered around the tower house of the local lord. Three roads met in her center square; one leading north to Korsiren, another southeast to the Sister Cities, and the third southwest to the Narrows. It was in this center square where Theel discovered the fate of the defenders of Calfborn.

A well had been dug where the three roads met, the reason for the intersection. The well was the reason why the town grew on this spot, supplying water to the people, their animals, their crops, and to countless travelers who'd passed through over the years. Just beyond the well, at the south end of the square was a large, multi-level inn called the Marigold. Several headless corpses hung by their wrists from the inn's uppermost windows, serving as symbols of Iatan supremacy.

They were barely recognizable, blackened and bloated by the sun, and picked at by carrion birds. Rasm threw a pebble, scattering a dozen crows to reveal a large banner draped across one of the bodies. It was bloody and tattered, but depicting golden diamonds and oak leaves on a field of green.

Theel recognized the sigil as belonging to the Overlie family of Norrester, lesser nobility, Embriss-born and Embriss-loyal, sworn to the Alisters of the valley. This would explain why Calfborn seemed to be largely unprotected when the Iatan horsemen came down from the mountains. Most of the Overlie men-at-arms were likely manning the walls beside their liege lords at Korsiren. They must have taken most of the men of fighting age with them, because those who had remained to defend the town were mostly old men and boys. These old men and boys refused to yield their homes to the invaders, and they paid dearly for it.

The diamonds and oak leaves suddenly filled Theel's vision as juy exploded in his brain, bringing all the emotions attached to that banner. Beneath was the body of an elder member of the Overlie family, brother to the Lord of Norrester. He had taken three of the youngest of the family to Calfborn to keep them safe from the fighting, inadvertently putting them in greater danger. At the onset

of the attack, he put the two youngest ones on a horse and sent
them southward to Widow Hatch. Then he rushed out into the
street, where he and his men were crushed by the charge of the
Iatan horses. It was a quick death, and it spared him the torture that
was inflicted on many of the others who survived.

Such as the one whose body hung at his side, torn and
butchered and barely recognizable as human. This body ignited
strong juy, and Theel was unwillingly dragged into the past, into a
seen of barbaric torture.

He was the only man among the citizens of Calfborn who had a
fighting chance against the invaders. He was not a common man,
but the rarest of breeds; stout of heart and mind as well as muscle
and steel. It was he who stood among the ranks of the mightiest
warriors, who bore arms in defense of the Seven Kingdoms. He
was everything Theel was not. He was a Knight of the Southern
Cross.

"Sir Jarcet."

The grief in Yatham's voice was thick, and Theel knew why.
Jarcet the Sentinel was a friend of their father, and had often
mentored Yatham during his frequent visits to Fal Daran. Theel's
brother had learned spears and blades from his father, but his
training in mounted combat came under the care of Sir Jarcet,
known as one of the finest horsemen among the Knights of the
Southern Cross. Jarcet hosted Yatham during the brief time he'd
spent in Calfborn, when Theel and their father traveled south
without him. And Yatham was riding with Jarcet when Theel
returned with the news of their father's demise. Now, just months
later, Jarcet was dead as well.

The Iatan learned quickly how fearsome Jarcet could be while
fighting from the saddle. He slew or unhorsed a dozen of them
before his lance was broken and his mount slain. He continued to
fight them on his feet, using his battle hammer to kill another
dozen of them before he was subdued. The Iatan chose not to kill
him outright, not when there was revenge to be exacted. He was
tied and stretched between two horses, forced to listen as the other

survivors of Calfborn were brought to the town square and executed one by one. Then they heated his battle hammer in a fire until it glowed orange and seared each of his knight's tattoos of rank from his body, a process he didn't survive. Then he was beheaded and hung from the inn. And Theel was witness to it all. In just a few frightened breaths, he saw the entire story unfold as though he was there among the Iatan as it happened.

"This one was a knight," Hoster said, looking at the desecrated body of Jarcet the Sentinel. "Either of you boys know who this was?"

"No," Theel lied, refusing to look up at the body. "I didn't know him."

His eyes were on the piles of severed human feet scattered around the square, heaped mostly next to the well. Dirty feet, clean feet, hairy feet, big and small feet, cut off at the ankles and left to rot in the sun or feed the dogs.

"All the town's feet, sorry bastards, God help them," Hoster said, wiping his face with a handkerchief. "I heard they did this, the Iatan, leaving this to be found to warn any who would resist them. I didn't believe it when I heard it."

Theel didn't believe it even as he saw it. Once again he looked to the east, to the horizon where he knew the Iatan had taken the children, squeezing the grip of his sword as though he meant to break it off.

"We can't stay in this town," Theel said. "I can't sleep in this town tonight."

"We won't stay." Hoster patted his shoulder with a rough hand. "We'll camp beyond, on the road to the Sister Cities. Or wherever you choose."

Theel nodded, staring at the ground, trying to spare himself any more of what had happened in Calfborn. But his juy was boiling over with the horror of it all. He could still hear the screams of the men and boys who fought beside the Sentinel as their feet were cut, then their throats sliced open and their kicking, thrashing bodies dragged to the well and ...

"We can't drink this water," Rasm said, looking down the well. "There's people down there."

Theel went to the side of the well and leaned over to see the faint shapes of arms and legs and heads heaped upon each other in the dim light. He immediately looked away but could not escape the smell, and saw only more death, severed feet and headless corpses. He felt it in his stomach. His mind had seen enough and now his body was reacting. He was about to collapse, about to vomit, about to lose all control. The sound of Hoster's voice brought him back from the edge.

"By God, one is moving," he said. "One of those poor souls still breathes."

Theel was able to fight off the urge to wretch and forced himself to go back to the well, to look in again. Among the mass of piled limbs, he saw an arm move.

"You see that?" Hoster said. "Rasm, get some rope from the cart."

"Yeah, rope." He turned and ran to the mule cart.

Theel, still looking down the well, watched as the arm moved weakly, is if trying to wave, to capture their attention. Then he heard a soft moan.

"He's alive." Theel looked at Hoster. "Can we save him?"

"We can try," Hoster answered.

Yatham appeared at his brother's side. "I will climb down to get him."

"We are men of Embriss," Theel called down the well. "We're coming to help you."

"Rasm, where's that rope?" Hoster yelled.

"I won't need rope," Yatham said, climbing over the side.

"You crazy jackhole," Hoster said. "You want to climb into that without a rope?"

"You'll fall," Theel said.

"No I won't," Yatham insisted, sitting on the edge, looking down.

"It's too dangerous," Theel warned. "Use the rope."

"I don't need rope," Yatham said, lowering himself down. "Father once climbed into a well. He didn't use any rope."

"You are not Father," Theel retorted.

"Very true," Yatham replied. "But I don't need a rope to climb into a well." He was already disappearing into the darkness.

Rasm appeared with a coil of thin rope. "Here's the ... I got the ... uh."

Hoster took the rope, tying one end into a loop.

"Careful with him," the spirit trader called down. "We have rope. You want it?"

Yatham's voice echoed in the shaft. "Throw it down."

"Will he live?" Theel asked, as Hoster threw the rope into the darkness. "Can we save him?"

"We can save him," Yatham shouted back. "Get ready to pull."

"We're going to save him," Hoster said with a smile. "Get ready to pull."

"Slowly," Yatham called from the well.

Hoster and Theel took up the rope and pulled, slowly, just as Yatham asked. Hand over hand, inches first, then feet upon feet of rope emerging from the well. For once, the two did not fight against each other, but instead worked as one, pulling the wounded man out of the well.

"We're going to save this poor fool," Hoster grunted as he worked. "We're going to save him. Someone in this town is going to live, by God."

And Theel knew exactly how the old man felt. Something changed from the moment they entered the streets of this town. It was as if the air of the place was full of despair rather than oxygen, and there was no way to avoid breathing it in. The futility Theel felt, the inability to help or to change what happened, gnawed at him. The entire town was dead, and his hands were empty, powerless to do anything about it.

But now his hands were no longer empty. Now they held a rope, and they worked to pull a man back to life, the last survivor of Calfborn. Pulling on a rope was easy. Pulling on a rope was something he could do. Someone in this town is going to live, by God.

Yatham's head appeared above the well wall. "One more good pull."

Theel leaned back, pulling until he could see the hairs of the wounded man. Hoster wrapped the rope around his waist, bracing to hold the weight. Yatham jumped over the wall and took the man under his arms, pulling him over the side as gently as could be managed.

It was then that Theel saw this wasn't a soldier, or even a man. He was no more than a boy, fourteen or fifteen seasons from his nameday at most. He was richly dressed in a green tunic embroidered with silver diamonds and golden oak leaves.

"He's just a boy," Rasm said.

"And nobility," Hoster added. "He's born of Norrester. Look at his clothing."

Theel looked at the boy as he lay on the ground, weakly grasping at the scraps of his life. He was white as a ghost, and shriveled like a corpse, missing an eye, an ear and both feet. He was dripping wet, soaked in the ghastly soup of the tainted water of a dozen other men, splintered shafts sticking from his chest where arrow heads were broken off inside him.

It was too much for any sane man to bear. For a few brief moments, Theel had entertained a feeling of usefulness, of personal value. He held it in his hands just as he'd held the rope. But it was a tenuous grip. And now it slipped away, burning his hands in the process. The smell hit Theel's nose, the rank of death and rot flowing forth from that hellhole of a well. The boy was marinated in it. He'd managed to control his stomach for a small time, but now that control was gone.

He turned away just in time to vomit. He fell to his knees, alternately sobbing and retching as his body and mind reacted to the horrors of Calfborn, as if he could purge his mind as he purged his stomach.

"Yatham, grab his ankle," he heard Hoster saying. "Tightly, like this. Rasm, get over here. Squeeze tight, boy, and don't let go. Just like Yatham."

Theel's head was swimming, his nose and mouth burning. He kept his eyes pinched shut, not wanting to see anything, but tears still dripped from his eyelashes.

"Amazing that he still breathes, the poor bastard," Hoster was saying. "A blessing from God, for certain."

"Is there anything we can do?" Yatham asked.

"I got noose tourniquets," Hoster said. "And a bottle of butterfly wings."

Theel could hear the scraping and banging of boxes and casks being moved in the wooden cart.

"Rasm, where the hell are the tourniquets?" Hoster asked.

"What's a tourniquet?" Rasm asked.

"Here they are," Hoster said. "Theel, take this bottle. Are you done heaving yet?"

Theel didn't want to speak, or move, or do anything. He stayed on his hands and knees, eyes closed, trying to breathe without smelling. Slow breathes, slow and easy, through the mouth, not the nose. No more vomiting.

"Theel?" Hoster said. "You finished puking?"

"Yes," he managed to mumble. "No," he quickly added. "I don't know."

"You better find your manhood, boy, and do it now." Hoster plunked a bottle full of yellow liquid on the ground next to him. "Swallow your puke and dry your eyes. This boy is going to die while you cry like a maid."

It was a strangely familiar place Theel found himself in, weeping and berated, hating his chastiser, hating himself more.

"I know," he said. "I know."

"Fight your weakness, boy. Stand and fight. Find your manhood."

Stand and fight. Hoster was saying these words, but it was the voice of his father that Theel heard. He didn't say anything, but felt the familiar shame. The shame of inadequacy. He bathed in it, his only friend.

"Here, put this on his ankle," Hoster was saying. "Like this. Pull it as tight as you can, like a slipknot."

"Can we save him?" Yatham asked.

"It'll take a miracle," Hoster answered. "Get him drinking those butterfly wings. Rasm, you do it. Theel's worthless."

Worthless. The word was like a dagger. Theel had hoped the daggers would go away when his father died. But they didn't. And they were as sharp as ever. Daggers everywhere. Daggers where they weren't intended. Daggers of his own creation.

Fighting every urge to stay put, Theel forced himself to his feet, his head swimming, his chest wound throbbing as if someone was punching him there. He kept his eyes closed, too frightened to breathe.

"Are you well, Theel?" he heard Yatham ask.

He nodded slowly as he turned and opened his eyes.

The Overlie boy lay on the ground where Theel last saw him, a shriveled corpse that somehow still drew breath. But now tourniquets on his ankles stopped the flow of blood there. And his head was rested on Rasm's lap, where the young man held a bottle of yellow liquid to his lips.

"Drink this, uh ... butterfly ... uh ..." Rasm was saying. "... um ... drink this shit."

"How are you alive, you poor boy?" Hoster asked. "You must have lost enough blood to fill two men."

"I did?" Rasm asked. "When?"

"Not you, lumberhead," Hoster said. "Theel? You okay? Can you make a fire?"

"Yes," Theel said as confidently as he could, though he was not confident at all.

"Make it hot," Hoster instructed. "We need to burn the arrows out."

"We don't have time for that," Yatham said. "He'll die first."

"He should be dead already," Hoster said.

"We don't have time to make a fire," Yatham insisted.

"What else can we do?" Hoster said. "All we have are prayers now."

"We have more than prayers," Yatham replied.

"And what is that?" Hoster asked. "What do we have?"

"Theel?" Yatham said. He looked at his brother, who looked back, and said nothing.

"What do we have?" Hoster asked. "Why are you looking at him?"

"Theel?" Yatham pressed. "Do it."

"Do what?" Theel asked, staring at his brother, his eyes narrowing.

"Help this boy. You know you can."

Theel shook his head. "No I don't. No I can't."

"What are you weedheads yammering about?" Hoster asked. "Why aren't you building a fire?"

"Brother," Yatham said. "Help him. He will die without help."

"I can't help him. He will die either way."

"Heal him."

"You do not command me," Theel said, coolly.

"Heal him, brother."

"Heal both your shriveled brains!" Hoster said. "What are you talking about?"

"He has the power to heal," Yatham answer.

"Quiet yourself, brother," Theel said.

"The power?" Hoster looked at Yatham, incredulous. "You mean Theel's a juy priest?"

"What?" Rasm asked. "Theel's a... what?"

Theel shook his head. "I am not a priest!"

"Heal him brother," Yatham insisted.

"No. It is too difficult. I can't."

"But you can use the Method?" Hoster asked.

Theel stared at the ground. "I know of the Method, but I cannot control my juy." Then he mumbled, "It controls me."

"You must try," Yatham said.

338

Slowly, Theel moved his eyes to the Overlie boy. "It might kill him."

"He's dead anyway," Yatham said.

"I will fail."

"No you won't."

"It will help nothing."

"It will hurt nothing!" Yatham shouted. "You must try. Listen to me. Theel!"

Theel did not move, only stared at the boy, the last survivor of Calfborn, lying motionless, looking sightlessly at the sky, lips barely moving, delirious, oblivious. The boy didn't know where he was, who he was, or what happened to him or his family. His wits were weakened by pain, blood loss, and the spirit trader's devious mixture. But Theel knew it all. The juy flooding his brain showed it to him, despite his wishes.

Theel saw how the boy refused to be sent away, wanting to fight beside the men of the town, insisting he was old enough. He wanted to make his father proud. He wanted to show the smallfolk of Calfborn that he was an Overlie, and an Overlie did not flee from battle. An Overlie defended his people, and defended his family's lands.

The boy emulated Jarcet the Sentinel, following the knight into battle. He saw his friends die, and continued to fight bravely. He suffered a wound to his arm, and witnessed his uncle's death, and still fought on. He wanted to make his father proud.

But then he saw the Sentinel fall. And the moment the knight was overwhelmed and defeated, the boy's spirit was overwhelmed and defeated as well. That was when he ran, as fast as he could, eyes blinded by his tears. But he could not outrun the truth of what was happening. He couldn't outrun the defeat and the death that surrounded him. And he could not outrun the Iatan horses that chased him down.

He was dragged back to the town square, where he was tortured and filled with arrows. Theel felt every bit of the boy's suffering and despair, every bit of his pain at losing so many of his friends and family, seeing the town destroyed, losing his eye, his ear, his feet, spending hours in the well, gasping, suffocating.

Theel felt all of the boy's emotions as though they were his own. He felt so much more than he ever thought he could bear. He'd seen enough of the horrors of Calfborn, while being powerless to change any of it. He looked to the northeast, the direction the children of the town were taken. He drew his father's knife, looked at it, and turned it over. He looked at it hard, while everyone looked at him. Then he looked to the northeast again. His father's words echoed in his mind.

Stand and fight. Find your manhood. *Stand and fight.*

"What's he doing?" Rasm asked.

"Shut up," Hoster scolded. "Lumberhead."

Stand ... Theel rose to his feet. ... *and fight* ...

"Someone in this town is going to live," Theel proclaimed. "Someone in this town is going to live."

"By God's grace," Yatham added.

Theel walked to where the boy lay and knelt at his side. He took a broken arrow shaft in one hand, while using the other to dig into the boy's chest with his father's knife. After a bit of wiggling, he was able to pry the bloody arrowhead out of the wound and press two of his fingers inside. He pushed them down, through the soft, slippery flesh, past the ribs, until he could feel the weakened tremors of the boy's heart against his fingertips. Then he closed his eyes.

To heal. A skill beyond the abilities of all but the most proficient practitioners of the Juy Method. It required the highest level of awareness, the highest level of personal control—true mastery of one's own juy.

Theel could hear the whispering voice of the Keeper of the Craft, instructing him on the art of healing, the manipulation of the body by joining life forces. He'd heard these instructions a thousand times as he'd practiced, as he'd tried to learn, but as he'd constantly failed, as he'd lost control of his juy again and again. He must not fail this time.

Very slow, shallow breaths. Heart beating heavily. Theel took that first tentative step. Reaching out with his thoughts, he sought his psychic nexus. It was the well of energy, of life force that propelled his mind and kept his body whole. It was difficult to find, and nearly impossible to hold. This was his struggle, his soft, delicate, excruciating struggle—to hold the power, to allow it to fill his body without taking too much, or too little. Without losing control.

And just like the slow turning of a spigot, he felt the juy come. A very gentle flow, growing heavier, filling his body with warm, sizzling ecstasy. He had it. Just the right flow. He smiled. And breathed. And felt the weak heart flutter beneath his fingertips. It fluttered, and stopped.

No heartbeat.

"Don't panic," he whispered softly, his words thundering in his own head. "Still alive. Still a chance."

Relax your mind. Calm your fears. The Keeper's words.

Stand and fight. Find your manhood. His father's words.

Juy filled his body with warmth, and he knew that for that moment, he had some control, even if it was not complete. He knew he should stretch forth his hand to seize complete control, to complete the healing of this boy, the saving of his life. But to stretch out for complete control was an uncertainty for someone of his limited ability. Theel wasn't sure he had the discipline to do this properly, to take that first step. The first step was a dangerous one. To strive for more might be to lose everything he already had. Then the boy would die for certain. And so he tried to proceed with what control he had, to heal the boy without taking the proper step forward to complete his control. It might be enough. It had to be.

He directed the flow of his life force directly into the boy's heart. A steady flow of drops, hot, golden life, more than he'd ever given before, dripping out of him, into the boy. Drip. Drip. He could feel the drain, feel his own heart thudding heavily under the strain. Drip. Drip. His head began to pound, then it began to swim. A hot buzz filled his ears. Drip. Drip. He was giving too much of himself, but he couldn't turn it off. Not yet. The boy's heart would beat again. Drip. One more. Drip. Theel's vision failed. Stars exploded in his brain.

Drip. The boy's heart wasn't beating. Drip. The boy's heart wasn't beating.

Theel's control began to slip. Much like a toddler learning to stand on his own two feet, learning to balance weight, and often failing, Theel tried to stand, but felt himself falling, and hadn't the experience to catch himself. The baby could not stand on its own, and fell. And Theel fell as well, control slipping through his fingers. It was a familiar feeling, and in that instant he knew precisely what was wrong. His fear of losing control was precisely *why* he was losing control. His fear of failing was causing him to fail. Theel could not yet stand on his own. He didn't have the discipline or the maturity. He knew this with bitter certainty.

And he also knew that as he lost control, the juy would begin to control him, as had happened so many times before. He knew his mind was about to descend screaming into living nightmares once again. But this time, it wasn't merely his own failure he must face. It was the consequences of that failure. This time, a boy would die because of him.

Heal! Theel's mind screamed. *Heal!* What minor control he did have was now lost in desperation. In an instant, he felt himself washed over a waterfall of juy. In his desperation to force the boy back to life, he threw open the spigot and emptied himself of juy, pouring it into the boy's body by the bucketful. But it was too much. The boy could never withstand so much. Healing juy was to the body much like water was to flora. The proper amount will give life, but too much will only drown it.

Theel's juy, loosed from his control, danced wildly, like a serpent contorting in his hands and striking out at him. His heart thumped one more time. His brain throbbed in answer. Then silence, and emptiness. His body went numb. All senses disappeared, creating a great vacuum of silent blackness.

Then the Sight came, rushing in to fill that void, assaulting his mind with unwanted images—sights, sounds, smells, feelings, and emotions. He relived all the horrors of Calfborn, the pain and anguish of every citizen of the town, living or dead, all at once. It was overwhelming and unstoppable. He could see the past, the present, and the future of that very spot where he knelt over the dead Overlie boy. He could see himself, with fingers inside the boy's chest, head tossed back, screaming, eyes pinched tight, tears streaking his face. He could hear himself screaming for mercy. He heard his own voice begging for the juy to stop, to release him, for the Sight to end.

But it didn't end. It was too powerful, too strong, and so he succumbed. It wouldn't leave him, so he left the world and joined it, all the images. They absorbed him. The world was gone, and the delusions became his new reality.

The boy he tried to save was dead. He would not come back. This was Theel's last thought before his body failed him, before he passed out and collapsed upon the corpse, upon the proof of his most recent failure.

Again he slept. And again, the nightmares came.

CHAPTER 29

Theel found himself in a familiar place, lying on the edge of a rocky precipice high above the world. He couldn't see anything below but endless fog, as if he was miles above the tallest mountains, even higher than the clouds. There was no such place in all the Seven Kingdoms, and yet he knew exactly where he was. He'd visited this ledge countless times in his dreams, ever since his father's death.

He couldn't escape this dream. Just like his Sight, it came to him at random times. It was inevitable and unavoidable, tormenting him with a vision he desperately wished to avoid. No matter how he fought it, it forced its way into his slumbering mind, even when he drank himself to sleep. Even when his blood was so full of seraphim angels that he shouldn't have awakened for days, this nightmare haunted him, terrified him, and shocked him to cold, sweaty wakefulness.

It was always the same. He lay on his stomach, his arms stretched out beneath him, holding his father's life in his hands. The great Knight of the Southern Cross hung by one arm from his son's grasp, with nothing beneath his feet to support him, nothing but an endless drop and certain death should he fall.

"Give me your other hand," Theel grunted, straining.

His father looked at him with sadness, giving the same answer he always did. "I can't."

"Give me your other hand, Father," Theel pleaded. "I can save you. I can pull you up."

Theel's father shook his head. "Let me fall."

"Don't do this to me again," Theel said. "I can't bear it."

"I can't change the past. Neither can you."

"Why must I relive this agony?"

"You can't save me. You must save yourself. My life means nothing. Yours means everything."

"But we can mend this," Theel insisted. "There is still a chance for us to be father and son."

"There never was a chance for us," his father said. "I ruined everything. I am to blame for your pain. I was a terrible father. I deserve this fate."

"The fault is mine," Theel wept. "I was a terrible son."

"I was no father to you," his father said. "You deserved better."

"You were a good father. You did your best."

"I punished you, mercilessly, for wrongs you did not commit," his father said. "I tried to make you strong with cruelty. Such a fool I was. I am so sorry. Forgive me."

Then Theel heard his own voice echoing across the heavens like a peel of thunder, shouting familiar words.

"I will never forgive you! I hate you!"

His father had no verbal response, just a face of anguished acceptance. He looked old and beaten, like a weathered old tree, gnarled from years of stress and strain, tortured by the wind and rain of his own mistakes, and the knowledge of how badly those mistakes hurt his son. Now it was the father who wore the marks of countless beatings, the scars of emotional neglect. The guilt he felt was more than any man could bear.

"I know," he said sadly. "I know you won't forgive me. I know you hate me. I am a weight dragging you down, destroying your future. That is why I must die. So you might live."

"No!"

"Good-bye. I love you."

Then he slipped out of his son's fingers and was gone. Even though Theel knew this was going to happen, there was nothing he could do to stop it. And there was nothing he could do to stem the horror that filled his heart at the sight of his father falling to his death.

Just as he fell that day on the bridge. Just as he'd fallen so many times since.

And just like in every other dream, Theel wept bitterly. "Good-bye, Father," he said. "I love you."

Chapter 30

Theel reached out to fight something, to punch something. He clawed desperately at the air, searching for something he could feel in his hand, something he could hurt, or strangle. He needed a tangible object to visit his anger and frustration upon. He only accomplished getting tangled in his blankets and feeling the sensation of falling. He tried to catch himself, reaching out to grasp at the crates and barrels of Hoster's cart. Instead, he came up with handfuls of dirt.

"Yatham's not here," Theel heard a familiar voice say. "He's off searching for clean water."

Theel sat up, and once again felt the familiar thump of pain in his brain, bringing a wave of wooziness. He chest wound throbbed again, his swollen cheek joined in, but Theel angrily shoved these nuisances away by force of will, staying in his upright position even though his weary body begged him to lie back for more rest.

"What did you say?" he asked groggily.

"You were yelling for your brother. You well, boy?"

It was Hoster, sitting nearby, his big rump planted atop his rickety camp chair. The old spirit trader sat near a freshly built fire, burning kindling that was snapping with sparks and smoke. A large iron pot sat upon the ground between Hoster's legs, catching the chunks of a carrot he was dicing.

"No, I'm not fine, but do you really care?" Theel said, rubbing his neck.

"I suppose I don't care, my boy," Hoster said. "But I don't need any sick heads near my supper. Bad for my fragile health, and my fragile temperament."

"I'll do my best to respect the needs of your fragile temperament," Theel said, "if you will stop calling me *boy*."

Hoster sniffed, finished his carrot, and picked up another while Theel took in his surroundings. He wasn't surprised to see Chigger and Ragweed lounging nearby, unhitched and lying near the cart, calmly chewing on some dried alfalfa, looking about as content as two mules could look. The camp appeared to be on the crown of a wooded hill, with aspens all around, their branches dancing in the cool breeze. Theel himself lay on a bed of moss near a rotting log, a cool but soft and comfortable resting place, no doubt chosen for him by his brother.

His nose caught a smell that was out of place in these woods; out of place in fact, for their entire trip thus far. It instantly brought thoughts of the feast hall in the belly of the Hall of Seven Swords in Fal Daran. He could almost hear the clamor of the soldiers as they lined the benches, spooning hot, greasy water to their lips.

But this smelled liked something so much better; like the food served at the high table when the king dined with his knights. This was a feast he smelled, cooking and bubbling and hot with spices, whose scent hit his nose first and then his stomach. Theel suddenly realized he'd never been so hungry in his life.

"What is that I smell?" he asked.

"That, my boy, is our supper, yours and mine," Hoster said, now dicing a celery stalk into the pot. "Tonight we will feast in ways the road life rarely allows. You'll find this old spirit trader can cook more than just booze. I can boil some damned tasty soup, if you'll allow me. And that's what you're smelling right now."

"Where did you find vegetables?" Theel asked.

Hoster's face darkened, but only slightly. "Tonight we dine courtesy of the good folks of Calfborn, God rest their souls. And may he bless those who still live, the poor bastards, wherever they are."

Theel looked at the ground, his face darkening as well. "God gave no blessings to that town," he muttered. "Or its people."

"May seem that way, if that's how you choose to see it," Hoster said. "Many awful things to see in that town; things that bad dreams are made of."

Theel coughed. "Yeah. Bad dreams." He began to dig in his pack.

"It's what war looks like," Hoster mumbled. "Better get used to it. There's lots more war coming. Those Iatan are here to stay."

Theel found the object of his search, a pipe and a pouch, wrapped in a large, green leaf. He opened the pouch and turned its contents into the pipe.

"Ever see anything like what they did to that town?" Hoster asked.

Theel shook his head, packing the bowl, sticking the pipe stem between his teeth. "Fire?"

"Rasm's not here." Hoster smiled. "But don't fret. I got more traditional methods of setting things afire."

The old spirit trader pulled a stick from the campfire, one with a flame dancing on its end, holding it out for Theel to use with his pipe.

"You're a squire of the Southern Cross, so I figure you've seen some battle," Hoster said, putting the stick back in the fire.

"Some." Theel took a huge puff, and shook his head again. "But nothing like this."

"I know what you're saying," Hoster said, shaking his head sadly. "There's enough zoths in the world to destroy a town like that, if they could get organized. But they don't do it. Only humans marching in armies can do that."

Theel only looked at Hoster blankly, smoking.

"You don't say anything and I know why," Hoster said. "It's because I'm feeling what you're feeling. I'm thinking the same thing as you."

"What are we thinking?" Theel asked.

Hoster sighed, looking sad. "We're not going to win this war. Not the way we're fighting it."

Again, Theel was silent, puffing on his pipe.

"We've been fighting zoths forever," Hoster said. "We want to live, but the zoths want to fight. Everywhere there is zoths, there is war. You know it's true. Your knights always do the hard lifting, fighting the zoths on every frontier; but they don't fight humans. The knights want to protect human life, not destroy it."

"That's what they say," Theel mumbled.

"These Iatan are different," Hoster said. "They're not like us at all. They don't want to live in peace. They want war. They raise huge armies and go out and burn everything down. No sense in that at all."

Theel shook his head. "None at all."

"You hear the stories from the Eastern Kingdoms?" Hoster asked.

Theel stared into the fire. "I have."

"The whispers say they killed Adionthel of Sidon without a fight," Hoster said. "He died with his sword still sheathed, meeting their generals to talk peace, but they murdered him. Then they burned his knights alive. You heard that?"

"I heard," Theel mumbled into his pipe.

"They say Sidon fell after only a month of fighting," Hoster said, no longer cutting the vegetables, but hacking at them angrily. "They say there's almost nothing left of Sidon. Those Iatan armies lay waste to the countryside everywhere they go. They burn the grain stores and anything that's still growing in the fields. They slaughter the animals and leave them to rot in their pens. And they ruin every source of water they find. Shows you what talking peace with those bastards will get you."

Theel sniffed and cleared his throat, and went on smoking.

"Why would they burn the grain and kill the cattle?" Hoster asked. "Why do they despoil the well water? Iatan have no need for food or drink?"

"I don't know."

"They kill every man of fighting age and enslave every woman of birthing age," Hoster said. "The young are murdered in their beds. The old are buried alive. Anyone who resists loses their feet."

Theel felt an unwelcome chill. "I've heard the stories. I don't need to hear them again from you."

"These Iatan bastards, they don't want to conquer—they want to destroy." Hoster nodded his head angrily, the veins on his neck standing out. "That scene in Calfborn is proof to me the whispers are true. These bastards don't want to rule us. They want to destroy us. This isn't any war for wealth or land. It's a war of genocide."

"It's a war of souls," Theel muttered.

"It's the Second War of Souls," Hoster said. "How do we deny it after that scene back there?"

"I don't deny it."

"Then why do you refuse our only chance to live?" Hoster asked. "Why do you quit on our salvation?"

The question grabbed Theel's attention firmly. He looked up to see the old spirit trader staring at him accusingly.

Theel took a pull off his pipe and said, "Drink your booze. Cut your carrots."

"Don't hide from my questions," Hoster stated, his voice uncharacteristically firm.

"You intend to be serious with me now?" Theel asked. "You who inhales liquor like it's air, curses all living things, and mentions scatter with every other word?"

"I'll talk of my flaws," Hoster said. "I know my ass stinks more than most people's. I'll tell you about it. I'm not ashamed. I'll talk all day."

"Please don't."

"Same with Rasm and Chigger and Ragweed, and even your brother," Hoster went on. "We're all ugly and dirty before God, there's no denying it. But what about you, my boy? Are you ready to face who you are?"

"What do you wish me to say?" Theel asked.

"I wish for you to answer me," Hoster answered. "Why do you quit on our only chance to survive this war?"

"What chance is that?" Theel asked. "What do I quit on?"

"You know what I speak of," Hoster retorted. "What is this quest of yours about? What will earn you Warrior Baptism?"

Theel only glared angrily. "I do not quit my quest for Warrior Baptism."

Hoster threw his knife on the ground. "Oh, that's a heap of scatter and we both know it. You're not even trying to get to the Outlands. You're going to the Dead Man's Bridge to die."

"I have good reason to go to the Dead Man's Bridge."

Hoster shook his head. "You'll find nothing there but the Crowlord."

"Perhaps I mean to find the Crowlord."

"Then you mean to die, because the Crowlord means death," Hoster accused.

"I have my reasons," Theel said. "Reasons beyond your knowledge."

"Dying on that that bridge will not bring you Warrior Baptism," Hoster said. "You would not be going there if you cared about this quest. You don't even wish to be a knight at all, do you?"

Theel clicked his teeth on his pipe stem. "No, I don't."

"So what are you doing out here on these roads, then?" Hoster asked. "Me and Rasm have good reason. There's the king's work to be earned. What about you?"

Theel looked off into the trees. "I don't know what you are asking me."

"Why are you wandering stupidly, with a stupid look on your face?" Hoster asked. "Dragging your brother across the Western Kingdoms, talking about finding a place to sit down and die?"

"I don't travel to the Dead Man's Bridge to die," Theel sputtered angrily. "And I do not quit on this quest."

"Oh, you quit on everything." Hoster looked back into the fire. "You never started nothing you haven't quit. Sometimes you quit before you're started."

"That's not true."

"Why do you even strive for knighthood at all?" Hoster asked.

"That's none of your concern," Theel answered.

"You're just pretending," Hoster stated.

"That's not true."

"You are a squire, ready to be a knight any day now," Hoster said. "I know the knights. I know what it takes to make a Knight of the Southern Cross, and I know what it takes to make a squire. It is not for the weak. Only those with strong minds and strong backs answer that call."

"So?"

"So, I know you've been through hell to make it this far," Hoster explained. "Yet you've no heart for this."

"How to you know what is in my heart?" Theel asked.

"A blind man could see it," Hoster answered. "You're not especially quiet about your anger toward your father, or toward the knighthood."

"I choose not to speak of the knighthood."

"But you don't espouse any of their creeds," Hoster said. "Your beliefs and their beliefs are not the same. You wear that glove and you carry weapons with markings of the knighthood, but inside you have no faith. Looks to me like your brother is more suited for knighthood than you are."

"You presume to know so much about me," Theel grumbled. "The all-seeing spirit trader."

"So why would you go through all the trouble to become a squire, only to quit while on your quest for Warrior Baptism?" Hoster asked.

"I told you," Theel said. "I do not quit."

Hoster looked Theel square in the eye. "Is this quest of yours to find the Blessed Soul of Man?"

Theel stared back at the old spirit trader, causing many moments of tense silence. Then he asked, "Did Yatham tell you this?"

Hoster went back to his cutting, satisfaction etched across his face. "Yatham told me nothing of the sort. But I know. I'm no fool. I learned a thing or two all these years pounding the stones. I know people. And I know you."

"What do you know about me?" Theel asked.

"I know your quest is to find the Blessed Soul," Hoster answered. "I know because you just told me."

Theel threw his arms up. "Then my secret quest is a secret no more. I don't care who knows."

Hoster snorted. "Don't care about much, do you?"

"Perhaps it is better this way," Theel said. "Now you can know, and the world will know with you. The knighthood is a sham. Their creeds are worthless, because their religion is dead—based on an empty promise. There *is* no Blessed Soul of Man. Would you like to hear how I know this?"

Hoster sighed. "Because you're smarter than the rest of us?"

"I know this, because you are correct about one thing," Theel said. "My quest for Warrior Baptism is to find the Blessed Soul. It is true. The hopes and dreams of all God-fearing Thershoni rest on what I find in the Outlands. All their prayers are with me. Every night, as they lay their heads down, they are crying out for their Lord to deliver them from the Iatan. They are begging him to send their Blessed Soul to them, to fulfill the prophecies and lead the Seven Kingdoms to victory. Their only hope is that the Blessed Soul will be found, and it is I who must find him. Me. You aren't laughing, spirit trader, but you should be. These people are relying on someone who cannot bring their Blessed Soul to them. I am not prepared for this. I am not sufficient to the task. You are all placing your hope on something that is hopeless—a hopeless quest, undertaken by a hopeless person."

Hoster stared at Theel, thinking, his face tinged with pity. "It's a shame you think that way."

"Don't you look down upon me, spirit trader." Theel puffed hard on his pipe. "Know this, and know it well. I will not find the Blessed Soul in the Outlands. Not only because he is not there waiting to be found, but because I don't intend to search for him. Why search for something that can't be found? I will never find the Blessed Soul of Man, and I will never become a knight. Fal Daran will fall to the Iatan and we will lose this war. All the prayers in the world can't change that."

"Yes, they can," Hoster insisted.

"No, they can't, because those prayers are heard by a cruel and uncaring god, who makes promises he does not intend to keep," Theel said. "If the Blessed Soul was really out there, waiting to be found so he could save the world, do you really think he would tolerate the knights sending *me* to find him? This quest was meant for a Knight of the Southern Cross, or a squire who is firm in his faith, who knows in his heart that the Blessed Soul is real, and that this quest will succeed. Instead, it is all up to me. And I don't plan to search for the Blessed Soul. I'm going to the Outlands for the same reasons as you—to hide from this war, or to die, I don't care which. The Blessed Soul is not in my future, because I refuse him. I refuse you!" Theel shouted at the sky. "No loving god would answer the prayers of his followers with a blasphemer like me. Forget your faith, old man. Lie down and wait to die. Or go throw yourself at the Iatan. Both actions are equally useless. And both actions have as much value as holding out hope, having faith in your prophecy, and praying for the arrival of some savior of the Seven Kingdoms, who won't show himself, who sits around *waiting* to be found."

"Oh, and your time is precious?" Hoster calmly asked. "All that time you spend smoked and stupid?"

"Drink your booze," Theel growled. "Cut your carrots."

"I'll drink my booze, and I'll do it with pride," Hoster said. "I'm not ashamed of who I am. I'm not ashamed of my beliefs."

"Glad for you," Theel muttered, fuming. "Take another drink."

"You must do something to kill that bitterness in your belly," Hoster said. "You must learn forgiveness, not for those you think done you wrong. Not for the knighthood, or the Blessed Soul, or your father. You need to forgive them for *yourself*, or your heart will never heal."

Theel waved his pipe. "Meaningless words."

"Secure those smart lips, boy, or I'll do it for you," Hoster warned. "You said your mind, now I'll speak mine."

Theel shrugged. "Why listen to words that have no value in them?"

"My words have no value?" Hoster asked. "You woke up and said to me you will not quit your quest. That was just before your little sermon where you said you've quit on your quest. Having trouble deciding?"

"I don't make my decisions to suit you," Theel grumbled.

"You don't make decisions at all," Hoster accused. "I'll never know why the Keeper of the Craft sent a snot like you to search for the Blessed Soul. Why didn't he send a *real* man to do it? Someone with a strong mind, and strong faith? Why didn't he send a Knight of the Southern Cross? Why you?"

"You ask me as if I know the answer," Theel said. "Perhaps the Keeper has lost his mind."

"Stop your talking about the Keeper," Hoster ordered. "No more talk of anyone else—not the Keeper, not me, not your brother nor Rasm. Talk for a moment about yourself."

"No need to," Theel said smugly.

"Oh, the need is there," Hoster insisted. "There's plenty of need for that. Forget the Blessed Soul. Forget the war. You don't believe in them anyway. What are you doing with yourself? Why are you here?"

"I decided to come here," Theel answered. "I go where I wish. No one commands me, not anymore."

"That is a mountain of scatter balls," Hoster said. "You didn't decide to come here. You don't even want to be here. You don't know why you do anything. Your whole life, you've searched for meaning by disapproving of others. Am I right?"

Theel stared at the spirit trader with anger in his eyes.

"I am right," Hoster stated. "I hear you piss about your father. I hear you piss about the Knights of the Southern Cross. You gripe and whine so much, you don't even know anything else."

"That's not true," Theel said with very little conviction.

"Your father is no longer here to command you," Hoster said. "You are out on the trails, free of the demands of the knighthood and there is no one to guide you. You alone must decide which path you will walk. Only you are afraid of decisions. You are intimidated by choices, so you shrink away from them." Hoster pointed at the sky. "You couldn't decide if that's the sun or the moon. Now you got some hard decisions to make, and you don't know what to do. You can no longer define yourself by condemning the actions of others. Now you must define yourself by what you *do*. Now you must find out who you are by choosing your own way."

"A sudden burst of eloquence from the drunkard," Theel said half-heartedly.

"Complaining doesn't get you anywhere," Hoster went on. "You're seeing that now, even if you won't admit it to me. Stop standing *against* everything. Start standing *for* something. Stop hating everything. Start loving something."

Theel's eyes smoldered but he remained silent, absorbing the words.

"You keep complaining by habit," Hoster said. "You keep talking about what other folks are doing. You don't talk about what *you* are doing. Don't tell me what other folks *shouldn't* do. Tell me what you *should* do. What should you do? What will you do?"

Theel stared into the fire, a very miserable look on his face.

Hoster kept going. "Life is punching you in the face and booting you in the ass. How are you going to react? Will you sit and complain about it? Or will you grow up and be a man? Will you quit and run? Or will you stand and fight?"

Theel didn't bite back with his usual angry words. Instead, there was a brief moment where the anger and resentment were replaced with something else. His eyes were those of a child, a child who was hurting, full of fear and uncertainty.

"What would you have me do?" he asked.

"What would I have you do?" Hoster said incredulously. "Why are you asking *me* that? My words getting into that hard head of yours? You finally listening to me?"

"It was a simple question, asked in honesty," Theel stated.

"An honest question deserves an honest answer," Hoster admitted. "So I'll give you one. Stop your pissing and moaning. There's too much good in this world to piss all day as you do. Your brother is as faithful and loyal a friend as I've ever seen. Yet your mouth spits nothing but scorn at him."

"Should I follow your lead?" Theel asked. "Should I take your treatment of Rasm as an example?"

"Yes."

"What?" Theel looked very confused.

"You can't believe in anything until you believe in yourself," Hoster said. "You can't love anything until you love yourself. For me, there's Rasm; that damned, log-headed idiot. I hate him, but I love him. And those stinking flea farms over there looking at me stupid. It's not like Rasm, but I love my mules, too. They and Rasm are all I got, and I love 'em."

"I'm glad of that," Theel snorted. "What are you telling me?"

"You don't have a care for anything going on around you because you don't have a care for yourself," Hoster said. "You don't have a care for the knights or your father—"

"Don't speak of my father," Theel warned. "You don't know. You don't understand."

Hoster took a deep breath. "Very well, then. I won't speak of your father," he said. "I'll speak of my father instead. You think you're the only boy ever to take a beating?"

Theel didn't say anything, but he stopped puffing on his pipe. Instead he held it on his lap, listening intently.

"The only difference between you and me is your father apologized," Hoster said quietly. "Mine didn't. He died hating me, probably regretting that he didn't wallop me more."

"I'm sorry to hear that," Theel said.

"I'm not asking for pity," Hoster said. "Many folks got it worse than me. That's the thought that keeps me sane. That, and the occasional nip of pig swill. You got to remember, it could be worse. You got to remember, it can always get better."

"I don't see how," Theel said.

"It'll get better if you just keep going," Hoster said. "Stepping feet warm the blood, and the heart. I learned that when I took up the spear and marched against the zoths for Yarik. I hid myself among the foot soldiers for years, but my father's ghost still followed me. I learned from the warrior's life that you can't run from your problems. I also learned to cook booze. And how to drink it. I couldn't count how my times I almost drank myself to death. But I never did. No matter how I tried, I still woke up afterward. God refused to let go of me. Then he gave me Rasm. And Rasm changed my life."

"How?" Theel asked.

"He taught me how to love something, the damned fool lumberhead. You see? Hate destroys, but love will save your soul. You have to stop hating everything and start loving something."

Theel still wasn't smoking, only staring into the fire. "I don't know how."

"Because you don't love yourself," Hoster said. "Earn your self-respect, and you will earn respect from others. You will learn to respect others. You will learn to believe, and you will learn to love. I see you shaking your head, but listen to me. This old fart has walked every road that cuts through these Western Kingdoms, greater and lesser. I got a lot of dust on my ass, and I've seen a thing or two. This is something I know. You'll not learn these things from listening to me. But you'll learn them from life. You can't be told this wisdom. But you can learn it on your own. From life."

"From life?" Theel shook his head. "You're making no sense."

"You'll never learn if you give up," Hoster said. "You'll never learn if you lay down and die. You will learn by striving. You will learn if you stand and fight for something."

"But how?" Theel asked.

"Just keep going," Hoster answered. "Keep your eyes and your ears open, and you will learn. I can't teach you with words, but life will teach you with experience. God will give you the lessons. He will be your teacher. Just keep walking and wisdom will come, in time."

"You tell me to wait for something to happen," Theel grumbled. "You tell me my hands are tied. This I already know."

Hoster shook his head "Your hands aren't tied."

"When I rise from bed tomorrow, what should I do?" Theel asked.

"You want to quit on something? Start by quitting with all these damned fool notions about crossing the Dead Man's Bridge," Hoster said. "I swear to you. You will find nothing but an early grave on those rocks."

"I have valid reasons for taking that route," Theel insisted.

"You should walk with me and Rasm to the Outlands," Hoster said. "You should find the preacher, Father Brashfor. Talk to him. He's a whole bucket of scatterbrains, but a good fellow in the end. Talk to him, and he might help you. Don't do it looking for the Blessed Soul. Do it looking for yourself."

"For myself?" Theel asked. "That sounds very much like what the Keeper of the Craft says. Or what my brother, Yatham, says."

"What do they say?" Hoster asked.

"They say this quest isn't for the Seven Kingdoms," Theel explained. "It's for me."

"That's true. That's good wisdom."

"They say I don't search for the Blessed Soul as much as I search for myself," Theel mumbled absently.

"Do it for yourself," Hoster said. "Believe in yourself."

"I believe in myself."

"There's room for more," Hoster said. "Stop the talk about dying. Stop the talk about quitting. Keep stepping, one foot in front of the other, like I tell my mules. Keep walking. Watch and listen. Before you know it, we'll be in Ebon South, far from the war. We'll talk to Father Brashfor, and who knows what will happen then?"

"Perhaps nothing will happen," Theel mumbled into the fire.

"Perhaps," Hoster said. "Maybe it will be for nothing. But you can't say it's worse than dying. And getting your brother killed, too. Maybe you can start a new life in the Outlands. No knights. No wars. Maybe you can find a woman. Maybe there will be a nice little lady who will let you put a baby in her belly? Someone to grow old and fat with, eh?"

Theel rolled his eyes.

"But maybe," Hoster smiled, "maybe you will find the Blessed Soul of Man. What's good for you just might be good for the Seven Kingdoms. What is the risk in that? Just walk on down to Ebon South with me and Rasm. Just walk that far. I'm your friend. You can trust me."

"You're my friend?" Theel chuckled. "I've heard that before."

"I'm your friend. You can trust me," Hoster said again. "Old Hoster's word is as good as ... well, I lie like hell, but only when I'm trading. I don't lie to my friends. You're my friend. You can trust me."

"All right then," Theel said. "I'll trust you."

Hoster held out his hand. "Shake?"

Theel reached out and shook the old spirit trader's hand. "I still must go to the Dead Man's Bridge."

"Not this again!" Hoster exclaimed. "Have you been listening to me?"

"I've listened to every word."

"There's too many zoths down there," Hoster insisted. "They'll catch us and skin us."

"You don't have to follow me," Theel explained. "Yatham and I will go alone."

"But you can't go alone. You won't survive."

"We go alone. Without you and Rasm. I have my reasons."

"They better be good reasons," Hoster said. "They'll mean your death. Both yours and your brother's."

"Don't worry about my brother and me," Theel said. "We will be fine."

"You wish to die."

"I do not wish to die," Theel said. "I am merely prepared for it. You must understand, I'm only doing what I must. The Dead Man's Bridge is necessary to me."

"Necessary to you? How is that?"

"You spoke to me honestly about your past. Now I will return the favor," Theel said. "You tell me to go to the Outlands for myself, but I tell you, the Dead Man's Bridge is where I must go, for myself."

Hoster raised an eyebrow. "You've made that decision? You are walking toward that goal?"

"I am walking toward that goal," Theel said. "I must. I cannot allow this opportunity to evaporate.

"What do you mean?"

"I never expected to come this far," Theel answered. "I never expected to leave Fal Daran, but my hand was forced. I nearly drowned, but Yatham saved me. You saved me, and your mules brought me this far against my will. And now that I'm this close, I will finish what you and Yatham started. I will finished the journey. I do this willingly. I am choosing it. I am putting one foot in front of the other, as you say."

"What of Warrior Baptism?"

"That can wait."

"No, it can't," Hoster said. "This war is happening now. There will be more Calfborns every day. The world can't wait around for you."

"You forget something, spirit trader," Theel said. "If the prophecies are true, then they will be fulfilled, no matter what you or I do. To say otherwise is lack of faith, is it not?"

"Perhaps."

"And perhaps you and my brother and the Keeper are not considering something," Theel went on. "Perhaps the prophecies are ready for me, but I'm not ready for them. The Keeper says the time for Warrior Baptism is now. I say it is not. Not yet."

"Not yet? What do you mean?"

"You've said it yourself," Theel explained. "I don't deserve to be a knight. I have no faith. I have no heart. My brother seems better suited for it than I do. Knighthood is the realm of men, and yet you persist in calling me *boy*."

"I didn't mean—"

"I'm not ready. No one knows that more than I," Theel said.

"When will you be ready?" Hoster asked.

"I may never be," Theel answered. "All that is important is that I am not ready now. I have no faith in myself, and I do not care about Warrior Baptism. There is something more important for me."

"And this thing that is so important," Hoster asked. "You think it can be found on the Dead Man's Bridge?"

"It is there. And I will find it."

"I guarantee you. All that awaits you on that bridge is the Crowlord and death," Hoster persisted. "So again I will ask you; is it your own death that is so important to you? Is that what you hope to find?"

"No, spirit trader, it is not," Theel said. "But if death finds me on that bridge, I will be content with that."

"Then what is on the Dead Man's bridge that is so important you'll risk death?" Hoster asked again. "What is it you seek there?"

Theel tapped the still-burning contents of his pipe onto the ground. "Judgment, spirit trader," he said, crossing his arms. "I seek judgment."

CHAPTER 31

The elderly priest knelt before the stone prayer altar at the front of his church, head bowed, lips moving silently in prayer. His arms were raised, hands pressed firmly against the altar, as if he found comfort in the cold stone, as if he drew strength from the church building itself. Sweat beaded on his forehead, trickling down a face reddened and stressed. Tears formed on his eye lashes as he shook his head with the passion of his prayer. Though it appeared as if this man was making the most fervent appeal of his life, few bore witness.

It was not church day at the Chapel of God's Grace. There would be no singing, no sermon. The benches were filled, but not with the usual church day congregation. They were filled with the bodies of the dead, and those who were soon to be.

The Chapel of God's Grace served the Outlander town of Ebon South. Positioned on the southern frontier of the Kingdom of Embriss, Ebon South was often the target of zoth attacks. This day, the zoths brought their worst.

The church, always a sanctuary for the spiritually needy, quickly became a refuge for the physically needy, a destination for those who'd fallen in the defense of the town. First it was a trickle of soldiers helping brethren whose wounds prevented them from fighting on. Then it became a flood, men and women of Embriss and Yarik stumbling through the front doors, crawling, or being carried, screaming, crying and gushing blood. The church became an impromptu hospital, with dying townspeople lying on every bench and chair, covering every inch of floor space, all but the center aisle. This was kept clear to allow easy movement for the women who'd come to help tend to the wounded.

The elderly priest remained kneeling on the stone floor long past the point where his knees were numbed. The windows of the church were shuttered, but that didn't spare his ears the sounds of the battle outside, the crackling of the flames as the town burned, the ringing of sword and shield as the fighting raged on. He could smell the stink of the smoke. He could hear the screams of the dying, zoths and clansmen alike. His church was filled with the cries and groans of a hundred men, and the weeping of a few women overwhelmed by their inability to help each one. Blood and death were everywhere, on everything—soaking the carpet, soaking his clothing. It was more than enough to cause any God-fearing soul to cry out to his maker.

None of this is why the priest prayed.

Just that morning, the priest had laid eyes on the one whose coming heralded a terrible darkness, as prophesied in the holy book of Sun Antheus. The Blessed Soul of Man. The priest saw the little boy with his own eyes. All his life he'd studied the Chronicles of Sun Antheus, all the prophecies concerning the Day of the Seven Eyes. All his life he felt it was his duty as a child of God to prepare the world for the coming of the Blessed Soul to the best of his ability. He never dreamed the war would be fought in his own lifetime.

He knew it the instant he saw the little boy with the golden skin and the white hair, all the signs he was born of a race foreign to the Seven Kingdoms. The knight called the Zealot brought the boy to him that morning, and he knew just by looking into the eyes of little Eleod that he was truly something special. Gavin told the priest the story of how he'd acquired the boy, and the old man listened intently, not surprised by a single word. He'd always known how the Blessed Soul would come. Now he had come.

The knowledge brought both joy and sorrow.

Joy, because the Blessed Soul of Man had come. Because the old priest delighted in witnessing God's will made manifest. Because the Blessed Soul was destined to one day ride forth as

God's champion among mortals, to deliver the Seven Kingdoms from evil, from endless war, from sin.

Sorrow, because the Blessed Soul of Man had come. Because he'd chosen the Seven Kingdoms, birthplace of the old Clans of the Silvermarsh to make his home, to live his life, and to fight his war.

The realization brought fear to the old man's heart—fear for his land, his people, and fear for the children of Embriss. For God had chosen their home as the battleground. It could not be denied. The old priest had seen the little boy with his own eyes. To deny it would be to deny his own faith.

The prophecies said the Year of Revelation would come during that little boy's lifetime. The gate would open for the Dark One's champion, the Serharek, to emerge at the vanguard of his armies of darkness. Awaiting him, challenging him, defying him, would be this little boy, God's Blessed Soul of Man. And this was where he'd chosen to make his stand, on the soil of the ancient clans. The Seven Kingdoms would be his battleground. The children of Embriss would make his armies.

The Blessed Soul would be victorious, the priest knew. The forces of evil would fail, as the prophecy stated. But the prophecy also said there would be seven battles. Six of them would end in defeat for the armies of goodness. Six of the Seven Kingdoms were meant to die. They would be sacrificed to win victory, to purchase freedom from the darkness that the Serharek was sure to bring. Salvation would come as the prophecies said. But the priest knew it would not be a deliverance of hope or joy, but one of fire.

The priest told Gavin the Zealot all he needed to know, confirmed the boy's identity, and stressed the importance of safeguarding Eleod's well-being. Now that the Blessed Soul had arrived, all the forces of evil would come looking for him. The devils wanted his blood.

But not a drop must be spilt. Not until God allowed it.

The knight took the child away, stating he would seek the counsel of the great wizard of Fal Daran known as the Keeper of the Craft. He took the boy with him to the small fortress in the center of town called Storm Hall. Then the zoths struck the town.

The fighting continued all day and into the night. The priest was not frightened for little Eleod. The prophecies said the Blessed Soul would die by Gilligod, the Devil Device, not zoth spears. And he knew the little boy was in the protection of one of the more able fighters among the knighthood. But all this couldn't stop the worry in his heart.

He feared for the safety of his daughters, the two orphan girls he loved and cared for as his own. They disappeared soon after the fighting began. He knew they would want more than anything to be at his side, helping with the wounded, praying with those who were dying, aiding him as he administered to the spiritual needs of the people in this time of crisis. He knew they would want to be with him if the zoths brought war to the Chapel of God's Grace. They would willingly do their part if the wounded soldiers needed protection.

But both of his girls were gone. They went missing soon after the priest met with Gavin the Zealot. He told them nothing of what transpired during that meeting, but strangely, the eldest took particular interest in the knight's whereabouts. She left, her little sister in tow. Then the zoths attacked, and they never returned. The priest tried not to dwell on it, but he knew there was a good chance they were caught up in the fighting. He knew there was a good chance one or both were hurt or dead.

With so much on his mind, he hardly noticed when the doors in the back of the Chapel of God's Grace were swept open so hard they banged against the rear-most pews, rattling loudly on their hinges.

The sounds of women screaming caught his attention. He stood and turned his head in time to see his eldest daughter rushing into the rear of the church. She came in from the hellish streets turned orange by the fiery sky, snowflakes swirling about her body as she ran down the center aisle toward him.

At first, he felt relief. At first, he smiled, happy to see his daughter safe. But the words of greeting died on his lips when he saw the look of hatred carved into her face. It was a face of evil, of murderous intent. It was a look his daughter was incapable of.

He knew it instantly. This was not his daughter.

One of the windows of the church exploded; painted glass, shutters and all. Something like a burst of golden sunlight crashed through, smashing a wooden bench to pieces, exploding on the stone floor amidst a storm of dust and splinters. It was like a comet had exploded in the middle of the Chapel of God's Grace. But as the dust and broken glass tinkled to the floor, a small figure rose to its feet, making it clear this was no comet.

The priest gasped when he saw her, the small woman standing naked in his church. But it wasn't just her nudity that shocked him. He could see that this woman was of the same race as Eleod, the Blessed Soul of Man. She shined like a golden-skinned angel, with pale lips, white hair, and eyes to match. They had no color; no irises and no pupils. Just two pools of milk. And though there was little breeze within the walls of the church, her snowy locks whipped about her head as if she stood in a hurricane.

As she stood and surveyed the room, her eyes changed from white to a smoldering red, like two glowing coals, distorting the air with their heat. When she saw the priest's daughter, she scrambled across the pews on all fours, the look on her face no fairer than that of the girl she rushed toward. There was nothing but murder in her eyes.

The priest looked back to see his daughter running toward him, shocked to see knives in her hands, horrified to see her throwing them at him! He fell back against the altar, raising his arms up defensively, shouting in dismay, calling for God's protection. But the knives did not strike him. Instead, there were multiple whooshing sounds like a dozen swinging whips, and the knives clattered to the floor.

For a moment, he cowered against the stone altar, covering his face in his hands. He felt his body reacting to the terror, even if his mind didn't. His heartbeat thundered in his ears. His breath came in gasps, and shivers racked his body. But his mind seemed to be in a place of calm. He knew strange things would happen the day the Blessed Soul came into the world. The prophecy warned of widespread strife, chaos, and war. The zoth attack on the town, the worst attack the priest had ever seen, now seemed to make perfect sense. His adopted daughters disappearing, one of them now returning to kill him. Then another woman with golden skin and white hair, the same race as the Blessed Soul, smashing through the wall into this church as if she'd fallen from heaven.

There was reason for all this.

The world had changed with the coming of the Blessed Soul. All the rules were different. Everything was turned askew, and it wouldn't right itself until the Day of the Seven Eyes, when the Serharek and the Blessed Soul of Man would confront one another. The war had begun, and two of its combatants had come to fight the first battle. Right there. In his church.

All this raced through the old priest's mind in a matter of moments, the time it took him to draw a few shaky breaths, the time it took him to force his trembling hands away from his face. The knives had not touched him, but lay scattered about the floor. Not far away he saw the golden angel holding his daughter by the throat. White, snake-like appendages sprang from the woman's body, striking at his daughter with the speed and viciousness of vipers.

It all seemed like a dream to the priest. Everything seemed to slow down. He knew he should be terrified, but calmness reigned in his mind. This was the most intense and overwhelming experience of his long life, yet he felt very removed from it all. He felt a stabbing pain in his chest, but was only dimly aware of it. His knees had given out long ago. He could feel himself falling, his heart thumping loudly, streaks of pain shooting down his left arm. He didn't feel a thing as his body hit the floor, his head bouncing off the stone. It was as if his struggle was over. His work was done, and now God was protecting him from the pain, taking him away into peacefulness.

He reached out, and felt someone take his hand, a warm and gentle grasp, leading him home.

Then for one brief moment, the fog lifted and sight returned to the old priest's staring eyes. He was lying on his back, looking up into the face of the golden woman. She looked down upon the old priest with anger and frustration in her white eyes. She seemed to be saying something, her lips moving as her eyes once again turned red, then back to white again. The priest realized that this woman was trying to revive him.

But he didn't want to be revived. He continued to hold the guiding hand. A simple thing, this grasp, but so full of kindness and love. He wouldn't let go of that love. And it would not let go of him.

His time had come, and he was at peace with that. No matter what anyone says, a man's life will go on until the moment God is finished with him, and not before. The priest had done all that was asked of him. His purpose on this earth was done. And now God was calling him home. The warm embrace of the Almighty awaited.

His face was numb, but his mind was smiling as he looked up at the golden woman.

You will lose this war, the old priest thought. *The Blessed Soul will slay you and all of your kind. He will squash you like the bug you are. You wish to know the identity of the Blessed Soul? You want to slay him before he grows to manhood? You cannot defy the prophecies. You cannot change the Lord's will. I know where the Blessed Soul is. But I won't tell you. That knowledge dies with me. Dies with me ... dies ... with ...*

"Wake up!" a voice screamed in the old priest's mind. "You must breath!"

Praise God.

Chapter 32

"Wake up!"

While walking through his dreams of realms that were, and some that were not, he heard a voice calling to him.

"You must breathe!"

He heard the words but didn't listen. Instead he tread upon wet, spongy rock, waved to kindly sea creatures who reached out to him with white tentacles, and he breathed the vibrant colors of the magical air.

"Wake up!"

The voice was very insistent, calling out to him repeatedly, but he ignored it. He chose to suck seraphim and lay in the hot sand while giant leaves bounced in the ocean breezes and tickled his bare chest. He didn't care what any voice had to say. He preferred to sink into the cushions of his father's giant chair, feeling the warmth of the fire, inhaling the scent of polished wood and old books. The voice grew in strength, became high pitched, and strangely familiar.

"Wake up!"

He heard the soft, slow beating of bird's wings, and this captured his attention. But only for a moment. No matter. He looked in the palm of his hand, staring in wonder at a white mask with too many eye holes. He counted the eyes. Seven.

Then the voice was screaming, hurting his ears, high-pitched, inhuman. The image of a large, colorful bird appeared in his vision—the tropical variety with a curved beak, thick and black. The bird flew toward him at a rapid pace, shrieking at him, calling out the same words repeatedly.

"Wake up! Wake up! Wake up!"

The bird seemed angry, flying straight for his face, seemingly on a mission of vengeance.

"Wake up! Wake up! Wake up!"

He cried out, throwing his arms up to protect himself, certain the vile creature aimed to peck his eyes out.

"Wake up!" the bird cried. "You must breathe!"

"No," he answered. "Breathe?"

Breathe. He tried to inhale, but his lungs were filled with water. He choked, and his mind screamed for air. Lungs full of water. Can't breathe. Need air. Dying.

"Wake up!"

He reached out with his hands and found a wall of wet sand in his face, packed in his nose and mouth, even under his eyelids. He pushed against the sand with all his might and his head splashed from the surface of the water. He was on a beach, he realized. He'd almost drowned. He might still drown, unable to breath. Then he retched, and warm liquid spewed from nearly every orifice in his head. The sand was pushed from his nose and mouth as he vomited, and vomited some more, until it seemed he'd ejected a lake of water from his insides. After coughing until his throat was raw, he sucked in a hefty helping of dank, nasty air. But it was air nonetheless.

Gasping, choking, and coughing, he crawled forward onto the beach until the top half of his body was out of the water. Then he rolled onto his back and lay in the wet sand, desperately thankful for the ability to breathe. But still he couldn't see. Though he stared with eyes open and wide, he was met with impenetrable blackness.

"I'm blind," he said.

"Mistress?" came a voice from inside his own head.

"Mistress?" he mumbled. "Who is speaking to me? Who are you?"

"It is Jass Armir," the voice said. "Son of Yarik."

"Son of ... Yarik?" he asked. "Who is Yarik?"

"Yarik is one of the Seven Kingdoms descended from the old clans on the Island of Thershon," Jass explained. "You came here. To Ebon South. In the Outlands."

"Yes I remember," he said. "I went to live in Ebon South after my fifty-fifth nameday. I keep my church there. I am a priest."

"Mistress?" Jass said. "A priest?"

"It is true," he said. "I went to the Outlands to escape the intrigues of the northern church. I retired to Ebon South to pursue my studies, and to await the coming of the Blessed Soul of Man. There I founded a church called the Chapel of God's Grace. I adopted two orphan girls."

"I don't understand," Jass said. "None of this has happened."

"It has," he insisted. "I remember these things."

"You are not a priest."

"Yes I am. I'm Father Brashfor."

Jass was quiet for a moment, then, "Father ... Brashfor?"

"My daughter!" he cried, feeling a touch of pain in his heart. "She tried to kill me. Why did she betray me?"

"I don't know, mistress," Jass replied. "I don't understand."

"Someone stopped her from hurting me," he said. "A golden angel. What is happening to me?"

"I don't know, mistress," Jass said.

"The Second War of Souls has begun!" he shouted into the darkness. "The Blessed Soul! I remember!"

"You remember wrongly," Jass said. "Mistress, you are injured."

"I remember," he repeated. "I must tend to my congregation. I must return to Ebon South."

"You have no congregation," Jass said. "You are not a priest."

"I know who I am!" he shouted. "I am Father Brashfor."

"This isn't right."

"I must return home," he said. "Where are we? Why can't I see?"

"There is no light here."

"No light?" he said. "Where are we?"

373

"You are in a cavern beneath the ground," Jass explained.

"Beneath the ground?" he asked.

"Beneath the ruins of Castle Illengaard," Jass answered.

Fear gripped his heart. "Illengaard? Among the creepermen? How did we come to be in this place?"

"Mistress, you must listen to me," Jass said. "Your name is not Brashfor. You are not a priest."

"Yes I am."

"You call yourself Aeoxoea," Jass went on. "You have come to Thershon in search of the Blessed Soul of Man."

"Aeoxoea?" he said, confused. "Blessed Soul of Man?"

"You followed the Blessed Soul to the Kingdom of Illengaard," Jass said.

"I followed the Blessed Soul?"

"Yes, mistress," Jass said.

"Why do I seek the Blessed Soul?"

"Mistress," Jass said. "Have you forgotten? You are a killer."

"A killer?" he said. "Of course. Tell me of this Blessed Soul."

"He is a young boy named Eleod," Jass answered. "He is in the care of a Knight of the Southern Cross called Gavin the Zealot."

"Where is this knight now?" he asked. "Where has he taken the Blessed Soul?"

"They travel deeper into the earth in search of Gilligod, the Devil Device," Jass said.

"Gilligod," he groaned. "The Blessed Soul will die by this weapon. I remember."

"The knights have taken the boy into the mua giou lair," Jass said. "It is the large tunnel to the east. They are not far. We must follow them, my mistress."

His robes were gone, as was his shirt. He reached up to rub his head and was shocked to feel his formerly bald head was now lush with hair.

"My mistress?" he moaned. "Why do you persist in calling me this?"

374

He scratched his chin and found it perfectly clean-shaven. His beard was gone. And his chin wasn't the only thing that was bare. It was then that he truly felt the sand of the beach beneath him, the grittiness of it biting into his back, the tickling of the waters of the lake as it lapped against his skin. He was completely naked.

"I call you this for good reason, mistress."

Jass was right. She was not the priest of the dream. She was the golden angel.

"Yes, my puppet," Aeoxoea said. "For good reason."

She lay still for a long time, doing nothing but staring at the black nothingness. She knew she was hurt badly. There wasn't an inch of her body that was pain free. Some of it wasn't even there, most notably her left arm, which ended in a mangled stump just below the elbow. Large portions of her left flank were torn open, exposing ribs so cracked and splintered they did nothing to protect or even contain the internal organs now touched by air for the first time. Her neck was broken so badly it was filled with crumbled splinters that no longer resembled bones. A crack in the back of her skull leaked something sticky. Her breath wheezed and bubbled from a crushed throat and a punctured lung. A large slit in her chest gaped where her body had been impaled, slicing away a large and important chunk of her heart muscle. She had more broken bones than she could count, and a number of cuts sufficient to drain every drop of blood from her body. She had suffered no less than four mortal wounds. Yet she remained alive long after she had no right to be.

"Jass," Aeoxoea muttered.

"Yes, mistress," came the reply.

"I nearly drowned."

"Yes, mistress."

"You saved me from death."

"I know, mistress."

"Why?" Aeoxoea asked.

"It is what God commands of me," Jass explained. "It is what my oath of knighthood requires."

"To preserve the lives of your enemies?"

"To preserve life," Jass said. "Even yours."

"You are a fool then," Aeoxoea said.

"A fool who believes in following God's commands," Jass corrected.

"And a hypocrite who cherishes life with a sword at his side," Aeoxoea said. "I've seen you shed blood, knight. You do it with a practiced hand."

"I fight to protect life," Jass said. "Even yours. And no one else needed to perish in order to save you."

"And yet you've chosen to condemn all those who have yet to die by my hand," Aeoxoea said. "I promise you, there will be more deaths before this is done."

"You will be judged for the blood on your hands, not me," Jass asserted.

"Suppose one of the lives I take is your precious Blessed Soul?" the assassin suggested. "What will you think of your actions then?"

"The prophecy will be fulfilled as God wills it, regardless of what I do."

"The fact remains," Aeoxoea said. "You saved the life of a killer, who intends to go on killing."

"You will answer for all the lives you take," Jass said. "I will answer for all the lives I save, beginning with the two I saved today, just now."

"Two?"

"Yours isn't the only life preserved today. I saved myself as well."

"I see."

"I am not dead," Jass said. "My life was taken, but you took it back."

"True words."

"Now it is your life that must be preserved if I am to go on."

"Well spoken."

376

"I have given you a second chance at life," Jass said. "Now you must give me a second chance at mine."

Aeoxoea said nothing. Jass had no eyes, so he could not see her smile.

"You can restore my life," Jass said. "You told me this, mistress."

"I spoke those words," Aeoxoea admitted.

"You will restore my life," Jass stated.

"Will I?" Aeoxoea asked.

"Yes, you will," Jass answered.

"You must have much to live for."

"I do," Jass said. "I intend to live. I will draw breath once again."

"What will you do with your second chance at life?" Aeoxoea asked.

"I will fight for the Blessed Soul of Man," Jass answered. "I will kill those of your kind."

"Very bold of you, sir knight. But perhaps one of my kind will kill you."

"Perhaps," Jass said. "But then I will die in the service of the Blessed Soul, fighting for the side of goodness."

"Perhaps the war will already be decided. Perhaps I will restore your life to be lived in a world of darkness, ruled by the Serharek."

"The prophecy says the Blessed Soul will defeat the Serharek."

"The prophecy also says the Serharek will slay the Blessed Soul," Aeoxoea retorted. "He will use the weapon Gilligod. Even your Keeper of the Craft believes this."

"The prophecy is correct on both counts," Jass said.

"How do you reconcile this?" Aeoxoea asked.

"The Blessed Soul will defeat the Serharek through his death," Jass explained. "His death and his victory will be one and the same. And I will live to see it."

"You have strong faith, my puppet."

"I am a Knight of the Southern Cross," Jass said in explanation.

"Then I must admit I owe my life to a Knight of the Southern Cross," Aeoxoea said. "You saved me from death, Jass Armir of Yarik. I draw breath because you woke me."

"Woke you from what?" Jass asked. "How do you live after all that has happened?"

"Some forces in this world are beyond your understanding."

"Help me understand."

Aeoxoea smiled. "You demand much for a slave."

"I am a slave to no one," Jass said. "Not even to you."

"You must serve someone."

"No one but God," Jass said. "My faith has set me free."

"Then you are a slave to your God," Aeoxoea suggested.

"As you are a slave to the limits of your mortal flesh," Jass retorted. "So in need of food and water and the fresh air you breathe only because I saved you from death."

"This gloating does not become you, honorable sir knight," Aeoxoea said.

"Weakness does not become you, dishonorable assassin," Jass said. "You are lying in pieces, unable to move; a moth with your wings torn out. How is it you still live? Tell me."

"I have ways of accomplishing the improbable."

"The impossible, you mean."

"It behooves a being of my nature to prepare for situations such as this," Aeoxoea said.

"Situations such as what?" Jass asked. "How does one prepare for death?"

"It is not death one prepares for, but life," Aeoxoea answered.

"You speak in riddles."

"I do not," Aeoxoea said. "The process of healing requires life. The process of living requires life force, the heartbeat of your soul, which is called juy."

"I know of juy," Jass said. "Though I cannot control it as some do."

"Yes you can, my puppet," Aeoxoea said. "Every being can, even animals. Some more than others. Some better than others. I simply do it more and better than anyone."

"Modesty is clearly your most endearing quality."

"It is not," Aeoxoea corrected. "But honesty is."

"Then tell me true," Jass said. "How is it you survived? There are practitioners of the Juy Method among my people. Some are even accomplished to the point that they can heal themselves and others."

"I have seen this," Aeoxoea said. "And your knighthood has uncovered a process by which this ability can be stored within a tattoo."

"That is true."

"I witnessed Elkor the Hound healing himself," Aeoxoea explained. "He is not knowledgeable in the ways of the Method, and yet he was able to tap his own juy to accelerate the healing process."

"The tattoo is called the Life Sign, mistress," Jass said. "Its creation is very difficult, a day's long process requiring the skills of the Keeper of the Craft and the most skilled priests of the Temple of Juy. Only the greatest lords of the realm may receive it, the rulers of the Seven Kingdoms and the highest ranking Knights of the Southern Cross."

"And I presume this fraternity of distinguished persons excluded you, my puppet?"

"As I said, mistress. Only the greatest lords—"

"Yes, as you said," Aeoxoea cut in. "Then you understand how it is I still live. It is through a similar process of manipulating and expending juy. If a person has enough juy contained within their body and mind, they can sustain life after the heart and lungs fail."

"How is this?" Jass said. "No one is born with that much juy."

"The body requires juy to live," Aeoxoea explained. "This can be supplied by means both conventional and unconventional. The flesh does not know the source of its sustenance."

"But what is the source of this excess juy?" Jass asked. "Surely, you do not create it."

"Only God can create life."

"Then where is this life obtained?" Jass asked. "Was it stolen from Father Brashfor?"

"Perhaps."

"From the doppelganger assassin?"

"Yes."

"From me?"

"No," Aeoxoea said. "You had no life to give."

"Can I believe you?" Jass asked.

"Believe what you wish," Aeoxoea stated. "It is I who sustains you. I can kill you with one thought, do not forget. I've chosen not to."

"But you would," Jass pushed. "Once my value to your cause has expired."

"Perhaps not."

"Perhaps so."

"You saved my life, dear puppet," Aeoxoea said.

"I saved my own," Jass corrected.

"Yes," Aeoxoea said. "You are not dead. Your life was taken, but I took it back. One day, you might live again. One day."

"You will restore my life?" Jass asked. "Truly?"

"Perhaps I will."

"You would raise me from death only to continue my slavery?"

"I am many terrible things, but never a slave master," Aeoxoea said. "If I give you life, it will be your life to live. I will not hold dominion over your actions."

"I would be free?" Jass asked. "To do as I choose?"

"Free," Aeoxoea confirmed.

"If you restore my life, I will thank you sincerely," Jass said. "Then I will slit your throat."

"If that is what you wish, then you will die a second death," Aeoxoea promised.

"In the service of my Lord," Jass added.

"Admirable," Aeoxoea said. "I'd enjoy seeing that."

"You will see it," Jass stated. "I promise."

"You are in no position to make promises, my puppet," Aeoxoea chided. "The promises of dead men are hollow."

"Fulfill your promise," Jass said. "And I will fulfill mine."

"I promise to restore your life."

"And I promise to take yours."

Chapter 33

Aeoxoea lay on the beach next to the underground lake for many hours. She stared into the darkness and listened as the ripples of water slowly faded, until the surface of the lake was once again a perfect calm. She couldn't see a thing in the sunless cavern, but could hear many things. The innards of the island of Thershon were alive with creatures of every size and shape possible. She could hear them with her overly-sensitive hearing; footfalls both large and small, clopping, thumping, shuffling, and slithering. There was heavy breathing, light twittering, chirping and crackling noises, low rumbles, high-pitched keens and hisses, and everything in between.

The corruption of Illengaard was still there, but was far away, a great blackness hovering above like the night sky. Whether she was free of its evil, she did not know, but this hardly mattered to someone who could not move. If the creepermen came and took her, then so be it.

Unable to stand or do anything of value, she did the only thing that required no physical effort, allowing herself to fall into periods of deep, healing sleep, sometimes for hours. Each time she awoke, she could hear her own heartbeat as it grew stronger, as the heart muscle mended itself. She listened as the hole in her lung closed, the wheezing softened, and her breath came easier. It was just the beginning, yet it was essential. Her body must heal to the point of self-sustainment as quickly as possible, for the well of juy that sustained her was not bottomless. With her heart thumping and her lungs inhaling on their own, the healing process would be accelerated.

So she slept more, and for longer periods of time. Wounds closed and bones healed. Warm blood no longer spilled into the sand. Now it coursed through her veins, filled her limbs and fed her thirsty organs. But even at this accelerated pace, Aeoxoea knew days were passing by. Each minute that passed carried her quarry farther out of reach, carried away by the arms the knight Gavin the Zealot.

Aeoxoea knew there was no time to waste, so the first moment she awoke and felt she might be well enough to crawl, she began the slow process of rolling onto her stomach. She lifted her head from the sand and felt a slight pressure on her neck, and a soft weight upon her chest. There was something attached to her throat, something she hadn't previously noticed in her alternating bouts of agony and numbness. She raised her remaining hand to feel around her neck.

She felt cold flesh—not her own—with bones beneath, ending in a stump of hacked, shredded meat. It was the severed appendage of the creature of technology who'd attacked her, who'd nearly killed her, whose body exploded beneath the surface of the lake. Its hand still hung from her neck, fingers gripping her throat tightly.

She tried to pull the thing off to throw it away, but it would not release its hold on her. She tried peeling each finger loose individually, but they felt as though they were made of steel, they were so unyielding. In her struggling, Aeoxoea absentmindedly raised her left arm, the one with no hand.

A bolt of electricity shot through her entire body, so forceful it felt as if someone struck her in the head with a hammer, rattling her brain, and leaving her fingers, toes, and ears tingling. She was stunned, her body going rigid for a moment as she blinked and gasped in confusion. Dimly, she was aware of a series of buzzing and whizzing sounds, then a sudden pain in her left arm. It was terrible pain, as if a thousand needles were jammed into the end of her wounded arm simultaneously, very long needles that reached the length of her arm up to her shoulder, into her neck, into her head, into her brain. Needles jamming into her brain, into her eyes, into her eardrums. Her ears crackled and buzzed and stars exploded in her vision. She screamed in agony.

Aeoxoea had been hurt in a great many ways in her life. She'd been stabbed and cut a hundred times. She'd been poisoned, and tortured, and drowned. She'd felt the pain of creeper blood devouring her flesh. It was a rare time that she ever cried out in pain. Even as the creature of technology nearly destroyed her with its invisible weapons, broke her neck and impaled her heart, Aeoxoea spoke not a whimper.

But this was a new kind of pain. This was nothing she'd ever felt before. And she let out a wail of agony that filled that underground cavern and many more, possibly making its way all the way to the surface. Certainly, all the creepermen heard it. Possibly, the Blessed Soul of Man himself heard it.

Thankfully, mercifully, the pain only lasted seconds, ending in a rush so intense, Aeoxoea felt her head might burst from its inability to contain it. Needles were everywhere—on her skin, her scalp, her tongue. Then, nothing. No pain. No screaming. Just quiet.

Lights began to flash in her vision. Sounds began to beep in her ears. They were strange, artificial. Aeoxoea knew her body and mind well. She knew this didn't belong. These were lights her eyes didn't see. They were sounds her ears didn't hear. They were unwanted sights and sounds, forced upon her from within, not without. They were forced upon her brain from her left hand.

Aeoxoea looked at her left hand, looked where she should have seen a mangled stump, but did not. She hurriedly shifted her vision to see variations of heat. She saw her arm as a blazing red against the blackness of the cool air. She could not see her hand because it produced no warmth. The flesh of her arm, appearing as a pulsing red to her heat-sensitive eyes, ended just below the elbow.

Quickly, she shifted her vision to the spectrum which perceived the Craft. She saw the colorful Craft weaves swirling about her, and this time she could see her hand, appearing as total blackness, as though it was a hole in space. She moved it around, curling her fingers, making a fist, watching in amazement as the hand obeyed her every command as effortlessly as her own once did.

It appeared as a black silhouette to her heat-sensitive eyes. It appeared as the same to her Craft-seeking vision. It appeared so because it was not warm flesh. It was not a creation of the Craft, nor of the Method. It was a thing of technology.

The creature's hand had attached itself to Aeoxoea's arm.

She pushed herself into a sitting position and switched her vision back to normal. Once again, she saw the total darkness of the sunless cavern, broken only by the lights flashing in her vision, pale blue lights that emanated from her new left arm. She looked at them as they blinked, constantly changing shape and size. Then she realized they were words, or characters from different alphabets, cycling through different languages. There were eight different languages, one of which she recognized. It was an ancient human language, now dead. Darhan historians called it Sye.

"I ou sil," she said.

A female voice boomed in her head, finally speaking words she understood.

"Thank you for purchasing your new DoomFist Elite Hand Cannon Model F-12b," the voice said. "Brought to you by Celkow Cybersystems, the leader in cybernetic small arms technology."

Again the words came from within, not without. Her brain heard the voice, not her ears, just as the blinking lights filled her mind and not her eyes. Now she could see more words blinking in her vision. They read:

Welcome.

Your DoomFist is registered!

Tutorial.

Use my DoomFist now.

Frequently Asked Questions.

About Celkow Cybersystems.

Aeoxoea, for a short moment, wondered what the words were telling her, wondered what to do. Her left hand seemed to respond, as if it heard her thoughts.

"This is the Welcome and Orientation screen for your new DoomFist Elite Hand Cannon," the female voice said. "Here you may choose to do any of the following: Hear about the DoomFist line of military and civilian-use hand cannons by Celkow Cybersystems. Hear about the history of the DoomFist line of weaponry and the superior service record that has made reliability, versatility, and performance synonymous with the DoomFist name. Hear how the most respected Research and Development team in the industry has redefined the standards of small arms safety and accuracy with innovations such as the S.I.L.K. User Interface, and the new Seek and Destroy targeting system, features that make the latest F-12b model your easy weapon of choice. You may register your DoomFist hand cannon with required local and combined law enforcement arms databases via the S.I.L.K. user umbrella. Learn to use your new DoomFist with the fast and simple-to-use Tutorial. If you are familiar with the DoomFist line or the F-12b model in particular, you may wish to skip the Tutorial. You can do this by choosing the 'Use my DoomFist now' option."

"Frequently asked questions," Aeoxoea said. "How do I remove this device from my arm?"

"Your DoomFist Elite can be disarmed and gene-mirroring disabled for removal at any Celkow Cybersystems distribution facility," the female voice said. "This service is also provided at many combined law enforcement air stations, and most licensed Celkow retailers. For a list of licensed Celkow retailers—"

"Can I remove the weapon myself?" Aeoxoea asked.

"Do not attempt to remove your DoomFist without the supervision of a certified technician," the voice warned sternly. "Removal of the unit without properly disabling gene-mirroring may result in serious physical injury, and possibly death. Therefore it is illegal—"

"Is it possible?" Aeoxoea asked.

"Do not attempt to remove your DoomFist without the supervision of a certified technician," the voice warned.

"But is it possible?" Aeoxoea asked. "Can it be done?"

"Removal of the unit without properly disabling gene-mirroring may result in serious physical injury, and possibly death."

"Perhaps I will cut it off," Aeoxoea suggested.

"This will result in certain death," the voice said. "Therefore it is illegal—"

"Shut up!"

The voice quieted.

Aeoxoea sat silently in the wet sand for many minutes, staring out across the smooth surface of the lake. Out in the center, a death blossom drifted aimlessly, its orange petals kissing the surface of the water as it slowly moved in circles.

Aeoxoea sighed.

"DoomFist," she said.

"Yes?" came the woman's voice. "How can I help?"

"Show me the Tutorial."

Chapter 34

"Mistress, why don't we continue into the mua giou lair in search of the Blessed Soul of Man?"

Aeoxoea sighed in exasperation. "Because, my puppet, I am composed of flesh and bone, just as anyone. Therefore, given the right circumstances, I can be subject to the same frailties as anyone else. Now is such a time. The Blessed Soul will have to wait."

The assassin sat cross-legged in the sand near the underground lake, her eyes staring sightlessly into the darkness around her. Upon her knees rested her two hands, one of them quite natural, the other a synthetic appendage called a hand cannon. Sitting in her lap was a charred shell, the remnants of a human head. It belonged to the former owner of the DoomFist.

Blue lights flashed across Aeoxoea's vision, thousands of them in succession, taking the shape of numbers and characters. They came to her mind courtesy of signals sent to her brain from the DoomFist, something the device called "code."

"Which circumstances are those?" Jass asked.

"What do you mean?"

"What circumstances will subject you to the same frailties as anyone else?" Jass pressed.

"You are curious to know this?"

"Of course I am."

"I see," Aeoxoea said with a smile. "Information to use when the time arrives where we will be at odds, when you will do me harm."

"Perhaps," Jass said. "Tell me what happened. What events led you to this?"

"I would be quite foolish to divulge such information to one who plans to slay me, don't you think, puppet?" Aeoxoea asked.

"Only if you fear me," Jass stated.

"Well then, you have me, dear sir knight," Aeoxoea giggled. "I am forced to assert my confidence of success should you raise arms against me, by answering your pithy questions."

Stop. The word was just a thought in the assassin's mind, but it was a command the DoomFist understood. The flashing lights filling her vision froze, showing her line upon line of characters of the dead language known as Sye. She looked at the line of characters second from the bottom, counting in four characters from the left, finding the letter cia. With the index finger of the DoomFist hand cannon, she drew the letter in the sand before her. Another thought: *Proceed.* And the characters began scrolling across her vision once more.

"Firstly, you must forsake your faith, my sweet puppet," Aeoxoea said, patting the blackened skull in her lap. "No creature such as this worships your god."

"No creature such as what?" Jass pressed.

"The creature who has rendered me incapable."

"Do you know what it was?"

"I cannot be certain," Aeoxoea answered. "I believe it to be a Trylon."

"A Trylon?" Jass asked. "What is that?"

"The word *trylon* is from the Darhan language meaning 'precursor' or 'forerunner,'" Aeoxoea answered.

"Ancestor?" Jass suggested.

"Perhaps," Aeoxoea answered. "Some say they thrive somewhere high above the clouds, but are prevented from descending to our level by some physical limitation."

"This one faced no such difficulties."

"No, it didn't," Aeoxoea agreed. "But this creature was not an organic being. Its body was synthetically created, built by another man."

"How is that possible?"

"The Trylons have built an extremely advanced culture," Aeoxoea said. "They are masters of all three of the divine talents bestowed by the Creator: the Craft of the fyral magicians, the Method of the kynir mindbenders, and the Technology of the human scientists."

"Have the myths come alive?"

"I don't know," Aeoxoea said. "This creature was of a culture very advanced in technology. That much is clear."

"And the Craft?" Jass asked. "And the Method?"

"I can't be certain," Aeoxoea answered. "It has chosen to destroy itself."

"Why would it destroy itself?"

"I can only guess, dear puppet," Aeoxoea. "Perhaps to keep its secrets, to keep knowledge of its true nature from us."

"Surely these are important secrets, if it would die to protect them," Jass suggested.

"Or perhaps the Trylons intend to keep their technology from being acquired by someone who does not share their interests," Aeoxoea said. "Someone who is dangerous, who poses a threat."

"Someone such as you?"

Aeoxoea smiled. "Yes, puppet, someone such as me."

A single thought directed at her hand—*Stop*—and the DoomFist complied, and again the stream of blue characters froze in her vision. She searched, found what she was looking for, and wrote the Sye character deo in the sand. *Proceed.*

"Why doesn't such a race rule the world?" Jass asked.

"Perhaps there are too few," Aeoxoea answered. "Some believe the Trylons thrive above the clouds, but there are others who think they are mostly extinct. It is possible that they achieved such great power that they destroyed the world, and themselves with it."

"If they are extinct," Jass asked, "then what was the creature that attacked you?"

"A remnant of a once-great culture, just as we are all remnants," Aeoxoea said. "Perhaps this was one of a precious few, who chose to come here at great personal risk, to pursue a goal of his own."

"What goal could that be?" Jass asked. "What would bring a Trylon to Thershon?"

"The Blessed Soul of Man."

Again the assassin found what she sought flashing across her vision. With a single thought, she commanded the DoomFist to freeze the numbers. She wrote the number mae in the sand. One more though—*Proceed*—and the characters started flashing again.

"You say they destroyed the world," Jass said. "What do you mean?"

"There once was a single world." Aeoxoea spoke slowly. "The Trylons destroyed it. Now there are many."

"Many worlds? What do you mean?"

The assassin smiled. "Surely you don't believe your island of Thershon to be all there is?"

"No, I don't," Jass said. "It is clear that there are other islands. Dark spots in the sky, both big and small. I've watched them since I was a boy."

"You see them," Aeoxoea said. "Yet you know nothing about them."

"I know they revolve around Thershon, rising and setting like the sun and moon."

Laughter burst from the assassin's lips. "Revolve around Thershon! Oh, my puppet. I so appreciate your underdeveloped perspective."

"You mock me."

"I cherish you, sweet puppet," Aeoxoea giggled. "Your earnest naïveté has made this otherwise tedious and stressful exercise a delight at times. A true delight."

"It is my pleasure to serve you, mistress."

"Then delight me further," Aeoxoea commanded. "Do you think Thershon to be the center of the world?"

"It is the only world I know. What else would I believe? Instruct me."

"I will not instruct you in belief," Aeoxoea stated. "I will instruct you in fact. Your world of Thershon is just another island like those you see in the sky. Thershon orbits another, much larger island, which orbits yet another."

"How do you know this?"

"It might be that I have many lifetimes of knowledge stored in my head, little one," Aeoxoea explained.

"Many lifetimes?"

"I must confess, not all of my knowledge is my own," the assassin said. "My memories are filled with sights seen through the eyes of others. Not all of my victims were so fortunate as you, my puppet. I have allowed you to live on within me. Others I have not."

"I am bested," Jass said. "Your understanding of the nature of the world, acquired through theft and murder, outshines my infant's perspective, learned from the experience of one single lifetime cut short."

"Very true," Aeoxoea giggled. "But your acceptance of that fact proves you are learning."

"I have learned that your murder victims include men of knowledge. I have not learned how they gained this knowledge. How can one learn about islands they cannot see? How can one learn about a place they've never been?"

Aeoxoea sighed. "I am attempting to teach reading to a child who has not yet learned his letters."

"How could anyone know this?" Jass retorted. "There is no way to travel between islands."

"Yet I have managed this, my puppet," Aeoxoea stated. "Somehow, I have done it."

"You've traveled to other islands?"

"I have not traveled *to* other islands," the assassin corrected. "I have traveled *from* other islands, to Thershon."

"You come from another island?" Jass asked.

"This is not plain to you?"

"People live on the islands that cross our sky?"

"Many people, in fact," Aeoxoea answered. "And though it seems there are many islands that cross your sky, your island crosses the skies of many more. Thershon is a tiny, insignificant speck in a sea of air, not even visible to most of the civilized world. It has been entirely forgotten since the Sundering, and likely would have remained forgotten, if the prophecies hadn't chosen your little rock as the home of the Blessed Soul. If not for that, you might have proceeded in your silly zoth wars for the rest of time, your boring little island unmolested by the rest of us."

"For all of Thershon, I apologize for afflicting you with boredom."

"I forgive you, for there is no way to remedy it," Aeoxoea said. "Your home is just puny, plain, and uninteresting compared to most."

"You've not seen all there is to see of Thershon," Jass said. "The Neversea Depths will show you wonders."

"I'm sure this is true," Aeoxoea said. "We both have much to learn, you and I."

"That is true."

"But you have more, therefore, I will continue your instruction."

Stop. The assassin looked at the characters, wrote the number teo in the sand, then thought, *Proceed.*

"Those islands you've been watching since your childhood; they are each their own world, just as your little island of Thershon, with your seven little kingdoms," Aeoxoea said. "There are races and cultures and religions, and nations and empires. There are millions of people, and many thousands of those blessed with the divine talents—the fyral wizards, the kynir mindbenders, human scientists. There is so much more out there than you know. So much beyond your knowledge."

"There are mindbenders living on Thershon," Jass said. "Wizards and theurgists."

"That is correct," Aeoxoea said. "But so few. There is not enough pure blood on this island. The gifts have been tainted. Your Keeper of the Craft may be impressive in his power. Yet he couldn't dream of the scope of the emperor, a pure-blooded fyral as ancient as time, whose mastery of the Craft is near perfection. He is the greatest wizard who has ever lived. He is ageless. His ambition is limitless, his will unstoppable. Your Keeper of the Craft is a mosquito by comparison."

Stop. The blue characters froze. After a moment of searching, Aeoxoea wrote the letter cana in the sand, then, *Proceed.*

"Does your emperor fear the Trylons?"

"The emperor fears nothing."

"Why does he not rule the world?" Jass asked.

"He does rule the world," Aeoxoea answered. "Even those who believe they are free are manipulated by him."

"He doesn't rule the Seven Kingdoms," Jass said.

"Your island was not worth the bother, my puppet," Aeoxoea said. "Not until now."

"Now your emperor cares about my island?" Jass asked.

"Oh, yes," Aeoxoea said. "Very much."

"Will he attempt to add the Seven Kingdoms to his empire?"

"There is nothing to add," Aeoxoea said. "Your kingdoms will be destroyed."

"We will fight you," Jass said. "The people of Thershon are strong. The Knights of the Southern Cross—"

"The Knights of the Southern Cross will die," Aeoxoea interrupted. "The Seven Kingdoms will be destroyed. The emperor's will is unstoppable."

Stop. Aeoxoea looked at the blue characters in her vision, then wrote the letter meot in the sand. *Proceed.*

"Why would the emperor wish to destroy us?"

"To fulfill the prophecies," Aeoxoea explained. "His wrath will fall upon this island, and you will see epic destruction. The Second War of Souls will end only after the Iatan Empire has achieved complete devastation of the Seven Kingdoms, the end of your people—the end of your way of life, forever."

"To fulfill the prophecy?" Jass said. "The prophecy says the Blessed Soul will be victorious."

"The prophecy also says the Blessed Soul will die by Gilligod, by the hand of the Serharek," Aeoxoea retorted. "The emperor wants Gilligod. He wants the Blessed Soul dead."

"Why?" Jass asked.

"Why? Because the emperor fears nothing and no one," Aeoxoea explained. "No one but the Blessed Soul. That little boy may mean the end of the emperor's reign. The Seven Kingdoms must die to save the Empire. That is, if I fail."

"And if you succeed?" Jass asked.

"Perhaps your island will be spared," Aeoxoea said. "No need to fulfill any prophecy if the Blessed Soul is dead."

"The Seven Kingdoms will live if the Blessed Soul dies?"

"A conundrum, is it not?" Aeoxoea said. "You must choose your side, then. Your people? Or the Blessed Soul?"

Stop. Another search, another character, this time the number su. Aeoxoea drew it in the sand, then thought, *Proceed.*

"The Blessed Soul will live," Jass said. "Gavin the Zealot will see to that."

"Then your people will die, and the Blessed Soul will be slain by Gilligod," Aeoxoea said. "The emperor will win. It is an inevitability."

"Then why have you come to this island?" Jass asked. "Why not let inevitability run its course?"

"Even those who would affect the course of the world sometimes hang from puppet strings," Aeoxoea said.

"You admit weakness."

"I admit nothing."

"You hang from puppet strings," Jass accused.

"I do." Aeoxoea shrugged. "There is a constant tugging on my strings, but there are only certain tugs I will obey."

"Why have you come?" Jass asked. "Who sent you? The emperor?"

"The emperor wants Gilligod," Aeoxoea said. "I am sent to retrieve it, to use it if necessary."

"You do the will of the emperor," Jass stated. "He is your puppet master."

"Every creature does the will of the emperor, by choice or otherwise."

"An excuse to do evil," Jass said. "You pretend to have no choice."

"What is choice in the face of the prophecy you so trust?" Aeoxoea mocked.

"You may choose to retrieve Gilligod for the emperor, or you may choose not to," Jass said. "That choice is yours to make."

"I have chosen to retrieve Gilligod."

"And the emperor trusts you will do this?" Jass said. "Strange that a being with limitless power would send a single assassin to accomplish his will."

"The emperor trusts no one," Aeoxoea said. "It is how he maintains his empire."

"Yet he expects that you will bring him Gilligod," Jass insisted. "He places great trust in you."

"The emperor trusts no one, least of all me," Aeoxoea said. "So many more than I have come to Thershon from the Iatan Empire, brought here by the re-emergence of the Blessed Soul. And many more will come, from many more islands. The emperor knows his disciples may struggle with other minions of evil for the chance to lay hands upon Gilligod, even to slay the Blessed Soul. He knows his goals are not shared by all those who fight for darkness, such as this Trylon. Thus, he has sent his greatest tool, a wizard name Azzrot, called the Icon of the Empire, the most skilled of his sorcerers, to see that the deed is done, to see at least one of the emperor's assassins successful in their task, even if it be the Icon himself. The emperor has imagined many contingencies. He has imagined no trust in me. His acts of redundance proves he has no patience for faith."

Stop. This time it was the number dia. Aeoxoea wrote it in the sand beside the others. *Proceed.*

"Should the emperor trust you to bring him Gilligod?" Jass asked. "Or to fight with those that would?"

"He is wise to mistrust me," Aeoxoea answered. "There is too much at stake."

"A miserable existence you and your emperor must share," Jass said. "Dishonesty, mistrust, disloyalty."

"Not everyone can be driven by faith and love as you gallant knights," Aeoxoea said. "For some, there is only fear and hatred, lust and vengeance."

"What drives you?"

"You will understand through observation," Aeoxoea said. "If you care to watch and learn, I may find pleasure in your education."

"You are a complicated person," Jass observed.

"That is why the emperor is wise to mistrust me," Aeoxoea said. "You knights delude yourselves with your childish simplifications, your adherence to the concepts of right and wrong. Often, there is no right or wrong, no good or evil."

"No good or evil? You speak nonsense."

"Either the master deceives his puppet, or the puppet deceives her master," Aeoxoea said.

"Or his mistress."

"Time will tell us which."

"So many puppets," Jass said. "So many strings."

"Some puppets need their strings, others do not," Aeoxoea explained. "Some puppets drop to the floor when their strings are cut. Others walk on their own, to seek revenge upon their masters."

"Even you do not understand how true your words are, my mistress."

"Oh, I do," Aeoxoea retorted. "And so will you. You will understand through observation. Watch and learn, my puppet."

Stop. The characters froze, and Aeoxoea sought out the letter ka, writing it in the sand. Her next mental command to the hand cannon was different: *Use my DoomFist now.*

397

A female voice, speaking the language of Sye, once again filled the assassin's head. "Please provide combined security authorization and ownership passkey now," said the female voice.

"Dia deo mae teo cana meot su dia ka," Aeoxoea said, reciting the characters from those she'd drawn in the sand.

"What did you say?" Jass asked, but was ignored.

"Access granted," said the female voice. "You may proceed."

Aeoxoea grabbed the head of the Trylon in both hands, throwing it out over the water. She extended her left hand, balling it into a fist. Blue lights flashed in her vision, a triangle with crosshairs.

"I said watch ..."

The hand cannon's Seek and Destroy targeting system mapped the distance to the target, determined proper discharge level, and adjusted Aeoxoea's imperfect aim. The DoomFist Elite belched forth a single burst of invisible fire, and the skull of the Trylon exploded into a million pieces of dust, which slowly settled to the surface of the water, causing tiny ripples all around the death blossom which floated there.

" ... and learn."

Chapter 35

Aeoxoea spent four days on the shores of the lake before she was well enough to travel. She wasn't healed to the point of being completely free from pain, but her body was whole enough to sustain itself through natural means. She was weakened and her mind exhausted, and it gave her an unwelcome feeling of vulnerability. She would have little chance of survival if another being such as the Trylon found her in this state. But further delay was unacceptable. The moment she was able to climb to her feet, she walked to the large opening in the eastern wall of the cavern and stared into its blackness.

"The mua giou lair, my mistress," Jass said.

"I see it," the assassin wheezed.

Her vision showed her a passage that stretched deep into the earth at a soft decline, bending slightly down, steeper and steeper. The two knights had walked into this tunnel with Eleod, the Blessed Soul of Man. And now they had a four-day lead on her.

The distance between the assassin and her prey was something Aeoxoea would have handled easily on another day, one that found her in better health. She had means of traveling great distances with little effort, but with her body and mind so exhausted as she was, and nearly bereft of life-giving juy, she had little choice but to move about through more conventional means. She would have to walk. It would be slow and painful, but she had no other choice. She could only hope the knights had done the same, that for the past four days they'd maintained the sluggish pace they'd started out with, rather than the sprinting they'd done on the surface of the island. If that were the case, the Blessed Soul would be a hundred miles away by now.

Aeoxoea stepped in the mua giou lair and followed, her bare feet falling quietly on the smooth stone. The earth floor of the tunnel was slick, wet, and slimy in some places. Some sort of acidic secretion covered the sides of the tunnel and patches of the ground, which made walking a slippery business. Even though a trickle of water flowed down its center, Aeoxoea was certain it was not erosion that cut this giant hole so deep into the earth. More likely it was the acidic substance, not water that did this. More likely, it was the creature that left the slime that covered everything.

She walked for an hour, then two hours, then a day. With endless passageway before her and behind her, with tons of rock above and below, she walked. With impenetrable darkness covering her face, filling her eyesight with its vast nothingness, she walked. She walked and walked and breathed the dank air, and smelled the slime and inhaled the nauseating stench of the bile-like acid that covered everything. She walked and listened to nothing but her own quiet footsteps for another day. Then another. Monotonous, rhythmic footsteps. Endless quiet. Endless nothingness.

A normal person would have gone mad at the lack of stimulation, the total absence of any clue that there was value in this ceaseless, plodding exercise. But Aeoxoea did not need any such motivation. This was important healing time for her, taking those easy, measured steps, as her flesh mended itself. Each step was a tiny bit stronger as she healed, and life returned to her body.

She needed nothing to remind her that she remained on the trail of the Blessed Soul, that those easy, measured steps carried her in the right direction. Much like a hunting dog, she didn't need sight or sound of her quarry to tell her which way to travel. Though the knights left no footprints on the hard stone, their trail couldn't have been any clearer to her eyes.

Aeoxoea had the ability to see the past when she chose to. If a person stepped on any one spot in the world, they left their unique imprint on the Craft weaves existing in that spot. The most skilled at covering their tracks would find it impossible to erase the mark of their own passing. Even time itself had no effect upon these footsteps left in the magic. Therefore, Aeoxoea knew she was walking the same path as the two knights. She placed her feet where they placed theirs, and she could see them. She could see how they were remembered by the Craft weaves, how they looked as they took each step deeper into the earth. She could see the Blessed Soul of Man. She could see Elkor's battle hounds. She could see how the humans and animals interacted, could hear the conversations that took place between the two knights. She knew what they ate and when they slept. She watched as Eleod played with Behe during a period where Gavin allowed the little boy to walk on his own.

She could also see that there were some minor changes in Behe's behavior, mainly her attention span, her ability to follow orders. She didn't walk or stay where she was told, and barked when her masters demanded silence. She also occasionally wandered away from Elkor when he commanded her otherwise. As a result, Elkor chose to hold her close with a chain he kept fastened around her neck. He continued wearing his magical torch strapped to his back, allowing it to cast its light over his shoulder. He did this to free both hands, allowing him to keep a firm control, which now held Behe's chain. It wasn't long before that decision would save his life.

On the third day of travel, Elkor walked with Behe ahead of the others. The knight and his animal were navigating a particularly treacherous stretch of ground in a place where the tunnel took a steep dip. The rocky floor was wet and slippery, and covered with slime in most places. Elkor chose his steps carefully, yet he couldn't be perfect, forced by a lack of better options to tread a particularly dangerous tract of slimy ground. He stepped off the dry rock, both he and his battle hound walking several feet through the thick, gooey stuff. Then he slipped. His legs flew out from under him and he fell hard. He landed on his back hard, knocking his torch off his shoulder, then began to slide down. Frantically, he searched for something firm to grasp, but he found nothing but smooth rock with no handholds, and copious goo squeezing between his fingers. Unable to stop himself, he quickly slid down the steep slope, out of the torchlight and into the darkness. Behe stood where she was, whimpering softly as she watched her chain lying in the slime, rapidly disappearing down the giant, black hole after her master. Behind her, Gavin walked down the slope with Kang at his side, both taking cautious steps. Behe turned around, looking to Gavin for guidance. Then the chain jerked taut.

She yelped and dug her claws into the slimy floor. The muscles in her legs tightened, and her head was pulled back rudely as her neck bore the weight of her master's body. Watching this scene, Aeoxoea could see that Elkor had fallen into a large crack in the floor of the worm hole. At that moment, the knight hung in midair by the chain, his life literally dangling from his dog's neck. But Behe too slipped, skidding a foot further down the tunnel before regaining her footing. She bared her teeth against the strain, every muscle in her body bulging, trying desperately to hold on. A slow growl of frustration came from deep in her belly as her head was pulled further back.

"Hold, Behe, hold!" Gavin said.

The Zealot quickly set Eleod down and took his leather shirt off. He planted his feet on a spot of the dry stone and threw one end of his shirt to Behe, yelling, "Catch, girl!"

The battle hound caught the leather shirt in her mouth and bit down hard. Gavin began to pull her back up the tunnel, pulling on his shirt, hand over hand. Her neck slowly bent back to its natural position. Then she walked up the tunnel, lifted by the knight pulling on the leather shirt she held in her jaws, pulled up until Gavin could reach out and touch her. He grabbed the chain around her neck and pulled, lifting the burden from her, taking the weight onto himself. Then he continued pulling, hand over hand, pulling Elkor back up the tunnel. Now, Behe panted and rested, and watched as Gavin did the work, as the muscles of his bare tattooed chest bulged. It only took a minute, but it required a good deal of strength. Slowly, a few feet at time, the Zealot pulled his comrade back to safety. Elkor reemerged from the darkness, sliding through the muck on his belly, the chain gripped in both hands. He was a little bloody, and a little bruised, but he smiled with relief. When he was safely on dry ground, the two knights sat down, breathing heavily. Elkor hugged Behe close, scratching at her ears while she licked his face.

"Good girl ... good girl," he breathed, his eyes wet.

Eleod giggled. "Good doggy!" he said.

Aeoxoea's attention was yanked from this scene back to the present by the feeling of slight tremors beneath her feet. The immediate impact was to cause her to lose balance, just as Elkor had. She slipped, almost fell, but managed to keep her feet with the help of a pair of white tentacles that slammed through the layer of slime into the ground, finding sure holds in the rock.

A brisk wind filled the giant worm hole, warm and sticky, carrying a foul smell from deep in the earth. Aeoxoea didn't recognize the smell, didn't understand the cause of the wind, but had strong suspicions, and strong fears. Back near the underground lake, Elkor had told Gavin that earthquakes on the surface were caused by the movements of the mua giou, a name derived from the dycleth words for "lizard worm." These tremors were familiar to Aeoxoea. They grew in strength in much the same fashion as the earthquake that struck at the onset of the attack of the creepermen. And she knew they would continue to grow until the world rocked beneath her feet. It was the mua giou. And it was coming.

Aeoxoea used her enhanced vision to stare down the giant worm hole for as far as she could see. It wasn't very far, due to the tunnel's curvature; probably only a mile. But it was enough to see a wall of white mist rushing toward her at lightning speed. The wind blew harder, and hotter, and Aeoxoea was almost knocked off her feet, even with help from her tentacles. It was time to retreat.

In one moment, many thoughts raced through Aeoxoea's mind. She wondered at the awful smell, the sudden increase in humidity.

She wondered what was behind that wall of mist, or perhaps it was steam? She wondered what had become of the knights and the boy Eleod who were so much farther down the hole. She was unsure of many things, but there was one fact that shone to her with perfect clarity: The mua giou would be upon her in only seconds, and she wasn't certain she wanted to meet a creature called a lizard worm who'd created a miles-long tunnel, and was big enough to cause earthquakes just by moving around its home.

There wasn't time to think. There wasn't time to search for a place to hide. There was only one option, and she took it. She retracted hers tentacles and dove forward into the muck, sliding quickly down the slimy hole toward the approaching mua giou. Just as she thought, it wasn't long before she reached the large crack that Elkor had fallen into, and with purpose, she fell into it herself, headfirst.

She tumbled head over heels, tentacles lashing out hopelessly, trying to find a grip on something to slow her fall. But the hot wind quickly became hot steam, blowing hard and pushing her fall harder than gravity pulled. She was swept up in the wall of heat and steam. She felt her skin burned and her lungs scorched by each breath. But finally, one of her tentacles found a hold in a rock wall. She was jerked painfully by the sudden stop, her body slamming hard against the stone. More tentacles lashed out, digging into the rock, making her tenuous hold a sure one.

For more than a minute, she clung to the rock wall as hot wind gusts hammered at her body. Her ears were filled with the heaviest of rumbles, rock against rock, groaning and crumbling. It began to rain thick globs of slimy acid, pelting her body and burning her skin. Soon she was covered in the stuff, gritting her teeth against the stinging pain.

Then suddenly the blowing wind stopped and reversed its direction, sucking Aeoxoea back up the tunnel. She felt herself lifted upside down, slammed against the rock wall once again, but managed to maintain her grip. She remained this way for another minute, feet up, head down, as in control as a butterfly in a hurricane. But eventually the sounds of the earthquake began to quiet, fading toward the surface of the island. Then the wind slowed, and Aeoxoea fell once again. She was left hanging in the darkness, clinging to the rock wall in the quiet, still air, wondering what had just happened.

She was hurt, but not badly. She'd been knocked around a bit, broke a finger, even lost a tooth. Her skin was burned in places, and she couldn't stop coughing. Still, she preferred the mua giou to the Trylon. After a minute or so her coughing subsided, and she was able to climb back up, using her tentacles to find firm holds in the rock, one over the other, like giant, white spider legs.

When she reached the top, her tentacles set her down on her feet on the other side of the large crack which had saved her. Aeoxoea looked down the length of the worm hole, changing her eyes to see the Craft, and to see the image of the past stored within. She could see the knights walking deeper into the mua giou lair, their dogs at their sides, Eleod on Gavin's back, completely unconcerned about what awaited them.

Again, Aeoxoea wondered what had happened to them. She knew they were four days of travel ahead of her; four days of travel closer to the mua giou when it came up the tunnel. Perhaps they tried to fight it. More likely they would have hid from it as she did. But Aeoxoea had been fortunate to find her hiding place in the mostly featureless tunnel, and still she endured an onslaught that would have killed or at least severely wounded any other man.

There was only one way to see if the knights had survived the mua giou.

Aeoxoea began to walk.

Chapter 36

The streets of Widow Hatch were cold and empty the day Theel and Yatham walked through. It was as dead and uninviting a place as Theel had ever seen. The clouds were heavy and hanging low, sucking the sunlight out of the air, sucking the color out of everything. The buildings appeared as decaying bodies, gray and forlorn and some collapsing, with black, unshuttered windows that resembled the eyes of skulls. Even the trees seemed dead, black silhouettes against the gray air, reaching for the sky with gnarled, leafless limbs. The only visible life in the town were the dozens of crows perched in the trees and atop the buildings, little black heads bobbing and cawing and wings fluttering about. Their constant, throaty calls filled the air and frayed the nerves. They ruled this town and they knew it.

Theel had been to Widow Hatch once, some months before, just prior to the death of his father. The masterknight and his squire had merely passed through, heading southward after leaving Yatham at Calfborn. In those days the town was still alive, and had reason to go on living. The Overlies had not yet marched their swords north to Korsiren. Back then, men-at-arms bearing the diamonds and oak leaves were ever present, in the streets and taverns, and manning the gatehouses at the entrance to the Narrows.

But that was before the zoths came, infesting the Narrows like an army of rats. Back then, the town still lived. But now it was dead. Killed. The place was something out of a nightmare. It wasn't as if the people had merely departed, leaving the town to rot. It was as if the presence of the zoths had somehow poisoned the ground.

The air was cold and the wind was harsh, sending leaves swirling around the brothers' ankles as they tramped along the road once so well-traveled, but now marred by patches of weeds. Theel pulled his coat tighter around him, surprised to finding himself craving the warmth and shelter that would be found in the confines of the Narrows.

"It would be nice to feel welcome somewhere in your own homeland," Yatham said. "I hope Herr Ridge, Calfborn, and Widow Hatch aren't the best Embriss has to offer by way of hospitality."

"War does things to a town," Theel said, his teeth chattering.

"War," Yatham agreed, "and the Crowlord."

The brothers had spent the morning and much of the afternoon walking from the road to the upper passes where they'd made camp the night before. The next morning, they picked their way down a steep, rocky slope, using an animal trail to head southwest through the forest until they came to the road, there heading south toward Widow Hatch. By late afternoon, they were nearing their destination. They were almost to the Narrows.

It was the first real walking Theel had done in days, after spending so much time riding on Hoster's ox cart. For the first time in many days, Theel could no longer rely on Chigger and Ragweed to haul his possessions for him. Once again he wore a backpack full of provisions, a tinderbox, a blanket and some food, supplies of seraphim and a wineskin, all gifts from the spirit trader to replace possessions lost in the Trader Cave. A water canteen swung from the straps of his backpack, and a pair of swords hung from his hips. One of the weapons, though sturdy, was rather battered and plain-looking. The other sword was clearly more valuable than its counterpart, shining brightly in the drab air. Its hilt and crosspiece were fashioned to resemble a golden angel, her wings spread wide as she silently sang the Battle Hymn for which she was named.

It was also the first morning in many days that Theel had strapped on his armor. It was made of rare and expensive leather, cut from the hide of the legendary, now extinct, white-horned bullosk. It was as supple as his cotton shirt, yet somehow provided protection as impenetrable as iron plate. Yatham had removed the armor to tend to his brother's wounds after the battle with the Overwatch in the Trader Cave. It had remained in Hoster's cart for days while Theel recovered, but as the brothers and the spirit trader went their separate ways, Theel knew it was time to wear the armor once again.

It was clearly taking some time for Theel's body adjust to the exercise—for his muscles to remember their use. His legs were stiff, and the joints of his knees and ankles ached badly. But this was nothing compared to the aching in this chest, the stab wound that still hadn't completely healed. His armor rubbed against the bandages with each step he took, a constant and painful irritation. He wanted desperately to undo his left shoulder buckle to provide some relief. But that would be the same mistake he'd made in the Trader Cave, when he undid his armor in an attempt to cool off. If he hadn't done that, he wouldn't have suffered the wound in the first place.

Thoughts of quitting constantly entered his mind. He wanted to sit and rest. He wanted to camp for the night. But he also needed the exercise, needed to get his body back into shape. He needed to get his limbs used to the idea of obeying his commands. And he wanted to reach Widow Hatch before sundown.

He got his wish. Just a few more steps and they'd be at the entrance to the Narrows. Not far was an inn called the Cask and Loaves, a place many travelers stayed the night before entering the tunnels. Theel had spent an evening there with his father when they'd passed through, and he'd found it comfortable enough. Even if it was abandoned like the rest of the town, Theel thought the Cask and Loaves would be a fine place to bed for the night—if the zoths hadn't destroyed it.

"Uncle Guarn might have had a friend in this town," Yatham said. "One of his contacts who could help us."

"Let me know if you see him," Theel muttered.

In that moment, Theel placed his foot on a specific spot of earth, and a burst of frozen wind passed through him. He gasped at the sensation, clutching at his chest. It felt like a giant fist had squeezed the breath from his body.

Yatham stopped walking and turned. "Theel? What is it?"

Theel didn't respond. He just stood still in the middle of the road, panting. He placed his foot back on the same spot, pushing the sole of his boot into the dirt and into the Craft weaves that swirled there. The Craft spoke to him, spoke of someone who'd recently set foot on that very spot.

The banner of a noble house flashed in Theel's brain—golden diamonds and oak leaves on a field of green. A quick flash and the image was gone, but it was there just long enough to see the colorful sigil, and the equally colorful spray of blood splashed across the cloth of the banner.

The Overlies.

Terrible emotions crashed over him; not his own, but those of a person who had walked this ground only days before. The emotions lived within the Craft, and were fed to Theel by the magic, forced upon him against his will.

Fear. Pain. Despair. Oh, the children!

"Theel?" he heard his brother saying. "Are you all right?"

His juy sprang to life, responding to those emotions, and the fear and uncertainly that filled his own heart. He didn't want this. Not now. He fought it, and immediately his body fought back. His stomach sickened, his head throbbed. A lightning bolt of pain struck him in the chest, as if he was stabbed a second time in the very same spot. He was about to pass out. Again.

He tried to work with the signals that were pounding his brain, to bend them to something he could understand. The attempt was futile. He might as well attempt to sculpt the clouds with his hands.

You can't listen by talking, the Keeper had told him countless times. *You can't listen by talking.*

So Theel tried to listen. He stopped fighting, and the juy stopped fighting back. With no war to wage, he quickly felt better, and he knew he would maintain consciousness. He took another step, placed his foot in the dirt, and another cold breeze chilled his bones. This time, he did not fight it.

"No!" he shouted. "The children!"

It was his voice, but not his words.

"Theel, what is it?" Yatham asked.

Another step.

"We must save them," Theel said. "They are in danger."

"Who is in danger?" Yatham asked.

He allowed the juy to fill him up, flowing through him like the blood in his veins. He was so full of the power it caused his fingertips to tingle, as if it would burst forth from his skin. Now he began to walk as if following a trail. With each step the juy spoke more to him. And he listened to every word.

"The Overlie children," Theel said, walking, looking around like a bloodhound searching for a scent. "The two little ones who fled from Calfborn." He began to walk briskly. "They survived. They came here."

"The Overlie children? Here?" Yatham asked, following along.

"A boy and a girl," Theel answered. "They came here from Calfborn, fleeing from the battle. It's as clear to my mind as you are to my eyes."

"How do you know this?" Yatham asked.

"I touched the heart of the Overlie boy," Theel explained. "I wetted my fingers with the blood of his family. And now that blood speaks to me."

"What can you see?" Yatham asked. "Where did they go? Were they alone?"

"No," Theel said. "An elderly woman accompanied them." He stopped in the middle of the street, looking around. The crows were thick here, darkening the sky with their wings. The symphony of their shrieking absorbed and destroyed all other sound.

Theel Theel Theel, the crows called, *Theel Theel Theel*.

"What did you say?" Yatham asked.

"An elderly woman accompanied them," Theel repeated. "But she was hurt."

The birds were gathered around a particular house. They covered its roof with a carpet of black feathers and noise. A dozen of them fluttered through its windows and doors as the brothers watched.

Theel Theel Theel.

"An elderly woman?" Yatham asked. "Where?"

Theel pointed at the house. "In there."

Neither of the brothers moved, they just stood and looked at the building. The crows looked back, as if daring them to enter. But they didn't need to enter. They already knew the fate of the old woman because the crows told them.

Theel Theel Theel.

Theel tore his eyes away from the house, looking up the street. "The children continued on without her," he said. "This way."

He walked as quickly as he could, following the trail of emotions left in the Craft at his feet. He could taste the residue left by the children who walked there, could feel their fear as if it was his own.

They were hurriedly taken south from Calfborn for reasons they couldn't understand. But they knew there was danger. They could see it in the eyes of their uncle as he sent them away. They could hear it in the voice of their guardian as she tried to reassure them during the flight. But their horse was lamed by an Iatan arrow and died on the road, forcing them to walk. The old woman's heart wasn't up to the task. She made it to Widow Hatch, only to collapse.

Now the children were alone, and terrified, walking aimlessly, looking for an adult who would tell them what to do. Theel followed their trail down the main road and through the center of the town. All along the way, the children had tried every door, had peered into every window, looking for help, disappointed every time. Their confusion and fear continued to grow. These were privileged children, walking the streets of a town ruled by their family. They should have been welcomed, should have received help. But there was no help. And no one welcomed them but the crows.

The little girl was exhausted and falling behind, pulled along by the boy. She was very young, and had only lived through four harvests. Her pink baby cheeks were covered with tears. She was crying because she'd lost her earring.

They'd passed through the center of town, where the main road began to slope downward. Theel knew the road continued this descent all the way to the south edge of town where it finally disappeared into the mouth of the Narrows. He looked in this direction, and knew immediately this was where the children went.

Diamonds and oak leaves flashed in his mind. He saw the Overlie family, the Lord of Norrester, the Lady Mother, and three children, two of them quite young, the third ... dead. He was dead because of Theel; alive when they found him, but killed when Theel touched his heart.

Theel's steps quickened to a full run, his strides fueled by desperation. It was terrible enough that the two children unwittingly walked upon ground ruled by the Crowlord. If they entered the Narrows, they were entering his lair. Then, they were as good as dead.

"God, if you still care to listen to my prayer, I beg you. Do not allow those children to enter the Narrows," Theel said between heavy breaths. "Keep them from the Narrows. Keep them from the Crowlord."

The brothers rounded a corner in the road and saw a huge black hole gaping like a wound in the earth. It was fifty feet wide, a rectangular shape stabbed into the side of a rocky hill. Several feet into the darkness, a thick white wall could be seen running down its center, cutting the tunnel into two separate shafts.

It was the first time Theel had looked upon the entrance to the Narrows in months. The sight of it evoked chilling memories— thoughts of his father, of traveling south together, but coming back alone. And with the sight of those tunnels came the blackness, the hard ball of ice he'd been carrying around inside his heart. But he refused to acknowledge it. He thought of the Overlie children and their needs, the needs of the living. He thought of the boy in Calfborn, of watching helplessly as he died, literally feeling the boy's heart stop at his touch. And he used all this as a shield against the blackness. No more children would die. A squire must stand and fight.

The opening was guarded by tall wooden scaffolding on both sides. These were normally manned by a dozen swordsmen and archers, Embriss soldiers, or Overlie men-at-arms, but now every post was bare. Theel remembered much more impressive buildings standing on this spot; guardhouses and barracks built of heavy logs with a foundation of stone. The foundations remained, but showed signs of fire, scorched and speckled with soot. Undoubtedly, those buildings had been torched by the Crowlord, and the scaffolding that replaced them seemed hastily constructed, a shoddy framework of planks and slats, hammered together at odd angles by someone with little or no carpentry experience.

On the left side of the scaffolding, a half-dozen gibbets rose from the ground, supporting human-sized bird cages. All of them were occupied by the bodies of criminals captured in the Narrows. Some of them were alive when they were placed there, some of them were not. In either case, their rotting bodies bespoke a warning to any bandits and thieves considering plying their dark trades in the tunnels.

On the east side of the road stood the Cask and Loaves, the inn that had played host to Theel and his father some months before. It once was a beautiful building, and at four stories, the largest structure in Widow Hatch. Now, most of it was gone, consumed by fire just like the guard houses. All that remained were a few chimneys and four charred pillars reaching up to support floors and ceilings that no longer existed.

The children's emotions pulled him in the direction of the inn, a thick cord that tremored like a harp string, playing music only Theel could hear. He followed the notes of sadness, listened to the tearful sobs of the little girl who'd lost her earring. And he listened as those notes sprang from sadness to hope as the children walked past the front step stones of the inn. They'd found someone, an adult who might help. It was a man who called out to them.

"Hail, friends!" a voice shouted, jerking Theel back to reality. The voice echoed among the rocks, giving little indication as to its source.

"Did you hear that?" Yatham asked.

"Yes," Theel answered, his eyes searching. But there was no one there. Nothing but empty scaffolding and dead criminals.

"Hail!" the voice repeated.

One of the lowest-hanging cages rocked gently, catching Theel's attention. There was a man sitting inside, with his legs hanging through the bars. He waved at them, kicking his feet like a child.

The brothers made the short walk to the left of the scaffolding where the gibbets had been erected. The man's prison dangled only feet from the ground, allowing them a full view of his accommodations.

His time in the cage had not been long, but neither had it been forgiving. He was little more than skin and bones; starved, shriveled, and sunburned. His tunic had once been fine, covered with colorful embroidery and tailored to fit his body. But now the colors were dull, the cloth riddled with holes and ripped seams. It appeared he'd been wearing them for weeks or more without washing. His shirt might have been held together by nothing more than mud and sweat stains.

The only things bright and clean about the man were his teeth, and the shining smile he showed them.

"Welcome to Widow Hatch, gentlemen," he said. "My name is Pitchford Wicker, born of the noble House of Wicker, sworn to the greater clan of Aramorun, though you might choose to call me Pitch, as most do."

He extended his hand through the bars.

Theel looked at the man's dirty hand and his white teeth, and in that moment, his mind again flashed to the past. He could see the same man, sitting in the same cage, but now it was from a different perspective. In his vision, Theel was much shorter, looking up at the cage through the eyes of a child.

"My name is Pitchford Alister, born of the noble House of Alister, sworn to the greater clan of Embriss," the man said to the little girl, smiling with his white teeth. "Though you might choose to call me Pitch, as most do."

In the present, the man was still speaking. "It is an honor to make your acquaintances, good sirs." His hand continued to hover in the air, unshaken. "Might I inquire as to your names?"

"I didn't hear you," Theel said. "To which noble house are you born?"

"I am honored to call the House of Wicker of Clan Aramorun my birthplace and home," the man said, smiling.

"I am born of House Alister of Embriss, my sweetling," the man said to the little girl. "Only one earring you wear, but it is a truly beautiful treasure for a truly beautiful girl. What are those gems? Diamonds and garnets? Oh, oak leaves! Tell me, are you a child of the Overlie family?"

"Your name is Pitch?" Theel asked.

"Yes, sir, Pitch Wicker," the man repeated. "Of the noble House of Wicker."

"... of the noble House of Alister," the man said. "As an Overlie, you must know of the Alisters. We are called the Valley Lords because we rule all the lands of the Toden, which includes Norrester and Widow Hatch. We are the masters of House Overlie. I am your father's liege lord."

"Very well, Pitch of House Wicker," Theel said. "Have you seen two children walking this road recently?"

"I've seen no one on this road, though I've prayed to see someone, anyone," the man said. "I've begged my Lord in heaven to send salvation from this cruel injustice, and now my prayers are answered in the form of you two fine sirs."

"... in the form of you two wonderful sweetlings," the man said to the children. *"Now quickly, you must find the key to this lock and free me, so I can take you to your mother. You are so wonderfully smart. I know you can do it. Your father will be so proud that you gave aid to his master."*

"Why are you in that cage?" Yatham asked. "What crimes put you there?"

"I've committed no crime, dear sirs, but do confess to one great weakness."

"What is that?" Theel asked.

"The love I have for my brother the welsher," the man answered. "Curse my trusting heart. I agreed to be imprisoned to serve his sentence as he went south to the Sister Cities. He swore on the soil under which our dear mother rests that he would return with the coin to pay his debts and free me from this cage, and I believed him. I am such a fool. Oh, curse my trusting heart."

"They asked me to join in the plot to hurt your father," the man said. *"I refused them so they locked me in this cage. You must free me so we can warn your father. You must bring me the key!"*

"You're lying," Theel said. "Tell me the truth."

"Lying?" The man's smile was as bright as ever. "Certainly not. On my honor as a Wicker."

"On my honor as an Alister," the man said. *"But first you must bring me the key to this cage."*

"You asked them for the key," Theel stated. "What became of them?"

"Who do you speak of?" the man asked.

"The children."

"What children?"

"The two Overlie children," Theel said sternly, angrily. "You spoke with them. You asked them to find the key to your prison."

"The key? It will be found in that tunnel," The man said. *"The Narrows, you call it? Well, you must enter the Narrows and find the key. You must do it immediately!"*

"You have me perplexed, good sir." The man smiled again. "I know not of which you speak."

"Yes you do. You know precisely," Theel said. "You begged them to free you from your cage."

"I've seen no one."

"You saw two children," Theel said. "You told them to enter the Narrows to find the key to your prison. Did they do as you bade them? Did they enter the Narrows?"

"My humblest apologies, my liege," the man said. "But I don't know of what you speak, on my honor as a Wicker."

"Liar! Do not speak of honor," Theel spat. "Where did they go? Did they enter the Narrows?"

"My humblest apologies, my liege—"

"Don't call me that," Theel growled. "I am no one's liege. Where did the children go?"

"I do not know."

"Yes you do." Theel drew his sword. "Tell me or I'll kill you."

"It is clear we have some sort of misunderstanding."

"No, there is no misunderstanding," Theel said, and banged the blade of his sword against the cage bars. "I believe I am being perfectly clear." He hit the bars again. "Tell me where the children are."

"But I don't—"

Theel hit the cage a final time, now taking aim at the spot where the man's hand gripped the bars. A loud cracking of knuckles was heard, followed by a yelp of pain as the man jerked back, clutching his hand and grimacing.

"Tell me now or you die!" Theel roared. "Now!"

The man was quiet, rubbing his fingers, with a wounded look on his face.

"Now!" Theel jabbed his blade between the bars and the man screamed, trying to squirm out of the way.

"Mercy! Mercy!" the man shrieked. "Oh, God, help me. Mercy!"

"God won't help you," Theel growled, pushing the point of the blade toward the man's throat.

"I know where they went!" he shouted. "Don't hurt me. Oh God, don't hurt me."

"Where did they go?" Theel asked, his sword blade hovering.

"Free me from this cage," the man demanded.

"Where?"

"Free me and I'll tell you."

"Tell me or I'll kill you."

"Kill me and it's over," the man said. "Kill me and you'll never know what became of those children."

With those words came a roaring in Theel's ears, and another flash to the past. And once again he knew he was seeing through the eyes of another person.

"Enter the Narrows and find the key," the man said to the little girl with one earring. "Free me and I'll take you back to your mother and father."

"You'll help us?" Theel said in the present. "You promise to help us find Father?"

"Excuse me?" the man said, confused.

"If I bring you the key, you promise to take me to Father?" Theel said. "You promise?"

"Yes, I'll promise anything," the man said, still rubbing his fingers. "Just free me from this cage."

"I promise I will help," the man said. "I will take you to your father. Come closer sweetling. Don't cry."

He reached out and brushed the little girl's cheek, wiping the tears away.

"I promise to help you," he said, smiling with his white teeth.

His touch was tender and reassuring, and the little girl felt the tiniest spark of trust.

"I promise."

Then he drew his hand away from her cheek and he held her earring between his fingers, white diamonds and garnets cut like oak leaves. She gasped and felt at her earlobe. There was nothing there. He'd taken it. And now she'd lost both earrings. More tears filled her eyes as he waved the diamonds and garnets at her.

"Enter the Narrows. Find the key," he said coldly. "Or I keep your little bauble."

Theel was jolted back to reality by a rush of emotions so intense his hands shook. He was filled with rage at what he'd just witnessed, and not just his own. His fingertips tingled as if he could still feel the blood of the Overlie boy there. And the blood seemed to be crying out in anguish.

Theel didn't bother to look for the key. He walked around the cage to where the door was closed and locked, drew his father's knife, and jammed it into the key hole.

"Oh, thank you, kind sir, thank you," the man breathed.

Then Theel slammed his sword against the lock with a loud clang.

"Brother?" Yatham asked. "What are you doing?"

Theel didn't answer, only slammed the lock again. Sparks flew.

"At last, God above has answered my prayers," the man said, his eyes watering with tears of gratitude. "I will show you to the children. I won't disappoint you. I will show you."

Theel smashed the lock a third time and that was enough. The door fell open, and the man smiled at him for the last time.

"Thank you," he said.

"I freed you," Theel said. "Now show me."

"Certainly, I will show you," the man said. "Another day."

He pulled Theel's knife out of the keyhole and lunged at him with it. It was a clumsy, unpracticed stab, but it was enough to put Theel off balance. As he stumbled backward the man crashed into him, and they both fell to the ground. Those could have been Theel's final moments, flat on his back, vulnerable as the man knelt over him with his father's knife. But the prisoner had no taste for battle, only his new-found freedom. He dropped the knife, jumped to his feet, and ran.

"Stop!" Theel roared. He grabbed at the man's ankle, but ended up with only his shoe. The man was tall and skinny, and fleet of foot. Despite limping on one shoe, he was already across the road before Theel gathered his bearings.

"He's fast," Yatham said.

"Not fast enough," Theel said, jumping to his feet. He shrugged off his backpack and gave chase.

On the west side of the road, the man vaulted the waist-high stone wall of the burned-out guards' barracks, then climbed onto the lowest level of scaffolding.

"Mercy! Mercy!" he screamed. "God help me!"

"I'll kill you!" Theel shouted, right behind.

"Mercy!"

The man climbed to the second level, then the third. He was quite nimble for a man who'd spent many days starving and roasting in a crow cage, but he could not climb faster than Theel.

"Leave me be!" he shouted. "I've done nothing to you!"

He reached the top and Theel caught him from behind, tackling him onto the hard boards where they fought, muscle against muscle. The next few seconds saw a flurry of elbows and knuckles, kicking and grunting and bones thudding against wood. The man may have been a scrawny thing, but he was no weakling. Unfortunately, his attacker was a squire and son of a knight, trained for his entire life to stand among the elite warriors of the realm. Theel was on the verge of becoming a Knight of the Southern Cross. Therefore, this poor fool was on the verge of having his bones tied in knots.

Theel wrestled the man onto his stomach, forcing his arms back by his wrists. He then pressed a knee between his shoulder blades, tying his arms behind his back in a vice-like grip. He pushed the man's face down hard, scraping his cheek across the dirty wooden platform.

"You stole from her," Theel growled. "You stole from a tiny girl."

"Help! Mercy!"

"Diamonds and garnets," Theel said. "They were all she had and you took them."

"Oh God, help me!"

"Where is it?" Theel asked. "Where is the girl's earring?"

"I don't know," the man moaned.

"Give it to me," Theel said.

"I can't," the man said. "I lost it. It was stolen."

"Was it lost or was it stolen?" Theel asked. "Tell me."

"I don't know," the man said. "I woke up and it was gone, I swear!"

"What is your name, liar?" Theel asked.

"Pitch ... ford," the man grunted. "Wick—"

"Lies," Theel spit. "You are no Alister. Tell me true or I'll stuff you back in your cage."

"Pitch," the man grunted. "I swear it. By the ... by the soil under which ... my dear mother—"

"Worthless words, Pitch the Liar," Theel said. "Tell me where the children went. Did they go into the Narrows?"

"I don't ..." the man cried weakly. "I can't ..."

Theel leaned heavily into his hold, and the man screamed in agony. He face was purple, his eyes bulging.

"Your shoulders are about to pop, Pitch the Liar," Theel said. "You will never use your arms again."

"Narrows!" the man screamed. "The Narrows!"

Theel relaxed his hold, but just slightly. "How long ago?" he asked.

"A day," he moaned. "Just yesterday."

"Yesterday." Theel released the man's arms and stood over him. "Yesterday you stole from a girl only four seasons old?" He kicked the man hard in the ribs, prompting another scream of pain. "You stole this girl's last possession then sent her to her death, into the lair of the Crowlord?" He kicked the man in the face. "Is that what you did yesterday, Pitch the Liar?"

Blood ran from the man's mouth. "I was ... locked ... in a ..."

"I don't care!" Theel screamed.

"Theel?" Yatham called from below.

"I don't care, Pitch the Liar. I don't care, Pitchford Wicker. Pitchford Alister!" Theel roared. He kicked the man again. And again.

"Are you going to kill him?" Yatham asked.

Theel looked down at his brother. "Not yet." His chest wound had reopened in the struggle, and fresh blood flowed anew, causing his shirt to stick to his chest. But he didn't care about that, either.

"You might consider hurrying," Yatham said, "if we mean to help those children."

"I mean to help those children," Theel said. "We're not staying the night in Widow Hatch. We will enter the Narrows tonight. And you, you son of a bitch!" He bent down and grabbed the man by the throat with both hands. "You will lead the way!"

Chapter 37

Theel had traveled the Narrows before. It was only months since he'd come through with his father and masterknight, so he was already familiar with the many amazing and perplexing features that made the tunnels so unique. He'd already walked on the smooth, gray river of stone with its painted white lines. He'd already seen the tiled walls and the glass boxes on the ceiling which once illuminated the tunnels with their magical glow. No one knew what ancient civilization had built the Narrows, nor what need was fulfilled by having two tunnels running perfectly parallel for miles beneath the earth, when both were wide enough to accommodate two-way wagon traffic. What he did know was that the Narrows provided a more direct route to the lands of southern Embriss than any other for hundreds of miles in any direction. They did this by cutting deep into the belly of Thershon, under the western branch of the Great Dividers Mountains, and over the canyon known as Krillian's Cut by way of a span travelers had dubbed the Dead Man's Bridge. Since before the birth of the old clans, the Narrows had always been the smoothest, safest, and most direct path through the mountains.

As a result, it also became the costliest. The potential for profit offered by the Narrows was seized upon by the local lords who controlled the entrances. The Embriss-sworn house of Overlie ruled the town of Widow Hatch at the north end, while the Yarik-loyal Ducharmes controlled Wrendale at the south end. Tolls levied by the nobles varied according to season, traffic density, and whatever mood had seized the local lords on any given day. Entrance fees were never lower than a half-ten, or five hours of the king's work per person or wagon axle. That was when the popularity of the Narrows was at an all-time high, when the route under the Dividers and across the Dead Man's Bridge was the preferred method of north-south travel. It was a time when the Narrows were so safe that wealthy clansmen and nobles from the north came to Widow Hatch just to see this ancient wonder. But that time was long dead.

There were always those would not travel the Narrows for reasons other than the steep tolls, those whose superstitions kept them away. There had always been hushed whispers of the dangers lurking in the tunnels, stories of curses and hauntings and monsters, such as the spitting lizard children, and the Cave Kraken. But the most popular of these were vanishings, stories of travelers who entered the tunnels, never to emerge on the other side. These souls became trapped in the tunnels, it was said, condemned to roam the Narrows as shades or wights or any number of terrible things.

The most well-known was the legend of an elderly fortune teller whose phantom haunted the area north of the Dead Man's Bridge. In her mortal life, she walked almost the full length of the Narrows before sitting to rest. She fell asleep, and when she awoke, she forgot which direction she was traveling and went back the way she came. With no sun to gauge which way she should go, she repeated her mistake, traveling back and forth, until the endless darkness drove her insane. Supposedly, her ghost still roamed the tunnels, haunting the dreams of those foolish enough to fall asleep before their journey was through.

Though he enjoyed these stories, Theel always knew them to be just silly legends told to amuse children. Now, he knew, there was no need for campfire tales, for real horrors had replaced the imagined ones.

The first bodies were found a few months before Theel and his father had passed through. There were six of them, men sworn to Lord Overlie, who were butchered and boiled, their bones piled on the floor of the tunnel. Nothing remained of their possessions save the bloody Overlie war emblems torn from their chests and arranged among the bones as if they were meant to be found.

All the tell-tale signs were there. Any man who'd served on the frontier recognized these killings for what they were—not the work of men or beasts, but something much worse. And yet, the nobles refused to accept the truth, insisting this was an isolated attack, the work of road bandits. Once these bandits were captured and brought to justice, they said, the Narrows would be safe again. But the attack wasn't isolated. The bandits weren't captured. And the Narrows were never safe again.

Not only did the murders not stop, they increased, until victims were being found almost every day, killed in gruesome ways, hacked to pieces, their blood painting the white-tiled walls of the Narrows. Lord Overlie sent some of his best men into both tunnels to deal with the threat. None of them returned. Two knights of House Ducharme led a dozen men into the entrance at Wrendale. Only one of the knights returned, headless, his body still clinging to the neck of his horse.

Shortly after, some travelers spotted a deathmark hanging on the Dead Man's Bridge, a bloody necklace of fingers and eyes. This ended all question as to who was responsible for the killings. A zoth tribe had claimed the Narrows as their own. And they would have no fear or concern for the evil that lived in the Narrows, for they were now the evil that lived in the Narrows.

This zoth tribe was led by a chieftain of terrifying notoriety, a seven-foot monster known as the Crowlord. This nickname was given him because he chose to decorate his head with crow feathers, and stories were told of flocks of the black birds filling the skies preceding his attacks. This single zoth warrior was responsible for the deaths of countless people, soldiers by the hundreds, men, women, and children of all the Western Kingdoms, and even three Knights of the Southern Cross.

It became impossible to deny the danger of traveling the Narrows the first time the Crowlord emerged from the southern end, followed by a score of his warriors. They attacked Wrendale, murdered dozens of citizens, and burned much of the town, ceasing the battle only when each zoth had claimed a human being to drag away as a prisoner.

It was a terrible time for this to occur, with most of the Overlie swords facing the Iatan in the valley. The people of Widow Hatch knew they could not be protected. No one dared enter the Narrows any longer, so there was no reason to stay and wait to be slaughtered by the zoths. The business died. Then the town died. And the Narrows were abandoned to the Crowlord.

Only someone who wished for death would enter the tunnels now. Or someone hoping to stop two children from unknowingly walking to their deaths. Theel was one of these two. Problem was, he didn't know which.

He ran with his old, worn sword in his hand. His father's weapon, the golden long sword called Battle Hymn, remained in its sheath, slapping at his hip with each step. Yatham was behind him carrying a makeshift torch he'd created from a table leg taken from the Cask and Loaves. The man who called himself Pitch Wicker led the way, just as Theel insisted, running against his will, the tip of Theel's sword blade in his back as the primary encouragement to keep a good pace forward.

Theel ran himself to the point of exhaustion. His hair was wet and stuck to his forehead and could absorb no more, leaving little rivers of perspiration to run down his face, down into his eyes, stinging his vision. Every inch of his body was slippery with sweat. Every part of his body ached—not just the hole next to his heart, and his swollen pulpy face, which throbbed as if pounded by a hammer with each step he took. He felt pain in places that bore no wounds. But he was almost numb to it, only aware of an intense headache of exhaustion and thirst, of a dozen smithy hammers pounding in his head. He panted and coughed and stumbled, but forced himself to keep moving.

Theel was a squire to the Knights of the Southern Cross, and had suffered many years of strict education and conditioning. This work was less exercise than was expected by his father during most training days. But those were better days, in ideal conditions, with perfect health. These hours of running came at the end of a long walk down from the Calfborn road to the Upper Passes, a route which led to the Sister Cites–the safer route Hoster preferred to take his mule cart. It was a long day and a long night. It was almost too much for Theel to ask of his battered body, yet he pushed.

Yatham ran behind him, and had no trouble keeping pace. He ran heavy in breath and sweat, but with the usual strong legs and strong lungs that so often frustrated his older brother. It was one of many attributes Yatham had inherited from their father that Theel had not. Theel knew Yatham could run forever, a distance horse who was always in the first mile of a hundred-mile race. It was annoying, but Theel was often thankful for it. His brother had never, *would* never, slow him down. Now was such a time. Yatham stayed with him and didn't utter a word of complaint, just kept pace and watched Theel's back, as always.

Pitch was the complete opposite. He had no lungs, no wind, and no legs. He stumbled along, a hopeless, weeping wretch, with the exhausted and awkward gait of man past his limits. He gasped and wheezed and cried out, holding his head, holding his belly, tripping and falling and crying out for mercy to anyone who would listen.

Perhaps God was listening, but Theel wasn't. When Pitch slowed, he got the sword in his back. When he stopped, he was kicked and shoved and cursed. When he fell, Theel beat him back to his feet with kicks and punches and every oath imaginable, while Yatham looked on disapprovingly.

The white-tiled walls of the Narrows stretched away into darkness, both before and behind them. Yatham's torch burned large and hot, trailing fingers of black smoke, providing just enough light to splay their shadows about them in a mad dance against the pale tiles. It was just enough to show them some of the signs that this dark and quiet place, once so busy with life, was now perverted with death.

First, there was the occasional spatter of blood on the tiled walls, or a broken sword or spear lying in the road. Then piles of animal waste, human waste, and discarded trash, rotting melon rinds, a rabbit skin, a few animal bones, a shoe full of holes, a cracked iron pot. Then they passed the corpse of a horse, rotting and buzzing with flies, stripped of most of its flesh. Then Theel saw a hand. A human hand, gray and bloated and discarded at the side of the road like a piece of trash.

Theel wondered about the Overlie children, what they thought of seeing these things. He could no longer sense them, where they walked or what they were thinking. Yet he still felt the strange urgent tugging of the Overlie blood on his fingers. He was certain they'd been in this tunnel. But the visions that once bombarded his mind now refused to come back.

He wanted to bring them back by tapping his juy to employ his Sight. He wanted to look into the past to feel the children, to feel their thoughts, or see what they said and did when walking this ground. But he dared not. The visions that once came unbidden were now elusive. He knew he lacked the discipline to control his juy, knew his "gift" of Sight would only show him things he had no desire to see, things he wished to forget. If he sought information about the fate of the Overlie children, his mind would be flooded with unwanted memories of his father, of the torturous relationship he, as a squire, shared with his masterknight.

He didn't need his juy to help him remember the pain. This tunnel contained memories enough without using the Method. It was only months before, when his father still lived, and the knight and his squire walked this very tunnel. Theel had many unwanted memories of his father, but this was among the worst, and now he was forced to remember by retracing his steps.

They'd walked through the Narrows side by side, squire and masterknight, Theel and his father, for miles. And as the miles went by and the hours dragged on, not one word was said. Theel's heart was bursting with the years of pent-up feelings he yearned to express. Countless times they were on his lips; he even inhaled the breath needed to say them. But he always lost courage at the last moment, exhaling empty air.

He didn't know at the time that his father felt the same way, wanting to say something, but unable to find the courage. It seemed impossible from a man who was renowned for his strength of will, who'd faced down a dozen zoth chieftains and countless zoth warriors without faltering once. But this was the one battle for which he was ill-prepared, where his skill with a sword could not help him. So he walked this tunnel for hours, struggling with what to say, and how to say it.

Eventually the masterknight did break the silence, when they stopped to rest for a few hours. He decided he needed to address the bad feelings between him and his son, even if he was unprepared and unsure of how to do it. But these were thoughts and emotions that had simmered, waiting to explode, for years. Theel yelled at his father, relentlessly, cruelly, saying things he didn't even know were inside him. He almost didn't care what he was saying; he simply wanted to hurt his father as badly as he could. He wanted to exact revenge for what his father had done to him. But no matter how angry he became, or how hurtful his words were, it never seemed to be enough. He'd never be able to soothe his pain, or heal his wounds, not with all the screams and curses in the world.

The more time Theel spent in this tunnel, the more he was forced to face this memory. And the farther down the tunnel Theel walked, the closer he came to the place where this exchange had occurred. He dreaded that moment. He knew there was no way the extreme emotions of that place wouldn't ignite his juy and torment him with visions of what occurred there.

He couldn't bear the pain of these memories, so he tried to squash them as hard as he could, tried to bury them in a grave so deep and dark they would never be found again. He didn't want to think of his father anymore. He didn't want to remember what happened in this tunnel, no matter the cost.

He tried to focus his mind on the task at hand, trying to think of nothing but those children. Nothing but the sight of the endless tunnel before, and the endless tunnel behind; the heavy breath of three men, and the shambling steps of the exhausted man named Pitch. Much like the first time Theel had walked this ground, no one said a word for miles.

Then Theel got the distraction he wanted, and suddenly his father was the farthest thing from this mind. The three men came upon a wagon laying on its side, two wheels smashed, the other two missing. Wooden boxes lay about, scattered and smashed open, their contents spilled across the road amid heaps of packing straw. It appeared to be a trader of some kind, hauling textiles, spices, perfumes, and liquors, and ceramic kitchenware, plates, bowls, cups and pitchers, some of the finest of the north. They were all cracked and broken, discarded by creatures who had no use for finery. The trader himself, or what was left of him, was tied to the top of the wagon, arms held wide in a scene so gruesome Pitch fell to the ground in tears. The wounds were days-old, with blood darkened and dried, hundreds of cuts applied delicately and precisely in a process meant to extract maximum agony. But beyond the horror of what had been done to the man, was what had been done to his eyes—cut out, or torn out, and ... replaced.

Yatham walked forward slowly, holding his torch high. The firelight flashed in the man's eyes, reflecting like a cat's. Or a zoth's.

"Oh God no!" Pitch wailed pitifully. "We're dead."

A pair of black zoth eyes now resided in the man's skull, moving as if alive, glaring at the three men hatefully. From somewhere, a shaman was watching them.

"They see us now. They know we're here!" Pitch cried. "We're dead. We're dead. We're dead!"

"You're dead already, fool," Theel said.

He jumped up onto the wagon and seized the dead trader's head in his hands, lifting it so he could meet the gaze of the zoth eyes.

"Do you see me, Crowlord?" he whispered. "I'm coming. You can't have those children. I'm coming to take them from you. And when I do, one of us is going to die."

"Have you gone mad?" Pitch moaned.

"Perhaps I have."

"Do you yearn for death?" Pitch asked.

"Perhaps," Theel repeated. He drew his father's knife and used the blade to cut the zoth eyes out. He cast them on the ground, and crushed them with his boot heel.

"You've killed us," Pitch wailed. "We're dead!"

"Shut up!" Theel growled.

Nearby, Yatham was being resourceful, as usual. "Lantern oil," he announced, digging through the trader's possessions. "And food."

Theel stood over Pitch, who cowered on the ground, curled in a ball.

"Get up," Theel commanded.

"Please, don't make me ... we must go back," the man blubbered. "Back to Widow Hatch, please."

He shoved Pitch with his foot. "Stand up," he said. "Have you no manhood? Stand up!"

"No," Pitch whimpered. "I can't. No."

"Those two children continued on after seeing this," Theel said. "Does a little girl of four seasons have more stomach than you?"

Pitch covered his head, knowing what was to come. "Yes."

Theel knelt down and punched Pitch in the ear, causing more sobs of pain. "Get up you pathetic ... you pitiful, wretched ... on your feet!"

"Theel," Yatham said calmly.

"I hate you." Theel kicked Pitch in the back, then the front, then wacked him with the flat of his sword. "So help me, I hate your bones. I will kill you here and now."

"Theel, stop this," Yatham said.

"Kill me," Pitch pleaded. "End it now, please."

"No," Theel said. "Death would be too good for you."

Another kick. Then another. Pitch groaned and wept, so distressed he was unable to form any words.

"Foul wretch, get up!" Theel cursed, and kicked him again.

"Theel," Yatham said. "This doesn't accomplish—"

"Shut your mouth, brother," Theel growled. "I will not listen to you. Not now. There will be justice. It will come for this man on this day, or there is nothing true in this world."

"Justice?" Yatham asked. "What justice?"

"Justice for the Overlies," Theel answered. "And justice for Calfborn."

"This man played no role in Calfborn," Yatham said. "It was the Iatan."

"Those children may be the last survivors of Calfborn," Theel said.

"Why does that matter?"

"If those children die, Calfborn dies, forever."

"This solves nothing," Yatham said. "Leave him. We can save those children without him. He has only slowed us down."

"Yatham, do not question me," Theel warned. "I will do this as I see fit."

"This solves nothing," Yatham said again. "You will kill him."

"It solves nothing? It solves everything," Theel said. "It is not I who will kill him. This man will die, but not by my hand. He will die fighting the Crowlord. He will die fighting for those children, that little girl that he robbed and sent to her death. He put her in danger with his lies. So it is he who will fight to save her. And it is he who will return what was stolen from her. It's justice, brother. It's justice because I say it is."

"No it isn't," Yatham said. "No matter what you say."

"I don't care what you think about this," Theel growled.

"Only God metes out true justice."

"Only God metes out justice?" Theel asked. "Then why does our precious knighthood exist? Why do we prance around with our swords and spears, spouting treatises on justice, if there is none?

We're in the Narrows, brother. Not so far from Yarik, the old clan of justice. And we were born of Embriss, you and I; Embriss, the old clan of order. Our father fought for the Kingdom of Embriss, fought his whole life for the Clan of Order. How will we achieve order without justice?"

"You're speaking nonsense," Yatham said. "This has nothing to do with justice."

"Yatham, you don't know what was done to Calfborn," Theel retorted. "Someone is going to pay for that."

"I saw what happened in Calfborn," Yatham said. "Hurting this man will not bring those people back."

"You think you saw what happened there?" Theel said. "Oh, no you didn't, brother. You saw the aftermath. You saw what was left. You didn't see what truly happened. You didn't see the mother's faces as the soldiers tore their babies from their hands. You didn't see the eyes of those children as they were carried off by the cavalry, off to some horrible place to be slaves or worse. You didn't see what they did to Jarcet the Sentinel, did you? You didn't see what they did to your mentor."

"No, I didn't," Yatham said, flat-faced.

"I wish you had, brother. I never knew him before, but I know him now," Theel said. "I know him now better than you or father ever did, because I saw his last moments. I saw how he fought the Iatan, how they bested him with numbers, how he surrendered with some of his men, and how they were all tortured and executed. They burned his entire body. And I saw his face. I saw his eyes. Jarcet the Sentinel wants justice. I know it. I can hear his voice in my head. He deserves justice. He fought and died, and now we must fight in his place, in Father's place, for justice and order. We must stand and fight. It is time. It is finally time. I understand this now."

Yatham said nothing, only looked at his brother with concern.

"It's why you struck me in the face, is it not?" Theel said, pointing to his swollen cheek. "Because you want to find the Blessed Soul of Man? Because you want to win this war? Thank

433

you for striking me. I needed it. I understand now that I must quest for Warrior Baptism, to find the Blessed Soul. I must find the Blessed Soul and win this war. We must put a stop to this."

Yatham nodded. "You are right."

"There will never be another Calfborn," Theel said. "There will not be another town destroyed in this war. Not another husband killed, mother raped, or child stolen. It ends now. Starting today. I'm sick of complaining that there is no justice in this world. It's time I started making my own justice. Hoster taught me that. It's time to stop talking and start doing. He was right in saying that. Now I will start doing things.

"I want the world to know, there has been a change in the heart that beats in my breast. Nothing is going to stop me. Not this deathmark, and not these zoths. I have a quest more powerful, more important than Warrior Baptism could ever be. I'm prepared to run this road of darkness and shed as much blood as is necessary to achieve it. And I will drag this wretched fool with me. All the way to the lair of the Crowlord, if need be. We might only find death. But we might also save two babes. Either way, your God's will is done. Justice is done this day."

"What are you talking about?" Yatham asked.

"You know what I am talking about," Theel growled. "We will find justice this day, Pitch and I, on the Dead Man's Bridge."

Yatham thought for a moment, then said, "This has nothing to do with Warrior Bap—"

"Finally you understand!" Theel roared.

"No. I don't," Yatham said. "Saving those children is good and righteous. Warrior Baptism is good and righteous. Beating and cursing this man is not. Dragging him to the Dead Man's Bridge to die is not. It is only ugly and pointless."

"It may be ugly, but it is not pointless," Theel retorted. "Justice can't always be pretty. But it must be done. And he and I will do it, together."

"You can't fix anything by dying, brother."

"Yes I can."

"You must forget this and pursue Warrior Baptism."

"I will pursue Warrior Baptism, brother, I promise," Theel said. "I'm going to go to the Outlands and find the Blessed Soul, and I'm going to become a Knight of the Southern Cross, and I will be the greatest champion the Western Kingdoms has ever seen. But I begin that quest only when the deeds of today are done. Only when the wretched piece of scum called Pitch has fought and died for those children. Only when the wretched piece of scum called Theel has faced the Crowlord. Only when justice is done on the Dead Man's Bridge, brother. Only then will my quest for Warrior Baptism begin."

Yatham said nothing, only looked down to where Pitch cowered. The man, thinking he was unnoticed, reached out for something lying in the piles of straw spilled from the crates, a small glass bubbler, filled with a brown liquid. He clutched it to his chest.

Yatham looked back to his brother, who was panting, covered with sweat, and staring at him wild-eyed.

"I know you'll hurt to hear this, because my words will echo Father's," Yatham said. "But I have long yearned to see you take command of yourself, to take responsibility, make decisions and take decisive action. Now you are doing this. It is pleasing to see. So I won't try to stop you from the course you've chosen."

"That is good," Theel said.

"This means the outcome of our wager is settled," Yatham said.

"What?" Theel looked confused. "I'm being serious."

"As am I," Yatham said. "I've won the wager, have I not?"

"What wager is that?" Theel asked.

"You must now admit that Father was right about the Blessed Soul," Yatham explained.

"There is no time for this, brother," Theel said, suddenly defensive.

"I know there isn't time," Yatham said. "So admit this now, and we'll move on. And we won't speak of it again. Father was right about the Blessed Soul."

"This has nothing to do with Father."

"Then forget what father said," Yatham said. "Just admit the Blessed Soul exists and we must find him. Admit this is the Second War of Souls we are fighting."

"This may be the Second War of Souls," Theel said.

"And the Blessed Soul exists," Yatham prompted.

"And the Blessed Soul might exist."

"Does exist."

"Perhaps," Theel said. "Let's move."

"Admit Father was right."

"I'll admit nothing," Theel said. "And I'll wait for you no longer. Pitch, you've rested enough. Get up. On your feet. Yatham, give me the torch."

Yatham didn't give him the torch. "Father was right," he insisted. "He was not a liar. You will say it."

"I will say the Blessed Soul exists if we save those children," Theel said. "Then I'll know there is a God."

"Good," Yatham said. "It's a start."

"We won't save those children blathering about your petty wager."

"It's your petty wager," Yatham corrected. "Not mine."

"It doesn't matter," Theel said. "On your feet, Pitch."

The brothers grabbed the man under his arms and hauled him to his feet, where he stood uneasily, hunched over, still upset and clearly exhausted, hugging the glass bubbler to his chest.

"I didn't know there were zoths," he said weakly.

"Now you know," Theel said.

"Believe me," Pitch whined. "I didn't know."

"Shut your mouth," Theel commanded.

"The wager is won," Yatham said. "You are going to wash my clothes for a month, brother."

"We'll see if that happens," Theel said.

"Oh God, forgive me," Pitch moaned.

"We'll see if that happens, as well," Theel said. "Move."

He shoved the wretched man forward, and the running began anew.

Chapter 38

The tunnel had collapsed.

Only a few miles beyond the spot where the three men passed the wreck of the trader's wagon, they found their way blocked, with the roadway disappearing under a heap of rocks and dust. They stood together, no one saying anything, too tired to speak, just three mouths hanging open, panting from the exertion of the run. They stared at the pile of rocks with looks of confusion and worry. Pitch put his hands on his knees, gasping, his shoulders shaking.

"Oh no, oh God," he cried. "They're gone, Lord save me. They're dead." He coughed and spit, and fell to his knees, overwhelmed. "I didn't know ... "

"Quiet, Pitch," Theel said, forcing the words out, gasping for air himself.

He looked at the wall of rock and debris in the flickering yellow torchlight, the scattered white tiles, and the road beneath his feet broken into large sections by some force, an earthquake perhaps. And that wasn't all. Lying among the tiles was a broken spear and a dented half-helm. And dark spatters.

"Someone died here," Yatham said, sweeping his torch across the floor.

The flickering light fell across more evidence of battle; a short sword, another spear, and a green surcoat, shredded and blood-stained.

"Who died?" Pitch asked. "Was it the children?"

"No, not the children," Theel said.

Yatham picked up the surcoat, holding it to the torchlight. "Diamonds and oak leaves. They were Overlie men."

Theel picked up the helm, turning it over. There was a large dent in the top where a hole was punched. It was the strongest part of the iron helm, and yet it was split open like a melon. The force required to do this was more than any living man possessed. And yet, the proof was resting in Theel's hands.

It also rested in his memory, the black iron spikes that made that hole, and the zoth chieftain who wielded them. This was the work of the Crowlord.

Yatham walked toward the pile of debris, holding his torch high.

"This happened recently," he said. "I hope it didn't separate us from the children."

"Did it bury them?" Pitch asked.

No one answered.

Theel walked forward with Yatham, the two picking their way between the boulders, looking at the dirt and dust. Yatham began to pick his way up the rock wall, torch in hand.

"These rocks haven't been here long," Yatham said, as debris tumbled beneath his feet. "No more than a day."

"Pitch, how far ahead of us were the children?" Theel asked.

Pitch didn't say anything, only sat on his heels, staring at the ground, dry washing his hands.

"Pitch?" Theel asked. "How far ahead of us were the children? Answer me."

"I don't know," Pitch said, staring at the ground.

"You don't know?" Theel asked, turning to look at him. He couldn't see very well, but heard the man's voice coming from the darkness.

"I don't know where they are," Pitch said miserably. "Why haven't we seen them? This is not good. No."

Theel drew his sword and walked to Pitch's side, holding the naked blade before the man's eyes to emphasize his words.

"Pitch, listen to me," he said. "You need to think. When did those children enter this tunnel?"

"Some hours."

"Some hours?"

"Before us," Pitch added. "Just hours. We should have found them by now, but we ... Now it's too late. They're gone. What have I done?"

"Did you see them enter the tunnel?" Theel asked.

"Yes," Pitch said. "I think so."

"Are we in the correct tunnel?" Theel asked. "Did they enter the southward tunnel?"

"Which is the ... ?" Pitch asked.

"Which tunnel did they enter?" Theel asked. "The left tunnel or right?"

"Two tunnels?" Pitch said. "I've never been here before!" He dropped his head in his hands.

Theel threw his hands up and shouted, "A perfect answer from a perfect liar! Oh my dear son of Embriss, citizen of Widow Hatch, how is it you keep your home next to the northern opening, yet are unaware that two tunnels make the Narrows? How is that? Answer!"

Pitch didn't answer. Theel cursed a vile oath and kicked Pitch hard, knocking him onto his back. He screamed down the tunnel, a full-chested scream of frustration that bounced and echoed far away. He paced angrily, waving his sword while Pitch cowered and whimpered.

"The zoths might hear you yelling, brother," Yatham suggested, as he climbed among the rocks, looking for a way through.

Theel ignored him. "What will we do? What will I do?" he said. Then he looked at Pitch "Prepare yourself to dig, you filth."

"Dig? Oh God, I can't," Pitch groaned. "I'm almost dead. I can't move. It's hopeless."

"It's not hopeless, damn you," Theel said, and placed his foot on Pitch's chest. "There is still hope that justice will be served. Those children may be lost, but this can be made right again. If you will not dig, you will die."

"Theel?" Yatham called from his place high among the rocks.

Taking his sword by the blade, Theel held the weapon at arm's length, offering the handle to the heavens as a sign of allegiance. He closed his eyes.

"Lord, please bless me and forgive me for what I do. These actions are required of me by knightly duty," he recited, speaking words taught him by his father. "I act with what I believe to be adherence to your word, humbly beg your forgiveness if I err, and know I will be judged fairly in the end. And so I pledge:

"I, as a son of the Silvermarsh Clans, do commit myself, body, soul, and spirit, to the earthly warriors of the Southern Cross, to the Seven Kingdoms they protect, and to the one true Lord of all Creation, that I might do his will, to love God's children, to lead God's Children, to protect God's Children, and that by these deeds, the Lord's blessings be given.

"I will care for God's children, by showing his love.

"I will guide God's children, by speaking his word.

"I will protect God's children, by wielding his judgment," he finished. "Do you hear that, Pitch? God's judgment."

"Theel?" Yatham said, waving his torch. "What are you doing?"

Theel opened his eyes and took the sword in both hands, blade down, a killing posture aimed at Pitch's chest.

"As a servant of the Lord, a squire to the Knighthood of the Southern Cross, I shoulder the responsibility and the honor of preserving the Order of my Clan Embriss, to declare the judgment of the First Guardian Lord Britou, Champion of Order, and to fulfill God's will on earth by this act. Face your fate, Pitchford. May the Lord have mercy on your soul."

"Theel, stop!" Yatham shouted.

"No, no, no!" Pitch screamed. "Don't hurt me!"

"The next face you see will be Dehen Yaulk," Theel added.

"Don't do it," Yatham said.

Theel looked at Pitch's panic-stricken face in the dim torchlight, felt him squirming beneath his foot. Though he'd spent much of the night begging for death, Pitch seemed to feel a change of heart, now fighting to get away, striving very much for life. Theel held him in place with his heel, knowing the man was completely at his mercy. The time to strike was now. But was it right? Yes. Theel was certain it was. This execution was necessary. This man committed despicable acts. Liar. Thief. Murderer. The world did not need him.

But the blade did not fall.

"Theel, please," Yatham said.

"I am not a Knight of the Southern Cross," Theel said. "But as a squire, I speak for the knighthood. I act on behalf of the Keeper of the Craft. I speak for the kings of Embriss, old and new. The throne would approve of this."

Pitch stopped struggling, exhausted, and groaned, "Please ... "

"A knight would do this," Theel went on. "It would be a knight's proper duty. Justice for Calfborn. Justice for that little girl. Justice for the Overlies."

"Theel," Yatham said. "You must stop."

"I am as strong as any knight," Theel insisted. But he wasn't.

He stared at Pitch as the man struggled beneath him, knew the man was crazed, upset, and desperate. As crazed as he himself was, and desperate. But desperate for what?

Theel could feel the throbbing in his chest, and the throbbing in his fingers. There was blood on his fingers. Overlie blood. He was just as guilty as Pitch was. Guilty of selfishness and apathy, lying and stealing. Guilty of denying his father, denying God and his Blessed Soul of Man. Guilty of hatred. Guilty of failure, failure, failure.

Pitch did not kill that Overlie girl. Theel did not kill that Overlie boy. But they were both guilty. Theel was not clean. He was as filthy as any man. There was blood on his hands ...

Theel hurt all over. His chest throbbed. His face throbbed. His brain throbbed. Every muscle ached. Everything hurt. But nothing hurt as much as his heart.

"Brother, you must stop this," Yatham said. "This is not proper."

"I can do this," Theel insisted. "I can."

"But you shouldn't," Yatham said.

"Father would do this," Theel said. "Father would approve." But he knew the truth. Father would never approve of this. Because it wasn't right.

"This is not the way to prove yourself," Yatham stated.

"This is not about proof of self," Theel said. But it was exactly that. Yatham knew Theel better than Theel knew himself.

"Nor is this the time, brother," Yatham said. "Sheath your weapon."

Theel lowered his sword but did not sheath it. He stared at Pitch for many long and tense moments before speaking.

"Pitch, or whatever your true name is," he said. "You will die for your crimes; that is for certain. But it won't be today. It won't be by my hand. I won't do it. I can't, because I haven't the stomach. I am not the man I need to be. I am not a man at all. You see, my father never saw much in me, and he was right. I'm every ounce a worthless being. They mean for me to be a Knight of the Southern Cross; the Seven Swords, the Keeper of the Craft, even the First Guardian Britou, our king. They all agree I must quest for Warrior Baptism, the great and ancient clan tradition of ascension to knighthood. They believe I should wear the knight's shield because of who my father was. My father possessed many qualities that were great. He passed none of those to me. My brother, Yatham, has more in common with our father than I. Yet they all expect greatness from me. Why? Because I am older? Because I am firstborn?

"They expect me to wear by father's shield, strap on his sword, fight as he fought, believe as he believed. What if my father's shield is too large? What if his sword is too heavy? What if I can't fight? What if I can't believe? What if I can't do as my father did? What if I'm not half the man he was? Why am I the only one asking these questions? Why are there no answers?

"We were such different people, my father and I. We never understood each other. It's almost as if I wasn't truly his son. It's almost as if his blood doesn't flow in my veins. I don't have what he had. I can't do what he did. No matter how much I try, I can't be him. It's a worthless effort."

Theel took his foot off of Pitch's chest. An apologetic tone filled his voice.

"I didn't know what I was about to do," he went on. "I think I should make you pay for what you did to those children. I think I should bring you justice by the sword. But I only care to do it to prove I can. I'm so lost and afraid that I almost killed a man to soothe myself, to feel strong, to feel worthy of all that they expect from me. I don't know what you deserve, but I can't do this. I don't feel it's my place. Perhaps it is for other men; knights like my father. It's not for me. I'm not fit to judge you. I will leave that to better men. I'll leave it to God."

"Theel, you need to rest," Yatham said. "We all need rest."

"Yes, listen to your brother," Pitch said, lying flat on his back, unmoving.

"I'm unable to help a pair of children trapped in a dead-end tunnel with nowhere to hide," Theel sighed, looking around, speaking to the air. "We've been running all night. We should have reached them by now. How fast can a girl of four seasons move?" Theel laughed sadly. "We've been outrun by a tiny girl of four. Knights of the Southern Cross spend their days defending villages from zoth attacks. I'm unable to run faster than a little girl."

"Those children are in this tunnel, somewhere," Yatham said. "We will find them."

"The zoths will find them first." Theel shook his head. "If they haven't already. It's hopeless. Pitch is right."

"It's not hopeless," Yatham said.

"Look at that pile of rocks," Theel said, pointing. "There's no crossing that. We can't dig through. We know the children are not on this side or we'd have found them. They must be dead. Either way, we have failed."

"We have not failed," Yatham said.

"How do you know this?" Theel asked.

"Because they've been here," Yatham explained. "I can see where they placed their hands and feet in the dirt; small hands, small feet, climbing the rocks. We're not the first to search for a way past this barrier."

Theel walked to the base of the rock pile. He couldn't see much where he was. Yatham held the torch high above, casting sparse yellow light, creating little more than shadows down where he stood.

"A child climbed that rock pile?" Theel asked, hope in his eyes. "All the way up there?"

Pitch's voice came from behind. "The boy was bigger, nine or ten seasons," he said. "The boy might have climbed those rocks."

Yatham nodded his head, appraising. "It may have been the boy."

"Did he find a way through?" Theel asked.

"I believe not," Yatham answered. "If he found a way through, that is collapsed as well."

"I have to know," Theel said. "There is only one sure way to know. But I must rest first. We all must rest. Yatham, climb down and get some sleep. We'll make camp here."

As Yatham climbed back down the rock pile, the light of his torch grew stronger, falling across Pitch, whom Theel could see still sitting on the ground. The man held a little glass bubbler, the same one he took from wreck of the trader's wagon. The bottle was unstopped and the brown liquid flowed into his mouth. Pitch grimaced, coughed, then smiled.

"Be thankful," Theel said, putting his pipe between his lips. "That may be your last comfort in this world."

"There's much to be thankful for," Pitch said. Smiling, he raised the bottle in salute. "I'm still alive, am I not?"

Chapter 39

Theel sat in the absolute darkness of the Narrows, listening to his own heartbeat as it thumped in this chest, pumping steady pain throughout his body. The adrenaline of the long run, the excitement of prodding Pitch, and striving to find those children, had long ago worn away, leaving him nothing but pain and exhaustion.

There was a remedy for this pain and exhaustion that never failed him. The wings of seraphim angels fluttered in his memory, beckoning, promising to swift him away to the bed of Narssic of the Nightscape. And yet, when he retrieved his pipe from among his things, he didn't pack the bowl. When he put it in his mouth, he did not light it.

A few small puffs would have done wonders; just a tiny amount, just enough to ease his pain and help him relax his mind. But he resisted the urge. He knew he needed to be responsible. He wanted no accidents and no nightmares. He simply wanted to relax and ply the Juy Method. Naturally. Without the interference of leaf. So he took comfort in the familiar feeling of his empty pipe between his lips, and did nothing more.

He would not give up on those children. Despite the odds against it, he was certain they still lived. He knew they were somewhere in this tunnel. The Overlie blood called to him, pulling him forward. He must find those children. He must learn their fates. To this point, he had failed, but he intended to fail no longer.

He'd tried to find the children every natural way he knew how. He traveled the Narrows on his legs, listening with his ears, and looking with his eyes. Perhaps it was time to travel the tunnels on his juy, listening with his heart, and searching with his mind.

But then he felt hot breath tickling his ear. He heard the words of Narssic warning him, telling him he could not control the juy. If he tried, he would likely lose control and succeed only in conjuring up more waking nightmares, she said. Perhaps the tiny bit of seraphim would help him control this thoughts, help him focus. Perhaps just one puff would be fine, would harm nothing.

Perhaps not, Theel retorted. Everything smoking leaf provided was false. Theel knew this from experience. The inner calm was fake, the sense of clarity fake, the feelings of control a total illusion. Seraphim leaf didn't provide control. It took control away.

He didn't know what to do. All he knew was that everything he'd tried up until now had failed. Perhaps he just wanted to relax and pray that God would show him the way.

Everyone around him preached action. Now he was choosing inaction, as always. Was this the proper choice? Probably not. But it was the choice he was making.

Theel was such a sinful person, that sometimes he needed to sin to do good. What a horrible thought, that a man is so covered up in his own filthy imperfection, that his sin is unavoidable, and his only choice is which sin is the best. Theel's father told him, as a knight with a will to do good, this was a struggle he faced daily. A sword is not forged to create, but to destroy; not to give life, but to take it. The existence of a weapon meant to kill is an affront to God. But it is a necessary sin that must be committed. There are no perfect choices in an imperfect world.

Theel still remembered the day his father told him the Knights of the Silvermarsh, these holy warriors of faith who dedicated their lives to God, were actually the most sinful men of all. The very moment a knight's heart is most full of righteousness, he said, is very often the same moment he is committing the most terrible deed. Theel wondered how men whose motives were supposedly the most pure, could possibly be worse than thieves and liars.

No man is better than another, was the answer, because every man has fallen short.

"A man must not judge himself against others," Theel's father had said. "Only against himself, and against the standard that God has set for him. You must not concern yourself with the sins of others, only your own."

Theel let out a big sigh, fingering his empty pipe bowl. So many riddles. Would he ever understand all the nonsense his father spoke? Perhaps one day. That is what his father always said, that he would understand these things better as he grew older and wiser. The Keeper seemed to agree. And Hoster too, the old drunk. One foot in front of the other.

"If the collapsed tunnel separated us from the children," he heard Pitch mumble in the darkness. "Perhaps it separated us from the zoths as well?"

"Perhaps," Yatham said absent-mindedly.

Theel listened to their conversation, but could see neither one without the light of a fire. There hadn't been a need to build one for warmth, since one of the many things said of the Narrows was true: The temperature inside both tunnels was warm, a warmth, it was said, that came from deep in the earth. So the three men had their conversation in complete darkness.

"How can you work with no light?" Pitch asked. "I can't see my hand before my face."

"I do not need to see my hands to know what they are doing," Yatham answered.

Theel's brother was busy building a workable spear from a few broken fragments he'd found discarded on the road. Theel saw his brother do this, finding pieces here and there as they ran, dropping some fragments when he found better ones. Theel even saw him sorting through the bits of junk left by the Overlie men. He settled on two sturdy-looking pieces and set to work merging them into a weapon as soon as they'd made camp. For the point, he chose a two-pronged fork called a moon blade, named so for its resemblance to a crescent moon. The shaft was made from a flexible but strong length of wood, formerly the trunk of a tree native to the delta clan of Membaro called the gingo. The combination was nothing exceptional, but formed a passable weapon if wielded by a trained spearman.

"Why, may I ask, do you work at this?" Theel heard Pitch ask. "Why construct a weapon with the throwaways of others? Why not carry your own spear at all times?"

"I do not carry weapons," Yatham answered.

"You don't carry weapons?" Pitch asked. "Do you leave all the fighting to your brother?"

"Yatham does not carry weapons because he has no need for them," Theel cut in. "He, himself, is weapon enough."

Pitch chuckled. "Your brother mocks you."

"It is his way," Yatham said nonchalantly.

"I am not jesting," Theel said. "Yatham has no need for weapons."

"Is that right?" Pitch said.

"He is a very dangerous man, I swear it," Theel said. "His most terrible attack is his menacing stare of disapproval."

"Must you reveal my secret to everyone we meet?" Yatham asked.

"You are both fools, for certain," Pitch said.

" ... said the greatest fool of all," Theel added.

"So why do you toil to make a weapon when your brother carries two swords?" Pitch asked. "Why not take one of those?"

"Because the swords Theel carries belong to him," Yatham answered. "And, as I explained, I do not carry weapons."

"Why build a spear if you don't carry weapons?" Pitch asked

"The spear isn't for me," Yatham said. "It's for you."

"For me?" Pitch asked. "I'm not a fighter."

"You will be soon," Theel stated. "You will fight to save those children."

"If you insist," Pitch said. "I would rather have a crossbow."

"I cannot make a crossbow," Yatham asked. "I haven't the parts."

"You haven't the parts for a spear, either, and yet you work to make one."

"It is the best I can do," Yatham explained. "The moon blade is in good condition."

"How wonderful," Pitch said blandly.

"The gingo wood is from the merchant's wagon," Yatham went on. "He used it for his trading guidon."

"So you wish for me to fight with a fork on the end of a flagpole?"

"Yes, but it's a really big fork," Theel chuckled.

"It is a moon blade," Yatham corrected. "It would be deadly as a pole arm, or a long spear, or from horseback against footmen."

"How comforting," Pitch said. "Since I don't have a horse."

"When battle comes, you will need something more formidable than your charm to defend yourself," Yatham said.

"I'd rather have a crossbow."

"Crossbows are for cowards," Theel stated.

"Just the same," Pitch said, "I would prefer a crossbow. I have no experience in spearwork."

"I don't care what you would prefer, and I don't care where your experience lies," Theel grumbled. "I won't have you standing at the rear, aiming quarrels at my back. You will fight with a spear, and you will lead the charge."

"We'll have us quite a short charge then," Pitch sighed. "I'm not certain I'm the charging sort."

"You'll learn soon enough," Theel said.

"I may need you to instruct me on the intricacies of ... um, charging."

"Point your spear and run," Theel stated.

"That sounds excellent, friend." Pitch took a loud pull from his liquor bubbler. "With your tutelage, I cannot fail. Consider me an expert spearman. I will conduct demonstrations of technique before the court of Lord Britou when this adventure is concluded. After I've led our intrepid band to victory in the Narrows, of course. Gallant Lord Pitchford Wicker of Aramorun. Hero of the Seven Kingdoms. Champion of the Iatan Wars."

"Pitch," Theel sighed. "Shut up."

"Very well," Pitch said. "I will busy myself in discourse with your brother. Yatham, where did you learn to construct weapons?"

"Pitch," Yatham said. "Shut up."

"Must the situation be so uncongenial?" Pitch asked.

"Yes," Theel said.

"Do they not teach squires of the knighthood manners?" Pitch asked. "Or is it the rigors of Warrior Baptism that steals one's humor?"

"Warrior Baptism?" Theel asked. "What do you mean?"

"Unless my ears deceive me, I understand I am in the presence of a squire of the Southern Cross Knights," Pitch said. "One who is on his quest for Warrior's Baptism?"

"How is it you know that?" Theel asked.

"You were ranting about it just an hour ago in this very tunnel, if you've forgotten," Pitch explained, sipping from his bubbler. "You said you were on a quest. What is it you are seeking?"

"None of your concern."

"You made it my concern, friend, when you held your sword above my chest, calling out to your god and all," Pitch said. "Those were some frightening moments you put me through."

"There may be more of those," Theel retorted. "And soon."

"What brought you to Widow Hatch?" Pitch asked. "Is it this Warrior Baptism?"

"Shut your mouth," Theel ordered. "You're drunk."

"A man has to pass the time somehow." Pitch sighed. "Am I to sit here with you in this darkness for hours without a single word?"

"Do you wish to talk, Pitch?" Theel asked. "Let us talk then, and let us start with this: What is your real name? Where are you from?"

"My proper name was never said," Pitch said. "I was orphaned before my nameday, of both my family and my homeland."

"Where is your homeland?" Yatham asked.

"The Greater Clan of Aramorun is my ancestral home, though I've not walked that soil in years," Pitch answered. "It is the birthplace of the Noble House of Wicker, or so I've been told."

"You still claim nobility?" Theel said.

"I am banished from my homeland," Pitch said. "A lesser lord, in exile, but a lord I remain."

"A lesser lord," Yatham said.

"They don't come much lesser," Theel added.

"No, they don't," Pitch said mournfully. "The Wickers lost everything in the War of the Eastern Scepters. Our gold and our lands were seized, all of us killed or banished. The Wickers are a dead house. I am the last."

"How do you know this if you were orphaned so young?" Yatham asked.

"He doesn't know," Theel said. "He's lying."

"I don't lie," Pitch protested. "They say my mother was a whore. Lord Wicker supposedly planted me in her belly before he died. But I can't prove any of it."

"You may or may not be the heir to a dead house, with no holdings, in a land from which you are banished," Theel stated. "Depending on the word of a whore."

"You have a keen eye for these matters, my liege," Pitch replied. "A keen eye."

"Do not call me liege," Theel said. "I am no one's lord."

"I owe you my life, my liege," Pitch said. "It is you who freed me from that crow cage, and in doing so spared me a slow death of thirst or starvation. My family owes you everything. House Wicker lives on because of you."

"House Wicker is dead," Theel said. "If it ever existed."

"The noble bloodlines of House Wicker were nearly severed due to the cruelty and injustice inflicted by the greater Lords of Aramorun," Pitch said. "But the blood of my family beats strongly within me, and House Wicker will live again, because of your kindness. You are my liege lord from this day forward."

"No, I am not," Theel insisted.

"All that is House Wicker is now yours, by the oath of fealty I speak," Pitch went on. "I swear on the blood of Wicker that flows through my veins that I will always be loyal to you, my lord, will never bring harm to you or your family, or to the good name of your ancestral house, and will observe my homage to you completely against all persons in good faith, and without deceit."

"The oath of a liar is worthless," Theel said.

"My sword is yours."

"You don't have a sword," Theel retorted.

"My gold is yours."

"What gold?"

"All the lands and holdings of House Wicker are yours."

"Pitch," Theel said. "Shut up."

"It is done," Pitch announced. "I am now your loyal servant for all time."

"God help me," Theel said.

"How may I serve you, my liege?" Pitch asked.

"You may stop calling me your liege."

"If you wish, my liege," Pitch said. "I am your faithful servant."

"You are not," Theel said. "Don't you understand? I don't want you as my faithful servant."

"Are you certain of that, my liege?" Pitch asked. "One day you may need a servant."

"I will never need you."

"Only a foolish lord would say such things," Pitch said. "Now is a time of peace, but when war comes, a lord invariably needs his vassals. A man without allies is only one sword."

"Where have you learned this nonsense?" Theel asked.

"I am born of noble blood, if you recall," Pitch said. "And you know I speak wisdom, my liege. One day you might find yourself on your back with no one to help you, and I will be there. You will reach out for help and I will give you my sword. You'll see."

"I will never reach out for your help," Theel said. "And I don't want your sword."

"You may not want it, my liege, but you may need it."

"Why were you in that cage?" Yatham asked.

"And tell the truth this time," Theel added.

453

"If I must," Pitch said. "It was a great injustice, I swear it. I was beaten and robbed by Overlie men. Two of them, wearing the diamonds and oaks. They stuffed me in that cage, and were quite rude about it."

"Who were they?" Yatham asked.

"Sellswords, they said," Pitch answered. "Travelling south from Korsiren."

"Deserters," Theel spit.

"I wouldn't doubt it," Pitch said. "They did seem to be riding south when the war is to the north. And they didn't seem to hold much regard for the diamonds and oaks they wore on their surcoats. I have grave doubts Lord Overlie would approve of their treatment of me."

"What became of them?" Yatham asked.

"I believe their plan was to accost travelers fleeing south from the war," Pitch said. "When they saw a wagon coming through town, they hid in the Narrows for an ambush. They didn't come back out. I never saw them again."

"That wagon coming through town," Yatham said. "Was it driven by the merchant?"

"The poor fellow who lost his eyes, yes," Pitch said. "That was him."

"The zoths found him," Yatham said. "I wonder if they found the Overlie men as well?"

"The Crowlord has them all," Theel mumbled around his pipe stem. "Merchant and deserters both. They are all dead. Don't doubt it."

"Then what of the children?" Pitch asked.

"All you can do is pray," Theel answered.

"My, you are the cheerful sort, aren't you?" Pitch said.

"What's to be cheerful about?" Theel asked. "All is nearly lost. Because of you."

"You are correct, my liege," Pitch admitted. "There is no cheer in that."

"You should be happy that I haven't killed you yet," Theel said.

"Despite your best efforts."

"I haven't taxed myself fully yet," Theel said. "When I truly want you dead, Lord Pitchford, you will be dead."

"That's cheerful, my liege."

"Don't call me that."

"Why did you send those children into danger?" Yatham asked.

"I saw no danger in what I did," Pitch said. "I didn't know the zoths ruled the Narrows, I swear it."

"Yet you knew bandits were hiding in the Narrows," Theel said. "You did nothing to protect the children from that danger."

"Those two fellows were Overlie men," Pitch said. "They'd find no gain in harming the offspring of their lord."

"You hoped," Theel added.

"I knew," Pitch protested. "Only great fools wouldn't see the potential for reward in offering their protection to the children of a man as powerful as Lord Overlie. I was thinking of the safety of those two wonderful sweetlings."

"How noble of you," Yatham said.

"Yes," Pitch responded. "Nobility is in my blood, you see."

"Truly a selfless gesture," Theel said. "Stealing from a little girl of only four seasons for her own betterment."

"Life presents many unfortunate choices, my liege," Pitch said. "It was the only way I could compel those young ones to listen to me. Children can be so willful."

"But why did you need them to enter the Narrows?" Yatham asked.

"I needed them to find those Overlie men," Pitch answered. "I felt it was the only way those children might find salvation."

"And those Overlie men also had the key to your cage," Theel said.

"A minor detail," Pitch mumbled.

"You wanted them to find those men and bring back the key," Theel said.

"Perhaps," Pitch said. "Perhaps they might provide my salvation after finding their own. Why shouldn't we all benefit?"

"No one benefitted," Theel said.

"It was a gamble."

"You gambled and you lost," Theel accused. "You forced two little children to accept all the risk while you enjoyed all the potential for gain. And what has come of it? Those children may be dead. And soon you will be, too."

"My plan may not have resulted in success."

"It may not have," Theel said. "Because it may have been a terrible plan."

"It was a flawed plan, I'd admit," Pitch said. "But not a terrible one."

"You will see how flawed your plan was on the Dead Man's Bridge," Theel stated. "I am going to feed you to the Crowlord. And if he doesn't kill you, I will."

"As you wish, my liege."

"Do not call me that."

"I will die fighting the Crowlord, if you command it, my liege," Pitch said. "But please let me die with the good reputation of House Wicker intact."

"What reputation?" Theel asked.

"Whatever reputation we Wickers retain after all the evil that has befallen us," Pitch explained. "Please understand, I meant no ill when I sent those two sweetlings into the Narrows. My reasoning certainly was unsound, but I was in that cage for days, my wits ravaged by hunger and thirst. I wasn't my right self when I did those things."

"You still aren't," Theel added.

"I cannot undo my misdeeds," Pitch whimpered. "All I can do is beg the forgiveness of my liege lord and give myself fully to the effort of delivering those children safely from harm."

"Which you will do," Theel said.

"If it please you, my liege," Pitch said solemnly.

"It pleases me," Theel stated. "You will march and you will fight. And if you survive the Dead Man's Bridge, I will see that you live long enough to place those diamonds and oak leaves in the hand of the little girl you stole them from."

"Nothing would give me greater joy," Pitch claimed. "All I wish for is a chance to atone for my sins. And there are many."

"Very many," Theel said.

"No man is clean, least of all, I."

"That is true," Yatham said. "Father always said that."

"I've done the best I can with the meager tools allotted me," Pitch went on. "But some men are destined to wear ill deeds like a second skin. My sinfulness sticks to me no matter how hard I scrub at it."

Theel had no reply for that.

"I'm no worse than many others in these dark days," Pitch said. "This war has made scoundrels of many a good man. Every good thing must one day perish, and sometimes that good thing is a man's decency."

"That's not true," Yatham stated.

"Perhaps," Pitch said. "Perhaps not. But I was a decent person once, I swear it. Unfortunately, moral difficulties tend to arise when a person hasn't seen a meal in days. Hunger will drive a man to do what is necessary to see his belly filled, even things he might one day regret."

"What did you do before the war?" Yatham asked. "How did you spend your time when you were a decent person?"

"I am a performing man," Pitch answered.

"A mummer?" Yatham asked.

"At times," Pitch said. "Mumming is a narrow skill, while my talents cover a broader range."

"Such as storytelling," Theel said. "Many, many stories of questionable veracity."

"The best stories aren't completely true to every last word," Pitch retorted.

"Neither are yours," Theel said.

"My primary talent is the gift of song," Pitch said.

"Do you play an instrument?" Yatham asked.

"I play them all," Pitch answered. "Story and song were my primary winners of coin. I sang a hundred songs, told a hundred tales, but that wasn't all. I was also accomplished at some minor feats of acrobatics, tumbling, and juggling. I did some trick shooting for a time. I could handle a crossbow rather well."

"Ever shoot a man?" Theel asked. "Or a zoth?"

"Goodness no, my liege," Pitch answered. "Zoths were a rare sight at our performances. And the goal of trick shooting was to avoid hurting the other performers."

"What did you shoot at, then?" Theel asked.

"My fellows would juggle fruit, usually apples," Pitch explained. "I would shoot the apples out of the air. The crowd would give us the apples, but we didn't give them back. They thought they were providing us targets for our show. In truth, they were often providing our next meal."

"Ever handle a weapon other than a crossbow?" Theel asked.

"I juggled hammers once."

"Well then," Theel said. "If we find some hammers in these tunnels, you may juggle them for the zoths. If not, you will carry a spear into battle."

"As you wish, my liege," Pitch said.

"Your troupe of performers," Yatham said. "Did they have a name?"

"The Merry Midwives," Pitch said.

Theel laughed. "How foolish."

"Yes, Liege, foolish, but that is the idea," Pitch said. "Only hearing the name has changed your once-sour words to ones of mirth, has it not? And that, before the show has even begun?"

"I've never heard of the Merry Midwives," Yatham stated. "Where did you earn your work?"

"Up and down the roads of the Eastern Kingdoms," Pitch said. "We found plenty of work in Sidon in the early days, but preferred the lesser clans most recently; Sirrothar, and Magna Lil. We'd work the festivals and tent shows in the spring, the sheds and barns in the fall. Any of the inns or taverns that paid, we were there. You could even earn your work on the street corners of some of the great cities, if need be. It was a fine life."

"It was," Yatham said. "But no longer."

"Every good thing must one day perish," Pitch mentioned wistfully. "Wars have a way of drying up business, stealing the charity from otherwise kindly folks."

"Very true," Yatham agreed. "War can steal many things from a man."

"Folks lose their thirst for ale when the tavern's burned down by Iatan soldiers," Pitch said. "Can't sing along with pipe and lute with a spear in your guts."

"I suppose not," Theel said.

"Then the plagues came through," Pitch went on. "The traveling folk were hit hard—the traders, caravaners, mercenaries and army men, and the performing troupes like mine. The more folk a man meets each day, the more diseases he finds simmering in the belly to be carried to the next town. It was some variety of fever that took all of my brothers and sisters. But it spared me. Now I'm the only one left."

"You are surely a difficult man to kill," Theel opined.

"You will learn that I am served by a healthy sense of self-preservation, my liege," Pitch laughed.

"I've learned that already," Theel said.

"After that, I sold everything we had for food; our horses and wagons, instruments and props," Pitch said. "I ate well for a month, but soon there was no food left to buy. I found myself fleeing toward the Western Kingdoms like all the other poor smallfolk, all of us herded before the Iatan armies like cattle."

"Did you witness any of the fighting?" Yatham asked.

"Some of it," Pitch said. "I was headed westward as the lords and their knights and their armies came east. I crossed paths with hundreds of soldiers on the roads, clumps of men rushing to fight the Iatan, rushing to their deaths. I thought to join them many times, but I've never raised arms against another in my life, and those men were committing suicide. It was a slaughter; complete butchery. Thousands of men fell dead on those plains, for nothing. It was over before it started. It is a very sad scene over in the Eastern Kingdoms. This war has ruined everything. And it's coming this way, faster than you know."

"We know," Theel said. "We've seen."

"So much of the world we once enjoyed is now in flames," Pitch lamented. "The skies over our land are getting darker every day, and I don't see any way things can be mended."

"The Blessed Soul of Man will mend things," Yatham suggested.

"Do you believe that?" Pitch asked. "Do you believe in the prophecy?"

"I do," Yatham answered. "I believe the Blessed Soul has come into the world to fulfill the prophecy. I believe he will fight this war and defeat the Iatan."

"I hope that is true," Pitch said.

"It is true," Yatham insisted. "I do not doubt it."

"You are certainly a devout man," Pitch said.

"Yes, I am."

"Well, then," Pitch said. "The next time you pray to your god about the Blessed Soul, please ask him to make haste. If the Blessed Soul is coming, we need him today, not tomorrow. If he waits any longer, I fear this whole affair might be finished before he steps out his front door."

"The Blessed Soul is coming," Yatham repeated. "He will mend this."

"Your faith is admirable," Pitch said. "I hope it is not misplaced."

"It is not," Yatham said. "He is coming."

Theel said nothing, but felt himself nodding, partly agreeing with his brother.

The Blessed Soul must come soon, if he exists. Or all is lost.

Chapter 40

Twenty years earlier, men were making decisions, choosing courses of action that would influence the fate of the Blessed Soul and the outcome of the Second War of Souls long before Theel and Yatham joined in the struggle. What would one day become the concern of so many, now rested on the shoulders of so very few. Two to be precise—the knights Gavin the Zealot and Elkor the Hound, who walked for days and days down a giant worm hole, the lair of the mua giou, traveling deeper into the earth in search of Gilligod, the Devil Device. They brought with them Eleod, the little boy with the white hair and golden skin, the Blessed Soul.

Four days behind them was the assassin Aeoxoea, who tracked their every movement, walking day and night in an attempt to close the gap. Though she was far behind, she knew all that the knights did by watching the clues left by their footprints in the Craft weaves that filled the tunnel. She could see what they did on any spot she chose to look. She could see where they walked. She could see where they rested. She could hear every word that was spoken between them, when she chose to. She watched them eat, sleep, and pray. She listened to them sing and laugh and play with Eleod.

And she watched as Elkor's battle hound Behe began her slow descent into the madness of creeper's disease.

The assassin recognized the signs because the blood of the demon Miacnon lived in her as well. She'd felt the pain of the blood of the demon Miacnon as it burned through her skin, sank into her flesh and entered her bloodstream. She knew how it felt to be poisoned, to feel it inside her, gnawing at her health and well-being. But that was just a brief introduction to what the Angel of Disease had planned for her. The curse had fallen dormant within her ever since she'd left the audience hall at the center of the Castle of Teardrops. It still flowed in her blood, but it made no attempt to claim her health, to control her body and mind.

Behe enjoyed no such luxury. The disease attacked her with much greater enthusiasm, and the battle hound began to show signs she was cursed by Miacnon almost immediately. The demon enjoyed every moment of his conquest, grinding down her will like a blade on a sharpening stone. Aeoxoea knew Behe would be claimed by darkness any time the demon wished, but he didn't wish to claim her just yet, perhaps enjoying the anguish Behe's decline elicited within her master, Elkor.

The Hound knew his own animals well, and he noticed every change that occurred just as well as Aeoxoea did. He saw how Behe's eyes became sad and hurting, as if she was in pain, or carrying a difficult burden. He saw how she suffered from terrible thirst, constantly stopping to drink from the small stream that bubbled along the bottom of the tunnel. She didn't sleep much, and when she did, she howled and barked through nightmares haunted by the Angel of Disease. As the days went by, her waking behavior became even more erratic. She didn't follow commands as quickly, and sometimes not at all. She wandered off for periods of time. The playful nipping and pawing with her father no longer seemed so playful.

Aeoxoea could see that Elkor noticed these things, but wasn't certain if he recognized them for what they were: Symptoms of creeper's disease.

"The darkness is bothering your daughter," he once said to Kang, ruffling the old dog's ears. "No smells, no sounds, nowhere to run. No sun to warm the bones. Just a touch of Neversea madness. I'm feeling it a bit myself."

Gavin made no show of whether he understood what was happening either. But whether the knights recognized the signs, or were ignoring them out of love for the animal, Miacnon's subjugation of the battle hound was an inevitable thing. And on the seventh day of travel into the mua giou lair, Behe lost her battle with the Angel of Disease.

"Behe, stop," Elkor shouted. "Stay. No battle!"

The battle hound no longer cared for her master's commands. She snarled and drooled, staring hatefully at Kang, ears flattened, legs crouching and ready to pounce. Kang, initially surprised and confused by his daughter's outburst, reacted similarly to the threat. Hackles rose on both animals as the father voiced his displeasure with a deep and mighty barking that would have frozen any other animal in terror.

Elkor waved his torch at Behe, shouting. "Down, Behe!"

But the battle hound was not listening. For a moment her eyes flashed yellow in the torchlight. Then she jumped at Kang, teeth bared, forward claws leading. Elkor intervened, tackling her before she could strike, crushing her to the ground. The two rolled across the stone, struggling, with Elkor on the dog's back. The knight grabbed Behe's snout with both hands, wrapped his legs around her midsection, and bit down on her ear. This did not stop her struggles, or her enmity for everyone involved. She was no longer herself.

"Elkor," Gavin said, holding his own torch high, staring into Behe's crazed eyes. "This animal has creeper's disease."

"No, she doesn't," Elkor said. "She can't. It doesn't occur in animals."

Gavin shook his head. "You don't know that," he said. "She has all the symptoms."

"No," Elkor insisted. "It can't be."

"We can't allow this to worsen," Gavin stated. "We can't risk it."

Elkor firmed his jaw, unwilling to face the truth. Gavin was quiet for a moment as he watched Behe struggle in her master's grip. He turned and looked at Kang, who had calmed, and now watched curiously.

Gavin turned back to Elkor, drawing one of his knives. "You know what must be done."

"Perhaps," Elkor said.

Gavin shook his head. "No, not perhaps."

"It may be possible to beat the disease," Elkor suggested.

Gavin frowned. "It is not possible, you know that," he said. "There is no cure but the healing touch of the Blessed Soul."

Elkor looked at Eleod, and a moment of hope flashed in his eyes.

"The boy cannot help her, Hound," Gavin said. "He has not grown. He has not yet realized his powers."

"I know," Elkor said sadly. "I know."

"We can't help her," Gavin said. "It must end here, now. She may have already passed the curse to Kang. Do it now, or I will."

"I know. I understand," Elkor said. "I'm sorry. Take Eleod farther down the tunnel. He shouldn't have to see this."

"See what?" came a small voice from the furs on Gavin's back. "The doggie?"

"Do it quickly," Gavin said. "Do not tarry."

"Follow the Zealot, old man," Elkor said, gesturing to Kang. It was a small gesture, but it required him to take one hand off Behe for more time than she needed.

With fresh strength, she ripped her snout free of her master's grasp and clamped her jaws down on his hand. As she leaped away from him, Elkor grabbed at her tail, but missed. In two breaths she was out of his reach, then out of the torchlight, running with all speed deeper into the worm hole. One of Gavin's knives followed her into the darkness, whistling end over end. Then a soft thud, and a yelp of pain. But it wasn't enough to stop her.

"Kang, stay!" Elkor shouted, springing to his feet. "Zealot, keep Kang with you. I'll retrieve her."

Elkor rushed after his wayward animal, pulling his axe from his belt as he ran. Gavin stood quietly and watched, holding his torch high as Kang nuzzled his other hand, whimpering softly. The knight pressed his lips together in irritation.

"Where did the doggie go?" Eleod asked from his back.

Gavin didn't answer, only set off after his comrade at a brisk run.

Aeoxoea witnessed all of this as if she stood beside the knights as it had happened four days previous. She found herself frustrated by what she saw, and it had nothing to do with the battle hound. The knights were running again. This meant that even though she'd been walking day and night, she may not have gained any ground on them. And worse still, they were increasing their lead.

There might be a hundred more miles between her and the Blessed Soul for all she knew, but she was powerless to change that in her current state. All she could do was travel at the best speed her wounded body would allow, and suffer the fact that she was falling further behind. She could only hope to find time to make up the distance once she was fully healed.

The worm hole wound its way deeper into the earth, taking gradual deviations to the left or right, up or down, but always righting itself on its sloping course downward. Aeoxoea now noticed cracks in its walls, which appeared with increased frequency. Some were as small as her hand. Some were large enough for a man to fit his body inside. Most appeared to be dead ends, minor fractures in the earth, possibly caused by the earthquakes. Some of the larger ones were gateways to other tunnel systems. It was beside one of these that she stopped walking.

This was where the knights were standing when the mua giou came through on its journey to the surface. Aeoxoea felt the tremors again as the Craft weaves remembered them, just as she remembered them days ago, the early tremors of an earthquake that had heralded the coming of the lizard worm. And that wasn't all.

Behe attacked Elkor on this spot. She hid within the crack in the wall and waited for him to pass by. When he did, she leaped out and struck him in the back, knocking him to the ground as she'd been trained. She jumped on him, pawed at him and licked his face. He laughed and scratched her ears, and for those brief moments, Aeoxoea could see hope flash in the knight's eyes. He was certain she'd fought off the disease. He was certain his dog had come back to him.

Perhaps it was Behe who came back. Perhaps, for those few moments, she'd beaten the disease. But if this was so, her recovery didn't last very long. She looked at her former master, her eyes sad, almost pleading. Miacnon, the Angel of Disease, now owned her. The curse screamed in her brain, demanding blood. And she was compelled to answer.

Then the mua giou came. Just as the earthquake reached its peak of power, when the rocks were screaming and the earth was lurching, the look of Behe's eyes twisted from love to murder. Then she was snarling in Elkor's face, all teeth and claws. She went for his throat, and almost scored the kill, but he grabbed her by the jaws and forced her head away from him. She made him pay with rakes of her claws from all four feet. He responded by drawing a knife and swiping at her flank. But she only jumped away and disappeared once again into the darkness of the tunnel, running straight toward the approaching lizard worm.

Elkor climbed to his feet, clearly meaning to give chase, to follow the line of blood droplets left by his battle hound. But Gavin arrived with Kang just in time to stop him. The Zealot grabbed his comrade by the arm, shouting at him. Aeoxoea couldn't hear what was being said, the words lost in the din of the earthquake. But Gavin's concerns were obvious. Behe was running straight into the face of the mua giou, straight toward her death. Her fevered, disease-ridden mind didn't know any better. Elkor wanted to stop her, but it was too late. She was lost.

"We must look after the Blessed Soul!" Gavin's lips mouthed.

Aeoxoea could see the wall of mist coming up the worm hole, about to swallow Behe, about to swallow them all. Elkor finally seemed to gather his senses, and joined Gavin in crawling into the crack in the wall, to search for cover. Inside, they huddled together, men and beast, to brave the onslaught brought by the passing of the mua giou; the scorching winds, the suffocating heat, and the spray of the acidic slime. Gavin held Eleod close, covering the boy's body with his own, ignoring his panicked screams. He was able to protect the boy physically, but was unable to protect him from the terror brought him by the might of the lizard worm.

But they made it. When the earthquake was finished, when the sounds faded up the tunnel toward the surface, the knights crawled out of their hiding place, cleaned themselves off, and prepared to renew their trek deeper into the earth.

While they did this, Elkor healed the wounds he'd suffered from Behe's claws. Aeoxoea had seen him do this before, just after his battle with the zoth chieftain on the icy plain south of Arka Moor. As the shadow of Behe Kang approached, Elkor and his dogs had fought the chieftain to protect Gavin the Zealot's escape into Illengaard. They were successful, but Elkor suffered a broken arm and puncture to his shoulder in the process.

Now, just like then, Aeoxoea saw him pinch his eyes shut, murmuring something that sounded very much like a prayer. After that first time, Jass explained to her that it was the Knight's Creed that Elkor recited, a statement of belief for those knighted under the banner of the Southern Cross. Recitation of the creed was necessary to release the power of the Life Sign, a tattoo that reached from a knight's left elbow to his left knee, with branches reaching out to his lower back, his neck, and his heart. The Life Sign wasn't merely ink that was woven into the skin, Jass explained, it was Craft, a magical power that allowed the knight to tap the power of his own juy in order to heal himself. It was an incredible asset for men such as the Hound and the Zealot, who in their quest saw battle regularly but were far from home, and far from the aid of healers.

Aeoxoea understood the process of accelerated healing through the power of juy. In fact, at that very moment, she was undergoing the same process healing the wounds she'd suffered at the hands of the Trylon. Ever since that terrible battle, her juy had done things for her body it could not do on its own. Juy sustained her life while she was unconscious at the bottom of the underground lake. It allowed her to survive the assault on her nervous system by the

DoomFist hand cannon as it so unconventionally attached itself to her body and mind. It shepherded her sorely damaged body from the brink of death back to a level of health that allowed her to walk again, if not quickly or comfortably. And it was juy that continued to heal her, even as she followed the knights and the Blessed Soul deeper into the earth.

Aeoxoea was unique in that she could command her own juy and the juy of others innately, effortlessly, naturally. To her knowledge, none of the races of Thershon had this ability. Only the greatest practitioners of the Method could heal themselves and others, and then, only after years of study and meditation. Like most men, neither of the knights had the ability to command their own juy to heal themselves. The Life Sign gave them this ability.

But it came with a cost. The healing it provided was not as efficient as that done by those who plied the Method. It used more juy than necessary, and was a clumsy tool in the hands of the uninitiated. In the case of severe wounds, the Life Sign could be a dangerous thing. It could drain too much juy while attempting to heal. The loss of so much life force might be too great for the body to bear, and the knight could perish. Thus, the Life Sign must be used sparingly, and carefully.

Elkor clearly decided the claw marks on his chest and stomach were worthy of the tattoo's usage. Aeoxoea watched the wounds slowly closing as the Hound grimaced at the pain of the accelerated healing. And just as the first time, the experience seemed to drain the knight's strength from him. His chest no longer bled, and was now covered with pink scars. But he also looked old and tired. He breathed heavily, almost gasping as he struggled to his feet like an old man needing the aid of the young. But he didn't ask for help, and Gavin didn't offer any.

The knights started out slowly at first, but after only a mile, they broke into a run once again. Elkor struggled, limped, and gasped, but kept pace long after a normal man would have passed out. It seemed unreasonable that the knights would push themselves so hard, but Aeoxoea understood why they did this.

The comings and goings of the great beast known as the mua giou were entirely unpredictable. There was no way of knowing when it would come back through, and if there would be anywhere to hide when it did. Most stretches of the worm hole were completely featureless, with no rocks or side passages or cracks in the wall, offering no protection at all. The only answer to this dilemma was to be out of the creature's home by the next time it chose to show itself. So, as usual, the knights ran, and Aeoxoea walked, the distance between them growing ever more.

Many more hours passed, then another day, and it was during this time that Aeoxoea could see, by using the Craft to see into the past, that Behe had not perished. The assassin was unable to see how, but the battle hound had survived the wrath of the mua giou. And now the animal tracked her former master just as the assassin did. Now seeing them as her enemies, she kept her distance, but matched their pace, waiting for the call from Miacnon to attack. Kang seemed to know she was out there, seemed to know she still lived. He ran with the knights as he was commanded, but constantly looked back, sniffing at the air, very aware that something was following. Aeoxoea wondered if there would soon be a confrontation between father and daughter.

Aeoxoea continued to walk, and watched with frustration as the knights ran, and watched as Behe tracked them. This went on for more than another day before the assassin came upon a series of cracks in the floor. The first one was only five feet wide and was easily jumped, but a mile later she came across another gap, this one a dozen feet. She ran and jumped, but landed in a streak of the foul smelling slime on the other side. It was extremely slick, and she began to slide. The tunnel declined sharply, and she realized it would be difficult to stop. White tentacles sprang from her body with the intent of finding purchase on the stone floor, to cease or slow her slippery descent. But she came upon a large gap, was sliding straight down into it, so she slapped her tentacles down, launching herself high into the air.

She cleared the gap, but landed in more of the slime and continued further down. She managed to remain on her feet, sliding through the muck like a child playing in the snow. But then the shaft of the worm hole suddenly leveled off. She lost her balance and fell. Then it declined down sharply again, then leveled off, then down again. It was almost fun, except for the stink, and the sensation of little control. She was on her back, spinning slowly, down, down, down. She wondered if the knights had chosen to travel this section of the tunnel similarly.

She looked into the past, catching a brief glimpse of the knights. They were tying ropes around their waists like safety lines, as if they meant to do some climbing.

Then the floor of the tunnel dropped out from under her, and she realized she was falling. Instantly, she lashed out with her tentacles, slamming them into the stone wall, and her fall was jerked to a halt.

She hung there for a few moments, covered in the stinking bile that irritated her skin, trying to see where she was. The shaft of the tunnel had abruptly changed direction and went straight down. It was impossibly deep, further than she could see. She looked up and saw that she hadn't fallen far, and hadn't lost the trail. Stretching away from her, both above and below, was a clear trail left by the knights.

This was the reason for the safety lines. They'd climbed down here. She could see places where they'd scraped away the slime with knees and elbows and boot tips as they lowered themselves down. There was freshly chipped stone showing in the small fissures that marked the side of the shaft, showing where they'd found purchase with their weapons. Gavin used his knife blades, while Elkor used the sharpened backside of this axe as a climbing pick.

Aeoxoea had seen many times over what these knights were capable of, but this still impressed her. It was amazing enough that anyone would even endeavor to climb down this tunnel with its smooth, goo-covered walls. But the knights did it without using any real climbing equipment, just their weapons and a rope tether, carrying Kang and Eleod down with them the entire way.

Glancing effortlessly into the past, she could see them climbing down, slowly, deliberately, taking their time, trying not to rush. She was certain they'd made it. They were excellent climbers and they were careful. But their pace was slow.

This was a very good thing. She could climb down much faster than that using her tentacles. This was an opportunity to regain some of the ground she'd lost. She didn't hesitate at all, and began to descend as rapidly as she could, sending stone chips, dust, and worm ooze splattering about as her tentacles stabbed the rock walls of the giant worm hole.

The climbing was tedious. An hour dragged by, but just as she'd hoped, she was gaining ground. She looked into the past and saw Gavin climbing down, and was heartened to see that she was much faster than he. She didn't know how much further she needed to go. She couldn't see the bottom, but neither could she see the top with the way the tunnel wound its way down. What she did know was that she was descending more than twice as quickly as the knights had. After another hour, she was sure she'd cut their lead significantly.

Then she felt it; the last thing she wanted to feel in that moment. It was a thump, like the single heartbeat of the world, so deep she felt it in her belly. Then the walls of the worm hole began to shiver. Then they stopped, but immediately started again. This process was repeated several times, and each time the vibrations were longer and more violent, like the wall was trying to shake her off. It was an earthquake.

The mua giou was coming.

She looked up. There was no time to hide. She looked down. There was nowhere to go.

She could only laugh. It was the worst place she could possibly be, suspended in that vertical tunnel. But this was where the mua giou found her when it chose to appear, coming back down from the surface, coming right down, right then, upon her head. The timing was too perfect.

Then a new thought struck her. Had she fallen into a trap?

It was a terrible fear, but a legitimate one. She'd learned many times over that it was dangerous to underestimate these knights. The wizard Azzrot, known as the Icon of the Empire, learned this lesson just before the zoths tore him apart. The knights couldn't have known who was tracking them, but they made sure their pursuers would have to cross ground sacred to the bloodthirsty, merciless creatures. Aeoxoea might have fallen into that trap herself if Azzrot hadn't done it for her.

Now Azzrot was no longer around to provide that service. Was it possible she'd sprung another trap set by the knights? The fact that she was questioning it at all proved she hadn't been cautious enough. But in the end, it did not matter. Whether by the designs of two knights or by a plan set forth by Providence, she knew she'd fallen into this danger from her own carelessness.

What a debilitating disease it is, the arrogance that strikes at the common sense of the servants of the emperor! The Reflecting God was not a name she'd chosen for herself, but it didn't prevent her from occasionally gazing with fondness into the mirror.

The wind crashed against her body from above, just as a violent suction pulled at her from below. The earthquake increased in strength, reached its highest intensity, and caused a hailstorm of stones and dust and boulders of all sizes to come crashing down through the giant worm hole. The hot air pushed down on her and brought white steam, searing her skin. She had little time.

She continued to laugh. It couldn't be helped.

"Jass, my puppet. Awaken."

"Yes, my mistress?" came the answer.

"Give me all your attention, my darling plaything, for this is the moment you've waited for."

"What do you mean, my mistress?" Jass asked.

"We live or die, right now, together!" she screamed.

And then she jumped.

She did not merely release her grip on the wall and allow herself to fall. She used her tentacles to throw herself down with all her strength. She held her arms tightly against her sides, falling headfirst in a desperate free fall, like an arrow dropping from the sky. She could see the walls of the worm hole racing by at maddening speed. She could feel the heat beating down on her as the mua giou came closer. Her mind screamed in frustration. She had no idea where she was headed, she only knew she was going there fast. But she could not fall any faster than gravity could pull, and still the great beast continued to gain on her.

Billowing white steam filled the air all around, burning her, cooking her flesh until her skin peeled. Rocks and stones smashed against her body. Hot dust and sand pelted her body, filling her eyes, nose and mouth. And everywhere was the acidic slime, spraying in sheets, splattering all over everything.

A great roar punched her eardrums from behind, something like the sound of screeching metal. Aeoxoea knew it was the mua giou, knew she was about to be devoured or crushed. She threw her tentacles out to catch the air and slow her fall, to reorient herself. She turned over onto her back so she could look up and see through the wall of steam into the face of her death. She couldn't help but shudder with awe at the sight of it, an avalanche of green flesh filling the worm hole, roaring down upon her with such force, such unstoppable power—a great, green mass of inevitability. It was almost beautiful.

She did not know why this was happening to her. First the creeper's disease, then the Trylon. And now this. Perhaps God was enjoying her frustration, reminding her and her masters who was really in control. She might have preferred a nice, old-fashioned lightning bolt. That would have made more sense because she could have answered it with thunder.

She raised her left hand, balling it into a fist. "Arm DoomFist."

Flashing blue lights filled her vision as the weapon came to life. In one split-second, it read her mind, determining the maw of the mua giou to be the target. It mapped the distance, set proper discharge level, and directed her aim by placing the blue cross in the center of the wall of green flesh.

"Discharge level eight," said the soothing female voice. "Standing by."

"Fire!" Aeoxoea shouted. Her fist throbbed, and the tunnel lit up with a fantastic explosion. The earth shook, and rocks and dust flew everywhere. But it did nothing to stop the descent of the lizard worm. It came faster, closer, responded with another mighty roar, an ear-splitting shriek like grinding steel. It hit Aeoxoea's face and stabbed into her brain, but the aim of the DoomFist remained true.

"Four cell rotation. Sustained pulse at discharge level nine!" Aeoxoea shouted. "Fire!"

The DoomFist answered her command by shredding the air, spitting hot, invisible death into the face of its target with a sustained, throbbing beat. Again the lizard worm roared, and again the world lurched. More rocks and boulders crashed down, slamming against Aeoxoea, knocking her all around the passage. She couldn't see anything, didn't know which way was down, or which way was up. She crashed into one wall, then the other, as they crashed into her, and she tumbled out of control. But through all this, she kept her arm outstretched, the DoomFist maintaining its aim, and filling the worm hole with invisible fire.

"Keep it up!" Aeoxoea screamed. "Discharge level ten. Fire!"

And the DoomFist spoke, answering the lizard worm's unstoppable force with unstoppable force of its own. It blazed away at its highest discharge level, delivering a steady pounding into the face of the mua giou, and the creature's flesh yielded. Buckets of green blood splattered everywhere, covered everything, filling the tunnel, replacing the air itself with the lizard worm's insides. Aeoxoea was hit in the face with the awful sticky stuff, blinded, choked and gagged as it coated her arms and legs like spider webbing, rendering her immobile. She couldn't move, couldn't see, but still felt the dreadful sensation of free fall. She was unable to move her arms, so the DoomFist had ceased firing, unable to get a clear shot.

Her eyes were blinded, but not her mind. She switched her eyes to Craftsight, pulling into her mind an image of the great lizard worm. She saw the color swirls of the Craft weaves clinging to it. The creature seemed to inhale the stuff, swallowing pure magical energy and then expelling it to propel itself downward. But this process was slowing as the creature died. The lizard worm rapidly lost speed, fading back into the mists.

All around Aeoxoea, the rainfall of rocks and boulders and slime and blood continued, joining her in her helpless unstoppable fall, struggling, kicking, and screaming, trapped inside a giant glob of worm entrails. Then she crashed into one side of the shaft and stayed there, sliding along the wall as it changed direction. It gradually leveled off, and she was riding down a river rapids— only she was drowning in green viscera instead of water. Then the tunnel dropped again, went left, then right. She had no idea where she was going and had no way to stop, or even slow herself. She was entirely at the mercy of gravity and the direction the tunnel took her.

Then she was falling straight down again, and she could see the worm hole had ended in the ceiling of an immense cavern with thousands of stalactites hanging down. The cavern was so huge, she could not see anything in any direction, nothing but the impossibly long rock icicles all around her. They looked like they might be longer than the tallest towers on the tallest castles she'd seen.

Then she was smacked silly by a wall of water, her ears roaring with bubbles as she was swallowed by a cold and black underground lake. Thankfully, it was deep enough to break her fall, and thankfully, she was an accomplished swimmer. She didn't know which direction would be preferable, but she knew she must swim away from the refuse that surely followed from the worm hole above. so she stayed beneath the surface as long as she could, swimming as far away as she could. This also served to wash much of the slime from her body and cool her skin, for which she was grateful.

When she finally did come up for air, she wasn't surprised to find the surface of the lake rippling, rings of waves flowing out from an epicenter created by a steady waterfall of stones and dust and worm guts crashing down from the ceiling. Aeoxoea floated on her back, bobbing up and down, her skin tickled by the water as it lapped against her side. She couldn't help gasping from the excitement of what had happened, her breath trying to keep pace with the thundering of her heart. She tried to calm down, tried to breathe evenly, but found it impossible.

Blue lights flashed in the assassin's vision as the DoomFist continued to seek its target. The crosshairs moved among the stalactites above, searching in vain for the lizard worm. It found nothing but a deluge of blood and slime and worm guts being spewed from the ceiling above into the lake below.

"Sir knight," she panted.

"Yes, my mistress?"

"You said this island would show me wonders," she said. "You promised I'd see things I'd never seen before."

"Yes, I did," Jass said.

"You didn't know how true your words were."

"You are pleased by this?" Jass asked.

The assassin laughed. "Nearly dying is not a pleasure, though you might say I am amused by the variety of unique ways in which your island has attempted to kill me."

"Then you should expect further amusement, my mistress."

"Of course, my puppet," Aeoxoea giggled. She began a leisurely backstroke across the surface of the lake. "Let us continue our shared holiday, then, by seeking new and more thrilling amusements."

"As you wish."

As the knight said this, the DoomFist stopped searching for the lizard worm among the stalactites. The blue lights ceased flashing, and a soothing female voice spoke:

"Target eliminated."

Chapter 41

Elkor the Hound sat on a soft, warm patch of gungi moss, his back resting against a rock formation of bumpy limestone on the floor of a vast underground cavern. He breathed evenly, slowly, resting as best he could while still remaining awake to keep watch. The act of keeping watch consisted primarily of listening, since the vast, sunless gloom rendered his good eye nearly as worthless as his bad one.

There was not one ray of sunlight where he was, not even the tiniest droplet to enter his eye and give him sight. He hadn't seen or felt any sunlight in more days than he cared to count. Before making camp in this cavern, the knights spent what felt like a lifetime walking in the endless tunnel of the mua giou lair. That was after visiting the Kingdom of Illengaard, the land frozen in perpetual nighttime. This was shortly after seven straight days of battle under the orange glow of the sunless sky.

The knights did see some light during their descent from the mua giou lair, though it provided little comfort. This was the light of the underground, produced not by sun or fire, but by the processes of life. They'd seen jugger beetles and zoot flies, creatures not so different from their counterparts of the surface, save for their innate luminescence. They also saw glowworms, which Elkor knew were misnamed because they were really plants with wriggly appendages that grew on the walls and ceilings of caverns, shedding pale, green light down upon them. He knew this because he'd traveled into the Neversea Depths on a few occasions in his youth.

Elkor was born a son of the old clan of Yarik, and had grown to manhood in the mountain kingdoms beneath the peaks of the southern Dividers. The children of Yarik were the only humans who maintained trading relationships with inhabitants of the Neversea, most prominently the dycleth and shan ju of the Iksiout nation. Elkor knew a small number of Iksiout growing up; he'd had dealings with their leaders once he took his oath and received his knightshield.

As a result of this, Elkor knew more about the Neversea Depths than most humans of the surface. He knew the Iksiout believed that the world was alive, and like any living thing, it breathed and bled and spoke. They had fanciful names for the natural processes of the earth: The Demon's Breath. The Father's Blood.

There was no denying that the belly of Thershon was as complex a place as the innards of a living being. It contained thousands of tunnels and passageways; caverns and rooms and rock formations of every size, shape, and color imaginable. It was an entire world unto itself, a larger one, in fact, than the one on the surface, with its miles and miles of twisting and turning tunnels and caverns. Much of it was dark and quiet and empty, but much of it was not. Many varieties of fauna lived in these shadows; some that walked, some that crawled, some that flew, and others that did all three. There were the two-legged, the six-legged and the thousand-legged. Some were mindless, some were clever, many were deadly. They came in every shape and size, from the jugger beetles and zoot flies they'd seen to the mighty lizard worm of the Garnet Dens.

It was a separate world with its own ecology, with its own air, its own wind and weather, rivers, mountains, valleys and forests. Golden or purple rainfalls of earth blood, occasionally whipped by blasts of Demon's Breath, fed the underground rivers and lakes of the Father's Blood. This kept the lungs of the world moist for the gatt worms who lived beneath the dirt, and nourished beds of soft riptaw, patches of stringy and toxic thraki moss, or forests of mighty siptaw mushrooms. The gatt worms fed the durke while the riptaw fed the eidyu herds, who fed their predators, the spearheads, night fishers, miagno spiders, and occasionally, snapper weed.

Elkor had not witnessed all of this himself, but knew enough of it was true that he did not doubt the rest. The Iksiout themselves were proof enough that amazing creatures made their home in the darkness of the Neversea Depths. Elkor had never visited one of their subterranean cities, but had seen enough of Iksiout culture in his dealings with them to know that it was just as advanced as his own.

The knight had spoken with their representatives on many occasions. Emissaries of the Iksiout leaders and holy men representing their religion had visited the leaders of Yarik on many occasions. Elkor himself once traveled to the construction site of a small underground fortress that would serve as a trading post. He saw the Iksiout planners and artisans who worked on the structure, and spoke with the military men who protected them as they worked. Each of these encounters served to open Elkor's eyes a little bit more to the vast, ancient, and complex traditions of the Iksiout culture and social structure.

Most men would think it impossible that life could exist without the blessing of sunlight, but the existence of the Iksiout proved otherwise. They showed Elkor and his fellow brothers of Yarik that intelligent beings could not only survive, but thrive in the inky blackness of the Neversea Depths.

Elkor would have preferred that the quest for Gilligod would have taken him into the caverns beneath the Dividers, onto ground controlled by the friendly Iksiout. Instead, the Keeper ordered the knights to seek the Devil Device many miles to the south, in the tunnels beneath the mua giou lair. This was unknown territory to the people of the Seven Kingdoms. No human had ever come here and returned to tell their story, therefore it was impossible to know what sort of creatures lived here, or what intelligent races might claim this ground as their own.

The place where Elkor rested was on the high end of a gently sloping, oval-shaped cavern with a sandy floor. He faced northward, looking down upon a giant crack that gashed the floor in the lowest portion of the room. This crack was impossibly deep, and emitted a faint, almost undetectable orange glow and a rumbling that was more felt than heard. It also spewed a hot wind from deep within the earth that swirled within the room and buffeted the sandy floor. After only a few hours, Elkor could see his own footprints in the sand erased by this wind, the sand blown smooth as if they were never there.

This gave the Hound some unease, for it robbed him of some of his tracking ability. He had no way to know if anyone else had previously walked this ground before him; less chance of knowing if danger was near. Elkor had seen some evidence that intelligent beings were in these tunnels. During the descent from the mua giou lair, the knights had found evidence of slaughter; piles of animal bones bearing knife marks, as if hunters had cleaned their kills there. Elkor searched for any sign of who this might have been, but found no abandoned campsites or the refuse commonly left by living things. If the creatures left any tracks in the sand, they were long gone, likely blown away by the hot wind that swirled in these tunnels.

The only evidence the knights could find of the hunter's passing was a smear of luminescent fungus which could not be blown away by the wind. Elkor saw it on the stone floor of one of the tunnels, as if someone stepped in the stuff, then tried to wipe it off on the floor. It could have been left by any sort of creature, but Elkor thought it resembled the ball portion and long, blunted toes of a dycleth foot. As soon as this thought entered his head, he immediately laughed at himself. In all his dealings with the Iksiout, he'd never seen any that would leave footprints so huge. If this was a dycleth, it would have stood between ten and twelve feet tall. It was simply impossible.

Though Elkor didn't enjoy being in these unknown tunnels, he was happy to be free of the mua giou lair, which removed the threat of being crushed by the random comings and goings of that mighty creature. The climb down the worm hole was long and arduous, testing the knights both mentally and physically. Especially taxing was the portion of the tunnel that went straight down, forcing the knights to climb down the rock wall, a harrowing descent that took many hours to complete.

Elkor thought this climb was dangerous and unnecessary, but Gavin insisted. While Elkor felt they should travel back up the tunnel and search the cracks and fissures in the walls for another route, Gavin argued that they should continue down the worm hole as the Keeper of the Craft had instructed them. Thought Elkor didn't realize it at the time, there was also another reason the Zealot wanted to climb. He wanted to set a trap for their pursuer.

The old knight knew they were being followed ever since shortly after they'd left Ebon South. He knew this because of a special connection he had with his dogs, courtesy of a tattoo the Keeper had woven into his skin. It gave the Hound the ability to sense his animals' thoughts and moods, and occasionally share their senses. At times when the connection was strongest, he could see blurry images of what they saw, or hear the distorted sounds detected by their ears.

This was how Elkor knew someone was following them. Behe caught the scent on their first night of flight in the snowy Outlander forest. Elkor guessed it was a young girl, but then several days later, Kang discovered three men who were following them. The knights wished to throw these pursuers off the trail without having to stop to fight them, so they attempted to utilize the zoths' enmity toward humans to invite an attack.

They set their trap at a place called the Tombs of Shackler's Ford, the site of an old clan settlement built during the time of Elkor's great grandsire. In those days, it was called the Inn at Shackler's Ford, positioned on a bustling crossroads at the midway point between the holdings of House Stormdell and the Valley of Illengaard. It thrived for years until shortly after the fall of Illengaard, when it was destroyed and its buildings razed in a terrible zoth attack. Legend said the creatures celebrated their victory by building a monument to the Blood Goddess on the site, using the remains of the inn and its inhabitants as building materials. Whatever the truth, the earth beneath Shackler's Ford remained soured. Whether it was cursed by the Maiden of Chaos or haunted by the ghosts of those who died there, nothing could live or grow in the shadow of that monument but thorns. Nothing was nurtured there but a desire to commit atrocities in the name of the Blood Goddess.

The knights knew the zoths would be enraged if any humans were brazen enough to cross this ground so sacred to their goddess. Committing such a deed would bring a ferocious response from the tribes in the area. But that was exactly what the knights wanted. If the three men wanted to continue chasing the Blessed Soul, they would have to follow the trail through the Tombs of Shackler's Ford.

Just as the knights had hoped, the zoths were aware of the intrusion. By whatever arcane powers of Shia Ka or the Wind Magic of the zoth shamans, the creatures detected the presence of their most hated enemy befouling their sacred ground and rushed warriors there to defend it. When those who chased the Blessed Soul arrived, they found their way blocked by a zoth chieftain and his war party.

It wasn't a flawless plan. While the knights were able to throw the hunters off their trail, they were not able to escape undetected themselves. The zoths' thirst for blood is never satiated, and once the chieftain reclaimed his territory, he quickly turned his attention to the two knights. The ensuing chase lasted for days, taking them all the way across the snowy plain to the southern spur of Arka Moor. There it ended with battle, Elkor and his hounds defeating the zoth chieftain on the edge of the Kingdom of Illengaard.

The knights thought their plan was successful, that they'd neutralized those who were following them. But once they were inside the Castle of Teardrops, Behe caught the scent again. It seemed the girl was still following them. Elkor had no idea how this could be. He was certain he'd misread his dog's thoughts the first time. But it was the same scent of the same girl. Somehow she'd managed to travel many miles through the bitter cold of the Outlander winter, an endeavour that severely taxed the two knights, grown men in excellent physical shape. She'd done this while somehow avoiding detection by the zoths of the Outlands, then following the knights into Illengaard, as unwelcoming a place as there was on Thershon. Merely setting foot on the tortured soil of Illengaard gave tremors to a man's stomach, but this girl was apparently fearless. She was still out there, somewhere, even in the land of teardrops.

Elkor knew he would have been a fool to think this was an ordinary girl. He considered himself a gifted tracker. He'd spend the majority of his manhood under the boughs of the Outlander forest, trapping, hunting, fishing, and playing games of cat and mouse with the zoths of the area. He'd both been hunted and done the hunting. He was certain he knew every way in which a living creature marked its own passing. But this girl left no trail. If not for Behe's nose, the knight wouldn't have had the faintest notion anyone was following them. But Behe knew. And so did the Zealot.

He made no mention of the girl, but regularly warned Elkor that danger was near. He was constantly looking off at nothing, as if listening or smelling with whatever sixth sense he had. Gavin had superb instincts. For reasons Elkor didn't fully understand, the Zealot was more in tune with his surroundings than anyone else he'd ever known. It was as if he had a connection to the world. And the world told him things. Whatever it was, Elkor had learned to trust Gavin when he warned of danger, just as he'd learned to trust his animals. They just knew, and Elkor did not question it.

So he didn't question Gavin when he insisted they climb down the side of the worm hole. He somehow knew the coming of the mua giou was imminent. It was like he could smell it. He also knew that the window of time allowing safe passage down was small, just large enough that the knights would have time to climb down. There would not be time for anyone who tried to follow.

The Hound wondered if the ruse would work. He wondered if someone clever enough to have followed them all the way from Ebon South, across miles of land infested with both zoths and creepermen, could be tricked in this fashion, and be trapped on the side of the worm hole when the mua giou reappeared. The girl had not lost their trail thus far, even though they'd walked some of the most dangerous ground in Thershon. The zoths didn't stop her at Shackler's Ford, and neither did the creepermen in the Castle of Teardrops. A person who could surmount such obstacles was obviously very powerful, capable, and clever. Such a person might somehow sense the same things Gavin did; might know just as he did when the mua giou was coming.

What Elkor did know was that he'd not caught any sense of this girl who stalked them since the knights left the worm hole. Perhaps the ruse had worked. But perhaps it hadn't. Perhaps she was at that moment standing in the darkness only feet away, staring at him. How would he know? Just because Kang didn't detect her didn't mean she wasn't still there. Kang's nose was old, and not as sharp as that of his daughter, Behe.

Behe.

Where was she? Was she still out there somewhere? Would she ever come back?

If he did not have more pressing duty, Elkor would have taken Kang and gone to look for her. But he didn't have the luxury of that freedom. So again, he forced himself to not think about it, tried to put those thoughts out of his mind and focus on things he could control, like serving out his watch duty.

He took comfort in his old man, the large black dog with the white hairs around his snout, who now slept with his head in his master's lap. Kang's confidence was never shaken. He was always loyal, always ready, always delighted to serve his master. The old man was Elkor's connection to the life he'd left behind on the surface, the life he would return to when this quest was completed. He loved Kang for this, and all the other things his dog did for him. He cherished the old man, just as much as he mourned the loss of Behe, taken from him by creeper's disease.

Elkor scratched Kang's ears almost constantly, listening to the silence, and reminded himself that silence was a good thing.

Silence meant nothing moved in the darkness. Silence meant nothing approached to threaten the Blessed Soul.

But then Kang's ears perked up and he lifted his head, reminding Elkor that silence to his old human ears didn't mean what it once did. The battle hound's hearing was far more trustworthy than his master's, and now his canine ears stood up straight, turning to detect the direction of the possible threat.

Then Elkor felt a vibration in the floor, slow and steady, accompanied by a deep rumble. Though he couldn't see anything, he instinctively looked up as if he was about to see the lizard worm burst through the ceiling of the cavern and devour him. But that wouldn't happen. The lair of the mua giou was miles away to the west. This sound was coming from the south.

Whatever it was, it came fast. The smell of churned earth filled the air, then the scent of flesh, the musk of animal, and Kang began to bark. Elkor jumped to his feet just as the rumbling burst into the room, thundering in his ears. It sounded like a herd of cattle running straight toward him.

"Zealot!" he shouted, but if there was a reply, it was swallowed by the thunder that filled the cavern.

Gavin made his bed only feet away, also at the base of the bumpy rock formation. Only moments ago, he was sleeping with Eleod. Elkor couldn't see or hear him, but was certain the knight was awakened by now.

"With me!" he said to Kang, jumping onto the side of the rocks.

The limestone rock formation was the largest of a handful that speckled the floor of this cavern. It looked like a fifteen-foot-tall heap of multi-colored piano keys melted together. The sides were steep, but the bumps made it easy to climb, and in only moments Elkor was standing atop the formation with Kang at his side, looking south. The reason the knights chose this place to camp was the gungi moss growing beneath it, which provided an acceptable, if not pleasant sleeping surface. Now Elkor was thankful they'd chosen to sleep on the north side, because it sounded like hundreds of beasts were charging toward them from the south. If that was the case, the limestone would protect them, acting as a shield against whatever was approaching.

Elkor still wore his magical torch strapped to his back. One whispered word and it flared to life, casting its pale, white glow over his shoulder. The sudden light was jolting for a man who'd just spent hours in total darkness, and it now blinded him with light rather than darkness. He knew he wasn't the only one who disliked the light, because of the sounds of distress that answered its sudden appearance. He couldn't see, but could hear something screaming, one hundred voices cutting into his ears like a great flock of cranes. But these cranes weren't in the sky. They were on the ground, and as Elkor's eyes adjusted, he saw them coming straight at him.

He'd never seen one of these creatures before, but had heard descriptions. They were called durke, described by the Iksiout as prey animals who subsisted on gungi moss, giving their hides for clothing, their bones for tools, and their flesh for food. It was also said that the trail of the durke was always the surest route to water.

They were large, as tall as a man, and covered in short, brown fur. They ran on large and powerful hind legs with high hocks, taking great strides that almost resembled horizontal leaps as they grasped at the air with tiny front feet that ended with sharp talons. They had short necks that bobbed their heads with the motion of their feet, and elongated snouts, big ears, and glassy, black eyes. Elkor could see hundreds of durke coming into his torchlight, running together with single mindedness, like a herd of cattle. He was immediately thankful for the protection of the limestone rock formation. If not for this natural shield, they might have been trampled.

The Hound looked back and saw Gavin huddling beneath the rocks below, hugging Eleod with one arm, while gripping a knife with his other hand. Elkor knew he did this to be prepared, in case the Blessed Soul was threatened. The Zealot looked up at him questioningly, squinting his eyes from the light. Elkor only shook his head in response. There would be no threat from these dumb creatures.

Content that Eleod would be safe, Elkor looked back just as the tide of furry flesh reached the south side of the rock formation. The herd began to split to run around the rocks, then one of them bounded into the air, effortlessly leaping up to where Elkor stood. It was unbelievable jumping ability for a creature so large, and it took the Hound completely by surprise. More durke followed that first one, and the knight barely managed to get his shield up to absorb the horned head of the creature that barreled him over, knocking him off the rocks.

He was momentarily airborne, then felt himself falling. A wall of sand crushed his left shoulder, then he was tumbling head over heels down a sharp slope, northward, toward the huge crack in the floor. He was unable to stop his fall and gather his bearings as he tumbled down the hill beneath the feet of the herd. Every time he tried, he was run over again, kicked and stomped and shoved further and further down the slope.

He fell against the base of a small cluster of stalagmites and movement momentarily ceased. His brain was spinning inside his head and his breath eluded him, punched out of his body by so many impacts. He managed to crawl to his knees, gasping, trying to shout a command to Kang. Nothing came out but a wheeze.

The respite was short-lived. Another of the durke collided with him, knocking him head over heels, and again he was tumbling in the sand. He was kicked and beaten over and over again, losing his torch as it was ripped from his back as he rolled down the hill. The entire herd of creatures seemed to be taking their turn running him over, pushing him further down the slope. It was like being at the bottom of a stampede of cattle, kicked and stomped and mercilessly pounded into the ground by hundreds of animals running with one single mind, unaware of his presence, unaware they were killing him, but too dumb to care. He got to his knees again, desperately grasping for fleeting breaths. He managed a few weak words.

"Kang, protect the—"

He was hit and knocked down again. He could barely see, pelted in the face by sand and confused by the flashing light of his torch as it was trampled and kicked around by the animals. All he could see were churning durke legs all around him, crashing into him, trampling him, and pushing him down the hill. Then one kicked him in the head and his ears were ringing, and warm blood ran down his face.

He was pushed up against another rock formation, this one smaller than where he'd made camp, but still large enough to present an obstacle to the creatures. Again, the herd split to avoid the rocks. Most of them ran around, many jumped over, but thankfully, no longer did any of them trample him. He huddled at the base of this rock formation, covering his head with his buckler as his ears continued to ring. There he waited, the herd thundering all around him. The wait lasted several minutes, as more and more of the creatures filled the room and thundered past. There must have been thousands of them.

All he could do was wait. Elkor knew he should have stayed near the Blessed Soul, but also knew there was no going back. If he crawled out of his hiding place, he would be crushed. So he stayed where he was, wiped the blood off his face, and whispered a prayer:

"Give this child strength.

"That he might raise your banner.

"Cleanse this child's wounds.

"That he might carry your shield."

Eventually the roar of the animals' tread began to fade, which told Elkor the majority of the durke had passed by. Now only dozens filled the room rather than hundreds, few enough that he could now distinguish individual footfalls. Soon there would be only a trickle of stragglers trying to keep up with the main herd. He raised his head to look around, and saw nothing but his magical torch lying far away. It cast nearly no light, lying half-buried in the sand, with the silhouettes of the beasts still passing by.

Then Elkor heard a grunt behind him, and the splattering of cleaved flesh. One of the durke cried out in pain, then quickly fell silent. This was followed by the thud of a body hitting the ground, and the fierce roar of the hunter. It was an inhuman voice, and yet, it was familiar.

The Hound could hide no longer. He climbed to his feet and ran. The stream of durke running past was lesser than before, but they still remained dangerous. He tried to see them coming, to dodge when necessary, but it was difficult in the darkness. He was hit twice, knocked down once, but he continued running, the image of that luminescent footprint fresh in his mind.

He heard the roar again, and knew this newcomer had seen him. Battle was a certainty, but he continued to run, striving desperately to reach his torch. He knew he could run as fast as he wanted, but he would be caught if this creature chose to give chase. Instead, he heard the whipping of a sling being primed behind him. He rolled in the sand, snatching his torch just as the sling let loose, and the slug sailed high. Way too high. It would have missed even if he'd stayed on his feet. Elkor knew the slinger couldn't see, and was aiming for a target much larger than a human.

He came to his feet and continued running, working feverishly to fasten his torch into the sconce of leather straps on his shoulder. He had no hope of avoiding battle. The slinger wasn't preparing another throw but was running toward him, giving chase.

Elkor's axe and buckler were in his hands, just before another durke struck him and knocked him over. He crumpled and nearly dropped his axe, eating a mouthful of sand. He was beat-up and hurting, but remained nimble enough to roll to his feet.

Someone approached from his left, the opposite direction of the slinger. Large feet thumped on the ground, spraying sand at his legs. Battle rings clattered, and a large weapon whooshed past his head. This was Elkor's blind side, so he couldn't immediately see who it was, which of the three kin he faced, or what nation they belonged to, but he knew to duck. They always aimed high, especially when they were blinded.

As he did this, he shouted the command word for his magical torch to burn brightest. It began to suck all the Flame Bringers from the air, converting it to blazing-white magical fire. It was an explosion of light that was only seen in the midday sun. And now that midday sun burned in a subterranean cavern that had never seen daylight before, and into eyes that had never beheld anything so bright as even a candle flame.

Elkor sprang back to his feet, axe and buckler ready, his torch burning on his shoulder, brightly illuminating his new adversary. The large creature towered above him. It had reddish skin stretched tightly over bulging muscles, splashed with war paint, chitin armor, and jingling silver battle rings. It was a mountain of muscle supported by enormous multi-jointed legs, a barrel-shaped torso, and topped by a head with four horns poking out of a lion's mane of fiery orange hair. The Hound wasn't surprised to see the face that resembled a man's stretched and elongated into a snout with two jaws, or the six eyes that ringed the crown of the creature's skull, a pair for each of the ways in which it could see. The mouth gaped with a roar of agony, and all six eyes were pinched shut to block out the light of the magical torch.

Elkor had never seen one with red skin before, but he knew exactly what this was.

Dycleth.

Chapter 42

Elkor knew more about the Neversea Depths than most humans of the surface. He knew many inhabitants of the darkness could not process bright light, especially if it was created magically. In the absence of sunlight to give them vision, many creatures of the Depths innately used their juy to detect other things, which allowed them to "see" even in total darkness. Elkor knew the Iksiout could detect Craft, heat, and life, hear distances and smell emotion, without the use of spells. He knew the Iksiout disliked fire, for while the glow it cast ruined their regular vision, the heat it generated also ruined their infravision. But they especially loathed magical fire, because it ruined every way in which they used their eyes, blinding with its heat, its light, and its Craft. It was too much stimuli to sort out, like a hundred voices drowning out the single one you are trying to hear.

This effectively left them unable to see anything, while a creature of the surface, whose eyes could detect neither heat nor magic—a creature such as Elkor—could see perfectly fine.

Such was the case with these red-skinned dycleth. They were blinded by the Hound's magical torch, while he was not. He could hear their cries of shock and pain when he commanded it to burn as hot has possible, as glaring as a bright summer day. He could see them searching for him as he attacked, each of their six eyes squinting with the pain, darting here and there, but seeing nothing. While they were blinded, they weren't totally without their senses. He could see their ears twitching, listening for him, and their noses sniffing, smelling for him.

Even without the ability to see, they were extremely formidable, each one physically outmatching Elkor in every way. The smallest and weakest of them possessed the strength of three men. And even though they were much larger than humans, their powerful, multi-jointed legs made them just as nimble, allowing them to run as fast as a horse, and jump many times their own height. The Hound knew he needed to neutralize this mobility, so when he fought the first dycleth, he immediately attacked the legs.

The remains of the durke herd thundered all around as the two engaged one another. This dycleth was small for his race, only slightly larger than a tall human male. His black war paint spoke of ritual application, and the chime of his battle rings sang a song of many battles won as part of a brotherhood. He bore a sling, a horn, and a curved knife, which told Elkor he was probably a scout. He was fast, and he knew how to use that knife, but he was blinded.

The knife crossed the air with defensive zigzags, swiping at an unseen enemy. Elkor was elusive and careful as he moved in. The blade only hit his buckler once, just before his axe chopped the dycleth's knee. Then a durke, screaming and blinded, rushed into the torchlight and crashed into the creature's back. The red-skinned dycleth grunted and staggered, and Elkor chopped at his knee again. The creature roared and kicked sand in the human's face, then charged, leading with four horns. Elkor avoided impalement, but was struck by the dycleth's massive shoulder. They both tumbled, but now Elkor's enemy knew where he was, and his arm struck like a serpent, seizing the Hound by the shoulder straps of his armor.

Elkor fought, trying to resist or escape his enemy's clutches, but the dycleth's strength was god-like. He felt like a toy in the creature's hands as he was pinned to the ground, the knife blade slashing at him. Amazingly, the first attack missed, cutting a groove in the sand just above Elkor's head.

It was a blind and uninformed attack, unlike the response Elkor gave—his axe to the creature's neck. The splattering sound was awful, and the dycleth made choking sounds as his blood sprayed on Elkor's face. Another durke jumped over them just as the dycleth's knife darted in again, this time cutting across the leather armor of Elkor's chest and scraping the knightshield beneath. That attack would be this dycleth's last act, as Elkor's axe struck again at his exposed neck. Elkor wasn't sure it was enough, so he chopped the dycleth twice more to be certain, then left him dying on the ground, a squirting, gurgling mess.

This occurred just before the slinger arrived to join in the fight. Again, this one was smaller, a scout armed with a curved knife and sling, and fighting blind. It made little sense that they attacked one at a time. If they combined their strength against him, the fight would be over quickly, but their piecemeal approach allowed Elkor a fighting chance. Clearly, they still didn't know what they were fighting; they couldn't see a thing. They were probably searching for the source of the light in the hope of extinguishing it, then bumbling into battle with him by chance. If that was the case, they were finding the source of the light to be elusive. Even beat up as he was, Elkor was fast enough to avoid blind adversaries.

Although these scouts were small for their race, they were still greater physically than any human ever hoped to be, and nearly as quick. Their blindness was Elkor's salvation, and he was reminded of this when one of the dycleth's blind attacks nearly cut him in two. He was able to raise his buckler in time, but the old and sturdy shield that had blocked a thousand attacks before was now cut like a piece of parchment. With one slash of his knife, the dycleth shattered the symbol of Yarik to pieces, leaving the Hound with a broken finger and a handful of kindling.

Then he charged and bowled the human over. If Elkor had been the size of a dycleth, that attack would have resulted with him impaled on the creature's horns. But he was a human, and the slinger only fell over him like an adult stumbling over a child.

As they tumbled into the dust, he hacked at the back of the creature's legs, catching him twice in the heel. The resulting roar of anger was deafening. The curved knife whipped and slashed at the sandy floor all around him, and Elkor was forced to roll away to avoid losing his head. He twisted to his feet, watching as the creature writhed on the ground, clutching his leg, blood running between his fingers.

This dycleth, just like the other, made the mistake of fighting him as though he were an equal. His powerful, straightforward attacks were useless against someone so small and elusive, especially when he could not see his target. Likewise, his chitin armor was made to receive heavy blows delivered in a straightforward manner. Instead of small chinks in his defenses, he had gaps. These were easily large enough to accommodate Elkor's small, human blades. And they were in all the most important places, leaving his joints, his lower abdomen, and neck exposed. These were not difficult targets for the human's axe to find.

As long as his magical torch burned, Elkor knew he had a chance. Once these creatures could see who faced them, see his size and speed, gauge his strengths and weaknesses, he would be dead. But for now, they continued to behave as if they were searching for dycleth warriors of a rival nation. For once, Elkor appreciated being undersized and overmatched.

The knight advanced on the blind and wounded dycleth as the creature struggled to stand on his injured leg. This kill would be quick and easy, as long as the knight was careful. But Elkor never got the chance to finish the job. He heard the whipping of slings and was forced to dive to the ground as a volley of slugs zipped by.

He remained flat on his stomach as that first was followed by another, then another. Once again, he was saved by the blindness of his enemies. Their attacks were as effective as if they were throwing shots at the sun. They couldn't hope to hit anything, but he knew their strategy was smart. Unable to locate and neutralize the source of the light, they chose to fill the air with slugs. The slingers took low-risk attacks from a distance, and did it all at once, as if they shared one mind. Or heard one command. The Hound cursed silently.

This was military precision.

By now, the crush of durke bodies had slowed to a trickle, with only the occasional straggler rushing by. The thunder of their tread no longer filled Elkor's ears, and he could finally hear what transpired elsewhere in the cavern. The first thing he heard was

Kang barking. Elkor knew his old man, and knew every sound the dog made. Kang felt threatened, agitated, and angry. He saw someone he disliked. The Blessed Soul was threatened. Then Elkor heard the clash of arms as a battle raged at the top of the slope, and worse, the whipping of slings and the thudding of spears in sand. Chitin armor shifted and clicked. Battle rings rattled and chimed. Then the deep-chested roar of the dycleth echoed off the walls of the cavern, many voices joined in a complex battle chant.

Fear gripped Elkor's heart. This was all the proof he needed.

They were out there in the darkness—slingers, spear carriers— a scouting group, or maybe light infantry, perhaps even an entire company. This was not a band of random dycleth out hunting durke, which would have been terrible enough. These were soldiers, trained in combat, and accustomed to working as a team. Blind or not, they were a foe he couldn't hope to overcome.

Though he could not see, it was easy to guess what was happening at the top of the slope on the north end of the cavern. A dycleth battle company of red-skinned warriors loyal to an unknown nation had stumbled upon the place where the knights were camped. After some initial confusion and skirmishing by the advance scouts, the dycleth leaders were organizing their soldiers. From this point on, their attacks would be coordinated, cohesive. This was the worst thing for the two knights.

Elkor jumped to his feet and began running up the slope. His duty was clear. He must reunite with Gavin and Kang and protect the Blessed Soul, no matter how dim his chances of survival. Perhaps this was the day he would die, but that wasn't a unique possibility. The old knight had joined in many fights with terrible odds and had survived every one. He didn't fear battle, and he didn't fear death. His only fear was in failing the quest, failing to preserve the safety of the Blessed Soul. And so he charged toward an unknown fate, one of two humans facing a battle company of dycleth soldiers.

Two humans, yes; but not just any two humans. These were two Knights of the Southern Cross, with the blood of the old clans flowing in their veins. The Champion of Embriss. A Battle Lord of Yarik.

He flipped his eye patch over, changing the image from a glaring eye to the diamond-shaped war emblem of the Kingdom of Yarik.

"By this hand," the Hound said to himself as he ran, "justice shall prevail."

CHAPTER 43

Elkor could hear the screams of the dycleth at the top of the slope as they attacked the Zealot and paid for it. It wasn't long after the battle started that the slithering voices of the Silent Sisters could be heard amid the cacophony of battle, screams and oaths and ringing steel, and occasionally, Kang's barks and growls. Gavin always carried other weapons, usually blades, to keep his skills with conventional fighting styles sharp. And also to decrease his reliance on the Sisters, should the time come when he didn't have them, or if his ability to wield them properly was dampened by injury or age. If the Zealot used his knives at all against the dycleth, they were quickly abandoned in favor of the Silent Sisters.

"Kang!" he shouted, then heard his dog growling.

The old battle hound was near. He'd abandoned Gavin, despite what his master ordered.

"Damnit, old man, I told you …"

His words died on his lips as he heard the dog's paws striking the sand behind him, running fast. The battle hound jumped, as if trying to strike him in the back and knock him down. But Elkor didn't fall for it. He had trained his puppy to do this, so he spun around just in time to meet the attack face to face.

All four of the battle hound's paws struck him, and he was knocked onto his back. Jaws snapped at his face in the darkness, just as clawed feet raked his chest and stomach. Elkor knew these tactics, just as he knew this animal's smell, and recognized the sound of her growl. He didn't need to see the two canine eyes glowing yellow in the darkness above him, blazing with the hatred of Miacnon, to know that this animal suffered from creeper's disease. He knew which dog this was—the puppy he'd raised, trained, and loved. She was as much his daughter as she was

Kang's. The Angel of Disease had taken her from him. Now he was going to take her back.

Elkor was caught off guard when Behe first turned on him. He did not keep his wits as he should have, and allowed his fear and uncertainty to keep him from doing the right thing. In all the days since he'd last seen her, Elkor had thought a great deal about what he would do if they ever met again. He wouldn't make the same mistake twice. There would be no uncertainty. Behe must die.

He knew she would attempt to knock him down. He knew she would go for his throat. It was how she was trained. This meant there was a good chance they would end up exactly as they were, struggling on the ground, and he was prepared for it. He'd sharpened the knife, and kept it sheathed on his left wrist. He dropped his axe and seized her by the scruff of her neck, drew the knife, and plunged it into her side.

It wasn't the lethal blow he'd hoped for. Behe was too squirmy, too well-trained to hold still for such an attack to land properly. He expected her to keep fighting him, driven on by the madness of creeper's disease, but instead she yelped in pain and jumped off him. He was frustrated by this, wanting to throw his knife at her, but now he had bigger concerns. Her blood splattered on his chest, and now it sizzled and hissed on the surface of his leather armor. If it touched his flesh, it would burrow beneath his skin in an attempt to infect him with creeper's disease. He dropped the knife, frantically jerking on his armor. He loosened the laces on his chest, undoing the buckles on his shoulders, shrugging the leather off as fast as he could. All the while the blood sizzled and smoked, filling his nostrils with the stink of Illengaard, that place he never wanted to go, that place he knew he'd never forget.

Miacnon no longer used his puppy to attack him. Now he used her blood. The Angel of Disease did not merely attack the knight's flesh. He did not only attack his health. He also attacked Elkor's spirit. Ever since the Hound reported to his post at Storm Hall, he could feel the call of Illengaard, the whispers of the Woman in White who haunted the dreams of children. She promised him he would die in the Valley of Teardrops. And he believed it. He didn't know when, but knew it was true. He might have survived his first visit, but Illengaard continued to call to him. The Angel of Disease would never stop trying to claim him.

He threw his armor on the ground, and was now wearing only his woolen shirt. Inspecting himself, he was happy to see no blood stains on his chest. He was safe from creeper's disease. For now.

He removed his magical torch from its leather sconce on his armor and rose to his feet.

"You wish to watch us fight, Miacnon?" he asked aloud. "You wish for me to fight my puppy while you laugh and sneer?"

It was bad enough that this quest had forced him to walk the terrible, cursed ground of Illengaard. It was even worse that creeper's disease took his Behe from him. But now he was forced to fight in a foolish distraction from his quest. He could not do his duty to the Blessed Soul of Man because he was forced into this evil spectacle, to fight his puppy at the pleasure of the Angel of Disease.

But at least some good would come of this. Another soldier of Miacnon would no longer march in his army of the diseased. Elkor was determined that this encounter would not end until Behe was dead. She must die, and it but be her master who did the deed. No one else.

"Come here, baby," he said to the darkness. "Come here and die."

He stood defensively, knife in one hand, torch in the other. It was oddly quiet now where he was, at the north end of the cavern near the crack in the floor. The durke had all gone, and now the only sound was the faint echoes of battle coming from the top of the slope. He scanned the floor, searching for some trace of his battle hound. But, by the pale light of his torch, he saw nothing but sand and limestone.

"You do not belong to Miacnon, puppy. You belong to me," he said. "He does not command you. I do. Therefore, he will not kill you. I will."

Then he heard Behe's pained whimper behind him. He spun to face her, but saw nothing but more sand and limestone. He could still hear Kang barking further up the hill, and the clash of arms, the screams and oaths of the dycleth, and the hissing of the Silent Sisters.

"Let us finish this, baby," he whispered. "Let us finish it together."

Then he heard Behe approaching from his left side, his blind side. But he was prepared for this. He spun to face her just as she leaped at him. He swung his torch and smashed her in the head just as the two collided, tumbling to the ground. Once again she was on top of him, growling and snapping. He dropped his torch to push her head away, trying to keep those teeth away from his throat, gripping her snout as spittle ran between his fingers.

He knew she was about to rake him again, and now he wore no armor for protection. He could not let that happen, so he jammed the knife home again, this time in her neck. She yelped again, and he felt her body immediately and noticeably weaken. As quickly as he could, he threw her off him before she could shed any more of her blood on him. He rolled away as fast as he could, trying to put some distance between him and his hound.

When he came to his feet, he could see that the deed was done. She was struggling in the sand with his knife hanging out of her, yelping, blood pooling beneath her neck. She would die soon, but he still hadn't made the efficient cut he wanted, and now she was suffering. It hurt his heart to watch this. He wanted to hold her, scratch her ears and kiss her head. But he dared not. He still feared the disease, so he simply stood and watched as she limped out of the light of the torch, leaving dark spots of red in the sand behind her.

He was about to go to retrieve his torch when he heard heavy feet thumping in the sand. It came from his left, from his blind side, and so fast he barely had time to react. He twisted his feet, spinning and dropping to a crouch just as a giant white blade cut the air above him. That attack missed, but was followed by a fist as big as a man's head, a fist that met his face with a crack. It momentarily killed his vision, and caused the world to spin in all directions. He felt himself falling, the sandy ground smashing into his back, and he only had a moment to see another dycleth looming above him, looking down at him with all six eyes.

Though he'd lost his torch, it wasn't far. It still lay nearby, casting enough pale light to illuminate half the creature's body. The memory of the splotchy, luminescent footprint he saw in the nearby tunnel returned to him, the one in the shape of a dycleth foot. He thought at the time that if a dycleth made that footprint, the creature would stand at least ten feet tall. Elkor laughed at that notion then. He was not laughing now.

The creature that stood above him looked larger than any human, larger even than any zoth chieftain Elkor had ever seen. Like the scout and the slinger, he was a mountain of red-skinned muscle, war paint, and battle rings. But he stood much taller than they, and was much more heavily armored, wearing plates of some dark material resembling beetle shells splashed with even more painted dycleth symbols. He was armed with *szer kaa*, twin blades the size of two grown men attached to his right forearm. Among the Iksiout, *szer kaa* were reserved for the mightiest warriors of the heavy infantry, due to their immense size and weight. There were probably few humans alive strong enough to lift these *szer kaa* using the full strength of the back and legs. But this dycleth had no problem lifting them with one arm.

Elkor knew he could not hide. He'd lost his magical torch and the advantage it provided, so this warrior could now see him. Though the magical light was still blinding to him, the dycleth merely shielded his eyes as he looked down upon his adversary. Human eyes met the dycleth's stare, and now there was recognition on both sides. Unlike his comrades, this dycleth warrior knew what he faced, and knew where to place his attacks.

Elkor knew he didn't have long to live.

The dycleth brought his enormous blades down upon the human knight, attempting to punch them through his prone body.

With no weapon of his own, and no hope of blocking this, Elkor rolled left and right, writhing in the sand, dodging and twisting his body every way he could as blows rained down, the *szer kaa* stabbing large holes in the ground. Then the blade hit his head and clipped his ear. He grabbed his attacker's wrist and sunk his teeth into the thumb and the dycleth reared back as Elkor was lifted high into the air. Then he was flying with a piece of thumb in his mouth, the world spinning madly. When he finally did land, the back of his neck and shoulders bore the brunt. The rest of his body went numb, crumbling limply. The world stopped reeling, but his brain didn't. He was unable to move, lying at the edge of the glowing crack in the floor, and at the edge of consciousness.

He'd already experienced far too many blows to the head, and now his senses were spiraling away from him, disappearing into a fog. But just enough remained for him to comprehend the huge blurry form of the dycleth standing above him, raising his weapon for an attack that Elkor knew he could not avoid.

Then he saw Behe coming for him, her yellow eyes flashing in the pale light. She, too, had little time left, limping pathetically, tongue dangling, impending death in her sad eyes. Both the knight and his puppy would soon be dead. At least they'd be together when it happened.

The dycleth put his foot on Elkor's chest, crushing the air from his lungs, pinning him to the ground to better deliver the killing blow. Behe saw this and broke into a weak run, the best she could manage, racing the dycleth for the prize of killing her former master. The dycleth swung his blade, a sideways chop meant for Elkor's neck. The knight could only stare dully as the weapon fell like an executioner's axe, as Behe rushed toward him, eager for his blood.

Certain death approached from two directions. Yet Elkor didn't even whimper. He'd done his duty, and reconciled himself with his Lord. Death had no sting, for he knew eternal peace waited on the other side.

The hot wind bursting from the floor above his head seemed to wail, drowning out all other sounds. It buffeted his head and warmed his face, filling him with peace. It was almost like the peace and warmth of God's love, the love which awaited him.

He closed his one good eye, waiting, a prayer on his lips.

Then the light died. In that instant, the magical torch exploded. For too long it had burned with all its power, channeling more Flame Bringers than it could handle. Now it burst in one last gasp of brilliant light, leaving darkness, and no witnesses to what happened next.

In that instant, a change came over Behe. Elkor was correct about his puppy. She wasn't yet beaten by the curse. She didn't fully belong to the Lord of Disease. A portion of her remained loyal to Elkor, and it was enough to purchase one final moment of free will.

All she wanted to do was protect her masterknight. It was what she was trained her entire life to do. So when she was given a moment of free will, she used it to launch herself into the air, leading with all four paws. It was the last favor she would do for the one who had raised her, trained her, and loved her. She threw herself against his attacker with her dying strength.

The blow meant for Elkor's neck, once so precisely aimed at an unmoving target, suddenly became errant. It missed the knight's neck entirely, falling much higher. The tip of a *szer kaa* blade hit him in the side of the head, slashing across his left eye, slicing his eye patch into halves, cleaving the symbol of Clan Yarik in two. It continued through the bridge of his nose and through his right eye, cutting a deep groove across the center of his face.

The dycleth, with one foot on the knight's chest, was not properly balanced to react to Behe's attack. She struck with great momentum, knocking him further off balance, causing him to fall forward. It was little more than a stumble; the battle hound was not large enough to knock the huge creature over. But she didn't need to, because the dycleth stumbled forward to where a yawning chasm waited.

It was a large crack in the floor which glowed red, and belched forth hot air from the center of Thershon. And the center of Thershon was where this dycleth was headed, along with the animal who caused his headlong fall into doom. Both the dycleth and the battle hound disappeared into the gap, falling through the blistering wind currents, tumbling head over heels toward the red glow below.

The red glow swallowed them, and neither was ever seen again.

CHAPTER 44

Theel lay on his back on the stone floor of the Narrows, his neck and head cushioned by his backpack. Pitch had long since fallen asleep, after draining his little bubbler, and now snored his way through a drunken slumber. Theel didn't know if Yatham slept, but hadn't heard a peep from his brother in hours. If Yatham slept, he did so lightly, with one ear open for trouble, or if Theel needed him. Faithful as always.

Now enveloped in darkness and quiet, he tried to calm himself, tried to relax enough to tap his psychic nexus. Just as the Keeper of the Craft had promised, the process became easier each time he accomplished it, but it still remained an agonizing exercise.

He relaxed his body, breathing slowly and deeply, just as the Keeper of the Craft had instructed him. He reached out gently, slowly, as if sliding his hand between the soft, warm blankets of a bed. It was his own mind he searched, stretching forth his will to find and tap that elusive inner psychic nexus, the source of personal strength, the life force that fueled the powers of the Juy Method. He felt it out there, felt its presence; that delicate connection, the flow of power from within. It was so fragile, so hard to maintain properly for the undisciplined mind. But now he had it, held it, like a soap bubble in his hand, trying to keep the bubble whole, despite its desire to pop.

He held it. And it didn't pop.

Theel felt the power coming, soft and warm, pure molten delight. The urge was there to passively accept the flow of power, to wait for it and react. He wanted to lie back, feel the warm sand against his back, the bright sun on his face, and let the wonderful rush of vitality unleashed by his psychic nexus crash over him like a wave on the beach. Seraphim leaf had nothing on this. The drug was too dry and bland a euphoria, too fake. There was nothing true about it. But this was real life. The feeling was perfect, so … there, so undeniably his, that he didn't want to risk losing it.

It was that fear of losing control, of blundering forward before he was ready, that always caused him to do just that; to wait too long, to watch the bubble pop, lose control, and descend screaming into the chaos of uninvited visions. So many times before when he'd found himself in this moment of questionable control, he knew the answer was to take one step forward. But he was afraid of taking one step back, so he did neither, and in doing so, lost the opportunity. To move forward took discipline that he did not have. Now he knew this was the problem that plagued his attempts at control. He'd been denying himself control of his power through a selfish need to maintain, a foolish capitulation to fear of loss. It was clear he needed to grow, to risk all he had, and gamble that he possessed the faith and the discipline to step forward. One foot in front of the other.

So this time he did not wait. This time he blundered forward intentionally, of his own free will. It was much like a baby learning to walk; learning to balance weight on shaky legs, arms waving, but maintaining his feet, grinning brightly at this new sensation, the feeling of control, of accomplishment.

And he knew immediately that the Keeper was right all along. He knew he had it inside himself, the ability to control it. He just needed to risk partial control in order to gain complete control, and now he had it. He held the power in his hand, controlled it, when it previously controlled him. Now he was in command. Now he was the master. Then he lost it. The baby stumbled, swayed. He was about to lose his grip, about to crash on his face, but he sensed this, compensated, and held it again.

Then the visions came. For the first time, Theel was not assaulted by wild, flashing glimpses of random nightmares. For the first time, he was in control. He was acting, rather than being acted upon. He was telling the juy what to do, and the juy was listening.

He was seeking information. He asked questions. And the visions answered.

He reached into the past, tapping into the signatures of all those who'd tread this ground, the footprints left in the Craft. If those children truly came to this spot, if the older boy climbed the rock pile to find a way through, Theel would be able to see them, see if they made it through somehow. And if they didn't, he would see where they had gone.

Yet he could not find them. He'd experienced a great victory, only to run into another wall. Only hours before, he couldn't resist the pull of the Overlie blood, how strongly it called out to him. But now it was silent. He felt no connection to those children. He could not find them. He had no idea where they were.

It was a simpler task to find the signature of someone he knew. It was easier the better he knew the object of his search. But his ignorance of these children worked against him. He knew nothing of their names or appearance. And so it was a struggle to find them. He searched for a long time. Minutes became an hour. He saw countless unknown faces, both human and zoth, the travelers of the Narrows heading south toward Wrendale and Yarik. He saw mothers, fathers, children and army men, traders and merchants.

Then he saw his father.

A shiver slid up Theel's spine when he saw him. There he was, the famous Knight of the Southern Cross, walking through the Narrows, all tattoos and muscle, swords and spears. Theel could even see the hole through his knight's shield on his chest where it covered his heart, the hole made by an unknown weapon years before. Theel's father was known as the only man ever to be stabbed through the heart and live. He was the man who beat death.

Dread soaked into Theel's heart. He couldn't afford this now. He didn't want to see his masterknight. Didn't want to think about him. He needed to maintain control, to find those children. But he couldn't control the emotions that overwhelmed him at the sight of his father. And now the only thing his Sight chose to show him was his father, walking and walking and walking.

Theel's masterknight had traveled this tunnel many times in his life—many times alone, but also with other knights and soldiers, and once with his squire and son. It seemed that Theel's Sight was determined to show him every time his father had walked this ground, both when he was young, and when he was older, just before he died.

One of the visions showed Theel's father as a young boy, when he was a squire traveling with his own masterknight. Theel knew nothing of the man who'd trained his father to be a knight, only that he'd died long before. Theel was shocked at how much this man resembled his own father. He wore the same tattoos of knighthood, leather armor, and belts bristling with weapons, swords, and spears. He even walked similarly, the way in which he carried himself exuding a confidence earned by years of training and countless victories in battle.

But that wasn't all.

The man's facial features also resembled Theel's father. In fact, he was almost the spitting image of Yatham. Theel shook his head, speechless.

"Was my grandfather your masterknight?" Theel whispered. "Why did you never tell me that?"

Then he looked to his father as a young man, as a squire. He looked at the young man's face and knew instantly what he saw there, for he knew it well. Theel's father showed none of the confidence he projected in his older years. He was unsure, afraid, but struggling to be strong. Theel could even hear his thoughts as if they were his own, reaching over the years, flying to Theel's ears on the wings of Craft magic.

I must be strong. I must not be weak. I must do this, and earn my place in the knighthood.

Theel couldn't believe what he was hearing. His father had walked this very ground as a young man on his way to pursue a knight's quest, his very first.

If I succeed, I will achieve Warrior Baptism.

Theel had never once seen his father show weakness or uncertainty. His masterknight's confidence in his abilities and his faith in God always appeared unshakable. It was very jarring to see him like this, as a young man, not even Theel's age, terrified, and racked with doubt. It was almost impossible to not feel a kinship with that frightened squire who was facing the most daunting task of his life.

"I am amazed, Father." Theel said. "It appears you once were human, after all."

Theel saw his father again as he appeared several years later, walking down the same tunnel, this time traveling with a group of soldiers who wore surcoats with the war emblem of Embriss. He appeared a little more battle-worn than before; more tattoos, more weapons, and now a silver knightshield on his chest. The men joked and laughed as they walked, but Theel's father didn't join in, his face showing more of the rigidity Theel was accustomed to. But while the knight's face appeared stoic, his thoughts told a different story.

Please, God, let me lead well. These men may die fighting for me. Please do not let it be my error that causes their deaths. Do not allow me to fail them. Please let me lead well.

It was clear his men had no idea how frightened he was, how unsure.

"You need not have feared, Father," Theel whispered. "The histories say you led very well. The story of your first command has become a legend."

Theel saw his father again, years after that, now traveling alone, a completely different concern weighing on his mind.

Help her to understand that I cannot marry. I am sworn to my shield. My oath to the knighthood leaves no room for a wife. She would be alone. She would have no husband. Our children would have no father. She must find another, someone she can rely on.

"Who is this you are praying about, now?" Theel asked. "Is it the mother I never knew?"

Theel never learned what became of his mother. His father refused to talk about it in depth, which left Theel confused about the subject all his life. But as much as he craved to see more, this vision divulged no further information, and was quickly replaced by another one.

The visions continued coming, refusing to stop, to be controlled, or to make any sense. Only a few months later, Theel's father accompanied a caravan of wagons headed to Ravenwater.

Lord, I can't understand why you would do this to me. A son! I cannot be a father. I am not fit for child-rearing. This boy deserves better than me. Why would you give me a son, Lord? I've never wanted children. Help me to see the wisdom in this, because I am confused and feeling betrayed.

Theel gasped at the pain those words caused. He always knew his father never wanted him. It was a scab that would never heal, that was poked over and over his entire childhood. And now it was torn loose again, bleeding freely.

"You never loved me," Theel said, tears forming at the corners of his eyes. "You never loved me because you never wanted me."

The same old emotions came back, and the same bitter words were sure to follow. But right as Theel was about to scream curses at the image of his father, he was able to resist the urge. His father wasn't really there to hear his words. And his yelling would accomplish nothing more than to waken Yatham and Pitch.

When Theel was finished wiping his face, he saw his father and uncle walking the road together as young men. Uncle Guarn was barely recognizable. He was thin and healthy, and laughing, a far cry from the scarred and broken shadow of a man Theel left behind in Fal Daran. He was sharing a tavern tale with his brother and the knight was pretending to listen, but his thoughts were far away.

I am expected to raise a son alone while still doing my duty as a knight. I cannot do both. I will fail if I try. I am not fit to be a father. This child deserves better than I can give him. How could I have allowed this to happen? God, why have you allowed this?

In the next vision, Theel's father was much older, bearing more tattoos and more scars. And now his knightshield was marred by a large hole in its center. He was alone and walking slowly, as if exhausted, and barely holding the torch he carried. With no one else around, he allowed his face to reflect the turmoil he felt inside.

I fear I cannot shoulder any more of this burden, Lord. And yet King Britou asks more of me. The Keeper of the Craft asks for more. I fear I will fail. Give me the strength to do this. Give Theel the strength to answer this call. He doesn't seem to wish for knighthood, but the Seven Swords demand this be done. Theel will be a knight. And Yatham will follow him. No one can stop it. Not even me.

It was almost too much information to absorb, and too many emotions to understand.

"I was forced to become a squire because the king commanded it?" Theel asked the vision, but got no reply. "This wasn't your idea at all? It was the king, the Keeper, the knighthood. Why? Why me?"

His hands were trembling. He dropped his pipe on the ground, but made no attempt to retrieve it.

"You didn't force anything upon me, Father," Theel said, his eyes watering. "It was forced upon you, against your will. You didn't want your son to bear this burden, and yet you placed it upon my shoulders out of duty."

Theel dropped his head into his hands.

"And I hated you for it ..."

Theel wept for many moments, unable to cope with the emotions. But it brought him some relief. The weight on his shoulders lessened slightly with each tear shed. As dark as these memories where, as unbearable as this knowledge was, he knew he was already pursuing a righteous conclusion to all this. He was in the correct place, in this tunnel, to make it right. He was headed in the correct direction, the Dead Man's Bridge, to make it right.

He was going to make this right.

I don't know how to raise a son. I don't know how to train a squire. I am not prepared. Help me. Help me. Help me.

The knight was still a young man, but his eyes were starting to show the fatigue of the constant demands of knighthood. The tattoos on his chest and arms were now very numerous, symbols of battle victories and insignias of rank. Again he traveled alone, and the worry Theel could see in his father's eyes was crushing.

I know what to do with a sword in my hand. I don't know what to do with a baby in my arms.

Theel could not believe how much fear and doubt he was witnessing within his father. He'd never known his father to falter in anything, yet these visions showed that he was constantly questioning himself, and constantly looking to heaven for guidance. For perhaps the first time in his entire life, he felt sympathy for his father's plight. He knew this brand of fear and doubt as well as anyone.

Now the visions were coming so fast he could barely keep track of them. They flew at him like a volley of arrows, and he simply cowered before the onslaught, unable to deal with them.

I do as I'm told, but nothing changes. Nothing works. He doesn't wish to train for knighthood. He doesn't wish to learn of the prophecy. I don't know what to do!

He is not suited for knighthood. I cannot force him to be what he is not.

I cannot treat him as my masterknight treated me. He cannot learn from me if he hates me.

I am a failure. I am weak. I must be strong like my masterknight.

My father doesn't love me because I am not good enough.

I never wanted children because I hated my father.

I never wanted a son and now my son hates me for it.

My father destroyed my happiness.

I am destroying my son's happiness.

God, please fix it. Stop it. Save me. I am ruining everything!

Once again, Theel's face was in his hands.

You've given me a precious gift, Lord, and I've destroyed it!

"No, Father," he whimpered. "You didn't destroy anything. You did the best you could."

These revelations were too much to understand, too much to bear. His father resented his own masterknight? He never felt worthy in his father's eyes? It now seemed that Theel's father was just as unsure and afraid as he ever was, from the time he was a boy, to the day he died. Despite the ironclad façade the great knight displayed to the world and to his son, he carried just as much doubt as anyone.

Theel's father bore deep emotional scars from his childhood. For this reason, he never wished for the responsibility of children of his own. But despite these wishes, children came, and once they did, he strove to protect them from the pain he felt as a boy. Yet he failed, and failed again, helplessly watching as his mistakes multiplied. No matter how he tried, he made things worse.

It was a feeling Theel knew all too well.

Theel is ready. His arm is strong. His back is strong. It is time for his Warrior Baptism. But he doesn't know this. He doesn't understand his worth because of my mistakes. He has no confidence because I stole it from him with my selfish, childish cruelty. I am a terrible father. My sins are inexcusable. The damage I've done is irreparable. There is a penance to be paid for this.

This was a brand-new vision, as crisp and clear as any Theel had ever had. The great knight appeared just as he had some months before, the gray hairs about his temples now growing very thick, the lines of worry carved into his skin as deeply as ever. Theel's father carried an incredible burden in those days before he died, and he showed every bit of the strain.

I am a fool. I have been a fool all my life, and have done foolish things that hurt the ones I love. And now I must reap what I've sown. I must behold my son's pain, powerless to ease it. I must witness him struggling with the scars inflicted by my countless

*foolish mistakes, and know that I cannot heal him. I cannot undo
what I've done. My deeds, good and bad, are carved in stone.*

*I did the best job I could do. I did precisely as I was told. I was
commanded to sharpen him, to harden him, to make him a man
worthy of knighthood. And I succeeded. But at what cost?*

*I have given him everything he needs to succeed. Except the
will to succeed on his own. He hates the knighthood. He despises
the prophecies. He loathes me.*

He has every reason to.

This vision showed Theel's father the final time he walked
through this tunnel. It was not long ago, shortly before he died.
Theel remembered this day as much from memory as from what
his Sight was showing him, for he had accompanied his father in
the Narrows that day. It was the last day Theel would spend with
his father.

It was the day his father apologized. It was the day he asked for
forgiveness.

It was the day Theel spit in his face.

"I will never forgive you. I hate you!"

Those were the words Theel spoke to his father that day,
shortly after entering the tunnels. Now, all these miles later, they
were still fresh in the knight's mind.

*My son has every right to hate me. He has no obligation to
forgive me. I deserve this.*

Then Theel saw himself as he appeared that day, following his
masterknight's steps as his oath required. Theel could see the
smugness on his own face, and knew what it meant. He
remembered the joy he felt in refusing his father's apology, and he
remembered the hours of silence that followed. His father didn't
say word for miles, probably agonizing.

Theel loved it at the time, loved hurting his father. Theel had
been hurting all his life, wounded by this man's neglect, by his
demands of perfection and his emotional distance. Now it was time
for his father to hurt. Theel had the opportunity, and he took it.

His masterknight reached out to him, and he threw it back in his face.

Now Theel was witnessing the tense silence that followed that bitter exchange. He and his father walked for hours without speaking a word. Theel was boiling with anger at the time, unwilling and unable to consider the thoughts that weighed on his father's mind.

But now, all these months later, the anger was gone, for Theel was finally realizing it did no good to hate a dead man. Especially one who died for you. And now he was forced to consider the thoughts that weighed on his father's mind that day, whether he wished it or not.

Theel is now beyond my influence. I pushed him so hard that I pushed him away. And now I cannot embrace what is out of my reach. This was my most sacred duty and I ruined it out of selfishness, out of a fear of loving. I knew I would lose him again, so I would not allow my heart to embrace him.

I lost him once, and barely survived it. I would die if I lost him again.

Theel could see the anguish in his father's face, and a few steps behind, he saw himself staring angrily at his father's back. The wall between them stabbed at his heart, and he buried his face in his arms once again, refusing to look.

No sin cannot be forgiven, no matter how great. Yet, there is a penance to be paid for what I have done.

"No," Theel moaned pitifully.

I forsook my duties as a father while I attended to my duty as masterknight. I taught Theel to fight. I never taught him to love.

"Please stop," Theel begged the vision.

I forsook my duties as a father, therefore I do not deserve to be his father. He cannot grow as a man with his heart poisoned by my misdeeds. He cannot succeed while his hatred for me still burns. I am an anchor weighing him down. I am drowning him.

Then came the words Theel was dreading to hear, muttered softly from his own lips all those months ago, quietly, but just loud enough for his father to hear.

"I will never forgive you," he said to his father's back. "Not as long as you live."

His father looked straight ahead as he walked, saying nothing. Thinking the words were said too soft to be heard, the son spoke again.

"It is too late," he said, louder.

His father winced at the words. *I must be strong. I must not be weak.*

"I will never forgive you."

The knight didn't say anything for a time, his sad, tired eyes belying the anguish of his thoughts. Then, finally, he whispered, "I know this."

Theel saw himself smile in satisfaction. He was such a resentful, spiteful child that he wasn't able to see what his father was trying to do. He told his son he loved him, that he believed in him, that he trusted him. But Theel's negative reaction proved that words weren't enough. The knight knew he needed to support those words with actions.

That was why he took his son into battle later that day. He put his life in Theel's hands, trusting him to prove his worth, to show his mettle by doing what it took to pursue his Warrior Baptism. He gave his son a great opportunity. And his son failed him.

"You were wrong," Theel wept, tears soaking his sleeve. "It wasn't too late for us. We could have mended it together. There was still a chance for us to be father and son. But we didn't. We couldn't. There was too much pride at stake, the pride of two fools."

It wasn't too late. Not then. But it was now. Now his father was dead. No going back. So much regret.

Theel wiped his eyes and looked back at the image of the boy and his father, the squire and his masterknight. Normally, a third person would have been walking with them, the youngest of the three, his features so resembling those of the knight that he appeared to be a younger, if slightly smaller, version of the man. But Yatham hadn't traveled with them that day. Theel's father had ordered Yatham to stay at the Calfborn Crossroads with Jarcet the Sentinel. He wanted to travel alone with Theel, wanted to complete their mission as father and son. It was his last gesture. Yatham didn't understand why his father made that decision to take Theel into the Narrows without him. Yatham still didn't understand. But Theel did.

He wanted to accompany his son on his quest for Warrior Baptism.

I'm sorry, son, but this journey is necessary. I've done all I could to prepare you, and though my efforts were inadequate, they must be enough if you are to fulfill the prophecy.

You do not feel you are ready, but you will learn otherwise as you walk the road to your Warrior Baptism. You are ready. You are strong. You will learn this. God will teach you what I could not.

I must accompany you for as long as I can, but I know I will not be with you when you reach the Outlands. This is the right thing. As you say, you will never forgive me as long as I live.

I will die soon. And God willing, my death will free you from the burden of my sins. Without my presence holding you down, you will fly.

You will complete your Warrior Baptism. You will fulfill the prophecy. I can find no greater joy than your success at this. I will die, willingly and proudly, for this.

It was undeniable confirmation of what Theel had been suspecting for days. His father didn't merely hope he could find the Blessed Soul. He was certain he would. And his father's willingness to die for this cause was proof that the leaders of the knighthood, the Keeper of the Craft, even the king himself, agreed with him. They had much more than a desire for Theel to find the Blessed Soul. They did not just *want* him to complete the quest and fulfill the prophecy. They *expected* him to do it.

They expected him to succeed. They expected him to achieve Warrior Baptism. They expected him to become a knight. How could this be true? What did they understand that he could not? What was waiting for him in the Outlands?

Theel never found out. His father died before they could reach the Outlands. He died, and his son fled back to Fal Daran, like a coward. Theel wasn't sure he'd ever find whatever was in the Outlands. That was because he was not questing for Warrior Baptism, no matter what promises he'd made to his uncle, the Keeper, or the king.

"I am on my own personal quest," Theel mumbled, putting his empty pipe back into his mouth. "It is *Anora Jinn*, the Warrior's Burden, where a son must complete a task left unfinished by his masterknight, or, as in this case, avenge his father's death. This quest does not come to me from the Keeper of the Craft, the king, or the knighthood. It doesn't even come from my father. I've assigned myself this quest, to be fulfilled on the Dead Man's Bridge. It is my quest to mend myself, to undo all I've done, to make right what I've made wrong. And if I can't accomplish these things, at least I will find justice. Only when I find justice will this quest be fulfilled, and only then will I do as the Keeper wishes, and chase my Warrior Baptism. The Blessed Soul will simply have to wait."

But right then and there, an even bigger concern remained. He still hadn't determined what fate had befallen the Overlie children. He needed to find out where they went after finding their path blocked by the cave-in. He'd tried to find them by harnessing the powers of his juy, but as usual, his Sight refused to comply, only showing him things he didn't wish to see.

"Please, God," he whispered. "I want to find the children but I can't see them. Show me what I need to see. Please, God."

Theel didn't want to see his father anymore. He wanted to see the children. And so he prayed. He begged God to show him the children. He was so desperate, he thought he might do anything, make any promise, to find them. But again, all he could see was his father.

He saw his masterknight in the tunnel, walking toward him.

The disappointment was so overwhelming that he dropped his head in his hands again. He felt so alone and so helpless, sitting on the cold stone of the road, wrapped in the silence and darkness of the Narrows. He was unable to speak, unable to rise, unable to do anything other than to weep uncontrollably. Would his torment never end?

Then, someone put their hand on his shoulder.

"You can do it, son," a voice said. "I believe in you."

Startled, Theel looked up into the face of his father. His masterknight knelt over him, squeezing his son's shoulder. He looked Theel squarely in the eye.

"You can save those children," his father said. "You can find them and save them."

"But how?" Theel asked. "Where?"

The knight looked down the tunnel, in the direction from which Theel had come from Widow Hatch.

"They went beneath the road," the knight said. "Now go and save them."

"I will," Theel stammered. "I will save them."

Then his Sight was suddenly extinguished and his father was gone, but his voice lingered, echoing softly in the tunnel.

"You can do it, son. I believe in you."

Then Theel woke up.

Chapter 45

"Yatham?" Theel whispered, crawling around in the darkness on his hands and knees, searching. "Yatham?"

"Here, brother," he heard Yatham say. "What is it?"

"The children are still alive," Theel said, still searching. "They did not travel beyond this spot. They are in this tunnel."

His hand closed over his tinderbox, and the unlit torch beside it. A few strikes of the flint and the cloth burned, then the torch burned, illuminating his brother's questioning face.

"We passed them?" Yatham asked, climbing to his feet. "How? We'd have seen them."

"They're beneath the road," Theel explained.

Yatham was shouldering his backpack. "Beneath the road? How? Where?"

"Just trust me," Theel said. "Pitch, wake up."

The song man went on snoring, so Theel walked over and shoved him with his foot, eliciting a startled yelp.

"How did you see where they are?" Yatham asked. "Did you use your Sight? Did you employ the Method?"

"Yes," Theel said. "Somewhat."

"Somewhat?" Yatham asked.

"I had a dream. I'll explain it another day," Theel said. "Pitch, get up. We must go. There isn't time to wait for you."

The man was struggling weakly to his feet, shaking the sleep away. He bent and picked up his spear, rubbing his eyes. "Is it time for battle?" he asked.

"Yes, time for battle," Theel answered. "Quickly. We must go."

"Where are we going, my liege?" Pitch asked.

"The children are beneath the ground," Theel said. "We must search every bit of this road for a crack or an opening of some kind."

"We'll need more light for that," Yatham warned.

Theel frowned. His brother was right. They had only one torch. Searching the tunnel floor by its meager light would take hours.

"We'll need more torches," he said.

"We might build some," Yatham suggested. "I have lantern oil."

Theel looked around at the battle debris on the floor, finding a broken spear and an axe handle. He handed the two shafts of wood to his brother.

"Those will serve," Yatham said. "We still have need of fuel, cloth of some kind. I've burned all I have."

"The Overlie surcoat?" Theel suggested.

"Burned," Yatham said.

Theel thought a moment, then said, "Pitch, give me your tunic."

"Excuse my weak hearing, my liege?" Pitch said. "Did you say—"

"There is no time," Theel insisted. "Take it off."

"My ... tunic?" the man asked, looking down at the torn and dirty shreds of cloth that hung from his shoulders. "Surely you don't mean—"

"It's only a rag," Theel said. "Now."

"Please, my liege," Pitch protested. "Might I retain some scrap of dignity?"

"I'll cut it off," Theel said, and waved his sword for emphasis. "And I won't be careful about it."

Pitch firmed his jaw. "You won't have it," he said, raising the moon blade of his new spear. "I may be unskilled, but I have the proud warrior blood of House Wick—"

Theel smashed Pitch in the face with the flat of his sword. The song man folded up and crumbled to the ground where he lay flat on his back, staring blankly, his mouth hanging open.

"Is he dead?" Yatham asked.

Pitch's leg twitched.

"No," Theel answered. "Not yet."

He knelt down, placing one knee on Pitch's chest, then drew his father's knife.

Pitch blinked. "Are you going to ... um ..." he mumbled, "... kill ... uh ...?"

"No," Theel said, cutting away the man's tunic, then slicing it into strips. "Not yet."

"That is good," Pitch said. "Since I've made the decision to ... offer you my clothing ... if you insist."

"Thank you," Theel said.

"It's my pleasure," Pitch said. "... my liege."

Yatham took the strips, wrapping the ends of the torches, then sprinkling on the lantern oil he'd taken from the merchant's wagon. Then, one by one, Theel lit the torches from his own torch, and the tunnel was filled with light.

"Get up, Pitch," Theel ordered. "You have the lives of two children to save."

But the song man seemed unable to move. "I think I'd rather prefer to stay as I am, right here, thank you."

Again, Theel stuck his sword in Pitch's face. "I'd rather prefer to kill you as you are," he said. "Right here."

"Very well, then," Pitch said. "Your skills of persuasion are unparalleled, my liege."

"Get up!" Theel yelled.

Yatham sighed. "He can't get up. You scattered his brains, brother."

He handed his torch to Theel, then knelt down and lifted the song man by his arms, dragging him to his feet.

"I am well," Pitch said, pushing Yatham's hands away. "A Wicker will not be kept off his feet for long. He may at times be felled by the travails of life, but he ... he will ... um ..."

His words trailed off, his eyes rolled up, and he fell back into Yatham's arms.

"This is foolish," Yatham said, struggling with the song man's limp body. "We must leave him and go."

"We are not leaving him," Theel said. "He's feigning this."

Theel slapped Pitch's face, and the song man's eyes flared open.

" ... he will always rise again," Pitch said, pumping his fist. "In triumph!"

"Good," Theel said. "You and your noble warrior blood can lead the way."

"As you wish, my liege," Pitch said, rocking unsteadily, looking around. "Which way?"

A torch was thrust into his hands, then his spear. He looked at them confusedly, then looked down at himself.

"What happened to me?"

"Nothing," Theel said.

"You took my tunic, my liege," he said remorsefully. "It is ruined."

"Your brain is ruined."

"That was a performance tunic," he said. "That was a costly item of clothing, once."

"It was, once," Theel agreed. "Now it's fuel for a torch."

"That's the most expensive torch you'll ever burn."

Theel stuck his sword in Pitch's face. "Say another word about it, and that will be the most expensive word you've ever spoken," he warned. "Now shut up and move. Watch for holes in the ground. Yatham, walk to his left. I'll walk to the right. Pitch, in the middle. Lead the way, song man."

Pitch didn't move. He was truly a pathetic sight, with his bewildered eyes, holding his torch and spear as if he had no idea how to use them. Now shirtless, and standing in better light, it was apparent to the brothers just how unkind the song man's recent days had been to him. His flesh was filthy, streaked by dirt and sweat, covered with sores, cuts and bruises. He was emaciated, a sack of skin with bones and ribs poking out all over. Theel felt a moment of shame as he looked upon the man, seeing the fresh bruises and welts that covered his body, marks made by punches and kicks and whacks from a sword. He didn't realized how badly he'd beaten the man.

He quickly swallowed his remorse, firming his jaw. "Move it, Pitch," he commanded. "I won't say it again."

"Well, certainly ..." the song man replied. "At your pleasure, my liege. To battle it is, then. For the children." He turned around and began to march north, leading with his spear. "You are a most persuasive and decisive man, Liege."

"You'd be the first to say as much," Theel said. "Stay close," he said, holding the torch high. He watched the floor as they walked, examining every inch of ground the torch illuminated. He knew Yatham was doing the same on the other side of the tunnel. If there was a hole in the ground that led under the road, they must find it.

"See anything?" Theel called out.

"I see a rat, my liege," Pitch answered. "Nothing more."

"I see nothing," Yatham added.

On they walked, slowly plodding forward at a snail's pace. Theel wanted to move faster, but also wanted the search to be as thorough as possible.

"Another rat, my liege," Pitch announced. "A bigger one this time. I'll handle it."

"Shut up, Pitch," Theel said.

Then, from up ahead, they heard the sound of scraping metal, echoing loudly in the silent tunnel. The three men froze, listening. The scraping continued, metal grating against stone.

"Is it the enemy?" Pitch whispered.

Theel didn't answer, he just began to run toward the sound, holding his torch high. The grinding sound stopped, but he continued running, charging into the darkness. Ahead, on the right side of the road, something turned and looked at him, and he saw the eyes reflect the torchlight, glowing in the darkness like an animal. It was something Theel had seen before many times. He wasn't surprised at all when, as he approached, his light fell across a gnarled, gray face covered with scars, and a pair of beady, black eyes with no pupils.

"Zoths!" he shouted.

The creature screamed and launched itself at Theel, swiping at his face with a clawed hand, then stabbing with a short spear. Theel dodged and knocked the spear high with his sword, then smashed the creature in the face with his torch. He tried to hit the zoth again, but this time it seized his torch in its clawed hands. For a moment, they wrestled over it. The zoth tried another spear thrust, but Theel knocked the weapon from its hand. Now he had his opening, and was about to slice open the zoth's middle with his sword, when suddenly Pitch's spear appeared there.

Just as he'd been told, the song man pointed his spear and ran, burying his moon blade into the zoth's guts, pushing the creature to the ground. The zoth screamed and so did Pitch, or perhaps he was laughing, as he thrust his spear into its chest repeatedly.

"For House Wicker!" he shrieked.

Another zoth appeared at Theel's right hand, apparently climbing right out of the floor. This one was unarmed but didn't seem to care. It jumped on Theel, scratching and biting, gouging at his eyes. He fell back onto his rear, dropping his torch. He saw nothing but dancing darkness and firelight and lots of teeth. He heard hissing, and blocked swiping arms and claws. He pushed against his attacker with his empty hand, trying to use his sword, but it was too large, and the zoth was too close. Another moment of struggling and he felt its breath on his neck, its teeth on his ear, about to bite down and tear it off. But in that same moment, he was able to seize a fistful of hair and jerk the zoth's head away from his.

The zoth shrieked at him, gape-mouthed, spraying spittle in his face, but he held it in place long enough to bash it in the side of the head with the hilt of his sword. He hammered away, stripping skin, crushing bone, tenderizing the zoth's head until the creature's cries died in its throat, it's muscles relaxed, and Yatham dragged it off by the neck.

Silence fell. It was all over.

CHAPTER 46

"That was close," Yatham said, smiling. "That one almost had you."

"I don't deny it," Theel said, wiping blood and saliva from his face with his sleeve.

"Victory!" Pitch yelled, raising his spear above his head. "We have smitten them, my warrior brothers, for the honor of House Wicker! Your advice was sound, my liege. I pointed my spear and ran, and in doing so have made the zoth tribes of the Narrows pay for their foul bearing! Victory! Our victory is won! Though I must say, it was quite disgusting."

"We may have found your hole in the ground," Yatham said to Theel, pointing. Theel looked, and could see in the dim torchlight a perfectly round hole in the surface of the road. Beside it lay a large metal disk, the cover.

"They were working to move this lid off," Yatham said. "Might this be where the Overlie children went?"

"It might be," Theel replied. "There is one sure way to learn. Pitch, into the hole."

"Me?"

"Yes, you."

"There may be more zoths down there."

"I don't care."

"They might try to kill me!" Pitch protested.

"I don't care," Theel repeated.

"I see," Pitch said. "I now learn my true place in my commander's eyes, that of the fodder of this army, the expendable front line."

"This isn't an army," Theel said.

"I am the meat the master throws to the dogs," Pitch said.

"Pitch, get in the hole," Theel ordered. "Or you will be meat on the end of my sword. There isn't time for your complaining."

"Yes, my liege," Pitch mumbled. "I am your loyal servant."

He walked to the hole and knelt down, looking into the blackness below.

"There is a ladder of sorts leading down," he reported. "Metal rings in the wall."

"Climb down them," Theel said.

"Certainly, my liege," Pitch replied. "This one understands and obeys." He put his fist to his forehead in a sloppy salute. Then he set his spear beside the hole and climbed down into the darkness.

"What do you see?" Theel asked.

"Nothing to see, my liege," Pitch answered, his voice echoing. "But plenty to smell. And more rats. The climb isn't a long one, however."

Theel handed Pitch's spear down, then climbed in after. Yatham came last, taking a moment to pull the metal disk into place over the hole behind him. As Pitch said, the climb wasn't a long one, only a dozen feet or so, down a series of metal rings embedded in the wall. The rings were rusty and old, possibly a part of the original construction of the Narrows. The climb down took them into a wide corridor leading only eastward, eventually disappearing into a darkened archway. The corridor was warm and musty-smelling, with a wet floor and metal grates leading down.

"We're in a sewer," Pitch commented.

"A drainage sewer," Yatham guessed. "The water flows eastward, keeping the western tunnel of the Narrows from flooding."

Theel looked into the darkness. He couldn't gauge the length of the corridor by the torchlight, or make out anything but slippery stones and metal grates, and lots of dripping water.

"Do you suppose this leads to the eastern tunnel?" Theel asked.

"I'd wager it does," Yatham said. "There is likely another ladder just like this one on the other side."

"Then the children may be in the eastern tunnel," Theel said.

"Hello?" Pitch called out and was met with silence, only the sound of his own echoing voice.

"We may find them on the other side," Theel said. "In the other tunnel. Forward, Pitch."

"Certainly, my liege." Pitch saluted, and proceeded down the corridor, holding his torch high.

Beyond the archway was another empty corridor leading eastward, but now they could clearly hear the sounds of flowing water. Further on, they came to another archway. This one led into a square room with what looked like a small donkey wheel, the kind Theel had seen a miller use. But this wheel was clearly turned by the sweat of men. The room was too small for a donkey, and the wheel had holes, suggesting poles must be inserted so that workmen could turn it.

"What is this?" Pitch asked, walking around the wheel, his torch held high.

"It's not for grinding grain," Theel said.

"It looks new," Pitch pointed out.

"He's right," Yatham said, inspecting their surroundings.

The donkey wheel was made of oak hammered together no more than a few years before, and recently sealed with a fresh coat of pitch. The iron grates and torch sconces in the room showed nary a hint of rust, unlike all the others they'd seen to this point. The walls of the other tunnels were composed of stacked bricks of a uniform size and shape, ancient stonework, cut and placed by the hands of men who had been dead for centuries. But this room appeared to be carved with hammer and chisel, designed by a mind with an entirely different idea of aesthetics than the other tunnels they'd seen. The room was clearly a recent addition to the Narrows.

"Clansmen built this room," Yatham said. "And this wheel."

"What does it do?" Pitch asked.

"Turn it," Theel answered, walking across the room, "and you will learn what it does."

On the other side of the wheel, Theel found another archway, this one filled with the sounds of running water. He walked through and found a stair leading down. After descending the several dozen steps, he came to a wide doorway blocked by an iron portcullis. The floor was covered with water, inky black and rippling. When he stepped in, it came up just over his knees. He splashed his way to the portcullis and peered through the bars. He saw a large passageway running north to south, an underground canal of foul water built with the purpose of keeping the Narrows dry. Just like the square room and the donkey wheel, the iron portcullis that blocked his path was much newer than the rest of the tunnel, showing little signs of rust.

In the opposite wall, beyond the flowing water, Theel could see his torch light flickering upon metal bars. It was another portcullis, a twin to the one which now blocked his path. This confirmed his suspicions. If he could open this portcullis, and the other one across the canal, it would probably lead him to another square room with a donkey wheel, and eventually to the eastern tunnel. He was certain of it. He need only open this portcullis.

"Turn the wheel, brother!" he yelled up the passageway behind him. "Raise the portcullis. Turn the wheel!"

"Just a moment, brother," Yatham's voice echoed back.

Theel put his torch in a wall sconce and reached out to grasp the bars. And in that moment, as his fingers made contact, his juy came to life. A blast of cold wind pummeled his brain so suddenly that he shuddered and almost fell. Only his grip on the bars kept him erect. He saw his hands before him, gripping the bars; no longer gloved hands, tattooed or bearing the seal of the First Guardian of Embriss, but now the hands of a child. A child of the Overlie family.

Terror struck his heart as the screams of the zoths filled the tunnels. They were up above, on the road, searching for him and his baby sister. It would not be long before they found the hole, the metal rings leading down into this sewer, and follow, and find them, and hurt them. Brother and sister huddled together, waist-

deep in the cold water, shivering, sobbing. He wasn't strong enough to console her. He wasn't strong enough to pull the metal disk back into place. He wasn't strong enough to turn the donkey wheel. He wasn't strong enough to lift the bars.

Now the zoths had found the hole. They were coming up the tunnel, shrieking, banging their spears together. Not strong enough to fight them. Now his sister was screaming.

"Oh God, oh God, oh God, please help us, please save us! Send us help! Show us the way! Send us a savior, God, please!"

Theel knew the children didn't die here. They'd passed beyond this portcullis, and so must he. He tried to rattle the iron bars to test their strength, but they didn't so much as budge. He tried to lift them, but might as well try to lift a mountain. It was hopeless. How did the children pass through here? He ran his fingers up and down the bars, searching for a weakness, and then he knew.

He felt the stiff iron bars sliding from the left side of his body to his right, crushing him as if he was going through a ringer sideways. He felt the little girl's pain as she got stuck with the bars on her little belly, but the older boy helped by pulling her through.

"Of course," Theel said to himself.

They were little children. They didn't need to lift the bars. They simply turned sideways and squeezed through. They crossed the canal, squeezed through the bars on the other side, and fled to the eastern tunnel. The zoths could not follow, not without turning the donkey wheel. And neither could Theel.

"Turn the wheel!" he shouted again, frantically.

His cries were answered by the screeching of metal on metal, then the clanking of a great chain. The wheel was turning, he knew. He could feel the walls rumbling, counterweights pulling chains over gears, turning screws. And raising the portcullis, or so he thought. But nothing happened.

He waited, listening to the clanking and rattling and groaning of this great mechanism. Something was happening. But what? The portcullis did not move.

Confused and frustrated, Theel rattled the bars again, cursed and kicked them. He drew his sword and smashed the blade against the unrelenting iron, over and over again, throwing sparks into the tunnel. His father would have been embarrassed for him. He would have chastised his squire for acting like a child. He would have told Theel to stop his antics, relax, and think.

The portcullis wasn't raising. So what was the purpose of that wheel?

Yatham splashed into the water at Theel's side, holding his torch high. "You can't bash your way through, brother," he said.

"I've discovered that already," Theel replied. "You're welcome to try something yourself."

"Pitch is turning the wheel," Yatham said. "It must accomplish something."

And then Theel saw. With the added light provided by Yatham's torch, he could see the large passageway beyond the portcullis much clearer. He could see the torchlight flickering on moss-covered bricks, the black water rippling in the canal. And beyond all this, he could see the portcullis on the far side of the passageway, rising slowly, inch by inch.

Yatham pointed. "Look, across the canal."

"I see it," Theel said. "So we've determined the wheel raises *that* portcullis. How do we raise *this* one?" For emphasis, he banged the bars with his sword again.

"There must be another wheel over there, just like this one," Yatham suggested. "We have to turn that wheel somehow. That will raise these bars."

"That is clearly the answer, brother," Theel replied. "But how do we turn that wheel when our path is blocked?"

"I don't know," Yatham said.

"Who would design such a pointless mechanism?" Theel asked. "No one coming from the eastern side may cross the canal unless someone on the west side turns the wheel. It means no one can pass these bars without aid from the other side. It makes no sense at all."

The noise of the mechanism ceased. On the other side of the canal, the portcullis hung in the air, wide open. The tunnel quieted, and again, there was only the constant whispering of the canal water.

Actually, it made perfect sense. Theel realized it just as the words were leaving his lips.

"The Overlies and Ducharmes," he whispered. "They built this."

"You're right," Yatham said. "It is commonly known how much mistrust there was between the two noble families who ruled the Narrows. Each of them had claim to one tunnel. They clearly would not allow any men loyal to the other family free access to their side."

"So they built this," Theel added.

"No one was allowed to enter the other tunnel without permission," Yatham said. "There must be Overlie and Ducharme men turning both wheels, or no one could pass."

"Which means we cannot pass. Damn them!" Theel cursed.

"We have to find another way," Yatham said.

Theel sighed heavily, then turned up the tunnel. "Pitch!" he yelled. "Come down here!"

The song man's voice echoed down the corridor. "Leave the wheel?"

"Leave the wheel!" Theel yelled. "Let it drop!"

The resulting noise was even more ear-splitting than before. The portcullis fell unchecked, and splashed down into the water with enough thunder to shake the walls.

"What can we do?" Theel asked. "How do we raise these bars?"

"Perhaps there is no need," Yatham said. "If we can't raise them, the children certainly couldn't. Perhaps they weren't even here at all."

"Yes, they were," Theel insisted. "They were here."

Then Pitch arrived, holding his torch and spear. "I live to serve you, my liege," he said. "Is there another enormous and cumbersome wheel you wish me to break my back upon?"

"The children were here," Theel said. "And they passed through these bars. We must find a way to follow."

"How did they pass through?" Yatham asked. "Two little children wouldn't have the strength to turn that wheel."

"There was no need for them to turn the wheel," Theel answered. "They were small enough to squeeze between the bars."

"You're right," Yatham said, looking at the portcullis, nodding. "That would work for them. But not for us. No man is that skinny."

"I am," Pitch said softly. "I can fit through."

The brothers looked at each other. Then they looked at Pitch.

The song man was naturally narrow of frame, and his time in the crow cage had shrunk him further. Now as he stood shirtless in the flickering torchlight, his shriveled skin stretched tightly over each of his bones, Theel could see that Pitch was more skeleton than man.

"I will fit," Pitch said again. "Allow me to try, my liege."

"It might work," Yatham said.

"It will work," Theel agreed. "Pitch, you can do it. Squeeze through, and turn the wheel on the other side. Raise this portcullis."

"As you wish, my liege." Pitch saluted. "I live to serve you."

"Don't serve me," Theel ordered. "Serve those children. Raise this portcullis, and we might spare them from the Crowlord."

"Then it is clearly my duty to raise this portcullis," Pitch said. "So we might save those two wonderful sweetlings."

The song man handed his torch and spear to Theel.

"This will make a splendid verse in some future epic ballad," Pitch said. "The one about the son of a whore whose heroic deeds lifted the once great house of Wicker from a place of ruin back to a place of prominence."

"And who will tell this splendid tale?" Theel asked.

Pitch stuck his head between the bars. "Me, of course," he said with a smile. "Who else?"

"Of course." Theel smiled. "Who else?"

The song man fit one shoulder between the bars, then began to push his chest through. He grimaced as the cold iron scraped painfully across his ribs.

"I never thought I'd be thankful for so many missed meals," he said. "This will surely be the only instance in my life where being starved will prove beneficial—oof!"

He stopped, apparently unable to move any further.

"I seem to have found a tight spot, my liege," he groaned. "Very tight indeed."

He was stuck fast, his body only halfway through, hanging sideways with the iron gripping his hips.

"This is very uncomfortable," he said. "I won't fit. Help me back out."

"Take a leg, brother," Theel said. "Push."

"I'm not sure that is a good idea, my liege."

But no one was listening. Each brother took a leg and pushed.

"Oh God, please stop. That is painful," the song man whined. "Please stop!"

They didn't stop. They made no progress, so they pushed harder.

"Oh God, help me! Mercy! Mercy!" Pitch screamed. "You are killing me. Please God, save me from these two unmerciful, soulless beasts!"

"Shut up, Pitch," Theel grunted.

"Please, my liege," Pitch said. "Take me back to Widow Hatch and throw me in the cage for a few more days. I swear I can starve some more and fit through these bars. Just spare me from this—"

And then he popped through. He tore his hose and left a good deal of skin behind. But he fell through the portcullis and splashed face down into the water.

"You see?" Theel said, when the song man emerged, shivering and dripping. "There is no need for further starvation."

"What a relief that is, my liege," Pitch said, hugging himself for warmth. "I think I've grown quite weary of starvation."

"Pitch, if you raise this portcullis, I will make certain you get a proper meal," Theel promised.

"How exciting," Pitch said. "And a new tunic? Clean and dry?"

"Clean and dry."

"Might you be able to grant me a King's Pardon?" Pitch asked.

"No."

"How unfortunate," Pitch said.

"But do I promise I won't kill you," Theel added.

"That's the most exciting news of all," Pitch said, smiling.

"Now move," Theel ordered. "You have one more portcullis to get past. Those children are waiting."

"Yes, my liege," Pitch said, taking his spear and torch as Yatham handed them through the bars. "One more portcullis to get past, and this nightmare can finally be over."

"Now go over to the other side, and turn the donkey wheel," Theel said. "Raise this portcullis, Pitch. You can do it."

Pitch gave another sloppy salute, turned, and began to wade across the canal. He walked slowly, poking at the water with his spear, testing his footing before each step. The water wasn't flowing swiftly, but it was enough to keep him off balance. He fell twice, but managed to keep his torch above water.

As he did this, Yatham went back up the stairs to turn the wheel and open the portcullis that would grant him passage. Theel gritted his teeth as the screeching and grinding of the mechanism again filled his ears. He could feel the stones rumbling beneath his feet as he saw the bars rising on the far side of the tunnel.

Once they were high enough, Pitch ducked under, then promptly fell into the water again. But he quickly emerged, smearing his hair back from his face and rubbing his eyes. Once he could see again, he flashed a quick smile, picked up his torch, and disappeared up the tunnel. Moments later, the light from his torch faded, and the tunnel fell into darkness.

"He is through, brother!" Theel shouted. "Let it drop!"

The sound was deafening as the bars fell, then splashed into the water, causing waves to roll across the canal.

Theel stood for many moments of anxious silence, seeing nothing, hearing nothing. He couldn't help but grip the bars of the portcullis with white knuckles, grinding his teeth impatiently. Then Yatham appeared at his side, breathing heavily from the labor he'd just undertook.

"We may never see him again," he panted.

"I know," Theel said.

"He may be running up the eastern tunnel right now," Yatham added. "Making his way back to Widow Hatch."

"Perhaps," Theel said. "But he won't get far. If he runs, the Crowlord will take him."

Just then, Theel felt the portcullis shudder beneath his fingers. The tunnel was filled with the sounds of screeching metal and the grinding of gears. The floor rumbled, and the portcullis began to rise, inch by laborious inch. Theel listened to the distant clanking of the great chain, watching as the spikes on the bottom-most bars slowly emerged from the inky water. He marveled at the mechanism, but marveled more at the cacophony of noise it made. Down in the tunnels it was somewhat muffled, but in the open air it would be heard a mile away.

"It's a wonder the zoths haven't heard this and come down here," Yatham said.

That was when they saw the light appear in the tunnel across the canal. Theel's blood froze. He feared it was zoths, but he quickly remembered that zoths didn't commonly use light sources because they can see in the dark. Besides, it wasn't weak and fluttering like the flame of a lantern or a torch. It was strong and constant. And where a flame would cast orange light, this was pale and bright like ...

Sunlight.

"Oh, no," Theel heard Yatham say.

The portcullis stopped moving, and the great mechanism fell silent. For a moment, all that could be heard was the rushing water and the crackling of their torch flames. The portcullis remained half-open, its bottom spikes dripping just inches above the waterline.

"Pitch!" Theel shouted, his voice echoing in the tunnel.

The response was a scream, distant but unmistakable. It was a zoth.

Then the portcullis began to fall.

"Stop it!" Theel shouted.

Both brothers grabbed onto the bars, trying to hold the gate open, but it would have required ten men to bear the weight. All they accomplished was to slow its descent, and only barely. It was a losing battle; the portcullis would fall shut in mere seconds and there was no stopping it.

Theel gave up the struggle and smashed his face into the water, trying to scramble under the portcullis before it closed fully. He was halfway through when he became stuck, with one of his sword belts hooked on the bars as the spikes descended, about to tear him in half. He screamed a stream of bubbles as he felt himself dying right then and there, kicking his legs and tearing at his sword belt. Then the buckle released and he squirmed through just as the portcullis fell into place.

He burst from the water, gulping in air and stumbling across the canal.

"Open it again!" he shouted to his brother as he splashed toward the other portcullis and the pale light beyond. When he reached the bars, they hadn't moved, but he was certain his brother would raise them. Yatham had never failed him and he would not now. While he waited, Theel listened. He could hear more zoths shouting. Then he heard Pitch.

"Oh God help me! Mercy! Mercy!"

Those words were swallowed by the grinding of the mechanism. The chain clanked, the gears ground together, and the portcullis began to inch upward. Theel pounded the bars anxiously, frustrated that they didn't raise faster. Without a torch, he could barely see anything, but gripping the bars, he could feel how slowly they were moving. Not fast enough.

He could just make out some movement in the tunnel ahead, shadows distorting the sunlight at the top of the staircase. It was zoths, he knew, and Pitch, probably fighting for his life. Or being eaten.

Theel felt under the water, finding the spikes with his fingers. As soon he felt they were high enough, he dove back in and kicked his way under the portcullis. It was much quicker this time, the gap wider than before, providing enough extra wiggle room to allow him to swim through. He emerged from the water stumbling, and scrambled up the wet stairs on his hands and knees. There was very little light here, forcing him to feel his way forward, upward, toward the pale light above. But the higher he climbed, the more sunlight spilled down around him, until he could see the outline of each stone step beneath his hands.

Now he sprang to his feet and ran as fast as he could, taking the stairs three at a time. He ran through the archway at the top of the stairs, bursting into the room containing the donkey wheel. Pitch's torch still flickered in a sconce above the wheel, casting just enough light to see that the room was empty. The butt of the song man's spear could be seen protruding from a hole in the side of the wheel.

Through another archway and up the tunnel Theel ran, the white sunlight becoming stronger with each step. Just as he'd surmised, these tunnels were a mirror image of those on the other side of the canal. And when he ran through the next archway, he wasn't surprised to see a round hole in the ceiling, with pale sunlight streaming down upon rusty iron rings set into the wall. And there was Pitch's limp body, hanging upside down and splattered with blood, being hoisted up through the hole by two zoths, one above, lifting him by the ankles, while the other was below, pushing up on his shoulders.

The zoth on the bottom didn't stand a chance, hanging from the iron rungs, exposed and unprotected as Theel drew his sword and plunged the blade into the creature's spine. It screamed and fell, hitting the stones with a limp splat. Theel jumped over it and scrambled up the rungs, grabbing Pitch by the wrist and pulling, but the zoth above held onto his ankles, refusing to give up the prize. Theel swiped at the creature with his sword but it was too far away, so he dropped the weapon and used both hands to grip Pitch's wrists. He jumped off the ladder, adding all of his weight to Pitch's, ripping the zoth's fingers off the iron rung.

The creature screamed and so did Theel as the three of them fell, Theel hitting the ground first, then Pitch on top of him, and finally the zoth. Theel's breath was punched out of his lungs by the impact, and when he tried to suck in more air, nothing happened. He couldn't move with the weight of Pitch's body on him, and the zoth on top of Pitch. The creature's shriek was joyous, knowing its enemy was pinned down as it pulled a spear from its back. Both of Theel's swords were gone, but he still had his father's knife somewhere at his side. He scratched with frantic fingers, searching for its handle.

He couldn't see the zoth's face, only the outline of its head as sunlight streamed down from the hole above. The perfectly round disk of white light formed a halo for the black silhouette of the creature above him. It was lifting the spear, pointing the tip down at Theel's face. And in that moment of doom, he found the hilt of his father's knife, bearing its blade just as the zoth brought the spear down. He twisted his neck to avoid the attack but could not—not fully. The point of the spear hit the left side of this head, tearing a groove into his flesh just above the ear. A second later, the blade of his knife slammed into the side of the creature's neck.

The zoth reeled back, choking and gurgling, raising the spear for another strike. It was dying, but not dead, and a dying zoth could be more fearsome than a healthy one. But again, its aim was imprecise, and the spear sliced through the bottom of the human's ear. Theel could feel the warmth of his own blood spraying against his neck and shoulder as he jerked his knife free of the creature's neck and jammed it in again, this time into the zoth's ear. That was enough to end the fight and the zoth slumped forward, the spear falling from its limp fingers.

Chapter 47

Theel tried to crawl out from under the bodies, but quickly realized he didn't have the strength. So he decided to take a rest, just a moment of lying on his back, staring up at the white circle above him. But that one moment became many, and as he lay there, the vision in his left eye slowly grew unfocused and fluttery, as if his eyelid was blinking uncontrollably. He pulled his glove off and felt the side of his head, surprised at the jagged groove he found there and the hot blood that flowed forth. It was long and deep, his flesh torn rather than cut, almost down to the bone. He was confused by the severity of the wound, confused by the lack of pain. His fingers felt around his left ear, and found that a large chunk of it was missing. And still, no pain. In fact, the entire left side of his face and scalp had gone numb, giving him the impression that half his head was missing. But he knew it was there because he could feel it with his hand. And he could feel the hot blood squirting onto his fingers.

He was dimly aware that he was in danger, from faint memories of men lying on past battlefields suffering from wounds like this one. He remembered what happened to those men, remembered the delirious eyes, the grasping hands, the nonsensical babble, the blood so bright and red all over the ground. He had the strength to move now, the strength to think, but that would not last. He had to fight this; had to find the strength to move, or he was finished.

But where was the strength to move? It was leaving his body, flowing unchecked like the blood running from the side of his head. Somehow, that gash in his scalp needed to be closed. Yatham would know what to do. He would be able to inspect the damaged area, determine its severity, and do what healing was necessary.

But Yatham wasn't here. Theel was alone, so it was up to him to solve the problem. He was certain he could not heal himself using his own command of the Method. That skill was beyond his understanding. The incident at Calfborn was proof. That left only one option. The Life Sign, the tattoo woven into his skin that gave him the ability to tap his own juy for the purposes of healing. It was painful, and exhausting. But it would work.

No, he realized, there was another option. He could do nothing. He could lay on his back and wait. He was so tired. Perhaps he didn't have the strength to heal. Perhaps he was dead already. And who would care if he was? He'd come all this way to die, after all. And now he was finally here. It seemed as good a place as any to die.

He decided to lay still, calm himself, and focus on something, like the circle of round light above him. But this was difficult with his blurry vision and fluttering left eye. That was when he realized he wasn't breathing, and hadn't drawn any breath since falling off the ladder. Where was the ladder?

He sucked in a huge breath, gulping air greedily, then choked and spit a stream of bubbles. It wasn't air he'd sucked into his lungs, it was liquid. The circle of light above rippled, so far away, above the surface. He was underwater! He kicked and screamed, but couldn't do anything, entangled in the bodies that kept him pinned to the floor, to the bottom.

To the bottom of what? A well?

Horror filled his belly. He was back in the well of Calfborn, at the very bottom, trapped beneath a mountain of dead flesh; dozens of bodies and severed feet. He pushed against Pitch, trying to free himself so that he could swim back to the surface, but only succeeded in flipping the song man over so the two were face to face.

Pitch was dead and rotting, and decayed nearly beyond recognition. His face was nothing but empty eye sockets, grinning teeth, and a hole where his nose should have been. He'd been dead for weeks. Theel didn't understand. How could Pitch be in the

544

bottom of the well? Pitch was alive and miles away, starving in a crow cage in Widow Hatch. Then Theel understood. This wasn't Pitch's body. It was the body of the Overlie boy who had died in Calfborn.

Again, Theel screamed and fought, trying to free himself. But no matter how he struggled and pushed and kicked, he couldn't push the boy away, couldn't avoid his eyeless gaze. So he pinched his eyes shut, anything to not look at that dead, accusing face.

He heard the boy's voice gurgle. "Stand up," it said.

"I can't," Theel choked.

"Yes you can," the boy said. "Stand up."

"I can't," Theel said, shaking his head. "I don't ... have the strength."

"You have the strength," the boy insisted. "You have more strength than you know."

"I don't," Theel whimpered. "I'm so sorry."

"You do not lack in strength," the boy said. "You lack in faith—faith in yourself."

"No faith ..."

"Have faith," the boy said. "We are not yet lost. We will live if you live."

"I can't," Theel wept.

"You must," the boy said. "Say the words."

"I can't."

"You won't," the boy said. "Yet you must."

"I won't," Theel repeated. "Yet I must."

"Give this child strength."

Give this child strength.

"That he might raise your banner."

That he might raise your banner.

"Cleanse this child's wounds."

Cleanse this child's wounds.

"That he might carry your shield."

That he might carry your shield.

Then Theel spoke aloud.

"I, as a son of the Silvermarsh Clans, do commit myself, body, soul, and spirit, to the earthly warriors of the Southern Cross, to the Seven Kingdoms they protect, and to the one true Lord of all Creation, that I might do his will, to love God's children, to lead God's Children, to protect God's Children, and that by these deeds, the Lord's blessings be given.

"I will care for God's children, by showing his love.

"I will guide God's children, by speaking his word.

"I will protect God's children, by wielding his judgment.

"With his mercy, I will care.

"With his compassion, I will give.

"With his wisdom, I will speak.

"With his word, I will guide.

"With his shield, I will protect.

"With his sword, I will defend.

"I will serve the Lord with my heart, my mind, and my voice, by learning and understanding his holy word, gratefully receiving his holy gift of faith, and always proclaiming his holy name. These things I hold dear. Amen."

"Stand now, and fight," the boy said.

"Stand and fight?" Theel asked.

Up above, peering into the well, Theel saw the face of someone looking down at him.

"Father?" he asked.

"Stand and fight, son," the knight said.

"Save me!" Theel screamed, reaching out for his father.

But his masterknight did nothing to help him.

Instead, he said, "You can do it, son. I believe in you."

"Help me!"

His father smiled at him. "I love you."

Then he walked away, leaving his son to die. Or to live. It was Theel's choice.

"No!" Theel screamed until his voice was hoarse. He began to kick and thrash against the bodies holding him down. He had to free himself or he would die. He had to find a way out of this place or everything he knew would cease—his life, his world—all of it would end. Nothing was more important than that round hole of sunlight above him. It offered fresh air, warmth, life. He focused on that bright circle. It was all that mattered. He would do anything to get there. He'd stand, and he'd fight. That circle filled his vision. Its light seared his eyes, burned his face, and filled his ears with sounds. The pounding of drums.

Boom ... Ba-boom. Boom ... Ba-boom.

The drums thundered in his ears. Or perhaps it was the pounding in his chest? The sound grew louder and louder until it became unbearable, as if someone was hitting Theel in the head with a hammer.

Boom ... Ba-boom. Boom ... Ba-boom.

This pounding wasn't his heartbeat, he realized. He'd heard those drums once before. They were drumbeats from his past, the pounding of memory, one memory in particular; his worst. He'd heard those drumbeats the last time he was there, in that place. And now he'd come back. He was no longer in the well in Calfborn. Now was he in the Narrows, about to walk the Dead Man's Bridge. The well in Calfborn was a dream. This was a nightmare.

The Dead Man's Bridge.

Boom ... Ba-boom. Boom ... Ba-boom.

He heard someone scream, a terrified, anguished cry. It was a small voice, that of a little girl. And it came from the circle above. She was alive. There was still hope.

"The Dead Man's Bridge," he whispered.

His fingers closed around the hilt of his sword lying next to him, and fresh strength filled his limbs.

"The Dead Man's Bridge!" he roared.

He threw the bodies off and sprang to his feet, climbing up the ladder as fast as he could. As he neared the top, a new sound joined the drums. It was a sound that had no place in the underground realm of the Narrows.

The cawing of crows.

Chapter 48

The first thing Theel noticed as he climbed out of the hole was the sensation of heat on his face. The eastern tunnel of the Narrows was noticeably warmer and more humid than its twin to the west. The road stretched away to the north, quickly disappearing into darkness. Hazy sunlight glared at Theel from the south, and a soft breeze carried warmth and moisture. It was almost inviting, and would have been, if not for the distant cacophony of crow calls.

Then he felt the warmth on his neck, and the dribbling of hot liquid on his left shoulder. Thinking he'd wipe some sweat away, his smeared it, then drew back a gloved hand covered in blood. That was when he knew he wasn't recovered from his wounds fully. The gash in his head was mostly closed, no longer posing a threat to his life. But his blood still flowed as if to remind him that the Life Sign was no substitute for caution. It was meant to give him aid, not make him invincible.

He rubbed his glove against his leathers and ran toward the sound of the crows, sword in hand, down the center of the gray roadway, with its smooth surface and its painted stripes. The wreckage of battle lay all around—broken swords and spears, and bits of armor. The light grew brighter and the sounds of crows grew louder, and to his right he saw a line of animals tied to rings in the wall; a few oxen, a mule or two, but mostly horses. Nearly all of them were dead, mere skeletons picked clean of their flesh. But two horses were still standing and tugging on their reins. They were saddled, bearing bags containing provisions and weapons—two swords, an axe, and a crossbow, as if their owners were taken without a fight. One of them, a large gray gelding, was caparisoned in the colors of the Southern Cross.

Theel briefly considered taking the gray, but thought better of it. Though a competent rider, he'd never come close to his brother's skill in the saddle. And he'd never quite learned to fight on horseback, despite his father's best attempts. To him, a horse was a means of transport, not an instrument of battle. And it was battle that awaited him.

Still, he couldn't leave them to feed the zoths, so despite his urgency, he took a moment to untie their reins from the rings in the wall. The big gray immediately ran, as if it smelled the danger and wanted nothing of it. Theel didn't wait to see what became of the smaller one, only turned and went the opposite direction, toward the smell of danger.

He ran with all the speed his legs could muster, his boots pounding on the gray stone, his footfalls echoing off the tunnel walls. It wasn't long before the ceiling split into open air and the sun shone down, scorching Theel's eyes. Here the gray stone of the road was broken up, split and eaten by erosion, allowing bare earth to show through. The road deteriorated more the farther out into the sunshine, eventually disappearing into a stretch of trampled earth flanked by wagon ruts. To both his left and right, the white-tiled walls of the Narrows showed their age, with fewer and fewer tiles, until they were replaced by exposed gray rock that crowded the sides of the roadway.

This wasn't how Theel remembered the tunnel openings. The rock walls were once covered with thick brown vines of multiple varieties, including one species that grew purple flowers and yellow, bumpy-skinned berries that tasted sour on the tongue. But the vines were gone, and now the rock walls were bare.

Eventually these walls flanking the road fell away, and Theel was running across a small field. This was once a lush and green place, home to a variety of plants and flowers that grew among the weeds. He remembered waist-high grass and bushes of bell crowns, arm fatch, and red dusk. But no more. Just like the vines, all of this was gone.

Now the field was covered with thorn bushes, black and twisted and growing outward rather than upward, as if reaching out to scratch at Theel as he passed by. Just like the streets of Widow Hatch, this place felt empty and dead, the ground so cursed that nothing good would ever live or grow. The first time Theel walked this ground, the air was full of the sounds of nature, the chirping of birds and insects. Now, all he heard was crows. And drums.

Boom ... Ba-boom. Boom ... Ba-boom.

The ancient road and the field of thorns continued onto an outcropping of rock, jutting out into the canyon known as Krillian's Cut like a giant stone tongue. As Theel approached the cliff edge, he could see the great canyon stretching away to the east and west, impossible to cross, endlessly wide in most places, endlessly deep everywhere. It was quite a sight to behold, the giant rock walls changing colors—stripes of light gray near the top of the canyon, which became yellow then orange in hue, then red, and deeper to crimson, and finally a deep brown the farthest down anyone could see, where it disappeared into a haze of grayness and fog. But beneath that fog, the canyon went deeper into the world, into places where the sun could not reach—some said all the way to the bottom of the Island of Thershon.

It also went straight up, so high it hurt the neck to look up so far, reaching toward the sun, toward the blue skies and fluffy clouds. Eventually it became the snow-covered peaks of the Dividers Mountains, the mighty range that was sliced in half by Krillian's Cut.

Theel slowed to a walk as he reached the edge of the rock outcropping, to the point where the road fell away into nothingness. A hot wind hit him there, pushing and tugging on his hair and clothing. He could feel the heat and moisture from below, from the guts of the earth, bringing with it the odd scent of bad eggs. At the edge of the cliff stood two large stone obelisks, poking up out of the tangle of thorns on either side of the road. They were covered with carvings that may have been legible at one time, but were since wiped nearly clean by years of wind and rain.

This was little noticed however, because beginning from the dirt at his feet and reaching all the way across to the other side of the canyon loomed the great skeleton of the Dead Man's Bridge.

Theel had just emerged from a tiny hole in one side of the canyon. On the other side, barely visible, was another tiny hole where the Narrows continued south toward Wrendale. In between was an enormous structure made of rusting metal beams, many of them hundreds of feet long and several feet thick. It almost looked to Theel's eyes like a spider web of steel, with larger beams connected by zigzagging smaller beams. But the spider web also appeared torn, as if by a fierce wind, abandoned by its creator, and barely clinging to the rock walls, with loose strands hanging down. The bridge deck was also crumbling, with holes showing all over its surface. In the very center of the bridge was a large gap where two dozen feet of roadway had crumbled and fallen into the canyon. All of these things Theel expected to see. But there were also many things which had changed since his last visit to the Dead Man's Bridge.

Back then, the zoths had gained a foothold in the Narrows. Now, the zoths called the Narrows their home. Back then, they'd made their presence known by hanging a deathmark from one of the crossbeams of the bridge. Now they chose to decorate all the beams with the symbols of their slaughter, a hundred pieces of human beings taken as battle trophies and lashed to the metal framework. The deathmarks took many forms—eyes, ears, arms, legs, heads, or just scalps. But there were also complete corpses. Most of these were warriors, men of Overlie or Ducharme who'd entered the Narrows on a quest to end the Crowlord's brutal reign. Some of these were the best men of the Western Kingdoms. Theel even saw a corpse bearing the war emblem of the Southern Cross. All of them came to kill the Crowlord, and all of them failed in the effort, their quests and their lives ending on the Death Man's Bridge.

Boom ... Ba-boom. Boom ... Ba-boom.

The sound of the drums came from the far side of the canyon, beyond the gap that split the bridge in two. Theel could see movement over there, and smoke drifting westward from the mouth of the Narrows in a lazy plume that was eventually dispersed by the canyon winds.

Boom ... Ba-boom. Boom ... Ba-boom.

The drums were accompanied by hoarse shouting, the voice of a zoth holy man. Each of his words was answered by the voices of his followers, all of them engaged in a ritualistic chant. Theel recognized these as the sights and sounds of a zoth religious ceremony. He'd seen another like it just months before when he last walked onto the Dead Man's Bridge, just before his father died. It could mean many things. But it could also signify something terrible—that now, just like then, the Crowlord would be supported by the magic of his shaman. His strength would be enhanced, his speed would be enhanced—heart and lungs and muscles bursting with Craft. His ability to fight and his ability to kill would be superhuman.

Boom ... Ba-boom. Boom ... Ba-boom.

But though the shouting and drums of the zoth ceremony were loud, they were not the dominant sound echoing within the walls of Krillian's Cut. This was the screeching of the crows, thousands upon thousands of them flying into the canyon in a snaking black line. It was as if they were guided by a single mind, which commanded them to congregate in the air directly above the Dead Man's Bridge. There, they circled endlessly, a giant black ring of fluttering feathers, their voices joined into one constant scream.

Theel, Theel, Theel, Theeeeeeeeeeel!

The birds called and the drums pounded, and then Theel heard a new sound that brought him back to reality. It cut through the din, cut into his ears, and cut into his heart. It was the weeping of a little girl. He knew that sound from his dreams and visions. He knew who it was, and what it meant. The children of Overlie were alive and they were here. But where? Theel's eyes followed the sound to the center of the bridge, where he saw a group of cages hanging from chains just above the gaping hole in the road surface. They were similar to the ones he'd seen in Widow Hatch where he'd found Pitch, hung from gibbets to display criminals and to make a spectacle of their punishments. Just like in Widow Hatch, these cages contained humans, both living and dead. And thankfully, the two Overlie children were alive.

They huddled in the bottom of their cage, swaying slowly in the canyon breeze, clinging to one another. They were so young, little more than babes. They were dirt-smudged and sunburned, their once fine clothing ripped and torn and covered with stains. But other than their terror, they appeared to be unhurt.

Their cage was suspended by a chain, and Theel's eyes followed that chain up to the top of the bridge, where it was attached to the highest point of the metal gridwork. This was where he saw the Crowlord, the zoth that had caused him to walk all this way, crouching on the topmost beam of the Dead Man's Bridge.

The Crowlord had taken his latest victim up to this perch, a soldier of Overlie, perhaps one of those who'd imprisoned Pitch in his cage. The man was clearly dead. The Crowlord was up to his elbows in the man's blood, methodically cutting, and eating.

The famous zoth chieftain looked little different from the last time Theel saw him. Theel remembered the black crow feathers that decorated the zoth's head, the source of his name among the people of the Western Kingdoms. Theel remembered the patterns of human teeth imbedded into the skin of the zoth's chest, forming an intricate design which could not be comprehended by any mind save those given over to the Blood Goddess. Theel remembered the Crowlord's face, and how it was frozen in a constant half-grin, the result of a battle wound that took away a portion of his jaw and most of his lower lip, permanently exposing the teeth beneath. And as the chieftain stopped what he was doing and turned to look at Theel, the squire remembered those black eyes and remembered how there was no life in them, no soul, and no mercy.

The Crowlord rose to his full height, gazing down upon Theel with blood dripping off his chin. The crows continued to circle above him, the black ring forming a crown in the sky for their lord, or perhaps a halo.

As the human and the zoth locked eyes, the Crowlord removed his weapons from his back, gripping them in his fists. Theel remembered these as well—a pair of thigh bones blackened by fire, with iron spikes where the ball joints once were. The Crowlord wielded his bone spikes like hand axes, with devastating effect. Theel remembered how fast the Crowlord was with his attacks, and how strong. He remembered how those spikes pierced armor, split bone, and tore flesh. And he remembered how those weapons were used to kill, how men, women, and children died screaming under the onslaught of those spikes. But mostly, Theel remembered how, as he looked on, the Crowlord had used those spikes to take his father from him.

That was when Theel saw it, the Crowlord's most prized battle trophy. On the zoth's chest, directly over his heart, he wore a hand-sized silver shield in the fashion of the Knights of the Southern Cross. Its once shiny surface was now dulled, scratched, and dented, and covered with dried blood spatters. Even from this distance, Theel could plainly see the hole in its center, punched clean through the steel by some unknown warrior of terrifying strength. Such a blow should have killed the man wearing that shield, should have pierced his heart and ended his life forever. But miraculously, it did not. Even though impaled, the heart continued beating. Theel's father survived that battle and went on to live for many more years. Until he came to the Dead Man's Bridge, and fell at the feet of the Crowlord.

Theel remembered. He would never forget. It was branded on his brain, burned there by the white-hot agony of watching his father die. It was the moment that shook his faith. It was the moment that broke his will. It was what afflicted him with ceaseless, soul-eating doubt. It was the memory of that moment that had brought Theel back to this place.

The First Guardian and the Keeper of the Craft had called on Theel, but the Dead Man's Bridge called him first. They'd assigned him his quest for Warrior Baptism just weeks before, but the Dead Man's Bridge had always beckoned. This was the place where Theel's father had died at the hands of the Crowlord. And now the knight's squire had returned to the scene of his master's death to die as well. As he should have the first time, instead of fleeing like a coward.

As the Crowlord looked down from the top of the bridge, with his servants circling above his head, Theel now saw the goal of his own personal quest, the means by which he might slay the demons who gnawed at his soul. The Blessed Soul was forgotten. This did not involve the Keeper of the Craft, the First Guardian, or the Southern Cross. It didn't even involve the will of God.

This was all about Theel and his will, his desire to make a decision and act upon it, and thereby right the wrongs of his life. If he couldn't do those things, then his Warrior Baptism and his quest to find the Blessed Soul of Man meant nothing. He decided that the Overlie children would be saved. He decided his father would be avenged. He decided he would earn forgiveness for his past cowardice by standing his ground on the Dead Man's Bridge. When all of these things were accomplished, *then* he could pursue Warrior Baptism. And all these things could be accomplished through one act: Killing the Crowlord.

Theel drew his sword.

He was glad he he'd come. Standing where he was in this horrible place, and facing the most daunting task of his life, Theel never felt so terrified. But he also never felt so at peace with the choice he had made.

"I've come for you, Crowlord," he whispered. "And one of us is going to die."

CHAPTER 49

Yatham stood in the darkness of the drainage sewer beneath the Narrows, listening to the sounds of running water and the crackling of his torch. He did his best to remain calm, to breathe slowly and evenly, despite the fact that he wanted to scream and bash his head against the bars until the portcullis opened. But it would not open by any effort of his. It was too heavy to lift, and its bars were too thick to bend. Its very purpose was to bar access to the eastern tunnel to any who didn't have aid from the other side. Unless someone turned that wheel, the portcullis would not raise, and Yatham was stuck where he was.

"Theel!" he screamed. "Pitch!"

There was no answer, just like all the other times he'd screamed. There was no point, he knew. Theel was no longer close enough to hear. He'd climbed up to the eastern tunnel and continued on to the Dead Man's Bridge, choosing to fight the Crowlord alone. It was an act of inexplicable rashness from his usually indecisive brother, truly an inconvenient time for him to find his backbone.

"Theel!" he screamed. "Pitch!"

Pitch was his only hope. Even if Theel was able to turn the wheel to let Yatham through, it still wouldn't get him past the portcullis on the other side of the canal. He needed Pitch for that. He needed the song man to squeeze through the bars again, go back beneath the western tunnel and turn the wheel there. Pitch was his only hope.

His heart nearly stopped when he saw movement on the other side of the canal, shadows shifting in the pale sunlight. *Please, Lord, no more zoths.*

"Pitch!" he shouted. "Turn the wheel!"

He hoped it was Pitch. If it wasn't, the song man was surely dead. But someone was over there. The movement continued. *Please, Lord.*

"Pitch!" he shouted. "Turn the—

The tunnel erupted with the grinding of the mechanism, and Yatham began to sing silent prayers of thanks as he watched the bars raising up. The second he saw the spikes at the bottom of the portcullis emerge from the water, he dove in and swam beneath them, then splashed his way across the canal. As soon as he reached the portcullis on the other side, he gripped the bars.

"Pitch, come down here!" he shouted. "Let it drop."

And he knew the song man heard him, because the portcullis dropped and slammed shut with a splash, sending waves across the surface of the canal. The shadows above continued to shift, then the pale light turned orange, dancing on the water. Yatham saw a torch coming down the staircase, and saw the face of the man carrying it. It was Pitch. And he looked confused.

"Where is your brother?" he asked through the bars.

"You don't know?"

"*You* don't know?"

"Never mind," Yatham said. "You must raise these bars. Go back to the western tunnel and turn the wheel. Quickly."

Pitch frowned. "Are you suggesting that I—"

"Yes," Yatham said.

"Again? Between these bars?"

"Yes!" Yatham shouted. "With haste!"

"I'm not certain I can—"

Yatham reached between the bars and grabbed the song man by the throat. "I am certain you can."

"Well, perhaps I could try," Pitch coughed. "If you insist—"

Yatham grabbed the song man's wrist and pulled his arm through, then grabbed a handful of hair, using it to turn his head sideways to make it fit.

"Yes, your aid might prove beneficial, thank you," Pitch grunted. "Ouch."

Once he had the song man's head through, Yatham grabbed both wrists, put his foot against the bars, and pulled with all the strength he had. Pitch cried out in pain as his entire body was jerked through the bars in one giant tug. That cry of pain was swallowed by the splash, as both men fell backward into the water. They quickly emerged, Yatham dragging the song man back across the canal by his neck.

"I'd always thought you to be more compassionate and reasonable than your brother," Pitch choked. "Perhaps I was mistaken."

"Shut up," Yatham said.

"Are we in a hurry?" Pitch asked.

Yatham ignored the song man's question, stuffing him through the bars in an effort akin to forcing a squirming cat into a burlap sack.

"Pitch, if you turn that wheel, you are free to go," Yatham promised, as he forced the man through. "Open that portcullis and run for your life."

Pitch fell to the ground with a splash, where he sat, rubbing his eyes.

"Run for my life?" he asked. "To where?"

"Anywhere," Yatham said, holding Pitch's torch through the bars. "Go back to Widow Hatch and climb back into your crow cage, if you like. Just turn that wheel."

"Perhaps I will go back to Widow Hatch," the song man said, taking the torch. "The cage was more comfortable than this experience has been."

"Go," Yatham ordered. "Raise the portcullis."

"Please give my compliments to my liege lord, your brother," Pitch said. "And convey my deepest sympathies that I will not be available to serve him in this most trying time."

"Go!" Yatham shrieked. "Now!"

Pitch didn't say another word. He turned and ran up the staircase.

CHAPTER 50

Theel could see the zoths, dozens of them, climbing up the gridwork of steel beams above the bridge. He could hear their shouts of glee, knew they felt he would be an easy kill. He would have nowhere to go once they were above him, once they began to drop down around him. It was a fight he could not win, even if the Crowlord did not join their attacks, even if they weren't strengthened by the magic of their shaman.

Theel knew he must find that shaman and kill him. As long as that vile creature worked his evil magic on the far side of the bridge, Theel didn't stand a chance against the Crowlord. It was a painful lesson learned on his last visit to the Dead Man's Bridge, as he watched his father's blades strike at the zoth chieftain many times, with no effect.

He needed to reach the opposite side of the bridge, to attack the shaman before the Crowlord and his warriors cornered him. He couldn't accomplish this by climbing up toward them. And the hole in the center of the roadway prevented him from running across the bridge. That left only one option.

He immediately ran for the side of the bridge, to a walkway made of steel gratings running parallel to the roadway. Here he knew he would find a ladder which led both upward and downward. He chose to go down. He didn't use the rungs of the ladder, instead he slid down in a speedy descent of several stories, until his gloves were so hot from the friction they felt like they might catch fire.

The steel gridwork supporting the bridge from beneath the roadway was just as intricate as that above it. The ladder took Theel down to a small structure built among these beams which contained two rooms, both filled with metal boxes and pipes. One wall and a portion of the floor was missing in the second room, giving Theel access to the outside, out onto the beams beneath the bridge.

He jumped out into the open air above the canyon, and before his boots struck the steel beam, he was slapped by a stiff wind. He stumbled and fell to his knees, but managed to hang on. Beneath him was nothingness—the walls of the canyon and their layers of earthen colors falling down into a bed of mist leagues below. The distance was so great he could see birds flying beneath him. If he fell from there, he might never stop falling. Just as that thought struck him, another burst of wind nudged him toward the edge.

He gripped the steel so hard it hurt, as if he might break the bones of his fingers. He must not fall. He must keep his strength, even as his wounds conspired to rob him of it. He felt a hot finger of liquid run across his left cheek and into his eye, turning his vision pink. He tried to rub it away, but that only made it worse. Another stream of blood ran to the tip of his nose where it dripped like a leaky faucet, leaving pats of bright red on the rusty beam between his hands.

He rose to his feet and walked across the narrow beam as fast as he dared, his arms waving like an unpracticed tightrope walker. Far beneath him, another beam rose up, eventually joining with his. That one was much larger, better than four feet wide, and therefore, much safer. He jumped onto it and ran. The beam took him gradually upward, a giant arc of steel with its highest point at the center of the bridge. Here was another small building surrounded by another walkway with handrails. And just above it was the hole in the roadway, allowing a large swath of sunlight into this shadowy realm.

It seemed half a world away. The smoke told him the shaman was on the other side of the canyon, near the southern end of the bridge. Could he make it that far before the Crowlord forced battle upon him?

One minute flew by, then several more, just like the spider web of metal beams that whipped by as he ascended the giant arc of steel. He was panting heavily, sweating buckets. But he didn't seem to make any progress. His precarious balance was constantly challenged by the canyon winds. He was sure he was going to fall several times. And despite all the effort, he wasn't even halfway up the arcing beam before the crows hit him.

They appeared below the bridge deck, a flock of hundreds, moving together like a school of fish. They grouped their bodies together to form a giant cloud of bird flesh and slammed into him, all their voices screaming one thing.

Theel, Theel, Theel!

They struck his head and chest, arms and legs, a flood of feathers with a single mind. They smashed into him and everything around him with no regard for themselves, even exploding into bloody poofs on the steel beams.

Theel, Theel, Theel!

He was pounded relentlessly, crushed to his knees, then knocked on his back. The sky was consumed by a hailstorm of beady black eyes descending upon him, hundreds, thousands, all screaming with the rage of the Crowlord.

Theel, Theel, Theel!

By the time it was over, he was hanging from the side of the beam, covered with feathers and bird guts, his feet dangling above the canyon. His left eye fluttered again, filled with blood again. With much effort, he climbed back up and found his feet, angrily trying to rub away the red blur. When his vision cleared, the Crowlord was standing in front of him, not more than a dozen paces away.

Theel had only a second to comprehend this. He saw the silver shield on the zoth chieftain's chest, and saw the hole in its center.

Then the crows hit him again.

Chapter 51

Yatham heard the portcullis slam shut behind him, and knew that he would never see Pitch again. But he didn't care. He had much more important worries.

He ran up the staircase toward the eastern tunnel and into the room with the donkey wheel. There he saw the song man's spear, the shaft of gingo wood topped by the moonblade, still protruding from a hole in the side of the mechanism. Yatham stopped just long enough to pull the spear out, and took it with him down the corridor. It wasn't long before he came to the source of the sunlight; a round hole in the ceiling, casting a pale stream of light down upon the ladder and the two dead zoths beneath it.

The bodies were still fresh, and Yatham knew instantly that his brother had done this. The zoths died in close combat, as if grappling with their killer. The mortal wounds were small, the size of a knife, and were aimed at the weak points, the neck and the ear. It was just as his father had taught him. Theel was always better with blades than he would admit.

But he wasn't skilled enough to stand alone against the Crowlord, so Yatham spared no further time. He scrambled up into the tunnel above. The sunlight came from the south, and cut into his eyes painfully. After so many hours spent in darkness, it should have been a welcome sight. But it also brought with it many sounds. Drums. And crows.

Those sounds told him he was near his destination, that he and his brother had finally arrived at the Dead Man's Bridge. But there was no joy in that knowledge. Instead, the thought filled his heart with frustration and fear.

The brothers had traveled so many miles to reach this spot. Throughout their entire journey, Yatham had never left Theel's side once, knowing his brother would need his help and support in every step he took toward his goal of Warrior Baptism. But now, at this crucial juncture, when the danger was greatest, the two had become separated. Yatham could not believe that his chronically hesitant brother had gone to the bridge without him. He couldn't believe Theel was so foolish as to willingly enter the domain of the Crowlord alone. If they survived this, he would punch Theel in the face again.

Please, Lord.

He knew God was listening, so he prayed hard and fast. He meant to fill his Creator's ears to overflowing. He prayed for strength, not for himself, but for Theel. He prayed for his brother to find his faith, to strengthen his heart as well as his sword arm. And to give him not only the knowledge, but the will to do what needed to be done.

What needed to be done? Yatham didn't know himself, but he knew there was something here, some unfinished business that gnawed at his brother day and night. And it wasn't just the Overlie children. Theel had been resolved to travel the Narrows long before the brothers set foot on the streets of Calfborn. So Yatham prayed that his brother would finally find the thing that drew him to this place, and that he kill whatever demons lived on the Dead Man's Bridge.

Perhaps such a victory might aid Theel in other battles, ones he'd been waging internally for years. Perhaps, with this victory, his brother might finally slay his bitterness—toward his father, and toward God. And toward himself. Perhaps then, he would be ready to undertake Warrior Baptism. Perhaps he would be ready to face the Blessed Soul of Man.

Yatham prayed some more. *Please, Lord.*

As he ran toward the sunlight, the debris on the floor of the tunnel grew thicker; broken weapons and armor, which indicated past battles. Then his nostrils filled with the stench of putrefaction. It wasn't long before he came upon the source of the smell. On the right side of the road was a line of dead animals tied to rings in the wall—horses, donkeys, and oxen. As one who had spent his life training with and caring for animals, the sight of it sickened him. Many were the war horses of knights and men-at-arms who'd come to the Dead Man's Bridge in search of the Crowlord and his minions. Instead, the Crowlord slew their masters, and the zoths butchered these once noble creatures with the delicateness of wild dogs, leaving their bones to rot.

It was a terrible waste. The frustration of it only hurried his steps further.

Just beyond this, the ceiling of the tunnel opened up and the sun blazed down, cooking his skin. The road cut down the center of a field of thorn bushes, black and twisted things too sick to grow upward. He ran through the middle of this, the thorns whipping in the canyon winds, almost lashing out at him. But he paid them no mind, bulling his way through as they sliced at his skin and snagged his clothing. He was too focused on the sounds he heard; the drums, the crows. And the smell of eggs, and of death.

He heard zoths shouting. He heard children crying. And he heard steel, the distinct sounds of battle. It wasn't the cacophony of armies clashing, but of two warriors locked in single combat. Yatham knew who those warriors were.

Then he was there, at the far side of the thorn bushes, with the great canyon and the huge structure of rusty metal beams looming before him. Yatham stood at the foot of the Dead Man's Bridge.

What he saw there terrified him.

CHAPTER 52

The Crowlord cared nothing for defense—always advancing, always attacking, his weapons swiping at Theel unrelentingly. Theel could not keep up, could not match speed with the zoth, in strength or skill. He never attacked once, only retreated, using knife and sword to throw up a weak defense. It was soon clear to Theel that he had no business trying to fight the zoth chieftain. This was the realm of men such as the Knights of the Southern Cross. It was not the realm of lazy, unmotivated boys who wore the title of squire only because of their fathers' standing in the knighthood.

Theel had lost his shield at the bottom of the waterfall in the Trader's Cave, forcing him to match the zoth's spikes with two weapons, which never was his strength. The canyon winds constantly kept him off balance, and his fluttering, blood-filled left eye was of virtually no use. Bloody and wounded, stumbling and half-blind, he was no match for any opponent, let alone a zoth chieftain.

The Crowlord was strong and tireless, and buoyed by the Craft runes woven by his shaman. His attacks were crushingly strong. Each time one of his weapons slammed against Theel's defense, the impact jolted his arms up to the shoulder. The Crowlord was pounding the strength out of Theel, and was doing so effortlessly. For some reason, the chieftain hadn't yet gone for the kill, even though Theel's poor defense gave him many opportunities. In fact, he used both of his weapons as clubs, holding the spikes backwards so he was attacking with the blunt ends. It was almost as if the Crowlord was protecting him from those spikes, trying to wound him, not kill him. Theel didn't know what to make of this.

This was nothing like the battle the zoth had given Theel's father. That was a fight in which both combatants put all of their strength toward trying to kill each other. This fight was like a cat slapping around a wounded mouse. Theel's father was a fighter the Crowlord respected as a threat. Theel posed no threat at all, and sensed he might still be alive only because the Crowlord allowed it.

The chieftain pushed him backward across a large beam, feinting left, attacking right. Theel was confused. He couldn't see with this fluttering left eye, and wasn't fast enough to react. He was fooled by the feint each time, barely maintaining his balance, losing more ground with each thrust.

Then he saw an opening in the rhythm of the Crowlord's attacks, the same attack over and over, feint left, attack right, leaving an unprotected left leg, over and over. Theel timed his sword thrust for the opening, planning to go for that leg. The Crowlord feinted again, attacked again, pushing him back against a railing, and Theel lashed out with his sword.

And missed.

The opening was no longer there. And the feint was no longer a feint. The Crowlord blocked the attack so hard he knocked the sword out of Theel's hand. Then he spun his bone spike and slammed Theel's unprotected left shoulder. The attack was no longer playful but vindictive, and Theel's armor did nothing to stop it. The hide of the bullosk split open just like his skin, just like his flesh, and was crushed, just like the bones of his shoulder. Theel felt the impact, but not the pain. He became aware that he couldn't feel his left arm at all. Then the Crowlord kicked him in the chest, and his legs flew straight up into the air as he tumbled backward over the railing.

In that instant, every prayer his father taught him flashed through his mind. It was a moment of pure helplessness as the beams of the bridge flew away above him, and death rushed up to enfold him in its arms. His mind was empty. He felt nothing. He saw nothing but the Crowlord looking down at him, and the bridge around the zoth growing smaller as he fell.

This was it. Nothing could save Theel but luck. Nothing could save him but fate. No one could save him but God.

Something rushed up to smash his back, punching the breath from his lungs and the blood from his head. His arms and legs flopped limply, draped over the sides of the steel beam that had stopped his fall. It was a shaft of broken steel, detached from the bridge at one end, hanging at an odd angle where it shouldn't be, as if placed there for the sole purpose of catching his fall.

He did not move. He could not—paralyzed by the shock of what had just happened. All he could do was gasp in quick, nearly uncontrollable breaths, his lungs celebrating that they still possessed the capacity to inflate. Then his left eye fluttered again as if to tell him yes, indeed, he was still alive. He could feel his heart thumping in his head, and his lungs sucked in more air. Yes, he was alive!

But he could also feel blood running across his face, still flowing from the wound in his head. And now he couldn't move his left arm; couldn't even feel it at all. He reached over with his right hand and felt the hole torn in his armor, drawing back a bloody glove. It was bad. He was now one-armed. And he'd lost his sword.

But it wasn't over. He was still alive. And he meant to fight. But though his mind was determined, his body was incapable. So again, he called on the Life Sign. He closed his eyes, and tried to force his frantic breaths to slow down. Then he recited the words of the Morning Supplication of the King's Cross, followed by the Knight's Creed.

Give this child strength.
That he might raise your banner.
Cleanse this child's wounds.
That he might carry your shield.
I, as a son of the Silvermarsh Clans, do commit myself, body, soul, and spirit …

Immediately he felt the pain in his shoulder, the pain of his healing. He gritted his teeth at the agony of the bones crunching as they shifted back into place, the flesh closing and the skin knitting itself together.

The pain didn't stop—it might never stop, he realized. The wound was only partially closed. Just as with the gash in his scalp, the Life Sign could only do so much. But it would have to be enough. Blood still ran from his shoulder, but he knew he would live.

He rolled onto his side and saw his left arm hanging limply, completely dead and unresponsive. He couldn't feel a thing, yet could see that his hand still held his father's knife. Just as he feared, the damage done by the Crowlord was permanent. It would take the greatest healers in the Method to return his arm to him now. But he had more pressing needs.

"Stand now, and fight," he said to himself. And he did, rolling over and crawling to his knees. Only twenty feet above was another beam, wider and more sturdy, and from this beam was the ladder that led up to the small building at the center of the bridge. He could make it. He knew it. It was going to be a long and laborious trip working with only one arm. It might take all the strength he had left. But he was prepared to give that strength.

"I'm not dead yet, Crowlord," he said. "I'm not dead yet."

He began to climb up the beam. Then he heard a sound.

Theel, Theel, Theel!

And the crows hit him again.

Chapter 53

Yatham stood at the north end of the Dead Man's Bridge. It was the first time he'd ever seen the ancient marvel, but he felt none of the wonderment and awe which struck so many others who'd stood on this spot. Instead of wonder, he felt dread.

He felt dread because of the smells of blood, and smoke, and the stink of a hundred corpses. Because of the ceaseless pounding of the drums, and cries of the crows and the shouts of the zoth shaman. Because it hurt to breathe the air of this place so poisoned by evil. Because his brother had willingly set foot on this bridge to challenge, to taunt that evil. Because his brother was out there somewhere, fighting, and alone.

Yatham knew it to be true. His scalp tingled and knew exactly where to look. His attention focused like water in a funnel, swirling around and narrowing to a tight spot below the bridge, where he knew his brother was fighting for his life. Against the Crowlord.

The zoth chieftain would be strengthened by the magic of his shaman. The shouting and chanting and the plume of smoke on the far side of the bridge told Yatham that. The shaman was holding some ceremony, some unholy ritual designed to support his chieftain, to support the Crowlord's attacks, while weakening Theel's defense. Defeating the zoth chieftain in this environment would have been an impossible challenge for any swordsman acting alone, even the most accomplished warriors among the Knights of the Southern Cross. And this was an environment that Theel had walked right into.

It immediately became clear to Yatham. His brother must no longer fight alone. If the Crowlord benefited from a shaman's aid, then Theel would benefit from his brother's aid. If the zoth shaman supported his chieftain through the magic of some unholy ritual, then Yatham would support Theel by disrupting that ritual and killing the shaman.

But the ceremony was taking place on the opposite end of the bridge, which seemed like miles away. Even worse, there was a gap in the bridge deck, where a large section of roadway had crumbled and fallen into the canyon. His only option was to climb up the intricate gridwork of steel beams above his head, to use them to climb over the hole in the road. But those steel beams were crawling with zoths.

There were no zoths on the bridge deck, nothing between him and the shaman but that hole in the road. If only he could find a way to cross it without climbing. It was too wide for him to jump across, and even if it wasn't so wide, it was too far away. Even the fastest sprinter would find himself stopped short this goal, trapped and cornered by zoths jumping down upon him from above. A horrible sense of futility closed in on him like the worst claustrophobia.

What could he do? He couldn't run fast enough. He couldn't jump far enough. There was nothing he could do but pray.

Please Lord.

Then he heard heavy footsteps thumping on the road behind him. He spun around, spear in hand. He was ready to fight no matter what faced him, if it was five zoths or five hundred. But it wasn't even one zoth.

It was a horse, a big gray gelding bearing the war emblem of the Southern Cross.

Chapter 54

Theel felt his resolve slipping away. It was leaving his body just like the blood leaking from his head, flowing from his arm, and falling into the canyon, drip by drip. He was able to reach the ladder by shimmying up the steel beam, hugging it with his one good arm as the winds tried tirelessly to tear his grip loose. It was almost impossible to hold on.

He was exhausted, almost completely spent. It wasn't merely his recent exertions, running for days with little food or water, and absolutely no rest, followed by battles with the zoths and their chieftain and the multiple wounds he suffered at their hands. It was cost of using the Life Sign twice in such a short time. The tattoo was created through the Craft, but the process of healing was fueled by his juy. Treating grave wounds like the ones he suffered required large amounts, drawn from the well of his mystic will, which was the very vitality that kept his heart beating and his lungs breathing. Calling on his Life Sign had taken so much of his energy, he feared he might pass out any second. He needed to rest to replenish his strength, to replenish his store of mystic will. But there was no time.

And then there was the pain. After the pain of the healing subsided, it was quickly replaced by the the pain of his wounds, almost as if he'd healed himself just enough to realize how hurt he was. Both his wounds were healed to a point where they no longer threatened his life, but that didn't stop the throbbing hammer blows striking him in the head and left arm. His shoulder was a ruin of shredded leather and scar tissue that still seeped blood. It felt like someone stabbed him with an icicle, then broke it off inside him. Every movement of his body, every breath drawn, felt like the Crowlord's spike hitting him again. He was able to pull himself up the ladder, slowly and painfully, with his left arm hanging limply, but each step and each rung was accompanied by a cry of agony. It hurt so much, he feared the pain might kill him before the Crowlord could.

Theel knew he was not going to kill the zoth chieftain. He might climb to the small building beneath the bridge, but then what? He could not fight. He could barely maintain his grip on the ladder. Even if he chose to quit and run, he didn't even have the strength to flee.

And yet he felt his trip to the Dead Man's Bridge was a success. This is what he expected to happen, and he accepted it. Justice would be done here on this day.

Theel deserved to die for his failures. He deserved to die for his cowardice. He should have died on his last visit to the Dead Man's Bridge. If he stood and fought beside his father like a man, he would be dead now. But he fled like a coward, and because of that he survived . He didn't deserve it. His father should have survived that battle, not him. If Theel had attacked the shaman immediately as his father ordered, things would have been different. The Crowlord would be dead, and Theel's father would be alive. But he didn't do as he was ordered. And his hesitation cost his father's life.

It was cruel fates or bad luck that caused the knight and the chieftain to meet on the bridge that day. The Crowlord shouldn't have been there. There shouldn't have been any zoths in the Narrows at all. Theel and his father had no reason to expect trouble when trying to cross the span.

He didn't know it at the time, but his father was taking him to Ebon South to search for Father Brashfor, and the Blessed Soul of Man. Theel's father was planning for him to begin his quest for Warrior Baptism, but that plan was short lived. The Crowlord intervened, the knight died, and his squire fled like a coward.

Theel failed his test on the bridge that day, but worse, he ran back to Fal Daran rather than continue south as his father wished. There he hid from himself, trying to drown in his liquors and smokes, and when Quiddip Kile called him a coward, Theel killed him for it.

Two men were dead because of him. And when the City Overwatch came looking for Quiddip's killer, Theel again fled like a coward. He told everyone, even tried to tell himself, that Quiddip's death was an accident. He told everyone he was going to Ebon South to quest for Warrior Baptism, not to flee justice. But no one believed either of those lies, and neither did he.

The Keeper of the Craft ordered him to go to Ebon South to search for the Blesssed Soul of Man, but Theel had his own quest. He would go to the Outlands and he would pursue his Warrior Baptism, just as he was ordered, but he would go there by way of the Narrows. His personal quest would first take him back to the Dead Man's Bridge to do what he should have done the first time. He would follow his father's orders. He would kill the shaman, and he would kill the Crowlord. Or he would die and justice would be served. Justice for Quiddip, and justice for his Masterknight.

Theel had passed judgement on himself. And now he was carrying out his sentence.

He was prepared to die. But he was also prepared to live. Either way, he would do it by standing up and fighting like a man. Not for his father. Not for the knighthood. And not for their God. But for himself.

And for those children. He could hear them crying as he pulled himself up the ladder. They were so far way, so high above him, their cage suspended from the highest point of the bridge. Theel didn't know how long their cries would continue. The zoths were up there, climbing in the steel gridwork surrounding them. He didn't know if the creatures intended to do harm to the children, and wasn't sure why the zoths had allowed them to live as long as they had. But as long as they lived, there was still hope to save them.

Theel knew he could not fight the Crowlord, but he could climb a ladder. He could climb all the way up to the top of the bridge and free those children from their cage. At least then, they would have a chance. Perhaps Yatham might take them back northward while Theel faced the Crowlord one last time, in a dramatic confrontation worthy of a bard's song—as long as the zoth chieftain did nothing to stop him before he reached that cage.

Curiously, the Crowlord was nowhere to be seen. Perhaps something else had taken his attention away. Theel chose not to question his good fortune, and chose instead to climb. And though it felt as if it took him all day, he finally reached the top of the ladder, where it ended on the side of the small building in the center of the bridge. The structure had a stone roof with a metal railing around it. Theel climbed onto the roof by sliding under the railing.

He lay on his back for a few moments, gasping and groaning in pain. Directly above him was the giant hole in the bridge deck. Through it he could see the spiderweb of steel beams in the sky so far above him, and the cages swaying in the canyon breezes. He could see the zoths up there climbing among the beams. Then he saw another one standing at the edge of the hole in the bridge deck, looking down at him with its beady black eyes.

The creature immediately jumped down upon him, leading with its spear. Luckily, it was a rash attack, ill-timed and ill-coordinated. Theel was able to roll so the spear tip missed, then he kicked the zoth off its feet. It fell on its back, but quickly rolled over and scrambled on all fours toward its spear. Theel made a desperate grab, seizing the creature by its heel, then its calf, then its thigh. He jumped on its back as it wriggled, trying to reached for its spear. But its spear was too far away and it was still reaching as Theel grabbed a fistful of its hair and smashed its face down against the stone as hard as he could. Then he did it again. After a third time the creature stopped moving, as black blood pooled beneath its head.

Another zoth replaced the first one, jumping down through the hole at Theel just as he rose to his feet. This one did not miss, stabbing Theel in the thigh, but his armor of the bullosk saved him.

Another downward thrust missed, connected with the stone roof of the building, and the spear tip broke off.

Theel knew he had an opening, but couldn't see it with his left eye, couldn't exploit it with his left arm. He tried to punch the zoth but missed, just as it swung its broken spear shaft and cracked him in the head.

Theel's brain did a backflip inside his skull, and the building began to spin beneath his feet. Then the stone roof smashed him in the face. Everywhere, he could see his own blood, streaks of it all over the stone. It was bright red, almost beautiful. He grasped around, looking for a weapon, but accomplished nothing more than smearing his blood around. He rolled onto his back, looked up at the zoth who would be his killer, and wondered why the blow hadn't yet fallen. But the creature seemed distracted; it was looking up at something.

Here was Theel's chance. He climbed to his feet, staggered, and fell to one knee. There were more of the creatures now. He could hear them up above, on the road. Soon they would be upon him, and then it would be over. He couldn't keep his balance. He could hardly see. But he also didn't care. He bull-rushed the distracted zoth, smashed into it and shoved it back against the railing at the edge of the roof, pinning it there. It grabbed him by the neck, trying to choke him as he punched it in the face repeatedly with his right hand, slamming its nose with his knuckles. He heard a roar that sounded like his own voice screaming as he pounded on the zoth. It grabbed at his face, perhaps to gouge at his eyes, but Theel was slippery with blood. It couldn't get a grip on him, and soon it stopped trying, its body bending further and further backward over the railing. And suddenly it fell, bouncing off a steel beam and tumbling into the canyon.

Theel could hear the other zoths above him. There were five or six of them from the sound of it. Any moment they could jump down and finish him, and yet they didn't. He turned to look at them, holding himself up by the railing, trying to rub the blood from his eyes. Two of them stood at the edge of the hole in the road, but were not jumping down to fight him. They weren't even looking at him. What were they looking at? Then Theel heard the sound.

Hoofbeats. And the whinny of a horse.

Something like a gray shooting star cut across the sky directly above Theel's head. But this star wore horseshoes, and trailed a caparison emblazoned with the black and white war emblem of the Southern Cross. It was the big, gray gelding, and it was flying through the air as if it had wings. Riding this winged shooting star was his brother, Yatham.

"Fly Southern Cross!" someone screamed, and Theel realized it was him.

The powerful warhorse slammed into the first zoth, then the second, scattering their bodies like they were leaves in the breeze. A third zoth tried to run, but was trampled to death. Yet another zoth fumbled with its spear before being crushed.

"Kill them, brother!" Theel shouted. "Kill them all!"

The last two living zoths stood their ground as Yatham charged straight at them. One of the creatures lifted its spear, poised to throw. But Yatham had a spear of his own; a long shaft of gingo wood topped by a moon blade. He carried it under his arm like a lance, lowered the point, and slammed the zoth in the chest with enough force to send it flying out over the canyon. The spear should have broken from the force, but the flexible gingo wood merely rippled as Yatham directed its point at the other zoth. This one lost its nerve and jumped.

That was the smart one, avoiding death by avoiding the charging horse. The creature saved itself by grabbing one of the beams beneath the bridge with its hands and feet. It clearly felt it was out of danger, but could not know that it was not alone in the shadows beneath the bridge deck. The zoth immediately began to climb back up the beam, but remained exposed to attack. It was an opportunity that Theel could not ignore. The instincts his father had drilled into him now guided his hand. He could almost hear his masterknight's words of instruction whispering in his ear as the zoth spear leaped into this hand, and just as quickly leaped out, striking the creature in the head and knocking it off the bridge.

Theel looked up to see that Yatham was already out of sight, the broken zoth corpses and fading hoofbeats the only proof his brother was ever there. Yatham was headed toward the south, to the far side of the bridge, which told Theel that his brother intended to challenge the zoth shaman. Perhaps the Crowlord's advantage was about to evaporate.

A savage roar burst from Theel's lips, an animal sound full of challenge and defiance—defiance of the zoths and their shaman, a challenge to their Crowlord. The sight of Yatham on that horse had given Theel his resolve back, had filled him and flushed his face with new hope.

This was not over yet! The battle on the Dead Man's Bridge would indeed one day be told through song. But all of the final verses were yet to be written.

"Come to me, Crowlord!" he screamed, hobbling across the roof of the structure.

He drew in a deep breath and screamed it again.

"Come and kill me!"

Chapter 55

In the sewers beneath the western branch of the Narrows, Pitch held the donkey wheel in place, keeping the portcullis open much longer than necessary. Once he'd raised it, he needed only hold it open for seconds to allow Yatham to pass through on his way to the Dead Man's bridge. And yet Pitch held the donkey wheel, held the portcullis in place, for what felt like minutes. It was almost as if he didn't know what to do next.

But he did know. He took his hands off the wheel, allowing the portcullis to drop, and the mechanism roared. The wheel spun unchecked, turning cogs and spinning screws, all this noise ending in one deafening crash as the portcullis in the eastern tunnel slammed into place.

When he heard that sound he winced, then smiled. He waited many minutes more, listening to the silence, as if he didn't believe it, as if it was impossible. But it wasn't impossible. It was true.

"You are free, Pitchford Wicker," he whispered to himself. "You are finally free."

He snatched his torch from the wall and ran from the room, jumping down the staircase which led to the canal. Wading through the water, he grabbed the bars of the portcullis and peered through.

His torchlight splashed off waves of dirty canal water rolling across the tunnel. The bars on both sides of the waterway were closed and quiet. There was no one to be seen—no zoths, no Overlie men, no Theel, and no Yatham. No one at all.

"That's it, then," he said. "One fool rushes to his death and the other follows, leaving their poor servant trapped in a moment of terrible indecision. Does he walk the foolish yet loyal path, and rush to the aid of his liege lord, saving him from being skinned by the Crowlord? Does he follow, not with warlike intention, but to play the role of onlooker? If the master should succeed, his servant might share in the victory. If the master should fail, his servant might savor the butchery."

The waves rolled past his knees, the water hummed, and Pitch tapped the iron bars, pleased at their stoutness.

"But, my dear liege lord," he said. "These wretched bars block my path. And so I must consider a third choice. To run. And to run like the devil himself is nipping at my heels. Because he is. It is you I have to thank for this. It is you who has brought me to the devil's door. And now you have chosen to enter his house, chosen to place these bars between us. You chose prison over freedom, leaving your faithful servant free to do as he chooses, to choose prison or freedom for himself."

Pitch's laughter echoed in the tunnel, mixing with the bubbling canal water. He put his torch in its sconce and pressed his face against the bars, as if getting closer, so Theel could hear as he whispered.

"The choice between prison, or freedom? That is no choice at all," he said. "This humble servant will never choose prison. Never. Perhaps this humble servant should run. Perhaps this thoughtless and bumbling servant is wise enough to recognize the beautiful, fragrant flower of opportunity when it blooms in his hand. A man once beaten and caged and condemned to death cannot turn from life. Not after he was dragged to the lip of his grave, to peer inside, to see and smell the fresh soil of its bottom, only to have his gaolers purchase his freedom by descending into the earth, taking his place in the grave."

Pitch glanced around to be sure no one was eavesdropping, then gestured with his hand, as if asking Theel to come closer, to listen closer.

"And that isn't the only gift you've given me, my liege," he whispered. "In your zeal to die, you also condemn to death this servant's guilt, for you and your brother are the final witnesses. You walk to your deaths, and carry with you all knowledge of what transgressions this servant has made. No one will ever know of the role Lord Pitchford Wicker played in sending the Overlie children to their doom. No one will ever know of the theft of the little girl's earring. No one will ever know who was present in Widow Hatch that fateful day, when the children of Overlie entered the Narrows and the brothers Theel and Yatham rushed after. No one will ever know what role the lesser Lord Pitchford Wicker played in this great tragedy, because now, the lesser Lord Pitchford Wicker will cease to exist."

He stood up straight, then bowed to the portcullis as if the bars were someone he'd just met.

"Why, hello! Whom do I have the honor of meeting on this fine day, in this foul place? Why, Danforth Stannis, a pilgrim hailing from the Silver Star, City of Dreams. And whom do I have the honor of meeting? Pitchford Wicker, displaced lesser lord of Clan Aramorun. It is a pleasure to make your acquaintance. Hello Danforth Stannis! Farewell, Pitchford Wicker!"

He bowed to the portcullis again.

"You are free of your past, Danforth," he said to himself. "Your new life awaits."

He turned away, turned to walk toward that new life, but quickly stopped, looking curiously at the inky water rippling around his knees.

"What have you stepped on, my dear Danforth Stannis?" he asked himself.

He plunged his hands beneath the water and fished around, scraping the bottom with his knuckles until he found something. It was resting on the stone floor, between the bars of the closed portcullis. When he lifted it into the torchlight, when he saw what he held in his hand, a gasp burst from his lips. He was so shocked that he nearly dropped it back into the water.

"My goodness, what is this?" he asked. "How can one man's fortune change so drastically, in so short a time?"

In his hand, he held Theel's leather belt by its buckle, and dangling from the belt was a sword still resting in its sheath, its hilt glittering golden in the torchlight.

Any man who laid eyes on this weapon would say it was the most magnificent sword he had ever seen. The hilt was fashioned in the likeness of an angel, her body serving as the hand grips, her wings serving as the cross guard. Her eyes were closed, and her mouth open in song. The water running off her face sparkled in a dizzying, almost blinding light.

"My goodness, what are you doing here, my sweet angel?" he said, then remembered the name. "My ... Battle Hymn. Why would Pitchford Wicker's liege lord leave you here in this dark place? Are you lost to him? Forgotten?"

He turned the sword over, inspecting the decorations of its hilt, marveling.

"Surely, you were his most cherished possession," he said. "But no more. Now you belong to another, a pilgrim of the east known as Danforth Stannis. Perhaps he will be forced to discard this final proof of Pitchford Wicker's encounter with the brothers Theel and Yatham. Surely somewhere in the northern cities of Thershon, there must be a dealer in precious rarities willing to trade his work for so fine a treasure as this."

He held the sword by its sheath, raising it high before the torchlight with both hands.

"No," he said. "Perhaps Danforth Stannis should not peddle you off to some street vendor for your material value, when there is a chance so much more could be purchased. Perhaps Pitchford Wicker should emerge from the Narrows, the last survivor of a party of brave souls who endeavored to smite the mighty zoth chieftain known as the Crowlord of Krillian's Cut. Perhaps Pitchford Wicker, loyal servant to the leader of this intrepid band, should return to Fal Daran with his liege lord's weapon, the famed Battle Hymn, speaking of the acts of faith and nobility and self-sacrifice which occurred on the Dead Man's Bridge; how his liege lord and his compatriots fell one by one before the Crowlord, and how he, Pitch, was helpless to stop it, but did his duty in returning to tell the tale, bearing his master's most precious possession as proof of what occurred. He could present the blade known as Battle Hymn to the Court of the First Guardian in Fal Daran, and beg the king's favor. Perhaps House Wicker might be restored to her former prominence, and lordship bestowed upon her sole surviving son. Yes!"

He dropped to one knee, splashing in the water, holding the sword forth in both hands. He touched the golden hilt to his forehead, then presented it to the portcullis in a gesture of fealty, as if the portcullis was his king.

"Great and noble King Britou, First Guardian of Embriss, Lord of the Western Kingdoms," he said. "All that is House Wicker is now yours, by the oath of fealty I speak—"

His words died as his eyes widened. It was as if he was struck by the grandest of notions, as if this new idea might improve his situation even further. He lowered the sword back to eye level, staring at it enthusiastically.

"What process was employed in the forging of your blade, my sweet angel, my Battle Hymn?" he asked, running his gaze over the angel's face. "If your scabbard contains a blade of common iron, no different than any other sword, then Pitchford Wicker could trade you for a lordship. But if that scabbard contains something else, something of considerably more value, such as a blade of shadowsteel ... well then ... Pitchford Wicker could trade you for a kingdom."

He took the hilt in hand, curling his dirty fingers around the body of the angel, and jerked the blade free of its sheath, holding it high, his eyes alight with joy and anticipation.

He never remembered whether he was able to see the blade, if he confirmed whether it was forged of shadowsteel or not. He never remembered anything of this moment, because when he pulled the sword from its scabbard, the strangest thing happened.

The angel opened her eyes.

Chapter 56

At the edge of the building, another ladder reached up through the hole in the bridge deck, rising up through the gridwork, from beam to beam, all the way to the top of the bridge. If Theel intended to save the Overlie children, this is where he needed to go. The area was crawling with zoths, all of whom would be eager to stop him, but Theel welcomed that fight. He was prepared to die.

"Come to me, Crowlord!" he shouted again, pulling himself up the ladder.

The ascent wasn't any easier than it was before, with only one arm, fighting fatigue and the canyon winds, but no zoths attacked him, and he made steady progress.

"Kill me, Crowlord!" he shouted repeatedly. "Kill me!"

But the zoth chieftain was nowhere to be seen. So Theel continued his taunts, and continued climbing. He made his way up through the hole in the bridge deck, then another fifty feet up into the gridwork above the bridge, where he found a walkway. This walkway led to another ladder, which continued upward toward the children.

He stumbled across the steel grating and was about to climb the next ladder when he saw the crows circling him. Up here above the bridge deck, there were hundreds of them, still flying together in a huge ring. And now, Theel was in the middle of that ring. Here they came, about to attack him again, to pummel his body as they did before. He braced himself for the onslaught and closed his eyes tightly, listening to their screams, thousands of voices calling out for his blood. And then the birds fell silent. Confused, Theel opened his eyes ...

And saw the Crowlord, up above him, among the beams. There was something flying through the air between them, toward Theel, spinning end over end. It was one of the Crowlord's blackened bone spikes, and it struck Theel in the chest so hard he heard his own bones crackle, even through his armor.

And he was falling. It seemed like he tumbled and spun hundreds of feet, the world spinning in all directions. He waited for the stone bridge deck to catch him, to stop his fall by crushing him like a fly being swatted. But instead, it was the steel grating of the walkway which slammed against his chest. He was still high above the bridge, face down on the walkway, his cheek pressed against the cold steel grating. He tried to rise, tried to draw a breath, but accomplished neither. Then the circling crows ceased their wait.

All at once, the quiet was split open by the shrieking of a thousand voices, and the ring of crows collapsed upon him. It was an unstoppable avalanche of avian hatred, and it slammed him down, crushing him against the floor of the walkway, pinning him there as crow after crow killed itself against his back. It seemed to go on for minutes; hundreds of snapping beaks falling upon him like spears from the sky. If it wasn't for his armor, they would have torn him to shreds, and as it was, his back felt like he was being punched a thousand times. Just when it seemed like this would go on forever, it stopped.

He couldn't wait. *The children.* He had to reach the children. He tried again to push himself up, succeeded only in rolling over onto his back. This motion reminded him of the wound in his chest. His bones crunched, stole his breath, and filled him with a pain so crushing, so overwhelming, that it washed away all thoughts but the desire to end the agony. But there was no way to end it. There was no way to breathe, or gasp, or cough. Every attempt died in his throat. All he could do was open and close his mouth impotently, his fingers twitching, as if all effort was beyond his reach.

He watched as the Crowlord fell from his perch, landing effortlessly on the walkway only yards away. The broken-faced monster still held one of his bone spikes, and Theel could see the blood glistening, saw the spike drip red. He couldn't say anything. He could only mouth the words:

"Kill me, Crowlord."

But the chieftain didn't move. He only stared at Theel with his dead eyes and his mangled half-grin.

Then the crows struck again, this time against Theel's chest and face. He was able to raise his right arm enough to cover his eyes, but it was the only defense he could muster as the birds stabbed and pecked at every bit of exposed flesh. They tore at his ears and scalp, his nose and lips. All the while, he could feel more of the birds hitting his chest and stomach, pounding bile into his throat, nearly causing him to retch. He could feel his chest wound, the one suffered in the Trader's Cave torn open, pouring blood as if it hadn't healed at all.

When the crows relented, Theel was little more than a heap of quivering flesh. Again he tried to rise, but again, his body failed him. He still couldn't find his breath. He felt as if he was drowning on air. He lifted his head briefly before it plunked back against the steel, and this effort took all the energy he had left.

All he wanted to do was stand. He did not have the strength to fight back, but he just wanted to stand. He couldn't bear the thought of dying on his back. Perhaps he could call on the Life Sign once again. Perhaps the Life Sign would give him just enough strength to rise and meet his end appropriately. There was the possibility he might drain his juy so severely that he killed himself. But if he did, it would still be the action of a man who wished to stand and fight. He would die trying to stand, fighting to do his duty. All he needed to do was stand.

And die.

He would find this end satisfactory. The Crowlord would cut him down, but Theel would die like a man, standing up, facing, and accepting, the justice he deserved. He may accomplish nothing on this bridge other than that; failing to save the children, failing to avenge his father.

If he died in vain, it was what he deserved, because he'd lived his life in vain. He'd made a practice of forsaking those who loved him, who believed in him. He'd cursed and denied the prophecy, the knighthood and their religion, his father, his brother, his uncle, and the Blessed Soul. Now, on this bridge, he tried to reverse what he'd done, but his efforts were meaningless, nothing more than filthy rags. God had forsaken him.

No. He had forsaken God.

No longer. Now was the time to appeal to his maker, to beg God to smile on him, just this once, and bless his efforts, just this once. Perhaps God would allow him to stand. Perhaps God would even allow him to fight. Maybe he could lash out at the Crowlord and draw blood, just once, before he was struck down in defeat. It was all he wanted, to stand and fight.

The Crowlord wore the armor of Wind Magic, woven by the fingers of his shaman. The chieftain's armor could not be cracked until these runes of protection were dispelled. Therefore, the shaman must die. Until that happened, the Crowlord remained unstoppable. This was a fact Theel had learned on his last visit to the Dead Man's Bridge, when he watched his father die.

Perhaps God would give him this if he asked for it. Perhaps God would forget all his past indiscretions, his lies, his curses, his blasphemies, and allow Yatham to defeat the shaman, and break his magical connection to the Crowlord. Theel knew this would not save his life. He was going to die even if the Crowlord became vulnerable. But at least then, he could fight. At least then, he might draw blood, and die like a man. His only hope was that Yatham was at that very moment riding the big, gray horse toward the far end of the bridge, riding toward the zoth shaman.

It all depended on Yatham.

Chapter 57

Yatham knew the gelding that carried him across the Dead Man's Bridge was previously the mount of a very wealthy and prominent knight, and not just because he wore the colors of the Southern Cross. Only the resources of the richest noblemen, or even the king, could produce an animal such as this.

Yatham had ridden hundreds of horses. He understood and respected them, from the lowliest flea-bitten plow horse, to the most magnificent thoroughbred found in the king's stables. This creature was special by any measure—not just powerful and fast, but also disciplined, likely trained by the finest horse masters of the Western Kingdoms. He took direction from his rider as if the two shared a mind. Yatham held the reins, but had no need of them, controlling the animal entirely with his knees and voice. This animal had never felt a spur in his life.

He recognized zoths as his enemy, barreling them over, crushing them with his hoofs. And he recognized humans as his allies, taking care not to touch them, to stay clear, even if that human no longer lived.

This is how Yatham reached the southern end of the Dead Man's Bridge, holding on while his mount did all the work. He was a battering ram of gray horseflesh crashing through the zoth army as if they were nothing more than a field of tall grass. It wasn't a direct path they took; they had to weave back and forth to avoid the wreckage of overturned wagons, jumping the corpses of humans and animals. And stomping zoth warriors to death.

Spears flew at them, from the surface of the bridge, and from the gridwork above, but most of the attacks weren't even close, as if the zoths couldn't compensate for the horse's incredible speed.

Then the crows came, an enormous, screeching black cloud, forming the shape of a spear, then slamming into both horse and rider. But the gelding just ran faster, as if trying to find the other side of the storm. It worked—the storm broke, and the horse burst through in a poof of black feathers. Waiting on the other side were more zoth warriors, a giant bonfire, and the zoth shaman.

There was no mistaking the shaman, with his religious facial markings, the strips of human skin hanging from his arms, and the shriveled face of a long-dead zoth that he wore mounted atop his head like a crown.

He stood above his followers like a priest at the front of his church, his pulpit the wooden box of an upturned freight wagon. Surrounding the wagon was a ring of several wooden posts. And lashed to these posts were the shaman's human victims. Many of them were dead, but at least one remained alive. Still clad in the diamonds and oak leaves of House Overlie, Yatham guessed he was one of the men who had imprisoned Pitch in his cage. Though the zoths had kept him alive, he seemed to wish they hadn't. He was screaming in agony, covered with wounds, and begging for death.

Yatham never saw this before, but heard descriptions from his father. That man bore all the wounds inflicted on some other creature that was being protected by the shaman's power. The Crowlord perhaps, or one of his zoth warriors. Whatever damage was inflicted on the zoth would be transferred to this human. If the zoth suffered a mortal wound, the zoth would live on, but this man would die.

This was the spot on the bridge where the stench of evil was most overpowering. Yatham had ridden onto ground sacred to the Blood Goddess, and he immediately felt the urge to retch. The distressed whinny of his mount told him the gelding felt the same. But the horse did not slow its charge.

The shaman was surrounded by zoth warriors and drummers, and they rushed to protect their leader. Yatham lowered his weapon and rode through them, spearing them, trampling them, scattering them. He didn't have to order his mount to hit the shaman. The gelding recognized his enemy and charged.

Yatham directed the moon blade toward the target, as he had a thousand times in years of horse training. The shaman was so engrossed in his chanting that he didn't even react to Yatham's charge, presenting an unmoving target, ripe to be killed. It was almost too easy.

Yatham lanced the shaman directly in the head with all the force of the gelding's powerful legs, and it felt like he had speared a mountain. The gingo wood bent into the shape of a horse shoe, and Yatham was thrown from the saddle. The bridge deck spun above him, then below him. Then he smashed onto the road surface, rolling with the speed of his momentum.

Once he came to a stop, he rose to his feet as quickly as he could, only slightly fazed. It was a painful tumble, but it wasn't the first time he'd been unhorsed, and it would not be the last. Somehow, he managed to keep his grip on the spear, which was good, because he would need it. A handful of zoth warriors had survived his charge and they now moved to attack him.

His options were disappearing. He was unhorsed and alone, with spear tips all around. The zoth shaman, protected by some magical, impenetrable barrier, was beyond the reach of Yatham's moon blade. And knowing this, the creature began to weave more Craft, summoning Wing Magic and Flame Bringers.

The shaman had no reason to fear. He was enfolded in the protection of his Blood Goddess, surrounded by the symbols of his sacrifice, men both living and dead. The Overlie man hung in the air above him, gasping and weeping, his body a crushed, bloody mess.

"Please, God!" he groaned, blood flowing from his mouth. "Kill me."

But God didn't answer his plea, and neither would the zoths. The shaman needed him alive for the ritual, and he would not die until they were finished with him.

They needed him alive.

The pieces of the puzzle began to assemble in Yatham's mind. The zoths needed fresh human victims for the shaman to work his sorcery. It was why the zoths of the Dead Man's Bridge did not instantly try to kill as so many others did. This was why travelers in the Narrows vanished without a trace, why citizens of Widow Hatch and Wrendale were kidnapped in the dead of night. It was why the Crowlord took the Overlie man without killing him, and it was probably why the children hadn't yet been harmed.

It was all so the zoth shaman could sacrifice them to the Blood Goddess. Each sacrifice strengthened the Crowlord. Each drop of blood spilt hardened the steel of his bone spikes. It was why a single zoth tribe was able to conquer the Narrows, and it was why the tunnels would inevitably fail to contain their ambitions. It was only a matter of time before the Crowlord's army burst forth from the tunnels to attack the cities and villages of southern Embriss. And with the Overlies and Alisters battling the Iatan, there would be no one to stop them.

Yatham held his spear high, ready to throw, as the zoths tightened their circle around him. He watched as the zoth shaman traced the runes, the intricate hand dance that resembled a man playing an invisible harp. Each finger movement left markings upon the air, carved into the fabric of existence, glowing and throbbing in the reds and yellows of Flame Bringers and Wind Magic. At any moment the runes would be complete, and the shaman would unleash some dark sorcery. There was no way to stop him from finishing the spell, no way to interrupt those hand gestures. The shaman's body was armored in Craft, the beneficiary of the sufferings of the humans hanging from chains all around. There was only one left—the Overlie man. Yatham looked up at him, the shaman's last living victim, and saw the agony in his eyes, and the delirium.

"Let me die," the man mumbled through bloodied lips. "Please, Lord."

Yatham felt pity.

"I'm sorry," he whispered, then threw his spear.

The moon blade flew above the ring of zoths, above the bonfire, and above the shaman's head. It struck the Overlie man in the chest, killing him instantly.

Chapter 58

"Kill me, Crowlord."

Theel's left eye was completely blinded, but he could still see quite clearly with his right. And what he saw was the Crowlord, now walking toward him. The chieftain was doing just as Theel asked. He was coming to kill him.

This was the moment Theel welcomed, and yet had dreaded for months, ever since the day his father died on this bridge. He knew he would come back to this place, and would likely die when he did. It was only right. Now the time had come, but it wasn't exactly what he had envisioned. He wanted to stand up, to rise and face the Crowlord and die like a man, but his body couldn't do it, no matter how much his mind screamed. It hurt his heart to know he was going to die helpless, lying on the ground, an impotent, beaten wretch. All his life, he'd never done anything on his feet. And now, he couldn't even die on his feet.

The Crowlord stood over him, staring down at him with those black, pupiless eyes, completely devoid of expression. To look into those eyes was to look into nothingness, to realize that the Crowlord was not a living being with cares or wants. He was merely a soulless tool of murder in the hands of the Blood Goddess. No matter how his victims met their end, whether begging and pleading, or silent and stoic, the Crowlord showed them the same thing. Empty black eyes, then bone spikes. Hundreds of humans had seen this, two Knights of the Southern Cross, and Theel's father.

And now it was Theel's turn.

As the Crowlord hovered, his head blocked out the sun, a dark silhouette of wind-blown crow feathers. The zoth chieftain didn't immediately strike. Instead, he held his weapon so the spike pointed down at his victim's head, allowing the blood to drip on Theel's face.

Theel grimaced and spit, unable to avoid the drops as they ran over his lips and splattered in his eye. He wanted to scream but could not, wanted to lash out, but could not. He didn't have any weapons left. His sword was swallowed by the canyon, and he had no idea where his father's knife was. Where was his other sword, the one called Battle Hymn? Had he left it in the sewer beneath the Narrows? It didn't matter.

He may not have any weapons of his own, but there was still hope. He knew the Crowlord's other bone spike, the one he'd thrown, was near. If Theel could reach it, he might use the chieftain's own weapon against him ...

Perhaps Yatham had succeeded in killing the zoth shaman. Perhaps the Crowlord was vulnerable. And if Theel could reach that bone spike, he might plant it in the chieftain's heel, might buy himself some more time. Time to live. Time to fight back.

He tried to gather every last precious drop of strength he had left, tried to channel it into his right hand, to reach out for that bone spike, to grasp at this last, final hope.

The Crowlord knelt, placing his knee on Theel's chest. The pain of this almost killed him. His mouth opened to scream, but no breath would come. Tears streamed down his face as his ribs cracked under the zoth's weight. Unconsciousness reached out for him, but he fought it off, still grasping for the bone spike. His eyes popped and his jaw clenched painfully tight, but even this agony didn't stop his hand from searching. Just as his hand reached out, his mind reached out, and suddenly the words to the Knight's Creed came to him.

Give this child strength.
That he might raise your banner.
Cleanse this child's wounds.
That he might carry your shield.

It was almost as if he could hear them, the words whispered in his ear, spoken in his father's voice. If he would die, he would die saying the words to the Knight's Creed. His lips could not speak the words, so instead he prayed them.

I, as a son of the Silvermarsh Clans, do commit myself, body, soul, and spirit, to the earthly warriors of the Southern Cross, to the Seven Kingdoms they protect, and to the one true Lord of all Creation ...

Theel felt the power of the Life Sign ignite within him, but only barely. It usually blazed like an inferno, but now was merely a candle flame, sputtering and threatening to die under the slightest puff of air.

The Life Sign could not heal him, or even provide enough strength to stand. There was simply not enough juy within him to do either. All the Life Sign could do was take what final drops of life he retained, steal it from his body, and take him away into death. But he welcomed this, and continued saying the words, clinging to them. The words of the Knight's Creed gave him the strength the Life Sign could not—the strength to die.

Theel reached out to his Lord, waiting to die, waiting for God to take his hand.

The Crowlord held Theel by the throat and raised his weapon to strike. He twisted Theel's head to the side, holding the spike reversed to attack with the blunt end. Theel knew what this meant. The Crowlord did not intend to kill him, but to knock him unconscious. The Crowlord wanted him alive. But Theel decided he would not be taken alive. He continued to recite the Knight's Creed in his mind, continued to feel the Life Sign drain his life away, and continued to hold his hand out.

Theel reached out to his maker, but God didn't take his hand.

Up above, among the steel beams of the bridge, a crossbow released its bolt. Theel never heard the twang of the bowstring, but he heard the sound of the quarrel thudding into the Crowlord's face, striking him on the bridge of the nose.

The chieftain's head recoiled, but otherwise the attack had no effect. He roared in anger, looking up, searching for his attacker. Theel followed his gaze, and saw the silhouette of a man, crouching on a beam above, a crossbow in his hand. Theel had seen that crossbow before, on the back of a pack horse in the Narrows, but he couldn't see the face of the one who held it.

Then the man rose to his full height, and Theel immediately recognized that tall and lanky body. It belonged to a certain displaced nobleman of Aramorun whose primary talent was the singing of songs. But this man was also known to earn some coin by staging exhibitions of crossbow trick-shooting. Lord Pitchford Wicker had sworn that he was a perfect shot with a crossbow. Now, he'd proven it.

"Liege!" the song man shouted. "Your weapon!"

Theel could see that Pitch held a sword by its sheath. He turned it upside down, allowing the blade to slip free. The weapon fell, hilt-first, sunlight flashing off something golden. Theel still held his arm raised, reaching out for God in a silent plea. But God did not answer as Theel had hoped. Instead, he answered with a sword.

The weapon fell into his hand.

The moment his fingers curled around the handle of the sword, Theel felt the Life Sign explode with power. It was so sudden and so overwhelming that Theel was briefly blinded, as if the healing magic filled him so full that it burst from his eyes. This was far more juy than was ever released by the magical tattoo before, more than he ever thought he had inside him. There was no relaxation, and no euphoria. It did not fill him with a gentle flow of healing fire. Instead, it struck him in the head with a lightning bolt so forcefully that his entire body recoiled.

At first he thought he was falling, because everything faded away. The sunlight and the crows, the zoths and the beams of the Dead Man's Bridge, all faded away so rapidly that he was sure the Crowlord had thrown him into the canyon. But there was no terror at this thought, no sense of falling or loss of control. Instead, he was held safely, supported by strong arms.

Theel knew instantly whose arms those were. His father was with him—he had never left him. He would never stop being

Theel's father. He still yearned to provide for his son's needs, even in death.

"Keep your grip, son. You will not fall."

Theel hung from the rope, reached for the next knot, and pulled himself up. But it seemed to take all the strength he had left.

"One more. You have the strength."

But Theel wasn't sure he had the strength.

"One more. You can do it."

He reached up, seized the next knot, and pulled. And with exhausted arms shaking, he pulled himself up. He'd done it.

"That's good. Now, one more. You can do it."

But he couldn't do it. He hung from the rope, trying to gather his strength, finding none to gather.

"One more. You have the strength."

Theel reached up. And pulled. He pulled until he thought his arms would fall off. And he did it. He was now only one knot from the top.

"One more."

Impossible. He had no strength left.

"You don't know your own strength."

Untrue. Theel did know his own strength. He knew how it would fail him.

"You will not fail. You will not fall."

But Theel knew he would fall.

"I believe in you, son. You will do this. You have the strength. Believe in yourself."

He pulled. His entire body shook with the strain. Almost there. Only inches away.

"You are my son. I believe in you."

Theel felt his father's arms around him, lifting him up, holding him tightly.

"I will not let you fall."

Almost there. His father's arms gave him support. But it was also an embrace. And the two prayed together, not as masterknight and squire, as they had so many times in the past. Now they prayed as father and son, finishing the task together with a recitation of the Knight's Creed.

... that I might do his will, to love God's children, to lead God's children, to protect God's children, and that by these deeds, the Lord's blessings be given.

Theel felt his father's breath tickling his neck as he whispered the words, as he lifted him up, supporting his weight.

I will care for God's children, by showing his love. I will guide God's children, by speaking his word. I will protect God's children, by wielding his judgment ...

Theel did it. He reached the top. With the strength of his arms, the strength of his heart, and the strength of his father's faith and love.

"I'm proud of you, son. I love you."

The words of the Knight's Creed, the words of the Life Sign, spoken together, by father and son.

The words burned brighter than they ever had before. They unleashed a torrent of raw mystic will. Previously, Theel's psychic nexus was cold and dark and empty, like a corpse—just like he was, bereft of hope, empty of life. But now, he felt as if he suddenly had a bottomless well of healing juy, as if the sun was exploding inside of him. The connection to his psychic nexus was complete. The door was open, the dam had broken, and through the breach flowed a river, an ocean, of mystic will, channeled by the Life Sign into healing energy.

... with his mercy, I will care ...

It all started when a sword dropped as if from heaven. Theel looked at the weapon he held in his right hand, saw its golden hilt fashioned in the shape of an angel with spread wings. The angel's eyes were closed, her mouth open, singing the Battle Hymn.

... with his compassion, I will give ...

The shadowsteel of Battle Hymn's blade seemed to hum, and he could feel a power emanating from it, as if it connected him to his roots, and gave him the strength of his homeland. And his homeland gave him the strength to heal. It gave him the power that fueled the Life Sign. This was his father's sword. It was his birthright. And it was his connection to his identity.

... with his wisdom, I will speak ...

The Crowlord, seeing this would no longer be an easy victory, flipped his weapon over, no longer wishing to wound or incapacitate. Now he wanted to kill, and he swung his bone spike with all his might. As the attack fell toward Theel's head, it carried all the power of the Crowlord's hatred, all the power of his shaman's sorcery, all the power of the Blood Goddess' rage.

The bone spike crackled with Craft as it descended. It was enough power to spray Theel's brains all over Krillian's Cut. It was enough to blast a hole in the surface of the Dead Man's Bridge. But it wasn't Theel's head that absorbed the power of the attack, nor was it the bridge. It was a blade of shadowsteel.

... with his word, I will guide ...

Theel couldn't be certain whether he blocked the Crowlord's attack or if it was Battle Hymn. Shadowsteel met bone with a thunderclap that shook the bridge, and both refused to yield. The human and the zoth were locked together with their weapons crossed, the air sizzling and smoking between them. In that moment Theel saw Battle Hymn, saw the angel's face and how it changed. All his life, her eyes were closed and her mouth open in song. But now she no longer sang. Now her eyes were wide open, bright, milky white, and pupiless, like two pearls. And her mouth was twisted in a snarl.

Then everything changed. In the time it took to draw a single breath, Theel's body was healed. In what could only be described as a miracle, he was bathed in the light of God's mercy, his flesh cleansed and made pure once again. Years later, when trying to describe this experience, all he could say was that God told him to heal, and he was healed. Then God told him to stand, and he stood. Then God told him to fight.

Theel's chest healed itself so suddenly and forcefully that the Crowlord was thrown off, flying through the air as if launched by a catapult. And in the same motion, Theel sprang to his feet, the sword in his hand singing one long, deafening note. Up to that point, hundreds of crows had filled the air, flying around him in a great ring. But now the song of Battle Hymn shattered that ring and the crows scattered, abandoning their lord.

Nearby, the chieftain climbed to his feet. Now he stood, staring at Theel with the same emotionless expression he always wore, those empty black eyes, that broken half-grin. Unlike his servants, the Crowlord refused to run. He raised one bone spike defensively, while gesturing with his empty hand to the other. It lay on the walkway between them, then leaped into the air, flying into the zoth chieftain's hand.

... with his shield, I will protect ...

Theel looked at his left hand and saw his father's knife. It had remained with him throughout this fight, locked in those deadened fingers that refused to let go. Now it would be a fair fight. Both warriors were armed, prepared for battle, and prepared for death.

... with his sword, I will defend ...

"Here I am, Crowlord," Theel said. "Come and kill me."

The zoth roared. Then the human roared. They charged at one another, steel flashing.

...and with his wrath, I will make war ...

Chapter 59

"Let me die," the man hanging from chains mumbled through bloodied lips. "Please, God."

Beneath the man, the zoth shaman worked feverishly, weaving battle runes with the tips of his fingers. The runes were nearly complete—Wind Magic and Flame Bringers, enough to transform Yatham into a heap of ash in an instant.

"I'm sorry," Yatham whispered, and threw his spear.

It struck the Overlie man in the chest, delivering the final death stroke he so desperately wanted. And in that instant, the shaman recoiled identically, as if he'd suffered the same blow. The moonblade pierced the human, but it was the zoth who bled. The human was killed, but it was the zoth who screamed, then staggered.

The shaman attempted to finish his spell, but his finger gestures lost all precision, now gashing the air with random lines of flame and wind that no longer obeyed his command. The half-finished Craft runes spiraled away from the zoth's fingers, exploding with random, unintended results. Beams of yellow light burst from the shaman's mouth as he screamed, then from his eyes and nose, and finally his ears, as if there was a tiny sun inside his skull. Showers of sparks sprayed off his body as if he was a sharpening wheel honing invisible tools. Then he began to spin like one, as he lost his balance and tumbled off the wagon.

Yatham winced as the sparks fell all around him like raindrops, as he watched the zoth holy man convulsing on the ground, his body smoking like a pile of burning leaves. Yatham wasn't sure what had happened, only knew the death of the Overlie man somehow crippled his enemy. The zoth was down, was wounded, and was vulnerable.

Yatham's hands were empty, but he was still capable. His father had taught him many ways to kill a zoth, and every one was currently on his mind. He would do whatever it took. He would strangle that shaman if need be. But plenty of zoth warriors still blocked his path; warriors who were now advancing to attack him. Yatham would have to fight through them, but was prepared to do so. There was only a handful. He would attack a hundred zoths if necessary. He needed to kill that shaman to aid his brother.

The zoths tightened their circle around him, moving in for the kill. They were glaring with their beady black eyes, menacing with a half-dozen spear tips. Yatham was about to rush them when he noticed an eerie quiet had enveloped the bridge. For the first time since he came there, the crows were silent, as if something stole their voices. Or as if the entire flock had scattered. He wondered if this was true, and wondered what it meant. But he dared not look up. He could not take his eyes off his enemies.

An explosion from above popped Yatham's ears, rocked the bridge, and knocked him off his feet. For a few moments, he lay on the stone bridge deck, disoriented and deafened, his body buffeted by fierce winds. He was so confused and unable to focus his senses that he wondered if someone had struck him in the head from behind. But then he saw the zoths on the ground nearby, crumpled, and in pain. They suffered similarly, wincing, and covering their ears.

What had caused this? Yatham couldn't be certain of anything. His head was swimming. He felt like he'd been kicked by a mule. Perhaps this was all a hallucination. That would explain the light he saw high above him, near the top of the bridge. A beautiful, golden light.

It was too high above, too far away for Yatham to determine its source, but the light was moving steadily up the bridge, higher and higher, as if traveling through the steel gridwork toward the top. All around this golden light, zoth warriors crawled across beams, swarming, their backs bristling with spears. They crowded in, converging on the light like moths to a flame. And then it began to rain.

It rained black zoth blood and gray zoth bodies. Everywhere the golden light flashed, zoths tumbled from the steel beams, a waterfall of screaming, gray flesh crashing into the bridge deck or falling into the canyon. But that didn't stop more zoths from crowding in, attacking the golden light, and falling to their deaths as well. In fact, the warriors laying near Yatham seemed to answer some unheard call, jumping to their feet as soon as they recovered their senses. They grabbed their weapons, and climbed up into the steel gridwork to join the battle.

Yatham could make no sense of this. He was struggling to puzzle it out as his hearing slowly returned. All he could hear was a ringing in his ears, one long bell tone so loud it overpowered all other sound. But the ringing slowly changed from a thin sound to something much fuller. It made no sense, but Yatham was certain now that it was a woman's voice. It was singing, and yet it maintained only a single note. One long, deafening note.

Yatham listened to this note as he watched the flashing golden light. It was beautiful to behold. It reminded him of his father demonstrating sword forms, how the knight's body moved with the grace of a dancer, his practice sword cutting the air not as an instrument in his hand, but as an extension of his body. It was a part of him. Seamless. Perfect.

In fact, the movements of the golden light seemed to mimic his father's sword forms, moving just as his blade once did. It appeared as if someone trained in the same fighting style as his father now practiced sword forms at the top of the bridge. But instead of a blade, this person held a beam of sunlight in their hand.

It was truly like a vision, something that simply could not be real. Yatham's eyes saw the light. And his ears heard the song. But his mind simply couldn't comprehend it. Finally, it was his heart that told him what was happening. It was his heart that believed.

Theel was still alive, and was atop the Dead Man's Bridge. For the first time in his life, he wielded the sword called Battle Hymn. And as Yatham looked on, he was fighting an army of zoths by himself.

And the most amazing thing was that Theel looked just like his father.

Chapter 60

Theel felt a calmness he'd never known before. All his life he'd felt alone, out of place, unwanted, unloved, and unworthy. Unworthy of all the expectations his father had, the Keeper had, and the knighthood had for him. He couldn't be what they wanted. He wasn't what they wanted. The pain of their dissatisfaction was constant. And as a result, he resented them, and hated them for wanting him to be something he was not.

Nothing was different at this moment. He hadn't changed. Nor had anyone's expectations of him changed. And yet, he was full of calm. And strangest of all, he was calm while doing the two things that always filled him with the most anxiety.

He was expected to be a master swordsman because of the training by his father. He was expected to learn the Method because of his training by the Keeper of the Craft. He had been an utter failure at both bladework and the Method, and therefore hated both, undergoing the training only because he was forced to.

But now he was calm while doing both. And capable while doing both. Perhaps because he stopped trying to be what his father wanted; because he stopped trying to resist what his father wanted. It seemed he finally just understood what he, himself wanted, who he was, and who he wanted to be.

The moment Battle Hymn fell into his hand, he finally felt a secure connection to who he was. And so he was calm, capable, relaxed, and fulfilled. He was happy with himself. And he knew his father was happy with who he was.

He could feel his masterknight with him, standing behind him just as he had all those years, helping him practice his sword forms. He could feel his father's hand on his wrist, directing his movements, the voice in his ear, explaining the importance of stance, and of footwork. Bend that elbow. Point that toe.

The calmness he felt, the inner peace that was always so elusive but now filled him up, was the perfect state of mind for plying the Method. And his juy flowed through him, his psychic nexus tapped by the Life Sign was now open and flowing. It was more juy than he'd ever released before, and it flowed freely. It should have been too much to control. It should have boiled his brain to unconsciousness, and drenched his dreams with unwanted torments. But he controlled it just as easily as he controlled his own body. He told his arms to move and they complied. He told his juy to act and it did.

Before he called on the Life Sign, he felt dead, and nearly was, beaten to a bloody mess by the Crowlord. But it wasn't just his body that was beaten down and crushed. It was also his spirit. When he recited the Knight's Creed, when he called on his creator, he knew his plea was not ignored. A gift was given to him, and it wasn't just a sword. He was given new life. His body was healed, filled with vitality. And so was his soul. His spirit was rekindled.

And now he finally understood something his father had told him so many times before. The greatest Knights of the Silvermarsh were no better than any other men, he said, because the moment a knight's heart is most filled with righteousness is often the same moment he is committing the most terrible deeds.

Theel never felt more secure in his actions as he did that day on the Dead Man's Bridge. The doubts that plagued him all of his life disappeared. He was confident in himself, confident in what he was doing. Just like a knight, his heart was full of righteousness. And just like a knight, he was committing the most terrible deeds.

The top structure of the bridge was swarming with zoths. They came at him from every direction—in front, behind, above, and below—attacking him face to face, launching spears from afar, or just throwing themselves at him in a desperate attempt to knock him into the canyon.

Theel knew they felt threatened. He knew the Crowlord and his warriors feared him. He knew this because of the respect they now showed, and the desperation with which they fought. This was the same fear and respect they had showed his father, the vaunted Knight of the Southern Cross, who'd never fallen in battle, who was stabbed through the heart and lived. The zoths feared Theel just as much as they feared his father. And Theel knew this was for good reason.

His heart was full of more than righteousness. It was full of juy. It filled his heart and lungs, muscles and bones. Even his armor. Even his sword. He and Battle Hymn were one—not a man and his weapon, but the physical manifestation of the juy that flowed from his psychic nexus. His legs did not run or walk. His juy did. His heart didn't beat and his lungs didn't breath. His juy did. His hand didn't hold Battle Hymn. And the sword didn't swipe and slash. It was all his juy that controlled and propelled every movement.

It was his juy that fought the zoths on the Dead Man's Bridge. It was his juy that fended off their ceaseless attacks, using shadowsteel to parry spear thrusts, knuckles to bash noses in, boot heels to crush knee caps. Juy filled his left hand and his father's knife, now turned backwards in a fighting style his masterknight had perfected, a style Theel struggled to learn, but now implemented with precision. And it was his juy that sang the hymn of battle through the mouth of a golden angel, her eyes wide and wings spread as she cut her enemies to pieces, painting the bridge with a storm of black zoth blood.

Theel's juy might have been strong enough to defeat every one of his enemies on that bridge. But it wasn't strong enough to defeat the Crowlord. He knew this because he could feel a power to match his own emanating from the chieftain's body. It was a raw power, magic or mystic will. Perhaps it was the protection of the shaman. Perhaps it was simple pure rage and hatred, the physical manifestation of the Blood Goddess' vitriol. Perhaps it was all of these things.

But whatever it was, Theel could sense it. He could also feel it every time their weapons clashed between them. Theel was executing the best fight of his life, an effort his father would have admired. He was putting on an exhibition of skill that would have impressed the most accomplished Knight of the Southern Cross. And he was doing so with each movement powered by the full strength of his juy, Battle Hymn's shadowsteel should have crushed the zoth's bone spikes, should have sliced the chieftain in half. But instead, the Crowlord's defense was just as stout as before. It felt as if Theel was pounding his weapons against a stone wall.

The Crowlord could not be unbalanced. The opposable toes of his feet gripping the steel beams provided a sureness of footing no human would ever enjoy. But Theel's balance was guided by his juy, a mystical hand that caught him when he fell, directing him when he faltered.

The two combatants leaped from beam to beam, covering impossible distances, the human chasing the zoth, the zoth chasing the human. Their weapons clashed between them. The bone spikes crackled and Battle Hymn sang, sparks and lightning and flame erupting between them. But there was no advantage to be found. Neither warrior could win, and neither warrior would relent. There was no end in sight.

The sun didn't suddenly move across the sky, but it felt as if they'd been fighting all day. The Crowlord's entire tribe seemed to be trying to intervene in order to break the stalemate. They attacked during every moment of lull, swarming at Theel each time he and their chieftain separated. But they were powerless against Battle Hymn, and were brushed aside like gnats.

Even the crows returned, a black, snaking line of them dropping down from the sky like a dark feathery tornado. But it wouldn't be as it was before. Theel now joined in the battle hymn, he and his weapon singing as one. The notes that came from the golden angel's mouth now exploded from Theel's lungs in a burst of juy that rose like a column to meet the point of the descending tornado. They met like two battering rams, fighting for dominance of the sky, and the line of crows exploded into a cloud of bloody feathers as wide as the bridge was long. Some of the birds were thrown clear, recovered, and simply flew away, but most of them were killed, and followed the rest of the Crowlord's slaves to the bottom of the Cut.

Theel was momentarily vulnerable as this happened. It was a perfect moment for the zoth chieftain to seize the advantage, but he didn't even try. Instead, he retreated further up the beams, closer to the top of the bridge. And Theel realized this was what the zoth had been doing all along, attempting to take this battle higher and higher. And suddenly, Theel understood why.

It was clear there was no advantage to be found in this clash of arms, of matching weapons in a contest of physical strength and speed. So the Crowlord was looking for an advantage in other ways. Finding no weakness in Theel's physical defenses, he would probe for weakness in Theel's emotional defenses. He wanted to fight at the top of the bridge, the place from which the cages were suspended. The Overlie children remained trapped in one of these, and it would take little effort for the Crowlord to break the chain that suspended their cage and let them fall.

Theel now realized the reason for the attack by the crows. It appeared to be a futile gesture, as did the attacks of the zoths that continued to converge on him. But now Theel could see they had a purpose. They were distractions that allowed the Crowlord to disengage and bait him, and pull him further up the bridge. The zoth chieftain wanted to force him to try to protect that chain, to force him to fight for the Overlie children. So far it had worked, and Theel knew it would continue to work. He had no doubt the Crowlord would kill those children if necessary. He'd killed half his own warriors already. He would not spare two human children. And so, Theel must follow. He'd come all this way to protect those children.

But there was more. This was also the place where Theel's father had died, at the very top of the bridge. It was where the

Crowlord bested the famous Knight of the Southern Cross, slaying the man who could not be slain. This was the spot where Theel's world was shattered, where he was dealt a wound far worse than the one that took his father's life. It was a wound that would never heal. And worse, it was self-inflicted, dealt by his own acts of incompetence and cowardice.

His father had fought for him that day. He did not return the favor. The Crowlord went into battle with the support of his shaman. But Theel's father had no support from his squire. No matter how skilled and precise the knight's attacks were, his weapons could not penetrate the zoth's magical defense, not as long as the shaman lived. And while it was clear what Theel must do, he did not do it. He did not attack the shaman. He watched his father die. Then he fled like a coward.

It was wise of the Crowlord to try to force Theel into this position. But what the zoth didn't know was that this was exactly where Theel wanted to be. Theel came to the Dead Man's Bridge to stand in that spot and fight the Crowlord. He was prepared to die. But for the first time since he father's death, he was also prepared to live. He would live or die and be satisfied with either result, as long as he did it standing up to the Crowlord, trying to avenge his father, and fighting to defend those children.

Theel should have felt crippling fear and regret, uncertainly and self-doubt. Instead, he was filled only with juy, and the confidence that came with his control of it. Theel knew his father was watching him, knew he was beaming with pride at what his squire had accomplished. Likewise, the Keeper of the Craft was surely watching these events through the Globe of Infinity, pleased with what he saw.

Theel now felt something happening that his masters had been praying for since he was a child. He was finding his manhood. He was finding his heart. And so the knowledge that the Crowlord was setting a trap gave him no pause. His nemesis awaited him at the top of the bridge.

Confidently, fearlessly, Theel went to meet him.

CHAPTER 61

Yatham climbed to his feet, his ears still ringing, his vision still blurry. But he couldn't take his eyes off what was happening at the top of the bridge. Theel's movements so mimicked those of his masterknight, they almost looked like they might be the same person. It was like watching the ghost of his father. His stance was identical. His movements were just as precise. He may not have been as quick or agile, not as naturally gifted as his father, but no one was.

It was clear those years of training had paid off. While Theel struggled and failed and appeared lost at times, his efforts did not go to waste. All those words his father spoke had sunk into Theel's brain. The masterknight instructed, and the squire was listening. Now Yatham was seeing the proof before his eyes.

It made his heart happy to see his brother achieve so much. No matter what Theel believed, he had the mettle inside him to make a knight. He just needed to understand that. He was a worthy squire. He did make his father proud. He was capable of achieving Warrior Baptism. And when he did it, when he completed his quest to find the Blessed Soul of Man, he would surely be one of the great knights of the realm.

But there were still obstacles to overcome. Theel couldn't complete his quest or become a knight until he defeated the Crowlord. And as Yatham watched, it was clear this remained a difficult task. The two battered each other atop the Dead Man's Bridge, trading endless flurries of swipes and thrusts, parries and blocks. Yatham could see that his brother was the better fighter, but was no match for the zoth's speed and strength. The Crowlord was stronger, but Theel had better technique. The Crowlord was faster, but Theel was more disciplined. They were perfectly balanced, complete opposites, and yet evenly matched.

"Yatham!" his brother's voice screamed inside his head.

The intrusion jolted his brain, and he staggered as if punched in the face. He was blinded and deafened and not just by the intrusion, or the sound of his brother's voice. It was the angel singing that accompanied it that was so crushing, the power behind it so overwhelming that Yatham couldn't see anything but a golden angel, couldn't hear anything but the angel's voice as she sang the Battle Hymn.

His scalp tingled as he saw fleeting images of the Crowlord before him, attacking him. And he knew he was seeing through his brother's eyes. It was jarring when this happened, when his brother's need was so strong that it was projected through his juy to Yatham's brain. It had happened before, but never so strongly. The thought that Theel held this much power in his hand, that this much juy was flowing from his brother's mind, was both amazing and terrifying. How could the Crowlord stand before this?

"Yatham!" Theel's voice came again.

But Yatham already knew the answer to that question. The Crowlord fought with the aid of Wind Magic, a blessing given him from the Blood Goddess through her shaman. Yatham could see the Crowlord before him just as Theel did; could see the fight that raged between them. His brother was the better fighter. The zoth chieftain relied on brute strength, on the power of his hatred. But Theel's patience and skill were superior to the Crowlord's undisciplined rage. The zoth was tiring, getting sloppy. He was giving Theel more and more openings as the battle wore on. Theel took advantage of each of these, but each time he attacked his sword or knife collided with Wind Magic. He could have cut the zoth's knee, or opened his wrist. He even delivered a forehand slash with his knife that should have gashed the bridge of the zoth's nose. But it didn't, because just like every other attack, it rang off the Crowlord's invisible armor as if the blades were striking stone.

"Yatham!" Theel's voice screamed. "The shaman!"

Yatham didn't need to be told. He knew what was necessary and was prepared to do it. His hands were empty, but his father had taught him many ways in which to kill a zoth, and not all of them required a weapon.

As the sound of Theel's voice faded, so did the singing of the angel, and Yatham was able to collect his senses. He could see clearly, hear clearly, and think clearly. He knew what must be done. But then he noticed something.

High above the bridge deck, among the crisscrossing metal beams, someone was climbing upward—not away from the battle, but toward it. He appeared to be a human, was rather tall and lanky, and held a large crossbow in his hands. He seemed intent on reaching the high point of the bridge, the point from which the cages hung, and the place where Theel and the Crowlord fought to a standstill.

Yatham shook his head, amazed at what he saw.

"Pitch," he breathed. "What are you doing?

Chapter 62

"Well, my dear Pitchford Wicker, you've carved out another delightfully horrifying emotional trauma for yourself. You're a coward, a terrible climber, and you're afraid of tall places. 'Just don't look down,' you told yourself. Here's a bit of advice, song man. Never take your own advice. Whoa!"

A strong wind gust pelted his body, blowing him off balance. He felt as if he was steady, and yet the metal beam kept dancing around beneath him, forcing him to wave his arms and raise a leg to keep his balance.

"Don't fall, song man," he cursed himself. "You're no good to anyone if you're dead, you foul wretch. Stop flapping your arms like a chicken. Lower your leg. You're not a dog attempting to relieve himself, are you? No, you're not."

After a moment, the song man was able to regain his balance, and shortly after, his composure. But it would take many more moments for him to muster the courage to continue forward. He made use of those precious moments by encouraging himself.

"Curse your bones, Pitchford Wicker. You've left whatever meager scraps of sanity you once possessed back in that crow cage, and now your brain is conjuring fanciful images. Birds are flying beneath you. Black rain is dripping from the sky. Blinding golden lights are flashing everywhere. And now an angel is singing so loud you can't hear your own thoughts."

He held still, breathing slowly, staring straight ahead. His goal was a ladder a few dozen feet away that led upward, which would take him closer to the fighting. At least he hoped so. He had been watching from a distance, but it appeared that Theel had gone up this ladder. If this was where Theel had gone, then it was where

Pitch wanted to follow. He just needed to get to this ladder. But he was still unable to move.

"But the grandest, most fanciful delusion you've enjoyed this day, song man, is the notion that you are brave enough to walk this bridge, that your balance is sure enough to climb through this gridwork, and that you would be able to accomplish either without coming frighteningly close to peeing yourself. Or retching. Or both. My wager is both."

He closed his eyes and took a few deep breaths through the mouth.

"Breathe, song man, breathe. Don't be sick all over yourself. Now walk."

And so he opened his eyes and began moving forward again, crossbow in hand, shuffle-stepping slowly across the metal beam, trying not to look down.

"No, no, no, never look down, Pitchford Wicker," he said. "Onward and upward. Think forward thoughts, not backward thoughts."

Instead of looking down, the song man chose to look above, to the place where he was trying to climb, to the place where he was certain Theel had gone. It was the tallest point at the center of the bridge, where the source of the golden light flashed incessantly. For a moment, he thought he saw the dark silhouette of the Crowlord against the pale sky. He quickly raised his crossbow and took aim, but the opportunity was fleeting, and he missed it.

"Wait for a good shot," he reminded himself as he lowered his crossbow and continued across the beam. "It must be a good shot."

Earlier, he was loosing bolts as fast as he could load the crossbow. Every opportunity he had, every glimpse of the enemy he saw, he said a prayer and loosed a bolt. But he might as well have been aiming for the sky, because that was all he was able to hit consistently. None of his shots were as lucky as that first one, when he was certain he'd struck the Crowlord.

Pitch couldn't see for certain, but he thought that first shot was true. It appeared the chieftain reacted to his attack as if he was

struck in the head. He was stunned briefly, and this purchased
Theel a moment to regain himself and attack with Battle Hymn.
Pitch wanted to do this again. He wanted to help. And so he
emptied his quiver, loosing quarrel after quarrel, hitting absolutely
nothing.

Once, he'd managed to hit the metal beam upon which the zoth
chieftain stood, but that was as close as he got. Now all of his
quarrels were laying somewhere in the bottom of the canyon. All
of them except one, the last bolt he had, now loaded and ready.

"Only one left, Pitchford Wicker," the song man said, as he
slung the crossbow on his back and began to climb the ladder.
"You have one chance remaining and you mustn't waste it. Just
one chance. Don't fall. Don't be sick, either. But don't fall."

He stared straight ahead, watching his hands as they pulled him
up, holding each rung of the ladder in a white-knuckled grip.

"Don't let go with the left hand until you've got a firm grip
with the right," he reminded himself. "And never look down. Just
keep climbing. Just keep—"

A zoth fell from above, screaming and trailing black blood. It
bounced off a metal beam nearby with a splat. The song man
pinched his eyes shut and gritted his teeth as he felt the ladder
shudder beneath his fingers, and tiny flecks of black blood tickled
his cheek.

"Now wounded zoths are falling on you," he moaned. "What a
treat that is. Zoth blood all around, hitting you in the face. That sits
wonderfully in the belly, so wonderfully it is trying to come back
up."

His stomach heaved, but nothing came out.

"This reminds me of fonder times, when as a child …"

He gagged again.

"… you proudly wore the mantle of Pitchford the Puker. Your
playmates at the orphanage were so wonderfully clever. I think I
hate children. Those children, at least."

A third heave, but it was as dry as the first two.

"Thank goodness for starvation, I say. Withering for days in that crow cage has proven beneficial so many times during this wonderful adventure. Are we done sicking ourself? No."

He heaved again, loudly and painfully. Sweat trickled down his forehead, despite the fact that he was shivering.

"A wise man might say this situation is the perfect opportunity for some accelerated character building," he said, wiping his mouth. "Said wise man would be invited to take a generous mouthful of this song man's ass."

He reached the top of the ladder, which led up to a walkway supported by steel grating. Pulling himself onto the grating was no small feat, as exhausted as he was. But he managed it, and climbed to his feet.

"This is as high as you go," Pitch told himself. "You are as close as you are going to get, song man. Now you must prove that first shot was no fluke."

He unslung his crossbow, gazing upward toward the top of the bridge. It was difficult to see anything with that blinding, golden light flashing in his eyes. But he was certain that was the spot where Theel and the Crowlord continued to battle each other, so this was where he aimed his last crossbow bolt.

"Now show yourself, Crowlord," he said. "Show that ruined face, and those pits you call eyes. Hold still for me, for just a moment."

But the Crowlord didn't hold still. And the winds would not relent. They constantly pushed and tugged on his body, denying him the clear shot he wished for. He held still for many moments, aiming the crossbow until his arms grew so tired he could barely hold it. But he didn't have the shot, and now his arms were shaking.

"This is impossible," he murmured. "You've reached your limit, song man. You laughing mad bag of bones. You're worthless and you know it."

He lowered the crossbow and fell to one knee, resting, attempting to gather his strength. He was exhausted, starved, and half-naked, sweating and shivering at the same time. He couldn't decide which discomfort was worse.

"A cloak would be especially welcome," he grumbled through chattering teeth. "Or even a tunic to cover this sunburned hide. But you have neither, foolish Wicker, so there's no use in dreaming."

He decided to stay kneeling, and raised the crossbow again, resting it on the railing to steady his aim and ease the burden on his tired arms. He need only wait. The time would come, and he would have his shot.

Then he saw it—what looked to be a clean shot. On the highest crossbeam of the bridge, the Crowlord separated briefly while Theel was distracted in fighting with some of his zoth warriors. And for the first time in a long while, the chieftain wasn't moving. He was just standing there as if he was tired and trying to gather his strength. This was the best opportunity Pitch had since this fight began. And he would not let it pass him by.

Fingers on the trigger. They began to squeeze.

"That's it, hold still. Good-bye."

Pitch was filled with satisfaction as he felt the mechanism turn, releasing the bowstring, just as another wounded zoth fell from the sky and struck the railing. All satisfaction vanished as the railing vibrated and threw his aim off. The quarrel was away, and if he was lucky, it might hit a cloud somewhere. After a string of terrible shots, this one was the worst.

That was it. He had no more quarrels. The frustration of this exploded from his lungs in a scream of rage. And that wasn't enough to satisfy his anger, so he began to repeatedly smash his crossbow on the railing as if he meant to destroy it. But he was a weak man and the crossbow was well built, so he turned toward the zoth who now lay on the walkway nearby.

"You!" he shouted, as if he recognized this particular zoth as the cause of every travail he'd ever suffered in his unfortunate existence. "I hate you!"

Instead of smashing his crossbow against the railing, he started to bash the zoth in the head with it. He didn't know how long he did this, or how many times he hit the creature. But he pounded it like he was pounding a stake into the ground. This went on until he was so tired he was forced to stop, sober up, and see the mess he'd created.

The front of the zoth's head was now missing, replaced by big glob of blood and brains with a jaw bone sticking out of it.

"Well, friend," Pitch said between heavy breaths. "If you weren't dead after your little fall, you certainly are now. Much luck in the afterlife. I may see you soon—"

Suddenly, the nausea came back and he fell to his knees, again racked by painful gagging.

"You sure … wish to sick up … Pitchford Wicker … Pitch the Puker … Aahh!"

After many painful moments, his stomach finally ceased twisting itself in knots. He continued kneeling, his head hanging, spittle dripping from his lips.

"There is nothing left inside you, song man. Stop now. Just stop trying. Stop trying to stand, trying to climb, trying to puke. Stop all of it. It's no use. Today symbolizes your wretched life boiled down to a few small hours, every second more forgettable and regrettable than the last."

He let out a big sigh, his shoulders heaving with a laughter he could not contain.

"What a wonderful growth experience this has been. I thought I'd gained so many fascinating insights while hanging from a gibbet, starving and dying. I thought I'd discovered the worst suffering that life can impose. I now know I was wrong. It can be worse—much worse. And if I persist in this dreadful life of mine, I'm sure it will get worse still. What a splendid thought!

"If pain and suffering nurtures wisdom, then, Pitchford Wicker, you should be able to start your own religion by now."

That caused him to laugh harder, but the laughter hurt, so he forced himself to stop.

"Even joy causes pain," he spit derisively, as he grabbed hold of the railing and pulled himself to his feet.

Once he did this, he reached into his quiver one last time.

"You must be certain before you abandon all hope, wretched, foolish song man," he said, reaching around inside. "You must confirm that you have spent all our quarrels before hope is truly abandoned. Perhaps fortune will smile and show you that there is one quarrel you missed. One more quarrel means one more chance. Yes!"

His fingers closed around something and he pulled it out. But as soon as he saw it, he was instantly disappointed. It looked like a crossbow bolt with a coil of silken line attached, and a large fishhook for a tip.

"What is the purpose of this? For scaling castle walls? For catching giant fish?"

His shoulders slumped and his threw the hook away, then slammed the empty quiver down on the walkway beside his crossbow.

"Many thanks to you, God!" he shouted. "I'm so delighted in my new, oversized fishhook. I have a grand idea. Perhaps I could throw a line off this bridge and reel in some sanity, or perhaps some dignity. If I'm patient, perhaps I might catch a good idea! You are so thoughtful to provide a fishhook for climbing walls when I beg you for a quarrel. So thoughtful. The only difficulty here is that you forgot to provide the wall! There is no wall here for me to scale with my trusty fishhook. Probably because you know if there was a wall here, I wouldn't hesitate in hanging myself from it. I pray for a wall to hang myself from, and you won't even provide me that. Thank you, Lord. You've always been so good to me."

He let out one more exasperated sigh, and thought a moment. Then, resolved to his decision, he walked forward to the railing. Seizing it in both hands, he threw one leg over, then the other. There, he hung out over the canyon, looking down. He could see the bridge deck below, and the large hole in it.

"This will suffice," he said. "I definitely won't survive this."

One more deep breath. He closed his eyes.

"Farewell, God above and world below. I understand you never truly wanted me at your table. I understand your wishes, and will not bother you with trifling protests. Instead, I now take my leave, humbly and quietly."

He was about to release his grip, to allow himself to fall to his death, when the winds brought a sound to his ears. It sounded like weeping.

His eyes flared open. "What? Who?"

He looked around for the source of the sound, but didn't see anything. There was an empty cage hanging in the air about two dozen feet away. Just below that was another cage containing a skeleton. It was almost as if it was looking at him.

"Quiet yourself," Pitch said to the skeleton. "Don't try to dissuade me from this course of action. It is my time to go."

But the winds blew and the sobs continued, louder and clearer now. They were tiny cries, like those of a child.

"Who is there?" he shouted, scanning the cages. "Where are you?"

Then he saw them, two small figures huddled at the bottom of a cage, hanging over the center of the bridge, far below him. He recognized them immediately—the girl and the boy.

The Overlie children.

Frantically, he looked behind him, searching the walkway. And there it was, the hook. He had tried to throw it away, but it stubbornly caught on the grating and now hung, its silken line dangling, swaying in the canyon breezes. Pitch could see it caught on the grate much like it might catch on the merlon of a castle wall.

Or on the bars of a cage.

He squinted at the silken line, studying it for a moment.

"About one hundred feet, I'd wager."

Then he looked at the cage below him and its precious contents.

"Eighty feet, give or take."

He could only shake his head.

"Shame on you, my dear Pitchford Wicker," he admonished. "Your doubts have been a waste of perfectly good thought energy. That frustratingly reticent and reclusive God above you did not provide you with the wrong tool. He provided the *correct* tool. You are simply trying to do the wrong job."

Pitch turned back, looking down upon the children, smiling at them with his white teeth.

"Why, hello, my wonderful sweetlings," he whispered. "Allow me to reintroduce myself."

CHAPTER 63

The Crowlord could retreat no further. Theel had chased him all the way to the top of the bridge, to the place from which the cages were suspended. This was where the fight would be finished, a single crossbeam well over a hundred feet above the bridge deck, offering a grand view of the canyons below and the mountains above. It was a very dangerous place, a narrow beam with treacherous footing, and buffeted by constant wind gusts, and it seemed to satisfy both combatants. It was as good a place as any to die.

Theel pounded away at the Crowlord relentlessly. The zoth blocked nearly every one of his attacks with a bone spike, but not all of them. Here and there, Theel was just fast enough to beat his enemy's defenses, just enough to deliver a strike that would have been crippling if not for the armor of Wind Magic. This should have been frustrating to Theel, but it wasn't. These opportunities were growing, occurring more often. This told him the Crowlord was tiring.

Theel had turned the tables. As each second passed, his strength and confidence grew while the zoth's was sapped. It was the opposite of what had occurred beneath the bridge, when the Crowlord toyed with him like a rag doll. It was the opposite of how the Crowlord treated Theel's father, showing no mercy as he pounded the knight into submission. Protected by his shaman, he need not fear defeat, and was never in danger from the knight's weapons. So he attacked relentlessly, pushing his enemy to the point of exhaustion, and killed him while Theel watched.

But now it was Theel who showed no mercy. Now it was Theel who pounded his enemy into submission. Theel was bolstered by the power of his juy and the strength of Battle Hymn's shadowsteel, and the Crowlord was powerless against it. The zoth grew tired, gasped for air, and Theel drank it up.

"I'm going to kill you!" he spit in the zoth's face. "Just like you killed my father. Right here. On the same spot. You are going to die."

There was a reason why the once tireless chieftain was showing fatigue. And Theel knew that reason.

"Your magic is weakening," Theel taunted. "Your shaman is hurt. He won't live much longer because my brother is going to kill him."

The Crowlord showed no indication he was listening; he just continued to fight, continued to block.

"And when that happens, your Blood Goddess will leave you."

Theel didn't think the zoth truly heard him, nor was he certain there was anything behind those eyes that knew fear, or could be intimidated in any way.

"You will be all alone."

But he didn't care if the Crowlord heard him because he wasn't talking for the zoth to hear. He was saying those words because he wanted to hear them. He was saying them for himself.

"But I won't be alone. My God will never leave me."

Another opening. Theel caught a bone spike with this knife blade, and swung Battle Hymn with all his might, connecting with the Crowlord's head.

"And he is with my brother, blessing his actions. Because he wants your shaman dead!"

But just like the other attacks, shadowsteel bounced off the chieftain's flesh harmlessly. Theel didn't care. He pressed the attack, too fast for the Crowlord to keep pace.

"God wants your shaman dead! And he wants you dead!"

He pounded on his enemy's arms and legs, his torso and head. And the zoth was too tired, too slow to stop him. But each attack was still stopped, with Theel's blades ringing off Wind Magic.

"Die!" Theel screamed.

Then he was struck in the back by another cloud of crows. It was the same treatment they'd given him so many times before, but on a smaller scale. It was only about two dozen of the black birds, probably all that was left of the Crowlord's once vast army. But it was still enough to knock him to his knees, then cover him with flapping wings, stabbing his face and scalp with their beaks. But Theel was only irritated by the distraction. He jumped to this feet, throwing the crows off him, screaming, chasing after the Crowlord, who was retreating again. He retreated all the way to the spot were a certain chain was wrapped around the beam, the chain which held the cage containing the Overlie children.

He raised his bone spike.

"No!" Theel shrieked, rushing at the chieftain, Battle Hymn flashing golden in his hand.

It felt like hours, running as fast as he could, but getting no closer. The Crowlord struck at the chain with his bone spike. The sun rose, Behe Kang drenched them in noondark, and the sun set in the time it took Theel to cross the beam. The Crowlord struck the chain a second time. It felt like Theel had all day to stop him. But all day wasn't enough.

The Crowlord hit at the chain a third time. The chain broke. And Theel watched helplessly as it unwrapped itself from the beam, the chain links clinking loudly as they spun around. The chain reached its end, the last links spinning free of the beam, then it disappeared below.

Theel looked down and saw the roof of the cage in freefall, trailing its chain. It fell through the hole in the bridge deck, bounced off the railing atop the small building with a loud clang, then fell into the canyon. It fell forever, as if it would never reach the bottom.

But Theel didn't wait for it to reach the bottom. Instead, he rushed the Crowlord, screaming in a rage, blood bursting from his eyes.

"Die!"

The zoth had no answer for the ferocity of his attack. He was driven backward, knocked off balance. He tried to block. He tried to counterattack, but he was exhausted and outmatched. And shadowsteel smashed him in the face repeatedly, driving him to his knees.

And Theel continued screaming as he rained crushing blows upon his enemy.

"Die! Die! Die!"

Chapter 64

Yatham knew what needed to be done as he walked to the place where the shaman lay on the bridge deck. The creature's body lay prostrate, writhing uncontrollably. Its head shook and its face shivered, cheeks twitching spasmodically. Eyes searched sightlessly. Lips moved wordlessly. The creature looked no more alive than the severed head he wore as a decoration.

Smoke still rose from the shaman's clothing, the stench of burned meat and putrefaction filling Yatham's nose, filling his heart will revulsion. The creature had done this to himself by playing with magic it couldn't control. The spell had gone wrong. And this was the reward.

It was a terrible fate, but Yatham felt no sympathy. In fact, he would have liked to allow the shaman to linger a little longer. He would have liked the shaman to draw a few more pained breaths, suffer through the agony of a few more seconds of life. It would be tiny compared to the pain this creature's magic had caused to so many travelers of the Narrows. Yatham might have enjoyed it. He might have allowed it. But there wasn't time.

Yatham knew what needed to be done.

His father had taught him many ways to kill a zoth, but in this moment, he opted for the simplest. He dropped his knee onto the creature's neck, crushing its throat. Yatham never took pleasure in killing a zoth, but this was the closest he ever came to it.

There was a cracking sound as he felt the shaman's bones crumble beneath his weight. Then the light left the creature's eyes.

The shaman was dead.

Chapter 65

Theel shrieked unintelligible rage, slamming his blades against the Crowlord's defenses repeatedly.

"How dare you show your face under God's sun, you wretched, cursed filth!"

He didn't care if anyone heard him, or understood him, least of all this abomination kneeling before him.

"How dare you take my father's shield, the symbol of his honor, of his oath to protect?"

There was no one nearby who could understand what Theel was saying, but these words would be spoken. They were too big to stay inside him, and so they burst forth from his lips of their own accord.

"You've earned no such honor. You've sworn no such oath."

Theel's curses and insults sprayed all over the zoth's face, just as his steel rained down, most of it unblocked. The Crowlord was pushed beyond his limits, so exhausted he could barely raise his weapons. But Theel's attacks were fueled by his juy. He would never tire, so long as his mystic will flowed.

"You protect nothing. You nurture nothing but strife. You make nothing but destruction."

The zoth chieftain must have been gathering his strength, because he allowed a series of strikes to connect, making no effort to block as his enemy's knife and sword bounced off his shoulders, head, and neck. Then he launched a counterattack, a desperate attempt to reclaim the advantage.

He sprang at Theel, swinging both bone spikes. For a moment, the Crowlord was his old self, pushing his enemy backward with the sheer savagery of his attacks. But Theel remained confident, and continued his insults.

"You cannot best me," Theel growled even as he retreated. "Not with my father's sword in my hand. Not with his spirit at my back."

While the zoth's flurry of attacks was ferocious, not one of them could breach Theel's defenses. The human's sword forms were precise, his footwork was perfect, just as his father had taught him. And every one of the Crowlord's attacks was knocked harmlessly aside. Theel stopped retreating, and quickly regained the advantage.

"You have not the strength to stand before me," Theel spit at the zoth's face. "Your shaman is dead. He cannot help you."

Then, as if in response to his words, Theel felt the power emanating from the Crowlord scattered to nothingness, like a trail of pipe smoke dispersed by a wind gust. One moment, the air tingled with Wind Magic, and the next moment, it was gone, snuffed out. Nothing stood between the Crowlord and Theel's weapons except scarred, gray skin.

"Your shaman is dead," Theel repeated. "You are forsaken by your god. Now you must fight on your own."

His sword smashed the zoth's fingers, and one bone spike fell out of his hand. The Crowlord swung his other bone spike, but Theel's knife blocked, and Battle Hymn countered, slicing the zoth's hand off at the wrist. The Crowlord's eyes widened as if he was surprised by this, as if it was impossible for him to be vulnerable, impossible for his shaman to die.

But Theel wasn't surprised. Yatham had never failed him.

"My brother has slain your shaman. His magic can no longer help you," he stated. "Your Blood Goddess is worthless. She cannot protect you."

Theel kicked the Crowlord in the knee, forcing him to kneel once again. As the exhausted and defeated chieftain bowed before him, Theel looked down at his father's silver shield, still strapped to the Crowlord's chest.

"Unfortunate that you've chosen to armor yourself with the ancient symbol of the knighthood."

It was the chieftain's finest battle trophy, the symbol of his destruction of the great Knight of the Southern Cross, the man who had beaten death. It was the most famous knightshield in all the Western Kingdoms, characterized by the hole in its center where the blade of some great weapon slammed through, piercing the shield, and piercing the heart of the man who wore it.

"So sad that all you have left to save yourself is my own masterknight's shield."

He aimed the point of his sword at the Crowlord's heart.

"For just like your shaman, and just like your goddess …"

He stabbed his blade directly through the hole in his father's shield.

" … it will not protect you."

Shadowsteel parted the zoth's flesh, slid through his chest, and slid through his heart. It did not cease until Battle Hymn was buried up to the hilt. But it didn't stay there long. Just as quickly as Theel shoved his sword in, he jerked it out. The Crowlord remained kneeling, glassy eyes staring, broken jaw hanging. Theel spun, delivering a backhand blow to the zoth's neck. The keen edge of the shadowsteel sliced through the chieftain's gray flesh easily and cleanly, sending his head spinning out over the canyon.

The headless body now slumped, threatening to fall, but Theel wouldn't allow it. He sheathed his sword and seized the corpse by the straps that held the silver shield in place on his chest. Using his father's knife, Theel cut the shield free, then kicked the remains of the Crowlord off the beam. The headless corpse bounced around the gridwork of the Dead Man's Bridge as it fell, but eventually it made its way to the bottom of Krillian's Cut.

Wherever it landed, it would surely be eaten by crows.

CHAPTER 66

The little girl was a splotch of vivid colors in a gray and drab world, a little bundle of bright-blue eyes and flaming red curls wrapped in a shiny emerald dress. Set against the deep gray of the cage bars, the rusty bridge beams and the cloudy sky, she almost didn't seem real. But the closer she came, the more genuine she seemed, the more detailed and colorful were her eyes, her freckles, her curls. Now she was only a few feet away, as close to Pitch as she was in their first meeting in Widow Hatch, when he was the one that needed rescuing from a cage.

Hand over hand, gripping the silken line with exhausted fingers, he pulled her closer, inch by excruciating inch, until the bars of the rusted cage thudded against the side of the walkway. The song man wrapped the line around his hand, braced his foot against the railing, and strained to hold the cage in place. It was shocking how heavy this thing was. He wasn't even holding its full weight, allowing the chain from which it hung to bear the majority of that duty. It hung out in the middle of the bridge, but it also hung below him, providing enough slack for him to pull it near. All he did was hook it and reel it in like a fish.

But now that he'd managed to pull the cage over to the railing, he could barely hold it in place. He was panting and sweating and sick with exhaustion. His shoulders hurt to the point where he was certain his arms were about to be ripped off. The line was cutting into his fingers so painfully, he feared he might lose one or two of them before he was through. Perhaps he was starved, or ailing from thirst. Perhaps Theel had beaten him nearly to death. Perhaps he was never that strong to begin with. Perhaps his brain was sunbaked, and none of this was really happening.

"That's right, Pitchford Wicker, you may have created a delusion in your madness, one in which you might attain forgiveness by saving these Overlie children who, in reality, died long ago as a result of your crimes. But a delusion can't be true unless it is embraced, and so this wretched, hopeless song man will save these hallucinations resembling the sweet children he so wronged, so he might achieve spurious redemption."

These words did nothing to earn the trust of the children, who only stared wide-eyed as if he were more threatening than the Crowlord.

"Forgive me, my darlings," Pitch said, straining desperately to hold the cage in place. "Cover your ears to ravings of this impotent, mad fool before you. I beg you, please come out of the cage. Let us end this nightmare."

The most difficult portion of this rescue should have been over. Clearly it wasn't.

It took more tries than he could count to hit his target. Loose the hook, miss the cage. Pull the hook back in, reload. Loose the hook, miss the cage. Pull the hook back in, reload. It seemed he might take all day attempting to hook those bars without success, but he did it. Then it seemed he might take all week to pull the cage over to the walkway, but he did it. It should have taken a strong man with shoulders and back accustomed to bearing heavy loads to hold this cage in place as long as he did. But the starving, half-dead song man did it, somehow finding the strength and stamina. The most difficult portion of this rescue should have been over. But it wasn't. The most difficult part was persuading the Overlie children to trust him.

"Come, little Lady Overlie," Pitch grunted, trying to smile. "Your coach awaits."

He was offering salvation, offering to free them from the danger they were in, to end the onslaught of horrors they'd lived through these past few days. But the girl only responded as if he was the worst horror of all, crawling to the opposite side of the cage and refusing to look at him.

"I know you have no reason to trust me," he said. "But you must. I will help you. I will take you away from these zoths, if you'll let me. We can survive this. We can live on together. I will prove to you I am not the man you saw back in Widow Hatch."

The little girl's brother was more receptive. He was a few seasons older, also with red hair and too many freckles to count. He was dressed in green like she was, a smaller version of the Overlie surcoat bearing the diamonds and oak leaves. It was probably his play clothes from a better time, when all the war he knew was a child's game.

"I beg you," Pitch groaned. "Squeeze between these bars and my friends and I will spirit you to salvation. I promise."

"Your friends?" the boy asked, a tiny glimmer of hope in his eyes.

"Did you see the man with the sword?" Pitch asked. "And the man on the horse?"

The boy's eyes brightened.

"Yes, you saw the man on the horse," Pitch said. "You recognize the Southern Cross, don't you?"

The boy nodded.

"These men are knights," Pitch lied. "They are knights and they've come to save us. They are protecting us right now, keeping the zoths away so we might escape."

The boy's resolve was breaking. He threw a glance out of the cage, looking northward, as if searching for the two knights.

"You don't trust me, but you trust them," Pitch said. "You know men of the Southern Cross can be trusted. I came here with those men, and we will all leave together. We will share our food and water. We have blankets. We'll build a fire. And tomorrow, we'll take you home."

"They'll take us home?" the boy asked. "The knights will take us to Norrester?"

"We will take you anywhere you wish," Pitch promised. "But we mustn't tarry. Please—"

At that moment, a pained scream cut the air.

"No!" someone cried.

It was a full-throated shriek, filled with desperation, and it came from above, near the top of the bridge. Pitch looked up, but couldn't see anyone.

Then the cage shuddered, rocking alarmingly. Something had struck the chain.

"Come to me!" Pitch yelled. "Now children! Now!"

He shook one of his hands free of the silken line and beckoned. Neither of them came, so he reached out between the bars, seized the boy by the wrist and pulled. The boy screamed. Then Pitch screamed.

"Now!"

But it was no use. He could not hold the cage with one hand. His arm was too weak. His back was too weak. He felt himself being dragged over the railing. They would all be pulled to their deaths.

He had no choice. He released the boy and grabbed one of the cage's bars. Then he did the same with his other hand, dropping the silken line so he could get a firm hold of the cage with both hands. Then the chain vibrated again, the cage dropped an inch, and almost tore itself from the song man's hands.

"Now!" Pitch screamed. "Or we all die!"

It was no use. Neither of the children were listening. Now free of the song man's grasp, the boy pulled away, crawling to his sister's side at the far side of the cage, and now both of them were out of reach. Pitch looked back up, trying to see what was causing this, but only saw the chain stretching up toward the golden light, vibrating like a strummed lute string.

"I will not release you. If you fall, we all fall. Come to me now!"

He looked back to see that the boy had grabbed his sister, holding fistfuls of her green dress and was dragging her across the floor of the cage. She fought him, kicking and scratching, but he was bigger and stronger and he forced her against her will. She was suddenly within reach and Pitch didn't hesitate, seizing the sleeve of her dress with one hand, holding the cage with the other. Now she was fighting him but he ignored it, ruthlessly jerking her arm out between the bars. She responded by sinking her teeth into his hand. He screamed at the pain, but didn't let go. He pulled on her as hard as he could but she refused to let go of the cage bars. He had the chance to save her. But he just didn't have the strength with one arm.

He could not save her without releasing the cage. He had no choice but to do it, so he did, grabbing her arm with both hands, allowing gravity to pull her free by pulling the cage down and away. And his heart was torn into halves as he saw the eyes of the boy, staring at him in shock, staring at him in horror as the cage fell away, swinging like a giant pendulum hanging from a shaky chain.

Pitch fell backward with the little girl in his arms, squeezing her tightly as his back hit the metal grating of the walkway. He should have been overjoyed to save her, but he could still hear the cry of distress from her older brother as he fell to his doom. The song man could not tell if the boy was screaming or weeping from the strangled scream that cut into his ears. He could not tell if he was screaming or weeping, himself.

He jumped to his feet. He was desperate to see, though he knew witnessing the boy's death would make him sick. He could already feel it bubbling in his belly. He was about retch all over himself, but he still forced himself to look, even as he crushed the little girl in his embrace, holding her so she couldn't see.

He, and he alone, deserved to see this, to see what his sins had done to a precious, innocent child.

The chain continued to vibrate as the cage swung away. It was about to break at any time, about to drop into oblivion. But somehow it didn't. Somehow it held, despite someone above trying to break it. The chain vibrated and the cage rocked and the boy screamed all the way to the other side of the bridge.

Then it began to swing back toward the walkway where the song man stood. And now he was screaming too, Pitchford

Wicker, the worthless song man, belching forth his joy as he saw the chain swinging and the cage spinning, bringing the boy back toward him.

"You can't do it, zoths!" he screamed. "You can't break that chain because it is not time for this little one to die!"

The cage had swung away from him like a pendulum, and now it was swinging back like a pendulum, down toward the center of the bridge, then back up to the walkway where he stood. He leaned over the railing, thinking to seize one of the bars when it came close, hold it in place, and get the boy out.

But the cage was losing speed. It wasn't going to come close enough. He could see this was true already. The boy had already squeezed partway out of the cage, was holding his hand out, reaching for Pitch, terror and hope and desperation flooding his eyes. But he wasn't close enough. They strained for each other, but neither could reach.

Then the chain finally broke.

Now there was nothing to keep that cage suspended. Just a few more seconds and it would fall. But in those few seconds, it continued its momentum and now that the chain had gone loose, it was flying straight at the walkway. Pitch had to lean back to avoid being crushed as the bars slammed into the railing with a crashing thud. But he kept his hand out, and so did the boy.

Their two palms clapped together.

The cage bounced off the walkway and fell. It nearly took the boy with it, and nearly took Pitch with it, but he held onto the railing. He didn't let go of the boy and the boy didn't let go of him. The boy cried out in pain as his body was torn through the rusty bars.

Beneath his feet, Pitch could see the cage dropping away, trailing its chain. It fell through the hole in the bridge deck, where it crashed onto the roof of a small building beneath the bridge, then fell to the bottom of the canyon.

Pitch sucked in a big gulp of air and heaved the boy up over the railing. For the second time, he fell backward onto the walkway with an Overlie child in his arms.

He did it. The children were safe.

CHAPTER 67

Yatham could see that the effects of the zoth shaman's miscast spell were lingering. Pools of blue flame spread out across the bridge deck with the zoth corpse at the center. It was almost as if the shaman had torn a hole in the wall that separated the world from its Flame Bringers, and now Craft was leaking through, pooling beneath him, spreading out all over the bridge, ready to erupt. The air snapped loudly, as if Yatham stood in the center of a giant crackling cookfire, and the road beneath his feet began to vibrate as if the bridge was humming. The air was so thick with Craft that it gave him goose bumps, and the hair of his neck raised up. Then he saw cracks forming in the gray stone beneath the zoth's corpse, spreading out like a spiderweb.

He didn't see anything else, as he was already turned and running with all the speed his legs could muster. He didn't look back as the trembling beneath his feet became a lurching so violent he nearly fell multiple times. He didn't look back as his ears filled with a grinding sound, then the crumbling of stone. And finally, the most alarming sound: The groaning of buckling steel.

He wasn't looking back so he didn't know what it was that stole his breath, caused him to go deaf, or created the burst of the wind that was so fierce it threw him to the ground.

He still didn't look back as he rose to his feet, continuing toward the center of the bridge where he knew his brother was. All he looked at was the gray horse up ahead, the large gelding draped in the war emblem of the Southern Cross. His eyes never left that horse because he knew it was his best, and probably only, chance of survival.

The gelding chose not to tarry once it lost its rider in the attack on the zoth shaman. All of its instincts told it to flee, to escape the south end of the bridge and the air so befouled by smoke and sacrifice and dark magic. Its instincts told it to run, but its training told it not to abandon its master. For this reason, the animal kept its distance, but it did not flee.

Now the time had come for the gelding to employ its incredible speed. This creature was built to run, and now it must do so. Yatham knew this with a certainty so complete that the word was already on his lips as he jumped atop the frame of an abandoned wagon, then launched himself at the gray horse.

"Run!" he screamed, as he landed in the saddle.

The gelding heard this command and understood, speeding quickly to a full gallop. Much like his first trip across the bridge, Yatham kept his head down and held on with white knuckles, trusting the horse's instincts and training to save him.

The Dead Man's Bridge was falling apart, threatening to drop him into the mouth of the canyon, and yet despite this, Yatham's thoughts were consumed with worry for his brother. He knew Theel was at the top of the bridge, the worst place to be at that moment. He wouldn't have time to climb down. He'd have no chance of running to safety, even if he could. If the entire structure collapsed, he would certainly fall with it, and Yatham would be helpless to stop it.

But at that moment, he was also helpless to do anything to save himself. His life depended on the speed of the mount beneath him. All he could do was hold on and say prayers and hope that God was listening. But he made the mistake of looking down again, and his prayer died on his lips. The road was falling away beneath him, literally crumbling beneath the gelding's hooves. It appeared as if the horse was running up a waterfall of gray stone fragments that were rapidly peeling away and tumbling into the canyon.

He pinched his eyes shut and didn't look down anymore.

"Lord, please," he breathed. "I am at peace with this. Take me if you must, but please preserve Theel's life. Please, somehow, save him from this. Please."

He felt the muscles of his mount tense and spring as if in one last desperate lunge. The gelding let loose with a stressed, anxious whinny and stopped running, now only kicking its legs as both horse and rider flew through the air. Yatham hugged the animal's neck as tightly as he could, whipped in the face by its mane, still praying.

"Please, God. Please save Theel."

When he opened his eyes, he wasn't surprised to see nothing beneath him but the yawning chasm of Krillian's Cut; nothing but tons of bridge fragments tumbling into the canyon, nothing but air to support his weight. And he felt the tug of gravity pulling him down, pulling him to his death. It was dizzying and nauseating all at once.

But then he saw the roof of a small building appear beneath him, then the northern half of the bridge deck. And then he realized he wasn't falling.

He was flying.

Four horseshoes sparked as they struck the road surface, and the gelding continued running. The animal whinnied and its rider joined in, letting loose with a roar of triumph. He threw his head back and raised his arms, screaming, tears streaking his cheeks. Even if he wanted to, he couldn't stop the joy exploding from this chest.

"Fly Southern Cross!" he shrieked. "Fly!"

And it felt like he was flying. The wind smashed his face and whipped his hair as the horse ran. The exhilaration of living, of surviving, gave him the feeling that he was soaring with the eagles. He felt as if he could do anything on this horse. Together, they could accomplish anything in the world.

Once he was satisfied he could yell no more, he grasped the reins and slowed his mount to a stop. The gelding's horseshoes skidded on the bridge deck and the animal stood still while Yatham hugged his neck, his lips moving in a silent prayer of thanks. When he had finished, he patted the gelding's flank, pressing his face into his mane.

"You couldn't save your master," Yatham whispered. "But you saved me. And you saved my brother. Thank you."

After a few more seconds of thought, and several deep breaths, Yatham dismounted, looking around. The northern half of the bridge appeared to be intact, looking just as it did when he first laid eyes on it. He was surrounded by an intricate spiderweb of metal beams that held strong in the canyon breezes. The road beneath was as sure as it ever was, not trembling, not cracking, just hanging off the cliff face as always.

From where he was, he could see that the entire southern half of the bridge was gone. It was somehow destroyed by the Craft unleashed by the zoth shaman, ripped off the canyon wall and thrown down to the bottom of the world. The gap in the bridge deck was once a mere twenty feet. Now it was nearly half a mile of empty air. Far away, on the other side, he could see the tiny black hole in the southern wall of the canyon, framed by a few twisted beams that looked like gnarled fingers digging into the rock, desperate to hold on. This was where the Narrows continued southward to Wrendale. But now there was no way to get there. Half of the Dead Man's Bridge was missing, leaving a gap so wide it was impossible to cross.

No one would ever travel the Narrows again.

But Yatham could not dwell on that. Now he had to find Theel and ensure his safety. He knew his brother had survived his battle with the Crowlord, as well as the bridge collapse. He was still up in the gridwork high above the bridge deck, somewhere. Yatham didn't know exactly where, and knew he would need to climb up and find him. But as soon as that thought entered his head, he heard someone yelling.

"Ouch! No, stop it! Mercy! Mercy!"

Yatham looked up and was surprised to see someone laying on a metal walkway, high above the bridge deck. He was shirtless, and very skinny, with bones poking out all over. And he had a very familiar voice, that of a song man.

"Ouch! Mercy! Oh, God help me!"

Standing on the walkway were two children, a boy and a girl, both dressed in green. The girl seemed angry with the song man, and persisted in punching and kicking him as he curled up in the fetal position, attempting without success to protect himself.

"Ouch! Stop it!" Pitch whimpered. "I know you have good reason to be cross with me, young one, but this is an unnecessary amount of aggression, don't you agree?"

She didn't agree, and punched him right on the nose.

"Ouch!" Pitch whined.

"Pitch!" Yatham yelled. "What are you doing up there?"

"Hello, Yatham!" the song man called down. "It's a most fascinating story. It would be my pleasure to regale— Ouch! Please, my sweetling. Do be a proper lady and cease in striking me in the face."

"Are you in need of aid?" Yatham asked.

"Why, yes, I need aid. A mountain of it, in fact," Pitch said. "Would you be so kind as to climb up here and help us down? I think the young one should be carried for her safety, but she doesn't seem to trust— Ouch! She doesn't seem to like me— Ouch! She hates me. A lot."

"Certainly," Yatham said.

"Oh, thank you. You are a fine and decent man. Ouch! Please, do not tarry. I'm not certain I can survive much more of young Lady Overlie's ... um, gratitude. Ouch!"

"Hold on," Yatham said, smiling. "It will take me some time to climb up."

"Oh, thank you. Please do hurry," Pitch said. "Ouch! Certainly I deserved that, my sweetling, but at some point you must be satisfied that you've caused sufficient pain. Have we reached that point? Are you finished punishing me? No? Ouch!"

CHAPTER 68

The wind blew just as hard and hot as ever, pelting the top of the Dead Man's Bridge, swirling around the beam upon which Theel sat with his legs dangling down. The view from his perch was dizzying. If he looked down at his boots, he'd see nothing beneath them except thousands of feet of air, the occasional bird, and a blanket of fog thick enough to give the appearance that he was above the clouds. It was a view previously obstructed by the bridge deck, but now made possible by absence of the entire southern half of the bridge.

Theel didn't fully understand how or why, but only seconds after he slew the Crowlord and cast the zoth chieftain's body down into the canyon, the Dead Man's Bridge began to fall apart. The southern end tore itself loose from the canyon wall, twisted itself into knots, and fell, piece by piece, down through the fog below. The stone of the bridge deck crumbled as it lost support from the superstructure, and Theel watched impassively as it fell like a line of dominoes, from south to north.

He was certain he had only moments to live, and knew there was no way he could save himself even if he tried. So he stood flatfooted, Battle Hymn in one hand, his father's shield in the other, watching as the bridge fell out from beneath him.

Then he saw a man on horseback riding northward across the bridge deck. He saw the gray coat of the gelding and the black and white caparison bearing the war emblem of the Southern Cross, and knew he was watching his brother riding for his life.

Only seconds before this, Theel didn't care that the bridge was falling, or that he would fall with it. There was nothing left for him to do here anyway. He'd fought his way to the Crowlord's doorstep. He'd faced the zoth chieftain and killed him, reclaiming his father's shield in the process. Considering the fate of the Overlie children, that may not have been enough. But there was no going back, no undoing what was done. Perhaps those children would be waiting for him in the afterlife, and offer him forgiveness for his failing. He would see them soon enough. All he had to do was wait and accept what was coming.

But when he saw his brother, he suddenly began to care again. Yatham didn't deserve to die. Yatham deserved life. Yatham deserved to survive this and go on to pursue his dreams. He deserved to continue his training with horses, or to pursue knighthood if he chose to. Perhaps Yatham wanted a more modest life, to find a wife and make a family. This was a real possibility, and if it was what Yatham wanted, it was what Theel wanted. Now that Yatham would be free of the burdensome yoke of his brother's existence, he could do as he chose, and walk his own path, whatever it may be.

Theel smiled at this thought. He never realized it before, but he now knew he wanted to die so that his brother could be free. Yatham was the best person Theel had ever known, and the only person alive that Theel loved. He deserved to be free. And though Theel didn't want to die, he accepted that this was likely to occur here long before he set foot on this bridge. Now he accepted it as inevitable. This left him free to embrace what his death would mean for Yatham. It would mean freedom—freedom from his oath, from the shadow of the knighthood, from the shadow of his father, from the responsibility imposed upon him by the Keeper of the Craft. And freedom from the responsibility that he imposed upon himself, to carry a brother who could not, or would not walk on this own.

Theel was certain for years that he felt pain more intensely than most people, both mentally and physically. He knew his burden was surely among the heaviest ever required of any man. But now this quest had taught him otherwise. The fact that Yatham didn't complain as Theel did was no indication that his burden was less. It was merely proof of the superior mettle in his heart. Yatham had the same father as Theel. He had the same upbringing. He had just as many challenges to overcome as his older brother. Yet he cheerfully bore his own responsibilities and most of Theel's, and he did it without complaint, even as his childish, simple fool of a brother berated him constantly out of envy.

Some men brought no good to the world, and therefore the world was not harmed by their passing. Such men were the opposite of Yatham. They made nothing better. They deserved to die because their lives meant nothing. These were men such as Quiddip Kile. These were men like Theel.

Yatham was one of the good people who walked the earth. Theel even believed he was a better man than their father. Yatham was so good, he made others better.

Yatham deserved to live.

And so as Theel watched that gray gelding run, he could not contain his desire that it capture a bit of Wind Magic within its legs.

"Run," he heard himself say. "Run!"

There was no way the gelding or its rider could hear him, but he shouted it anyway.

"Run!"

The bridge was falling apart much faster than the horse could run. It was crumbling twenty feet behind, then ten feet behind, then directly beneath its hooves. Theel felt himself squeezing the steel of his father's shield, squeezing the handle of Battle Hymn, raising his arms above his head as if he could hold the bridge together, or lift the horse up by the sheer force of his will.

He knew he couldn't. But he still tried to will his brother to safety by pure instinct. And he cheered when the horse jumped. And he cried when he saw it land, when he saw it carry his brother to new life.

"Fly Southern Cross!" he heard his brother scream.

"Yes," he said to himself, wearing a smile his face could not contain, tears blurring his vision. "Fly."

But then he realized that he was so jubilant that his brother lived that he hardly noticed that he didn't die. He looked down at the beam beneath him as he felt the tremors lessen and die, and was shocked when it didn't fall; even more shocked when *he* didn't fall.

The entire southern half of the bridge was gone, but the northern half remained intact. And so Theel was left standing there, Battle Hymn in one hand, his father's shield in the other, alive.

Alive.

When he undertook this quest, he told the Keeper of the Craft that the Blessed Soul of Man was the goal of his search. That wasn't true. The truth of the Blessed Soul, and the Revelation spoken of in the prophecies, had been miles away from his mind. Even he didn't realize it the day he fled from Fal Daran. His father's knightshield was the goal of his search all along. And now the goal of his search rested in his hand.

He'd avenged his father's death and reclaimed his father's shield. This quest was complete, and therefore freed him to pursue a new quest, one that was assigned him, one that he was groomed for. The quest for the Blessed Soul of Man.

Theel stared at the shield of his father, worn on the man's chest for more than twenty-five years of life. It was in poor shape after spending so much time on the chest of a creature of evil who cared nothing for its welfare. It was beaten, battered, and scratched, its once shiny surface dulled by months of abuse. But this was nothing compared to the damage it had received years before, when the blade of some weapon stabbed clean through its center and into his father's heart.

Every day of his masterknight's life, Theel saw that shield strapped to his father's chest, every day until this one. Now he held it in his hands for the first time. Now he could put his fingers through the hole that fueled the legend, and he could not deny its truth.

It was the first time the great Knight of the Southern Cross was ever defeated in battle, so the stories went, the day his heart was pierced but continued to beat defiantly. Theel's father decided not to have the hole mended. He chose instead for it to remain, and for its jagged edges to cut into his flesh every time his chest expanded with a breath of air. It was a reminder, he said, that every breath he took that day forward was a gift to him from God, another opportunity to serve his maker.

Theel ran his fingertips over the worn surface of the shield, over the words and symbols engraved in the once-shiny steel, now filled with dried blood, the blood of zoths, the blood of his father. In the center of the shield was carved the outline of a therac, a winged lizard native to the Silvermarsh. Upon the therac's breast was the character of the ancient Thershoni language meaning Order, indicating allegiance to the Kingdom of Embriss, the old clan of Order. Above the therac's head was the war emlem of the knighthood, the Southern Cross, made up of seven interlocking swords representing Embriss and his six sons, the fathers of the old clans. Across the top of the shield were engraved these words:

My God. My Clan. My Shield.

More words were carved across the bottom of the shield:

By This Hand Order Shall Prevail.

Theel stared at the shield for many long minutes, absorbing the words as best he could, remembering his father's words as he imparted the doctrines of the knighthood. Theel could still hear his father's voice in his head. He read the words aloud.

"By this hand order shall prevail."

Theel understood now more than ever what it took to be a knight. And he understood a little better each day. He understood how powerful and rare this combination truly was, this wedding of faith and steel that made his father among the greatest knights alive, that made him able to withstand a stab to the heart and continue fighting. Theel no longer doubted that the legend was true. He now believed his father was stabbed through the heart and lived. He believed it as if he'd seen it himself. He would doubt no longer. He would not doubt his father, and he would not doubt himself ever again.

"My father beat death and lived," Theel said. "If he was able to accomplish this, I will find the Blessed Soul of Man. There is no room for doubt. I will rise to knighthood. I will be a Knight of the Southern Cross."

To become a knight, one first needed to become a man. That was the reason for his quest. That was why he was denied knighthood until he found the Blessed Soul. He needed to grow inside. He needed to learn wisdom and maturity. He needed to find the man inside himself.

"Find the Blessed Soul of Man, and you find yourself," the Keeper had told him.

"I will find the Blessed Soul of Man," Theel said.

The surface of the shield was patted gently with the impact of falling tears.

Epilogue

The battle had occurred days before, but there was still enough physical evidence to tell Aeoxoea what had happened, even without tapping her juy to see the past. The battlefield was a cavern with a sloping floor and a large crevasse that emitted heat and a constant, red glow. The slope was covered with sand and pockmarked with limestone rock formations here and there—some large, others small, some colorful, others dull. The cavern was swept by a brisk breeze, both warm and constant, which moved the sand, smoothing it, and giving it ripples that mimicked the surface of a pond. It also erased much of the evidence of battle, covering the footprints of the combatants, burying weapons and armor that were broken or dropped, and soaking up their blood. But the drifts could not conceal their corpses, dozens of them, frozen in death and half-buried in the sand.

They were very large, red-skinned creatures, some as tall as two men, with extremely long arms and powerful-looking, multi-jointed legs. Each of them had four horns and six eyes on a face with a mouth that resembled a lion's, but with a lower jaw split into halves. Aeoxoea found the ears to be most interesting—tall and pointy, and perched atop their heads like those of a feline, but continuing down the sides of their heads to their necks. The assassin touched one of them, feeling the membrane between her fingers, and she pulled it out to see its true size. It looked as if their ears were composed of more than simple cartilage, containing a good deal of muscle. This appeared to allow the dycleth to expand or contract their ears as needed, or perhaps even turn them slightly in different directions. Aeoxoea guessed these creatures could hear a good deal more than sound.

Smile Bathes in Fire confirmed this.

"Sound as you explain it, is the smallest thing I hear," came the voice from inside her head.

"You hear nothing, dycleth," Aeoxoea said. "For I have taken your ears from you."

"It is you who hears nothing, human," the dycleth retorted. "Since I've tried to hear through your puny, worthless ears, I can confirm this."

The assassin put her finger in the mouth of the creature and pulled it open, inspecting the inside. The bottom half of the mouth was split into two jaws that moved independently of one another. Each contained rows of pointy teeth, including longer canines. The creatures also had two tongues, one on each side.

"What would you hear if your dycleth ears were returned to you?" Aeoxoea asked.

"I would hear your size, shape, location, and proximity," the dycleth answered. "As well as the textures of your skin, clothing, weapons, and hair."

"Echolocation," Aeoxoea said.

"You give name to an ability you do not understand, human."

"I understand it well enough," the assassin said.

The eyes of the dycleth laying before her were also noteworthy. Three individual pairs crowned the creature's head, three pairs that Aeoxoea guessed would detect three individual spectrums. She pulled one of the eyelids open, finding glossy, black orbs with no pupils or irises, not unlike the zoths she had seen. These clearly detected whatever sparse light could be found in this sunless realm.

"We see light just as you humans see it, but more acutely," Smile Bathes in Fire said. "The dycleth can see as humans do in the realm of the sun, but the humans cannot see as dycleth in the realm of darkness."

"Have you been to the surface?" Aeoxoea asked. "Have you seen the sun?"

"I have not."

"Then it is you who speaks of things you do not understand … dycleth."

She opened the middle eyelid and saw something resembling an average human eye, but for the orange and yellow tones of the iris.

"Used in seeing the warmth of your flesh, human," Smile Bathes in Fire explained. "The flow of blood throughout your body is plain to me. I can see your vitality. I can see the strength of your heartbeat."

"Infravision," Aeoxoea said. "A unique and wonderfully useful ability."

"An ability humans do not possess."

"Very true," Aeoxoea confirmed. "Humans are such fragile creatures, after all. But, I am forced to admit, your ability to see variations of heat is far less interesting to me than this."

She opened the creature's third eye, revealing a surface that was milky and white, and otherwise featureless.

"The third eye," the assassin said. "The white one …"

"I am able to see the breath of the Stone Fathers, the Thousand Sires whose spirits dwell within the Deep Stone."

"Craft weaves," Aeoxoea stated.

"Craft weaves? I don't understand."

"Your people have the ability to see magic."

"It is the breath of the Stone Fathers," Smile Bathes in Fire insisted.

"It is magic," Aeoxoea said. "And the ability to see it naturally, innately, is an extremely rare gift previously only found in animals."

"In animals?" the dycleth laughed. "Foolishness."

"Many users of the Craft, and practitioners of the Method, are able to use their powers to grant this ability to themselves and others," Aeoxoea said. "But there is no intelligent race which sees magic innately. Some of the most accomplished wizards to ever live have labored to create this ability within sentient beings. They have never found success."

"You are wrong," Smile Bathes in Fire said. "Magic is a myth created by the liars among the Iksiout. There is no mystical power other than the will of the Stone Fathers."

"It is a precious gift given to your people," Aeoxoea said. "It has allowed your race to prosper in the most inhospitable of places. And you don't even know what it is."

"You are a fool to believe this."

Aeoxoea smiled. "If I am a fool, then it is fortunate for you that I am a patient fool."

"What do you mean?"

"The time you have until I find another who might provide the same knowledge as you is rather limited," the assassin warned. "Be careful that you do not exhaust my patience before that time comes. But for now, I grow tired of inspecting your corpse."

"*My* corpse?"

Aeoxoea did not answer. Instead, she stepped over the dead heap of flesh that used to be a dycleth and continued to walk the battlefield, her small feet making slight dimples in the rippled surface of the sand. She was careful where she walked, placing her feet in the specific places where the combatants had, allowing the Craft to fill her with the thoughts and emotions of those who'd struggled and died on this ground. She felt every shred of their rage and frustration and fear as the sand squeezed between her toes, and watched the battle as it unfolded, as if it was occurring right there before her eyes.

"What are the symbols you wear?" Aeoxoea asked. "What does your war paint mean?"

"It says many things. It says I am blessed by the Gray Hand, our Most Favored God Preist. My sire was declared Quiet With Fast Hands, son of Climbs With His Voice. I have slain forty enemy warriors. I and my brothers have won eighteen battle victories. I run with the First Honored Battle Company. It is commanded by the Kuri Kii, declared Hand Shines of Pain, who wields the mighty Sen Kil. I have never been bested-"

"Until now, sadly," Aeoxoea said. "You have my sympathy."

"I do not wish for it."

"I cannot help but give it," Aeoxoea giggled. "I fear I've always lamented the fortunes of the vanquished, those who've proven themselves the weaker, the lesser."

"The First Honored Battle Company is neither weaker nor lesser than any other unit of infantry above the ground or below it."

"Perhaps that is true," Aeoxoea said. "But it was not a unit of infantry who bested you. It seems you brave and stalwart warriors have proven yourselves to be collectively weaker, and lesser, than a single human man."

"Not true," Smile Bathes in Fire said. "No single human can stand before any dycleth warrior and live."

"And yet this single human defeated your entire unit."

"With the aid of evil spirits," the dycleth insisted. "That human was a devil."

"*Is* a devil," the assassin corrected. "He lives on, while you do not."

"That is impossible. Our commander, the mighty Kuri Kii, is the most accomplished fighter in Youghiot. He would not allow the human to go on living."

"The human does live," Aeoxoea said. "And I seem to have found the place where your commander, the mighty Kuri Kii, fell before him."

She watched as the struggle between these two played out before her. Seeing that the Zealot was more than a match for his dycleth brothers, the Kuri Kii made the fateful decision to challenge the knight to single combat. Aeoxoea had seen the Zealot accomplish many amazing things, but his battle with the Kuri Kii was truly special. This particular dycleth was a gifted warrior in his own right, unique in his incredible strength and speed, even among his race. Though he was nearly three times the size of the human, he was almost as fast, moving about on his powerful, multi-jointed legs that allowed him to jump and run better than any human could hope to. He wielded a dual-tipped spear with hooked blades at the ends, and he did it with a speed and ferocity that Gavin the Zealot had never seen before.

Aeoxoea was certain she would never in her lifetime see a fighter as gifted as Gavin the Zealot, but the Kuri Kii almost made her question that belief. He was as skilled with his weapon as the human was with his, and he also benefitted from his size and speed and strength, all of which dwarfed the natural abilities of the human. If it wasn't for the blessings bestowed upon Gavin the Zealot by the Craft weaves, the ways in which the magic aided and supported his every movement, this may have been a fair fight. But as Aeoxoea had witnessed before, and was now seeing again, there simply was no such thing as a fair fight with Gavin the Zealot.

Things started out well enough for the Kuri Kii. His arms were long, and his reach was made longer by the length of the Sen Kil. The knight couldn't hope to get close enough to use his tiny knives. For this reason, the knight was pushed around and herded by the whirring blades of the Sen Kil.

The Kuri Kii also had dycleth slingers as his allies, and he used this to his advantage, calling for volleys of slugs to fill the air any time the human threatened to gain any advantage. None of these attacks found their targets—every one was dodged or blocked by the knight. Seeing this, the Kuri Kii called for other forms of ammunition—breakable orbs which contained dangerous substances. These could not be dodged or blocked.

"Dro'qua pods, made from the bile of the mua giou," Smile Bathes in Fire explained. "The substance is alive in its appetite for all things. It devours flesh and bone just as the mua giou devours stone."

Aeoxoea watched the dro'qua pods flying at the Zealot, breaking on his blades when he tried block them, exploding in the sand at his feet when he tried to dodge them. In both cases they splattered their acidic contents against his leather armor, where it sizzled and smoked.

"Venom of the jugger beetle," Smile Bathes in Fire said, as another volley of pods exploded all around the Zealot. "The jugger stuns its victim, sedating his mind and numbing him to pain, but also paralyzing his limbs."

The knight should have been able to save himself by dodging, but the Kuri Kii would not allow him to, using the Sen Kil to drive him into the face of these attacks. And the attacks of the slingers proved effective. The acid burned holes in the Zealot's boots and armor, through which the venom found access to his skin. The human's stride slowed and his breathing became labored. And for the first since Aeoxoea set eyes upon him, the Champion of Embriss showed weakness.

This occurred just before the Kuri Kii signaled for another volley of pods; these were imbued with Flame Bringers. For a few brief moments, the Zealot's body was engulfed entirely in a blazing inferno that burned at least twenty feet high. The fire was black, with a purplish hue. It cast no light, and it burned cold. Aeoxoea knew what this meant:

Necromancy.

The knight was burning alive. It seemed the battle should be over, with the Kuri Kii and his warriors victorious. But Aeoxoea had her doubts. She'd seen too much of this man to believe he had no contingency for this. And her assumptions were proven correct when the fire died, and Gavin the Zealot stood unhurt, his pink skin whole, as if nothing had happened.

The assassin sensed the pop and release of magic, and wasn't surprised to see a spot on the knight's arm glowing softly to her Craftsight. It was another protective rune, similar to the Life Sign, but with a different purpose. Aeoxoea found herself smiling.

Fire resistance.

But while the Zealot was a better fighter, it was clear to Aeoxoea that the Kuri Kii had other strengths to draw from. He was a superb battle commander. He'd created a strategy to defeat the invincible warrior, a method of combining the attacks of the Sen Kil with those of his slingers to wear down the human. It was a sound strategy. It should have worked. And it almost did.

The Kuri Kii was undeterred by the human's resistance to Flame Bringers. Shortly after the magical fire dissipated, the Kuri Kii was upon the Zealot once again. The human was clearly weakened. The bile of the mua giou was burning his skin. The venom of the jugger beetle was slowing his movements. The Kuri Kii kicked sand in his face and smashed his wrist with the shaft of the Sen Kil, knocking his knife out of his hand.

The dycleth leader surely thought this would be his moment of triumph. In any other battle with any other foe, it would have been. But this was not just any battle. This was not just any foe.

As a military commander, the Kuri Kii had faced many different sorts of enemies who posed a variety of threats. He was excellent at sizing up the strengths and weaknesses of his foes, and anticipating their thoughts and actions. This was knowledge gained through the vast experience of countless battles. But none of those battles could prepare him for what was coming. He had no experience facing a man such as the Zealot. And no creature alive had experience against the Silent Sisters, because no creature who faced them survived.

The Kuri Kii would regret knocking the knife out of the knight's grasp, because that formerly empty hand how wielded a silver tongue. It was very long and impossibly thin, and it hissed like a snake as it licked at the Kuri Kii multiple times before he could comprehend what was happening. No matter how many times Aeoxoea saw the Zealot ply the Silent Sisters, she still found the sight of it to be stirring. All of the Craft surrounding the Kuri Kii listened to the knight's wishes and obeyed. Tiny, delicate fingers of Wind Magic guided the ribbons of silver past the dycleth's defenses, finding the gaps in his armor, seeking out the most vulnerable places on his body.

It took less than a second, and the Kuri Kii's left knee gave out beneath him. Unable to catch himself, he crumpled to the ground, the Sen Kil flying from his fingers. He tried to rise, but his body wouldn't obey. He tried to reach for his weapon, but his hand wouldn't work.

The Zealot was already gone, spending no further time with a foe who could no longer threaten him. Leaving the Kuri Kii sitting on the ground, staring in shock at the blood pooling beneath his left leg, the knight turned and rushed to attack the slingers. They had seen their leader fall, and answered this with a fresh volley of slugs. The human produced another stream of silver as he rushed at them, now using both weapons to deflect or catch every missile thrown at him, discarding many of the pods, but throwing many back. Then he was in their midst, and the whispering song of the Silent Sisters was joined by the cries of dycleth warriors being cut to pieces.

While this was happening, Aeoxoea noticed a new dycleth, unlike any of the others approaching. He was elderly, showing his advanced age with each labored step, leaning heavily upon two canes of black wood. He walked on old legs with twisted joints that could barely carry him, and a backbone so bent his chest was almost parallel to the ground. This may have been caused by the multitude of necklaces he wore around his neck, composed of many shiny black stones. Half of these necklaces were so large they dragged upon the ground between his legs.

"The Gray Hand," Smile Bathes in Fire said. "The Most Favored God Priest."

The priest looked like a demon with his large eyes glowing softly, white with Craftsight, and red with infravision. He also looked like a ghost, with his wrinkled skin coated entirely from head to toe with a fine white powder that caused him to leave fingerprints all over his canes and his clothing.

"The powder is made from a special recipe of medicines meant to ease the burden of his age," Smile Bathes in Fire explained. "He is older than the oldest of my people by many times."

"A clever trick."

"It is not a trick," Smile Bathes in Fire corrected. "It is said he is ageless, that death does not come for him. No one knows when he was born. He was elderly in the time of my great-grandsire."

"Death does not come for him?"

"He cannot be killed by any means. Even time is powerless against him."

"Why do you think this is?" Aeoxoea asked. "What do your people say?"

"He is the Most Favored God Priest," Smile Bathes in Fire stated.

The assassin laughed. "Is he? You say those words as if they hold meaning."

"You dare deny the truth told you by your own eyes?"

"What truth is that?"

"The Gray Hand has been granted the gift of agelessness by his standing in the eyes of the Stone Fathers. He is the Most Favored God Priest."

Aeoxoea giggled. "Did he tell you this, himself?"

"It is known."

"I know otherwise."

The ancient priest's clothing appeared ceremonial, but gave no pleasure to the eyes. His garments consisted of strips of black cloth wrapped around his arms and legs, hanging from his shoulders in tatters, giving the appearance of a burial shroud. The strips of cloth were covered with words embroidered in gold, words that were sacred to the priest's religion, and whose meaning were known only by a cherished few. Aeoxoea was one of these.

"You know otherwise?" Smile Bathes in Fire asked. "What do you know?"

"I know there is only one thing you've said about your priest that is accurate," the assassin answered.

"What is that?" Smile Bathes in Fire asked.

"Death does not come for him."

A retinue of three dycleth trailed in the Gray Hand's wake. Two of these were larger and muscled, armed with spears and dressed in chitin armor. But where the Kuri Kii's warriors wore the war paint of the First Honored Battle Company, these soldiers bore markings showing allegiance to some other entity. They wore shortly cut robes beneath their armor, which hung to their top knees and elbows with dark and thick fabric embroidered with runes that glowed to Aeoxoea's Craftsight.

"They serve the Temple of the Stone Fathers," Smile Bathes in Fire explained. "The Church keeps its own soldiers to serve as protectors for the clergy and peacekeepers among the brothers. These two were sent with the Most Favored God Priest to safeguard him in his travels."

"Your priest had another task for them," Aeoxoea said.

"The human knight will be defeated," the old dycleth whispered to his guards. "He will be subdued, and made a prisoner. He will not be slain. Now."

The two temple guards nodded and obeyed. As these two rushed to attack Gavin the Zealot, Aeoxoea's attention focused on the last of the old priest's followers. He was a smaller dycleth, much slighter of stature, bearing no weapons or armor. Like the Most Favored God Priest, he was dressed in robes.

"An acolyte of the Most Favored God Priest," Smile Bathes in Fire said. "He is declared Fifth Among Brothers. He is a constant presence at his master's side."

The Gray Hand now gave orders to his acolyte. He spoke softly, but Aeoxoea heard every word.

"The human child will be found," the old priest said. "He will be made a prisoner by your hand. Go."

As Fifth Among Brothers moved to obey, the ancient priest continued walking forward by himself, slowly and painfully, approaching the place where Gavin the Zealot battled those few who remained of the First Honored Battle Company. The Most Favored God Priest looked so frail, it appeared the human could swat him like a fly, yet the old priest showed no fear as he walked closer and closer.

Finally, he stopped a short distance away from the battle, taking a moment to regard the Zealot with his intense, burning eyes. He released his grip on one of his two canes and it remained upright, in perfect balance as he took hold of one of his necklaces.

Then the old priest gripped the handle of his cane in one hand, and a tangle of his necklaces in the other, wrapping them around his wrist. He glared at the knight, fingering the stones, and speaking in puffs of white powder. As he did this, he reached out, forming a fist in the air, squeezing the stones tightly. The stone crushed to powder in his grasp, releasing a burst of golden Wind Magic.

The old preist's lips peeled back, revealing four rows of clenched teeth. A burst of wind exploded from his mouth, blowing more air than any lungs could possibly contain. It was a stiff breeze, stronger than those that occurred naturally in the cavern, and it buffeted the knight's body, causing his hair to whip around his forehead.

Otherwise, the Zealot didn't react to it at all, continuing to fight as if nothing had changed, as if it was just another of the many breezes that swept through the cavern. But while it looked and felt to the knight like any other breeze, Aeoxoea's Craftsight told her it was much different. The gust of air was full of Craft harnessed by the old priest. The assassin expected golden Wind Magic, but saw something else, something unnatural, something dead.

It was more necromancy, the cold black magic of Death. It acted as a dispel rune, scattering the naturally occurring Craft that surrounded the knight, the yellows, greens, reds, and blues withering before the plume of blackness that blew from the dycleth priest's mouth. In one breath, the Craft runes that guided and aided and obeyed the knight were gone. In one breath, the Most Favored God Priest blew them all away.

"You devilish old man," Aeoxoea whispered. "That's not fair."

It only lasted a moment, the dycleth ran out of breath, the wind died, and the colorful Craft weaves would quickly rush back in to fill the emptiness. But in that moment, the knight was surrounded by a vacuum of Craft, abandoned by his magic, and that moment was more time than the Most Favored God Priest needed.

The old priest crushed another shiny stone in his grasp. Tendrils of green Earth Sorcery squirted from between his fingers as he punched his fist down into the sand at his feet. At the same time he did this, a hand reached up from the ground at the knight's feet, a hand composed of deep stone, the flesh of the world. The hand was perfectly formed, showing veins and knuckles and wrinkles, an exact duplicate of the dycleth's own. It looked like the work of a master sculptor, yet it moved as if it were alive, moving just as the old preist moved his, and it seized the knight's ankle in its stony grasp.

Gavin the Zealot clearly did not anticipate this attack. Momentarily without the aid of the Craft weaves, he suddenly wasn't as fast or as aware. Weakened by the bile of the lizard worm, slowed by the venom of the jugger beetle, it was almost too easy for the old dycleth. The knight went down instantly, his back splashing in the sand in a moment so spectacularly ungraceful, so completely unworthy of his own standards that it forced Aeoxoea to laugh.

"Perhaps you are fallible after all, my sweet butterfly," the assassin whispered.

The knight cried out in pain, his leg bent so awkwardly that it was clearly broken, but he had worse problems. He lost control of his limbs as he fell, and lost control of his weapons. He crashed into the sand, the Silent Sisters whipping around him unpredictably, like angry snakes free of their master's control, striking at everything. He could put no more effort into fighting his enemies, or defending himself against their attacks. Now he was forced to swing his arms in an effort to save himself, to keep the blades away from his skin. As always, the Craft weaves aided him, and the silvery blades mostly avoided him as he crumbled to the ground, but he still suffered a nasty cut to the back of his scalp.

That was when it became clear to Aeoxoea why the knight so often relied upon his knives past the point when she thought the Silent Sisters were the better option. Jass told her the Sisters were the deadliest weapons in the world, and the assassin had seen enough to know this was true. But while they were deadly to the

Zealot's enemies, they could be just as dangerous to him if they ever escaped his control.

"Of course," Aeoxoea said. "The greatest fighter in the world. He can't be defeated, unless he defeats himself."

"The Kuri Kii is the greatest fighter in the world," Smile Bathes in Fire said.

Aeoxoea ignored him.

The Zealot had whittled the First Honored Battle Company down to two slingers, but now they were joined by the temple guards, and the human was forced to defend himself while flat on his back with his ankle broken and encased in stone. Much of his armor was damaged from the acid pods, and it was clear he still suffered from the effects of the jugger beetle venom. It was the most vulnerable Aeoxoea had ever seen him. But the knight's resolve wasn't broken, and the Silent Sisters remained hungry for dycleth flesh. One of the silver blades assaulted the stone hand gripping his leg while the other lashed out at his attackers.

A temple guard approached with a spear but had it torn from his hands by one of the Sisters. Then he was tripped and thrown to the ground, the side of his neck spurting red. A slinger threw a pod charged with Flame Bringers. This was caught and whipped into the face of the other temple guard, who was instantly engulfed in cold, black fire.

The Zealot managed to cut the stone hand off. It still held onto his ankle, but he was free, momentarily. Then the Most Favored God Priest thrust his fist back into the ground, and another stone hand reached up, seizing the knight's right arm. The hand was controlled by the frail priest, but it derived its strength from the earth, deep stone stronger than any living flesh. Its grip was crushingly strong, and Aeoxoea could hear the bones of the Zealot's forearm cracking as the stoney fingers squeezed. He cried out in pain, his weapon falling from his limp fingers.

The human was now at an extreme disadvantage, struggling against unyielding bonds and physically hobbled by his wounds, but also pinned to the ground as the two slingers attacked him.

Another hand composed of stone reached up, clutching at his right leg, but he fought on with his left hand, lashing out at the slingers with the lone Silent Sister.

The Most Favored God Priest's voice was raspy and weak, but so emphatic were his words that they boomed in the cavern, carried by the wings of Wind Magic.

"The knight will not be slain," he commanded. "Yet he will be subdued by your hand. His weapon will be seized. Now."

"You needn't worry, priest of death," Aeoxoea said. "They will not slay him. They cannot."

The dycleth slingers had as much chance of obeying the priest as they had of killing the Zealot. They could not subdue him. They could not disarm him. Flat on this back, immobilized, wounded, and weakened by jugger venom, he was still more than a match for them. One hand was free. One Silent Sister still whispered. Gavin the Zealot would not give up.

One of the dycleth lost his sling when he lost the hand that held it. Another hand burst out of the ground, seizing the human by the throat. The satiny ribbon hissed angrily, no longer delicate, no longer precise. Now the Sister lashed out wildly, hacking at the knight's enemies with the subtlety of a woodsman's axe. The attacks were savage, the wounds large.

One of the dycleth fell, his limbs rigid, his back as straight as a board, and his head attached only by a narrow strip of flesh. The old preist punched the ground and another hand appeared, another to seize the human's throat, joining with the other by lacing fingers, and pulling the knight's head back. But this couldn't save the last slinger. He didn't even realize he was dead, looking down at himself with a calm face at the gash in his gut, at the heap of viscera lying at his feet.

When the last dycleth fell, there was no one standing between the Zealot and the Most Favored God Priest. The First Honored Battle Company was down, completely defeated. The temple guards were down, completely defeated. Most every dycleth who'd entered the cavern had sacrificed himself to subdue this single knight, and now, finally, it was done. As if to emphasize this, one more stony hand reached up from the ground, crushing the knight's left wrist, ripping the weapon from his grasp.

Now Gavin the Zealot was helpless, unable to move, unable to stop himself from being strangled. His face was purple, his eyes bulging as the stony hands squeezed his neck. He was entirely at the mercy of his enemy, a fact proven when the old dycleth priest loosened his grip, allowing the knight to breathe.

"To the Fifth Son, give praise," the Gray Hand said. "You come, chosen warrior, to lay down the prize, Man's Blessed Soul, at the feet of Dehen Yaulk."

"It is him," Aeoxoea said. "He is found."

"Who is found?" Smile Bathes in Fire asked.

"The time has come," the Gray Hand said. "For the Fifth Son to birth his child. For the Fifth Son to grant this gift of Hell. By your sacrifice, frail human, the seven eyes will open. By your blood, the slayer of your Blessed Soul will live, as it is prophesied, in many tongues told, in many languages written."

"Your old priest," Aeoxoea said. "He is the father of Gilligod."

"Gilligod?" Smile Bathes in Fire asked.

"The Devil Device," the assassin explained. "The ancient weapon of evil prophesied to slay the Blessed Soul of Man."

"What are you talking about?" Smile Bathes in Fire asked.

"My knightly friends of the surface journeyed a very long distance, and risked very much to find him. It seems he was waiting. It seems he found them first."

"The humans came here seeking the Most Favored God Priest?"

"No," Aeoxoea said. "They came seeking the father of Gilligod. Your priest was born for this purpose, to forge the ancient weapon of evil."

"Why would he do this?" Smile Bathes in Fire asked.

"To serve his lord," Aeoxoea answered.

"The Stone Fathers?"

"No," Aeoxoea said. "Dehen Yaulk. The Angel of Death."

The Kuri Kii limped up the slope, grimacing in pain, gripping the Sen Kil in one hand, clutching his leg in the other. His eyelids were heavy from blood loss. His jaws hung open with fatigue. He was badly hurt, one side of his body glistening with blood. He didn't appear as if he could remain standing much longer.

The Kuri Kii's warriors had fulfilled their mission, but did so at the cost of their lives. The knights were defeated, but the dycleth leader resembled no conqueror Aeoxoea had ever seen. He looked more defeated than the Zealot, limping pathetically toward the Most Favored God Priest.

Then the Kuri Kii saw the knight, his eyes widening as they focused on his fallen foe. A fire was ignited within his glare, defeat and exhaustion swallowed by rage and hatred. And Aeoxoea could see why.

This human warrior had beaten him as he'd never been beaten before, crushed his pride by humiliating him in personal combat. And worse, he'd destroyed the First Honored Battle Company. He'd taken the Kuri Kii's brothers from him, comrades he'd led into battle, fought beside, bled with, sacrificed for, loved. Some of those corpses rotting on the sand were brothers who grew to manhood with the Kuri Kii. The spirits of these comrades cried out for vengeance, for justice, for the restoration of their honor. The Kuri Kii heard these cries as he staggered to the place where his enemy lay helpless.

He stood over the Zealot, the Sen Kil raised, poised to strike. The eyes of the two warriors met, the dycleth's gaze filled with his intentions, the human's eyes filled with understanding of what those intentions were.

"Stay your hand, Kuri Kii," the Gray Hand whispered, his voice booming magically in the cavern. "The human knight will not be harmed. He will live on as my prisoner."

These words reached the Kuri Kii's ears, but not his brain. He did not hesitate. He did not flinch. He thrust the Sen Kil down like a spear, striking the human in the chest, in the direct center of the silver shield he wore there. He drove the blade clean through,

through his chest, through his heart, through his body, through his life. The attack carried so much force that the tip of the Sen Kil was jammed deep into the sand floor until it hit the stone beneath. When the Kuri Kii released his grip, the weapon remained upright, protruding from the knight's chest.

With this single thrust, the Sen Kil became a part of legend, forever known as the weapon that pierced the heart of Gavin the Zealot.

"This life is not yours to take, Kuri Kii!" the Most Favored God Priest shrieked, shuffling forward, leaning on his canes. "This was not your choice!"

The Kuri Kii didn't seem to hear the priest's words. He only stood over the human, glaring at the knight's body with equal parts shock and sadness, the look of someone who'd committed a desperate and hateful act, only to realize it did nothing to ease his pain.

He reached out with a shaking hand and pulled the Sen Kil from the knight's body. This left a gaping hole in the Zealot's chest, and in the center of his knightshield, from which bubbled gleaming red blood. It ran in rivers over the surface of the shield, filling the words engraved there.

My God. My Clan. My Shield.
By This Hand Order Shall Prevail.

The Most Favored God Priest dropped to his knees, casting his canes aside. Wailing as if in pain, he clawed at his chest, tearing his robes open.

"Dehen Yaulk, my father, blessed Angel of Death, Lord of the Dead, you must now heed my prayer!" the old priest shouted. "This man will soon be free of your grasp, protected, and made holy and claimed by God. As the Fifth Son, as the Death Angel, your unholy duty you must forsake. Leave this man's house untouched. Imprison his spirit within his dead flesh. Do not allow his soul to fly to his Lord in Heaven. My prayer is this. I beseech you, Death Angel, Fifth Son, Lord of the Dead!"

When these words were spoken, the flow of blood ceased from the hole in the knight's shield. The flesh beneath closed, the wound in the heart healed, and the muscle began to beat strongly once again, pumping life through his body. He breathed again. His fingers twitched, and his closed eyelids fluttered.

Aeoxoea had seen many unusual things since coming to this island, some that had shocked her. But nothing was so amazing as what she was now witnessing—a slain man restored to life by the Angel of Death's refusal to take him. Despite being stabbed through the heart, he would go on living. He would survive, and recover to fight again.

"I don't believe it," she breathed.

Gavin the Zealot had beaten death.

To be continued in

Wither the Waking World

Book Two

About the Author: Jonathan Techlin lives in Kaukauna, Wisconsin with his wife and two daughters. He enjoys reading, traveling, and following the Green Bay Packers. He is currently at work completing the second novel in the Wither the Waking World saga.

●

This book is dedicated to Mom. You always believed. I love you. I still miss you.

●

Thanks to my brother Mike for letting me write on his computer.

Thanks to Dad, Rick, and Adam

Very special thanks to Jennifer, Anna, and Lucy for being beautiful.

Made in the USA
Charleston, SC
16 December 2015